ANDREY RUBANOV was born in 1969. After studying at Moscow State University he worked as a driver, journalist and bodyguard before becoming a successful businessman. In 1996 he was convicted of fraud and imprisoned. Three years later he was exonerated on appeal and released. This is his first book, based on his own experiences of life in prison.

ANDREW BROMFIELD is a British editor and translator of Russian literature. He is a founding editor of the Russian literary journal *Glas*, and has translated works by Boris Akunin, Vladimir Voinovich, Irina Denezhkina, Victor Pelevin, and Sergei Lukyanenko. In 2007 he translated Leo Tolstoy's *War and Peace: Original Version*.

DO TIME
GET TIME

ANDREY RUBANOV

TRANSLATED BY ANDREW BROMFIELD

Old St PUBLISHING

First published in Russia in 2006 by Limbus Press, St Petersburg, as *Sazhayte I Vyrastet*

This translation first published in Great Britain in 2008 by Old Street Publishing Ltd

This edition published 2009 by Old Street Publishing Ltd
28-32 Bowling Green Lane, London EC1R 0BJ
www.oldstreetpublishing.co.uk

ISBN 978-1-905847-75-4

10 9 8 7 6 5 4 3 2 1

A CIP catalogue record for this title is available from the British Library.

Typeset by Old Street Publishing and Martin Worthington.

Printed and bound in Great Britain by J F Print Ltd., Sparkford, Somerset

PART ONE

1

They picked me up early in the morning of 15th August 1996. In Moscow.

Two of them came for me. They walked up, asked to see my ID and politely ushered me across to the car. They opened the door smartly and correctly, with all the airs and graces of a commissionaire, but then shoved me inside without any ceremony.

The first one, who smelled of onions and old socks, got into the driving seat, turned to me and said, with a glint of a cheap gold tooth:

'Now, tell us where the Lefortovo district is in this Moscow of yours. We're not locals, you know.'

I was dumbfounded. I didn't understand. Was a newly apprehended villain supposed to show the sleuths the way to jail? And then, why straight to jail? What about proof?

The capital of an empire is a special kind of city. No curious crowd gathered instantly. People hurried past, averting their eyes. Only one, a youngish man, slowed down and bent his head slightly to look in through the windows of the car at the pale-faced arrestee. But the palm of a hand was abruptly slapped against the transparent barrier from inside:

'Move along!'

The curious youth gave a violent start and hurried on, tugging down his jacket. My jacket cost about fourteen times as much.

'Turn right at the traffic lights,' I said despondently. 'Then keep going straight along the embankment …'

And so the victim led his executioner to the scaffold. I would have relished the absurdity of the moment, but I was feeling too afraid. After all, it was the first time I'd ever been arrested. At the very least I was being taken in for intensive interrogation. And in the worst case, I was being transported from the realm of freedom to the realm of compulsion.

From a world of Japanese computers, Cuban cigars, French cognac, genuine port from Portugal, Swiss watches, gold cufflinks, whispering air-conditioners, two-hundred-dollar fragrances, linen trousers, crocodile-skin briefcases, silk shirts, glamorous magazines, bullet-proof glass, polished limousines and seven-figure bank accounts – straight to a place where they fed you coarse gruel.

But if they'd managed to get to me, that didn't mean they would get to my money. They'd been looking for me for two months, on suspicion of embezzling a million American dollars from the state treasury. And now they'd caught me.

I hadn't stolen the million. I don't like stealing and I don't know how to do it. So now I didn't completely lose my presence of mind. These were changed times, they didn't put innocent people behind bars any more. Changed times, gentlemen! On my way to Lefortovo prison, I was surrounded by the noise and bustle of the hot, nervous summer of 1996. Only a couple of weeks earlier the country had re-elected its first president for another term. In doing so, it had chosen democracy. And in democracies, as far as I was aware, only a court could deprive a man of his freedom.

The morning had turned out bright and very warm. We drove for a long time through a city that was barely awake and gradually growing warmer, drove through the quivering air, through the thick yellow sunlight slanting down from the dusty crowns of the trees that lined the road. Jammed fast in the herd of traffic, our car moved slowly. I was sitting all alone in the back and could easily have jumped out as we drove along: tried to escape, made a run for it through the courtyards and the side streets. But why should I? I hadn't done anything. I'd just explain everything to them and before lunch I'd be back in my office, where the computer screens glittered as money, shifting and shimmering, appeared and disappeared.

Along the way I was deliberately rude to them. They had addressed me too familiarly and I told them what I thought about that. The police were furious and for a while they said nothing.

The car dodged through traffic for a long time before it finally drove into a series of yards and stopped in front of a massive building with no sign.

'Looks like we're here.'

Suddenly, one of them turned to me and grabbed my nose between his crooked fingers. The August heat had made his hands and my nose moist and slippery, so the prank was only half successful. I jerked back and freed myself from his grasp, but even so the sudden pain and humiliation brought tears to my eyes.

'Now we're going to take you in there with us,' I heard. 'And then we'll see who's the polite one.'

Behind the massive doors there was a large lobby. An embrasure in the wall, covered with metal mesh. A pale functionary in a grey cap looking out curiously from behind it.

'Face the wall,' the one who had attacked my nose said briskly. 'Stand facing the wall! Move!'

He chuckled to the pale-faced duty officer and nodded towards me:

'Just look what a fine Rockefeller we've caught.'

He was obviously talking about my suit. The jacket and trousers looked pretty expensive, and they were.

They led me along corridors with complicated twists and turns and shoved me into a room that was large but extremely stuffy. There were several dour-looking men in shirts with rolled-up sleeves, sitting on the chairs and tables, smoking. All of them were older than me, and much bigger. I suddenly felt rather uncomfortable.

Several hoarse voices spoke at once.

'Oh, so you've caught him, have you?'

'Well, what did you think? We caught all the rest and we've caught this one too.' And then, speaking to me again: 'Face the wall!'

'We haven't searched him,' said the second one who had arrested me, concerned. 'What if he's got a weapon?'

'That's right! Up against the wall! Spread your legs!' That was to me again.

I stood as I was told, and spread my legs.

I didn't like the wall. Rough, lumpy plaster covered with streaky, old green oil paint, it had a depressing, almost obscene look. The kind of wall Pink Floyd ought to have sung about.

They went through my pockets expertly and quickly, extracting three mobile phones, a passport, a notebook, a heavy bundle of keys and about half a kilogram of money in two currencies. They flung the money on the nearest table with genuine indifference, but the notebook aroused great professional interest. Continuously dosing themselves with nicotine, the sleuths leafed through that precious item of material evidence, handing it back and forth to each other, and then took it out of the room, evidently for a more detailed analysis of the contact details of my friends, acquaintances, relatives, colleagues, business partners, clients and all the other men and women who fell within the orbit of my carefree life.

'Sit down!'

The door opened and another two men rushed in, followed by a third. They'd obviously come running to catch a glimpse of the newly captured criminal.

'At last, Andriukha! If you only knew how tired we are of running around after you.'

I didn't say anything.

'Where do you think you are?' they roared in my face. 'You're not in your office now! Sit over there, nearer the light!'

With an effort, I managed to distance myself from the situation and see these men as amusing monsters. They were trying to look frightening, jangling their handcuffs and battered Makarov pistols. They strode around the room, clomping heavily, with their elbows sticking out, as if they had extra sets of male genitals dangling under their armpits, one on the right, one on the left. The way long-serving army men walk. Or cowboys in classic westerns.

I had to admire their attitude, it was simple and honest: compared to them I was shit, a pup, a little kid, an unscrupulous liar. A bad man. A lover of easy money, Mercedes cars and girls. The state paid its servants poorly, and the servants felt a natural class hatred for nouveau-riche juveniles.

'I know where he's headed,' one of them said to another. 'He's going down for a long stretch. And that's right!'

They were trying to intimidate me with the idea of prison, but I'd been ready for it for a long time. I'd prepared for it in advance. And what I felt now was not so much fright as a bizarre combination of exultation and horror.

I thought the most amusing detail of the interior was the ashtrays. They were made out of matchboxes with the foil from cigarette packs painstakingly glued over them – handicraft work by prisoners.

It soon became clear that the entire investigating team consisted of provincials on assignment to Moscow. The detectives and criminal investigators had been transferred to the capital from Saratov, Penza and Chelyabinsk, given rooms in a hostel and ordered to work. To seek out criminals who had embezzled money from the state. By creating a team formed entirely of strangers, the militia chiefs had intended to exclude the possibility of graft. After all, their local Moscow people were corrupt, fused inextricably into a system of relatives, friends and lucrative acquaintances. But the newcomers didn't know anyone, they had no family or friends here. And what's more, a provincial assigned to the capital works like a demon – if his efforts are appreciated he might just avoid being sent back to Penza!

And the result of all this was that I was now bearing the full brunt of their xenophobia and profound contempt for a pampered inhabitant of the pampered capital.

But I didn't let that bother me: I myself had only come to this city five years earlier – I was a newcomer, just like them. An alien. A visitor. The son of two teachers, raised in the country.

The atmosphere of the large, gloomy building found appropriate expression in their grimly abusive language. The monotonous drone of crude peasant obscenities filled the corridor and the office. As harsh as the blow of an axe against a tree, the slang grated on my ears and set my nerves on edge.

I estimated things were moving at a pretty mediocre pace, and I noted that down as their mistake. A guy like their newly apprehended suspect should have been made to talk quickly, no time wasted. Wham bam – and there's your client already providing evidence!

But no. They circled round me, taking my measure. Walked in and out of the room. One of them would come in, yell some crude insult at me, give me a kick and then disappear; another would reassure me, question me ingratiatingly, slap me on the shoulder, offer me a cigarette, but then also withdraw into one of the adjoining rooms; a third would come on all aggressive, a real brute, yelling and abusing me, a putrid stench belching from his mouth, and I could see that his teeth were rotten and his cheeks were covered with pimples.

The detectives spent a long time softening up their newly captured villain; too long. They ought to have broken me in half an hour. Subdued my will straight away. Gone for the Gestapo approach. Ties and white shirts. Clever, terrifying questions. A lamp in my face. No time to think or analyse what's going on. Who? Where? The circumstances? The facts! The truth! The real truth! Stick to the point!

But no – they wasted time, gave me a chance to observe, correlate and draw conclusions. And to figure out that the servants of the law knew a great deal about me, but not everything. Including what was most important.

I'm twenty-seven years old.

I'm a businessman. A banker. More precisely, the joint owner of a bank. Even more precisely, a junior partner. I'm rich. And I've just been arrested for misappropriating state funds.

My bank is a very small one, not many people have even heard about it, but – an important point – it is entirely independent and perfectly stable. In addition – and even more importantly – it is expanding rapidly. This bank sprang up out of nothing in about three years. My bank. My brainchild, my offspring, the meaning of my entire life, the devourer of my time and my nerves, a source of incredible profit. Its name doesn't appear on advertisement hoardings, those model types with wide mouths don't announce it to people from their TV screens. And thank God for that.

Of course, the principal of the entire business, the founder of the firm, the number one, is not me but someone else. My senior colleague, the boss, the chief. Mikhail Nikolaevich Moroz.

He was the one who agreed the terms for the transit of that cursed million dollars. I'm only a subordinate. A clerk. A technical operative. I was told what to do and I did it. Implemented the boss's decision.

They've picked up my boss Mikhail too. Today. Half an hour after me. Outside the door of our offices. I've gathered that from snatches of conversation. But they'll let my boss go. And my job is to do everything, absolutely everything, to make sure they do. To accept the burden of guilt.

Arrest, interrogation and possible imprisonment are an integral part of my work. And I perform this, as I do any other, to a high standard. My boss pays me for meeting my targets. He has already paid me a substantial round sum. And he will pay me more. My boss Mikhail is a lot richer than I am, he's a millionaire, in dollars, and he can easily afford the services of a specialist like me.

It's three years now since Mikhail and I met each other, talked and found that we held the same views on life and its values. We started working together. To our mutual benefit. My boss Mikhail looked for clients and he found them: people who wanted a tax haven for their money. And I helped him. I covered his back. I took care of the details. And prepared to answer to the full severity of the law some day, when the time came. After all, not paying your tithe into the state coffers is a criminal offence.

What was the threat I faced if we were caught or went bankrupt? Three years for non-payment of tax, a year or two for falsifying documents. But I'm no lowlife. I have no previous convictions. I have a good background. I'm a married man, with a young child. Under the right circumstances, I could actually get off with a suspended sentence. And that's chicken-feed. People go through worse things than that for money.

Perhaps there had been a time, many years ago, when I took decisions too hastily, thought too cynically, overestimated my own courage. But there's no point dwelling on that now. I've been in business for a long time, I'm stuck in it. And business doesn't recognise the provisions of Criminal Law.

The charge of embezzling from the state will be dropped, of course, and very quickly. After all, neither I nor my boss have stolen anything. Just imagine that one man buys something from another. He transfers the money, receives his goods and disappears. A year later it turns out that the money he transferred was stolen. He'd failed to mention that. Now he's on the run, it's the seller who's arrested as an accomplice.

Of course, some people might find it disturbing that the goods sold had a somewhat unusual appearance, being wads of green paper dollars, cash. In other words, all I did was to cash a bank draft. But that doesn't change the essence of the matter. I am prepared to face the full severity of the law for having put through an illegal transaction and issued paper banknotes to villains, thereby violating the legislation that applies to financial operations, currency exchange and taxation. But I will not allow myself to be branded an embezzler of state funds.

I'm no more immoral than a hundred thousand others just like me, young men doggedly keeping the wheels of business turning in the hot, cramped offices of Moscow. They may blithely disregard the state's stupid, antiquated rules for the game of business, but they will never resort to blatant theft. They don't want to take what belongs to others – what's important for them is to earn something of their own.

I'm not some ignorant son of a bitch who dreams of pocketing a bundle and then blowing it all in seedy dives. I'm a capitalist, do you understand that? I believe in the power of cash the way children believe in Santa Claus.

While I was running higgledy-piggledy through these disjointed arguments for the benefit of the excited sleuths, I realised they were all waiting for something. Whether they were laughing at me or abusing me; listening attentively or interrupting me in mid-word; joking in a way that was almost friendly or kicking the leg of my chair; slapping me on the shoulder or spewing out curses – these armed men in their cheap, down-at-heel shoes were clearly in no hurry to draw up any statements, inventories or other ominous documents. The top brass must be due to arrive, I guessed.

The arrest had taken place at about eight in the morning. Now my gold Longine watch showed almost ten. Just the right time for the senior ranks – the people everything depends on – to arrive.

Eventually, from somewhere far off in the distance, there came a heavy tramping of feet, a cry of 'Attention!' and then, less loudly, 'At ease!' In the corridor on the other side of the wall a large number of voices suddenly began talking excitedly, mingling together and drawing rapidly closer.

'The general's here,' one of the gumshoes said to no one in particular and stubbed out his cigarette.

The rather elderly man who entered the room with a firm, energetic stride roused my fellow feeling straight away. The jacket and tie, the cold gaze of those transparent eyes, the touch of grey in the hair, the severe curve of the dry lips, the magnificently moulded hands, that distinctive stoop of the high dignitary – everything indicated that he belonged to the caste of the masters of life. The police agents immediately readied themselves, adopting less casual poses and freezing in anticipation. One of them – the one who had shouted more crude abuse than the others – quickly dragged a chair across from the wall to the centre of the room and the high-ranking gent slowly sat down, crossing one leg over the other and displaying an excellent pair of summer shoes in light-coloured suede (my shoes cost at least three times as much). Then he shuffled his fingers and everyone except me left the room without speaking a word; the last one out closed the door carefully behind him.

The militia big daddy was as fresh as a currant bush in the morning dew. He exhaled the fragrance of eau de Cologne, which set him in striking contrast with his subordinates, who diffused into the atmosphere the mingled scents of potent male sweat and shoe polish. I concluded that the general must have sped on his way to work – straight through that muggy, humid Moscow August – in an air-conditioned automobile. Which meant he knew the taste of comfort. And that was good. That was potential common ground. I also loved and understood the pleasures of life. Perhaps I should offer him money immediately, straight from the off, while we were alone? No, it was too soon. First I should listen to everything he had to say. They might even let me go without any bribe. Surely this mature, respectable, reasonable-looking man, who was clearly very experienced, could not fail to understand that I hadn't stolen anything …

The general unhurriedly lit a cigarette. Through the veil of tobacco smoke I was studied, slowly and very attentively. The grey-haired big boss peered especially long and hard at my forehead, as if he were trying to read something on it.

'Well, pal,' this master of life finally enunciated in a pleasant, gentle baritone, 'you're in big trouble. You're in really deep shit. Say just one wrong word, and I'll have you banged up for ever. Do you understand me?'

'Yes,' I replied and made a gallant attempt to withstand the general's gaze. I failed.

'This case is being handled by the General Public Prosecutor's Office of Russia,' the militia boss enlightened me in a quiet voice. 'I report progress in the investigation to the government on a daily basis. Do you understand that too?'

'Yes …'

'That's good,' the grey-haired man said, nodding benevolently and recrossing his legs. 'It goes without saying that you didn't steal the money. It was stolen by someone high up, a high official. A minister. Not a federal minister, of course. Republican. From the provinces. But a minister nonetheless! He colluded with his own brother, who colluded with a distributor of pharmaceuticals. A huge sum of money was allocated. Supposedly for purchases. And then the pharmacist colluded with you. Is that right?'

'No,' I protested heatedly. 'It's not right. There was a pharmacist all right, but there wasn't any collusion!'

The general screwed up one eye.

I suddenly had the feeling once again that he was trying to read something written above the bridge of my nose – some kind of inscription on my suspect's forehead that had been concealed only a moment earlier, but now stood out in large, clear letters.

'So it *was* the pharmacist who came to you?'

'Yes,' I admitted in a quiet voice, after a pause.

Only it wasn't me he had come to.

I'd given the general the most important piece of information at the first time of asking, I'd named a name, blown the gaff – but I didn't feel any pangs of conscience at all. It was the man referred to only a moment earlier as the 'pharmacist' who had dropped us all in it – me, my boss and our business. He was the one who had embroiled us in this catastrophe by sending us *dirty* money. Why would I want to cover for him?

I had only seen the pharmacist twice. The first time we introduced ourselves: a handshake, a smile, an exchange of run-of-the-mill pleasantries. The second time I handed him a million US dollars in cash. All the other matters had been sorted and settled by my boss Mikhail.

Anyway, it wasn't my function to keep quiet. I could talk or not talk, but either way I had to achieve my goal. I had to lead all these sleuths, plain-clothes men, investigators, interrogators and generals as far away as possible from one simple question: exactly who was the head of my business.

Big daddy shrouded himself in yellowish-grey smoke again and his gaze turned sombre. That gaze gave me such a bad feeling I almost panicked. The sensation was something absolutely new: it was the first time in more than twenty-seven years of life that I had ever experienced genuine, intense, undisguised human contempt.

Up until that moment the emotions I had aroused in people had been quite different – and, for the most part, positive. Interest. Respect. Sometimes envy. People wanted to be friends with me. They took me as an example. At first in school. And then at university. And again in the army. And in the editorial office of a factory newspaper. And, of course, at the bank.

Year after year, ever since I was a child, I had been granted continuous proofs that I belonged to a superior breed, that mankind needed me no less than it needed air to breathe. And now this elderly gent, enveloped in his aura of invincible might, had made it clear that this just wasn't so.

It wasn't malice I read in his eyes – in that case they would have glinted. And it wasn't loathing – in that case his features would have been twisted into a grimace. No, what I saw was contempt in its pure form. As candid as a porn film.

And that was when I became a prisoner, when the instantaneous transition from one life to another occurred. The general put me behind bars with a single glance. At the moment he walked in, sat down on the chair, lit up and started to talk, I was still a free man, brought in on a misunderstanding. Now, having experienced the animosity of a man at the top, I realised that I was in way over my head: after my conversation with the grey-haired high priest of the militia, I wouldn't be going back to the office or home to my wife. I'd be going to a cell.

'Think,' the general said in a voice that suddenly sounded grating and old. 'You could go down for a long stretch. And so could your Misha.'

I turned cold. The general and his squad had a good chance of putting me away. But I had to keep Misha, my boss Mikhail Nikolaevich Moroz, safe at any price!

My boss Mikhail and I had agreed everything in advance. If things went as far as a criminal investigation, then I would declare at once, unflinchingly, that I was in control of the business. And the boss would be left out of things; he would keep our capital safe, take good care of it and use it to make my punishment as lenient as possible. To have me released, or get me a short sentence with every possible comfort. In other words, I kept him free and out of harm's way, and he looked after my money. Simple, elegant and effective.

Yes, I was proud of the fact that my boss Mikhail and I had foreseen every eventuality! Given serious thought to defining our precise roles. It was an indication of how highly organised our business was, and our business was worth it: in three years of unrelenting work it had earned both of us an entire fortune.

But if I didn't manage to get him off, we were done for, both of us.

Alarmed at a powerful trembling in my knees and my hands, I broke the silence:

'I beg your pardon, er …'

'General Zuev!'

'Comrade general!' I immediately exclaimed, pronouncing that universally familiar, magical word 'comrade' in a single, rapid breath, slurring the consonants – the way it's pronounced by men who have served their time in the armed forces, who have uttered the word innumerable times in the course of a single day: 'comrade lieutenant!', 'comrade major!', 'comrade warrant officer!'

Only someone who has carried an automatic rifle on his back and worn shoulder straps is capable of rapping out that short, vigorous 'comrade' and at the same time imbuing his tone of voice with the necessary reverence for a man of superior rank.

'Comrade general. This whole business is absurd! I didn't steal any money! I don't need to! I have enough to feed my wife and son! I'll pay a fine … Any amount …'

And so in a single hastily uttered phrase I managed to inform big daddy Zuev that the man facing him had served in the army (that is, he wasn't some kind of delicate namby-pamby weakling), that he was a family man (that is, he was reliable and prudent) and that he was prepared to pay for his freedom.

'Go on, go on,' the general said, observing me with interest.

I perked up a bit.

'This man … the one you call the "pharmacist" … he didn't say anything to me about his money being stolen!'

'Of course he didn't,' the grey-haired high priest agreed magnanimously. 'Why would he?'

'So you understand that I'm not guilty?' I exclaimed exultantly.

'We'll see about that …'

The price tag on my question was written in years of imprisonment. For putting through illegal financial operations I faced a three-year *suspended* sentence, but for thieving billions of roubles from the federal budget it would be ten years of *real time*. I started trembling even more violently.

'I can see you're a decent enough young guy,' the general told me approvingly, lighting up his third cigarette in ten minutes. 'I'll tell you what we'll do. The investigator will be here in a minute. You're going to dictate your testimony to him. In detail. Who, when, how, who with and so on. The investigator will take it all down. On the basis of the record of the interrogation I, as the head of the investigating team, will take a decision on your future. Is that clear.'

'Pretty much, yes.'

'Pretty much ...' the general said contemptuously, mocking me. 'Don't do anything stupid, son! The slightest hint of a lie or any attempt to deceive us – and you're finished. Completely. You'll vanish without trace. You'll be doing time for the rest of your life. And don't forget to sign the statement ...'

'The statement?' I echoed after a brief pause. 'No problem. But I'll need a lawyer.'

'He's already waiting for you,' General Zuev replied sternly. 'I repeat. Don't even think of lying, not a single word!'

'I promise,' I lied.

2

The same brutish sleuth who had positioned the general's chair for him a moment ago now clutched my elbow painfully with fingers of iron and led me out into the corridor.

I saw several bulky boxes lying on the worn linoleum on the floor. They were filled to the brim with bundles of all sorts of documents and floppy disks. Only yesterday both the documents and the disks had been my personal property, kept in my private room at the office.

They've searched the place, I realised. Everything's been confiscated! I had to give the foul-mouthed detectives their due, they moved fast … So there was no office any more. It had been pillaged. The documents had been removed. The computers had been sealed. The employees were in shock. No doubt they had all been interrogated. The firm's business activity was paralysed. Losses were guaranteed.

I pictured my assistants, the managers Semyon and Sergei, quiet young guys who worked the computers, standing facing the wall, with their arms held out and their feet spread wide – and I realised that something really bad was happening. Something categorically vile and nasty. When everything calmed down and they let me go, it would take me many weeks to put everything back together … And who would remunerate us for our losses? How was it possible to blitz a businessman's work place in such an offhand fashion? It was an outrage! I would complain …

They bring you, frightened but still struggling to keep your spirits up, to the investigative wing of the Lefortovo prison, and there you suddenly see your own papers. The documents that you personally drew up and signed with your own hand. In your absence, without your permission, they have all been packed tidily into neat boxes by some punctilious individual, so that they can be exhaustively analysed. You will be visited by strange feelings. You will sense that an important period of your life is coming to an end in this place; and in that infinitely brief moment of transition another, equally important twist in the spiral of fate is beginning; a page is being turned. Where is that fortunate man whose luck held out for so long? He has vanished, never to return.

I barely had time to cast a mournful sideways glance at my property before those iron fingers dragged me on further – through a door opened by a powerful blow of the hand into a poorly furnished room with bright rays of sunlight slanting across it from one side to the other. But despite the bright light, the room seemed unbearably gloomy to me. A good room for making full and frank confessions to all sorts of violations of the law, then leaving and forgetting everything that had happened, as if it had all been a terrible dream.

Squinting against the light, I made out two men who were obviously suffering from the heat. They both instantly turned their sweaty faces towards me. One of them was my lawyer, Maxim Stein – a young man inclined to corpulence with a mane of fiery-red hair and watery eyes that gave no indication whatever of even the slightest vestige of conscience.

Until that day I had only seen my lawyer once – when we were introduced. There had been three of us in the office at the time; my boss Mikhail was there too. In fact, he was the one who had arranged the meeting.

Any serious banker is always willing to buy – and does buy – information about himself. He doesn't have to go looking for it: at the right moment well-informed people appear of their own accord to inform him about possible police investigations.

And so my boss had received timely warning that his junior associate was wanted by the Public Prosecutor's Office. And he had promptly found an experienced defence lawyer. And arranged a consultation, with just the three of us.

Despite their more or less identical ages and backgrounds – all about thirty, all from the intelligentsia – the three individuals present behaved quite differently. The bankers were tormented by nervous tics: my cheek was twitching, while for Mikhail it was his shoulder and jaw; we both smoked incessantly, wrinkling up our foreheads and toying affectedly with our expensive cigarette lighters and fountain pens. Two guys with big bucks and big problems.

The lawyer, on the other hand, seemed complacent in the extreme, frequently stretching his plump cheeks into the cautious smile of a man who never lets the little things get him down.

'This is Andrei,' said Mikhail, indicating me with a jerk of his massive square-cut beard. 'Sort of my right hand. And my left. More like my left, you know, considering his range of duties. But my right hand too …'

'I get it, I get it,' Red said hastily, nodding as he adjusted the magnificently formed knot of his expensive tie. My tie cost at least three times as much.

My boss winced. He absolutely couldn't bear to be interrupted. Mikhail's interaction with other people always proceeded in the form of monologues (he was the boss, after all). The monologues always began awkwardly and inarticulately. But as his thought process picked up speed, the phrases he uttered became more well-rounded and intelligible.

'The moment they pick him up,' said Mikhail, jerking his beard in my direction again, 'you go to work. Swing – you know, into action. Spending whatever it takes. And when I say spending, I mean dosh, hard cash, as well as anything else it takes to get my man released from custody as rapidly as possible. Let me emphasise that: you will be obliged to take *every possible measure!*' The boss raised his voice emphatically: 'Complaints! Petitions! Phone calls from offices high up in the administration! Articles in the newspapers! Reporters with TV cameras! And so on, up to and including street demonstrations with people carrying placards and chanting slogans …'

Red cast a curious glance in my direction. Who was this kid he was supposed to knock himself out for? That keen curiosity, with a hint of zoological interest, stuck in my memory. Visitors to the zoo look in that timid but almost ecstatic way at a young beast striding energetically around its cramped cage, lashing its powerful tail to the right and left.

'But are you sure they're going to pick him up?' the lawyer asked.

'I've seen a copy of the resolution authorising his detention,' Mikhail growled. 'With my own eyes.'

Red paused and then asked:

'Maybe it will all blow over?'

The boss started breathing heavily through his nose. He had one significant shortcoming: he thought he was cleverer than all the other six – or however many it is – billion human beings in the world. He pressed his pale lips together and told the lawyer:

'Don't you try to calm my nerves. Don't! I graduated from Moscow University. I have a degree in psychology. I worked on the telephone helpline for a year. Calming the nerves of people who were suicidal ...'

The lawyer lowered his eyes.

'If I wanted, you know, to calm my nerves,' the boss said, still pressing his point, 'then I'd calm them down myself! You'd do better, Maxim, to calm him down.' Another jerk of the beard in my direction.

I suddenly felt annoyed. They were talking about me in my presence as if I wasn't even there.

'He was the one,' my boss said in a quiet voice, 'who oversaw the whole deal with that lousy million bucks. He drew up and signed the contract and the other documents ... It's him the Prosecutor's Office is really after, not me at all. Officially I'm nobody in this firm. But he's a marked man and they'll do him over good ...'

Maxim Stein suddenly demonstrated his resolve. He stood up and buttoned his jacket.

'I'll make enquiries about your case immediately,' he said dryly. 'I have contacts of my own. I'll consult my senior colleagues. I'll check the literature. This evening I'll be ready for a second, more detailed discussion. But for now permit me to take my leave ...'

'He's gone running off to think it over,' I suggested when the red-headed lawyer had gone, pulling the steel door closed behind him with an effort.

'Yes,' Mikhail agreed. 'Looks like he's sort of ... scared ...'

'We shouldn't have talked *here* ...'

The walls in our basement were peeling, the floor was chipped and the furniture was cheap and threadbare. But standing in a neat row along one wall there were four Magner bill-counting machines, the latest model, carefully protected by plastic covers, and beside another wall there were two document shredders. Each of them could reduce the Sunday edition of the *Kommersant* newspaper to fine confetti in a second (I'd checked). There were two huge TV monitors blinking beside the door, with switchers linked to sixteen video cameras watching the exterior of the premises. The steel door with its titanium reinforcing strip around the edge weighed two hundred and fifty kilograms. Nestling against the wall across the room from the door was a safe that weighed three times as much. It had been hauled in by four porters on a special trolley with a hydraulic lifting mechanism. The entire operation had cost about the same as three pairs of my shoes. After all, we'd had to pay the men afterwards to make sure they kept their mouths shut.

In a place like this, conversations about the theft of a million dollars were bound to start a well-informed man, even a criminal lawyer, thinking, if they didn't actually frighten him. Maybe it wasn't really worth taking the risk?

'I don't think he realised who I am.'

The boss snorted.

'Do you even realise who you are?'

'Of course! I'm a promising young Russian entrepreneur. A financier. A smooth operator. And apart from that, I'm the one who covers your ass.'

Mikhail looked at me without smiling. We were friends, but our friendship had developed as a relationship between two intelligent and serious people. There was no place for backslapping bonhomie. Especially at work.

'All right,' the boss said with a nod. 'But when you explain yourself to the militia, don't tell them you're a smooth operator. And don't mention my ass either. Focus on the fact that you're a financier and a ... what was it? ... a young, inexperienced one.'

'Promising!' I corrected him.

'Yes, and say that too.'

That was the way we joked with each other in the middle of the summer of 1996, when we knew the hunt for us was already on.

Here's a simple story. Two young dudes who didn't know each other came to the biggest city in the country to study. They were both lucky. They became students at the best university in the world. But during the last ten years of the millennium everything in their country was turned upside down. The once prestigious professions in the so-called humanities – including those of psychologist and journalist – no longer guaranteed even a crust of bread on the table, let alone any level of material comfort. With the decisiveness typical of both of them, the young men abandoned the careers they had studied for and started casting around for new areas in which to apply their energies.

What else could you do? Only yesterday you were a final-year student, a sportsman, a scholar and a joker, the boyfriend of a beautiful girl with soft, wavy hair, and today some crop-headed prick gets your girlfriend into his car with tinted windows and drives her off to a restaurant.

Basically though, the desire to get rich was stronger than the desire to copulate. But then, the former guaranteed the latter.

In the course of an almighty, relentless piss-up – you could call it a student gathering, except that almost everyone there was intending to give up their studies – the two young guys, Mikhail and Andrei, told each other similar stories about their girls who had given them the elbow for crop-headed rivals with tinted windows. They took a liking to each other. Mikhail's outlook seemed very jaundiced to Andrei, but Andrei put that shortcoming down to his new friend's age. Mikhail was older than he was. At twenty-two it's still okay not to have gainful employment, social status or a decent pair of trousers, but at twenty-six the doubts have already started gnawing. Who am I? What have I made of myself? What have I achieved? Those cursed questions, those remorseless blades of steel slashing away at your youthful self-esteem.

Andrei understood Mikhail and Mikhail understood Andrei. And both of them wanted a better deal from life, a deal that reflected adequately the effort, energy and talent they'd invested.

What exactly was it that Andrei and Mikhail wanted?

What did all of us – students, young men with brilliant degrees and holes in our shabby sweaters – want back then, in '91?

Everything, and right now.

Success. Victory. Advancement. Self-realisation on an absolute scale. Honour. Glory. Status. And money.

We wanted to make names for ourselves. To make mankind happy. To improve the universe. To convert our personal genius into evidence of its reality. To discover the secret formula that would guarantee happiness to everyone. To win a Nobel Prize for it, an Oscar, a Booker, a Pulitzer. And money.

We wanted women, cars, fine cognacs. We wanted adventures, fights, journeys to the edge. Risk. Devious stratagems. Success. And money.

We wanted to set the entire planet down in front of us like a hot, bloody steak, carve it up and devour it.

With wine.

Anyone who wasn't at least a bit of a megalomaniac at the age of twenty would be no one at the age of thirty.

And we didn't try to see any further than that.

Our gang of half-wild provincials had almost conquered the capital – we had swept straight into its best university. Obviously, things would go on like that. Onwards and upwards, ever upwards! Climbing further, without ever doubting or faltering. Never taking it easy, never sleeping or applying the brakes …

Neither Andrei nor Mikhail – for all their degrees, their highly trained intellects and bodies – had any clue about what to do or how to do it. Then one day Mikhail came up with an idea.

He asked Andrei to be his partner, and he started buying and selling money.

Three years of unrelenting effort were spent on establishing the business and acquiring experience.

Then some things started going right. Then, with a crash and a jangle, they were in profit. Then everything expanded. Then their circle of contacts changed, the number of enquiries increased; then they had expensive timepieces adorning their wrists; then the profits became super-profits, and their protruding Adam's apples were drenched in the very finest of fragrances; and then it seemed like ANYTHING WAS POSSIBLE; and everything except money – free time, wives and children, friends, holidays, health, interests, hobbies – was put on the back burner, and in grateful response the money multiplied, growing and expanding: all they had to do now was stay right there beside it all the time to monitor and manage it …

And now this finely tuned business might crumble, get sluiced down the tubes. What else could Mikhail and Andrei do but crack sombre jokes?

From a distance of four paces, the second man in the interrogation room looked like an apprentice pensioner. He was dressed in a heavy-duty checked shirt and trousers that were badly worn but perfectly clean and painstakingly pressed. His forehead was cut across from side by side by deep wrinkles. He had a massive pair of black-framed spectacles with large bifocal lenses perched firmly on his nose.

As I got closer, however, I saw that this wrinkle-faced four-eyes was only forty years old at most, and the premature wilting of his complexion was obviously the result of a sedentary lifestyle.

Standing on the table in front of the man in checks was a portable computer, with a portable printer beside it. A sheet of paper was already set in the printer. Nestling innocently between the two devices was a skinny-looking document folder, light-grey and well-thumbed round the edges.

Eight letters printed on the cardboard in bold black type conveyed an ominously terse message:

CASE FILE

The words were followed by a long string of digits.

I reached into my pocket, took out a handkerchief and mopped up the heavy sweat that had broken out on my forehead.

'Oh! Hi there!' the prematurely wilted individual greeted me in a calm, friendly voice, pointing his thick lenses towards me. 'So you must be Andrei, right?'

I gave a cautious nod.

'And I'm an investigator from the General, you know, Prosecutor's Office. Your investigator.'

'Mine?' I echoed.

'Yes, yours. My name's Khvatov, Stepan Mikhailovich Khvatov. I'll be working with you.'

Khvatov, from the verb *khvatat*, 'to catch', I thought bitterly. Excellent. You used to have your own driver and masseur, and now you've got your own investigator. And he's called 'Catcher'. Who was it your distant ancestor used to catch, dear Mr Khvatov? People just like me, no doubt.

'You don't need to work with him,' my lawyer said in a tone that sounded calm but determined, giving me a wink of encouragement. 'All you need to do is question him and release him! Nothing else! Let's get started, so as not to waste the man's time! He has a business to run! A lot of work to get through. He's already lost almost half a day thanks to you.'

'That's fine by me,' four-eyes replied, quick as a flash, and gestured to me invitingly. 'Have a seat ...'

He pointed to a stool that was anchored to the floor beside the desk so that it couldn't move. I sat down, sideways on to him.

Every banker knows that when you question someone, you make him sit in profile to the man in charge. It's a psychological trick. Seated sideways on, the client feels awkward, he's forced to move, to twist his body; it's harder for him to concentrate and, consequently, to mislead his questioner.

But as I sat there at that badly scratched desk in that poorly furnished room with the high ceiling, wriggling my skinny but firm backside around on the stool set into the floor, facing an investigator from the General Public Prosecutor's Office in the interrogation room at the Lefortovo pre-trial prison – I was intending to lie.

'It's hot in this Moscow of yours,' the investigator complained unexpectedly. 'And noisy. Very noisy …'

'It's not my Moscow,' I snapped back. 'I'm not even registered to live here …'

'How about you,' Khvatov asked, turning his thick lenses towards the lawyer, 'are you from out of town too?'

The red-headed advocate gave a dignified shrug.

'Not me. I'm a native Muscovite. Third generation.'

'So how come you live here without, you know, a certificate of domicile?' the man in checks asked in surprise, training his specs on me again. 'Hasn't anyone ever checked your documents?'

'Many times,' I replied amicably. 'But I give them money and they let me go. I'm not greedy. I always pay the going rate. And just like you, I'm not very fond of Muscovites … Where would you be from, Stepan Mikhailovich?'

'Ryazan.'

'Well, would you believe it!' I exclaimed. 'Ryazan! Why, we're almost neighbours!'

The investigator squinted at me distrustfully.

'Neighbours?'

'Practically. The Severno-Prudsky District,' I said, referring to myself. 'Down at the south end of the Moscow Region. It used to be part of the Ryazan Region. That's where I grew up …'

In informing the man with the wrinkled forehead that he and I both came from the same social group – provincials, in other words – I'd been counting on gaining his sympathy, and I was clearly not mistaken. Now not only General Zuev but the investigator too knew that I was prepared to pay for my freedom. At the going rate. To celebrate my first little victory, I lit up a cigarette.

'The boss told me,' Khvatov began, fastidiously pushing towards me a little cardboard ashtray exactly like the ones I'd seen in the office next door, 'that you're ready, you know, to provide testimony …'

'Quite correct,' I replied hurriedly, shaking the ash off my menthol light. 'Honest and exhaustive testimony! I testify, and then I immediately leave this sinister institution of yours.'

'Did the general promise you that?' the man in checks enquired cautiously.

'In person.'

The investigator became thoughtful. He opened the CASE FILE, glanced into it, leafed through a few pages, tapped his fingers on the keyboard and sighed.

'I see. Right then, let's get started. A great deal depends on your, you know, testimony … You're a suspect. If you prevaricate or try to lie, we'll put you in a cell …'

'Just a moment!' exclaimed Red, leaping up off his chair and charging into the fray. 'What do you mean, a cell? That's psychological pressure! A threat! My client is an honest man! He pays his taxes! He creates jobs! He's a banker! And banks are the circulatory system of the economy! After questioning he'll be going home in any case!'

Khvatov smiled.

'And what if he, you know, makes a full and frank confession?'

'To what?' the lawyer and I both bawled simultaneously.

'To embezzlement.'

'There wasn't any embezzlement!'

'Yes there was,' the man from Ryazan retorted, turning his thick lenses on me again. 'The stolen money passed through an organisation, you know, under your personal control, Andrei. We've already assembled a body of evidence. Payment instructions. Bank statements. Other documents. Documents, you know, with your signature on them …'

'Show me!' Red demanded rudely.

The investigator frowned.

'In good time we will, you know, produce all the documents for you … Under the established procedure.'

'Why drag things out? Let's solve this problem right here and now!' The lawyer sat down again. He was smiling, but he articulated his words with great emphasis. 'It is quite obvious to me and my client that there has been some kind of misunderstanding. Let's just clear it up, shake hands and all go home!'

'He knows his job,' I thought, mentally praising Maxim, and with him my far-sighted boss, who hadn't found me some white-headed old man but an energetic young guy who went at his job hard. But things still didn't look too good for me. After all, I wasn't the most law-abiding of citizens. I'd had my hand in the cookie jar. I'd put through plenty of illegal financial deals. Faked other people's signatures. Drawn up fictitious documents. Involved numerous other people in this improper activity. The man from Ryazan with the powerful specs was clearly no ignorant beginner. In two shakes he'd have me fitted up for tax evasion, forging documents, and maybe something else as well …

Suddenly I felt a cold, prickly sensation spreading rapidly through my chest. The jacket that had cost so much no longer kept me warm, and the exclusive printed silk shirt no longer held in the smell of body odour escaping from its collar. The feeling of anguish and shame was simply too strong – I just wanted to get up and run away from that terrible place. And never break the law again. Work for a fixed salary, raise my son, stay cheerful and serene, forget my ambitious dreams forever and never look around me – so that I wouldn't see those who *had* managed to satisfy their ambition …

But my repentance lacked any substantial impetus. Its energy was drained completely in a few brief moments. I gritted my teeth, dabbed at my tense features once again with the crumpled handkerchief and forced myself to remember that the most important thing in my life now was money.

'Okay, you shit, calm down,' I told myself. 'Put on a smile, don't drag so greedily on your cigarette. And sit up straight!'

'Do you know, Mr Investigator, what is the most important condition for the brain to function properly?'

'No,' Khvatov replied cautiously, 'what is it?'

'An erect spinal column.'

The investigator involuntarily straightened his back and squared his shoulders.

That's my favourite joke, one I thought up myself; it has always helped me take control of a conversation, even put a bit of psychological pressure on the other person, whoever he might be. Seeing this move work even here and now, during my interrogation in the terrible, legendary Lefortovo prison, made me feel almost cheerful and lent me strength.

'How are we going to proceed with this, you know, conversation?' Khvatov asked after a brief pause. 'How are you going to provide your testimony? In the form of questions and answers?'

'I need to think about that,' I replied.

'Think then,' the investigator said generously and began tapping his fingers on the keyboard. 'Only don't take too long. And meanwhile we'll clarify your, you know, biographical details …'

The twenty-seven years of my life fitted into five minutes. I was born. I finished school. Worked on a construction site. Went to university. Served my time in the army. Left university. Got married. Went into business. Chose the financial market as my field of business activity …

Now at last the moment had arrived when I ought to mention the boss. After all, it was Misha Moroz who had involved me in the aforementioned financial market, damn him. It was my boss Mikhail who had taught me everything I knew. Shown me what to do and how. Explained the rules. Taken me on as the co-owner of a profitable enterprise. Lent me money. Transformed me from a half-baked, indigent nitwit to a high-flying Moscow yuppy.

I tensed up. My throat went dry. The delicate muscles in my groin started twitching. It was my body's way of protesting against the deception that was being perpetrated. It had activated its self-defence system. I had to summon up every last ounce of self-control.

Every moment of truth was matched by its own moment of falsehood. There was a critical point. A threshold had to be crossed. And I stepped across it. I said nothing about the man who ought to have been sitting there, sideways on, on that hard stool, instead of me.

'In 1993' – I coughed to clear my throat and took a deep drag of foul smoke – 'I … that is, I set up a financial company. It engaged in operations on the stock market. Now, three years later, the company is in the process of reorganisation. Transformation into a genuine commercial bank …'

'Are you the sole, you know, owner?'

'Naturally,' I responded impressively, swallowing more smoke.

'And what functions,' the man in checks droned monotonously, 'are performed in your, you know, structure by Mikhail Moroz?'

I managed to raise my eyebrows in a very natural fashion and turned towards the lawyer, who backed me up splendidly with a bewildered shrug of his shoulders.

'What has he got to do with anything?' I asked.

There's nothing in the world more repulsive and disgusting than telling a deliberate lie, and at first I felt constrained and awkward. I was afraid my hands would start shaking or sweat would start streaming down my temples. But it was absolutely sweltering in that room and all three of us – me, Red, and the wrinkly, native son of Ryazan – were sweating copiously, clutching our handkerchiefs in our hands and using them to mop our soaking foreheads and necks as we gasped for breath. That was my salvation – I disguised my increasing agitation with small, rapid movements of my hands, crumpled up the damp scrap of cloth in my fist, crushed my cigarette into the bottom of the ashtray, took another one out of the pack, lit up and exchanged eloquent glances with the lawyer, realising in horrified relief that now there was no way back. The most important thing had already been done. The boss had been kept out of danger.

People study the technique of interrogation for years. In special militia schools. It's taught like a complex science. The students have to take tests and they're given marks. And the discipline is constantly being advanced by quite brilliant minds.

People accused or suspected of crimes, naïve criminals and harebrained lowlifes, have no way of resisting scientific methods. They haven't created their own science of resistance. Where would you start? How you should behave? How you should listen to the questions and formulate your answers? What your facial expressions should be like? Your gestures? Your posture? Your tone of voice?

'Answer the question, Andrei,' said the investigator.

I shrugged and spread my hands:

'Well, Mikhail Moroz is my employee ... A kind of office supplies manager. Why, has he been arrested too?'

'Yes.'

I feigned amused surprise and slapped myself on the knee.

'But that's plain stupid! My subordinates have absolutely nothing to do with all this! What grounds do you have for dragging totally innocent people into prison? Misha Moroz buys faxes and photocopiers for my bank! Office equipment! That's the only job he does!'

Khvatov spread his own hands peaceably.

'If that's true, we'll release him. And now let's move on to the embezzlement ...'

The red-headed lawyer leapt to his feet and opened his mouth to protest indignantly, but I stopped him with a wave of my hand and snapped haughtily:

'I repeat! I know nothing about any embezzlement! I do not engage in stealing money from the state treasury. I do not like that kind of business! The risks are too high and the moral damage is too great! Do I make myself clear?'

The investigator nodded coolly. He gave the impression of being an exceptionally well-balanced individual.

You'll never fit me up for embezzlement,' I continued, raising my head proudly. 'For the simple reason that I didn't do it! That would have been clear to any man of intelligence after three minutes of conversation. Instead of arresting me and my subordinates and plundering the private office that I don't even let the cleaning lady into, you could simply have come to the company's premises and asked me your questions there ...'

'Your office is *your* office,' Khvatov declared sententiously. 'And my office is *my* office ...'

He glanced round the walls with a satisfied expression to show me that he was quite content with his workplace. Although to my mind, there was absolutely nothing to be proud of. A safe from the late Brezhnev period, a windowsill with peeling paint, a warped door, dirty linoleum, windows that needed washing, and specks of dust suspended in the air, gleaming silver in the shafts of sunlight – it all looked rather pitiful.

'By the way, about your private office,' the man from Ryazan said. 'During the, you know, search there, they confiscated the keys and documents for three cars. All registered in your name. But they didn't find your driving licence anywhere.'

'Do you mean,' I asked in a low voice, 'that you opened my safe?'

'Naturally,' the investigator replied with a shrug. 'We're, you know, obliged to open it, so we did.'

The safe had cost twice as much as a house in the town of Ryazan and I felt angry and upset that it had been opened in only a few hours! The people who sold me the steel monster had guaranteed that it was absolutely impossible to break into. I'll call them today and raise hell, I decided. I'll demand my money back.

'You had no right to open the safe,' I declared. 'I'll submit a complaint.'

'Four,' Red put in.

'Yes, of course,' Khvatov said, nodding absentmindedly. 'But I was talking about something else. We didn't find your driving licence.'

'That's right,' I said with a nod. 'I haven't got one.'

'Then how did you, you know, drive about?'

'I just did,' I said with a nonchalant chuckle. 'Without any licence. If anybody stopped me, I paid the going rate. I told you, I'm not greedy. And I know what the rate is. And apart from that, I have my own driver.'

'Where is he at the moment?' the man in checks asked quickly.

'I won't tell you,' I parried in delight. 'Or you'll arrest him, like my office supplies manager …'

My boss Mikhail and I had made up the story of the 'office supplies manager' together, two weeks before my arrest. After a couple of glasses of Chivas Regal. It had a good ring to it: 'Moroz the manager'. We'd drawn up a back-dated contract of employment and a labour book, and a salary statement and a pass with an official seal and a photograph.

'Don't worry,' the investigator said compassionately. 'Your office supplies manager won't come to any harm. Although we have information that he was involved in the embezzlement too …'

I suddenly felt numb, but I forced my lips to stretch out into a smile.

'It would be interesting to take a look … at your information …'

The investigator cautiously lowered his bony hand on to the folder and stroked it.

I felt a sudden urge to offer him top dollar if he would allow me just to leaf through the materials of that CASE FILE. But I thought better of it. Instead I slapped my hand down on the table.

'To hell with the office supplies manager! I'll hire another one. Let's stop wasting time! At five o'clock today I have an extremely important business meeting, so let's get a move on …'

'It's a pleasure to work with you,' Khvatov declared thoughtfully. 'And what exactly was it, you know, that your financial company did?'

'My financial company,' I replied, 'engaged in operations on the financial market.'

The investigator took this scoffing riposte exceedingly calmly.

'Then that's what we'll write,' he muttered as he tapped on the keys. 'What kind of operations exactly?'

'Mostly buying and selling securities – stocks and shares, bonds and bills of exchange. On the exchange and the secondary market.'

'And in more detail?'

'Detailed information,' I replied rudely, 'is insider information. A commercial secret. Not to be divulged under any circumstances!'

'All right.' Khvatov nodded. 'And what about exporting, you know, capital? Converting funds into cash? Sheltering money from taxes?'

'There was some of that too,' I admitted imperturbably and mopped my wet neck again. 'I inhabit a competitive environment. In order to survive, I'm obliged to offer any client a complete range of services, even some that are not entirely legal.'

'That is to say,' the man in checks said provocatively, pursuing his point, 'that anybody could have sent you a bank draft, and in exchange taken, you know, the money in cash.'

'Not just "anybody". I wouldn't have spoken to just "anybody". I only work within my own circle.'

'Then that means,' said Khvatov, squinting at me, 'that you have a distinct circle of clients, all entrepreneurs, to whom you regularly, you know, provide illegal financial services?'

'Outrageous,' the lawyer laughed. 'What kind of question is that? That's an assertion!'

'Never mind,' I said with noble condescension. 'It's okay. I'll dictate my reply, slowly. In the initial stages of my business activity, about two years ago, I occasionally, in exceptional cases, provided the aforementioned services to two or three individuals. I don't remember the details of the deals any longer …'

The lawyer started squirming, but I didn't look in his direction.

Sooner or later I was going to say what they wanted. General Zuev had already got me to that point an hour earlier, in the room next door.

Yes, there had been a certain man, a dealer in pharmaceuticals, with features that possessed an agreeable Semitic charm, and yes, he had asked me to provide a service; he had transferred several billion roubles from the account of a small pharmaceutical company that no one has ever heard of, and asked me to convert those roubles into American dollars and transfer them to several European banks. In Latvia and Austria. And hand him half a million in cash. And that was what I had done, retaining my commission.

According to the law, I was obliged to pay substantial taxes on an operation like that. But I hadn't paid them. And the punishment stipulated for that by the Criminal Code was three years' imprisonment. I was prepared for that. The money was more important. I'd do a year at most, then I'd be released early. For good behaviour, as they say. Throughout that year the boss would keep my job open for me. I'd go back to a chair with the imprint of my backside still warm on it, to my own desk, to the steering wheel of the air-conditioned automobile with the big wheels. I'd go back to the saunas, the restaurants, the jacuzzis, I'd dive into the glasses of fine liqueurs, jump into the Kenzo trousers and Lloyd shoes, and start living my old life again. The logic of it seemed extremely simple to me.

My way of thinking was probably immoral. But I hadn't always sat on a soft seat in an expensive set of wheels. When I moved here to the capital of the Empire, I started from nothing. I used to spend the night on friends' floors and eat macaroni with margarine. In five years I travelled thousands of kilometres in the capital's metro system. I could remember the day when the old women first appeared in the underground pedestrian crossings, weeping and holding out their begging bowls in their wrinkled hands.

They appeared as soon as the communist leaders were overthrown. And they'd never gone away again. They were still there.

'Better to suffer for one year, while you're still young, than for twenty years in your old age,' I thought to myself one day, as I dropped yet another coin into a trembling palm. 'Better to cut loose and take a risk, but at least secure yourself and your parents and your children against poverty. Even if you end up in prison, it's still better than a poor and hungry old age … Damn it all. God forbid.'

Then I gave the investigator Khvatov a long and wordy explanation of what a powerful businessman and all-round great guy I was. And after that I started holding forth about money, about family, about politics, about the law and justice – about everything in the world, anything at all in order to bury the subject of the 'office supplies manager Moroz' as deep as possible. I lied convincingly and eloquently, embellishing my blather with figures, details and proverbial sayings like 'the deeper you go into the forest, the closer your own shirt is to your back'. I gesticulated, smiled and lowered my eyes diplomatically. I put everything I had into half an hour of the very finest dissimulation of my entire life.

But the man in checks was absolutely unaffected by my flamboyant monologue – right in the very middle of it he suddenly stood up, excused himself and went out. The same uncouth detective from earlier immediately appeared in the doorway. He folded his arms across his chest and watched in silence as the lawyer leaned his head down to mine and whispered fervently:

'Don't worry about a thing! From what I've seen, they don't have anything on you. No proof. But the law allows them to hold you for a full thirty days without bringing any charges …'

'Thirty days!' I exclaimed in despair. 'A whole month! What about my business? It's a disaster! Everything will collapse! I can't be away for thirty days! Go and cut a deal, think of something!'

The lawyer only shook his head sadly in reply. I swore as foully as I could.

'By the way,' Red asked quietly, 'are you familiar at all with the specifics of criminal case procedure?'

'In general terms,' I muttered. 'As far as I'm aware, they're obliged to serve me with an official indictment signed by a public prosecutor. And at the time they select the "restraining measure". That will either be a written undertaking not to leave the area, that is, I wander about free but show up for questioning when I'm subpoenaed; or the other thing – arrest and imprisonment: I sit in prison and they bring me to the investigator from my cell …'

The lawyer tugged on the cuffs of his shirt. My shirt cost about seven times as much.

'Not actually in prison,' he corrected me, 'in the pre-trial detention centre.'

'So what's the difference?'

'To be honest, none,' Red admitted. 'None at all.'

'So I sit in prison for thirty days, and then they charge me?'

'Yes.'

'Aha!' I chortled, feeling relieved. 'But I'm not guilty of embezzling state funds! There's no proof and there won't be any. All they'll be able to accuse me of is tax evasion. That's a low tariff offence! Three years. They're hardly likely to keep someone accused of that in solitary confinement!'

'You're right.'

The lawyer's face and hands were very white, covered with a thick sprinkling of freckles.

'Thirty days!' I exclaimed, suddenly horrified again. 'A month! In that time my business will collapse! The clients will all go running to the competition! I'll suffer losses!'

'We'll sue them,' Red suggested.

'Who?'

'The Public Prosecutor's Office.'

'I'm going to bring an action against the General Public Prosecutor's

Office of Russia? That's absurd.'

'You're probably right again.'

'Thirty days in prison,' I thought bitterly. 'For what? So much for a fair trial!'

I was burdened with a shortcoming similar to my boss's: I assumed I was the brainiest of all the six – or however many there are – billion human beings in existence. And so I felt ashamed to have to ask the next question:

'But isn't it the court that decides where I'm going to spend the entire period of the investigation – behind bars or at liberty?'

The lawyer smiled sadly.

'Unfortunately, in this matter our Russian jurisprudence … how shall I put it …'

'Is a shambles.'

'Basically, yes.' Red wiped the sweat from his forehead again. Nowadays they put people in pre-trial detention on the prosecutor's say-so. And the suspect waits years for his fate to be decided. A man can spend a year or two inside while the investigation is going on, and another year or even two until he hears the verdict on his case. The courts are overcrowded, there's a queue. There are too many people waiting to be tried. Not enough judges. They say they're going to make changes to the law soon. But that won't affect you and me. You'll be deprived of your freedom by a bureaucrat at the Public Prosecutor's Office, not by a court. And the prosecutor will act to suit *his own convenience*. He'll compose a little resolution saying that if you were at liberty, you might abscond and jump bail …'

'I have a business!' I cried. The detective at the door started and shifted his pose. 'I have a family! A child! An old mother! Where am I going to run to?'

Red raised his open hand.

'And apart from that, if you're at liberty you might bring pressure to bear on witnesses and hinder the investigation. I'm only quoting the official formulations …'

I started snarling indistinctly in my frustration, but managed to get a grip and ask hoarsely:

'So what am I looking at?'

'For now – one month.'

'And then?'

'They'll release you,' Maxim said confidently. 'They'll hang a charge of tax evasion on you, give you a three-year suspended sentence, and that will be the end of it …'

'All right. If it's a month, so be it. I can do that.'

I turned my face away and pressed hard several times on my eyeballs with one thumb and forefinger so that they would turn red and my eyelids would swell up bit. When Khvatov came back, I immediately complained that I was feeling tired and unwell and tactfully requested him to end the conversation.

'Very well,' the wrinkle-faced four-eyes said with a nod that was almost indifferent, 'we'll carry on tomorrow. And now, I'm sorry but we have to, you know, register you both …'

'Both?'

'You and your office supplies manager,' the man in checks explained in a humdrum tone of voice. 'Under the terms of the Presidential Decree on measures to combat organised crime and, you know, racketeering, we're detaining both of you temporarily for thirty days!'

'Why detain my office supplies manager?'

'Just for company.'

I stood up.

'So you're going to jail us, then?' I asked after a pause, feeling my final faint hope shredding away to nothing at a point somewhere just below and to the right of my heart.

'Yes, we are,' Khvatov said in his humdrum voice.

'That's not legal!' my lawyer cried belligerently, also rising to his feet. 'I shall lodge a complaint. Today. And not just one.'

'That's your right,' Khvatov replied, almost yawning. 'Don't let it bother you, Andrei. While you're inside you'll catch up on your sleep, get some rest …'

'Tonight, Mr Investigator,' I declared darkly, 'you're going to suffer terrible nightmares. You're putting an innocent man in jail!'

'I sleep badly here anyway, Moscow's such an awful place,' the man in checks laughed. 'It's much too, you know, noisy ... Cars honking their horns ... But tonight you just think about maybe providing some genuine testimony. With details. So far you've said no more than a few words about the real substance of the case ...'

'Please don't take this the wrong way,' I protested with aplomb, 'but I have a business. All sorts of things happen in my office, just as they do in yours.'

'I repeat,' Khvatov said resentfully, 'let's not get your office and mine confused!'

'My office,' I continued, 'has been visited by some people I'll never tell anybody about. During any interrogation. In your office or any other. If I do, they'll have a skewer through my guts pronto. Even in a cell, even in a prison camp barracks. That's the way my life is. Sometimes the cheap option is to do the time ...'

They led me off to start doing just that.

In those days there were terrible stories circulating about businessmen who ended up in 'places of confinement'. It was said that the criminal community did not take kindly to men of commerce. It was said that the criminal world – well organised and closely knit in its beliefs and customs – regarded these new people with great hostility. It was said that entrepreneurs were beaten and humiliated, their food and clothes taken away from them. It was said that a rich man who ended up behind bars, in the company of thieves, murderers and rapists, was surrounded by an atmosphere of universal malevolence; that he was constantly showered with insults, despised and shunned.

But then, at various different times they used to say the same things about militiamen who were sentenced to jail, and about deserters from the army, and about foreigners.

On the whole, as I strode along between two stalwart detectives into the depths of the Lefortovo fortress, I wasn't really feeling all that nervous. If it came down to it, I had dollars on my side! And my lawyer! And my boss! And my influential friends! And finally, *I* was on my own side – sinewy, artful, intelligent, decisive, one of a kind. A poor student who in a few short years had risen to unimaginable heights, to contracts worth millions. A prosperous self-made man. Prison? Bring it on: the cell, the detention centre, the penal colony, the prison camp, hard labour – bring it all on.

I did the most important thing in the world – I made money. And to do that I'd slice through any prison like a knife through butter.

3

I'd begun thinking seriously about prison a long time before. Not exactly since I was a child, but even then I'd been drawn to the idea. An institution with bars on its windows seemed to me like the most terrible place in the world, and the fear of it excited me.

I spent my childhood years in the blissful, daisy-strewn meadow of the Land of Soviets. Within its boundaries criminality had been conquered physically, ethically and morally. If some fools robbed a savings bank somewhere in the remote provinces, it was regarded as an exceptional event, measured on the scale of the Empire as a whole. Of course, the newspapers said nothing – but all the top men in the militia, the departments of state security and civil authorities in the area where the act of gangsterism had occurred immediately lost their jobs.

When two brothers by the name of Grach organised a group of criminals, got hold of a sub-machine gun and used it to kill a militiaman, it caused a sensation. They even made a movie about the unprecedented incident.

Totalitarian regimes exterminate all serious criminal activity, not to mention organised crime. Mussolini eradicated the entire Sicilian mafia in a couple of years – a fact well known to historians.

The leaders of the Land of Soviets took a similar approach. With the cunning appropriate to genuine Byzantines, they decided to keep their subjects in complete ignorance of criminals and their whereabouts. The official line was that crime had been liquidated. With painstaking thoroughness, a culture completely free of the criminal *idea* was inculcated. The heroes of books and films, radio dramas and theatrical productions were honest, entirely positive characters: men and women with no inclination toward shady enterprise. And the criminal world was depicted as inhabited by a few handfuls of totally inept, profoundly miserable troglodytes, with every second one of them dreaming of being transformed into a respectable member of society.

During the holidays the city children went to stay with their grannies in the country while I, as a country boy, travelled in the opposite direction. From the sweltering heat and dust into the cool, into the city, to civilisation. Ten cinemas, three sports stadiums, a library with a reading hall, a 'park of culture' and, right in the middle of all this magnificence – my granny's spacious flat, with windows overlooking a quiet courtyard. In the yard, a plaster ballerina; and on granny's bookshelves, ten yellow volumes of the *Children's Encyclopedia*, the 1958 edition. I could read the volume entitled *Science and Technology*, but I preferred *The Seas and Oceans*. And afterwards I used to get on my bike and go dashing to the cinema, to study the 'Coming Attractions' poster, eat an ice cream that cost me seven kopecks, race around the courtyards to my heart's content and come back to the seas and the oceans. And every day was like that.

That boy experienced happiness as something enduring.

Only we're not talking about the seas and oceans, but prison and criminals.

It was in the town, during my summer holidays, that I saw them for the first time. Every centre of population in my country had special places – beside the door of the wine shop and behind the stalls where people returned empty bottle and jars – filthy, trampled little patches of ground where the most degraded citizens gathered in groups, squabbling and scrounging small change from each other. One day the happy youngster clutching his ice cream saw some unusual people at one of these places. Loud and pushy, wearing baggy undershirts that exposed their pointy, tattooed shoulders to the public gaze. Craggy, unclean creatures with missing teeth who gave off a sickly stench of fortified wine. Their girlfriends looked particularly unpleasant – incredibly coarse, shrill women with swollen, heavily made-up faces.

Criminals, the boy realised in horror, and pressed harder on the pedals of his gleaming bike. Criminals! Evil-doers! Fiends! Bad, dishonest people! Oh, carry me, carry me away from them, my swift bicycle!

I was one of those boys who, if they find a purse with money in it on the pavement, immediately put up a notice on the fence: 'Found: a purse containing money'. My honesty, firm principles and decency were as boundless, as infinite as outer space itself. In those days I was absolutely crazy about space, spaceflight, spacesuits, laser cannons and other stuff like that.

At the age of thirteen and a half I had definitely decided I was going to be a science-fiction writer so ingenious that I would outdo my own favourite authors, the Strugatsky brothers. This brilliant duo had shown me that the meaning of human life and happiness lay in creative labour, artistic endeavour, understanding the world and developing your individual personality.

I set about my task with determination. From the very beginning I made it a rule to write every day. For at least two hours. And I spent the same amount of time in the municipal reading room. I studied world literature and persevered in ruining paper with my scribbling. My peers were already hugging and squeezing the girls in the alleyways, but I laughed at them – I was building my future. Sitting at the writing desk, polishing the parts of the secret weapon I needed to conquer the world.

By the age of sixteen I was already fully developed as a writer: I knew I was going to write prose with plots that were light and puckish. Bitterly humorous. Incisive and laid back. I had decided that my books would set guys' and dolls' heads spinning just like a twelve-year-old schoolgirl's first cigarette. I swore to myself that I would work without sleep or rest, until I collapsed unconscious, until my eyes went blind – but I would surpass everyone else. I was going to be the very best. Great. Unique. I was going to stand the entire literature of the last thousand years on its head. People would be engrossed by my novels, laugh and cry over them, they would be made into movies and quoted everywhere. My novels would explode like bombs. They would change humanity. They would lead people to the light.

All I had to do was acquire some experience of life.

And that was when I started thinking about prison and criminals again.

I wanted to write extreme stories that struck hard. Accordingly, they required extreme material. In my search for it I first of all took a job as a construction worker, pounding at the ground with a jackhammer in minus thirty degrees. After an hour's work, my face, my neck and my forearms were completely covered with machine oil. But I didn't discover anything genuinely extreme in this. In general, I don't find heavy physical labour too hard to tolerate: I was inured to it when I was still a child. My lunch breaks were spent writing a story with a hero called Kolyukha, who worked with concrete on construction sites, and a heroine who was the president of the trade union, known by the nickname 'Board of Honour'. At the same time I was studying for the entrance exams to the faculty of journalism at Moscow University and composing lively pieces of reportage for the construction trust's in-house newspaper, a militant publication in A2 format with the highly significant title *Lights of the Construction Sites*.

One day the photographer brought the editors a portrait that he'd taken in some foundation pit: an extremely handsome man, a worker with black hair, a serene, open face, a high forehead and a gleaming white smile, wearing his brand-new boiler suit left romantically unbuttoned and his helmet at a rakish angle. The photograph would have looked well in an exhibition or on the cover of any Moscow magazine.

I had the idea of putting the portrait on the front page and printing a short article beside it. I immediately phoned the personnel department of the branch where he was listed as working and knocked out thirty lines.

'It won't do,' said the editor-in-chief. 'This handsome guy of yours has a criminal record.'

I graduated from school as innocent as a gladiolus and made it into university at the first attempt, surviving the competition of seventeen applicants for every place. I had visions of brilliant prospects. The road stretching out ahead was broad and bright, and I was going to travel it happy and unconstrained. First studies, then hard but interesting work in a publishing office. Personal growth and all the rest of it. Prison didn't really fit into the picture anywhere.

But how could you really understand people and the processes taking place in society until you'd spent some time down at the very bottom?

My thoughts gradually assembled themselves into something like a plan. I anticipated dropping into that institution with the barred windows just for a short time – six months, say – in order to get to know my way around and understand both prison and the criminal idea. And after that I would walk among the people with a lugubrious air, radiating a mysterious, arcane power! Fortunately, however, things never got that far.

Before long the Motherland notified me that it was time to put on boots and shoulder straps. I had to discharge my military obligations in full. Serve out the entire two years. For me the army of the Land of Soviets turned out to be no worse than an ordinary collective farm, and yet again I failed to collect any strong material for my books. In the year I was demobbed, 1989, two or three young writers tried to make a name for themselves with their soldiering memoirs, dealing, in powerfully emotional terms, with the humiliation of certain boy soldiers by other identically dressed boys. But I sensed that producing that kind of prose was a mistake. In its barracks form, violence is of absolutely no interest to mankind. In the final analysis, when I served in the army I was involved in fights and got my face punched no more often than I did before I was a soldier. It's just what young men do.

Time showed that I was right. Less than a year later, videos arrived in the Land of Soviets, bringing with them the infinitely broad culture of international cinema. The public watched Kubrick's *Full Metal Jacket* and lost interest in the shallow military opuses of novice writers from their own capital.

Something else that arrived with video culture was the global criminal idea, as depicted in the masterpieces of great film directors. In essence this idea is very simple. A man remains good and kind only as long as he has enough sleep and is warm and well fed. Try to take away his life, his food, his comfort or his mate – and you will see him transformed into a wild beast with ferocious fangs and absolutely no interest in the law. In other words, every last one of us seemingly good, honest people will turn criminal if the circumstances are right.

The criminal idea is undoubtedly important. It has survived through the ages and will continue to do so. It has its own apostles, martyrs and evangelists. This idea will not allow society to forget that it, society, consists not only of good people but also of bad, weak ones, burdened with vices. Everyone knows that two criminals were crucified to the right and the left of Jesus. The criminal idea is the howl of the genuinely wretched: all those who lack conscience and compassion, all those who lack willpower and backbone, all the psychopaths, murderers, maniacs, rapists, monsters, conmen, gangsters and mentally ill, all those with no faith, talent or gifts. *Remember that homo sapiens is imperfect*, this idea shrieks at everyone who gets it into his head that he's a genius and mankind is just an open field where others like him can grow.

In the Land of Soviets the criminal idea was suppressed. Neither its supporters nor its critics had any voice. And therefore the prisons of my Motherland will be overcrowded for many decades to come.

When I emerged from those army gates with the red stars on them, the sight I beheld was astounding in its naked beauty: the caramel-sweet forest meadow of my childhood had been reduced to scorched earth. The country of buttercups and peasant shawls, the quaint Land of Soviets, had expired and a new state was growing up, thrusting its shoots through the decomposing corpse: a cruel, cynical state, but one that was brimming over with humour and vital energy. Exactly like the novels that I hadn't written.

But now I decided to let literature wait for a while. The first idea I had was to scrape together a million dollars. All my peers were busy trying to scrape together a million. Some of them were actually managing to do it.

American financiers have a saying: 'Before you buy shares, buy a house!' That is, think about yourself before you start getting adventurous. First make yourself secure, then take the risk. I invented a similar slogan for myself: 'before you write the books, make the money!' Provide for yourself and your family, then write as much as you like …

Making money is an extremely risky business, and I remembered about prison again. And not just once or twice. In the early 1990s, conditions in the capital of my Motherland were pretty close to active service under fire.

Five long years passed like that. Every time my business enterprises were becalmed and I was left with nothing to do and free time on my hands, I immediately sat down at my desk and started writing. This is what the writer Turgenev said about this situation: 'In the days of doubt and oppressive pondering, you alone are my hope and support, oh great and mighty Russian language!' But then, Turgenev was a nobleman, and he was never tormented by the question of where to get some money for a bite to eat. Anyway, a job or something else to occupy my time always turned up quickly and I never finished a single thing I was writing.

I never felt anxious for the fate of my manuscripts, never collected them together in some precious file. At twenty-two or twenty-three it's not possible to write real prose – all you can do is practice. Later the stories and novellas were lost as I moved from one flat to another – a process I went through a dozen times.

In the end a business turned up to which I devoted myself completely, and it brought me gold, gentlemen. I found the process of getting rich so interesting in itself that I gave up literature. There'd be time enough for that! I was gathering in money – and incredibly rich material for novels and film scripts – hand over fist! Business! That was where the passions and the dramatic conflicts were! Where the characters and personalities were. 1990s Moscow was clearly going to get even heavier than 1930s Chicago: they killed people for hooch and moonshine there, but here men were fighting over oil, gas and real estate …

At night the great shades of Balzac and Dreiser hovered over me. Just like them, I lived among bankers, industrialists and extortionists, surrounded by the jingle of coins and the rustle of banknotes, in a world where the old morality was being trampled into the dirt and its place triumphantly usurped by a new one: simple, clear and cruel.

Every month I promised myself faithfully to start a new text at last. A brilliant text. The very best. One that would stagger the imagination of even the most sophisticated reader. All I had to do was find just a few hours a week. My head was bursting with ideas. But the hours were never found. The nervous energy required for creative work was all expended in the office, there was nothing left over. In the evening body and soul demanded a slacker pace, relaxation. At the very least a dose of alcohol. I was absolutely unable to make myself set aside the commercial problems of the moment and give serious thought to my first great novel. And apart from that, they don't pay much for novels. And every worldly-wise businessman will tell you it's stupid to waste precious time on creating a commodity that no one pays much for.

Naturally, not one of my fifty or so business partners knew that I wasn't really a businessman at all, but a writer collecting material. If I had so much as hinted at anything of the kind, no one would have done business with me. In business they like hard-bitten realists, they respect plain speaking about concrete facts; there's no place for contemplatives and fantasists, for scribblers and others who are not really of this world. This impulsive, unreliable little nation apart is sometimes supported by business, but it is infinitely remote from its realities. And so I kept quiet, maintaining the appearance of a sharp, energetic wheeler-dealer with a calculator for a brain.

Later on the business grew. I got rich. The long-awaited and passionately desired million was dangling there, at arm's length. I made a dash forward, not even pausing to wipe away the drool of excitement. At the same time, the workload increased. My sleep was cut back to five hours a day. Envious enemies and competitors sprang up on all sides. At times I was seriously concerned that I might lose my reason in the intricate tangle of my own commercial dealings.

Then, at last, came the final act: they picked me up. Just half a step away from that million.

I never even started the novel.

And so the threads all came together – the million, prison and literature.

4

Special pre-trial detention centre number one stroke one positioned itself on the market as the very finest of all the institutions offered to the public by the Russian penitentiary system. A block of VIP apartments.

Here the very *idea* of isolation was embodied in a talented and sensible fashion. Here isolation was triumphant. It ruled supreme. It was taken to the absolute, to its glorious apotheosis. In the cells of this fortress every client was isolated totally and absolutely – in a way that could not help but inspire you with respect for a state that possessed such a strong and cunning prison.

In a cool room finished in green plastic I was asked to strip naked. A very polite, middle-aged man with a warrant officer's straps on his skinny shoulders examined every last stitch of my clothing, probing every seam thoroughly with his fingers. Then I was allowed to put my shorts on and was left alone. I waited for what would come next, pining in anguished uncertainty for an hour and a half, two hours.

Suddenly the warrant officer appeared, accompanied by another in a white coat who donned rubber gloves, snapping the elastic against his wrists with the swagger of a case-hardened anatomist, and requested me to bend over and spread my buttocks.

'Well, what can you see?' I asked when I'd done what I was told. 'Any sign of a free pardon?'

The warrant officers didn't laugh – they'd obviously heard the joke plenty of times before. Or perhaps they were wondering to themselves whether this man would still be laughing after two weeks spent in their cells. Would he ever laugh again? Or would he do nothing but laugh for the rest of his life?

They took away my shoelaces, belt and wristwatch. All they left me was my handkerchief. When I put my five-hundred-dollar trousers back on, they immediately started slipping down over my skinny thighs. I had to hold them up with my elbow.

'Hands behind your back! Forward!'

The moment I took a step, the trousers slipped down again and my shoes almost came off my feet. I had to grab hold of the cloth on my own backside in my clenched hands, tug it up high and spread my toes as wide as I could in order to deter my shoes from attempting to escape – in short, extemporise.

I was led up a broad stairway to the first floor, then to the second. Every now and then my escort struck the iron banisters with a bunch of huge keys the size of kitchen knives. When there was a similar clattering from somewhere up above us, the escort said.

'Stop. Face the wall.'

I turned round. The wall was similar to the one in the office. A generous, uneven layering of plaster, copiously daubed with dark-green oil paint the colour of grass.

Several pairs of boots went tramping past.

'Forward.'

In a dark storeroom smelling of soap they gave me a mattress, a blanket, two narrow sheets and a pillowcase with two immense stamps in the form of a five-pointed star enclosed in a rectangle. The last time I'd seen stamps like that was fifteen years earlier, when I was serving in the army. Even back then I had already suspected that the wide sateen underpants, long-johns and little honeycomb cotton towels, in the authorised style, had been produced in the Empire under Stalin and Khruschev in surplus quantities, sufficient for many decades ahead. Undoubtedly in those years the military genius of the leaders of the state had penetrated the dense strata of the future with ease.

'Want to get washed?' asked the quartermaster, another warrant officer.

I shook my head.

'That's a mistake. The next bath's not till Thursday. Five days away. But for now, welcome …'

And so I stepped into the inner space of the world-famous Lefortovo fortress. I saw a wide, brightly lit gallery that seemed to have no ceiling – the walls ran upwards out of sight. Nobody told me not to turn my head and, casting a few hasty glances around me, I saw four levels, four rows of doors. Stretching along the rows were steel gantries, fenced off by railings on their outer edge. Steel-mesh nets stretching right across the central space dissected the prison universe into several layers. Everyone knows why the nets are needed: if not for them, sooner or later some desperate inmate would throw himself down headfirst.

In a few places on the ground floor and first floor there were figures in green, lingering beside the doors.

With the tongues of my shoes hanging out, my trousers trying to collapse and the rolled-up mattress tumbling out from under my arm, I walked up the iron steps to the second level. Here the iron flooring was covered with a carpet runner. The hollow thump of my footsteps flew off sideways and upwards into the distance. In contrast, the functionary in a green uniform strode along behind me without making a sound.

'Stop,' he told me again.

This time I turned to face the wall without having to be reminded.

The steel tumblers of the locks rumbled through three distinct phrases, deep and powerful. The echo reverberated under the arching roof. In the distance there was the faint cry of a sparrow – the one that always lives up under the roof of any vast covered space. The bird's cry was repeated again, and then again. It was a greeting to the new inmate, or an expression of sympathy, or simply a brief statement: there's nothing to worry about, my friend, even here in jail you can still live and chirrup away.

I didn't see any wicked criminals.

The cell was empty: very light, very clean and beautiful. The stone floor was brown, the three empty iron bedsteads were bright blue, the walls were yellow. In the near corner, beside the door, I recognised an original receptacle for sewage, a conical cast iron pipe that widened at the top to the size of the statistically average human backside.

I laid out the mattress and collapsed onto it. In order not to see that blue, yellow and brown beauty, I turned to face the wall. And immediately I saw little letters traced on it with a ballpoint pen. *'Man' – that has a bitter ring to it.* And below that another three words: *Maxim the Proud.* A rephrasing of Maxim Gorky's famous saying.

Instantly the rectangular hole in the door, the 'feed-hole', clanged open. The screw clattered all his keys against its iron surface.

He wants my attention, I guessed, and raised my head.

'Everything all right?' I heard from the opening.

'Yes, everything's all right.'

'No lying with your face to the wall! No covering yourself with the blanket before lights out! No pulling the blanket up over your head,' the warder said in the quivering voice of a disciplined lout.

I didn't answer. The feed-hole slammed shut with a savage crash.

'Hey, captain!' I shouted. 'Give me a smoke!'

Not a sound in reply.

Light and air entered the cell through an embrasure in the end wall. I studied its construction curiously. The wall itself at that point was at least one and a half metres thick. A steel casement set into it held a rectangular piece of thick opaque glass with fine steel reinforcing wires running through it. Behind the glass, by the bright light of the evening sun, I could clearly make out the forms of massive bars. Vertical rods three centimetres thick with strong flat crosspieces.

I hate bars, I thought miserably.

The upper section of the window was hinged and could be lowered to open it. Grabbing hold of the edge of the frame with my fingers, I hauled myself up, hoping to find out if there was a open gap above it through which I could see something going on outside the building – but there was another loud clatter of metal behind me.

'No climbing up on the window!' the sentry shouted.

I jumped down on to the floor. The hole in the door slammed shut again with a deafening clatter.

Well, what did you expect? I asked myself. The carpet wasn't laid along the doors for aesthetic reasons, but practical ones. And the overseer had special soft footwear – not boots, not shoes, but slippers of some kind, like sports shoes. Everything arranged so that he could move from door to door without making even the slightest sound. Walking carefully, approaching silently, sliding open the shutter of the peephole without making a sound – and watching. Then creeping on to the next door.

After a little thought, I decided that the screw's professional occupation had its interesting side. When he glanced in through the little hole, the overseer observed either a sorrowful, newly captured spy, or a homicidal maniac, or a top-level state functionary who had stolen billions. The Lefortovo isolation prison is intended for the elite, for the arch-villains, the especially dangerous; those whose fate is important to the state. The stories of those who lodge here are national sensations. The screw watches the latest TV news bulletin and then goes to peep at the key players eating their rations, playing a wild, passionate game of dominoes with their cell-mates or shitting thoughtfully.

Directly above the door I discovered a skimpily made black ebonite handle. I turned it and an extremely agreeable baritone voice boomed elastically into the space between the yellow walls:

'Here is the exact time signal!'

It was the state radio company *Svoyak*. I hadn't listened to any of its broadcasts for at least fifteen years – not since the first private FM stations had appeared in the country.

'The beginning of the sixth stroke,' the announcer continued with masterfully controlled intonation, 'corresponds to three p.m. Moscow time!'

I felt myself smiling. From the radio speaker I caught a breath of my childhood, the forgotten, colourful Land of Soviets. It breathed out stale alcohol fumes, sniffed like a geriatric, belched out a scalding odour of boiled sausages, vinaigrette, pickled mushrooms, fortified port and occasional Belomor Canal papyroses. The radio station of a country that had long ago ceased to exist was still broadcasting in the same old ideologically stable voices, to the same uniformly cheerful music. Slowly, tendentiously, in emphatic phrases with impressive pauses.

I immediately turned the handle again. It was fifteen years now since I'd realised I couldn't bear to hear these stressed-out retards trying to tell something to other retarded, dopey, weak-kneed citizens of their native Land of Soviets. I paused for a moment and turned the volume back up.

'Our correspondent,' a female contralto announced blithely, 'recently visited the honoured worker of the arts, professor and winner of many international awards …'

Horrified, I turned the sound off again. Nothing had changed. The information was conveyed too slowly and pompously. It was radio for those who were incapable of thinking.

Left in silence, I sat down on the mattress (prison property), then lay down – and unexpectedly fell asleep. After all, during the previous five months I had rarely slept more than five hours a night. After a while the screw knocked loudly on the iron spy hole, waking me up. He asked something about supper, but I just shook my head and went back to sleep.

Later a group of functionaries in khaki opened the door, entered the cell and woke me with a cry of 'Check!' They forced me to assume a vertical position, asked if everything was in order and went straight back out.

I lay down again, but now the light prevented me from falling asleep. I got up, found a switch on the wall and pressed the button. The lamp on the ceiling carried on glowing. I clicked it again, and again. With no result. Was it broken then?

The aperture in the door came to life again.

'What's wrong?' a stern voice enquired. 'You pressed the call button!'

'I thought it was the ceiling light. Switch it off, please!'

'Not allowed.'

I had to shade my eyes with my hand.

This time I slept right through until morning, only coming to when my stomach started aching from hunger.

I could hardly wait for breakfast. I heard the noise of the trolley from far off in the distance. Its movement along the steel flooring past the row of doors was accompanied by the sparse sounds of voices and a rumble of iron. When the steel plate was finally lowered I was right there, clutching the aluminium bowl with its battered rim.

'Breakfast,' the sentry announced in a low voice.

On the other side of the door, against the background of the opposite wall, I saw a brisk-looking woman in a white coat. She cast a curious glance at me as she stirred some kind of intensely steaming gruel in a cyclopean saucepan with a massive ladle. The saucepan had an inventory number crudely daubed on its side. She grasped the bowl that I held out to her, filled it to the brim and gave it back to me. It was followed by bread, then sugar.

There was a wooden table standing in the very corner of the cell, beside the door. I put my rations down on it, waited until the feed-hole closed and hastily set about my dainty repast.

And so, mesdames et messieurs – skilly!

The food was a brownish-grey colour. It looked like semolina. I sniffed it. The smell was not encouraging. But the food was hot, and the bread was fairly fresh. I ate it all.

I should say that I'm not in the least bit choosy about food and believe that this attitude – strictly utilitarian – is the only correct one. For those citizens who doubt this, I suggest a simple experiment. Take a volunteer and persuade him to fast for, say, two days and nights. Then serve him black bread and water – as much as he wants. Let him eat his fill. Stuff his stomach as much as he thinks appropriate. Just bread and water, nothing else. The very moment the experimental subject sighs in satisfaction and sets down a half-eaten crust, offer him a full five-course dinner: fiery-hot, subtly flavoured soup and a piece of meat marinated in spices and perfectly roasted, and cheeses, and dessert, and coffee. What will happen? That's right: the volunteer will refuse. He will announce that he is full. Spicy aromas will not excite, steam rising from the food will not make his mouth water. Sated on bread and water, a man will not want anything else. This clearly demonstrates that culinary science is a mere pseudo-science and should be regarded exclusively as an amusement for idlers and snobs.

After dining on the state's humble fare, I felt spiritually and physically uplifted. I wanted a smoke very badly, but I'd finished my pack of cigarettes the day before. I searched the entire cell for a dog-end, but failed to find one. Nothing. Not a single crumb of tobacco.

Searching and peering into every last nook and cranny gradually led me to thinking about the place I had ended up in and how I could get out of it. It's a poor prisoner who doesn't make up his own plan of escape, even if only for the mental exercise. Naturally, I had no intention of escaping. What for, when they were going to release me on legal grounds after twenty-eight days? But I couldn't exclude the possibility that those twenty-eight days would be one long string of taunts, torments and beatings. If Shalamov's books were to be believed, you could expect absolutely anything from the authorities of the Empire. So I simply had to prepare an exit route.

After running through several possible variants in my mind, I admitted to myself that escaping from the Lefortovo fortress was inconceivable. There was no way out through the window, everything was sound and solid there. The wall round the window was thick, and the opposite wall, with the door in it, was exactly the same. It was only logical to assume that the two other walls were also indestructible. I drummed on one with bent fingers – the sound was dull and forlorn. I struck them with the edge of my fist, hard: no effect at all. I might just as well hammer on the great pyramid of Cheops.

No one responded to my call sign from the cell on the other side of the wall. I crossed to the right wall and repeated the experiment. No reply. Either the walls were too thick or – and this was more likely – the cells on each side were empty.

It would be great to have my own boss as a neighbour just behind the wall, I suddenly thought. We'd soon set up an exchange of messages and send each other greetings by tapping Morse code or some other kind of signalling system …

But almost immediately I was brought to my senses: there was a squeaking and a quiet rustle at the door, and a human eye peered in at me through the hole. I hastily sat down, assuming a pose that expressed a humble resignation and absolute acceptance of my circumstances.

How could you escape? How could you, if you were observed every ninety seconds or two minutes? How could you, if you were constantly being monitored? How could you escape from a cell where you weren't even allowed to hide your head under the blanket, where you had to keep your face in the screw's line of sight all the time?

No, I told myself. Playing the Count of Monte Cristo will only make things worse. There's not going to be any escape! What's going to happen is that in four weeks, on 15 September I shall proceed in triumph through the main vestibule, holding in my hands the official documents stating that I have been granted my freedom on legal grounds.

It was a shame about the Kenzo suit. I'd have to throw it away. Wearing your prison clothes on the outside is regarded as very bad form in Russia.

Maybe they wouldn't let me out in a month, but a bit later? Maybe I'd be detained here for another day or two. But that was the absolute maximum. They *were* going to let me out! First they'd let the fake office manager Mikhail out. And then me. My boss needed me. After all, we were partners. Associates. Neither was any good without the other.

My friend was somewhere here now. Maybe the same overseer looked through the hole at me, then took a few soundless steps and could see my boss. He could watch him feeling miserable without cigarettes and suffering for himself, for me, for our money, for the business …

I turned the tap on and washed my bowl as well as I could under the stream of cold water. There were spots of grease left on the dove-grey metal surface. The sight of the dirty bowl disgusted me, and I almost flung it against the wall.

To a certain extent it was harder now for the boss than it was for me. In the first place, he didn't have a lawyer. We'd arranged things that way. Where would a lowly office supplies manager in a small commercial firm get the money to pay for the expensive services of a professional legal specialist? And most important of all: what would an office supplies manager need a lawyer for anyway? The office supplies manager didn't know anything. He was innocent *a priori*. His job was buying paper and cartridges for the printers and copiers. Felt-tip pens, pencils, petrol for the cars – that was his province.

So my boss Mikhail didn't know anything. He didn't know what testimony Andrei had given. What if Andrei had suffered a moment of weakness and immediately given a full and frank confession to everything? And now he was sitting in a restaurant instead of an isolation cell?

I imagined my boss dashing from corner to corner in his suffering. The boss was a tough, experienced man; he would quite certainly have thought through all the possibilities, including the very worst. What if – a terrible thought – Andrei was playing his own game? What if he had dumped everything on Mikhail, painted himself whiter than white and kept himself out of everything? And now he wasn't even sitting in a restaurant – he was in the office! Planning to grab all the capital for himself! And they would put Mikhail away for an eight-year stretch!

It's a pity I'm not telepathic, I thought. I could have sent the boss a thought message, short and simple. Don't worry about a thing, boss! I've covered for you. Told them officially that you're not the boss, but the office supplies manager. And I signed the statement. And I've been put away inside.

They'll let you go. And then what you do will make them let me go too.

A new day, a new screw. This one introduced himself by thrusting a wet rag in through the feed-hole.

'Wipe down the spy-hole please.'

'Go to hell,' I replied glibly. 'It's your spy-hole, you wipe it down.'

'You'll go to the punishment cell,' he parried indifferently from the other side of the door.

I walked over to the door and without saying a word ran the rag over the piece of transparent acrylic set into the heavy wooden door-slab, bound in thick sheet metal.

'Thank you,' the sentry said politely, giving me a glimpse through the feeder hole of a pale face with a pointed nose and a large translucent ear sticking out at each side.

'Come back any time,' I just managed to get in before the feed-hole closed.

Never let your opponent have the last word.

Feeling proud of my small verbal victory, I began striding along the very longest route available to me – from the door to the edge of the iron bedstead set against the end wall of the cell. The entire distance was only five broad, energetic man's steps and four and a half back: half a step went on the turn.

'Come on guys, come on! Bring it on!' I encouraged my opponents lightheartedly. 'What have you got here? Bars, locks, walls? Doors with holes for spying on people? Skilly? What else? No knives and forks? Sleep with the light on? And you think you can defeat me, when that's all you've got? You want to crush me? Break me? I'm not afraid of you! I'm not afraid of your prison!

'I'M NOT AFRAID OF YOUR PRISON! I'M NOT AFRAID OF YOUR PRISON!

'YOU'LL NEVER, EVER STOP ME!

'We'll see what song you're singing a month from now!' I chuckled, clapping my hands together. 'No – twenty-eight days from now! When my friend, my boss gets out, when he organises everything and pays for pressure from every side, when the lawyers, Duma deputies and reporters all pounce on you! My friends and my money will pluck me out of this prison in the twinkling of an eye! No one will be able to stand against the overwhelming power of the dollar. I'll corrupt you so thoroughly it'll shake the world to it foundations! I'll buy every last one of you!'

It was also true, of course, that I didn't know what the process of buying someone actually involved. There wasn't any institution where you could officially pay money in through a little window to secure your personal freedom. I didn't know what concrete actions I had to take in order to buy it.

But I'd find out. I'd come up with some idea and think it through. I'd find the man my fate depended on. Whoever he might be – a militia general, a top-level state functionary or a minister – I'd strike a deal with him. I'd give him so much that he'd be shocked. I'd bury him in money. I'd hand him five times more than he asked for. Ten times more!

After all, it was only a game. They caught me, took their share and let me go. They always had a share. Anyone who forgot that was a total idiot. You should never forget that they had a share. They had families, children. Wives who coveted furs and gold. Grandchildren whose education had to be paid for. And so on …

I respected the law. I was going to buy its representatives with all due respect. I would corrupt them, not because I was a bad or vicious man. And not because I was a criminal; the reason I was going to corrupt them was that they had put an innocent man in a cell.

And then someone invisible, very big and very stern, punched me straight on the forehead, not really hard, but forcibly enough to offend. You're the one in prison! You're the one who's been put away! Stuck in a cell! You're under suspicion of something terrible! Come to your senses! What business! What money! Have you given any thought to your family? Your nearest and dearest? How will they survive something like this? What's going to happen to your wife and son? To your mother and father? How are they going to get along now without you? What have you done? What have you done? What have you done?

5

The last time I'd seen my wife was two days before the arrest.

We'd had a row. Right there in the doorway. In the hall of the three-roomed flat that I rented for crazy money from a hoyden of an old-age pensioner who was passionately devoted to Stalin and fruit yoghurts.

I still hadn't acquired a home of my own, despite all the super-profits. I just hadn't found the time.

'You never spend the night at home!' Irma reproached me. 'And if you do come back, it's at one in the morning, and always drunk! You go out chasing women!'

'I'm don't go chasing any women,' I protested, trying to breathe away from her.

'You do chase women!'

'I don't.'

'You do! You do!'

'I don't! I don't!'

We had tried as hard as we could to maintain a high standard in our relationship. Agreed from the very first days of marriage that ours was the very best family in the world. Not like all the others. We hadn't come together just to spend the rest of our lives juggling nappies and saucepans, but for the sake of a great love, a transcendently great love – that was our slogan.

However, this striving for sublimity of feeling was accompanied by superlatively sublime rows. The noise generated by our active family life carried for kilometres. Reproaches and complaints flowed in torrents from both sides, punctuated by resounding slaps to the face, spitting and terrible curses. On particularly stormy occasions I used to punch a hole in the toilet door and my wife loved to fire an air pistol at the window or slyly purloin the money I had stashed away in a volume of Edward Limonov.

Sometimes in the middle of the night the neighbours – may God grant them good health – would tap on the radiators in an attempt to bring us to our senses. But they didn't dare take any more decisive action than that, for, even though I came from a cultured family, I always looked like an out and out criminal: I wore black leather, combed my gelled hair back from my forehead and didn't shave for three or four days at a time. Decent, respectable citizens in the grip of popular stereotypes were wary of tangling with such a suspicious character. What if he suddenly pulled a revolver out of his pocket and blasted them?

'That's not the way it is, my darling!' I began, speaking from the heart and spreading my arms wide in a gesture of extreme meekness. 'Women have got nothing to do with it! What time have I got for women? I'm hiding! The militia are looking for me!'

My wife waved her hand wearily. She looked unhappy. 'There's always someone looking for you! The militia, or gangsters, or creditors, or some of the other idiots you're always getting yourself mixed up with! I'm tired of it! I'm sick of your cloak and dagger games!'

I straightened up proudly. There was a roaring in my head from all the drink I'd taken.

'Yes, I live life to the full.'

'That's not life,' Irma declared. 'I don't see you for weeks at a time. And when I do the sight of your ugly drunken mug makes me feel sick!'

Both of us were hissing in a coarse half-whisper. Our child was sleeping in the next room.

'You have to understand,' I went on patiently, 'we're controlled by our natures. I have to go out and bring down my mammoth every morning. And you have to roast it. That's all there is to it. If, in the pursuit of that mammoth, I'm detained at work and I take a drink – what's so terrible about that? And anyway, this is a banal argument. That's enough.'

I prevented myself from hiccupping with an effort.

My wife married me when she was eighteen years old. She never studied at university. She used to work as a hairdresser. For several years she was convinced that 'banal' was an indecent word meaning 'like a banana'. On the other hand, a certain degree of ignorance was more than compensated for by her natural drive and love of life. Not to mention her appearance. And then, in five years of marriage she had come on a lot; her vocabulary had increased substantially, and now she protested energetically:

'It's your fairytales about mammoths that are banal! Don't take me for a fool! If you're out chasing women, at least have the courage to admit it!'

'I'm not out chasing women!'

'You are!'

'I'm not!'

I leaned down to tie my shoelace. Banknotes came tumbling out of all my pockets and fell on the floor in chaotic disorder – wads of notes with elastic bands round them and separate notes, carelessly crumpled and creased. The very money for which I had sacrificed my own equilibrium and my wife's. My helpmate furiously prodded the thickest wad with the toe of her slipper.

You could drop women like that on the enemy instead of a nuclear bomb, I thought.

'Get out,' Irma said spiritedly, but rather theatrically, which greatly reduced the impact of her instruction.

'That's just what I will do,' I said, nodding calmly. 'I have to … I'll sit it out for a couple of weeks in a different flat, and then everything will settle down and I'll come back … You know me … And Misha too … We'll give them as much money as it takes and then they'll leave us alone …'

'There you go again,' my wife laughed dolefully. 'You give everyone money to get them to leave you alone. You even give me money just so that I'll leave you alone!'

I suddenly felt guilty.

There's no doubt that in the final analysis it's always the man who plays the part of the destroyer of love, the family and the very idea of matrimony. That's because he's a destroyer by his very nature. And anyone who doesn't understand this simple idea is not a man at all. After every row

I was always the first to seek reconciliation, to repent and beg for mercy, to go down on my knees, run off to buy flowers and so forth. And a hefty fine was also paid in hard currency.

But every time it became harder and harder to exonerate myself. I left all my verve and my strength behind in my private office. The more money there was deposited in the safe, the less spiritual energy there was left over for my family. It wasn't only my wife who understood this, even my eighteen-month-old son did: while he treated his mother just like a mother, he regarded the father who put in an appearance on one evening out of four as some kind of walking fairground attraction. A clown hung all over with toys.

'Get out,' my wife repeated firmly and burst into tears, twisting her full lips into an ugly grimace. 'Go away. Go away!'

I took hold of her shoulders, but she pulled away sharply, turned her back on me and slouched off, dragging her slippers across the brand-new, thick woven carpet. I stayed put, stuck my hands in my pockets and leaned back against the door.

It wasn't really safe to stay there. The militia could easily be lying in wait for me at the entrance to the building. My boss Mikhail had warned me two days earlier that an arrest was imminent and given me strict instructions to keep my head down temporarily. Not to spend the night anywhere except at the secret apartment and not to come out of the office during the day

I walked through into the room anyway – stooping down on the way to pick up the money scattered on the floor – and said in a quiet voice:

'I feel really sorry for you. I know I'm hurting you … I'm in pain too … But the two of us can't act any other way.' Irma didn't say anything. She was looking out of the dark window. Her shoulders were heaving.

'All right,' I corrected myself meekly, clutching the dishevelled wads of multicoloured notes in my hands. 'It's my fault. I'm the one who can't act any other way. It's not us, it's me, personally. But you have to understand me too. At a moment like this I have to work a lot. The more the better! Round the clock! I'm earning super-profits. Every day I make us secure for another year ahead. Our future's right there for the taking. As soon as I earn all we need, I'll drop everything and devote myself completely …'

My wife put her hands over her ears. I stopped talking, put a pile of crumpled banknotes on the first horizontal surface that came to hand and walked back to the door.

And I went away, leaving a crying woman all alone with nothing but money.

I substituted one thing for another.

Lying there on the hard Lefortovo mattress and running over my last conversation with my wife, I cursed myself with the most gruesome of medieval curses. I grabbed hold of my tangled, already slightly greasy hair, bit into my lower lip and drew in the drop of warm blood mingled with saliva. Fifty times I called myself a scumbag and a hundred times I called myself a bastard, a bombastic imbecile and a pompous shit-head.

What had I done? Why had I betrayed the people dearest to me? What if I ended up stuck in here for months and months? Or even for years? How would they survive without me? My wife couldn't do anything. Since the age of seventeen she had been used to me deciding everything, bringing home the money and the food. What was she going to do now? She would have to go through hell. I had been her entire support. I had built a crystal palace around her. I had given her material comfort. And for what? In order to abandon her now, leave her all alone? Surrounded by the collection of cunning and cruel reptiles that was 'the world around us'?

An appalling guilt complex for what I had done to the people I loved consumed the core of my being. When I went back home, everything was going to be different, I swore to myself. No more boozing. No midnight vigils in front of the flickering computer screen. No working for a hundred hours a week. Only someone who was a born idiot like me, and cruel as well, could inflict pain on his own wife.

But I was wise now, I'd been cured with a medicine that was called gruel – as soon as I went back, I was going to put my life in order without delay, and everything would be fine for everyone – my wife and son, my sister, my mother and father – all the people I loved …

There was a little mirror, no larger than the palm of a hand, set into the wall of my residence, above the washbasin. Moving closer and glancing into it, I saw a face floating in a yellow broth of electric light: pale and unshaved, with its lower lip bleeding.

'Swearing oaths is stupid,' said the yellow-faced fool on the other side of the mirror. 'Never swear. Don't make promises. Never promise not to do anything again.'

Yes, I knew that. Making promises was the last thing you should do. At least that was the way clever people saw things. But I had to, there was no way I couldn't promise myself – right here and now, in the holding cells, in solitary – that I would go back to my family a completely different man. Calm, cheerful, considerate.

'First you've got to get back,' the yellow-faced man remarked.

I stuck my hands into the pockets of my subsiding trousers and started striding from wall to wall, stopping every now and then to scrape at my prickly cheekbone with my fingers. And sometimes in my fury I punched the impregnable stony walls of the cell. The wall offered serious resistance. We'd see who came out on top.

I had the brains, I had the money. All I had to do was come up with a plan.

6

The last time I'd given a bribe to a representative of the law was just six hours before my arrest.

On the evening of that final day my boss and I did some serious drinking. Right there in our office. In the metal-clad, securely guarded basement, protected by alarm systems and video cameras, under the old Moscow town house just a kilometre from the Kremlin. Joint Staff HQ on the left, the Cathedral of Christ the Savour on the right and there, exactly halfway between them, our very own underground bank. An office without any signboard or licence, without any public face or name.

After walking through several communicating rooms (all the doors were steel, with locks like safes), in the very last room of the 500 square-metres basement, you came across several armchairs of cheap imitation leather and a black office desk, cluttered with empty and half-empty coffee cups, huge ashtrays and even huger calculators. You could gladly sink your firm backside into an armchair and put your tired feet up on a littered desk, then pour yourself the alcohol your soul was craving and sink into a state of beneficial relaxation.

The soles of my shoes were bright yellow, practically virginal. How could I possibly do them any damage, when everywhere there were pile carpets, woven rugs and parquet floors – here, and at home, and in the car, and at the dacha?

The desk didn't exactly look cheap either. There were Zippo and Dunhill lighters lying on it. Packets of Parliament cigarettes, boxes of Davidoff cigars. There were bottles of Chivas Regal standing on it. The very best brands were literally scattered everywhere, gentlemen. The most popular, prestigious and chic labels caught the eye whichever way you looked on that desk of ours.

Seeing the strung-out state I was in – that's what happens when your portrait is about to be pasted up all over town with the words 'wanted by the militia' under it – my boss and partner Mikhail advised me to try visiting some whores.

'Go on,' said the boss, taking a good swig of expensive Irish poteen, 'cut loose, have a fling. It'll freshen you up. You're drinking too much.'

'You drink more,' I remarked.

'I'm allowed,' said Mikhail, taking another gulp and crunching a piece of ice in his teeth. 'I'm the one, sort of, in charge. The founding father.'

I had to lower my eyes modestly and look into my glass. Peering into my face, the boss wouldn't have discovered even the slightest trace of protest, rebellion or disagreement.

Actually, we both used to drink a fair amount. Only Mikhail was substantially built, with a forceful temperament and willpower, and people like that drink a lot, but don't get very drunk. It was no problem for him to down a full 75 centilitre bottle of spirits in an evening, and still be in good shape. So naturally I tried to keep up. But the boss put me to shame every time.

'I drink as much as I want, where I want and how I want,' he said with obdurate indifference. 'But you shouldn't drink a lot. Change your drug. Switch to women.'

'What about my wife?' I objected drunkenly.

'It's got nothing to do with your wife.'

'I doubt that somehow.'

'Okay. As the senior partner here all I can do is give you advice …'

The boss often gave advice. In the three years we'd worked together, I must have heard a thousand pieces of advice from him.

Mikhail Moroz was four years older than me, twenty-five kilograms heavier, ten centimetres taller, three years of university more educated and a million dollars richer. And as well as that, there was absolutely no doubt that he was far more talented when it came to commerce. Insatiable, hard-bitten and intelligent, he was skilful at bending people to his will – something I couldn't do.

I had to admit the boss had a perfect moral right to advise me how to act in order to shake off the stress and fear, to lose that horrible, aching emptiness inside.

Once again the two bankers' shared fear hung in the air between them.

We could be arrested any day. The case had already been opened. The search was ongoing. We ought to close down the business immediately, gather up all our bits and pieces and disappear. For two or three years. Take off to some remote provincial spot. Or even better, somewhere right outside the country.

It had all gone too far. From naïve, reckless fools who had scraped together a few thousand roubles, we had turned into fools of a different kind, handling billions. We ought to call it a day and make a run for it, otherwise they wouldn't just put us in prison, they'd take our billions away as well. Okay, if they took back their own money, then we'd simply end up right back where we started from. That is, at point zero. But what if other people's money disappeared as well as ours? What then? A bullet through the forehead?

But instead of running for it, we were still working sixteen hours a day, because neither I nor the boss had the strength to tear ourselves away from the broad, shimmering rainbow of that conveyor belt bearing along that bright stream of gold.

In the morning we plunged our work-weary hands into that stream, and by the evening we had drawn out two kilograms, counting at four hundred dollars per troy ounce. And the same thing every working day. Naturally, the very idea of shutting up shop seemed absolutely crazy to both of us and we had never discussed it even as a joke.

'Do you drink at home too?' the boss enquired indifferently, toying with the end of his tie.

His tie was at least three times as expensive as mine.

'All the time,' I replied. 'I never go to bed sober.'

Mikhail probed me with his bleary eyes.

'You really do drink a lot?'

'Yes.'

'You look wretched. You're no use to me like that, get it? Play the same way you work. No holds barred. The whores are a must.'

'Give me a holiday.'

My boss Mikhail gave a sombre smirk.

'Sure, by all means! Start packing right now, Andrei! Tahiti, Mauritius, Goa, Barbados, the Seychelles, anywhere you like! Buy yourself an aqualung and a Hawaiian shirt. But you can only go when the cops are off your tail … Not before. Got that? In the meantime I advise you to make your own, you know, little Mauritius here at home. You'll feel better for it.'

'I'm not so sure.'

'Have yourself a fling,' the boss instructed me. 'Relax. Get yourself a girl. Two girls. Get three girls! Take a ride into the centre and get yourself the very best, sort of, girls there are! The best! There are hundreds of them at night in every club. They'll name their, you know, price. Pay them twice as much, or even three times – and you'll get something that will relax you, take your mind off things …'

As he uttered these phrases, the last thing Mikhail looked like was a salacious tempter – his expression was gloomy and he kept wincing all the time, as if he was suffering some sharp internal pain.

'Okay,' I said, with a yawn I couldn't suppress any longer. 'But why pay over the odds?'

'It's important, my little child. The triple fee will be a pleasant surprise for the girls and they'll, you know, put everything they've got into it. Three quarters of their clients are crude gangsters and perverts. But the girls prefer cultured and generous men. So they'll *work*. And work very well. To make sure you enjoy it. And come back to them the next time …'

'Interesting,' I said with a nod.

Maybe it really was worth giving it a try?

'And how come you know all this? Do you do the rounds of the night clubs?'

'Sometimes,' the boss admitted. 'When I fall out with the wife. Just as soon as I get into a quarrel, I go to a club …'

'But those places are full of gangsters! And you hate them.'

'That's true,' Mikhail agreed, taking another greedy swig. 'I hate them.

With every fibre of my being. But I put up with them. It can't be helped. Where there are girls, there are gangsters. And vice versa.'

I didn't say anything.

'Believe me,' said the boss, 'when a man of our stamp quarrels with his wife, a visit to the professionals is one of the most powerful remedies for calming the nerves. They can all be bought. All of them. Including the wives.'

'Maybe.'

'It's no secret. You go and you'll find out just *how* venal they are … Everyone loves money!' Mikhail spread his arms wide and stretched powerfully, cracking his joints. His ribcage expanded until it was a broad as a barrel. 'In a country with women and representatives of the law for sale on every street corner, it's impossible to believe in anything except money! So believe in it, Andriusha, and calm down! We've got two million in our pocket! We'll buy them all! Every one! You sit there whining – ah, what's going to happen, I'm wanted by the militia, they'll, you know, put me away – just stop whining and calm down! The most they'll give you is a year. Maybe eighteen months. You'll do your time in every possible comfort. Good salami, magazines, books … I'd go and do the time myself, but how can I? Who can I leave in my place? You? You'd ruin everything. You're too impulsive and kind-hearted …'

'No need for you to get jittery,' I said magnanimously. 'I'll do the time and come out. Just as long as the business survives …'

'Yes,' Mikhail said confidently. 'That's the important thing.'

'And as for women, you're wrong there. Women are only for sale as long as there are men who want to buy them.'

'Indeed.'

I rubbed my eyes hard and stuck another cigarette in my mouth.

'And your wife,' I began – the question just slipped out – 'does she know you visit hookers?'

'I don't know for sure,' the boss said harshly. 'I think she has a good idea. She's no fool.'

On the whole, he set a lot of store by his wife. I'd noticed that plenty of times. Unlike me, the boss Mikhail never shouted at his wife on the phone or insulted her if the call caught him at an awkward moment.

'And?' I asked

'Nothing. So that means she tolerates it.'

'Mine won't tolerate it.'

'That's your business,' the boss summed up. 'Let's get up and go!'

'Let's finish the bottle.'

'No. That's enough.'

'Just one more each.'

Neither of us stirred from the spot. A fourteen-hour working day had drained our final dregs of energy. My head felt like cast iron and my legs like cotton wool.

'Let's get up,' said the boss.

'Let's finish the bottle,' I suggested.

'Get up!'

'Finish the bottle!'

'Get up.'

The senior comrade won. Yet again. He tore himself out of that moment of physical weakness before I did and jumped to his feet, rising up in a single, powerful, energetic movement. He didn't stand up, he leapt up. Setting an example for me, his feeble subordinate. The snot-nosed jerk he had once fished out of the dirt and set to work.

However, the boss's attempt at dynamic movement ended in unexpected disaster – he staggered hard to one side, throwing his arm out in an attempt to grab something he could hold on to, and his ninety-kilogram body went crashing to the floor. I was about to dash to his aid, but Misha Moroz had already recovered his self-control. And now he stood there, rubbing his wet mouth with his hand. Of course, I'd realised already that he was totally ossified, drunk as a skunk – it was only his willpower that had prevented him from losing consciousness.

In the course of the past month the senior partner and founding father had gone downhill very badly. Acquired a drawn, haggard look. Stopped visiting the gym. Smoked too much. He had adopted new gestures: for instance, at times he would start scratching hard at his Adam's apple with his nails. That looked really primeval, feral almost. Even his voice had changed. A month earlier this massive, broad-shouldered creature's voice had been a booming, velvety, imperious bass, but now the sound produced by his throat was a squeaky falsetto. Yes, I thought sadly, he's seriously frightened by everything that's going on and obviously more afraid of prison than I am. The dollar millionaire, owner of a bank and ninety-kilogram boxer Mikhail is afraid.

Drunk and tired, in our expensive but ruinously creased jackets, clutching cigarettes in our teeth, rubbing at our foreheads and cheeks with our fingers, we walked over to the desk and started thinking. There were keys, many bunches of them, lying in a jumble in front of us. Each bunch was decorated with an absurd, immense, eye-catching trinket of some kind, purely and simply to avoid getting confused in those thick deposits of nickel-plated metal. Every key had its own door, its own space behind that door, its own piece of property. It was important not to forget.

Those were the keys of the flat where my family was, those were the keys for the flat where there was no family, those were for the door of the office, those were for the second door of the office, and those were for the third door of the office, the most important one. Those were the keys for the car, the garage, the second car, the personal safe, the corporate safe, my private office, for the computer, for the personal bank box, for the corporate bank box. Those were the keys for the archive room. It contained a ton of documents, and it was more than my life was worth to lose a single one. Those were the keys for the flat where the record-keeper himself lived. And those were the keys for my country house – this summer my eighteen-month-old son would be able to breathe the fresh air outside of Moscow instead of the carbon monoxide of the megalopolis.

Eventually I located the keys I needed and set off towards the exit. I said goodnight to the security guards, two cheerful young guys with student passes for the General Staff Academy, with the rank of at least captain, with combat experience. The military officers of the Russian state nodded in reply and turned their gaze back to the screens. Sixteen screens. Sixteen points covered by cameras. The view from the left, the view from the right. From the façade. From the back. Keep your eyes peeled, lads. God forbid that some intruder should break through, some bold villain dreaming of getting his hands on our hard-won billions.

Eventually I crawled out into the warm, electrically charged city evening, filled with all the very best smells. It felt good emerging into that evening in my white linen trousers! It felt good walking along, parting the thick, sweet darkness of Moscow with my chest. And it felt good thinking to hell with my boss Mikhail, who was despatching me to prison with a wave of his mighty hand, and to hell with this all-consuming business that was sucking out my soul and rotting away my conscience, which was already worn full of holes in any case ...

But no, I couldn't; I wouldn't know how, I wouldn't dare. Pawns don't move backwards. They either go under or move on to be transformed into mighty queens.

I unlocked the car, got in and set off. Tverskaya Street was close – only two minutes of rapid driving along the half-empty roads.

Both of them were inciting me to visit the harlots – my wife and my boss. So okay, I'd try it.

What came after that was almost like a comic strip, gentlemen. Crude, stark kitsch. Zippy and zesty. A bit like Japanese manga, guys, only even heavier. In his fast car the drunk, smug, conceited cretin with his pockets full of money hurtles off into the depths of a city gleaming with bright neon advertisements. Not particularly well-muscled, but with a predatory gleam in his narrowed eyes and a cynical grin on his lips. He spits on the hot asphalt. The atmosphere is electric. Something's about to happen any moment now. He's either going to get himself arrested or get himself sucked off.

He sees a group of the bodies he wants. Standing there smoking, with their backsides stuck way out. One or two have them stuck out in expert fashion, the others are clueless, but they're trying hard. All of them, however, have shapely figures, long legs and the most incredible high heels. The cynical nouveau-riche type brakes rakishly to a halt. The madam instantly comes bounding across. The regulator of this uncomplicated process of exchange, bodies for gold. A fat, ugly, mature jade in tracksuit trousers with stripes down the side.

It's noisy on the pavement, and she's almost shouting. So is the client as he checks out the price. After all, while he was driving along he'd been playing music loud enough to knock himself out.

'Eh? What?' the woman yells hoarsely. 'Two hours – a hundred and fifty! All night three hundred!'

With a nod at once dignified and jaunty the client steps on the gas and streaks off into the darkness.

Hurrah! The first step has been taken – *I've got the price.*

On towards the centre, down along Tverskaya Street, leaving the hotel Intourist and the Central Telegraph behind on the right, we hang a left, skirt round the hotel Moscow, leave the Bolshoi Theatre behind and drive on up towards Old Square ... A turn to the right past the Polytechnical Museum, up to the base of the massive hotel Rossiya, along the front of it, right again – and there I am on the embankment. On my left is the black water of the Moscow River, on my right is the red wall of the Kremlin. I turn up just before the Bolshoi Kamenny Bridge.

Cast-iron railings go flitting past – the Faculty of Journalism, my own dear alma mater, wreathed in ancient myth and legend, the one and only.

There had been a time when I was proud of being a student there. But everything is different now. A long, long time ago, in a former life, during the time of the Land of Soviets, working for a newspaper was regarded as prestigious and it was well paid. Nowadays a reporter is a pauper dressed in rags. I had abandoned my beloved profession, so why didn't I regret it? Because the profession was no longer lucrative? So it wasn't the profession I had loved, but the money? Yet again, for the thousand and first time, I had to admit that I couldn't imagine my life without money and success; it made me furious and I flattened the accelerator against the floor.

But beware! The enemy is ever vigilant. A figure in blue comes leaping out of the ink-black shadows of the night, waving aloft a striped baton. For the convenience of citizens driving along in the flow of traffic, the baton glows in the dark. It's impossible not to notice him. I obediently stop and make a dynamic exit from the car.

The fashion nowadays is to do things American-style: sit at the wheel without moving, wait until the militia officer gets close, and then talk to him through the open window. The guardian of the law stands there, shifting from one foot to the other, while the driver wallows in his soft chair. But we're not in California, we are proponents of a different style of human relations – the imperial style. We respect the law and its servants. And we're always ready, with all due respect, to give these poor guys with the red, weather-beaten faces a little bit of money. And anyway I'm drunk.

I swing the door of the car wide open, deftly and imperceptibly ridding the interior of alcohol fumes.

But the guy in the blue uniform turned out to be no fool after all: one whiff was enough for him to see the way things stood.

'What's this then, comrade driver?' he asked reproachfully. 'Been indulging, have we?'

It's noisy in the street. The guardian of the law is almost shouting, and so is the apprehended transgressor. After all, while he was driving along he'd been playing music loud enough to knock himself out.

'Sorry!' I confessed, inflating my chest manfully. 'I am at fault, comrade captain! I'll pay the fine on the spot. At the usual rate.'

The officer toyed with my ID.

'And where's your driving licence?'

'I don't have one!'

The guardian of the law laughed a predatory laugh.

'Go get in the car,' he ordered, pointing backwards into the thick shadow out of which he himself had appeared only a minute earlier.

There, in a poorly lit spot, in an alley between two monolithic five-storey Stalinist blocks, I finally caught sight of the cunningly concealed militia Zhiguli. I approached it cautiously. There was a second traffic cop sitting in it. The dialogue was repeated almost word for word.

'What do you think you're doing, eh? In control of a vehicle while under the influence? In a state of alcoholic inebriation.'

'It happens sometimes, comrade major.'

'I'm a lieutenant. Where's your licence?'

'I don't have one.'

They all really love that short reply I give: 'I don't have one'. Basically, if you're prepared to pay the going rate, you should keep it brief and to the point.

Concerning my state of inebriation the naïve guardian of the law was seriously mistaken. I was intoxicated all right, but not with alcohol. It was money that had intoxicated me. I had earned six or seven thousand dollars that day. The precise amount would be calculated over the following weekend. A good day, a successful day – the boss and I always wound up days like that with a glass of whisky. Our business was really hard on the nerves. But it was profitable. And it was that profit, constantly materialising in our safes and pockets in the form of plump bundles of banknotes, mostly American, that had intoxicated me, titillating my nerves and jangling those special, secret, subtle inner strings that clouded my mind more thoroughly and profoundly than any strong liquor.

'What have you got to say?'

'I'll pay the fine right here. At the going rate.'

They pondered on that. The guardian with the wide face took off his peaked cap and extracted a white rag out of the crown – carefully folded thin and flat, its function was obviously to absorb excess sweat – turned the piece of wadding over and pressed its dry side against his law-enforcer's brow.

'A fine's all well and good ...' the guardian muttered. 'But how can I let you keep going in that state? There's another stake-out up by the Metropole, and then one further along Tverskaya Street ... And you're drunk, and you don't even have a licence ... Got a lot of money, then, have you?'

Without wasting any time, I showed him the specially prepared plump wad that I kept for such occasions, all small denomination dollar bills, for the most part fives and tens. Brand new, every last one. Only a few hundred, but it looks impressive.

The traffic cop cast a lecherous glance at the foreign bills, but he maintained the honour of the uniform to the last. His monthly salary was equivalent to what I earned for about half an hour's work. Both of us understood that, and the transaction that was in process seemed entirely fair and just both to me, the snot-nosed yuppy, and to him, the fifty-year-old servant of the law.

'Stick to the middle lane, son,' he advised me amiably in farewell. 'Take care ...'

In all fairness, I ought to mention that even in the swirling vortex of individuals jockeying unceasingly to prostitute themselves a certain order was observed, also imperial in character. While the available women strutted their stuff some distance away – about a kilometre, in fact – from the fortified territory of the Kremlin, the representatives of authority acted more boldly and openly, levying their baksheesh only about a hundred paces from the very tower where the light once used to burn by day and night in comrade Stalin's legendary window.

Little by little the thoughts of the prisoner of Lefortovo on the subject of corruption began slipping back to his smutty but vivid memories of the search for an amenable girl.

But just then reality intruded to inflict a terrible punishment – for my deeds and my thoughts.

The hatch in the door opened. A woman's voice asked.

'Rubanov in here?'

'Yes,' I replied.

'There's a delivery for you. Here, take it ...'

A list was held out to me. I saw my wife's writing on it.

They started shoving packages, bundles, paper bags and individual items in through the rectangular opening. Taking each tranche in turn, I tossed it onto the blue metal frame of the bedstead closest to me and hurried back for the next portion of riches. I got all hot and bothered. I scurried backwards and forwards, counting everything twice over. There was sack after sack. Everything neatly wrapped in a woman's style: for safety's sake the sugar and tea, coffee and cigarettes had all been put inside two plastic bags, carefully tied with tight little knots. I caught glimpses of fruit and underwear, matches and notepads. I accepted trousers and slippers, crockery and soap, notebooks and pens, as well as all the food that a man sitting behind bars is allowed to have, including fruit. I accepted fatty bacon and bread, onions, garlic and salami, cheese and apples, oranges and bananas.

The last little package, the smallest of them all, tied with two knots, contained several lacy woman's handkerchiefs – absolutely tiny, yellowish-pink: I ripped open the transparent plastic with my teeth and caught the fragrance of her perfume – my beloved's perfume: sharp, intense, bitter.

I finally broke down at that and sank my tense, bluish-grey face into that perfume, cursing myself. I started howling – at my powerlessness to put everything right, to turn back the pages of that hellish comic book, at my inability even to weep over all this endearing frippery that my woman had touched with her own hands only two hours earlier.

But God would not give me tears.

I was a loathsome profligate. A turd. An odious troglodyte. A cur. A brute. An apocalyptic cretin. A human ass-wipe. A brainless blockhead. A lunatic lowlife, falling endlessly into the pit of his own debasement.

I was a sublime wanker. A primordial dickhead. A man who sold and bought his own immortal soul. A conceited sheep-shagger. A schliemazl, corpse-eater and degenerate. An unwashed savage. An ape. A reptile. A slimy belly-creeper. A dolt and a scoundrel.

I was the lowest of the low. I had devalued my own currency to the ultimate. I had betrayed my love, and with it everything that was brightest and dearest. I would go to hell.

If, on some warm summer weekend evening, as you stroll along the pathways of the park of culture and recreation in any small provincial Russian town, you should decide to risk calling into the public toilet, that very instant your eyes will be assaulted by multitudinous heaps of shit. They are huge. It is impossible not to feel a powerful rush of pride for our national gene pool – only truly healthy and strong young bodies could possibly expel such wondrous, potent excrement. The shit covers every square centimetre of the wooden floor. The older, rock-hard faeces, overgrown in many places by a special kind of grey mould, are layered over with soft, lighter-coloured new ones. And there, circling above this genuinely picturesque excrement worthy of the brush of a Toulouse-Lautrec, are the flies: two or three big dung flies with shiny, emerald-green bodies, and a dozen ordinary, livelier, blackish-brown ones.

Well then: I was worse than those multiple, variegated layers of shit, far worse. As much worse as the shit itself was worse than its own total absence.

The depths to which I had fallen were monstrous, and I myself was a monster.

Not only had I abandoned my wife to the whim of fate by ending up a suspect under investigation in a prison cell. In addition, as a special bonus, I was betraying her by sitting in that cell and comforting myself with memories of my amorous street adventures. I had not simply betrayed the woman I loved, I had betrayed her twice over, in spades. Betrayed her in deed and in thought. Betrayed her like no one had ever betrayed anyone before.

Suddenly all this disappeared. The man of excrement froze. His eyes, which had been roaming aimlessly over the heap of clothes and food, had stumbled across a tempting little package, tightly stuffed so that the smooth cellophane glittered merrily.

I didn't stop showering myself with curses. But now that just seemed to continue automatically, of its own accord – every last scrap of attention was riveted to that little bag filled with something brown. I dashed to the table where I kept my tableware, filled a mug with water and lowered the heating coil's dull-grey stinger into it. Then I hurried back to the package, picked it up and toyed with it for while, kneading it in my hands, listening to the little granules rustling under the plastic. And I felt my lips spontaneously stretching out into a dry smile.

Caffeine was one of my closest friends. I'd been using it regularly for six years. First three times a day – in the morning, at lunch and in the evening. A cup at a time. Then I had acquired a certain amount of taste and money, so I didn't drink instant coffee any more, only the fresh-brewed stuff, Turkish-style: I bought packets of it, whole beans, and ground it myself. In the morning I made myself two cups, one after the other, at lunch I drank another two, and then one more in the evening. And before bed I always drank a little cup too. It was at that stage that the office appeared. My own room, my own door, my own desk, chair, cupboard, computer, telephone. Tag a coffee-maker on to that little collection – and it was heaven on earth. My dosage shot up – I was switching the machine on every half hour. The longer it went on, the more I drank: two years later I was still drinking at the same rate, still nothing but Turkish-style, only now the secretary brought it to me. Every morning I used to order her to count the number of cups I drank in a day. Then I worked out the statistics. It turned out I was consuming enough poison to kill a horse. But that didn't stop me.

A year later, working from eight in the morning till ten at night, I was gulping down brewed and instant with equal voracity, every fifteen or twenty minutes. In the morning and late at night, at home, I prepared a special strong brew: I poured mineral water on to a double portion of well ground powder, brought it to the boil and added salt instead of sugar – the drink this produced was almost suicidally bitter, but it lashed the nerves into frenzied activity. Exactly the way a stimulant ought to.

My teeth were covered with an amber yellow coating that was impossible to clean off. I could even smell coffee when I urinated.

Now, as I generously sprinkled the drug into the water, stirring the spoon round in a circle of snowy-white foam on top of the steaming liquid and lowering four lumps of sugar into that circle, my nostrils trembled as I drew in the beloved aroma and laughed lecherously.

I took several large swallows straight away. Emptied half the mug. Gulped it down like water. Several long, agonizing seconds passed, and then there they were – a million little needles jabbing into my brain. A dizzy feeling; a light sweat breaking out on my forehead. My eyes went dark. I felt for the wall with my hand, leaned against it and sat down. Dozens of bright-coloured stars started spinning in front of my eyes, glittering and leaving tortuous, twisted trails that faded immediately.

Caffeine is the best poison I've ever tried. You don't have to breathe it in as smoke, mutilating your bronchi and lungs. You don't suck it up into your nostrils. It doesn't transform you into a doltish beast, the way alcohol does, or into a slow-creeping plant, like cannabis. It doesn't carry you off into contorted spaces crammed with tortuous thoughts, like a hallucinogen.

There's a certain nobility in its preparation and consumption. If some brilliant intellect ever draws up a periodical table of poisons, then caffeine will be right there at its centre, the golden mean.

The poison instantly jolted my mind into action. A number of very useful thoughts went rushing through it, like noisy trains. I grabbed hold of the last one, lowered my hand into the glittering cellophane of my treasure trove, found a pen and a note book, ripped out several pages with a sharp crack, moved my empty mug to one side, sat in a comfortable position and wrote:

To the head of the investigative team, general Zuev.

A little lower, after a moment's thought – inside my brain everything had started zooming about like crazy again – I traced out in big letters:

Personal.

Comrade general! Circumstances oblisge me to request a meeting with you, at which I intend to provide you with important information concerning the criminal case that you are investigating.

This declaration would be sent twenty-eight days later, I thought. When my month was up. Perhaps the general would let me go anyway, without any one-on-one, without any bribe – simply because he had no proof of my guilt. But if he only let my boss go, and put me away, then my declaration would hit his desk the following day.

The general would pick up his phone and give instructions to bring the prisoner to him.

They would bring me, and I would begin. More or less like this:

Comrade general! There's a good song that contains the words: 'No one will grant us deliverance – no God, no Tsar, no hero …'

I remember the song, the high-priest Zuev would reply benignly. Carry on, my son.

After that the song goes: 'We shall secure out liberation with our own hands! And those hands will not be empty! The hand that gives will not give grudgingly…'

No, I said to myself. That's not right. I shouldn't come at it from a distance like that. Better get straight to the point.

I know I'm in the wrong! I've broken the law many times, and I'm prepared to take my punishment. I'll pay the fine. It doesn't matter to me whose pocket it goes into. I'm not interested in trying to figure that out and I don't have the time. I can pay into two pockets, I can pay into three. I'll do whatever you say. Pay it to the state, or a private individual, or into a fund, or an account in a Swiss bank – it's all the same to me. All I want is to be left in peace.

Yes, I thought with a nod, closing my eyes and trying to picture the entire scene. The right way to treat the general was like the traffic cop who had accepted my dollar bills in exchange for his forbearance. Put the proposition directly, simply, comprehensibly, with a friendly gleam in my eyes.

I gave in, made myself a second mug of coffee and drank it in large, greedy gulps. The metal of the mug was hot, it burned my lips. I blew on it and spat out the pain, but I didn't stop until I'd drunk the lot. Then I immediately lit a cigarette. In the slang of consumers of poisons, this is known as 'topping up'. First putting one poison into your body, then following it straight away with another.

Now, to proceed: don't look anywhere except in his eyes! Should I smile or not? That would become clear when I was there. I definitely ought to crack some little joke or other. But not right at the start. Otherwise the general would think I was trying to ingratiate myself. And I'd make my gestures forceful, but keep them within moderation.

The mirror on the wall was absolutely tiny – I had to move my face right up close to it in order to see my reflection and form an opinion on whether I was convincing or not.

Would a man whose trousers and shoes were falling off him be convincing? A boy prisoner looking like some disgraceful, unfunny clown from a cheap sideshow? What if the general saw before him not an uncompromising, hard-bitten capitalist, but a pitiful, unshaved youth with crazy hair sticking out in all directions?

Every few minutes I heard a light scraping sound and a knock from the direction of the door – that was the shutter being opened – and the guard on duty looked at me through the thick piece of transparent plastic covering the hole.

I definitely had to drink three or four mugs of coffee before I went to see Zuev. Never mind if I looked agitated. Never mind if my hands shook and my voice trembled. That didn't matter. How else should a young boy who has ripped off a bundle look when he's offering a bribe to a big militia boss?

Surely you understand, general, that I'm going to give you money anyway? If not you, then your subordinates. Or your subordinates' subordinates. Your vassals' vassals. There's bound to be one coarse brute who'll take my money and ease my fate. Betray you all for dollar bills. I'll search for that scumbag energetically, tirelessly, but carefully, cautiously – until I find him. And my boss will look for him. And my lawyers, friends and patrons will look too. After all, I didn't make my money alone, on an uninhabited island. I'm built into a system, and it will support me.

You were wrong to treat me this way, comrade general! I don't make money in order to squander it in Nice, Barbados, Florida and other such places. I don't have that kind of sweet tooth. I don't even have a passport for foreign travel. I don't travel anywhere. And I won't go away. I won't just scatter the money to the wind. If you take it all away, I'll earn more. Don't you worry, Zuev. All the capital has been and will be invested right here, in my country, right under your nose. My money will stay in Russia, because I want my grandchildren to have intelligent and interesting friends and soulmates who speak the same language as they do! So you see, I'm not crap, I'm not scum. You made a mistake, general. Take the money and let me go home.

Such were the oaths, the doubts, the fog of pointless thoughts, the torments of conscience that filled my first full day in my pre-trial isolation cell.

7

I couldn't give a damn for prison. I was strong and tough. Too tough for these Lefortovo cells that were as sterile as a maternity ward. That much became clear on the third day.

The prison that had so impressed the bearded classics of Russian literature proved on inspection to be a sanatorium. Every day here they fed me boiled grain made with milk. They wished me goodnight in the evening. They brought me the catalogue of books in the local library. They took me up for my walk – from the first floor to the third – in a special lift. The lift was divided in two by thick steel mesh: the guard in one half and me in the other.

I could sleep all day long if I wanted. When I caught up completely on my sleep – that took about twenty-four hours – I realised I had absolutely nothing to occupy my time. The only form of activity accessible to me was thinking, and for the greater part of the day I strode around engrossed in my thoughts, wearing just my shorts and slippers, moving backwards and forwards across the narrow space of my abode behind bars. In thirty days I would get enough sleep and rest to last for many long years, I calculated happily. It might be jail for some, but for me the Lefortovo pre-trial detention centre was a genuine rest home. Quiet and sunny. Sit, drink tea, smoke. Make plans.

Maybe six hundred years earlier, in some medieval dungeon, suspended on the rack with my sex organs clamped in red-hot pincers, I would have given in. But outside the prison the twentieth century is just coming to an end. The supervisory prosecutor visits my cell and asks considerately whether I have any complaints or demands. I smile – I feel ashamed. The prosecutor is fifty and I am twenty-seven. He is a servant of the law and I a nouveau-riche smooth operator. My food parcel includes smoked meat and red fish, bananas and kiwi fruit. I can barely stop myself inviting the prosecutor to join me for breakfast.

The prosecutor is an experienced man, and he clearly realises that I ought to be dealt with more strictly. I ought to be tortured, patiently and skilfully. By three or four men. The mysteries of torment ought to be painstakingly revealed to me. My nails should be torn out. First on my hands. Then, if necessary, on my feet. They ought to kick me in the face. File down my teeth. Inject sodium pentathanol into a vein. Then I would probably tell them something. I'd provide the investigation with every last scrap of information. Confess. Break. Testify on the true substance of the case.

But no. It's all very different. The servants of the law are smiling, cultured individuals. At six in the morning the screw on duty says good morning and at ten in the evening he says good night.

I am equally polite in reply. It's not hard. Your jail is no jail to me …

In the morning the hole in the door opened up.

'What's the name?' I heard a voice ask.

'Rubanov.'

'You're wanted.'

'I don't understand …'

'Put your trousers on and come out.'

'Where to?'

'To where you're wanted.'

'Where are you taking me, captain? Who's sent for me?'

'No talking! Face the wall!'

I walked over the steel decking of the second level as far as the middle of the gallery, where it expanded into a wide hall. Looking down, I saw the control centre of the entire prison. There was a man in a camouflage suit sitting with his elbows propped on a massive grey-metal console that looked like the jawbone of an ancient mammoth: jagged and angular, with rows of huge, different-coloured buttons, it must have been manufactured at least fifty years earlier. The reliable, hand-built technology of the old Land of Soviets. Buttons of super-strong plastic, each one as big as a horse's eye-ball. Thick wires of absolutely pure copper. Terminals the size of a Communist Party ticket. A device like that would carry on working forever. It wouldn't stop even if it was flooded with water, blood or vomit. It could be controlled by any little eighteen-year-old soldier. He would never hit the wrong button. Even if a nuclear bomb exploded close by in the Lefortovo Park, the electricity would carry on running through the wires, keeping the doors securely locked. God forbid that the minor commotion of a nuclear war should allow the enemies of the state to scatter and run.

Turning off the gallery, I found myself in a completely empty room with no windows, where I was subjected to a thorough search. The checker patted down my entire body through my clothes; he made me remove my slippers, crumpled them up and examined them; he gave the elastic waist bands of my shorts and trousers a thorough fingering, each one separately; and to finish with, he even looked into my mouth.

The heat still refused to leave the great city, raising its stone blocks to incandescence, searing and thickening the air, pressing down heavily on people's heads. I caught the smell of my guard's sweating body. The corridor of the interrogation block was ventilated by a feeble draught; I could still breathe there, but in the office everything suddenly began trembling and shimmering, slithering slowly downwards in front of my eyes. The features of the two men who were most important to me now were mirages adrift in the stifling haze. One had made it his objective to put me in prison, the other to save me from it. One was smiling with professional courtesy, the other was grinning self-confidently in an attempt to inspire me, his client, with hope.

But the client didn't really feel much like being inspired.

'Everything all right?' Red asked me straight away.

'Fine,' I replied, sitting down sideways on to him. 'I've had enough sleep to last me for the next three years. And how well-rested are you, boss?'

Khvatov pursed his lips.

'Don't try to make fun of me. I'm not your enemy, Andrei. You might well have nothing to do with this business. It's possible you really were set up. I won't lie to you: the evidence against you isn't, you know, massive. But I do have to answer to my own, you know, bosses. They give the orders and I do the work, get it? My job is to put that, you know, statement on the desk. And express my own ideas about it.'

'It's not a joke,' I protested. 'It's a question. What am I in here for? Why did you put me in prison? Because you were afraid I would run away? Well, I won't. I have a family, a small child, a father and mother. I have nowhere to run to …'

Through the bars of the wide-open window that overlooked the inner courtyard of the building there came a breath of hot wind and the sounds of the prison's internal economy: people calling to each other, car engines starting up, someone swearing crudely as he dropped a crate, the hoarse, ear-splitting barking of the guard dogs, the rumble of doors being opened and closed.

I suddenly felt as if I hadn't been in there for just two days, but for a long, long time, and I wasn't going to stay there for a month, but for many years, until I was old and grey. These obscenities shouted in the distance, these badly scratched desks and rough windowsills, these dark, depressing colours – brownish-green, dirty yellow, light brown – these sagging floorboards, these cracked door lintels, that strident roar and clatter of decrepit engines – they were all an extension of the universe that had once produced me too.

Lethargic Asia. Crudely daubed in the savage tribal colours of the Land of Soviets.

'Tell me, Stepan Mikhailovich,' I asked with real feeling, 'why do you want to put me away? There's no advantage in it. Just figure out all the money owing to the budget. Add in the fines. And I'll pay it all. Perhaps it will take all my money, down to the last kopeck, but to hell with the money. I'll earn some more. Why put me away, eh? Why take away my freedom? Once you put me inside, I'll never pay anything back! Not a thing, do you understand? The criminal code prices my offence at three years of maximum security detention. I'll survive that somehow. And I'll come out – angry, disgraced, but still with money. And I'll finally turn into an enemy of the state, a lifelong opponent of the authorities, an embittered, dyed-in-the-wool villain. Why put me away?'

'Because it's right,' Khvatov replied patiently. 'I think your tricks have earned you more than three years. You ran an unlicensed business. That's a separate, you know, offence. Up to five years, as a matter of fact …'

'Yes,' I agreed morosely. 'I didn't think about that.'

'Don't bother. All the thinking's been, you know, done for you. Five years.' Khvatov looked at me. 'Why didn't you, you know, buy one? With all that, you know, money of yours?'

'A banking licence?' I asked in surprise. 'Who needs it? It costs tens of thousands of dollars, and you have to spend a year running around trying to get it, collecting signatures in all the offices. It's simpler and cheaper to fake the documents. To pretend I'm not a bank at all, that I trade in Pampers and Snickers. If I spend years going round the official channels, collecting licences and permits, I'll never earn anything …'

The native son of Ryazan shook his head censoriously.

'But you can't, you know, do that either! Not pay the state anything, register everything through false nominees. It's getting too greedy that finishes you.'

'Ah, I get it,' I said with a smile. 'You're offended because I didn't buy a piece of paper giving me permission when I should have. A little royal charter. I didn't make my contribution! I didn't share. Okay, well now you've caught hold of my hand and given it a good slap, hard enough to make it sting – I respect that. I probably do deserve it. Maybe I was a bit too greedy. But now what? Instead of making me pay up in full, you lock me away? What for?'

I put on an honest, open expression, radiated positive energy, tried to transmit a charge of cheerful strength and confidence in my own rightness from my eyes straight into the forehead of my check-shirted compatriot.

You can't deceive someone if you're sitting sideways on to him. Two days earlier, at the first interrogation, I'd had a hard time. But now I discovered a narrow crack between the side of the desk and my stool that was screwed to the floor, a crack just slightly wider than a pack of cigarettes, and I stuck my right leg into it from the knee down. Thanking God as I did so that all the men in my family were gaunt and thin, with the minimum of solid flesh on their slim bones. Now the lower part of my body was no longer poised on the stool in a sideways-on position, it was half-turned. All I had to do was make a half-turn to the right from the waist in order to achieve my goal and confront the other man head-on. The way a TV anchorman sits facing the camera.

Once I had arranged myself properly, I could carry through my deception in total comfort: pull back my shoulders into the 'I have nothing to hide' position and put my hands on the desk – the investigator definitely had to see them. Open hands are good for sending concealed signals. To do this you have to hold them on their edges, perpendicular to the surface of the desk, repeatedly opening them up and moving them towards the other person, as if you are gathering in the air or pushing a large sphere. Forcing your deception forward into space, endowing the words you speak and the sound of your voice with additional impetus. At the same time I didn't forget to apply pressure with the upper part of my body as well as my hands – leaning towards Khvatov, bringing my face closer to him.

There was no smell coming from his mouth. Which was a clear indication that this smart guy never forgot to eat breakfast and lunch at the right time. So he was a calm man who was temperate in all things, with a penchant for strict order, and his brain was the same – it functioned precisely, without deviating from the primary task that had been set.

And that brain, I admitted to myself with an inward shudder, was dangerous. It would expose me as a desperate liar the moment I made the slightest mistake.

'Tell the person who decides things,' I went on hoarsely, under the tense gaze of the red-headed lawyer, 'that the suspect Rubanov is ready now. He wishes to write a frank confession of failure to pay taxes into the tsar's pocket. And he is prepared to pay everything immediately, even if it reduces him to a beggar. But only when he's free!'

Khvatov gave an official nod.

'But you can't implicate me in theft from the treasury,' I said firmly, once again raking in air with my hands and leaning forward, drilling into the investigator with my glance, smiling slightly, hypnotising him, implanting the suggestion of my words in his mind. 'I didn't know anything. I was set up, period!'

The CASE FILE lying on the table had a tempting look.

I immediately tried to remember exactly how many dollars there were in the plump wad I'd left for my wife. I supposed there would be about ten thousand. If the red-headed lawyer met Irma today and got the money from her, and gave it to Khvatov, then tomorrow I would already be reading everything I wanted to see. Maybe I ought to suggest this plan to the short-sighted phlegmatic from Ryazan there and then? A simple deal: this evening – five thousand dollars in cash, tomorrow afternoon – five minutes alone with the case documents …

No, I decided, I have to get out of this myself and not drain my family dry. The boss will be out in twenty-eight days – and then I'll have all the dollars I need.

'Are you going to provide testimony?' the man in checks enquired cautiously.

'There won't be any testimony,' I said. 'That's absolutely definite. Try hassling the people who set me up. The minister, the pharmacist, anyone you like. But I'll give it a miss.'

Khvatov took his time before he spoke.

'Andrei, you're a, you know, pretty heavy guy. We looked at your bank statements, you know … studied the documents. Billions of roubles passed through your hands every day. How come they weren't afraid to set you up? I don't quite understand that. I'd be afraid to, you know, go head to head with someone who controlled all those billions …'

The question was a pointed one, awkward, it made me appreciate the militia functionary's sober and rational mind even more – far removed as he was from the habits of Moscow's business world, he still thought about it in the right way, as a pack of predators in which everyone fears the strong and the weak are torn to pieces.

'Don't exaggerate,' I replied hastily. 'My billions aren't really mine, they belong to other people. My job is shifting them about, deftly rearranging them here and there. Investments, foreign currency, bank deposits, state securities and so on. Money loves to circulate. One man comes to me and says: buy a bill of exchange. Another says: change deutschmarks to pounds. Yet another wants to transfer funds to his daughter in England, for pocket money. And another has quarrelled with his business partner and wants his entire share up front, cash straight into his pocket.'

I wasn't lying. That was the way it was. It was stupid to deny the obvious. I could babble on about the details of my work for hours. The deception consisted of the actual subject of conversation. I had to keep throwing up the subjects, one after another, without any pauses. Otherwise Khvatov would eventually get around to asking me directly if I'd been working alone or with someone else.

'You shouldn't think about me being so big-time,' I said and smiled. 'There are hundreds and hundreds like me in the city. Maybe I am pretty big-time, but I'm not irreplaceable. I've got no one behind me. That makes it cheaper and easier to bring me down.'

Khvatov nodded seriously and started gathering up his things.

'So you've answered your own question,' he said suddenly.

'Which one exactly?'

'Why we should put you away. Maybe it's, you know, safer for you in here? Haven't you thought about that?

I shook my head, perplexed.

The lawyer asked quickly:

'Do you have any concrete information?'

The investigator picked up the case file carefully with both hands and started shoving it precisely, starting with the corner, into his baggy, artificial-leather briefcase.

'Of course not. But if I were in Andrei's place, I'd be on my guard … That's all, gentlemen! I'll, you know, leave you alone together. Will ten minutes be enough?'

Red and I both nodded with equal impatience.

As I pondered how best to deceive one man and the state machine standing behind him, the machine that was supposed in principle to protect all honest people, I didn't feel like some rat or devious bastard at all. They wanted to take away my freedom – so I was going to defend myself as hard as I could. What else did you expect, guys? I asked, mentally addressing my provincial opponent as he watched me through his spectacles, peering apprehensively through narrowed eyes. What did you expect from a man who has been flung into jail just like that, without even being charged? He hasn't killed anyone, or robbed anyone, or raped anyone – it's just that he's too young to have all that money. A man like that will defend himself. Use his hands, his feet, his teeth, his nails. He'll snarl like a dog and try to strike like a snake. He'll use cunning and exploit logic. A man like that will call on all his resources in order to save himself.

Don't expect me to give you an easy time; you won't get it.

Left alone, the lawyer and I smiled at each other: my smile was crooked, his was excessively cheerful.

'How are things?'

'I'm in jail,' I replied in the same tone.

Red smiled again. Of course, how could things be in jail?

I'd taken a liking to Maxim Shtein from the first moment we met. From my point of view, this intelligent and rather determined young man had only one serious shortcoming: his official domicile in Moscow. As a native resident of this well-fed, clean-swept, brightly lit, well-guarded capital city, he could never fully understand the raging, bloodthirsty passion for money and a better life experienced by me, his client.

He had lived in a rich European city ever since he was a child. His entire appearance testified to that. His clothes, his manners and his facial expressions. But I had come from a drowsy, dusty little provincial town, where for centuries the main amusements for young people had been drinking the local moonshine, brawling in the street and chewing sunflower seeds. Red-headed Maxim was no fugitive from the back of beyond. He hadn't arrived in the centre of the state carrying a bag in which two or three pairs of socks and shorts jostled with two or three clever books. He had never gone hungry, he had never gritted his teeth and promised himself he would do anything he could to make it in this new place.

Looking at Red, I saw a possible version of myself – someone who had not abandoned his studies out of sheer hopelessness, but calmly gone on to earn his degree and then gone to work in his own chosen profession. If I hadn't left the university five years earlier, then perhaps by now I would have been a respected author and dressed like the red-headed lawyer, in neat suits that were low-key, but without a sign of wear. Worn a Japanese watch and gazed into the future with cool-headed optimism.

Yes, in the early nineties, when my boss Mikhail and I, and another ten thousand young men like us, had come here to the capital, work had been found for everyone; if he pulled a few tricks, an intelligent and intrepid newcomer could always find himself a decent job. But it was always paid monthly, unofficially, in 'black cash'. And the money was just barely enough to rent a place to live. You inevitably found yourself caught in a cleft stick. As if the flat-owners and the employers had conspired: if you want to live in a separate flat, give the owner all your money! Moscow pays, but it immediately takes all its cash back again!

All the newcomers, to a man, dreamed of breaking out of this closed circle. The young bachelors clustered together into small groups, with two or three of them living together. The married ones, especially those with children, wept and groaned, but they paid out the rent on time.

But the lawyer I saw sitting in front of me, with his perfectly shaved, round, ruddy cheeks, dressed in his fresh, pleasant clothes, twirling a rather neat fountain pen in his fingers – he had never been tormented by the question of where to get money to pay for a place to live. Where? Where? How can I get hold of those damned two hundred dollars (later it was three hundred, then four hundred)? Practically the same age as me – well, he was three years older, but anyway we were the same generation – he looked like a level-headed individual, with those relaxed, slightly lazy movements. Laid back. But I was wizened and dark in the face, exhausted by the constant battle for survival. I regarded him ironically but enviously. When he found a job for the same pay as I did, he didn't have to pay anyone anything simply in order to live in the capital. His cash had gone into his pocket. He had bought appetising food and beautiful clothes. Taken girls out dancing. Bought books and records.

At that time the sullen, provincial Andrei Rubanov, who had grown up and become aware of his own individuality in the village of Uzunovo, was also living in Moscow. Skinny, raw-boned, nervous, he gritted his teeth and grabbed at any offer that promised to put a little extra capital in his pocket. Always taking risks, always tormented, always spoiling for a fight.

But he always fed his landlords their rent on time.

These were sprightly pensioners with cars and dachas on standard plots of land. Possibly even this young lawyer's parents. As a rule these people were rational with their money, spending half on themselves and investing the remainder in their rural estates. And they also passed a bit on to their children. Without forgetting to remind me that I, their tenant, had no right even to hammer a nail into the wall of their home.

I nodded and agreed and slaved like a lunatic in order to pay the rent on time. And year by year, I gradually became more and more brutalised.

Even my advocate's handkerchief, which was yellow, to match his tie, and protruded elegantly from his breast pocket, seemed to me aware of belonging to the select group of inhabitants. Unlike me, Red had always felt perfectly at ease. He wasn't busy deciding the urgent problems of the moment, but acting with the longer term in mind. He had graduated from the law faculty and gone to work in a law firm for a mere pittance, but with the chance of professional advancement. And he had advanced! It had taken him, perhaps, ten years, but he had risen to membership of the municipal college of counsellors at law, and then the serious clients had appeared: people like me, like my business partner, young and fierce, with low social origins, from the semi-indigent or totally indigent stratum of the Russian intelligentsia. Relentless, energetic, prepared to take risks, to deceive people and buy them, prepared to do many things if only they could get gold.

After waiting patiently for the door to close firmly behind Khvatov, the lawyer shook his head, gave me a frightening glare and whispered:

'Don't forget, they listen to everything in here …'

I nodded.

The lawyer leaned even closer:

'What are you doing? Why are you mocking him? That's a strategic error! The investigator's just a stooge, he doesn't decide anything. He's a little man, not the one we need. Don't waste your nerves on him. Relax and take it easy. Be patient …'

'Is there any news?' I asked, also speaking in a whisper and ignoring his advice.

Red shook his head without speaking.

I was quite certain that the office was bugged from top to bottom. After seeing the main control post of this tidy, well-organised state institution, I had come to understand the place better. No doubt about it – the room was bugged expertly, in several locations. With old, carbon-button microphones, made by hand, with a soldering iron. The solid technology of the 1960s was still operating in the interrogation office of the Lefortovo fortress. Pretty much the same kind of mikes as the ones into which Elvis had crooned 'Love me tender' and Marilyn Monroe had chirped 'Happy birthday, Mr President'.

Nowadays equipment like that – with securely soldered circuit boards, valves and thick wires – was sold in the shops in the *high end* category and it cost big bucks.

'There's only something from your wife,' Maxim whispered and took a letter out of his briefcase.

I read it. Two pages, and on the second Irma had traced the outline of our eighteen-month-old son's hand. A little infant's hand. The heartache I experienced at that moment was so intense that the blood rushed to my eyes. If I hadn't squeezed them shut for a few seconds, I would have wept bloody tears. But I didn't.

'Bring me some news, from Mikhail,' I said with just my lips.

The lawyer nodded. As he did so, he gave me a brief, probing glance, lowered his eyes and started thinking, but then immediately looked at me again, with a look of charitable sympathy. He can't understand, I guessed, why a client would be worried about his business partner and not himself.

It was very simple: Mikhail Moroz had far more chance of slipping through the hands of justice unscathed. My own chances weren't too good.

I'd done all the dirty work. All the clues led to me. That was the way everything had been planned from the very beginning. My boss's safety was sacrosanct, since he knew how to make money and he made it. Not a single hair must be harmed on the head of a man with that kind of skill. It was a purely Asiatic way of putting the question. The samurai way. After all, Moscow isn't really a European city. It's an immense Mongol camp. Where every lackey seeks a master and is willing to fight to the death for him.

As soon as my boss Mikhai was let out, he would get the money together – that would only take a couple of days at most – and I would request a meeting with big daddy Zuev, and he would let me go. It was simple. A general who liked air-conditioned cars couldn't possibly refuse money!

Yes, they had put me in prison. But that was the way everything had been planned, the possibility had been foreseen, it had been discussed, an agreement had been reached about possible lines of behaviour, about what each of us would do in an unpleasant situation. Mikhail and I both thought in simple business terms: there was a business, it brought in big profits, it had made us rich. It was our sacred cash cow. Our chicken that laid golden eggs. It was our everything. The chicken and the cow had to survive at any price. Business *über alles*.

Maxim the red-headed lawyer didn't need to know about that. And he wouldn't understand it anyway. He hadn't arrived in this city from the dark, distant, icebound expanses where wolves howl in the night. He didn't really have any idea what it was like to go soaring upwards. He intended to obtain the good things in life without risking anything. But did that ever really happen? Not here, at least, in the capital of the Empire. Not now, at least, and not to me.

'So you don't have any complaints?' the supervisory prosecutor asked me again.

I had already guessed that young people didn't often turn up inside this strictest of political prisons. And the prosecutor was examining me with great curiosity.

'None at all,' I reported briskly.

'Any applications? Requests?'

'One request.'

'What would you like to request?'

'A cigar, a bath and some cognac!'

The prosecutor said nothing, allowing the rapid movements of his pupils and twitching of his cheek to express his negative emotions.

'No chance!' he replied rudely, thrusting out his chin, and walked out, stomping heavily across the brown concrete floor in his worn, light-coloured shoes.

He had the last word, and he was right. I sadly admitted that to myself, lowered my backside on to the blanket and dropped my head into my hands. Maybe there really was no chance at all? Maybe I ought to have stayed a hungry and honest reporter? Maybe I was wrong? Maybe I really was a bad man?

8

The point about the cigars was this: the last time I'd dreamed about a cigar was three years before my arrest. In the spring of 1993, during the warm, languorously humid Moscow May, my friend Mikhail and I, benignly inclined and physically strong young novice capitalists (I was twenty-four, he was twenty-eight), were sitting in a car parked at the kerb and waiting for the man we needed to see. We were listening to the radio-cassette playing one of the anthems of those turbulent times, 'Hotel California' by the American band The Eagles.

'Welcome to the Hotel California' the lead singer drawled, that special hint of hoarseness in his voice making it clear that the invitation was by no means addressed to everyone, but only to the most progressive, sharp, decisive, risk-taking, serious, strong, confident, cool and at the same time subtly sensitive of men. The very group in which Mikhail and I classed ourselves.

We were looking for an office. We required premises. A room. With a telephone. With a door that could be locked. With heating. At a reasonable distance from the metro. A middleman had been found who had promised to line up something suitable. He had phoned that morning. Named the address and set a time.

When we reached the place, we had realised it was an option that suited us perfectly. Not a Californian hotel, of course. But basically it was just what we needed. The building was a seven-storey grey concrete box owned by a certain scientific institution. In the days of the Land of Soviets science had flourished to a quite exceptional degree. Soviet scientists used to work in bright rooms with big windows. Now the spacious halls and studies that must have made such a sweet setting for solving the problems of inorganic chemistry or nuclear physics were being rented out to entrepreneurs whose minds were exercised by problems of a different kind: supply and undersupply, hand-outs and back-handers, conversion and deconversion, getting goods into customs and getting them out of customs – that was the standard set of problems currently being resolved, with excruciating effort, beneath the high ceilings of the former shrine of science.

All the approach roads to the building were crowded with expensive motor vehicles. There were young men darting about in all directions, their neckties casually knotted and their facial muscles set in tense expressions. Gold watches, bracelets, rings and spectacle frames glinted on every side. And at the same spot the resourceful representatives of petty street commerce had organised their ancillary trading activities by erecting a tobacco kiosk.

After waiting for an hour, we realised that nothing was going to happen – we weren't going to see any intermediary or any premises.

At that time proper business etiquette was only observed on the real estate market by those who were working with solid, substantial clients. Those who sought the company of fat cats with thick wallets. But Mikhail and I had not positioned ourselves as fat cats, which was quite understandable: if you don't happen to have a thick wallet, there's absolutely no point in positioning yourself as a fat cat.

Nonetheless we – and especially Mikhail – knew the taste of money, we knew the right way to behave, and we dressed quite presentably.

But even so, the middleman had dumped us.

If it had been the year two thousand and something, this disreputable individual would obviously have called our mobile number and at least apologised to his clients for the deal falling through. But back then, in the rough and tumble year of '93, only the chosen few were familiar with the pleasures of mobile communications technology. The other ragamuffins like me and my friend Mikhail used the public phones on the street.

The broker didn't turn up.

Mikhail and I couldn't understand it. At the first meeting with the middleman we thought we'd done everything right, covered all the finest points. We'd dolled ourselves up in coarse pigskin jackets and black jeans. Our cheek-muscles had twitched and our eyes had glittered with a steely glint. Heavy diplomat-style briefcases had weighed down our arms. But that swine of a middleman had still spotted us for beginners. Poor provincials. Young fools.

So now my friend Mikhail and I were sitting in the modest interior of our modest automobile without speaking, each thinking our own thoughts about the same thing.

I felt annoyed. The broker had spurned us. That meant the forty-year-old gent with the birdlike movements hadn't been impressed by the tough-guy elements of my wardrobe: the club jacket and the belt with metal studs all the way along its edge, and the devastating crimson cowboy boots with pointed toes. I drummed my fingers against the shabby steering column and admitted to myself that my expensive war paint, which only one year earlier would have convinced any citizen that I was a real heavy guy, was no longer working too well. Any entrepreneur who was even slightly well off, even a broker on the property market, could easily recognise me as a young man who was practically a pauper.

I assumed that Mikhail, my reliable partner and soon-to-be boss, was wrestling with similar problems. He looked exceedingly respectable for his twenty-eight years. He weighed very nearly a hundred kilos. His spoke in a deep bass voice. He only had to tie on a basic necktie made in Russia, and he already looked like some Mr Big: at the very least a former secretary of a regional committee of the All-Union Leninist Komsomol. But if the tie was from Italy and the jacket was tweed, then the entire world gave way to Mikhail. He wasn't a boss yet, but he already looked like one. Looking at him, I grasped an amazing truth about Russian commerce, and all commerce in general: if you want to make yourself into a boss, the first thing you should start with is dressing like a boss and talking like one.

But even so, the impressive tweed on Mikhail's shoulders had failed to make an impression on the broker. And the broker had not turned up to parley. He'd realised he wouldn't get a decent commission out of Mikhail and his friend Andrei.

In fact Mikhail and Andrei hadn't been planning to pay any decent commission. They'd been planning to sting the broker. Right from the off. Not give him anything at all. It was simple: we only had to pretend we didn't like the room we were offered, say a polite goodbye to the middleman and leave, but then come back an hour later and sign a contract with the owners of the building directly.

The broker had got it right. His instinct had not deceived him. And now Mikhail and Andrei were idling away the time, fuming in dejected silence.

'Let's go,' Mikhail said eventually. 'We're not going to get a bite in this stream.'

'Agreed,' I replied, switching on the ignition and starting to swing the wheel.

Maybe we'd have sworn like troopers and vented our rancour by acoustic means, if we hadn't been surrounded on all sides by the glorious month of May, assertively insinuating itself into the car over the tops of the half-lowered windows, caressing our cheeks with warm currents of air from the right and the left, pacifying our hearts, mellowing our souls and instilling them with faith in goodness, love and humanity – even though it did consist in part of unscrupulous property-market middlemen ...

Suddenly an immense German sedan cut right in front of my boxy little car and stopped, settling heavily on its suspension just two metres ahead. The gleaming body of this urban torpedo swayed, the massive doors swung open, and two men stepped out on to the asphalt – both young in years and wearing expensive threads.

One of them, the size of a huge fridge, had to struggle to get out of the car. He straightened up with difficulty, in several stages, and it became clear that his body was only slightly less wide than it was long. It had almost no neck, but up at the top there was a naked shaven head, with a little Quasimodo face decorating its front facade.

The second individual looked like an updated version of the first, faster-moving and more adaptable. His solid figure, attractive gold bracelets, tracksuit trousers with stripes down the side and smooth gait – which, by the way, even had a certain spring to it – were impressive. But the strongest impression was produced by the cigar: thick, light-brown and belching out copious smoke. At the precise moment of his emergence from the leather-bound innards of the automobile the sporty youth took a puff and a serious dollop of ash detached itself from the end of the colossal cylinder of tobacco, landing on the asphalt pavement. Both men had flattened noses and cauliflower ears.

These young lions had arrived on their own business. They had nothing at all to do with Mikhail and me. They had simply performed their dangerous driving manoeuvre out of habitual loutishness.

Undoubtedly, these colourful individuals were far from stupid, they clearly understood that the offence they had committed was not so much a contravention of the rules of the road as of the unwritten code of driver's etiquette: thou shalt not get pushy! Thou shalt not cut across everyone else! That was why the cigar-lover glanced in our direction and even gave his neck a brief interrogative jerk, as if to say: no complaints, are there? And he released another cloud of smoke. His car cost ten times as much as mine, and he looked at me the way a young lion is supposed to: with an air of superiority.

I replied with a movement of my head, neck and forearms that was basically hostile. The meaning of the pantomime was very clear: two serious guys had cramped two far less serious guys' style.

Quasimodo and friend set off towards the tobacco kiosk.

The extreme humiliation of the moment was felt very keenly by Mikhail and myself: the caramel-sweet springtime was all around us, with the clattering heels of a girl in a mini and the scent of fresh young foliage setting your very soul yearning to soar up into the blue heavens – and in the middle of this riotous festival of life, two brazen-faced cretins had tried to pick a fight with us.

'Let's smash their faces in,' Mikhail suddenly suggested with a resolute air. His solid western-Slavonic neck turned red. He even reached out his hand to open the door.

I thought about it. My friend had a good boxing grade in the heavyweight category. There was no doubt he would easily flatten Quasimodo with a few crosses to the jaw. Meanwhile, I'd be measuring up to the other guy. He was taller than me and he was wearing comfortable trousers – but he was obviously a junky. His arms dangled like ropes. His movements were jerky. That was why he smoked a cigar: he required a larger dose of poison than the average nicotine user. Maybe victory would be ours. But what if they had guns?

'They're gangsters,' I said and drove off.

The right way to leave the scene after a fight that never happened is slowly, maintaining your dignity. It's even helpful to brake slightly at the last moment and look back, as if you're having doubts: maybe you shouldn't let the insult go after all? Maybe you should swing into action? Let your potential opponent have a few more nervous seconds – then, if not a moral victory, at least you'll have a moral draw.

'Gangsters?' Mikhail echoed defiantly. 'So what?'

'Gangsters are gangsters,' I replied philosophically. 'Criminals. Why tangle with them?'

'No,' Mikhail objected, jutting out his square chin. 'That's wrong. Shaving your head and riding round town in a stolen Mercedes isn't a crime. It's stupidity. Some criminals they are! I could get myself a Merc like that tomorrow! I can collect all my money together, borrow a bit and buy one, easy! And I'll hang gold chains, you know, all over myself! And shave my head. And start shaking down petty street traders. What's so heroic about that?'

'Did you see his cigar?' I asked, shifting into third gear.

'Did you see his trousers?' Mikhail squirmed on his seat. 'A cheap cretin, leading a cheap lifestyle! A cheap man riding around in an expensive automobile. When I see people like that it makes me sick!'

My friend wound the handle on the door furiously and spat crudely through the open window.

'Pay-backs,' he exclaimed in disgust. 'Shoot-outs. Shoot-ups. Raids. Meets. And all the time trying to act like they know something I don't! Konchalovsky was right: there is no animal worse than man.'

'He's only a director,' I corrected him. 'All he did was direct *Runaway Train*, but the final quote is Shakespeare's.'

'Who cares?' Mikhail shouted angrily, passionately. 'I'm talking about jerks and bastards, not Shakespeare and Konchalovsky. I'm talking about moral rights. What moral right has that insolent lout got? None! He can shave his head as much as he likes, you know, and bend his fingers in that gangster way, but he can't frighten me. The only reason I don't tangle with a caveman like that is because I haven't got the time! I'd have flattened him, fuck it, never mind Shakespeare! Turn the bloody car round!'

My friend was talking about something that was a sore point. We both had considerable experience of contact with representatives of the criminal world. A novice businessman can never avoid encounters with the professional extortioners more widely known simply as bandits. These extortioners lie in wait for the bold hero inside the entrance to his building and out on the road. But at some point the beginner ceases to be a beginner – he grows bigger, rents an office with a guarded entrance, and the shaven-headed hooligans pretty much stop bothering him. I knew it was the failed attempt to rent an office that had thrown Mikhail off balance, not the behaviour of a smug idiot with a cigar. If the broker had been a man of his word, we might already have been sitting in our own room, with a high ceiling and a window right down to the floor, figuring out where to put the coffee machine and the fax.

But unfortunately the two of us were still out on the street. And we were obliged to swallow insults from its barbarous denizens.

The lack of a little office with a desk, a chair, a computer and a telephone was a torment to my older friend. He was gradually emerging from the ranks of the beginners. And I was counting on him to drag me out after him.

Apart from Mikhail, I didn't have any friends in the world of business.

'Did you see his cigar, though?' I asked again, trying to improve my friend's mood.

But Mikhail still didn't calm down.

'I have a third-level, you know, education, right?' he roared. 'A degree! In psychology! I have a current account in the bank! I have a business, damn it! Last month I laundered almost a hundred thousand! I'm expanding, looking for an office, I can't keep up! So I hired someone! You! But I don't ride around in a Mercedes! That's not my level! That cap doesn't fit this fool! And who's he? What has he got, apart from a stolen car? What does he know? What can he do?'

'You're too intolerant,' I said. 'And that makes you frustrated.'

'Oh ho!' Mikhail exclaimed heatedly. 'Just hark at that terminology! And maybe I'm tormented by fundamental anxieties. Or simply subconsciously suppressed. Or maybe I'm in a state of emotional anazagnasis?'

I stopped speaking.

'Don't come the intellectual heavy, my son,' my friend advised me. 'Otherwise one day you'll sink into a reactive state. Save the clever-clever stuff for the gangsters' sort-outs.'

'Are we expecting any?' I asked quickly.

'Maybe.'

'Then you'd better not be there in person.'

'Why's that?'

'You despise gangsters too much.'

'Yes, I do,' Mikhail said with hate in voice. 'They're animals. Creatures with no brains or culture! Cheap garbage!'

'They're society's garbage men,' I objected.

'You're the garbage man!'

'Why are you shouting like that?'

'And why are trying to be so smart?'

I shrugged.

'Sorry,' my friend muttered after a moment's pause.

Yes. Mikhail was a rather high-strung young man. He could be rude and even insulting, but he possessed willpower and had a rather good education; he always found a way to regain control quickly.

'We're the real garbage men,' he said in a calmer voice, low and heavy. 'When we make our money, we'll clear up the space around ourselves, humanise it. Idiots with gold chains, you know, they won't be allowed into it. The more rich people there are in society, the safer it is. It's a direct relationship. Let's go and make money, Andrei! Let's go! Turn here! We'll drop in on an interesting young guy who's got something fine and juicy on offer ...'

'So which way do I drive?'

'I'll show you. Now take a left. Do you know anything about the financial market? About the banking business?'

'Almost nothing.'

'You'll learn,' Mikhail assured me.

His fit of despondency and spleen was replaced by furious activity. Obstinate guys like that always take every new defeat as a pretext for redoubling their efforts to bring victory closer.

I stepped on the gas and turned the wheel. The engine roared. The tyres squealed.

And that, finally, broke the chain of events, the multiple sequence of cause and effect in which the gangsters had ego-tripped at our expense and then Mikhail had shouted at me and ego-tripped at my expense, and I'd been forced to ego-trip at the expense of my automobile.

'But did you see that cigar he had?'

'Don't let it bother you. Soon we'll be smoking cigars just like that!'

I pressed a button, turned up the sound, and the car was filled with the passionate hollering of the American singer inviting everyone who had commitment, courage and strength to the Hotel California.

On the evening of the day when Mikhail and I were insulted by underage criminals, I bought a cigar in an expensive shop.

Back then I thought that I despised dreamers and respected only those people who knew what they wanted and got it. I went to an impossibly expensive supermarket and bought the very biggest, thickest, longest Havana that I could find. And I shelled out for a special metal case as well. I could smoke the cigar, stub it out and put it away in my pocket until the next time. Cigar butts smell horrible, but still not as bad as cigarette butts.

The money I had left over was enough for a pack of pelmeni and a Snickers for my wife. My pockets were completely empty. But I'd acquired something that would sharpen up my image. Lend it a bit of weight. Make it more serious. You can't get anywhere on the financial market without a good cigar.

9

On my fifteenth day in the solitary cell I started talking to myself for the first time. First in a whisper, then in a low voice, then in a normal voice. It wasn't actually a dialogue between a first me and a second me. If it had been I would have realised I was coming down with schizophrenia, and that wasn't part of my plan at all. As Salvador Dali said, the whole trick is not to go insane. No, I started recounting the story of my life.

Turning to the washbasin, I declared:

'Now, dear friend, I shall tell you about the cars in which I have ridden.'

Or:

'And now I want you to learn about my favourite books.'

Or:

'Now listen, brother, to how I raised my very first money.'

And then there followed graphic narratives, oral thrillers replete with multitudinous details – intimate, heart-rending and original. Naturally I had to exaggerate slightly, lay it on a bit thick. The hero of my stories, my protagonist, was Andriukha the nouveau-riche smoothie – a cheerful character, always slightly drunk, sharp-tongued and dressed by Kenzo. He was a little bit cleverer and luckier than the author, and he always emerged from any scrape unscathed. There should always be a happy ending. It always helps to dilute the truth of life with a little bit of invention.

The washbasin was silent but very attentive. This useful enamelled pan attached firmly to the wall had been chosen as my conversation partner for a very simple reason. In Russian grammar the names for almost everything around me were either feminine or neuter. But I wanted to talk to a man.

To a friend, you might say. Or an accomplice. Grammatically speaking, there were only five of us men languishing in the cell: me, the washbasin, the teapot, the heating element and the mattress. None of the others present – the pillow, the sheet, the pillowcase, the rag on the floor, the towel, the soap in the soap dish, the toothbrush – were members of this gentlemen's club.

The floor and the ceiling also reckoned themselves among the men, but we were holding them in reserve on the waiting list, as candidate members. A real club always consists of full members and candidates on the waiting list. Things look more respectable that way. The candidates are first set a period of trial membership and checked to see if they're worthy or not. Only after that, at a special induction meeting, are they solemnly promoted to full membership.

'I believe, gentlemen,' I would declare after a break for lunch or supper or after a couple of mugs of coffee, 'that you have not found my idle chat overly wearisome. So, with your permission, let us continue.'

The audience remained silent, but with my sixth sense I could tell that my listeners, both members and candidates, were eager for the continuation. A drop of water oozed slowly out of the tap and splatted tactfully against the metal surface.

'Don't worry,' I would chortle in the middle of my latest tall story. 'I shall soon relieve you of the burden of my company. Two more weeks and everything will change! They'll let my friend and boss go, and he'll hoist me out of here pronto. The two of us have lots of money, lots and lots of it. We're rich, get it? Rich by international standards, not just by local Russian ones. We're rich on a huge scale! Hundreds of thousands of dollars will be thrown into saving me! And that's no joke!'

The gentlemen silently agreed: yes, that was no joke! Certainly no joke! Hundreds of thousands was clearly no joke at all.

In general, there are no more patient and appreciative listeners than inanimate objects. It's just a pity they don't ask questions to clarify points.

Every three or four minutes the warder outside the door would open the shutter with a quiet rustling sound and watch me striding around the cell muttering something excitedly and making oratorical gestures. I didn't take any particular notice of him. I was holding forth, pontificating. Painting in the vivid details. Striving for a light, precise touch and clear, simple presentation in the telling of my tale. Not lying, but not telling the whole truth either. Such, in my view, was the art of the short story. Or of giving testimony in a public prosecutor's office.

In the evening the members of the club were joined by a visitor, always the same one and always alone: General Zuev. With only a slight effort I could easily picture the militia grandee sitting there facing me, wreathed in cigarette smoke, his watery eyes always looking down or off to one side. A big boss always looks off to the side, never at the person he's talking to. He is burdened with concerns of crucial importance for the life of the state, he is thinking of what is most central, important, fundamental. He is not greatly interested in bankers and other greedy modern businessmen who have become the subjects of criminal investigation. He is willing to hear me out, but he is in a hurry, he has a lot of work to do, and I understand that I must express my thoughts clearly and succinctly.

'Comrade general!' I begin.

It goes without saying that he is no 'comrade' of mine. What would I want with a 'comrade' like that! He is a general of the Interior Ministry, the MVD, and I am a director of an underground bank. A light-fingered speculator. But soldiers whose youth and mature years were spent in the blessed Land of Soviets are extraordinarily fond of being addressed in that way. Take any aging, greying traffic cop burdened with a family and address him as 'comrade senior lieutenant', and he will be positively inspired with subconscious love for you. 'Mr Militiaman' grates on the ear. The code word 'comrade' is simpler and clearer, it establishes contact, reminds him of the heroic past. It has a whiff of the dust thrown up by the wheels of old machine-gun carts, of tank fuel and tunics soaked in sweat, of feats of heroism and commissars in dusty helmets. It's a password.

And I shall use it.

'Comrade general!' I shall say. 'Why have you put me in jail? Why the solitary cells and the barred windows, what's the point of the gruel and all the rest of it? What am I, a murderer, a gangster, a looter? Or am I a maniac who drools as he rapes little girls in an alleyway? Or maybe I'm a terrorist? A bearded militant come down from the mountains in the name of Allah, may peace be with Him, to blast away with my grenade launcher? No, I'm a modest toiler! I work fifteen hours a day! I have broken the law, I didn't share, I didn't pay money into the treasury of the Motherland, but I'll turn over a new leaf. Why put me in prison?

'I'll give you as much money as you like,' I will continue in a quiet voice, possibly in a whisper, looking at the bridge of the comrade general's nose. 'I'll give you it. I'll pay. At the going rate. Deposit it wherever you say! I'll blithely part with the money earned by the sweat of my own brow, the banknotes that mean so much to me. Just as long as I can leave prison and go back home. Tell me how much and where, in what form, dollars in cash or pounds sterling by electronic transfer. Just tell me and it will all be done …'

The general thinks. He's interested.

'I understand what you're saying,' he will say in a quiet but firm voice, pronouncing the phrase in such a way that the distance between him and me remains the same as ever, that is, immense; he's a general and I'm a little shit. 'I'll let you have my answer very soon. You understand?'

'Yes, sir.'

The general slowly melts away into thin air.

I know I'm definitely going to convince him.

On Tuesdays and Thursdays I was called out for interrogation, and then my audience underwent a qualitative change: I was no longer inventing for the mattress and the water-heating element, but for a living, thinking being, the investigator Khvatov.

I didn't provide any testimony. The imperturbable fellow from Ryazan added four identical pieces of paper to the CASE FILE one after another, with four refusals. Signed by the suspect and his lawyer.

But *outside* of the minutes all sorts of different things were said in that sunny, dusty little office in the Lefortovo fortress. The principle followed was this: I mixed together details, amusing facts and factlets, added a humorous story or a gag and concluded by proposing a basic thought that sounded like an outburst of fury addressed to the entire universe:

'How did it happen, gentlemen, that Andriukha, an intelligent, decent young guy, an energetic and active member of society, a soldier, journalist and banker, by no means the least of citizens, has found himself behind bars? Is this really the right place for him?'

The closer the end of my month inside came, the more melodramatic the question sounded. But no one gave me an answer – neither the animate investigator, nor the inanimate iron washbasin.

It was only on Tuesdays and Thursdays that I had genuine contact with living people and could observe the reactions of my companions. Twice a week. Ten minutes of talk with the investigator and then the same brief period of conversation with the red-headed lawyer. About an hour and a half in a fortnight. The rest of the time I had as much silence and solitude as I could endure, but I was already beginning to realise it wasn't likely I would be able to endure it for long.

On the days when there was no interrogation, my contact with the living world outside was limited to a dozen words or phrases falling at fixed intervals into the silence surrounding me, like the heavy drop of water falling from the tap on to the enamelled body of my speechless friend.

The morning began with the flat word 'reveille'. An hour later I heard the word 'tea' and I thrust my second friend, the metal teapot, into the hole in the door and brought it back in, filled to the brim with a hot, clear-brown substance with a taste and a smell that really were strongly reminiscent of tea. Soon after that, with a multitude of metallic sounds, the door opened to its full extent and the doorway was filled by the advancing front bumper of a steel trolley on little wheels – it had a tin rubbish bin attached to it. By the trembling light of the new day, in my half-wakeful state, I could make out behind the trolley the gloomy features of a convict from the domestic services section. He uttered the word 'rubbish' or 'dump'. I tipped out the plastic bin with the waste products of my life in the cell: a few apple cores and a dozen cigarette butts.

Then came 'breakfast'.

During the interval between eight and nine in the morning the door opened again and the senior warden came in: he was distinguished from his juniors by a more democratic, not to say frankly slovenly appearance, as well as a red armband with the letters DDHPTP, which decoded as 'Duty Deputy Head of the Pre-Trial Prison'.

'Everything all right?'

'Everything's all right.'

And again I was left alone.

An hour or an hour and a half later the silence was broken by the word 'walk', and after that came 'lunch', then 'supper'. Between eight and nine in the evening there was another check, the second in twenty-four hours, and the final dialogue, in the form of that same five-syllable question and the same indifferent answer. Finally, at ten clock, came the finale: 'bed'.

I also received certain live signals from living people during the process of being taken out for the walk ('stop', 'face the wall', 'move on'), or the weekly expedition to the bathhouse, but overall the prison communicated with me by using no more than a dozen brief commands.

In the minds of the prison's organisers, it was Radio Svoyak that was intended to save the inmates from nervous breakdowns as a result of their isolation, but I found myself unable to appreciate it adequately. Most of the time I kept the volume turned all the way down. Sometimes, to lighten the mood, I took a risk, turned the sound up and made an honest effort to listen to a piece of some reporting. But after only a few minutes, horrified, I turned the handle anticlockwise again. The programs broadcast by the radio station that had once served the whole Soviet Union sounded flat, talentless and depressingly dull. Less than ten years ago this same Svoyak had been the monopoly broadcaster to an audience of thirty million – and now what a dusty, tedious, yawn-provoking outfit it had become …

The window of my cell looked out towards the west. From midday until the evening, even through the double layer of opaque glass the sun generously warmed the walls of the cell, with all the air and the objects in it, including myself. On windless days it became genuinely hot. I went to bed in nothing but my shorts and didn't cover myself with anything.

But on the twenty-first day I woke very early, before dawn, trembling from the cold. Hastily wrapping myself in a sheet, I dozed off again, but not for long. Soon the temperature dropped still further. From outside the window I could hear the monotonous drumming of lashing rain. Creeping under the blanket this time, I finally got warm and slept through until late morning, only getting up when I heard the word 'walk'.

The door was already opening, and I was still pulling on my trousers. On the way out I managed, with a single swift movement, to turn on the tap, scoop up a handful of water and moisten my leaden eyelids.

It was only when I found myself in the small exercise yard and saw with my own eyes, that I realised summer was finally over. Out in the open it was fresh and cool. My arms and shoulders immediately felt chilly. The pitted ground was covered with small puddles. This was autumn. And then there would be winter, and the New Year!

If you're young, healthy, strong and full of confidence, the departure of one more jolly summer doesn't cause you too much suffering – no more than a fleeting sadness, a painless sigh of alarm in the far distance. However, as I celebrated the arrival of my latest autumn, my twenty-eighth, in such original style, in this place that was both terrible and romantic, I hugged my own elbows and shuddered as I stepped over the puddles reflecting a bright-blue sky that seemed to be forcing itself down through the bars of the grillwork above me – and dejectedly admitted that my youth was approaching its finale. That austere date, the big 3-0, was looming ever closer up ahead. The boundary line! How would I celebrate it? Who would I be?

When I got back from the walk and saw the members of the club eagerly awaiting the next tale from the adventures of the elusive Andriukha, I realised I was fed up with entertaining teapots and lumps of stitched cotton padding. There wouldn't be any more high-tension plots. The mood was gone.

Something's not going right, I realised on that first day of autumn. Events are not unfolding as I anticipated. My silence at the interrogations doesn't bother anyone. The investigator puts the blank sheets of paper away in his file with no sign of concern. And I've already done two-thirds of my time. They only have nine days left to come up with the clues to convict me of embezzling state funds. But instead of intensive, relentless interrogation, instead of daily intellectual battles lasting for hours at a time, instead of pressure, persuasion and threats, there's nothing but polite indifference, four ten-minute rounds. Is that it?

Something was wrong.

Autumn is very good for clearing the mind. On hot days the head doesn't work too well. Dehydration, fatigue – the brain doesn't produce good ideas in summer. But just let the temperature fall, the pressure rise and the sky turn a brighter blue, just let the atmosphere be infused with melancholy, and the mind is populated with clear, simple realisations. They had already decided everything about me.

'All right,' I sighed. 'Sod you, gentlemen. Here's another little story for you.'

The mattress and the washbasin were silently delighted.

'Only be sure not to interrupt!'

10

The last time I had associated with an individual of the opposite sex was just five hours before my arrest.

After parting from the traffic cop whose pocket was now weighted down with my payment at the going rate, I lit another cigarette, drove back up Tverskaya Street, performed a dashing U-turn opposite the statue of Mayakovsky – flagrantly violating the Highway Code and blatantly ignoring the State Road Safety Inspectorate – and cruised up once again to the kerb of a pavement populated by semi-naked women.

'Looking for a girl?'

'That's right,' I replied jauntily.

'What sort do you want?'

I tossed my cigarette butt out through the window.

'How do you mean?'

The aunt gave a weary frown.

'Skinny? Plump? Blonde? Brunette? Older? Younger?'

I hesitated ingloriously, taken aback by the level and scope of the offers available on this unfamiliar market in illegal intimate services.

'Regular,' I eventually specified and lit another cigarette.

'Two hours, a hundred and fifty dollars! All night for three hundred! No …'

I interrupted her offhandedly.

'I know, no anal sex or S&M.'

'Money up front.'

'Whatever you say.'

I put the cash into the aunt's hand and it was instantly probed and analysed by nimble fingers, before disappearing into the semi-darkness. After a brief consultation, a youthful creature set out towards me from a large group of girls who were flocking together: she walked with an almost insolent stride, her skimpy bottom tightly bound in comical shorts. She had a good neck, though, and her smile was enchanting.

Overcoming my awkwardness, I pushed the door open from the inside.

'Good evening,' the girl said politely, instantly filling the interior of the car with a powerful smell of sickly sweet perfume. 'I'm Nina.'

'Hi,' I said. 'You get into a car the wrong way.'

'So what's the right way?' my temporary girlfriend asked.

The girl could hardly have been more than twenty. After looking her over more closely, I immediately decided that paid copulation was quite out of the question. On the priestess of love's skinny left hip, the one closest to me, I could clearly make out an extensive bruise, and there was a very obvious, fresh, fiery-red scratch visible on her neck.

Everyone knows where scratches and other marks like that come from. It's the pimps using the fist and the knife to keep their labour collectives under control.

'First you should lower your backside on to the seat,' I said with a scurrilous laugh, 'and then swing round on it to the left, simultaneously drawing your head and your bent legs in through the opening of the door.'

'Shi-it! And what did I do?'

'You got into the car like a bear climbing into its den. First your head, then your legs and then all your other body parts.'

'Fascinating. So where are we going?'

'Nowhere,' I answered. 'We'll take a little ride, have a little talk, and that's it. I don't want anything else from you. I swear.'

She wasn't surprised.

'What are we going to talk about?'

'Anything you like.'

'You're very tense.'

'I'm always that way.'

'What's wrong, got nobody to be with?'

'On the contrary.'

'Are you married?'

'Yes. Five years.'

'Shi-it! Aren't you bored with your wife?'

'The moment I get bored with my wife, I'll put a bullet through my head.'

The priestess laughed tunelessly.

'Pardon me, of course, but I've heard that from lots of men. They all say that. To their wives. And themselves. And then they dash off to buy themselves a girl.'

'Speaking personally, this is the first time I've ever done it.'

My temporary girlfriend looked at me incredulously with her round, heavily made-up eyes.

'Shi-it! This is the first time you've ever bought a woman?'

'Yes.'

'That's not possible!'

'Why do you find it so surprising?'

'Well,' she shrugged. 'Such a respectable-looking man, and a cool car …'

You're obviously flattering me, I thought. As if I haven't seen myself in the mirror recently. Respectable is the very last thing the reflection is. What I've observed in the magical looking-glass just recently is a pale, bluish-grey face, swollen and basically not very attractive. Purple bags under bleary eyes. And a neck so thin it's almost dystrophic, irritated by rapid, careless shaving. And brown, flabby eyelids, under which Vizin eyedrops are applied twice daily. And teeth that are yellow from coffee and incessant smoking. And a small, crooked mouth with sore corners. And long deep wrinkles along the wings of the nose.

Alas, despite that immense income, to look at I'm still nothing like a respectable yuppy, I look like what I am in reality – a cheap, pushy jerk from the provinces.

In using a strong term like 'pushy jerk', I have in mind the kind of people who, owing to their youthful and impulsive natures, always want to have everything and to have it right now. Their goal is to get rich immediately, this very moment. They have keen eyes with constantly roving pupils. Sunken cheeks, thin necks, skinny shoulders. They often dress gangster-style. They love black.

The craving for money is what drives them on. They struggle and strain, they put up with things, they take real pains. And sometimes they manage to do something right.

The expression on the faces of these pushy jerks is extremely serious, often quite frankly glum. The corners of their lips are turned down. The general picture suggests that the guy is on his way either to a funeral or to a meet with his gang brothers. Or both at once. Although in reality I'd just set out on my way to get my son from the kindergarten, and from there to the grocery store.

'So you think,' I asked, making the right turn on to the embankment again, 'that all successful, respectable men buy girls?'

'All of them,' the young girl replied in a clear, ringing voice. 'If they've got money, they've all tried it at least once.'

'I know lots of rich men who are never unfaithful to their wives.'

The priestess looked at me and smiled.

'Sh-it! You can't really be that dumb! They just say they're never unfaithful! It's just promoting their own image! But really they make use of every convenient moment. Men are all secretive! And liars too. Shi-it – they're just full of crap!'

'Yes,' I said provocatively. 'The males of the species are all cunning. You can't bring a mammoth down without cunning. In these troubled times you have to know how to lie.'

'But you make hopeless liars!' the girl laughed. 'Let me tell you, straight up! This guy comes to me on Friday evening in a good car, gold chain and all the rest, acting the big-time hood. During the day he puts the draughts board up on the roof and hacks for fares … And as soon as he earns two hundred dollars, he comes straight to me. Takes off the draughts board and goes to see his little Sveta …'

'And who is this Sveta?'

'Me, why?'

'I thought you said you were Nina.'

'For him, I'm Sveta,' the girl explained imperturbably. 'What damn difference does it make anyway? They trick me, I trick them ...'

We said nothing for a while.

Night-time Moscow is beautiful and capricious. During a weekend afternoon or evening, as you stroll through the heart of town, it's possible to take the sum total of facades, bright shop windows and clean pavements for something entirely European. But at night, seen through the windscreen of a car, this city reveals its true face. It is immense, smoothly curvaceous, opulently developed, but chaotic. Lavishly flooded with electric light – then instantly plunged into impenetrable darkness. Everything spacious and roomy, everything a little bit crooked – Asia, gentlemen! Damn me if it isn't Asia.

'Don't be sad,' I declared briskly to my suddenly melancholy companion, 'it's exactly the same in my business. There's one character who comes round for a cup of coffee in his hundred-thousand-dollar Mercedes. At the end of the conversation, he borrows fifty dollars. Two weeks later he pays it back, on the nail. Another cup of coffee, a chat about this and that. A month later he borrows a hundred. Then he gives it back. It's been going on for a year and a half now. He's got about twenty guys like me, he goes round all of us in turn, and that's the way he lives. He thinks he's more cunning than anyone else too ...'

'And you know what happened to me once – shi-it ... one of my friends spent three days with me. A nice man he was, kind, not a bastard. Afterwards he told me how he went back to his wife after three days on the spree, drunk, with condoms and casino chips falling out of his pockets. You know what he told his wife?'

'Well, what?'

'That he was kidnapped by gangsters, and then they deliberately got him drunk and stuffed all sorts of garbage into his pockets, so his wife wouldn't believe him ... Shi-it! And his wife smelled my perfume too, but he told her, that's the gangsters, they poured perfume over me! And she told him perfume like was way too expensive for gangsters to go buying it! And he said they were real big-time gangsters, they had lots of money ... shi-it! And she went and let him in. She believed that stupid nonsense! Crazy crap like that! She didn't even bother to ring the militia. See what kind of shit happens. And you talk about men not being unfaithful to their wives …'

'My clients,' I admitted, 'are no better than yours. One of them always comes for his money by metro, in an old tracksuit and tattered sneakers, and he carries a string bag, you know, the kind they had back in the seventies, stuffed full of old newspapers, and he hides the wads of cash between the newspapers. Then he goes back home like that. And he just happens to own a big supermarket …'

'Shi-it! And one of my best friends has this client who's really rich, and cultured too, but just imagine, he only comes if you take a swing with a hot barbecued chicken and smack it against his bare backside just at the crucial moment …'

'But where,' I asked, astonished, 'do they get a grilled chicken? Just at the crucial moment?'

'They buy it earlier, then heat it up in the microwave.'

'That's really something,' I said and smiled. 'But another client of mine – he was rich and cultured too, as it happens – once turned up to collect his fifty thousand dollars with his sister, and his sister was at least a hundred kilograms live weight! And a metre and a half round … I counted it all out for him, and then he said to me: excuse me, but could you leave the room for a minute. I realised later they must have loaded the whole fifty thousand, five wads of a hundred bills, straight into her bra …'

'Shi-it! And there was this other client of mine …'

I suddenly sobered up and realised that instead of sleeping peacefully in my conjugal bed, I was driving a woman of the street round the city in the middle of the night, and the contempt I felt for myself was like a fearsome sword piercing my soul.

'And what about me?' I interrupted her. 'Are you going to tell the others funny things about me too'

'No,' said the girl, offended. 'I don't tell everyone about things … If a man's decent, then I'm decent with him … But if you get stuck with some gangster, you can't do much talking with him …'

'Do you end up with many?'

'What? Gangsters?'

'Yes.'

'Lots,' the girl sighed. 'Lots and lots. Shi-it, there are so many of them. All the creeps end up here, in the capital, from all over the country ...' She pressed her thin hands together. 'Animals ... I hate them ...'

'That's what my boss says too. He despises their kind.'

'And you?'

'I don't mind them. I reckon it's better to be a gangster with a vicious attitude but stay active, than turn into a fat slob and rot in front of the television with a bottle of beer ...'

'You're wrong,' said the girl, 'it's not better.'

'That's my personal opinion. Maybe some day I'll change it.'

'And you're wrong to compare my clients with yours, too. You don't work out in the street. You sit in a bank, in a nice soft chair. It's stupid to compare.'

'Don't be envious,' I said didactically. 'Sure, it all looks so fine from the outside. A bank, a car worth twenty thousand, a watch worth three, a suit worth two ... But from the inside, it's all the same. And there are plenty of cheap hoods in my business too. Pardon my plain-speaking: you sell a certain part of your body, but I've sold body and soul and everything else. I only sold myself once, but everything was thrown in. A package deal...'

'Even so, it's great to be rich.'

'Ugh. For the first two months. Then you get used to it. And then it's just mind-numbing drudgery.'

'So why don't you give up your job and so something more enjoyable?'

'Give it up?' I said, amazed. 'That's impossible. It's like a prison ... Where shall I drop you off?'

'Have you got fifteen minutes?'

'Yes.'

'Then take me back to where you picked me up, all right?'

'The cops have traps everywhere round there, and I'm drunk.'

'You can pay them off ...'

I'd completely lost interest in the conversation, and in my companion.

'I've already paid. I don't want to pay them any more. Once is enough. I've laid out a lot of dough today already. I give them money every damn day God sends. And there's no end in sight. Like I said, it's like a prison …'

After rubbing his puffy face hard with his hands, our mammoth-hunter reached into his pocket.

'I'd better … here … I'll give you a bit, there, that much …'

He pulled a bill, or three, out of a wad, the one on top tore slightly and the girl looked at it with regret, and at him with pity. The pushy jerk dropped the pieces of paper on his companion's bare knees.

'Pay the fool with the draughts board. He'll take you where you need to go!'

'All right, then, be seeing you!' Nina, a.k.a. Sveta, said very prettily. 'Thank you for a pleasant evening!'

I nodded without looking, lit yet another cigarette and drove away – a real hotshot, as hot as the steam from a locomotive. But steam locomotives, as everyone knows, became obsolete ages ago. They generate lots of noise, but not much traction. Their efficiency's too low. In short, nothing but show.

Five hours after that conversation I was in a real prison and I realised how wrong I'd been to compare the prison of gold and the prison of stone. The paradox was way too shallow.

And now I was planning to pay out money again. So that they would leave me alone. Send me back from their stupid prison to my own, just as stupid.

11

On the twenty-eighth day there was an unfamiliar command I'd never heard before.

'Name?'

'Rubanov!'

'Seasonal!' said the door's wide-open mouth.

'What?'

'Seasonal!'

I jumped up off the mattress and ran over to the feed hole.

'What's that?'

'For going out,' he explained patiently. 'They're taking you out for a ride. Take outside clothes, okay?'

'No,' I replied. 'Where are they taking me? Why are they taking me there?'

I was trembling like a frightened hare.

'They'll tell you when you get there.'

'Where?'

'The place they're taking you to. Get ready. Ten minutes!'

As I hurriedly pulled on my trainers, my incomprehension expanded into alarm, and then fear. What kind of trip was this? What was *seasonal* all about? Where was I going? What for? Why hadn't they told me anything that made any sense? What should I take with me? Would I be coming back to this cell, or even back to the prison at all? And what if freedom lay ahead? Or what if my mighty boss Mikhail had taken some radical action in order to decide my fate? The damned uncertainty of it all! Such excruciating torment! Not knowing what's going to happen to you in an hour's time – what torture could be worse?

The cosy gentlemen's club went into liquidation. Its little world, built up brick by little brick inside my head, collapsed. Burst, scattering its wretched fragments like jangling shrapnel. I must submit to someone else's implacable will. I am nobody. I don't belong to myself. I don't decide anything. My life is in other people's hands.

For a long time they led me up and down dark stairways and along dark corridors, until I suddenly found myself in the same part of the building where I had first been introduced to the confines of Lefortovo – in a short little corridor with a dozen doors. Two or three of them were standing half-open. For a while I sat in the same box-room where four weeks earlier the prison's functionaries had scrutinised my back passage. Then I was led out again, only this time, instead of a puny screw I found myself facing a two-metre-tall dog of war, wearing a brand-new khaki camouflage suit and a black mask. His huge hands were cradling a stub-barrelled automatic rifle. There was a pistol swaying in a holster on his hip. The soldier was breathing loudly through his nose.

A second soldier, less heavily armed, appeared beside him. With the gesture of a conjuror, he took out a pair of handcuffs, deftly coupled my hand to his own and, without any unnecessary words, dragged me forward. The machine-gunner stomped after us, jangling and clanking.

A door opened. Sunlight struck me in the face. Taking a step forward, I caught the scent of perfectly fresh air, and saw, just three metres away, the open door of an angular armoured car. Its engine was running smoothly. My nose was assaulted by the forgotten smell of exhaust fumes. Standing on my right and my left with their feet planted firmly apart were two more soldiers, armed to the teeth. Their tense, unblinking eyes gazed out at me through the slits in their masks. Their thumbs lay on the grips of their automatic breeches. I liked the look of their pieces – absolutely brand new AKSUs with folding stocks, still 'in oil' as they say, like sardines. If I'm going to be shot today, at least it will be with the best gun in the world.

'Move!'

A solid palm thrust hard against the back of my head and at the same time a second one, equally strong, twisted my forearm. I dived, rather than stepped or climbed, straight into the gloomy interior of the meat wagon – the very first of my life.

The minibus was actually no less comfortable than the prison itself. The air was conditioned. There were neat rubber mats lying on the steel floor. Half of the space was taken up by two steel kennels – a metre wide by a metre and a half long. Each had its own separate heavy door. One door, trimmed round the edges with thick, soft, black rubber, slammed behind me with a dull thud and I was left in silence and semi-darkness. I couldn't stand up in the kennel. Or stretch out my legs either.

We set off.

Where are they taking me? To kill me? To torture me? To shoot me? To take away all my money? To set me free and apologise?

We didn't drive for long, but we moved slowly, braking frequently. The body of the armour-plated minivan quivered gently. After about an hour, we arrived, they opened the kennel and the lightly armed soldier shackled my wrist to his once again and dragged me out of the van's dark innards.

I jumped down on to the warm pavement and found myself on a street. I suddenly had a very strong feeling that the space around me was wrong – it felt inordinately large. Panicking, I looked around, searching for the familiar close walls, but didn't find them. The ceiling was missing too – instead, there was a vast, boundless, piercing-blue sky that immediately started hurtling down towards me.

A few civilians in bright clothing stopped and turned curious eyes in my direction. The echoes of a multitude of booming sounds filled my brain. Thousands of different, powerful energies pierced me through and through. Dozens of window-panes glittered unbearably. The living city – moving, exhaling moisture, smelling of petrol, foliage, perfumes, dogs, cats, tobacco, fried chicken and hot asphalt, covered by a gigantic blue dome – surrounded me from all sixteen points of the compass. The teeth in my lower jaw all began aching at once.

Deafened, blinded, disorientated, with a lump in my dry throat, I swayed and would have fallen, but my guard held me up by the shoulder.

'Easy now, easy …' he reassured me, the way a sober man tries to calm a drunk. 'Not used to it anymore, eh? Been inside long?'

'A month.'

'That's no time. We had one who'd been inside six months, then we brought him out, took him into the street – and he puked …'

Massive double doors.

There are doors like that – three metres tall, made of dark varnished wood, scuffed and worn, with immense handles. They open with great difficulty. Just looking at them, anybody, whether he's a banker or an office supplies manager, understands this is a place that's very easy to enter, but much, much harder to get back out of. These doors were exactly like that.

Beside them on the wall there was a sign. Yellow letters on a black background: 'General Prosecutor's Office of the Russian Federation'. Inside there were guards. A spacious vestibule. Men in jackets darting about. White shirts, red folders under their arms. The lightly armed soldier dragged me up a stairway. The machine-gunners covered our rear. Two or three grey jackets pressed back against the wall to let the procession past.

After knocking politely on a door, the lightly armed guard led me into a room where I saw familiar faces: the red-headed Maxim and Khvatov. There were strangers present as well. In the corner, fiddling with a video camera attached to a tripod, there was someone quiet wearing tattered jeans, and sitting on a row of chairs along the wall there were two other men, shaking their cigarette ash into the same ashtray.

'Sit him with them,' Khvatov ordered my escort, 'on the chair in the middle.'

From what was said next – an agitated phrase from the investigator and a reassuring one from Red, I realised that the occasion in which I was involved was what is known as an 'identity parade' and I was destined to play the leading role. The two dejected smokers were the extras and the witnesses were going to identify one of us three, i.e. me.

So the execution with the brand-new automatic rifles is cancelled – at least for today. That's good.

Evidently in honour of the videotaping, Khvatov had decked himself out in a fairly decent wool sweater instead of his worn cowboy shirt. He cleared his throat, gave instructions for the camera to be switched on and then recited the date and the time into the lens in a loud voice.

The cameraman panned across the scene. When the crystal eye of the lens turned in my direction, I felt such a fierce urge to stick out my tongue that the strain of resisting it gave me cramp in my cheeks. But I managed to stop myself.

In obedience to the rules of the visual arts, the panoramic shot concluded at the same point from which it had begun, with a close up of Khvatov's face. He flashed the lenses of his spectacle and proclaimed:

'Now we will proceed to, you know, call the witnesses.'

The man from Ryazan hurried out into the corridor and returned in the company of a neat, fresh-looking young woman who walked like a B student from the sixth form who has been called up as usual to the blackboard to run through the lesson. The young maiden was biting on her lip, but on the whole she acted fairly confidently. Her modest trouser-suit sagged and puckered slightly, in this particular case concealing the good points of her figure rather than its deficiencies. Of course, the witness had been warned in advance that she was being summoned by the agencies of law enforcement to identify a dangerous criminal and she had dressed modestly so that the vulgar louts wouldn't stare.

'Do you recognise any of these men?'

'Yes,' the youthful creature said with a nod, chewing on her pink lips.

'Which one?'

'That one, in the middle ...'

'Please, go closer and point to him. Don't be afraid ...'

The girl hesitated, certainly, but the flush on her small round cheeks showed that she was excited, she was interested, and every man in the room could feel it; everyone, including the shabby cameraman, gave a gentle, condescending smile.

'This one ...'

I had only seen the young female in trousers once. It had all happened way over a year ago, our conversation had barely lasted more than ten minutes, and it had taken place as we were walking, along the corridor of the tax offices; the girl worked there, and I needed some urgent document or other, a certificate or something of the kind. The offices were closed to the public that day, but I had managed to persuade the doorkeeper to let me into the building, sought out the young creature in the extremely modest blouse and prevailed upon her to issue me the required document immediately – citing the extreme urgency and importance of the matter.

Now, fourteen months later, the female tax inspector pointed unerringly at me. Feeling nervous as she did it, but still examining the scene and the people in the office with obvious curiosity. I was completely staggered by the whole situation, and drew two important conclusions. The first was that a young maiden's memory is by no means as short as the Russian saying claims. The second, and more significant, was that there was no future at all for me in the world of criminal business, if people who had met me by chance and exchanged perhaps a dozen phrases with me, retained my face in their memories for years …

After that things started moving faster. Having explained everything that was required, the girl withdrew – with obvious relief, but also a certain disappointment – to the next office, and another, pretty much the same, appeared in her place.

From first to last, the witnesses all turned out to be ladies, seven or eight of them. They all pointed to me without hesitating for a second. It was hard for them to make a mistake: when the ladies entered the office and looked around apprehensively, they spotted a sullen-faced villain in a crumpled tracksuit sitting on the chair squeezed between the two clean-shaved extras. An unshaven villain, staring into empty space. Two hours earlier he had been dragged out of the solitary cell where he had spent four weeks, shoved into a metal box and brought here with automatic rifle-barrels trained on him. In sum, of all those present, I was the one who looked like a lowlife scumbag.

Give me back my Kenzo and Valentino, my Lloyd and Longine, take me to the hairdresser's and the solarium – then the fingers won't be extended in my direction quite so confidently.

Generally speaking, when people point their fingers at you and say: 'That's him, I recognise him,' you start feeling guilty of every crime ever committed in the whole wide world, up to and including the assassination of President Kennedy.

I hadn't done anything bad to any of these people, but even so I still felt terribly uneasy now. There had been occasions when I chatted for ten minutes or so about various interesting things with the women who identified me, and they had taken me for an honest, straightforward guy, but now it turned out that I was a bastard, and associating with me was likely to get you called in by the militia to give evidence.

All the numerous ladies (with the exception of the first, the tax inspector) were members of a profession popular with the young people of the capital – legal agents, or *law-mongers* in the vernacular. Their business consisted of obtaining from agencies of the state all sorts of permits, certificates, licences and other beautiful, coloured pieces of paper with monograms, watermarks and embossed golden stamps.

Without a set of such licences, no citizen can even think about starting his own business. Long weary perambulations along the dark, crowded corridors of the state licencing offices, queues lasting hours, muddle and confusion lie in wait for any novice businessman who decides, after long and painful reflection, to risk setting up on his own account.

After paying one visit to a certain branch of the State Registration Chamber and discovering that people started queuing up there at four in the morning, so that by lunchtime there was a crowd of several hundred, and there were fights, a certain young businessman felt saddened. But then he opened the newspaper, found an ad, and hired a law-monger to solve his problem.

The law-monger would register the legal entity, taking a fee for the job. He or she was the one who languished in the queues or, more likely, paid the going rate for expediting the passage of his or her documents through a long sequence of offices. He or she took a substantial sum for services rendered – three or four times the monthly earnings of a doctor or a teacher. Meanwhile the businessman took care of more urgent, day to day matters. He only had to turn up once, with his passport. Or sometimes just the passport itself was enough. And in other cases even a photocopy of the document was acceptable. Every day hundreds of new firms passed through the hands of the unfortunate servants of the state. Nobody paid any attention to petty details. Surname? Rubanov. Name of the firm? 'Vasya and Co.' Has the state duty been paid? Next!

A month later the law-monger would hand the happy businessman his new certificates and warrants and also a round seal. Now he could conduct business on a legal basis. Now the state had officially approved his intentions. Of course, if the new boy expressed a wish not simply to trade, but to buy or sell money, oil, gas, timber, tobacco, alcohol, diamonds, automobiles, real estate, medicines or weapons – in other words, if he aspired to any kind of serious role in this life – then he had to move up to the next level in the pyramid of permission. To obtain a special licence. That meant going round the circle again: another law-monger, only this time more expensive, more waiting; and the actual cost of the document itself and other concomitant expenses were enough to render any entrepreneur taciturn and irritable.

But anyway, the day arrived when the wheels of the brand-new business started turning. People got richer, the state received its share in the form of taxes. Then one day our cunning businessman (he didn't really want to give away that share), came up with a simple trick. He abandoned the firm he had only just founded, 'Vasya and Co.', and immediately registered another one, 'Vanya and Co.', through a law-monger. And after that came 'Grisha and Co.', 'Sasha and Co.', 'Natasha and Co.', and so on. After turning a few profitable deals, the cunning individual scuppered his latest 'Sasha' or 'Natasha' – he already had 'Masha' and 'Lyosha' ready and waiting.

In order to avoid trouble with the authorities, the crafty entrepreneur concealed his place of residence from the tax inspectors. They tried once to find him but failed, and then forgot.

By the mid-1990s there were about eight hundred firms for every inspector of taxes in the capital. It was physically impossible for the tax-collectors to keep up with every unscrupulous taxpayer.

The boy and girl law-mongers developed their sector of the market. They began offering completed sets of documents and permits for sale. Companies, associations and corporations already registered 'for future use'. Selling ready-made firms brought in good earnings. Now the cunning businessman was able to go to the law-monger's office, drink a cup of coffee, put someone's passport on the desk, and half an hour later he was no longer a simple businessman, but one with a business for which a completely different person was accountable.

The artful young capitalist was not wasting any time either. He was moving forward, he started putting through big deals, and accordingly spending more on his financial security. After another two years he was buying up fictitious corporations by the dozen. All of them were registered on passports that had been lost or stolen. He also had his own volunteers, fake company chairmen. In the mid-90s the capital of the Empire was overflowing with desperate, impecunious saps. For fifty dollars they would put their signature to any document.

Our businessman never visited the tax inspectors' offices at all. Now, as far as the tax administration's computers were concerned, this man didn't exist. If some pernickety pen-pusher did decide, out of professional zeal, to seek out the owner of one or other suspicious firm, then as a rule he turned out to be some young student shooting up fifteen cc's of pure heroin every day of the week; an individual well known to the local military commissar and the militiaman on the beat.

Everything was going very well until the moment when, in the effort to build up his business, the crafty wheeler-dealer got involved in a clearly dubious undertaking with a bad smell to it, something involving the transfer of large sums of money to accounts in European banks. The terrible realisation came suddenly: his new, respectable business partners were embezzling state funds. And 'Masha and Co.' was registered at a fictitious address, and its official owner and director was a nominee, a mere boy, a drug addict!

The businessman fell into a depression. Day by day the situation became more and more threatening. The fraud was exposed and the Public Prosecutor's Office started looking for the money that had gone missing. The firm Misha also came to light (or was it Vova? – it was hard to remember, since the adroit financier had more than a hundred ephemeral companies under his control). They found the director. The moment the sleuths laid eyes on the eighteen-year-old junky, their very worst suspicions were confirmed: the mysterious founder of this dummy corporation was one of the brains behind the gang! *He* had set up the fictitious firm in advance, especially to facilitate the theft of billions of roubles from the budget!

And now the mystery man was sitting on the artificial leather covering of a hard militia chair, enjoying the gentle play of the draught from the window on his neck and feeling rather pensive.

He had paid many thousands of dollars to nominee directors, idiots and drug addicts. He had not set foot in the tax administration's offices for years at a time. In fact only once, in four long years, had he called in there for half an hour – and he had been remembered. And when the occasion arose, identified.

Members of the intelligentsia make the worst criminals. That top brand in the Russian novel-writing business, F. M. Dostoevsky, was right about that.

For all his apparent rusticity, the Ryazan provincial Khvatov conducted the identification parade quickly and adroitly. As I watched him walk through into the adjoining offices, lead in the lady law-mongers and then lead them back out again; as I heard his quiet instructions to the cameraman, it occurred to me that the short-sighted investigator must have handled hundreds of procedures like this one. Stepan Mikhailovich of Ryazan had brought criminal and witness face to face a whole host of times. And he had exposed the truth of his CASE a host of times too.

A lucky man – he knew how to isolate his truth. If only I did.

It took more than an hour to question the ten or so witnesses. Then I was led out into the corridor, and there I sat down on a chair, right beside the door. The lightly armed guard perched on the chair beside me and immediately sank into a light doze.

I barely had time to make myself comfortable before there was a tramping of feet from round the corner. Immediately a procession consisting of two machine-gunners and a prisoner appeared and hurriedly filed past. The prisoner was a thickset, elderly man with his hands shackled. We glanced briefly at each other. The villain (his tracksuit cost twice as much as mine) suddenly winked at me. I didn't have time to make any sign in reply. While I was pondering the possible meaning of the stranger's genial wink, another mini-convoy passed by, moving from right to left. The detainee was another large man with grey hair, wearing trousers with stripes down the side. He also greeted me, this time with a friendly nod.

When they led the third one past a minute later – he was unshaven, with a confident air – I anticipated things by looking into his face and winking first; in reply I received a brief, bitter smile.

And so I sat there in the corridor of the national General Prosecutor's Office, a criminal greeting his *confrères*, until General Zuev walked by. That gave me a real start. I have to say something quickly, I thought anxiously. Something clever and interesting. Give the general some extremely subtle hint that I will soon be requesting a face-to-face meeting with him.

The day after tomorrow my thirty-day term will be over. My boss Mikhail, saved by me, will be released. That's as clear as day. After all, it was me, not him, who purchased the girl law-mongers' wares: brand-new firms all ready to go, officially registered, with a full set of documents and a blue seal: all sorts of corporations and all sorts of limited companies. They may have identified me today, but they would never identify the boss.

As soon as he was out of those iron doors, the boss would call a few people on the phone and give instructions to get some cash together – for a start, about two hundred thousand. That same night he would convene a council of legal specialists. They would decide everything: how much to give to whom and who would conduct the negotiations. The boss himself couldn't get involved in the dialogue – officially he had nothing to do with anything. He was only the office supplies manager! That just left me – and the red-headed lawyer. Maxim Stein was the one who would come running to me in my prison cell the next morning, for a meeting, with instructions from the boss: what I should do and how.

I would respond with my own plan: I was going to speak with Zuev myself.

'Good morning, comrade General!' I said, enunciating the words with all the buoyancy and self-confidence I could muster. I even tried to get up, bowing slightly at the same time. But my guard woke from his stupor and forced my chest back down with his hand, so that I half-rose in a slow, dignified manner, but fell back hastily, with my shoulder blades slapping against the back of my chair.

The militia big daddy cast a bewildered glance in my direction and walked past without even slowing down. He walked with a firm and gentle stride, hunched a long way over, like a very elderly man, but moving his feet with exceptional sprightliness, even skipping slightly as he walked along, jiggling the two halves of his bony backside.

I watched him until he disappeared round a bend in the corridor and thought what a long time it was since I'd felt so stupid. I had been prepared for anything. I had spent four weeks in intense deliberation. I had envisaged every possibility. I had brilliantly foreseen the most subtle nuance. Every evening the same picture had appeared before my eyes: General Zuev, in his general's office, smoking, screwing up his eyes cunningly, drinking tea from a glass in a silver glass-holder – and waiting for the suspect Rubanov to request his own interrogation.

And now it turned out that the general had forgotten about the suspect. Completely.

Unable to control myself, I put my elbows on my knees, lowered my face into my hands and howled – inaudibly, soundlessly, with just my insides: all my dry throat produced was a long, grating wheeze. Zuev hadn't even recognised me! For more than two weeks I had been rehearsing my dialogue with the grey-haired militia boss, and he had forgotten that I even existed! I had thought through every minor detail, selected the right words and intonations and then, when I finally had my assault objective in my sights, he hadn't even remembered me.

Against my own will, I laughed out loud.

'What's wrong with you?' the lightly armed soldier asked me suspiciously.

'Nothing,' I replied. 'Just my nerves playing up …'

You idiot, I told myself. You naïve, conceited idiot! You were forgotten ages ago, the general's not interested in you. He probably never did find you particularly interesting! You're just one out of hundreds to him! Four weeks have gone by, the general's been preoccupied with new CASES for a long time already. Maybe he's caught a dozen other big-time crooks, maybe even dozens upon dozens! And he hasn't given you a single thought! You never entered his mind even once! This is an automated production line they have here! Always looking for some, catching some, pinning CASES on some – you can't remember every single reprobate. Given your testimony? – get in the cell. Next! And you can be quite sure that every single reprobate is dreaming of buying his freedom at the going rate! So how are you going to talk with the militia boss, what are going to say to him, if his eyes are already dazzled by unprincipled millionaires?

It's a big country. A lot of people. Some want to do business, others want to steal from the public purse. You have to be able to keep an eye on all of them, monitor them, pull them up short when necessary – and mete out exemplary punishment to some of them.

These men in grey jackets with red folders and ties that were out of fashion clearly didn't have enough time for every single banker.

12

There, outside the bars, in the realm of freedom, existed a warm, transparent September.

Here, inside, it was merely a sensation at the very borders of my mind – a fragile emanation of obscure, intangible sorrows. In the same way the anticipation of death enters into human souls and the premonition of winter enters into nature.

Today they will let me go, I thought, breathing in the subtle scents of the fading summer through the narrow chink in the barred window. I had heaved myself up, clutching the upper edge of the massive steel transom with my hands and bracing my feet in the lower corners of the window recess – and now my nose caught the very weakest and most distant aromas.

That's damp laundry – in the next building someone has brought out some sheets and hung them up to dry on the balcony.

That's savoury smoke. They're burning leaves.

That's engine oil. That's cats' urine. I suffer from a congenital allergy to animal fur. I can sense animals from a distance. If there are cats and dogs anywhere in the vicinity, it's never a secret to me.

That's cosmetics.

Shoe polish.

And that, quite definitely, is vodka being drunk out in the open air, on a bench somewhere very near, in Lefortovo Park …

Tomorrow this will all be mine again. There's hardly any time at all left to hold out now.

I greeted the morning of the final day in a mood of elation, almost as if it was a holiday. One of the most important moments in my twenty-seven years of life was already approaching, forcing its own bundle of transparent yellow-white light in through the window. Immense sums of money and people's lives were at stake here. Yes, it was that big. There were families at stake – mothers, wives and children; and also a business that had swallowed up three years of gruelling work. Everything I lived for was at stake.

I opened the tap as far as it would go and spent a long time washing, splashing the water on to my shoulders and chest. I rubbed myself down thoroughly with two towels; I dried my body with a standard piece of coarse flannel (prison property) and my face with the soft fluffy towelling my wife had sent. Then I went on to shave. I heated some water with the coil and used it to steam the firm skin of my cheeks, then I lathered them up and slowly scraped them clean, taking three goes. I washed my face again – it smarted and stung where there were cuts, and pink blood welled up in one place on my throat, but that only added to the grim charm of the situation. I climbed into a new pair of shorts and realised that I was ready.

The floor is spattered with water. Should I bother cleaning up my cell on the day I was leaving it?

'Definitely,' I mumbled.

At this important moment everything around me will be clean and beautiful. And I myself, calm and collected, smiling resolutely, will face any blow of fate with dignity …

At this point I had to straighten out the pathetic Andriukha, that infantile tearaway and lover of sound-bites squatting inside me. I seized hold of a rag and sedulously restored order.

Stop babbling, Andriukha! Do something useful.

I tore one of my old tee-shirts into strips and washed the state tableware and the open metal hand of the washbasin with soap. I boiled up some water and scalded everything. Disinfected it, kind of. When they put a new man in here tomorrow, he'll be amazed. A good man lived here before me, the newcomer will think, and he'll take heart.

Then I moved on to the walls. Puffing and panting in my zeal, energetically replacing dirty scraps of cloth with new ones, running with water from the tap to the corners, climbing under the horizontal metal planes of the three beds, I became perfectly calm. The process enthralled me. Dirt turned up in the most unexpected places. It all had to be eliminated. I'm going to leave this place immaculately clean, gleaming, like an operating theatre or a millionaire's kitchen.

'Name?'

'Rubanov,' I replied, wiping the dust out of the corners of the windowsill.

'You're wanted!'

Strange, I thought. It ought to be a different phrase. 'Get your things!' – those were the right words, if you could believe Solzhenitsyn's books. Your things! Take all your property and be ready to leave the cell! But they hadn't said anything to me about things. That meant something was wrong. Aren't they going to let me out today? Is the investigator going to tell me that and order me to be brought back? Whatever – I'll find out soon enough.

In the doorway I looked back. God only knows when I'll ever be in a cell in the legendary Lefortovo prison again! But an attentive glance round my humble abode forced me to admit that a prison cell is really the most unromantic place in the whole wide world. Looking at its colours, smelling its odours, this was just a perfectly ordinary prison. A place that had soaked up the deadly fears of hundreds of men. That radiated energy on the wavelength of suffering. I felt a momentary revulsion, first for the prison, and then for myself, for having got into this mess out of sheer youthful folly. I clasped my hands behind my back and walked away.

As I entered the interrogation office my heart was pounding furiously. I screwed up my eyes. The scantily furnished room was flooded with sunlight. The stage set of my freedom was brightly illuminated.

Khvatov was sitting in his usual place at the desk. Standing beside him with his hands in his pockets was a man I didn't know: a massive, rugged individual with short legs, dressed in a worn leather jacket of a comical orange colour and black trousers, also of leather. His round, close-cropped head was inclined forward, as if by its own excessive weight.

Looking around, I failed to spot my lawyer and that put me on the alert.

'Hi, Andrei,' Khvatov said warily. 'Come in. Sit down.'

'I'm inside already,' I joked.

The man in leather watched without speaking as I took a few steps forward and sat down on the stool. Then he took his hands out of his pockets. I saw a red ID card in his right hand. Approaching me from the left, he opened the folded ID and lifted it up to my face, as if he was about to smother me with a rag soaked in chloroform. His hand astounded me – huge, crimson, with rugged fingers and yellow peasant's nails. No doubt when firmly clenched this gigantic hand was transformed into a fist of formidable size and solidity. With a sledgehammer like that you could stave in my feeble ribcage without any real effort, I thought in passing as I struggled to make sense of the contents of that little red booklet – photograph, stamp, name, position, an institutional name that was a string of long words, all starting with capital letters. I wonder if the average citizen presented with a militiaman's ID is capable of reading even a single word in it just at that moment?

'Captain Svinets,' the hulking stranger introduced himself in a pleasant, rather flat voice. 'Criminal Investigation Department ...'

'What?' I asked.

'Svinets,' the leather man repeated. 'It's a kind of metal.'

So it is, I thought; the Russian word for lead.

'Perhaps I should leave the room?' Khvatov asked.

The captain from Moscow CID loftily dismissed the idea with a wave of his thick, stubby hand.

'What for? I have no secrets from anyone, in the first place, and in the second, it won't take any time at all. We'll just chat for five minutes and then I'll hit the road. No time to waste! I've got a woman waiting, you know how it is. And you can carry on searching for your billions ...'

'How are we going to find them now?' Khvatov complained. 'The money's long gone.'

What was happening was nothing at all like the procedure for release from detention. The darkness inside my head thickened. So I'm staying, then? They aren't going to let me out? Or is it still too soon to start getting upset? After all, the calendar month only ends at six o'clock in the evening. My lawyer mentioned that yesterday (he'd come specially – to offer moral support). And it's still morning now. Yes, they still have time to work me over one last time.

'Listen, er … Andrei,' said the captain with the metallic surname, still standing at my shoulder, 'when was the last time you saw Genka Farafonov?'

I strained my memory, but I couldn't remember a single thing about the name he'd just mentioned.

'I've never heard the name before,' I replied honestly.

Svinets walked across to the wall with his trousers creaking and looked at me in great surprise. Then his face hardened and he said in a weary voice:

'Let's just look at the situation we've got here. We haven't even started talking properly yet, and you're already trying to trick me …'

'I've got no reason to trick you,' I objected rather nervously. 'Why would I? I honestly have no idea who this Fafaronov is.'

'Farafonov!'

'There, you see!'

The leather-bound sleuth hid his massive hands away in his pockets and rapped out several beats in rapid rhythm with the toe of his shoe.

'Well, I suppose there is a certain buzz in hoodwinking someone,' he suddenly declared, and winked at me.

'I've never given it any thought,' I lied.

'Oh, there is,' Svinets said with a smile. 'A fantastic buzz! Almost like sex! Maybe even better. And you know all about it. I repeat my question: Do you know a certain Gennadii Sergeevich Farafonov?'

'No.'

'No?'

'No!'

'Excellent. Maybe if you think about it for a moment you'll remember?'

'Unlikely.'

'What's the problem? Can't trust your own memory?'

'I don't know any Rafa…'

'Farafonov!'

'Right!'

'You don't know him?'

'Yes! No! I don't!'

'Yes or no?' the captain thundered. 'Speak more clearly!'

'I don't know him!' I sighed.

Captain Svinets turned crimson and took two abrupt steps in my direction. I flinched.

'Farafonov's passport,' the detective bellowed like one of the trumpets at Jericho, 'was found in your office! With the documents of a firm registered fifty days ago! In his name! But Mr Farafonov, thirty-seven years of age, with a degree in engineering, departed this world six months ago! He was murdered! A blow to the head with a blunt instrument! Tell me, why and how did you register a fictitious corporation on a dead man's passport?'

I suddenly felt tremendous relief.

'Why didn't you say so straight away? Yes, there could have been a passport like that. In with all the others. I always had about thirty of those passports lying in the bottom drawer of my desk … I've already explained here what they're needed for. Off the record. Shall I go over it again?'

'Give it a try,' he agreed.

'Off the record,' I specified sullenly.

'By all means.'

'Every month,' I began, 'we used to set up fifteen or twenty firms. Officially, through the standard procedure. I always used other people's passports. Then I opened a bank account for every firm. Anyone who wanted could make a transfer to any of these accounts and then get banknotes from me in exchange. Hard cash. It was basically a matter of converting one form of money into another. Roubles into shares. Shares into dollars. Dollars into bills of exchange. Bills of exchange into bonds. And so on.'

Svinets listened to me very carefully, then narrowed his little eyes and asked:

'So you're a money-changer?'

'Exactly.'

'Then why the fake front-men?'

'So I could stay clear of your system. The administrative machine.'

'And what don't you like about the system?'

'It works too slowly,' I replied immediately. 'And it charges too much. It makes me pay big money for all sorts of licences and permits. And wait for years. I don't want to support a system like that. And I won't …'

Svinets nodded.

'I see, I see. But you have to be checked, don't you? Tax inspections and all that sort of thing … Or am I wrong?'

'He was checked,' interjected Khvatov, who had so far been stroking his keyboard with crooked fingers and saying nothing. 'In this country every new firm has to present accounts to the state three months after registration.'

'Three months?' the captain asked incredulously, striding across the room again and filling it with the loud creaking of his inflexible, tough-guy trousers.

'Yes,' I replied. 'Work for three months and then, if you would be so kind, submit accounts and pay out to the treasury … Four quarters. Pay four times a year.'

'A bad law.' Svinets shook his head and looked at the investigator, who nodded in agreement. 'How can you get a business off the ground in three months? I know lots of businessmen. It took them years and years to get anything properly set up and start earning …'

'It surprises you,' I declared, 'but it depresses me. It's thanks to that law, and others equally divorced from reality, that I'm sitting here now.'

'But his firms,' said Khvatov, continuing with his explanation, 'only lasted a few weeks. Then he dumped them, withdrew every last kopeck from their accounts and abandoned them, you know, to the whim of fate. When the time for the audit arrived, the tax inspectors were faced with a total shambles. There was a firm, but it didn't do anything, it had no office, no contact telephone number, the director was nowhere to be found, the postal address was, you know, cancelled and so on …'

'Nowhere to be found,' muttered Svinets. 'And what about these directors of yours, the front-men – how did you persuade them to get involved in a shabby little deal like that, eh?'

I shrugged.

'I didn't persuade them. I didn't even see any of them in person … The middlemen did all that … I paid well for every document …'

'How much?'

'The going rate. Some passports were bought, others were loaned for temporary use. You can always get hold of a passport that someone has lost or sold for drink.'

'Where?'

'On the black market,' I replied primly.

'Ah, yes the famous black market …' the man from Moscow CID said pensively.

Then suddenly he smiled, revealing a gold tooth and instantly becoming indistinguishable from the popular clichés of the criminal type; those narrowed eyes and that cheek twitching in a crooked smirk.

'If only someone would tell me the address of this famous market! Whisper it in my ear, will you, eh?'

'You know it yourself.'

The massive detective suddenly turned crimson again.

'Listen, creep! Don't you go getting funny with me! I'm not some soft-hearted gent from the department for combating economic crime! I catch *murderers*, is that clear? Who did you get the passport from? The name? The address?'

A good question, I thought. Straight and to the point. And he obviously expects the same kind of answer.

'I have to remember.'

'Then remember!'

'Can I smoke?'

'Yes!'

'Show me the passport.'

Svinets reached deep inside his leather armour and pulled out a badly crumpled, dark-maroon, standard Russian identity document with gold claws on the cover. The claws were squeezing an entire planet in their clutches. Firmly, but gently. Gently, but firmly. I leafed rapidly through the document, handed it back and said in a low voice:

'I can't remember anything right now.'

The sleuth snorted loudly through his nose, evidently on the point of getting really furious, and I hastily put in:

'But all the passport records are kept on my PC! You must have the computer now! It was confiscated in the search! All the information's in there! I'll tell you the password and the name of the file. You won't be able to understand a thing, because the texts are encrypted. You'll have to print out the entire file. Five pages at most. Bring me those pages, I'll go through them with you and find the record of Ferapontov's passport.'

'Farafonov.'

'Yes, right, him.'

Svinets hesitated for a moment.

'If you're lying, you're toast.'

'I already guessed that.'

The captain paused. He looked at me, then at the quiet Khvatov, then back at me.

'By the way, they told me that today … you just might … be released … So I'll find you myself the next time we meet. Don't even think of doing a runner – try it and I'll put you on the wanted list as a murder suspect.'

In a fit of rapture my soul tore itself free of my body, circled boisterously above my head and returned to its proper place.

They are going to release me! They might release me today! They just might.

'By the way,' Svinets went on. 'Are you a rich man, Andrei?'

'Relatively. Why?'

'How are you on clothes, shoes, ties, colognes?'

'So-so.'

The captain stuck his hands back in his pockets.

'Listen, how do I look? Okay? Not like a total scruff? I've got a date in two hours. I want to get married! I've found a good girl, kind, intelligent … She really stands out, too, a double D bust … A natural blonde.'

'Congratulations.'

'Well, and so?'

'Meaning?'

'How do I look, eh?'

'Quite presentable,' I lied, really enjoying myself. 'But there are a few weak points. Too much leather. A matter of taste, of course … And as well as that – the socks.'

Svinets seized the creaking leather of his trousers in cyclopean fingers and hoisted them up.

'Yeah?' he asked in amazement, gaping at his feet. 'What's wrong with my socks?'

'They're white.'

'So?'

'Just forget all about white socks. Throw them out and never put another pair on again. Not under any circumstances. White socks are only good for one place – the tennis court. Shall I continue?'

'Mmm.'

'Well, here's something: don't tuck your sweater into your trousers.'

'But then it sticks out from under my jacket!'

'Wear shirts, not sweaters. A sweater's like wearing a sack.'

'I get it.'

'Change your cologne, it's no good. You can't buy a decent fragrance for anything under fifty dollars. And change your watch too. And another thing: you cut your hair too short. In my opinion …'

'That's enough,' the captain growled and glanced at the watch I had just condemned. 'I get the idea. You can continue your lecture when we meet next week. I hope you're not planning to change your home address?'

'I have to get home first.'

'That's not going to be a problem,' the metallic detective remarked encouragingly. He shook hands with Khvatov and walked out.

'What's going on?' I asked immediately. The spectacles from Ryazan were trained on me and I spoke straight into them.

'Nothing special,' was the reply. 'Standard investigative procedure.'

'And what about letting me go home?'

'No decision's been taken yet,' Khvatov said in an apologetic voice. 'The boss will, you know, get round to it some time later today. So you go back for the time being. To the cell. And don't get the jitters. Your lawyer's already been summoned. Personally I'm on your side. Everything's going to be okay …'

'Thank you,' I said sincerely.

The investigator nodded and reached into his little attaché case. He took out a vacuum-sealed pack of tablets, popped one out, stuck it in his mouth and followed it with a swig from a small plastic bottle.

'Painkiller?' I asked.

Khvatov nodded and swallowed.

'It's so noisy here,' he complained artlessly. 'How can you live here, in the capital of our Motherland? With all this racket?'

'I've got used to it.'

The investigator took off his spectacles, pulled a clean handkerchief out of his back pocket and began carefully polishing the lenses, but then suddenly put everything down on the table.

'What sort of life is this you have here? Every second person has no ID, no residence permit. The criminal lifestyle, the suspicious faces, accidents on every street corner, everybody shouting, everybody running …'

'A big city,' I declared laconically.

Khvatov smiled sadly.

'The city's big, but the people aren't. Go to your cell, Andrei. And wait. Of course I'm not, you know, certain that you're not implicated … Maybe your status will remain unchanged. There's no way we can transform you from the accused into a witness. But you'll be going to the interrogations and the court from home …'

As I walked back, my vision of reality was slightly distorted. I could feel an unpleasant, hot, tickling sensation inside my chest. Instead of going home I ended up at a scandalous interrogation, complete with shouting and insults, and now I'm going back to my cell! And I have to wait for General Zuev to make a decision! Why is fate tormenting me like this?

As I walked along the iron gantry past the rows of identical doors, I calmed down slightly and promptly recalled the finest, the most promising phrases: 'they're going to release you today', 'everything's going to be okay', 'you'll be going to the court from home'. When I got back to my sparkling-clean cell I was already smiling.

I'm only a few hours away from freedom! I declared confidently to myself, then resolutely made a cup of coffee, drank it, walked to and fro and switched on the radio. A rich soprano voice was singing some classical canzone or operatic aria. The effect was rather sensual. It was a concert recording – I could hear the rustling of the singer's sheet music being turned and her abrupt intakes of breath.

Suddenly there was a small, pleasant explosion somewhere inside my head, followed by several more. I looked down and saw that I was desiring my freedom physically. Like a real, live woman.

I immediately grabbed hold of myself with my left hand and set to work. The arousal was all the stronger for having come on in just a couple of moments – as if all the blood had suddenly rushed form my brain to my loins. Realising that I was standing in the middle of the cell, with my mouth open and my trousers half-lowered at the front, I laughed silently, turned my back to the door and carried on, for greater convenience stretching out the elastic of my trousers with my right thumb, turning my face to catch the light from the window and closing my eyes – the sun made my eyelids semi-transparent, and what I saw was not darkness, but a red space illuminated by slow flashes and populated by hundreds of large and small black spots.

Prompted by my will, a screen rose up out of the scarlet depths and unfolded. A picture appeared on it, then another, and another. My artful brain presented me with the most hard-core scenes, full-colour movies. I saw absolutely fantastic naked bodies, faces with dyed hair sticking to their foreheads, moist mouths half-open, manicured nails, cool, slithering gold chains. I glimpsed pink curves, distended pupils clouded by passion, svelte legs and lips and sheets, everything hot and damp. My mind conjured up smells and sounds – groans, screams, sighs and especially provocative little details like a thin rivulet of sweat glittering like glass between two breasts. Even the appropriate music started to play – Sting, and then Sade. A sleek, up-market sound-track, inciting the inclination to take a woman roughly and adroitly, but without any acrobatics, and then watch the inner surfaces of her splayed thighs trembling in the final orgiastic paroxysm of bestial gratification.

At this point I tightened the grip of my palm a little and increased the speed. In principle, you can use just the thumb and the forefinger. Even just their tips. It all depends how high the onboard voltage is running. In my case, gentlemen, it was very high indeed.

It was years since I had indulged in self-pleasuring. I could even date the last occasion to 1989: my time in the army just about to end, hormones rampaging through my twenty-year-old body – that was the real thing, true-life, explosive masturbation sessions, powerful demob jerk-offs. Not some little boy's childish touching, fiddling with his willy, but rugged copulation with the dream of adult life about to come true.

Of course, acts like that can't even come close to genuine sex, and when I eventually got to grips with a real, warm body, I forgot for a long time that a hand can serve as a replacement for a woman. But masturbation is like riding a bicycle – once you've learned how to do it, the skill stays with you for the rest for your life. It only took me two seconds to recover the skills – stroking, squeezing, tugging and rubbing until I made that warm feeling appear in the right part of my body. The back and forth movements of my hand communicated an oscillatory impetus to my balls, and they started swaying regularly, striking against the upper edge of my trouser waistband, against the cold synthetic fabric. That lent added acuteness to the sensations, and a series of stupendous shudders ran through my entire body.

I was shafting the entire world. Today they're going to let me go. Today, now. Right now. There it is, my freedom. Right there beside me.

Once, in a previous life, seven years before my arrest, I was sitting on a stool in the service basement of a military airport, and when I picked up the phone I was told I could go home the next morning. I whooped like Tarzan in my elation. And in the evening of that same day, just before lights out, I withdrew into some out-of-the-way bushes, hastily unfastened my complicated military flies with all those buttons and committed a savage act of love with the entire universe. I took life itself – not out of aggression, not in an attempt to subjugate it, but out of love.

Seven years had gone by. I had definitely come full circle and returned to the same point. Once again I was walled in, and once again I was grappling with my genitals in anticipation of leaving those walls behind me.

The shameful performance was brief, only about twenty breaths, in and out. Everything expanded rapidly, started shimmering and glittering, burst into a flash of bright colours, then shrank rapidly towards a single point, and the first shudder ran up through my body.

But it was not to be! Behind me metal clanked against metal, hinges squeaked as they turned, and I heard the warden's voice.

'What are you doing?'

'Tossing off!' I answered in a loud voice full of hate, and shuddered. The sperm shot out of me, straight on to the prudently positioned standard prison towel.

'Turn this way!'

With a feeling of white-hot fury I took a step back with one foot and swung round, covering my groin with the material. The screw gave me a glance of contempt and paused for a moment, then the hatch in the door slammed shut.

And that was how it happened, gentlemen, that I was unfaithful to my wife, not with another woman on a soft divan, but with the ghost of naked freedom – in a solitary prison cell.

I refused my lunch. Why take lunch in prison if you're going to have dinner in a restaurant? Soon the ever-punctual Svoyak droned through its celebrated comedy routine about the time being three o'clock in Moscow and midnight in Petropavlovsk-Kamchatsky. An hour later I realised that I could barely hold out. There was less and less time left. The general was hardly going to carry on thinking about my humble personage until late in the evening. Everything was certain to be decided before the six o'clock deadline, the official end of the working day.

At five-thirty I was almost out of my mind.

At five-forty they gave the order 'You're wanted' again. I shouted out that I'd been ready for ages. The guard opened the deadbolts of the locks and we almost ran to the investigative wing.

This time I saw my counsel at law – but all on his own. Maxim Stein's face looked like the masks worn by ancient Greek women keening at a funeral.

'You're staying,' the lawyer said. He slapped his hands down on the table. 'They won't let you out …'

I collapsed despondently onto the stool.

'They'll bring the resolution on the choice of *detention under guard* as the measure of restraint to your cell. But that will be about eight o'clock. I deliberately came early so that you would know everything …' The lawyer switched to a whisper: 'Now for the good news …'

I gathered myself. My advocate pointed behind him with his thumb, and then with his index and middle fingers, he mimicked someone walking across the table-top. That meant my boss Mikhail had been released from prison, he was free. And consequently, in few days' time I would be free too.

No one will be able to resist the might of our money.

Everyone and everything will be bought.

Wholesale and retail, in small batches and large, on the exchange and the secondary market, the traders and brokers will buy up all the freedom.

For me.

13

'**A**nd then what happened after that?' asked the man in the white sweater.

'After that? It was all over. The end.' I replied. 'Mikhail' (I pointed at him, my motionless, pale-faced former boss) 'was let out of the prison, and he immediately did a runner. Seemingly he holed up in rented apartments at first … Then he got his head together, showed his face at the ruins of our bank, restored a couple of things to working order, grabbed every last bit of money he could lay his hands on and legged it as fast as he could. He left Moscow. Even left Russia. Settled down in his native Belarus. It's a separate country now, with its own laws …'

'I'm not talking about laws,' my second conversation partner said with a frown. The way he frowned made it quite clear the profound contempt that he felt for laws. 'This big-shot – you mean he didn't do anything with the money to help you? Never mind not sharing his own, he even stole yours too? So you're polishing a prison bunk with your backside, taking the blame for the entire crime, and he just took the money that belonged to both of you and disappeared? And since then he hasn't got in touch at all? All these years?'

I shrugged.

'Yes.'

'I still don't get it,' said the third participant in the conversation, who looked as though he had already got everything ages ago. 'So you – the two of you – made the underground bank together, right?'

'Right.'

'With no licence and no publicity, right?'

'Exactly.'

'That's a racket!'

They all made affirmative exclamations, very quiet ones.

'Then they caught you, and you decided to take all the responsibility …'

'No,' I replied patiently and politely. 'It was agreed almost from the very beginning that I would be the one who did time. Back in '94. When we started going up in the world. After about a year's work, we realised the business could be built up to an incredible level. Till it was worth millions. That's something worth fighting for, you get me?'

'Sure, sure,' everyone agreed again. Everyone except Mikhail.

I licked my dry lips.

'But in that business you can't get by without breaking laws: criminal laws, administrative laws, currency laws, tax laws and all the rest of them. Black cash, money-laundering and suchlike – that's what we were about. Mikhail was the boss, the senior partner, the man in charge. As the founding father he didn't want to do the dirty-work himself: looking for passports, setting up the fly-by-night firms, manufacturing the fake documents – all that came under my direct area of responsibility …'

The phrase sounded dry and bureaucratic. The second participant in the conversation winced slightly, twitching the dry wings of his small, pointed nose and gave me a swift glance of contempt. He'd spotted me for a highbrow.

'Go on,' Number Three told me, looking as if he could go on for me if he wanted.

I settled myself more comfortably in my chair and cleared my throat.

'If the agencies of law-enforcement decided to raid us, I was supposed to claim I was the boss. All the threads led to me. The go-betweens and the clients got their money from me. In any identity parades I was the one they would pick out, and when there were identity parades, that was what happened. According to our plan I was supposed to calmly go and do the time, and he was supposed to take care of the money and the business. It was big money. More than any chauffeur or doctor could earn in ten lifetimes.'

By and large the discussion was proceeding in a very seemly manner. No one was shouting or stamping their feet. My companions uttered their brief tirades in low voices, waiting patiently for the preceding speaker to finish.

There were five of us altogether in the conversation.

The one who had got everything straight away – he was the one leading the discussion – had a small body, totally ruined by prison. The blunt edges of his bones protruded under the skin of his face. The second participant, sitting beside him, looked like a more twisted and dehydrated copy of the third. Their throats, ruined by smoking and drinking chifir, made grating, croaking sounds. Their dark faces with diseased-looking cheeks gathered now and then into tormented grimaces.

The clothes all of them wore looked grotesque. I had to look long and hard before I realised what was wrong. My friends' outfits freakishly combined modern items with others that had gone out of fashion long ago. The main speaker, for instance, was kitted out in stylish trousers from the 2002 fashion season, coupled with a shirt that was out of date five years ago.

These men clearly bought their threads during the breaks between their stretches inside, which lasted on average four or five years. Then something presentable was put together out of the disparate items.

But then, my own clothes were even worse. The suit was threadbare. The ends of the sleeves were grimy and greasy. The trousers and jacket dangled as loosely as if they were on a hanger. My stretch in prison had cost me twelve kilograms of live weight, and in the three years of life outside afterwards, I still hadn't put any meat on my bones.

White Sweater looked different from his two friends – he represented a more advanced, modern type of bandit: his muscles bulged all over as he eloquently swung the brown, cracked, horny knuckles of his fist, which were well acquainted with the punch bag. There was no cigarette clutched in his hand, just a can of energy drink.

When we met two hours earlier, they had all told me their names, but they immediately slipped my mind. I don't remember names and numbers very well. A reporter's professional weakness: the blithe knight of the inkwell writes everything down in his notebook, there's absolutely no point in filling his head up with it. And in addition, this entire grave, nervous and lengthy conversation was so important to me that the evening before, as I tried to make my moral and physical preparations, I had reduced myself to a state of almost total exhaustion. I completely ignored the unimportant details. Forgot to eat anything in the evening and in the morning. I was anxious.

The meeting with Mikhail was supposed to set my life back on track. I had been waiting for it for three years. I had been intending to concentrate entirely and exclusively on a dialogue. To mobilise a hundred per cent of my intellect to demonstrate that I was right.

I'd spent all those three years searching for my former boss, who had run off with my (our) money.

My boss had done a good job of hiding, but he'd been found in Minsk, the capital of Belarus. By that time he had become an extremely staid and respectable citizen, the owner of a hairdressing salon. The Moscow millionaire banker was now a Minsk hair stylist.

'And all that time he was stealing from me,' Mikhail piped up. So far he had just sat despondently in the corner of the broad divan without saying a word.

Suddenly, in two rapid strides, the man in white was there beside him. He took a short swing and smashed a mobile phone over my former boss's head.

The blow was really only symbolic, but the phone fell to pieces. Parts of the case and microchips were sent flying.

Mikhail bore the assault patiently.

'Do you at least understand what you did?' White Sweater asked aggressively, ignoring Mikhail's remark about my stealing. 'Do you know what it's called, the thing you did? Eh? Or don't you understand? What? Nothing to say, then?'

Mikhail didn't utter a word.

'Wait,' said the second man, with a grimace of childish annoyance on his bony face. 'Not like that. It's got to be done right ...'

'It's got to be done properly!' the man in the sweater retorted.

'Done properly – for something like that, sawing him in pieces would be too good!' the third participant in the discussion declared emotionally.

'The man worked with him! He went to jail for him! He left his health behind in there! He did everything! And what did he get for it? A pair of horns?'

'What's wrong with your health?' White Sweater enquired, turning towards me and measuring me from head to foot with a curious glance.

'I've no complaints,' I replied sullenly.

'Tell it like it is.'

'Well, I lost three teeth, plus there's a curvature of the spine. I had meningitis. And, naturally, Koch's bacillus…'

'Naturally,' agreed the owner of the bony face.

The third man also nodded, understanding what we meant.

'I did some time in prison too,' Mikhail suddenly remarked in a quiet voice.

All four of us laughed. The bony-faced one turned towards Mikhail:

'Where? Which prison? A month in Lefortovo – call that doing time? What are you on about, my friend? Don't you ever say that to anyone again! Lefortovo! Some prison that is!'

'Anyway,' the Third Man asked, 'what was that you were saying about him stealing?'

'I've got documents,' Mikhail said in a breaking voice. 'They show that Andrei, sort of … he was skimming all the time. From our own business … For his personal use … That's why I didn't give him anything.'

Losing the thread and growing confused, sweating and stammering, my former friend tried to tell his tall tale. Who knows when he made it up? Maybe three years earlier. Or perhaps, on the other hand, only yesterday, the night before the conversation.

'You know where you should stick your documents?' asked the man in the white sweater.

'Let's not get coarse,' Bony Face declared amicably. 'There's no point. This isn't a gang meet, after all. Just a friendly conversation.'

Mikhail brushed the pieces of plastic off his ears and neck.

'Andrei was stealing my money,' he repeated stubbornly.

'Okay, supposing you're right,' said Bony Face, and from the pitch and tone of his voice it was clear that he was a man of great patience. 'Supposing you're right! Suppose Andrei did steal from you. Did he steal much?'

'According to my calculations, it's exactly the same amount that I owed him. That is ...' Mikhail gulped, swallowed. 'At first I honestly intended to give him back his share, but I suddenly discovered that my own man had been skimming off money ... on the sly ... the whole three years ...'

'So one thing balanced out the other,' said the Third Man, getting the point.

Mikhail jerked his head up hopefully.

'Ye-es,' drawled the Second Man. 'All right. He was stealing. Just suppose! And now tell us ...' The short pause seemed to hang, ringing, in the air. 'Please ...' The second pause felt almost unbearable. 'Tell us this: What did you do with the million that was left? You had a million for the two of you, didn't you?'

'A million and a half,' Mikhail and I replied simultaneously, in the same haughty, jealous tone of voice.

The men of crime smiled.

'So where's that million and a half now? What did you do with it?'

'I lost it all,' Mikhail muttered after a short pause.

'You lost it?' White Sweater asked, astonished. 'How do mean. Dropped it in the street, did you?'

'I invested the money in a few deals, and everywhere ... sort of ... anyway, the million kind of slipped away.'

'Tell us about it,' Bony Face suggested 'And stop squirming, don't worry, we're all friends together here. Just don't try to fool us. We're not easily fooled. We're like you. Tricksters, crooks. I work scams. And he' – a crooked finger with a dark nail was extended towards White Sweater – 'takes people's property and money away from them by force. A bandit. And he' – the finger moved on to the Third Man – 'is a thief. Has been all his life. Never does anything else. Steals and does time. When he's done his time, he steals again ... So don't go trying to fool us, my old mate, all right?'

Mikhail sighed – quietly and very affectedly.

I immediately realised he was up to something. Playing for time. Driven almost cataleptic by fear, he had decided to endure this painful conversation until it finally came to an end. And then run for it.

'Four hundred thousand,' my former friend began, 'I invested … in real estate … in non-residential premises in Moscow. The people handling everything promised a quick profit … But then the whole operation turned out to be a bluff. The money disappeared.'

'All six hundred thousand?' the Third Man asked.

'Yes.'

'So,' said the Second Man with a nod. 'What did you do with them?'

'With the offices?'

White Sweater gave a heavy groan, got up out of his armchair and started pacing around the room.

'With the people!' said Bony Face, getting a bit annoyed. 'With the ones who ripped you off. With those lousy swindlers, those bad men who stole the bread off your table – what did you do with them? Did you kill them? Chop them into pieces? Chain them to the wall in your cellar?'

Mikhail lowered his eyes.

'I didn't do anything.'

The taciturn Third Man hissed morosely through his teeth.

'I see,' Bony Face said with a nod. 'And what about the rest? One million, take away six hundred thousand – that leaves four hundred thousand. Where is it?'

'The same,' my former boss mumbled, 'it disappeared.'

'How did it disappear?'

Mikhail shifted his posture and sniffed.

'In Belarus,' he said almost in a whisper, 'these men came to see me – I'd known them for years and years – and offered me a chance to buy a large, sort of, consignment of textiles. Fabric. They promised to help me sell it at a profit straight away. In a month or two I was expecting to double my money …'

'And then what?'

'It turned out the goods were, you know, kind of … non-liquid.'

'They took you for four hundred thousand dollars for shop-soiled rags, right?'

'Something like that.'

'White Sweater stopped striding from one wall to the other. Suddenly moving close to Mikhail, he asked:

'Begging your pardon, but do you know anything about textiles?'

My former boss lowered his head.

'I do now.'

'And then?'

'I knew almost nothing.'

'Maybe you'd traded in them? Textiles? Eh? Manufactured them? Made blouses and bras out of them?'

'No.'

'Then why did you get into it?'

'I wanted, sort of, to earn some money.'

'And did you?' Bony Face asked, smiling.

My former associate shook his head. It was absolutely obvious he had never experienced such public humiliation and disgrace before, I thought, banishing a feeling of pity with an effort of will.

White Sweater heaved another sigh and swore in a whisper. Bony Face wagged a threatening finger at him and glanced into Mikhail's face.

'And what did you do, my friend, with the people who stung you so cruelly? For four hundred big ones! Four hundred big ones! That's huge money, an entire fortune! Four hundred thousand dollars. After the failure with the Moscow real estate you must have been really, really angry, right? And you told yourself: no more, that's enough, no lowlife's ever going to flim-flam me again!' Bony Face clapped his palms together hard and loud and rubbed them against each other. 'Well, tell me now – and we'll listen! – what was the cruel punishment you handed out to those con artists? Tell me how you sawed them up for sandal straps, those bastards. I can just imagine what you did with them! I can just imagine your blind fury. What did you do? What?'

'Nothing,' Mikhail whispered.

'Why?'

'Those people … sort of … disappeared.'

'Did you go to the militia?'

'Yes. Unofficially, of course … I made enquiries. I found out I'd been dealing with professional swindlers. They had fake passports, they were wanted by Interpol and so on …'

'And the fabric.'

'I've got the fabric. But it … It can't be sold. Not even at a give-away price. It's material that, sort of, went out of fashion a long time ago. And nobody wants it.'

'Hock it to a bank,' suggested the Third Man, who hadn't said anything so far.

Mikhail moaned feebly.

'I tried. It's no good. The bank brings in an expert, and he, sort of, valued the security. And the expert …'

' … Says your goods are rotten!' Bony Face concluded. 'Right?'

'Yes.'

'And now – look!' said the Third Man, suddenly raising his voice for the first time. 'You didn't do anything to the man who stole six hundred big ones from you.'

'You forgave him!' White Sweater boomed in a deep bass.

'Yes, you forgave him!' the Third Man went on. 'Just let it go. Or were you afraid to tangle with them? Time goes by, and you get duped again. Taken for four hundred thousand. And you did nothing again. You forgave them again! Ah, to hell with you guys, you said, *relax*. You forgave the first lot, then this lot. But Andrei here – you didn't forgive him a single thing! He worked for you. He did time for you. Then you decided he'd been cheating you and you threw him out in the street, fleeced him, turned him into a beggar! So what does that make you, eh?'

I realised with a shock of surprise that neither my ex-friend's wan appearance nor the conversation itself was giving me any pleasure at all.

Only five minutes earlier I had caught myself twisting my lips into a spiteful grin – but now the sight of this man suffering so acutely seemed loathsome in the extreme. My former boss sat there, huddled into the corner of the divan, with his palms pressed together and clasped tightly between his knees, only tugging his trembling limbs out in order to light yet another cigarette. He was smoking them one after another (I'd gone through an entire pack in two hours as well; the other debaters, including our host, were far less agitated and smoked less intensively. White Sweater didn't touch a single one.)

Mikhail's face, once pale-pink with a luxuriant growth of beard on the cheeks and clearly defined lips, could easily have been his own death mask now, and its colour was appropriate too: a dense grey, with a tinge of yellow. He hid his eyes from everyone and tried hard to maintain his self-control.

He was among the kind of people he had hated all his life.

It was painful to watch – I got up and walked out into the kitchen.

The criminal underworld in our country lives pretty poorly.

After I was released from prison I maintained several connections in criminal society. Out of curiosity, not necessity. And after I had spent a few evenings in the company of thieves and bandits, I was rather astonished to realise that they didn't often have money in their pockets.

The lads were barely scraping by, gentlemen.

Many of them didn't even have a rusty kopeck to their name. Others, a minority, more mature and more fortunate, were more or less poised on the edge of the lower middle-class: a small city flat, a car, perhaps even a garage. The cars were certainly notable for their power and comfort, but it was no secret where those gleaming mercs and beemers came from; stolen and repainted, with the chassis numbers hammered out. The headaches these polished rides brought their owners far outweighed the pleasure they got from using them.

Some gangs, a little younger, didn't have any property at all apart from a collectively procured automobile. Several of them lived together in rented apartments, amusing themselves with vodka and the video player; they couldn't see any clear prospects ahead of them at all.

Sad times had arrived. For armed robbery they gave you twenty-five years. Burgling apartments had become more difficult: rich homes, equipped with alarm systems and steel doors, with doorkeepers, no longer offered easy pickings. And worst of all, the businessmen, those bloody fat cats, no longer sought the brotherhood's patronage. Commerce no longer wished to pay for protection, for a 'roof' over its head. People had become clever, cautious, experienced, and they were well protected.

Of course, the home I was visiting today, where they were trying to convince my ex-friend just how wrong he was, was not exactly a bandit's den. But even so the small flat (on the edge of town, metro station Tyoply Stan), was far from a model of material prosperity. The host's extremely modest coat hung in modest solitude in the extremely modest hallway. The room where the conversation was taking place was scantily furnished. The leather armchairs, patched in many places, had an almost pitiful look. The windowsill was cluttered by an array of half-empty wine bottles.

'What are you dreaming about?' asked White Sweater, suddenly appearing behind me. He didn't smile. 'I wish you wouldn't smoke here at least,' he said reproachfully. His voice sounded young and vibrant. I threw the cigarette I'd just lit out through the window. 'Don't throw things out of the window,' my companion went on even more reproachfully. 'What are you dreaming about?'

'I'm thinking.'

'What's there to think about? Everything's clear. We'll wind things up now …'

'Do you think,' I asked in a low voice, 'that he'll give everything back?'

The muscular man in white stretched, cracking his joints, spreading his arms out wide as if he wanted to clasp the whole of existence in his embrace, and then slapped his broad chest with a booming sound.

'Where can he go to?'

His pectorals reminded me of the curved blades of old Soviet-style shovels. His fingers gave off a smell I had almost forgotten – gun oil.

'He'll trick all of you,' I said. 'He tricked me, and he'll trick you too. He'll wriggle his way out of it. That's the kind of operator he is, believe me, Igor!'

'My name's Yegor.'

'Sorry.'

'No problem.'

The young guy in white, Yegor, opened a new can with a picture of a buffalo on it, took a careful sip and held it out to me. I shook my head and he took a second swallow.

'In short, don't you worry,' he reassured me. 'We'll do everything, he's ours, getting your money out of him – well, in short, that's a matter of honour. How we're going to do it, you don't need to know. In short, all you do now is just sit at home, do nothing and wait for us to give you a call.'

'He won't give anything back,' I repeated. 'He'll either run for it, or go to the militia …'

'What?' Yegor laughed lightheartedly. 'What militia?' He turned and walked back into the room, calling out loudly: 'Hear that? Lads!'

'What?'

'Andrei said our friend Mikhail will go to the militia.'

I heard a chorus of jolly laughter. Left alone, I immediately took the chance to get out another cigarette.

'What's this, want to complain to the militia about us, do you?' I heard someone in the room ask.

'No,' Mikhail replied very quietly.

'Thank God for that. Or else then we'd have a real comedy on our hands!' the same grating voice said with a catch of humour. 'First you pulled all sorts of scams. Then you made another guy take the rap instead of you – for your own scams! Then you robbed the guy! And now you want to go running to the militia? A real comedy, straight up.'

The word 'comedy' was pronounced with a strongly accented 'o', which added to the humour of what was said. I heard more loud guffaws and couldn't help smiling myself.

At this point the powerful figure appeared in the doorway again. I had to move fast to stub my cigarette out in the ashtray and tip the ashtray into the rubbish pail.

In addition to a large number of cigarette butts, the pail contained fresh potato peelings and strips of cellophane from cheap sausages.

The people here lived frugally. I thought in annoyance that with his experience Mikhail understood that as well as I did. This poor flat is inhabited by poor people, their incomes are low, and that means they haven't had any real success in life. Perhaps they won't be able to handle Mikhail either?

'What are you doing skulking in here?' White Sweater asked amiably.

'Thinking,' I said,

'Think as much as you like – a hundred roubles still isn't money. What do you do anyway?'

'Nothing,' I admitted.

'Then how do you live? What on?'

'I get by,' I replied evasively. 'I borrowed some money from an old friend, that's what I feed my family on. And sometimes one of my friends tosses me a couple of hundred.'

'Yeah?' said White Sweater and raised his eyebrows, intrigued. 'What do you reckon, would one of those friends of yours toss a couple of hundred my way?'

I took this as a joke.

'Hardly. They all owe me.'

'So apart from Mikhail, you've got other people who owe you?'

'Half of Moscow,' I said honestly.

'Yeah?'

'The day I was picked up, about two hundred thousand disappeared from the office in the confusion ...'

'Dollars?'

'Naturally. People who just happened to be there took the money and hid it. Technical personnel. Employees.'

'Did you complain to them?'

'Of course.'

'And what did they say?'

'Every one of them confessed that the money was long gone. Spent. Used up. Invested in various commercial projects, deals, operations, businesses. And every one of them went bust ages ago ...'

'So what did you say?'

'I said: 'Pay me back any way you can.'

'And do they?'

'A little bit at a time.'

The body-builder pondered.

'That's good,' he replied. 'But in short, even so, you can still demand it back. Separately. Because they took what wasn't theirs and used it, and in the end they gobbled it all up, right down to the last kopeck. That's the way it was, right? While you were inside, they used it! And then they lost the lot! They ought to have put the lot straight down on the table for you! The whole amount! In the same bills! If someone else's valuables come into your hands by chance, then, take good care of them! And give them straight back, at the first opportunity! And especially – big money …'

'Yes,' I said with a nod. 'They took what belonged to someone else – and they spent it all on themselves. There was just one person, the only one, who did exactly what you said. Only one person put a wad down on the table in front of me and said: "This is yours, untouched, take it". Only one.'

'Who was that?'

'My wife.'

The huge bandit observed a respectful silence.

'Then,' he said after a pause, 'you really have been lucky in life, bro.'

In a gesture of powerful fellow-feeling he took hold of me by the shoulders, easily lifted me up (the soles of my feet parted completely from the floor) and immediately put me back down carefully and quickly.

'You'll get your money, I'm responsible. Let's go say goodbye. If you ever need to get anything from anyone anywhere, always come to me. Deal?'

'Deal,' I said with a sad nod.

They let Mikhail go, giving him two weeks to get the money together.

On the tenth day, early in the evening, I got my answer. They phoned me and told me that my former boss and associate Mikhail had gone straight from that terrifying apartment to the militia, where he said he'd been grabbed by extortioners; that it was a miracle he'd managed to escape from the criminals.

The gang had been arrested immediately. But since no evidence confirming the fact of extortion was found (where could it have come from?) the villains were immediately released.

My former friend and boss disappeared without a trace.

And that was the end of this Asiatic story.

If anybody ever asks me about the moment when I experienced the most intense rapture in my life, I shall tell them that one day the dazzling beauty of human depravity was revealed to me. And I saw that there is nothing in the world more beautiful than depravity, frank and undiluted.

PART TWO

14

At precisely six o'clock in the morning the opening above the iron door emitted a pompous musical phrase as radio Svoyak announced to the entire country that a new autumn day had begun.

The inhabitants of the cell in the Lefortovo pre-trial detention centre began to stir. Hardly even opening their eyes, they crawled feebly out of their beds, carelessly tucked their blankets of coarse, blue, great-coat cloth under the edges of the short little mattresses, pulled on their woollen trousers and lay back down again – this time on top of the blankets. They covered themselves with their jackets. Scratched a bit, snuffled a bit and then fell quiet.

The 'rules of behaviour for individuals held under arrest and convicted offenders' allowed every prisoner to sleep twenty-four hours a day if he felt like it. But from six in the morning to ten in the evening his bed had to look respectable. Failure to obey meant the punishment cell.

The third inhabitant of the three-man cell didn't bother to go to sleep. He sat on his bed for about a minute, with a gloomy air, staring at a single point with a fixed, almost insane expression. His hair was standing on end. His left cheek, crumpled by the flat, hard pillow (prison property), sagged slightly. Eventually he shook his head several times to drive away the remnants of his dreams and with the gesture of a boxer struck himself slightly above the temple with his open palm, inducing jangling, painful sensations inside his skull. Thus was vigour injected into the nervous system.

He slipped his feet into plastic slippers grown cold overnight, and stood up. He filled a mug with water, dropped in the electric heating coil and rapidly made the icy water hot; he washed his eyes thoroughly with it, copiously wetting his eyelids and then the whole of his face, alternating the hot water from the mug with icy water from the tap and, by making the abrupt switch from warm to cold, managed to achieve a resonant clarity in his brain.

Only recently, literally just a few days earlier, this sinewy but narrow-shouldered and slim-boned individual with dark hair, a certain Andrei Rubanov by name, had been planning grandly to buy the entire law-enforcement apparatus of the country. And then bound briskly and merrily out of the detention centre the way a rich yuppie jumps out of the open door of his private business jet, thrusting a tip into the stewardess's bra with one hand and slapping the pilot on the shoulder with the other.

He had been arrogantly certain of his money and his friend – his business associate and boss Mikhail. His boss had been released five days earlier. They obviously really *had* taken him for an office supplies manager, and not a banker. They had failed to put together any substantial evidence. And they had released him from detention. The head of the underground banking business had escaped punishment for his crime by putting another man, specially prepared, in his place. A retainer. A fake chairman. A boy to do the time.

When it finished tootling its little tune of morning greeting, the radio greeted the citizens of the country in a rich, exceptionally well-balanced male voice, a baritone oozing with optimism – and informed them of the date: the 20th September 1996.

The individual known in this text by the name of A. Rubanov picked up a pen from the table with a wet hand. Shuffling his feet, he walked over to the wall and made a mark on a homemade calendar – a page from a notebook stuck up with chewed bread. He crossed out the figure 'twenty', took a step back, gloomily studied the result of his labours, moved back close and crossed it out with a thicker line.

The month had expired on the 15th of September. His boss Mikhail had been released from the detention centre. But his retainer, the boy to do the time, had been handed an official document which stated that the boy was accused of a grave crime and would remain behind bars for at least another two months.

The following morning the prisoner was moved from cell No. 87, on the first floor of the prison, with yellow walls and a west-facing window, to cell No. 33, on the ground floor, with green walls and a north-facing window. There were already two prisoners in the cell. Rubanov was the third.

The move took place straight after breakfast, and immediately before supper the suspect was summoned to a meeting with his lawyer.

The red-headed solicitor shrugged and spread his hands: Mikhail had been released and he had immediately disappeared. No one knew where he'd gone. His whereabouts and telephone number were unknown. 'But he did come yesterday,' Red informed his client in a tense whisper. 'He came to see me at home. And gave me a note for you ... Here it is ...'

The scrap of bright-yellow paper (scraps like that, in various bright colours, lie in abundance on businessmen's desks for jotting down some important idea or sum of money) bore only four wildly scrawled words: 'KEEP QUIET. BE PATIENT'. It was my boss's writing.

The red-headed lawyer didn't understand much. From what he said, Mikhail had behaved like a man who was extremely frightened by everything that had happened. He had visited the solicitor very late in the evening, when it was almost midnight. He phoned from his car, on a mobile, and asked Red to come out. The entire conversation took only thirty seconds. The lawyer stood on the pavement, Mikhail sat in the driving seat of his car and spoke through the half-lowered window; the engine was running the whole time. Mikhail, thinner now and grey-faced, said that he would be away for a while and as soon as he got back he would be in touch; he handed over the note and instantly roared off, stepping recklessly hard on the gas.

No information, no money, no instructions. Nothing. Keep quiet, be patient.

There was nothing left to do but hope that after a dramatic and nerve-jangling adventure like a month in a pre-trial detention centre, the fake office supplies manager had simply decided to take some time out. Drink himself senseless, gorge himself on roast meat and beer, snort himself crazy with cocaine in a night club or simply spend some time alone with his wife – in other words, reward himself somehow for all his suffering and torment.

But a day went by, and a second, and a third – the boss still didn't get in touch. Everything pointed to the conclusion that the boss and friend Mikhail had betrayed his faithful retainer, his boy doing the time. The doleful suspicion surfaced every now and then from the depths of A. Rubanov's subconscious, like some loathsome octopus from the salty ocean depths.

His boss and friend wasn't going to finance any efforts to free his man from detention. His boss and friend had taken fright and run away.

In order to get his mind into gear he had to wash his face again. With cold water, then with hot. Several times.

Here's a picture from the past. In colour. A comic strip drawn with incredible skill. The picture shows an office, in the evening: two young men without jackets counting money. Both of them sniffing frequently. Sweaty faces. It's hot. There's a lot of money. Nothing but dollars. Brief glimpses of faces – transatlantic presidents with sausage curls. The process has already been going on for more than an hour. With cigarettes smoking and coffee steaming. Fan-blades whirling.

One of the two is larger and more imposing, the other is serious and yet fitful, fussy, almost theatrical. The capitalists' appearance is not particularly bourgeois. Open shirt collars, expensive ties skewed to one side. Unshaven cheeks twitching. They count without speaking, intently, deftly. The movements made by the quick fingers stained with blackish-green are like a cardsharp's.

The atmosphere in the spacious room has a faint hint of insanity. The immense television is switched on, but there's nothing on the screen except a grey rippling. The cyclopean safe is standing open. There are bundles of green paper inside it.

'One million, three hundred and forty-five,' the boss says with a heavy sigh.

'That's what I make it too,' the junior associate says with a nod.

'A good day.'

The junior shrugs his shoulders without the slightest sign of enthusiasm.

'All's well that ends well.'

The boss frowns.

'Don't be nervous.'

The junior smiles sadly.

'I can't help it.'

'Learn not to.'

'How?'

'By distancing the reason for anxiety,' the boss pronounces. 'You won't be inside for long. You'll get three years. You'll do a year and a half, two at most. I'll provide you with all the, you know, comforts. The finest food, books and all the rest. Why be nervous? Before you can even, sort of, blink, you'll be back out again …'

The blades of the fans circle and hum. The dishevelled wads of American money diffuse a magical emerald glow. The junior associate's ashtray is overflowing with butts and his head with dark thoughts. What lies ahead for him? Success? A cool million? A limousine? A yacht? A mansion on the Rublyovo-Uspensky highway? Filipino servants? A platinum American Express card? Or barred windows, crude skilly, friends who are criminals with protruding bones?

The junior catches his boss's eye. The boss is calm.

They've been together for three years. They started small and grew big. Grew into big deals, serious sums of money, clients from among the big-shots in oil and political wheeler-dealers. All that time the boss kept impressing on his junior the fundamental truth of their activities, the most important law, the basic rule: the business *über alles*.

For the sake of the business you have to be prepared to do anything. The business is the very same productive labour that turned a monkey into a man. The satisfaction of all our demands. It feeds us. It will guarantee the Sorbonne and Oxford to our children, a gracious old age to our parents, eternal youth and beauty to our wives.

Senior and junior look at each other. They are both young, intelligent and rich. Soon one of them, the junior, will go to jail. That's the way it has to be. There are moments when the imperial Moloch has to be offered a sacrifice. Then the other one, the senior, will get his partner out on the sly, for a bribe, and it will all be over …

Really, gentlemen, doesn't that make a really wild comic strip? Instructive and life-affirming.

If you splash icy water on to your eyeballs, and then hot water, the flickering picture will become sharp and inordinately bright, the faces of the heroes will stretch out into bloated caricatures. The senior, the boss, will be revealed as a cunning and greedy cheapskate and the reader will recognise the junior as a naïve, romantic fool.

No, we don't need any pictures like that now, the boy suspect thought, working away intently with his toothbrush and peeping at himself in the tiny little mirror. His own eye, rolled furiously back and up like a horse's, came diving out at him. What we need is complete calm and absolute composure.

So, the plans for buying generals have collapsed. The blitzkrieg has failed. Any rapid victory over the prison system is quite out of the question. But the boy banker is used to thinking of himself as a staunch, unbending individual. He has not abandoned his intention to conquer prison.

In that interrogation office, five days ago, alone with his solicitor, he asked for a pen and wrote his wife a letter. The basic sense of the two paragraphs was that he would definitely be back, and very soon.

The boy suffered minutes of torment as he wrote the letter to his beloved. There was no one closer and dearer to him than this extravagant, vociferous blonde with huge green eyes who he had once invited into his lousy life, promising her a great love. He hadn't promised money: at that time, in 1991, his entire fortune consisted of a shabby leather jacket, a pair of Cossack boots and a rattling old automobile. Also thrown in were a pair of lips set in firm resolution and a glance full of cool determination to achieve his goals. The eighteen-year-old girl had said 'yes'.

Now that he had ended up behind bars, the boy suspect realised he needed to be careful in fitting one word with another. The first version of the note was ripped to shreds. And the second. And the third. The red-headed lawyer waited patiently, sensitively averting his eyes. Eventually the right phrases were assembled.

The postscript contained an avowal that came from the very core of his soul.

I LOVED YOU, I LOVE YOU NOW AND I ALWAYS WILL LOVE YOU, MY ONLY ONE, MY DARLING BELOVED GIRL.

The letter ended in a list of books he needed and a request to send them to the prison just as soon as possible.

The boy was extremely obstinate. Now, after spending thirty-five days inside, after guessing that he had been betrayed, he did not despair – on the contrary, he felt his strength had been increased tenfold.

With the boss or without the boss, with money or without it, he was going to get out of jail. He had adjusted his tactics and his strategy. Now he intended to fill his enforced idleness with a continuous series of gruelling, subtle training exercises for body and mind, one following straight after the other. He had conceived the intention of tempering himself. Transforming himself into an indomitable warrior.

'I'm going to turn all the harmful effects of jail to my benefit,' he decided. 'And I shall triumph over the bars, the walls, the screws, the skilly, the need to sleep with the light on and all the other naive abominations of this institution with barred windows!'

He took off his undershirt and tossed a few handfuls of water on to his shoulders and chest, rubbed himself down with his hands, shuddered at the cold and dried his torso briskly with a narrow prison towel.

He tried not to make a noise – the others would get annoyed if he did. It was no part of his plans to cause any inconvenience to his cell-mates. He was always modest and polite. He was cautious. Often he simply didn't know how to behave. Many simple situations baffled him. But he learned quickly, he was quick on the uptake, he strove diligently to comprehend all the subtle points of this freakish prison life.

He squatted down on the meagre mattress (prison property) in a special pose, with his backside set on his heels, his back perfectly straight, his open hands resting on his knees – all this taken together is called 'zazen' – and began taking slow, deep breaths in and out. He closed his eyes and tried to separate his consciousness from himself, to purge it of chimeras and fears.

At that moment one of the two sleepers gave a dull groan, grated his teeth together hard and opened his colourless eyes for a brief instant, then licked his lips several times and fell asleep again. His knees tucked themselves up closer to his chin and his little feet wriggled about, so that the cats' faces tattooed on them just above the toes started moving and twitched their whiskers.

Half an hour later the betrayed boy emerged from his state of immobility, feeling that his mind was clear and sober.

Without making a sound, he took a book down from the shelf, opened it, then turned it upside down. And started reading it – slowly, one syllable at a time.

That was how the CASE FILE lay on the table in front of him, for half an hour twice a week. The grey folder kept growing thicker, swelling, its edges getting grubbier. The CASE FILE was being gradually filled out. The boy's fate might be concealed in it. Perhaps what the future held for the sullen, skinny youth with dark-brown hair – once a respectable financial functionary, and now a prisoner suspected of a grave crime – was eight or nine years of detention, standard regime? Or, on the contrary, an eighteen-month suspended sentence ...

The investigator's documents were an important target. The check-shirted man from Ryazan, Khvatov, began every interrogation by taking the thick volume out of his bag and setting it down in front of him. Then he laid out his office equipment and produced yet another set of minutes, peering into the screen and screwing up his eyes. Constantly checking against the CASE FILE. The cardboard-bound volume lay open on the desk for thirty or forty seconds. It was stupid not to take advantage of that, not to try to extract at least some scrap of information, no matter how small.

It is possible to learn to grasp a page of text instantaneously with your eyes – no matter how it's lying, sideways, on a slope, upside down – and remember it word for word. There are special instruction books. They're sold in the shops. The times are gone when the skills of speed reading and memorisation were only taught to spies. The country has democracy now, all information is accessible, all knowledge has been declassified. The guide books the boy has claim that anybody with even the slightest degree of self-discipline is capable of recording a mental image of a page of printed text in just a few seconds. The most important requirement is regular daily practice.

It also says in the foreword that the practice sessions are most beneficial if you do them at the same time each day, sleep in a well-aired room and follow a regular routine in general. The boy can certainly manage that. The conditions he is living in are almost ideal.

The betrayed boy wakes up, takes meals, goes walking and falls asleep at the same times every day. He has a table, paper and a pen. And plenty of time.

15

They woke up late in the morning.

The first to break the silence was Frol: he pushed off his blanket and scratched his sunken belly with a grimace of pain. The Virgin Mary tattooed there and the baby Jesus in her arms began to move. Her face seemed to come to life and the infant tightened his grip on the bared breast.

'Good morning, Fatty!' Frol wheezed. 'Why so sad, little brother? Your life shattered, ha?'

The words were directed at my second cell-mate, an extremely corpulent man by the name of Vadim; but I was the only one who called him that; Frol always used his nickname.

Fatty lay there without speaking, an expression of profound sadness on his face.

'I'm sick of being inside,' he replied laconically in a high voice.

'If you're sick of being inside, then hang yourself!' Frol advised him briskly. 'String yourself up, on the quiet, over there in the corner. With the lead from the electric coil. If you can't mange it all on your ownsome, just ask the people and they'll give you a hand …'

They laughed.

My two cohabitants had several variants of these gallows jokes that they shared. But the laughter they evoked was prison laughter: fierce, exaggeratedly loud, spilling over at the end into a fit of painful hacking and coughing. The two of them together looked like bosom buddies. They told me they'd been sharing a cell for four months already.

'And by the way, about the electric coil,' Frol went on with a yawn, scratching at his biceps. The mosquito wearing a militiaman's peaked cap and a major's shoulder straps that was tattooed on the muscles started to move, trying to stick its hairy proboscis into the ulnar vein, along which there was a slogan inscribed in Gothic lettering: 'no blood left, a cop drank it'. 'How about a spot of chifir, gents? Andrei, won't you join me?'

'No. I'll have coffee.'

'And I'll have salami,' corpulent Vadim declared.

'As you like,' Frol growled hoarsely and stood up.

His morning ablutions were a harrowing procedure to watch. This uncommonly stoop-shouldered, raw-boned man, tattooed all over his body, thrust his open hands against the edge of the washbasin, leaned down and began slowly hacking up phlegm, taking several goes, producing scraping sounds from his nose and throat. The low groans, the swearing and coughing lasted for several minutes. After that the angular little man filled his mouth with water and flushed it from one cheek to the other – that was a substitute for brushing his teeth.

When he finished, he hopped back up on to his blanket, crept closer to the table, which could well be called the kitchen table (we kept our tableware and food there, on several layers of newspaper spread out on the table top), and became absorbed in preparing his morning chifir.

He sprinkled fifty grams of loose tea into a hundred and fifty grams of boiling water and quickly covered the mug with a special little homemade lid.

In that moment when he was anticipating his morning fix – the most eagerly desired one – it was impossible to look at Frol without a feeling of pity. It wasn't just his hands that trembled, his forearms did too, and the head on that thin, sinewy neck.

Of his forty-eight years of life he had spent more than twenty in jails, prison camps and detention centres, in several stretches. In other words, he was a professional felon. Frol himself related the main milestones of his life to me during the first few hours after we met. In simple phrases. As he told his story, he shuffled his strong, short fingers and the thief's rings tattooed on their lower joints seemed to glitter with the non-existent diamonds described by their form.

But now the beverage is ready. The hot mug is concealed in his hands. It gives off an aroma that fills all the space in the cell – extremely bitter, dense and powerful. The first sip has been taken, the most important one; after all, caffeine is lighter than water and so collects at the very top of the receptacle.

The cigarette is lit. Several seconds pass in agonising torment – and the tattooed jailbird's face is distorted by an expression of suffering that is almost biblical in its profundity. For there is no poison in the world more bitter than prison chifir! Then almost immediately the agonised grimace is rapidly replaced by an indecent, wet, monkey-like smirk. The old lag looks up at me with eyes gleaming with tears and winks – the way a hundred thousand incorrigible optimists would wink.

'What I could do with now's a good puff of hash,' he said with yearning in his voice.

'That's right,' Fatty said with a nod and a yawn. He was still lying down. 'Some good Central Asian weed …'

'What do you know about Central Asian weed,' Frol chuckled.

'I served in a construction battalion,' Fatty explained.

'So?'

'So almost all the other guys in it were Kazakhs.'

'I get you.'

My new friends were different in every way. Above all in their corporeal geometry. Fat Vadim, massive and amorphous, with a Roman nose, pale-blue eyes, and a face and body that bore the traces of every kind of vice, consisted entirely of spheres and ovals. His head and his shoulders and his backside and his knees – everything seemed excessively round. Frol's body, on the contrary, was composed of right angles and triangular prisms. Everything protruded – the cheekbones and collarbones, the nose and chin, ear cartilages, elbows and knuckles.

When they turned their backs to each other and started making their beds, I had the feeling that any moment the puny recidivist's sharp corners would puncture Fatty's plump curves and he would burst like a balloon.

Their voices didn't go together either. Frol rasped and grated loudly, like some rusty old hoist, while Fatty span out quiet, melodic phrases.

These two completely dissimilar people were alike in only one respect: they both had a very bad stoop. I thought of them to myself as 'the curved spines'.

Fatty's immense frame shuddered as he washed noisily. He took out a piece of smoked salami neatly packaged in cellophane, unwrapped it and laid it on the clean newspaper.

'Salami!' he announced. 'Any takers?'

Frol shook his head – he was still in the grip of his morning caffeine rush, the heaviest hit of all. I said no too.

With a shrug of his shoulders, Fatty took a book down off the shelf and removed a long strip of rigid cardboard from it. Its actual function was not to serve as a bookmark, but as a ruler – there were precisely spaced notches along its edge. After measuring the salami cylinder in a very elaborate fashion, Fatty took a prison knife – a piece of plastic crudely sharpened against the metal edge of a bedstead – and sawed off several extremely thin slivers of the meat product, which he proceeded to consume. He disdained both tea and bread in the morning.

The semi-transparent meaty morsel was first sniffed voluptuously, then carefully examined, and only then placed in the mouth; the lips instantly closed together, the cheeks and chin moved right and left, the sounds of copiously excreted saliva could be heard, and then the slice of salami was demolished by several mighty masticatory motions of the jaw. The little blue eyes either glowed dreamily or, sometimes, probed the surrounding space suspiciously: is there anyone nearby who might seek to purloin our greatest treasure? Finally the thoroughly chewed substance passed into the alimentary canal, assisted on its way by a cautious but instantaneous swallow, accompanied by a hollow internal rumbling – and the fingers were already lovingly caressing the next crimson-brown fragment of food that looked like a pre-revolutionary coin.

Unlike the penniless Frol, Fatty had been a rich man in his past life on the outside: the head of a construction trust. His selection of provisions was in no way inferior to mine. His tracksuit had obviously not been bought at a market stall. Naturally, mine cost at least twice as much. But somehow that thought failed to excite me now. After spending a second month in the Lefortovo fortress, acquiring cell-mates, and sinking into the prison like a swamp, I found myself starting to forget many things. The ever-fortunate, jet-propelled Andriukha, the snot-nosed fat cat, had been left behind. The past was never coming back. And neither was the nouveau-riche Andrei. His position in space was now occupied by a quite different person: a cautious realist.

On the first day Frol explained to me with great patience and tact where everything's place was and how to organise my daily life.

The question was far from simple – three grown men passing their days in an area of ten square metres. Each of them had underwear, dishes, clothes. Each of them wanted to eat and drink, sleep, move around, defecate and keep himself clean. It was far from easy to arrange everything so that the cell-mates didn't butt foreheads together as they reached out for a pen or a towel.

When the screw glanced in every two minutes through his spy-hole – or, more correctly, his observation window – we probably looked like the occupants of a compartment in a long-distance train. The same slippers, tracksuit trousers and tee-shirts. The cramped space. The primitive, rigid male order. Toothpaste here, rubbish here, food and dishes here. But what destination was our train rushing towards?

After his hit of chifir, Frol became lively and started radiating joie de vivre and vitality. At such moments he simply couldn't keep still.

'Brothers!' he grated. 'I'm going to take a little stroll. I hope you don't mind?'

Hearing no objections, the grey-haired jailbird began striding to and fro along the narrow strip of free space between the iron bedsteads: from the side of the end bed to the door and back. Five steps to get there, four and a half to get back, and half a step for the turn.

Even I had acquired the habit of walking from wall to wall, although I had only been inside for a month. In my struggle against physical inactivity I had walked many kilometres in that way. And moreover, it was Nietzsche who said that no thought should be trusted unless it is born in the free movement of the entire body.

'Listen here, Fatty,' Frol called out. 'We forgot something yesterday.'

The construction magnate finished chewing his final slice of sausage and shrugged.

'The newspaper,' I suggested cautiously.

'That's right!' Frol exclaimed. 'The paper! Well done, Andriukha! A new paper came yesterday. And we didn't read it.'

'You're right,' said Fatty, nodding. 'We can't have that.'

The newspaper was immediately found. In a ten-square-metre cell every object – a newspaper, a book, a pack of cigarettes, or a stick of salami, or a box of tea – is within reach of an outstretched arm. The life of a guest at Lefortovo is spent in a lying position. He only has to reach out a hand, and he is already smoking, or chewing, or reading.

Outsize Vadim opened the black and white pages with a rustle.

'What's in it?' Frol asked impatiently, pacing out his short trail.

'The TV guide.'

'At last,' the hardened criminal croaked triumphantly. 'I was afraid they were going to leave us without one … Read it, brother!'

'Oho,' said Fatty, rustling the pages. 'Already the middle of September, is it? It feels as if summer's barely started …'

'I told you, time flies here. Well, what does it say? Any good films?'

'Heaps. On Sunday, for instance, there's a film about the American mafia. *The Godfather*.'

Frol grimaced without slowing down:

'Sod films about the mafia.'

'What's wrong with films about the mafia?' Fatty asked in surprise.

'Sod the American mafia,' Frol replied emphatically. 'Sod it! What do we want stories about the American mafia for, here, in Russia? You know what the American mafia is?'

'Tell me,' said Fatty, spreading his hands in acknowledgement of the other man's authority.

'A load of hucksters!' Frol said succinctly. 'Genuine, one hundred per cent, no-good hucksters! Bootleggers! What can hucksters and bootleggers have to do with the real criminal world? Absolutely nothing!'

The old lag kept striding impetuously back and forth, gazing into empty space, tossing out his words like cards dealt from the pack.

'Now just look what happens: the honest citizens watch films like that, about this father, about gangsters – and they think our Russian criminal world lives exactly the same way as the American mafiosi in the movies. Aha. By the same rules! Slobbering on the godfather's little hand! That's where the harm is – the central danger! Forget films about the mafia, Fatty! It's all garbage. Real life's not like that! In my country there aren't any godfathers, there never have been and there never will be. Carry on reading!'

'Channel four,' Fatty read out. 'From five o'clock until late evening, programmes about cops and criminals. First *Criminal Cases*, then *Full and Frank Confession* and after the news *Man and Law*. Then you can switch straight over to channel three and watch *CID, 38 Petrovka*. And at ten o'clock – *Prison and Liberty*.'

'You're joking!' Frol exclaimed.

'No, I swear.'

'Five programmes on two channels next to each other! All on the same subject! That's where the criminals are!' Frol exclaimed. 'In the TV. That's where the harm is!'

The old criminal's entire simple and radical view of the universe came down to the idea that the very greatest villains were not doing time in prison, but sitting in business offices, government offices and the editorial offices of newspapers and TV channels.

'It's nothing to do with the TV companies,' Fatty objected. 'You don't understand, Frol. TV presents the picture the viewers want to see. The public wants to be frightened by the sight of your face, but it wants to be reassured at the same time – everything's all right, the law-breaker was caught in time. So they show the public that picture. And during the breaks they stick in advertisements for washing powder.'

'Right, I get it. And everyone's happy,' Frol agreed pensively. 'The criminals thieve, the public watches and gets a bit of washing done and the lads collect money from the TV ... Listen, my old mate, don't take this wrong way, just scratch me here, will you, between the shoulder blades, closer to the right one ... yeah ... aha, there ... Thank you kindly. What else is in there?'

Fatty turned the page.

'A film about a cannibal.'

'About a cannibal?'

'Yes. American. The day after tomorrow. On channel two. At ten in the evening.'

'See, that's where the harm is! About a cannibal, you say ...'

'Where's the harm in that?'

'Don't you understand? They can't show that! No, of course, they can. That's what freedom's all about. Aha. But not on TV. Only for big money, in special places. Behind a big fence ...'

'Like porn films?' Fatty suggested.

'For instance. Aha. And there shouldn't be any bright-coloured pictures on the fence, and the notices should all be written in red!'

Fatty smiled condescendingly.

'Who's going to decide which films are good and which are bad?'

Frol flung his hands apart.

'The women! Our sisters and mothers! And the priests too. A special commission. All that garbage – junkies, cannibals, maniacs, godfathers – it can all go through the commission! Why not? A hundred well-respected women and a hundred priests. Secret voting. Aha. Everything's decided there: we show this movie in the usual place, and this one in a special private cinema ...'

'I see.' Fatty smiled again. 'And then who's going to select the women and the priests for the commission, Frol? Apart from anything else, there's money in films, big money too! They could slip in helpful people on the sly, the right kind, and then they'd vote the right way, for bribes ...'

'If they take bribes, shoot them!'

'Women and priests?'

'Yes! Yes!' Frol exclaimed with serious passion, halting his rapid stride. 'What else can you do? No, I can't bear it, you please yourselves, but I'm going to rustle up another little blast of chifir. They ought to be shot, Fatty, any way you look at it. In public. As a lesson. Aha. And shown on the news. So the whole country can see their disgrace, so it falls on their families …'

'You, Frol, are an idealist.'

'Maybe that's right. But they oughtn't to show wild crime and murdering out in the open. Let alone make up films about it. Carry on reading …'

Fatty put down the newspaper and muttered.

'You're a strange man. Had a hard time from the filth, spent all your life in prisons and you go calling for people to be shot …'

Frol turned serious.

'I'll tell you what I say to that, my old mate. My entire life is a bucket of shit. It would have been better if they'd shot me. The soldier boys. The proper way, up against the wall. Better if they'd shot me! Ask me now. What would you have chosen, my dear fellow: twenty years inside in five stretches or be topped? It's too late now, but I'd rather have been topped. Like some chifir?'

'No.'

'How about you, Buddha?'

'No thank you,' I refused politely and put down my textbook.

It was time for me to move on to something different. I pulled a large exercise book out from under the pillow, took a tattered old Rex Stout detective novel (prison property) down off the shelf and start copying the book out by hand.

'Don't fancy it, eh?' Frol joked. 'All right. Damn the pair of you. So I tell you, brothers: better take an honourable bullet in the forehead than lead a dog's life knocking about the camps. Straight up, that's how it is. When they don't shoot someone, take pity on him, afterwards he carries the bitterness and shit in his soul and spreads it round the whole wide world. And that includes making harmful films. About cannibals and hucksters, about all sorts of sleaze. There was this guy called Lenin, Vladimir Ilich, maybe you've heard of him? In our camps, out in Potma in the old days, back in seventy-five, the library only had two full sets of collected works – his, Lenin's that is, and Jack London's. I read them both. Shoot more of them! That's what Ulyanov-Lenin writes. In every third article – shoot more of them! He saw to the real root of things, a genius. He saw the cause. Rotten seed has to be pulled up, roots and all. And you talk about the cinema …'

Throughout the entire discussion I sat there without speaking, writing words in the exercise book.

On the very first day of my new life, having been granted two cell-mates – grown men of fifty – by the will of the prison authorities, I immediately made it a rule for myself only to break the silence when I was directly addressed with a question or request. The rest of the time I kept my mouth tight shut. The guiding principle of prison cohabitation that I had divined was easy to formulate: live any way you like, but without harming anyone else. Don't touch another man or the objects that belong to him. Don't obstruct him in any way. Don't bother him with advice. Don't express an opinion. But get on with the things that you need to do, your own business – nobody will ever hinder you or distract you, if you don't hinder anybody else.

'Andriukha,' Frol asked unexpectedly, 'what are you doing?'

'Copying out a text,' I replied amiably. 'Why?'

'Copying out the text from a book?'

'Yes.'

'What for?'

'I want to try something.'

'Such as?' Frol persisted.

'Changing my handwriting.'

A look of amazement appeared in the tattooed old man's grey eyes.

'And just how do you want to change it?'

'Completely.'

'No, you don't understand. What's your method?'

'It's very simple,' I said seriously. 'Every day I copy out a page of text from any book. I've already been doing it for eleven days. But I don't write in normal handwriting, I only use capitals. You see, I'm trying to make my hand forget its old habits.'

'I get it,' Frol wheezed warily. He stopped walking and sat down on his bed.

The effect of the caffeine had worn off. Now the prison-camp old-timer was turning morose before my very eyes. I knew already that in another twenty minutes his body would demand another dose.

'Why do you want to do that?'

'Just in case,' I replied evasively. 'Maybe some day I'll have to sling my hook for ever.'

'Go on the lam, you mean?'

'Sort of.'

Fatty knitted his white eyebrows together, compressed his lips into a narrow line and shook his head sternly.

'You've been watching too many films as well. Don't go crazy, son! How old are you?'

'Twenty-seven.'

My cell-mates laughed in unison.

'You're still a boy!' said Fatty, shaking his head. 'A boy, you understand? But I'm fifty. Now I have money, houses, a business, absolutely everything. And what's more – note this – at forty I didn't have a thing. No houses, no business, no money, no prospects. So don't be in a hurry, don't get fired up, don't just put your horns down and charge. And whatever you do after prison, don't go back to your old ways. Drop all that, forget it, start over. You have everything ahead of you. You'll do your time and get out, take up some normal kind of work. You'll earn money and raise children, live your life and breathe free and easy. What do you want with all this cloak-and-dagger nonsense? Going on the lam? Changing my handwriting?'

'Leave him alone, can't you?' Frol interrupted. 'Maybe the man stole so much, he made enemies of half of Moscow. Aha. Let him do his studying, if he wants to.'

Fatty fell silent. Frol turned towards me.

'So tell me, Andriukha, are you getting anywhere with this idea of yours?'

'No,' I said, shaking my head ruefully. 'The day before yesterday, on the ninth day, I tried going back to the ordinary way of writing – there weren't any changes.'

'Not everything's that easy,' Frol chortled. 'You can't cheat nature!'

'I'll give it a try.'

'You do that,' the jailbird said sceptically. 'Only this is what I have to say to you. There was this interesting guy once: Vladimir Ilich Lenin. Maybe you've heard of him? After the revolution, when he already had all the power, when life was more or less sorted, he got ill and started dying. Plenty of people ran off with money then too. They all went into hiding – some in Europe, some in Brazil. The ones who'd been in power with Lenin, who shot the bourgeoisie and pocketed their diamonds. Money, precious stones, foreign currency – they stuck it all away in Swiss banks. Plastic surgery and all the rest … And they changed their writing too. Aha. To cut it short, they covered every possible angle. Then Lenin died. Stalin came to power …' Frol paused dramatically. 'And he hunted down all of them. Every one! In Europe, in Brazil, he got them everywhere. He found them all and ordered them to be tortured. Put through the wringer, carved up. He got all the money back. And he used it to organise the economic recovery, the construction sites, Chkalov's flights and all the rest of it …'

'All right, Frol,' Fatty put in. 'Stop confusing the young lad. You were right, we shouldn't hassle him if his intentions are serious. Sorry brother, we won't bother you any more. It's just that we're quietly going crazy in here. There's nothing to do. Not even a television …'

16

Thirteen and a half years before my arrest I was sitting on a bench in the changing room of the Metallurgist sports stadium, lacing up my gym shoes.

The process required careful attention. A badly tied knot could let me down at the most crucial moment. At the very height of the training session. Then I would have had to stop and waste many seconds, disrupting my breathing and falling hopelessly far behind the group. And I didn't want to fall behind.

Not one of us twenty young boys wanted to fall back behind the rest.

I had been going to the cycling sessions for almost four months. Twice a week.

The bicycles themselves, ten of them, were hanging right there on the wall. But nobody rides bikes in winter. Not even the ones who have earned the title of Master of Sport. What a cyclist – especially a novice cyclist – mostly does in winter is run. Eight kilometres or, even better, ten in a single training session. In a freezing blizzard, over the snow. But the pedals won't come into use until closer to April, or even in May, when the roads dry out a bit.

All the novices in our section, including me, thought of themselves as highly experienced cyclists. We all had cool two-wheeled machines with saddles upholstered in rabbit skin and reflecting badges or 'cat's eyes' in the spokes.

But those chrome-plated sports machines hanging up above our heads – with their slim wheels, light frames and ornately curved handlebars – were as different from little kids' bikes as genuine running shoes are from rubber gym shoes, as different as an American action movie is from an Indian one: as different as any genuine item is from its surrogate.

At the age of eleven, twelve or thirteen, we could already tell the one from the other. Even if we had grown up in a country where the very concept of 'surrogate' had been elevated to the rank of a state idea.

True, in that very year of 1982, something important had happened to the state and its ideas. The permanently entrenched, virtually immortal General Secretary of the Communist Party, Leonid Ilich Brezhnev, had passed away. One sixth of the planet's land surface was plunged into a state of serious alarm. Our mums' and dads' faces took on anxious expressions. The telephone calls to friends in the capital started, the conversations in the kitchen, the subtle hints. The most sensible grown-ups all agreed on one thing: there isn't going to be a war. The Communist Party is as enduring as the diamonds on the cap of Vladimir Monomakh in the Kremlin, as the granite of Lenin's Mausoleum, as the launching pad at the Baikonur cosmodrome. It won't allow the system to collapse. Everything's under control.

Our trainer was absent that day, due to illness. The session was led by the second most important person: a small, strong girl with grey eyes. A Master of Sport of the USSR, in cycle road-racing.

'Right,' she said, casting a strict eye over the miscellaneous band of sports school pupils, from boys in darned jumpers to several youths in decent tracksuit trousers. 'The seniors take the training machines! The main group runs! With me!'

A gasp of horror ran through the cluster of short-cropped heads.

'Whoever comes in last,' the girl-master continued imperturbably, 'cleans up the changing room. Seniors – take care of that equipment! Training machines cost money. Everybody ready?'

Twenty young faces – the main group – were turned to gaze in envy at the seniors and the training machines: two frames set horizontally on the floor, with rotating rubber rollers. Put a bicycle on top and pedal away, without ever leaving the warm hall. It was good to be a senior, to own a sports bike and have two years of training experience! The entire group had the same thought.

We sniffed a bit, stamped our feet a bit, pulled on our mittens and went out into the stadium yard, where the sharp January frost immediately nipped at everyone's nose and cheeks.

'Fifteen degrees below,' someone said despondently.

Someone else swore roundly. Boldly and elegantly – the way only teenagers swear.

Outside the wall of the stadium, in the evening gloom, the stalks of the gigantic chimneys smoking the sky black to meet the requirements of secret industrial production were only vague outlines between the factory buildings. Above the door leading into our changing room, in the twilight left by the prematurely dark day, we could see a sign with the mind-boggling abbreviation: SCYPORSS.

Translated from Soviet gobbledygook that meant: Specialised Children's and Young People's Olympic Reserve Sporting School.

So all of us standing there beside the porch of the sport school in our sweaters, home-knitted mittens and fleecy trousers, were not just snot-nosed neophytes, not some gaggle of pitiful keep-fitters after all. We hadn't joined any old club, we'd been enlisted straight into the Olympic Reserve! With capital letters!

If, for some reason, all of the country's Olympic cyclists left the sport, fell ill, lost their form, got injured and ended up in hospital – then we were the ones who would come to the defence of the Motherland's sporting honour. The Reserve. This prospect, for all its obvious improbability, filled the hearts of twenty snot-nosed brats with pride.

'Why are we just standing here?' the Master of Sport shouted in a stentorian voice as she appeared on the porch. 'Let's see some jumping and loosening up! Warm up those calves and thighs!'

Two of the seniors followed the girl out. They were running with us today. They were advanced athletes, following individual training programmes.

The rabble of kids started bustling about. The Master performed a few economical warming-up movements of her shoulders and pelvis and then set off, her waterproof tracksuit rustling loudly as she ran. The two seniors dashed off in her wake. The novices scurried after them.

They set off in a jolly rush. Chatting as they went, swearing good-naturedly at each other, coughing to clear their throats and spitting into the snowdrifts. But very soon they stopped talking and their breathing became noisy as their legs started working harder. The girl-master was setting a good pace.

The first stretch of the route is the hardest. Simply because it is the first. And also because the route leads through the streets of the town, along a narrow pavement. Not only do you have to keep up the pace, you have to manoeuvre between the pedestrians while you do it. It's a good thing that when they hear the joint tramping of numerous fast feet behind their backs, they have the wits to make way. And apart from that, in winter the pavements are slippery: lose concentration and you fall, pull a muscle and end up dropping behind. And no one wanted to drop behind.

The little town languishes and fidgets in the winter evening. Men gasping heavily for breath and smelling strongly of cheap vodka are gathering outside the liquor shops. Young people dressed in the height of fashion – felt boots, padded work jackets, bright scarves and coxcomb caps are seeking adventure in the warm entranceways of the buildings, in the queues for cinema tickets. Squeaking, freezing buses carry women with broad, pale faces, dressed in grey and black, from one empty food shop to another.

But we ran past their empty, pale, grey life: a compact group of boys snorting strenuously, wreathed in clouds of steam. Swift, strong sportsmen. Best not to tangle with guys like that. You won't find them jostling in front of the liquor shop. Guys like that reckon it's beneath their dignity to sit for hours on the steps of a front entrance, expending their youth on idle tittle-tattle.

We ran on sternly, struggling for breath – and thought well of ourselves for our dedication and willpower.

Of course, I wasn't making any dash for Olympic honours. My thirteen-year-old heart had not been seduced by medals, laurel leaves and podiums. It was pretty obvious that the road to big-time sport was effectively closed to me. At my age it was a bit too late to be starting a serious sporting career. They'd already explained that.

It was six months since my parents had moved here, to this Moscow satellite town, from the country. Following a long-time dream, I immediately went rushing to the ice stadium, to the ice hockey school. Skates and hockey sticks were my passion. But the trainer didn't like the look of this skinny kid with the narrow chest of an asthmatic and, more importantly, I was the wrong age. They were taking in eight-to-ten-year-olds. Anyone else was rejected.

I wasn't upset. My mum and dad had chosen a special town to live in. Built immediately after the revolution on the direct instructions of the top leaders, it had a population of a hundred thousand – and three full-scale sports stadiums, two swimming pools and a dozen separate sports halls. It also had two immense factories where they made something very secret and subtle; nobody spoke out loud about it, not even at the beer kiosks. The party and the government had obviously decided to reduce the general level of the citizens' garrulity through the forceful inculcation of sporting activity. There were flourishing clubs for boxing, wrestling, football and ice-hockey, volleyball and basketball, athletics – both field and track – and swimming – both racing and synchronised performance events.

I had no trouble in choosing my own sport. Bicycle racing! What could be more glorious than this intoxicating flight along a ribbon of asphalt, on a gleaming racing bike, in a bright-coloured tee-shirt with little pockets sewn on to the back so that you could stick a bottle of water and a spare inner tube into them?

Who could ever have imagined that the passion for riding a two-wheeled mechanical friend would be realised in gruelling ten-kilometre cross-country runs through the wind and snow? But it was not my habit to give up without a fight.

The tortuous route through town, full of steep turns and frequent changes of step, concluded with a turn on to a highway that ran round the edge of town. Now we would run another three kilometres along firm, easy asphalt, and then turn on to a country road that led to the dacha settlement, continue through the forest for another kilometre, wait for the laggers to catch up – and cover the distance again in the reverse direction.

I didn't think about what lay ahead of me. Do that, and you might as well stop there and then, turn back to the changing rooms, collect your things and get the hell out of the club. Quit the glorious ranks of the Olympic Reservists. What's the point of thinking? You have to run. Take rhythmical breaths in and out, work that body, move those legs. It's not rocket science.

On the asphalt surface the girl-master and the two seniors gleefully speeded up, but the novices hung in there: no one dropped out of the pelleton. To loud honking from the rare trucks that drove past, the pedestrian cyclists hurtled on like hot, living cannonballs. Through the inky darkness – when and where in this country have the outskirts of provincial towns ever been lit up? – with the flickering soles of the runners' feet the only bright spots.

Just at this point the group started to flag. In tandem with the girl-master, the seniors started pulling away. The girl slowed down and shouted back behind her in a resounding school-ma'am's voice:

'Come on there, move it, move it!'

And then she speeded up, working her round backside with the aesthetically impeccable movements of a genuine Olympic Reservist.

Silently cursing the world and its mother, I started pushing a bit harder. Just as long as I have enough breath. Just as long as I don't start wheezing right here, in the middle of this freezing roadway, during the first third – the hardest – of the distance. Asthma is a disease of the nerves. The moment I stop believing in my own strength, it will immediately defeat me. It will defeat me if I let it frighten me.

When the sweat flooded my eyes and my lungs were already working at the limit of their strength, greedily sucking in helpings of the prickly air, as usual I started thinking about how good it would be now simply to stop. In Russian sport this is magnanimously know as 'not going the distance'. In reports on all kinds of sporting competitions, after the name of the loser who finished last, they write impassively 'so-and-so failed to go the distance'.

Failed to go the distance – that's okay, it happens; it means that today a certain athlete just the same as all the others, no worse than the rest, simply decided to drop out. No big deal. You'll win next time.

But every Olympic Reservist, even a kid who has hardly been in training for any time at all, knows you should never put anything off until the next time. Especially a victory.

'I could use cunning,' I carried on dreaming, staring fixedly at the regular swaying of the shoulder blades of the friend running in front of me, 'pretend to lose my footing, stumble, fall picturesquely, fall hopelessly far behind all of them, catch my breath – and jog gently back to the stadium, then show the trainer the bruises and scratches on my battered knees.' One young kid or another from our group regularly pulled a stunt like that if he felt he absolutely couldn't go on. But tricksters were not popular with the trainer, and the seniors regarded kids like that with grins of disdainful derision.

At thirteen years of age the mocking grins of your friends are extremely painful. And so I carried on running. I had already got through thirty training sessions. Started and finished thirty times. Not first, but not last either! A ten-kilometre cross-country run no longer seemed like the nightmare it was that first month. I had learned how to breathe properly and harbour my strength. I decided I could fail to go the distance next time. Not today.

A red-and-white boom cut right across the winter road that had been punched through the forest by bulldozers. Further on, in the black gloom, there were the vague outlines of log-built holiday homes. Here the group of sportsmen paused briefly. The girl-master stopped running, but she didn't stop moving. She stamped on the spot, swung her arms about and squatted down, inhaling and exhaling noisily. Everyone who had kept up with the leader repeated her movements.

They waited for the others to arrive.

All around the frozen forest crackled as the naked, crooked branches shifted sluggishly under the pressure of the slow wind. Two or three dogs yapped hoarsely, somewhere off in the dark distance, at the feet of the houses large and small whose owners had blocked off entry to their paradise of orchards and vegetable gardens with huge iron pipes.

'No standing still!' commanded the girl who didn't know what it was to be tired. 'Keep moving! We don't want to cool down! Has everyone caught up?'

'Yes, seems like it …'

'Let's go, let's go!'

To the disappointment of the kids who were half-dead from exhaustion, the break came to an end. Now the gruelling run over icy pavements and asphalt verges had to be repeated in the opposite direction.

The pelleton did break up after all. The group of runners stretched out for a good hundred metres. The girl-master and the two seniors kept hold of the lead, but a small bunch of the most stubborn and fastest kids held on close behind them. The others fell back a bit and the exhausted outsiders trudged along right at the very back.

I suddenly discovered that I was not among the last group, or even the mid-fielders, but directly behind one of the seniors. True, to reach this prestigious position, I'd had to strain my strength to the limit. The seniors were only trotting along at half-speed, and even talking to each other, as if this hellish dash was a mere lark to them.

I pushed myself still harder, dropped my chin – that makes it easier to summon up your courage – and overtook everyone.

'Oho!' the seniors laughed good-naturedly. 'A little squirt's made a break for it!'

Someone threw a snowball after me, but they missed.

Leading from the front turned out to be hard. I realised it was a lot easier to be led than to lead. It was easier to breathe into someone else's back and try not to fall behind than to force yourself, with only yourself to rely on, to run faster and faster.

In less than a minute the seniors had caught up with me, without really trying, still joking among themselves.

'What did you slow down for, squirt? Come on! Head down! Forward!'

I pretended I hadn't heard and made another effort to move my legs faster.

'Come on! Come on!'

The yells carried a long way into the black winter forest, but all I could hear was the starchy crunching of the snow under my rubber soles.

This time I thought I'd opened up a good lead. I wanted to glance round to make sure, but that would have cost me a precious second.

'Knackered again, squirt?' I head a voice say right above my ear. 'Work harder! Forward! Head down!'

They think it's funny, I realised. They're just having fun. Ten kilometres across the January snow is nothing to a trained sportsman. If they wanted to, the seniors could have run twice as fast. But advanced athletes don't strain themselves in winter, they just maintain their condition. In the summer they would cover ten times this distance in the saddle of a bike ...

'Go for it, squirt, go for it! Come on! Another break, little squirt, a spurt! Forward!'

The seniors were at least seventeen years old. In the changing rooms I had seen their thighs – clean and firm, rippling with chiselled muscles. Accustomed to turning the pedals for many hours at a time.

'A spurt, little squirt! A spurt! You can do it!'

The girl-master – the whole scene was obviously being played out for her sake – finally gave in and laughed melodically.

'You can do it, squirt!' the inspired youthful bass voice persisted. 'Speed up! Head down! Work!'

I picked up speed. The voices began falling back. Faster! Even faster!

Don't you worry, the squirt *can* do it! He managed it last time, and the time before that, he can do it now. You masters think the little snot-nose is trying to make an impression. *You* think it's all just posing, showing off. But I'm not tearing my sinews apart just for the sake of looking good. A year ago I couldn't even run a hundred metres without doubling over in a choking fit. I used to stop, lean forward, prop my hands on my knees and stand there in that shameful pose, with my backside stuck out, for several minutes, waiting for it to ease off. Or I used to reach into my pocket and take out my medication – an aerosol spray of Asthmopent. Sometime when I went out for a walk with my friends I discovered half-way that I'd forgotten my aerosol – and the fright would immediately trigger an attack. And now here's this puny asthmatic outrunning not only his own healthy peers, but masters of sport as well. Maybe it's not for long, maybe it's not much more than a joke – but he *is* outrunning them, running without stopping!

At this point my strength deserted me. It became perfectly clear that I could only take another ten steps, and then I was going to fall. I took those ten steps. But I didn't fall. I started the next ten. Another ten and now that's it, I'm falling. Speeding up and spurting ahead have exhausted my body. The calories have all run out. I'm not going to finish the run. I'm going to lose. I'll do another ten, and then another – this time it's the last, the final set of ten, and collapse, breathless, right here on the verge of this road that winds between the trees. That's it. I'm finished. I'm not a horse. I'm a human being. A weakling, unprepared for such intense loads. I've tried it and I've realised that bicycle sport is not for me. I think I'll give up training. Take up volleyball. My school friend Nikolai has been asking me to join the volleyball club for ages. It's a fine game that doesn't require any great physical exertion. Jump up in the air and hit the ball. A comfortable, well-lit hall, a net, squealing girls – nothing at all like ten kilometres along paths covered with snow …

'Wake up, squirt! Make a break! Go on!'

Gritting my teeth, I let the laughing athletes move in front and tucked myself in behind them.

'What's up with you?' One of my peers wheezed alongside me. 'Cool it, don't go busting your ass!'

'Aha,' was all I gasped out.

And I speeded up again. To spite them all. To spite myself.

One more kilometre of this hell – and after that it will get easier. The girl-master will slow down to gather her strength before the final spurt to the finish. And the spurt itself will be a real celebration. For there, at the end, is the well-heated changing room, dry socks, tea from a thermos flask. A sense of victory, as deep as the sea. Enhanced self-esteem. And after that – the road home.

Victory is very close now. Only a few minutes separate me from it. A few hundred metres, a hurricane spurt along an icy pavement. I have to speed up, put absolutely everything I've got into it.

Run – and you'll get there.

I got there. That time, and the next.

The winter passed. My asthma receded into the background. By the end of March I'd completely forgotten about my illness.

In April the snow melted. Ten novices – half of us had been weeded out – glanced often and lecherously at those chrome-plated machines. Any moment now they were going to let us have them. Any moment now it would begin, the thing we came here for, for the sake of which we had spent five months trampling the snow.

My friends on our block had started the season ages ago, hurtling in sweet delight along the asphalt pathways, still dark in places with the mud of winter. And I had also wheeled out my little steed of steel, dotted with efflorescences of rust. I pumped up the tyres, tightened the chain, oiled it, raised the saddle a bit. Of course, what I really wanted was not childish laps from one park square to the next, not rides on a kid's bike, but a genuine race on a genuine sports machine. Serious competition.

But new novices joined our club, a whole crowd of them, and at twelve years of age, they already knew perfectly well that nobody rides bicycles in winter. If you join up in winter – they'll force you to run! You have to wait until it's warm – simple.

Now there were twenty-five of us, for ten bikes. Each new training session began with quiet whispering through clenched teeth, arguments and instant fights. Today I'm riding the red one. Then I'm on the green one. No, the green one's mine, I booked it last time. You booked it? You mean you bought it, then? I told you, it's mine, so it is. Shove off. You shove off …

The trainer knew, but he just sniggered. Weak-willed characters are no use in sport. It's the hard-bitten, stubborn types you need, the ones with chins of stone. The kids will sort things out for themselves. Out of twenty just one will be left, a fanatic who has reached the standard of the first adult grade. After that – two years of unrelenting labour (with daily training sessions, and every week two intensive ones so hard that you faint), until he reaches the standard for Candidate Master of Sport. Only one in a thousand will get as far as the actual title of Master.

The seniors took no notice of us, they all hung about in the workshop, with their fingers smeared with grease. They assembled their own bikes. Spokes, saddles, rims, chains, handlebars, frames – for them, these sounded like the words of a poem. But not for me.

In the middle of May I finally became disillusioned with cycling. It really is a beautiful sport. But I didn't want to fight for bicycles. After all, I hadn't joined the boxing club, had I? One bicycle between three – there was something seriously wrong with that. And so I left.

The most important lesson I learned that winter could be summed up in a single word. A word of advice, a moral maxim or an order from the trainer.

Run.

If you want to achieve something – run. Train. Conquer yourself.

Manoeuvre between the fainthearted, the feeble and the drunk: between those whose breath has given out.

Run. Work. Spurt ahead. Defeat your own weakness.

Run past them all – straight to your goal. No resting. No dreaming. No pitying yourself. No looking around. No doubting.

That way, you'll win.

Run, breathe, push off hard from the surface of the globe. And, once having overcome yourself, will you ever run into anything that you can't overcome?

Never.

17

On the first day of October – so dry, transparent and transfixing that it set your ears ringing and your heart aching with melancholy – the walk was particularly successful.

We were given yard number fifteen. The widest, nicknamed the 'presidential yard'. I could even run round in a circle here. And what's more, the yard was located to one side of the building and it was swept clean by the wind in a way that was somehow special – all the way through. The fresh autumn air flowed into your lungs easily and freely. The concrete floor was new and smooth, with no cracks. Exercising the body in conditions like that is sheer pleasure.

I threw back my head, vigorously breathing in the *prana*, stood there for several minutes, then undressed to the waist, laid my tee-shirt down neatly on the wooden bench built into the wall, and started to run. Not in a circle, of course – that would have been a bit much; after all, I wasn't out on my own, there were three of us – but in a straight line, from wall to wall. And even so there was more than enough room. I could flail my arms and even my legs about as much as I liked.

My friends and cell-mates are with me today. Usually they're still asleep when I'm led out for a walk. But once in every few days the crooked spines do come out for a breath of air. Screwing up their eyes against the daylight, both of them have taken up positions by the wall: Fatty has leant his back against it, but Frol has squatted down on his haunches, lit a cigarette and started spitting rapidly and repeatedly on the ground near his feet.

I started building up the tempo. In order not to lose speed on the turn, when I reached the wall, I thrust both hands against it and pushed off hard. The faster you run, the more oxygen enters your body – everybody knows that.

From behind the high wall, twice the height of a man, from the next exercise yard, I could hear tramping feet and loud panting. There was someone else there moving about strenuously in an effort to vanquish the effects of physical inactivity and imprisonment. I sent a mental salutation to my unknown brother-in-arms. Maybe it was the minister who was involved in the same CASE as me. But I shall never know anything about my neighbour on the other side of that wall. In the elite pre-trial prison an inhabitant of one cell can never, not even for a brief moment, run into an inhabitant of another stone box. When I'm on my way to my walk, or to the bathhouse, or to an interrogation, the other prisoners are waiting their turn behind their doors. And if I'm on my way back from an interrogation, and someone else is being led towards me (I can only hear them), then the guard hastily shoves me into a 'cooler' – a kind of kennel, one metre square, that bolts shut from the outside. For the convenience of the staff, such kennels are located in many parts of the institution and at regular intervals along all the corridors.

I didn't find running easy. I was gasping for breath and my head was spinning, my knees and my calves ached and the sweat blinded my eyes. The breathlessness will pass, I told myself. It's because I'm out of practice. I'll soon get into shape. Twelve steps that way, twelve steps back. Breathe more deeply, more regularly! With your nose and your mouth! Don't let the prison have a single minute of your life. Don't allow anyone or anything to steal your time. And especially your freedom. Keep training. Make yourself stronger. Be obstinate and patient. Nothing must distract you. Everything's down to you – so do it!

I tried hard. I hurried. Sixty minutes is very little time. A cell is cramped and airless. It's impossible to exercise in it. I had only been allowed a single hour to strengthen my body. And I spent my energy and my time on just one thing – movement.

'Hey, Brumel!' Frol called. 'Want some chifir?'

I shook my head.

Today Frol has brought his precious prison beverage out on our walk.

How he could have carried a mug of scalding hot liquid in the sleeve of his padded pea-jacket past the watchful eyes of the controller is a mystery to me. And now the lifetime criminal is enjoying his caffeine in combination with the fresh air.

His face lit up in a sublime reverie.

'I could just smoke some pot now,' he sighed.

'Right,' the construction magnate agreed. 'Some good Tadjiki hash.'

'What do you know about Tadjiki hash?'

'I'm a builder,' Fatty said, offended.

'So what?'

'Half the labourers on my sites are Tadjiks.'

Frol suddenly gasped, grabbed hold of his side with one hand and winced.

'Does it hurt?' Fatty enquired cautiously.

The recidivist nodded.

The symptoms of the old convict's classical prison illnesses – stomach ulcer and toothache – usually became more acute as evening drew on. The tattooed recidivist often finished supper by getting up, pressing his hands to his throat, hastily staggering across to the corner of the 'hut' and puking up his food into the prison toilet, hawking loudly, spitting, blowing his nose and groaning. Then he would apologise to us politely and very sincerely for spoiling our appetites, lie face down on his bed and carry on suffering.

Frol treated his ailments with smoking. Neither I nor Fatty every heard him complain, but we couldn't just watch impassively while a live human being writhed about in agony and swore in a hissing whisper. One of us would press the button on the wall, the screw would come and we would demand a doctor. Frol objected. As a devotee of the criminal moral cose known as 'the rules', he didn't want to ask the administration for any kind of help. The construction magnate and I did that for him.

The doctor would cast a critical glance at the sick man through the feeder and dispense a tablet of Analgin painkiller.

I found it painful to observe this nerve-wracking scene, see the miserable criminal's convulsed and contorted face and feel just how malignant and wrong the whole situation was, and I used to fall asleep in a gloomy fury, with the darkness settling in my soul.

Frol used to start the morning with a massive dose of chifir, which clearly did nothing to assist the healing of the hole in his stomach. And once again, after the walk, after another of my runs, he would mockingly refer to me as either 'sportsman' or 'Brumel' or 'Olympic champion'. The names changed; the irony and sarcasm increased day by day. His ponderous friend merely guffawed.

Prison running, from wall to wall, is no strain on the nerves. It's not covering the distance that's important, but the process itself. You have to warm up the muscles and the joints and, even more importantly, ventilate yourself thoroughly. Refresh the brain. Oxygen is its food. In one hour I have to consume as much of the health-giving gas as possible. The more, the better! Breathe, breathe as hard as I can, grab the air with my mouth, make a real effort! Starting tomorrow, I'll go even further, improve the process, immediately after my warm up I'll stand on my head for two or three minutes – so that even more fresh blood can reach it. An expertly trained brain enriched with oxygen will help me to break out from behind these bars. One day I'll learn to read the CASE FILE and understand what I need to do in order to gain my freedom. Day after day I'm going to run and breathe, run and breathe, spending the rest of the time meditating and training my mind. My mind will learn to work like a perfectly adjusted machine for producing ideas – the most valuable and precious product known to humankind. And new ideas are essential. There are too many urgent questions demanding my attention, too many problems that have to be solved.

Where is my boss? Where is my money? What should I do? What testimony should I give, and should I give any at all? What is going to happen to my family if I can't get out of here? How long am I going to be in here? Is my business still intact? Did I cause anyone problems by disappearing so suddenly and outrageously? Have I made any enemies? What am I going to do when I'm finally free? Difficult questions, terrible questions, and I have to search for the answers with a cool, clear head …

The time ran out. The lock clanked. I tumbled into the corridor semi-naked, sweaty and red: there was steam rising from my shoulders and back.

'Stop,' said the guard. 'Get dressed.'

Hastily pulling on my tee-shirt, I smiled.

'Sorry, boss. I got carried away.'

'Hands behind your back. Forward.'

In the cell I moistened a towel. Rubbed down my shoulders, neck and chest. Changed my underwear. Cleaned up the splashes of water on the floor. Washed my hands with soap.

'I see you're an energetic young jack,' Frol said to me, watching my movements disapprovingly. 'You ran today, ran yesterday, ran the day before ... you going to run tomorrow too?'

I nodded without speaking

'You a sportsman?' the bony convict enquired.

'Sort of.'

'Good for you,' the tattooed man hissed through his teeth. 'Just don't overdo it. Or you'll use up all your strength in training ...'

I didn't ask him to explain what that meant. After drinking two mugs of very fresh, hot tea, I got on to my bed, pulled my legs up and opened a textbook.

In the order of my day, the second and final most valuable period had arrived – a period of a little over two hours between the walk and supper. A fresh head and an empty stomach. Ideal conditions for any intellectual activity.

However, to my annoyance, Frol distracted me again: after first politely asking permission, he leafed through the small volume entitled *Train Your Memory and Attention*. His face wore an expression of great interest, and it became almost beautiful.

'What do you need this for?' he asked as he returned the book.

I thought for a moment and kept my answer brief.

'I don't like it here in prison. I hate bars on windows.'

'Me too,' Frol grinned. 'But what's that got to do with memory and attention?'

'I have to occupy myself with something while I have free time. In prison your life's on pause. I'm going to read books here that I would never have read on the outside. Master skills and abilities that I would never have mastered in ordinary life ... They shut me up and tried to take away my time. I've decided not to give it to them. I'm going to use it in my own interests. Every second.'

Fatty chortled critically, with a twitch of his round cheek.

'I personally,' he declared, 'am employing the time inside exclusively for building up my subcutaneous layer. For eating salami!'

Frol deftly yanked up his track suit trousers and sat down on his blanket.

'It's not a matter of salami, Fatty,' he said pensively. 'In jail that salami of yours has turned more than one decent guy into a bad bastard ... Listen, Andriukha, how did someone as smart as you ever get caught?'

I shrugged. I couldn't tell everyone that I was just a boy doing someone else's time, could I? That I'd gone behind bars voluntarily, for money?

'He was unlucky!' Fatty answered laconically on my behalf.

'I suppose so,' I agreed.

Frol pondered that.

'But aren't you afraid of losing your mind? Of getting so advanced that ordinary people won't be able to understand you any more? What are you aiming for, in any case?'

'Enlightenment,' Fatty interjected again.

'No,' Frol objected, turning towards him. 'You don't understand, Fatty. This kid wants to be better than everyone else. Am I right?'

'That wouldn't be a bad idea,' I agreed, and joked. 'Then all the money and the women would be mine.'

Frol peered into my face.

'What if one day you retreat into this ... into Nirvana, and you get so stoned on it you can't get back out again? And then you won't want any money or any skirt?'

I smiled condescendingly. The old lag had failed to understand the most important thing.

'That's not possible,' I said. 'In general, sitting for hours in the lotus position is an exercise for beginners. The enlightened man doesn't meditate. The ideal meditation should be instantaneous. Breath in, focus your mind and zap! Behold the hidden mystery!'

'I get it,' Frol said seriously. 'Well then, carry on, old mate. Hold the banner high, enlightened man! You defying prison, that's really good. It's the duty of every one of us to hate these walls, these bars and this sky with squares on it. Only the strongest move into defiance! But don't you forget, brother, that in reply the prison will start to hate you. Ferociously ...'

Fatty nodded in agreement, knitting his brows sadly.

'By the way, your runs are a waste of time,' he told me after a pause, 'and bad for your health.'

'What harm do they do?' I asked in amazement. 'Why are they a waste of time?'

The big construction boss slapped his boundless stomach.

'Because you don't get any decent food. You don't get enough calories. You're losing your subcutaneous layer.'

'They feed us pretty well here.'

'That's what you think. Were you in the army?'

'Yes?'

'Remember the old soldier's trick for filling his stomach. Swallow as much bread as possible! Cabbage soup – plus two pieces of bread, boiled grain – another two pieces, and then a piece with your tea. And you feel full. On just bread, with no butter or meat. We've got the same situation here. The only meat, that is, protein and animal fats, that we have in this cell is ... what?'

'Salami,' I suggested.

'Correct. So now, if you don't object, let's carry out a simple calculation. Once every two weeks you receive a food parcel and so do I. There are two sticks of salami in each, right?'

'Yes,' I said, nodding.

'That's eight sticks a months, right?'

I nodded again.

'It's not possible to measure each individual stick of salami precisely,' the chubby-cheeked builder went on, gazing at me with a gloomy, serious expression, 'since the full sticks never get here, they arrive already cut into pieces, the controllers cut them when they're inspected – to check to see if there's anything forbidden hidden inside ... And so let's take the *nominal* length of one stick to be four hundred millimetres, and then we get a total of three thousand, two hundred millimetres, or three point two linear metres ... of what?'

'Salami.'

'There are three of us here,' the magnate reminded me in an even more serious and severe voice, 'so the total length has to be divided by three.'

'Naturally.'

There was no doubt that the well-padded Vadim felt the subject of this discussion was absolutely cardinal, pivotal, central. But I could hardly prevent myself laughing.

'So the outcome is that the net amount for each of us ...' – Fatty closed his eyelids for a moment and wrinkled up his forehead – 'one point zero six metres a month, or one thousand and sixty millimetres! By, the way, please forgive my odd way of speaking, I've worked in the building trade all my life, rose from foreman to head of the construction department, and that's why I'm in here ...'

'How do you mean?' I asked, confused.

'Because I calculate linear metres faster than anybody else,' Fatty explained vaguely. 'But that's all by the way ... Let's continue. Divide one thousand and sixty millimetres by thirty days, and we get the daily norm of consumption for each one of us, i.e. thirty-five linear millimetres of salami.'

In order to reinforce my appreciation of this fact, the magnate held out his homemade ruler to me – it consisted of numerous layers of paper from an exercise book, glued together, trimmed precisely along the edges and covered with fine, regular notches – and demonstrated exactly how much thirty-five millimetres was.

'And so,' he summed up, 'in order for animal fats always to be present in the body, each of us should consume a piece of salami seventeen and a half millimetres long twice a day!'

'Brilliant!' I said approvingly! 'How much is that in grams?'

'I don't know,' Fatty said with profound regret, 'but then, we don't need to know that. Our task is to calculate the correct norm. In grams or millimetres, it doesn't matter ...'

'But wouldn't it be easier,' I suggested, 'to consume all the linear metres straight away, so we could feel full at least twice a month?'

Fatty shrugged and spread his hands.

'Please yourself about that. Personally speaking, I've determined my daily norm and I take that as my starting point. I'm going to consume thirty millimetres in the course of the day, and five will go into the reserve. In thirty days that reserve will build up to a hundred and fifty millimetres! A piece fifteen centimetres long, almost half a stick! And I advise you to do the same. Otherwise you won't last long,' Fatty informed me authoritatively, and his massive cheeks set into a woeful expression.

'Why?'

'Because one linear metre of salami a month is very little ...'

'You're right,' I agreed. 'It's worse than that. It's a joke. But I'll think of something.'

'He didn't understand a thing,' Frol suddenly hissed through his teeth, turning to Fatty. 'Not a thing! *Tomorrow he'll go running again!*'

'Definitely,' I declared inflexibly.

'I'll tell you what I think,' the hardened criminal announced into space. 'I think you've done enough.'

'Enough what?'

'Running,' Frol explained, looking first at Fatty (who nodded in agreement) and then back at me. 'No more running ...'

'And why's that?' I asked bluntly.

My cell-mates exchanged glances.

'You mean you don't understand?'

'No.'

'You stink,' Fatty declared succinctly.

Frol didn't say anything, but he gave me a glance that made me feel awkward and ashamed. Damn! I hadn't thought about that. The enlightened man had forgotten that your own shit never smells. The men who lived side by side with me were now obliged to smell the fragrances of my body, covered with several layers of dried sweat. There were still two days to go until the bathhouse. The bathhouse was once a week. Six days – six layers of sweat.

'So what should I do?' I asked, feeling like an idiot.

'Drop all this stupid nonsense,' Frol snapped rudely. 'This isn't a sports hall! Stop running away from a heart attack, okay! It doesn't do much good, but it does endless harm! It's only good for you, and it's harmful for everyone else! Take a break, or you'll over-train and never even reach the start of the championships ...' He smiled at his own sarcasm, but a moment later the corners of his mouth turned down again, and I realised I had to make a decision right now.

I felt afraid. On all sides of me the dark-green prison-cell walls began moving and turned into jaws – they were closing together, intent on grinding up the puny boy-banker. My cell-mates – little and large, skinny and fat – assumed the air of monsters about to pounce.

But wasn't I coming on a bit too strong? After spending only a month and a half in prison, was I right to think of contradicting someone who had spent decades here and must surely have seen thousands of young, stubborn, insolent ego-trippers? I'd ended up in an isolation prison, with no support, no money, tumbled to the very bottom of the pile – was I really right to pick a fight with the resident population down there?

'No,' I said in a quiet voice, 'no, Frol. There's not much harm from the smell. This isn't some fashion show, we're not here to breathe in sweet fragrances. Smells aren't important here. A bad smell can't offend anyone's dignity here. Nothing bad will happen if you two put up with it for a while. That's my opinion, and I'm informing both of you ...'

'So you,' Frol said in a dull voice, 'have already decided to dictate what we can do and how? Your orders are to put up with it, are they?'

'I'm not dictating,' I snapped. 'And I'm not giving orders. I'm only objecting.'

Frol frowned.

'Can I ask a question?'

'On any subject you like,' I parried smugly.

'I'm sorry, what was it you did on the outside?'

I drew in a loud breath through my nose and snapped proudly:

'I made money.'

'Business, was it?'

'Yes.'

'And apart from business?' Frol asked, twitching his desiccated cheek. 'What did you do, apart from make money?'

'Nothing. I just made money. Sixty hours a week.'

The jailbird put on the air of a man who has just seen the light.

'Ah, so you're a *businessman*! Is that right?'

'You could say that.'

'But I,' said Frol, bowing slightly with singular dignity, 'live by theft and deception. I'm a criminal, is that clear? A homeless tramp. I don't know how to work. And I don't want to. I'm not capable. Aha. My health's damaged. So I steal other people's property. How else can I feed myself? The state and its servants, the cops, put me away and I do my time. This here is my home. I don't have any other home. And I don't have any money either. Or any business. Or any family either. Or any father ... Only my old mother, my only kin ... Do you see that?'

Frol stretched his leg out into the passage and pointed to the foot. The cat's face tattooed on its top surface wiggled its whiskers shamelessly.

This display of the prisoner's naked extremity was very offhand, almost offensive, but not so offensive that I felt it necessary to take offence. And anyway, ten days of regular morning meditations had rendered me imperturbable.

'Know what that is?'

'A cat,' I muttered.

'That's right,' Frol said approvingly. 'In Russian *kot*, K-O-T, and in Russian those letters stand for Native Resident of Jail!'

'I understand,' I replied. 'So the cat means you, Frol are at home here, and I'm just a visitor. And I have to pay careful attention to what you say. And behave accordingly ...'

'You got it,' the native resident said approvingly, then suddenly gave a disarming, mischievous smile. 'Okay, Andriukha, don't, you know ... don't get all worked up. You're a good guy, we could do with more like you ...

There's no beef between us. If you want to run and jump about, then go right ahead! Only not so as it damages the people around you! Isn't that right, Fatty?'

The immense magnate nodded stolidly.

'And the reason I mentioned the outside,' Frol pronounced the last word in a low voice, but with emphasis, 'is because sooner or later, in this hut or some other, in this prison or any other, in the Matroska or in the Butyrka, in the isolation cells, in a camp transport, in the camp zone, this conversation is going to happen, for certain. Aha. And you should always remember this … difference. Between you and the people who belong to the criminal world. Don't go getting above yourself. Be a bit more modest. Aha. Prison is the house of suffering, you get that? It's not a sports field …'

'I get it,' I replied, feeling my imperturbability draining away. 'The house of suffering. Clear enough. Only I'm sorry, Frol, but I don't intend to suffer. That's not what I was born for. I'm not going to suffer in this house or anywhere else. If anyone wants to suffer here, then let him suffer, by all means. But I'm going to do what I need to do.'

'You're stubborn,' the old lag said sadly. 'Young and stubborn. Okay. All I can do is warn you …'

I pressed one hand to my chest.

'Frol! I'm very grateful to you for all the advice and the warnings. I mean that for real. From the heart. And I realise this is no prophylactic clinic. Maybe some day your advice will be my salvation. In some other prison. Or this one. In some filthy, starving place. But right here where the three of us are doing time, the conditions are perfectly fine! Food, warmth, quiet! Why shouldn't I use the time for the maximum benefit to my body and brain?'

The native inhabitant lowered his head, and his affected criminal-aristocratic manner completely evaporated, leaving nothing but a sick old man with shattered nerves. Without saying a word, he picked up some newspaper or other that had been read at least ten times and opened it, cutting himself off from me with ostentatious disdain.

I lay down on my back and busied myself with a habitual occupation that I never tired of – the mindless examination of the ceiling. Rage and resentment were tearing at my soul. My pride had been wounded most cruelly. A semiliterate, inarticulate savage of a man, a 'crooked spine', had explained to me in clear, simple terms that the territory of the cell belonged in the first instance to him. And I, the capitalist, the journalist, the almost millionaire, was a being of a lower sort.

Why, I wondered, do these grown men who are so worldly wise, wax so ironical about me working-out to the point of exhaustion? What is the point of all these rapid glances and critical smirks? Maybe the fifty-year-old creatures with crooked spines are suffering from primitive envy? What if they actually wake up every morning with a burning desire to stop smoking and start doing exercises, but they can't make themselves do it any longer? They're always trying to find excuses for themselves. There's always something stopping them – the smell of sweaty singlets, worries about their subcutaneous layer, or something else.

But there's nothing stopping me. I've been robbed and betrayed by my own business partner – and even that must not stop me.

And then I was visited by a burning desire to tell the native inhabitant all about my business. I even sat up and reached my hand out for the cigarettes. Frol – who had long ago put down his newspaper and was now also lying on his back – cast a puzzled glance at me.

But I lay back down without saying a word and turned away from him. What could I tell him? How could I tell him? There was no way, absolutely no way I could tell him anything. Either of these two, or both of them could be witnesses, informers planted so that they could inform the prison administration of every step I took and every word I spoke. And the administration would inform the investigator Khvatov and General Zuev. And that meant I couldn't tell them anything! Let the tattooed Frol, and his friend Fatty, and the head of the pre-trial prison, Razrez, and the investigator Khvatov, and General Zuev all think that I genuinely was a peaceable businessman who had ended up behind bars through a misunderstanding.

Let's just assume, Frol, that you have a million dollars. Where it came from isn't important. You sold some oil, or gas, or shares, or rocket salvo launchers. And as they say these days, you cleaned up. Now you have to perform your civic duty and pay your taxes. After all, the state is obliged to build schools and hospitals, pay doctors and postmen. They order you to give away some of the money, they force to cut your jackpot in half, to share.

You don't agree. You don't want to give away the money. That's quite understandable too. And you decide to trick the tax inspector. It's not good, of course, but absolutely everybody gets up to tricks like that, and there isn't a single millionaire in the whole wide world who doesn't spend his own money on maintaining an entire gang of cunning individuals whose job is to think up ways of paying less. I'm one of them.

Your firm, brother, is flourishing, its name is up there on the advertisement hoardings, it's big news on TV. It's your child, your creation. But you just wave your hand and dozens of other firms spring up around it. Illegitimate offspring, bastard organisations. Some of them only exist in the form of round rubber seals, others only as wads of money, there are some that actually have an office with a telephone, but they are all the same in the most important respect: their business activity is a fiction, it is only conducted on paper.

Here, in the dark forest of fly-by-night firms, is where you and your men hide your million away. In the very densest thickets of this forest.

So that, dear native inhabitant, is my business: I come to work, sit down at the desk, switch on all the office equipment – and I draw up false documents. I handle bullshit. I fabricate. There have to be a lot of fake documents, very many. That is an invariable rule that I laid down and then followed unswervingly for three years. Not fifty contracts, or a hundred, not two or three cardboard files, but cabinets stuffed full of them. The more pieces of paper there are, the better! I used to produce fifteen or twenty kilograms of them a month, and I must have fabricated about three hundred kilograms in the course of my career. It would take ten experienced specialists six months to study this Mont Blanc or Fujiyama of bullshit. They would drown in this paper swamp. The specialists come to work at nine in the morning, they start at half-past, at ten they drink tea, then they have lunch, at six in the evening they go home. They do their job without straining themselves too hard. But I used to sit at my desk for up to a hundred hours a week, and use all the latest technology. My boss allocated an impressive special budget to finance me. There were three printing machines working simultaneously, with ten different sorts of paper and various inks. The pages were fastened together in various different ways. As if they had been produced by different people's hands. Every fake contract looked absolutely genuine. It was covered with the beautiful impressions of seals and ministers' signatures. And most important of all – there were cabinets full of them, all these accounts, invoices, orders, statements, receipts and so on. Just let the tax inspector or some other specialist try to check how the firm 'Vasya' offloaded gas, or diamonds, or tanks, when it was acting in the interests of the firm 'Vanya', via the firm 'Sasha', in the interests of the firm 'Grisha', on the instructions of the firm 'Natasha'.

The contracts, invoices and receipts gave telephone numbers and addresses for the organisations. Send a fax, write a letter or phone. The answer, given with all due respect and courtesy, will be that the boss is not there. Away on a business trip! Can I give him a message? Behind the polite voices and the imprints of the beautiful seals there is nothing – empty space. Entire concerns and holding companies are nothing more than what is referred in the modern language by the adequate if disharmonious term 'swank'. Beautiful, showy external packaging, without any content.

So, brother: I'm sitting there in a comfortable armchair in the middle of a basement that is dirty, but advantageously located in the centre of town, with a telephone, a fax, all the office equipment, an air conditioner and an FM radio, with money for food, cigarettes, alcohol, petrol and clothes, plus some spending money. If I need to add any office equipment to what's already there, I go straight for the very best, ultra modern.

I am creating a spider's web of dozens of firms. A certain amount of business is conducted between them, for show, a certain amount of money is transferred, various sums appear and disappear in the cash office or the bank accounts. And all in order to conceal someone else's million, either stolen or earned from the sale of something that it might or might not be legal to sell. Who the million belongs to, I have absolutely no idea. What difference does it make to me? The man in a Valentino suit who comes to see me in a Mercedes in order to give me personal instructions concerning the million could easily be part of someone else's system of cunning swank.

But the more advanced swank is when there's not just one million involved, but five or even ten, and the instructions are given by quiet, boring guys in modest threads who drive battered Zhigulis. With guys like that I am very careful.

The dusty basement where I graft for my dough ought to have been changed ages ago for a better one, more spacious and brightly lit, but I just can't get around to it. There's never enough time. There are more and more punters who want to stick their money into our underground bank in order to save it from the heartless tax collectors. Neither I nor my boss are concerned about petty details. We laugh at businessmen who spend their time on buying leather armchairs, carpets and aquariums. Our version of swank is far more austere. The bill-counting machines we bought recently cost more than our cars.

My desk drawer is stuffed with other people's passports. They have all been lost, stolen or bartered for a couple of bottles of vodka. The safe is overflowing with dollars or roubles. If the militia enter the basement at this precise moment, I won't be able to explain how I came by the passports and the money and I'll lose both. So everything I do is calculated to make me as inconspicuous as possible. The door of my basement has no sign on it, and there's no gleaming chrome-plated Buick, or other such crass heap of metal standing at the porch. I don't slam the doors of my car, I don't shout into my mobile phone as I walk to the porch. I pay the rent for the office just a bit late. Like a genuine middle-level entrepreneur. I trade in a showy fashion, with swank, in consumer goods. A small business, enough to hold my pants up …

That evening the enlightened man filled his belly with basic gruel and calmly fell asleep.

18

But in the middle of the night he woke up with an uneasy feeling, sensing an indistinct question maturing inside him – together with the answer.

During the day just past something important had been said. A certain word of truth had been found and pronounced – but what was it?

The silence of Lefortovo prison is not silence. Both of my friends were snoring obliviously. Fatty was lying on his back, with his belly quivering regularly in time with his breathing. Frol was in the foetal position, with his bony arms wrapped round his drawn-up knees. The expression on his face was very childlike, defenceless and ingenuous, and I immediately felt sorry for this man who had destroyed his own life by wasting it on stretches in the prisons and camps of my cruel Motherland.

'Unlucky!' I remembered, and sleep finally took flight. That was it, the formula, so simple and precise, that had been uttered a few hours earlier! Unlucky. That was it. 'He was unlucky,' a man who hardly even knew me had said. He had expressed – unconsciously, of course – his very first and therefore most accurate impression of me as a functioning personality. Unlucky.

The yellow forty-five-watt light bulb shed its meagre light down on the three motionless men. Objects cast complex shadows.

Where am I? Why am I here?

'Unlucky' – that's what they called me. What sort of word is that? Who invented it? Why do most people simply love to appeal to this ludicrous metaphysical category? Where is it, my own personal bad luck? Perhaps it was hiding in that village among the hills and copses, in that region of small, slow-flowing rivers, halfway along the road from Moscow to Ryazan, where my grandfather, a native of Nizhegorodsky Province was cast up fifty years ago?

There, in a large village of three hundred households, I spent the years of my infancy and childhood, but when I grew a little older, I realised I was too ambitious to stay forever in a quiet, boring place where the people shout and the birds call loudly, but not very often.

No, I declared to myself, crumpling the hard prison pillow as I tossed and turned. Not my grey, tight-lipped native village, swamped with snow in winter and mud in spring and greenery in summer – that's not where I'll find the reasons for my failures. Quite the reverse – I've always felt proud of being a country boy. A provincial.

It is precisely the provincials who grow the wealth of capitals. It is these energetic out-of-towners who play the most important roles in the turbulent bustle of these cities with their glittering lights. If God did not love me, he would have made me a Muscovite: passionless, grasping, secure, well-schooled in all the pleasures, a creature of comfort. The same as my red-haired lawyer.

But I am not him. I'm a provincial! An out-of-towner. An alien. I shove and I scrabble. I strain every sinew. I'm hungry and pushy. That is how the Creator wishes to see me. That is where his gift to me lies: my luck.

Finally realising that sleep had completely deserted me, I took the cigarettes. Smoking in bed is the height of ignorance. In that Lefortovo prison cell, in the middle of the autumn of 1996, at the age of twenty-seven, I did it for the first time.

Perhaps my bad luck is a result of the death of the Land of Soviets? Of a shift in the destiny of three hundred million people? I was fourteen when the Kremlin leaders started dying one after another. At seventeen I graduated from secondary school. Chose a profession. The party of communists still held power – but it had already given citizens permission to get rich. I rejected that option. I had already decided everything. I intended to act consistently. Without deviating from my course. If you've chosen a job for yourself, get on with it! What point is there in just standing there gaping around you?

However, by the age of twenty it became clear to me that my favoured profession had been devalued. By a factor of ten. Journalists, once the elite of society, had been transformed into hungry, emaciated lovers of truth with empty pockets and burning eyes.

By that time I had invested four years in mastering the fundamentals, the basic skills of my trade. I had published fifty articles, sketches, reports and investigations. I had got my hand in. I knew the theory.

Then a sudden blow. News reports aren't worth anything. They only pay kopecks for them. All that effort, nervous strain, talent – nobody needs it.

Meanwhile on all sides the thunderous message resounds: 'Get rich! Forget everything you've been taught! Learn all over again! Make money! Earn and spend!'

It is a well known fact that on this matter there are two opinions. One is European. 'Blessed is he who has visited this world in its moments of destiny,' said a great poet whose life was spent in a European capital.

But long, long ago in the centre of Asia, an entirely different saying was composed on this subject. A term of abuse. 'May you live in times of change.'

I finished the cigarette and stubbed it out in the ashtray – the same as the ones that adorned the desks in Lefortovo's investigative offices.

If I'm an Asiatic, then I really am unlucky. The period of my youth has coincided with years of change. But if I'm a European, then I am the most fortunate of mortals.

I just have to understand where it is that I actually live – in Asia or in Europe? Or tell myself that an inhabitant of a vast country whose borders are lost in infinite distance, is doomed to languish in eternal indecision between West and East, between calm and storm. Between structure and flow.

I am neither here nor there.

There lies my bad luck. Our common lot. Or, on the contrary, my good fortune.

Two monotonous prison weeks flew by as quickly as minutes. Frol became totally fed up with having to tolerate the presence of a taciturn individual with battered and bloody fists who alway has his nose stuck in exercise books.

The feeling was mutual. I was also tired of the old warped criminal wheezing and hawking and puking up brown prison bile almost every evening, but still taking his chifir every one-and-a-half or two hours. I decided that in the periodical table of poisons – if some brilliant mind were to draw it up some day – caffeine would undoubtedly end up in the bottom basement, in the group of especially terrible substances that transform any human being into a dried-up, twisted creature with blank eyes and uncertain movements.

Nicotine will go beside it, I thought, pursuing the subject. It was consumed in incredible amounts before my very eyes and with my own participation. The smoking went on ceaselessly, from the moment of waking right through until evening. We smoked as we talked, or drank tea, we smoked when we took a crap, and after our walk, and after lunch and supper, and before bed. We smoked for lack of anything else to do. And while Fatty and I smoked the expensive light cigarettes sent to us by our wives, Frol's pride drove him to avoid running up debts and at the same time demonstrate his independence by puffing on Prima ordered through the prison kiosk. As a result in the evenings the cell, even with its four-metres-high ceiling, filled up with blue-grey smoke, carbon monoxide and something I found especially irritating – the disgusting smell of burnt matches.

In prison there are no cigarette lighters, the regulations don't allow them, they can always be transformed into a weapon, a bomb. Fling a plastic cigarette lighter hard against the floor, and it will explode with an ear-splitting boom. Matches are permitted. If anyone wishes to find out (not for practical purposes but out of sheer curiosity), what a cell in the Lefortovo pre-trial prison smells like, strike a match, immediately extinguish it, raise it to your nostrils and breathe in the smell. What is it? That's right, sulphur! Just like in hell.

In this atmosphere of tobacco smoke, between the four green walls of a poorly lit, cold cell in the Lefortovo Fortress, the two crooked spines, devoted themselves to an ecstatic game of backgammon, tried to solve crosswords, talked 'about life', leafed through detective novels, sipped chifir and slept for twelve hours at a stretch.

Finally, on one of those days – very possibly the most overcast and dreary day of autumn – Frol moved from contemptuous glances to direct attack.

I usually washed my underwear immediately after lunch. I hadn't chosen the time by chance: a full stomach immediately privatises all the free blood in the body, and the brain works poorly after food has been taken. I was giving it a chance to rest while I manipulated the soap, the water and my rags.

The rags required daily attention. After every outing I changed my sweat-soaked underwear and put on dry, clean items. I washed the dirty underwear immediately.

It took a long time to heat the water in mugs and gradually fill up the plastic washtub (prison property).

But on that dreary, grey day, before I could even soak my socks and singlets, Frol suddenly stopped studying his fingernails, leapt up briskly off the bed, took several steps in my direction and resolutely grasped hold of the edge of the washtub with his fingers.

'Please, allow me …' he said politely.

I took my hand away. The tattooed old lag lifted the plastic container with an effort – under the thin, greyish-yellow skin of his arms, his biceps stood out clearly, catching my eye: they were small, but they looked very firm – and poured the water into the washbasin. He stood the plastic basin neatly in the corner. Wiped his hands unhurriedly on a towel.

'Sit down,' he said.

Obediently sitting down, I put my hands on my knees and prepared myself for something important.

'We understand everything,' Frol began amicably after he had gone back to his bed and settled himself comfortably. 'You're a young lad, hot-headed, strong. Aha. And you've got a temper and all the rest … But your antics are affecting us so badly that we can't keep silent any longer. Isn't that right, Fatty?'

The construction magnate, who had so far been dozing peacefully, roused himself and also sat up.

'Yes, that's right.'

'You once told me that this is your first time inside,' the native inhabitant continued ingratiatingly, 'and you would be grateful if experienced people – me, for instance – would tell you what you're doing right and what you're doing wrong. Isn't that so?'

'Yes,' I agreed in a steady voice, trying not to betray my agitation.

'So now listen. Every day you spend half an hour splashing about under the tap. And another hour washing your smelly foot rags every day as well. Then you hang it all up in front of people's noses.'

'I'm sorry, Frol,' I interrupted, 'but ever since I was little I've always preferred clean foot rags. I'm no slob.'

'Well, well,' said the native inhabitant, narrowing his eyes. 'And just what, by the way, is a slob?'

'It's a slovenly, dirty person who doesn't follow the rules of hygiene.'

'Where did you learn that?'

'From you, Frol.'

'Then learn another thing from me. This is a prison. There's tube everywhere.'

Tuberculosis, I guessed.

'Damp is our enemy, yours and mine. Aha. For a jailbird there's nothing more terrible than water in the air. Have you heard about Koch's bacillus?'

'I seem to recall something.'

'He seems to recall!' Frol smiled with the corner of his mouth. 'He seems to recall, Fatty! That very bacillus, a tiny little thing, is there inside you all your life. Right from when you're little. Aha. As long as you eat well and go walking in a fresh breeze, it's passive. Sleeping. Waiting for when they put you in jail. In a place where there is no decent food or fresh air. Where everything's rotten and wet! In the damp air it multiplies. And it starts eating you, brother! Devouring your lungs. First just a little bit, then more and more! And by the end you're spitting those lungs out in little pieces. And you croak …'

'All right, I understand ...' I began, but Frol stopped me with a gesture of his hand and stood up. His face turned red.

'You wash your pants, and I can hear it sitting there inside me, the bastard. And it's chomping away! Eating me up, understand? I told you once to stop your gymnastics, I told you twice, three times – it was all a waste of time! You've been told. Politely. We hinted, we made fun of you! Gave you every opportunity to guess for yourself! But all you ever think about is your books. Aha. You want to be some kind of James Bond! And you don't give a damn for the people around you! That's not right! I'm going to stop it! Stop it, no matter what! No more laundry sessions! Shorts, socks and other underwear are only washed in the bathhouse! In the morning when they're dry they're taken down off the lines straight away. So that the air can move freely round the cell! If you go hanging up wet rags every day God sends, it'll do us in, get it? Wipe us out! The tube! We'll go under in no time, just a few months!'

I listened with my head lowered.

A solution in principle had already been found.

'Well, that's all I have to say,' Frol concluded in a low, indifferent voice. 'Now you have your say.'

'No,' I sighed. 'I've got nothing to say. You're right. There won't be any more laundry sessions. Or any damp ...'

'He's thought of something,' Fatty put in. 'He's not going to stop.'

'No, I won't stop,' I agreed and lit a cigarette, because I still hadn't learned how to manage entirely without poisons. 'I'll write to my wife and tell her to send in more underwear. And towels, about a dozen. I'll wet them with water in the hut and rub myself down out there during the walk. Put the dirty wet underwear in a plastic bag and in the morning throw it in the rubbish ...'

'In other words he wants to throw his duds out straight away and not wash them,' Fatty explained. 'And get new stuff in from outside ...'

Frol clutched at his head and an expression of horror appeared on his face.

'And don't you feel sorry for your wife?'

'He doesn't feel sorry for anyone,' Fatty declared morosely.

I was suddenly furious. My wife had nothing to do with this. I looked at the construction big-shot.

'Vadim, do you know the most important condition for the brain to function normally?'

'No.'

'A straight spine.'

Fatty immediately pulled himself up and straightened his rounded shoulders.

'Why do you mention that?'

'Because every man goes insane in his own way. One gets hooked on salami, another on exercise. Agreed?'

'So,' Fatty said aggressively, 'you've decided to reproach me about the salami, right?'

At this point a new party interposed in this argument that was developing so dangerously. A party we often forgot, but he never forgot us. He approached the door from the outside, pulled back the shutter of the spy hole, put his key in the lock of the feeder and opened up.

'Rubanov!' he said loudly. 'You're wanted!'

I swore.

'You didn't understand a single thing again,' Frol declared mournfully and shook his index finger in front of my face. 'People talk good sense to you, tell you what's right! And your answer is to come the clever dick! Go on, the cop's waiting for you! When you get back we'll finish talking …'

'Definitely,' I said and walked out.

You should never let your opponent have the last word.

'Face the wall!'

So this is how things have turned out, Andrei? So now the crooked spines are going to tell you what to do and how. Impose their will. So now you only wash your shorts with their permission. You wanted to conquer prison, do battle for your freedom – so take your freedom to wash your shorts, go and do battle for that!

The rage and frustration made my nose start to itch.

As I stepped inside the interrogation office, I suddenly had an awkward feeling and for a second I couldn't understand what was wrong; I finally realised that almost all the daylight entering through the aperture of the window was blocked off by a broad figure. Someone with an impressive span of shoulders and a very solid, square backside, wearing baggy militia trousers and a shirt of the same ilk, was standing with his back to me and his hands stuck in his pockets, looking out through the glass into the yard.

At one side, in his usual place at the desk, facing his computer screen, was Khvatov.

'Hi,' he said and pressed a tablet out of a plastic pack with a crackle and a crunch.

'Headache?' I asked.

The investigator nodded. I thought he looked pale.

The massive man at the window turned round.

'Good morning to you, chief,' I greeted him in a low voice.

Captain Svinets said nothing in reply and the expression on his face didn't change: it radiated that specific blend of interest and pity that usually precedes a moment of extreme rage.

At our first meeting, dolled up in his leather trousers and white socks, the man from Moscow CID had looked like a blockhead, large but not dangerous. Now, dressed in the dove-grey uniform of an officer of the militia, Svinets appeared far more impressive. If he wanted, a captain like that could easily set the people around him trembling in the literal sense of the word. I thought sadly: I'm not going to have an easy time today. In the developed countries, block-built captains like this one make excellent sheriffs and commissars. They become colonels and protect presidents. And in Latin America they're not averse to joining juntas.

'How are you?' the captain asked in a quiet voice

'All right.'

'Still in a cell on your own?'

'No, there are three of us.'

'Cell-mates okay?'

'Just fine.'

'I suppose you spend days on end playing poker?'

'I don't play games of chance.'

'Why?'

'I'm too impulsive.'

Svinets nodded. He paused. Then he breathed in, filling his chest full of air.

'To be quite honest,' he said confidentially, almost affectionately, 'I could kill you. I swear to God, I'm fighting the desire to do it this very moment.'

Khvatov cautiously cleared his throat.

I carried on standing in the middle of the room.

'And in general,' the dangerous captain continued in a businesslike tone, 'shooting's less costly than prison. For every five men in jail in our country, two guards are required. I know the figures. And there are almost a million and a half of you doing time in the camps and the prisons … Keeping people is expensive. It's a terrible strain on the state's pocket.'

'But,' I objected quietly, 'what about the famous iron manhole covers on the sewers? Every second one has the logo of some corrective colony or other …'

'Damn you and your logos,' the captain replied in disgust. 'Convicts are very poor workers. Do you know what killed the Roman Empire?'

'It was led to its end by the logic of history.'

'No. It was because they used slave labour. Slaves!' said Svinets, savouring the word as he repeated it, and then continued: 'And our empire … will go under … from the same disease. Enemies of the nation and the state should be liquidated, not kept for years and fed for free. They should be shot!'

'One of my cell-mates said the same thing only recently.'

'There, you see!' the detective said, frowning. He had clearly not been joking about liquidating enemies. 'For instance: I can kill you any moment … I'll take the prisoner out for an investigative experiment … he will attempt to escape and will die after being shot in the back with an officer's handgun … What do you think, Stepan?'

Khvatov forced a smile.

'That's not my idea.'

Svinets smiled broadly.

'Damn it! These cultured types make life hard! But I'm stubborn, I'll manage … And now,' the broad-shouldered captain said in a voice of thunder, 'listen up, you little bastard! You tried to make a fool of me! Your computers are empty! All the information's been wiped! Destroyed! And, as it happens – you knew it!'

'I knew it?' I also had to raise my voice so that my tirade would sound convincing. 'What do you mean, destroyed? Why destroyed?'

'When they arrived to search your office, your people refused to open the door.'

'And they were right!' I responded vengefully, remembering Semyon and Sergei with gratitude.

'While they were cutting through that door and breaking it down,' said the captain, turning to Khvatov and starting to tell him the story instead of me, 'some person as yet unidentified by the investigation placed a five-kilogram chunk of magnetised iron beside the main server. All the information was destroyed.'

'Aha!' I exclaimed triumphantly. 'What did you expect? Did you think you'd just turn up and stick your automatic rifle in my employees' faces, and they'd hand you everything on a plate? Tell you all the details? Oh no, Mr Chief! Everything was arranged properly in my office! You know, every week on Friday I used to have a drill session! For everyone! Including the secretaries, the drivers and the office supplies manager! Every soldier must know his manoeuvre! Everyone learned what he should do when men in camouflage suits started breaking in the door. One demagnetises the hard disks. One flushes the record books down the toilet. One stuffs the current documents into the shredder … That's how it is! Exactly like that, Mr Chief! If my security measures aren't ultimate and exhaustive, then who's going to trust me with his money?'

'Money …' Svinets said pensively. 'Money again. That's why you ended up in prison, and that still isn't enough for you, you fool … And what about your people, the office managers and the drivers, didn't they ask you any questions at these drill sessions? Didn't they wonder what all these strict measures were for? Five-kilogram magnets, document shredders?'

'We live in Asia,' I replied. 'We don't have any employers here. We have masters. You don't ask the master questions. May I sit down?'

'You may not!' the detective roared. 'Where did you get a magnet that weighs five kilograms?'

'I bought it on the black market. Paid the going rate.'

'I see.' Svinets knitted his light eyebrows together menacingly. Right, sunshine, you'd better get ready. I'm going to make your life really sweet. I won't have you shot, of course … Not yet. But in the prison I'm going to put you in, you won't know what hit you. Thought you could play games with me, did you? You told me to look in your computer, when it was empty! And you knew it!'

'I didn't know.'

'You did!' Svinets rumbled. 'You knew, you bastard! You've just admitted that you taught all your people what to do in advance. But you still sent me anyway, so that I'd come up empty! Waste my time and effort! I won't forgive you for that, son. Never. I'll pay you back. As soon as I'm done with you here, I'm going to see my girl. And you, as it happens, are going back to your cell! To pack your things and get ready to move! They're going to take you out of this cosy sanatorium where you get butter in your boiled grain and sugar with your tea, to a real prison. The kind which is just where you ought to be! The Butyrka! Or over to Matrosskaya Tishina Street. Things are different there! Thirty-man cells with a hundred and fifty prisoners in every one, starving to death, washing themselves with their own bloody tears, feeding the lice!'

Svinets breathed out noisily and seemed to have calmed down. His face turned red and his nostrils flared. His grey eyes looked at me and through me – straight at the ideal, absolute criminal lurking inside every man alive.

'I took note of your comments about the white socks. As it happens, I had doubts of my own anyway … But never mind. My girl likes white. When it comes down to it, it's all for her, even the socks … But you tried to put one over on me, you snot-nosed kid. To have a laugh at a detective. Reckoned if I have white socks, I've got to be some kind of oaf, did you? Nothing of the sort! Maybe when it comes to socks, I am an oaf, but when it comes to working with suspects under investigation I know a thing or two! And I'm going to come down hard on you. Now you're going to testify, and then you're going back to the cell to pack your things and hit the road. And once you've settled in at the new place and spent a few days sleeping in four shifts, you'll start to understand what it means to lie to an officer of the militia! And you'll remember absolutely everything about Farafonov's passport. The full background. Where, when, at whose place. All in the minutest possible detail ...'

Svinets detached himself from the wall and came straight at me, crashing his shoulder hard into mine. It was like colliding with a railway locomotive – I was tossed aside. The militia captain walked straight out of the office without bothering to say goodbye to his colleague, and from the way he left, it wasn't clear whether he was coming back in two minutes or two weeks.

I suddenly remembered that after today's interrogation I wouldn't be able to have a quiet drink of tea in my quarters and think over what had happened. There was an enemy waiting for me there, spiteful, riled and dangerous, a lifetime criminal, and he had a bone to pick with me, and perhaps it would all end in a loud scene and a fight, followed by sanctions from the prison authorities.

This is my chance to open my mouth and utter a few phrases, and instead of the old cell, they'll take me to a new one, where I'll meet new men. They might be more tolerant of my lifestyle. Or on the contrary, they could throw me in with a set of bastards, cannibals and killers, for whom one more slit throat means nothing ...

The departure of the thunderbolt-wielding detective was followed by a significant pause. Khvatov swallowed another tablet and gave me a guilty glance.

'Do I understand correctly, Andrei, that you're not going to testify again?'

'Testify?' I felt a burning sensation in my chest and an ache in my temples. 'Fuck you and your testimony. Fuck you and your testimony, you understand? You're not getting any testimony! You're not getting anything! Not a word! No testimony! Nothing! Is that clear? I'm not going to say anything, not a thing.'

I kept on and on raising the tone of my voice, octave by octave, adding more force and expression. It happened against my will, the hot saliva simply came spurting out of my throat and my fingers reached up to tear at the collar of my sweater all of their own accord: resentment, bitterness, fury, disappointment, tears, heartache – it all mixed together and suddenly poisoned me, and I started yelling, slurring my consonants:

'Come on, take me back to the hut! Take me back to the hut! To the hut! What do you mean, testimony? Screw you, Mr Chief, no fucking testimony for you!'

It was only then that I understood what genuine prison hysterics is like. It comes over a man who has been arrested and put behind bars when he is under threat from all sides, at the interrogation and in the cell, when there are dangerous enemies lurking everywhere, when the threat never recedes by day or by night, when it is there every moment.

Where has my composure gone now, I wonder? Where is that harmony of thought, the result of regular meditation sessions? What if all that is a deception too and no matter what exercises I do I'll never manage to make my nerves genuinely strong?

My last chance to chicken out and say farewell forever to the crooked spines was on the way back, during the search. I could have whispered a few words to the guard – after an admission like that he's obliged to take appropriate measures. Lock me in a kennel, report to the governor ... But I didn't say anything.

In my eyes the native inhabitant, the old lag, the fully illustrated recidivist embodied all those who had knuckled under to prison. And lost out to it.

But I'm not like that. I want to win and I'm going to get what I want.

I stepped into the cell like a gladiator entering the arena of the Coliseum. God only knows how the ancient Romans actually made their entrance to the field of battle and death – but their brows were probably knitted in a frown, their lips pressed tightly together and their eyes shot lightning bolts as they sought avidly for the gaze of the enemy. Their palms were moist with sweat as they clutched their weapons ...

And by the way, about weapons. What am I going to use to defend myself if the chifir-crazed old man throws himself on me? I might do press-ups on my fists a hundred and fifty times a day, but I have no skill in prison fighting, while my opponent is experienced and cunning …

The picture that actually met my eyes puzzled me. My cell-mates were both sitting on their beds with their hands folded on their stomachs with an extremely peaceable air. Frol's face was genuinely radiant.

They didn't utter a sound until the screw had closed the door, turned the key and glanced in one last time through the spy hole. Then Frol smiled and said to me.

'Come here, quick.'

He leaned down and pointed with one finger at the angle between the two steel bedsteads.

'See?'

'Yes,' I said, when I'd taken a look. 'A spider.'

'A spider!' said Frol, perfectly happy, and slapped me on the shoulder. 'A spider, brother!'

All his aggression had vanished without trace.

I cautiously examined the little black creature as it wiggled its legs.

'This calls for a good dose of chifir!'

'But what's the cause for celebration?' I asked, realising that the conflict was exhausted, smoothed over, it had been relegated to the past by a new event, the significance of which was only fully comprehensible to native inhabitants of prison.

'A spider's a good sign. A very good sign. The best one that I know.' Frol stuck his head into the hole between the edge of the bed and the wall and started burbling affectionately: 'Damn, how I love you, brother! You're just the same as me! A cell-mate. Fatty, let's give him a piece of that salami you love so much! A little piece, eh?'

'No problem,' said Fatty, 'only do spiders eat salami?'

'What's up, too mean to spare any?'

'Not for you, or for Andriukha. But for a spider …'

'You crackpot. Your entire ration's not good enough for a neighbour like this, never mind a bit of salami. Cut some, don't be a miser.'

'It won't eat rubbish like salami. It's not a human being!'

'Okay.' The old man straightened up. 'Do as you like, but I'm going to celebrate ...'

The life-long criminal jumped up and ran to the table, which bore his greatest treasure, the box holding his stock of tea, a box made of pieces of cardboard cut out and glued along the edges with strips of paper.

Every time a food parcel came for Fatty or me, the first thing to be extracted from the heap of plastic bags and bundles was the tea. It was triumphantly tipped into the container and Frol proclaimed triumphantly:

'The box is full!'

He didn't know that he drank what was probably the very finest chifir in the entire history of humanity – made from Earl Grey tea mixed in London at the premises of Curtis and Partridge, the leading specialists in their line of business.

'A spider!' Frol exclaimed, wagging one finger in the air to admonish someone whose identity remained unknown to me and Fatty. 'A spider! That means we're getting on okay in here. We shouldn't argue! We should take it easy, calm down. Have a hit of chifir. Have a smoke. Have a chinwag, then have something to eat and get some sleep. Aha. Sleep to our heart's content. In the warm. Under the blanket. You fools!' he almost shouted at us. 'You don't realise what it means when a man has tea, a smoke and a blanket! It's everything, fuck me if it isn't! It's everything you need. It's life. All the rest is a bucket of shit ...'

Trembling, he grabbed a spoon, sank it into the box of tea, scooped out a heaped spoonful and deftly shoved it all into his mouth. He started chewing energetically collecting the black particles that fell from his chin in his free hand. Then he took a gulp of water straight from the tap. He chewed again, moving his jaws from back to front and side to side. His cheeks swelled out with saliva. He took another gulp of water. After the third time he turned his back to us and spat out a dense, black mass into the metal receiver for excrement.

'What do you now about spiders, Fatty? Its web is a thousand times stronger than the strongest steel. It's woven its little net and now it's waiting. It couldn't give a damn, it'll go on waiting for as long as it takes.

One way or another something's going to come flying in. Aha. It always has, every time! God will send the spider something to eat, no matter what. The important thing is to hang out the net and make sure it's strong as strong can be ... And you Andriukha, you're a fucking Buddhist and you don't understand, you can't see the real life in spiders or in people ...'

As I was falling asleep in the evening of that tempestuous and nervous day, I heard Fatty impressing something on Frol in a low voice:

'We pour the water from a mug into a plastic bag. A mug holds a hundred and fifty grams. And we get a weight, we can weigh things! We tie the plastic bag in a knot, hang it on a thread, there's a balance arm here, and over here – the salami. Then we can approximately determine the weight of the entire delivery of salami that comes in to us ...'

19

A week later they held a search of our cell. They took us out for a walk and while we were gone they gave the whole place a thorough going over. It's standard practice at the Lefortovo prison.

When he got back, Frol discovered that the web had been wrecked barbarically. Its remnants – semi-transparent, white flakes – were dangling between the corner of the bed and the wall. The little creature had disappeared too. Either it had escaped and run off, or it had ended its days under the soft sole of a warder's shoe.

Poor Frol grieved for a long time and searched for his cell-mate's crushed body on the floor. The way the long-term convict saw it, if the screw had killed the spider, he wasn't likely to have cleaned up the mess after himself. No dead spider was found, not even the form of a wet spot on the cement – so it must have survived, Frol reasoned and, having lifted his spirits with this piece of logic, in his great joy he took a powerful dose of chifir; and then he was sick again.

'No body, no CASE!' he wheezed, grimacing. 'The little spider's alive, I'll answer for that! He's hiding away somewhere. He was frightened. Let's be patient, Fatty. Our brother will put in an appearance again soon. He'll hang out a new web!'

But our arthropod brother had disappeared without trace. Frol became morose.

He wasn't speaking to me at all now. I was still running every day. I put the damp tee-shirts, pants and socks away in a special bag. My entire store consisted of three changes of underwear. For three days a week I could train, sweating and breathing hard, and then I waited patiently for

Friday and the regular trip to the bathhouse. In the bathhouse I washed my things – and then for another three days in a row I exercised intensively throughout the hour of the walk.

In formal terms the native inhabitant's request had been carried out: now damp washing only poisoned the air inside the cell once a week.

On the other hand, I wasn't feeling particularly upset about the argument with my tattooed cell-mate. Autogenic training every morning had altered my psychology. External pressures from outside had ceased to bother me. My consciousness had been normalised. My nerves had grown stronger. Even my fingers had stopped trembling – and I had had a tremor for the last few years.

There was nothing so very extraordinary about my dawn watches: after waking up at six o'clock and switching off the tiresome radio, I simply sat there, entirely without moving for an hour, sometimes for an hour and a half, with my eyes closed and my body held straight, trying not to think about anything. The thoughts – when I finally allowed them to appear – arranged themselves in regular rows and obeyed my will. The necessary thoughts were allowed to develop into ideas, the unnecessary ones were expelled into non-existence.

I no longer found my cell-mates irritating, they were more amusing. Now I saw them as good-hearted men who were probably not without talent, but were at the same time quite impossibly irrational.

In addition, by mid-autumn – and autumn in the Lefortovo prison is dreary, grey, oppressively quiet, sad, tinted with the wan glow of half-blind electric light bulbs, permeated with the smell of damp sheets – one of us three, Fatty, fell into a deep melancholy. He slept until midday, and then all day long he lay on his back, looking at photographs of his wife and children without saying a word: the only breaks he made were to chew another piece of his favourite food product. I watched him and pitied him. From my new viewpoint it was obvious that the construction magnate had allowed the wrong thoughts into his head, and now he was suffering because he didn't have the strength to drive them out.

I believed the cause of his decline to be a lack of salami. In one of his food parcels Fatty received only soap, tea, sugar and cigarettes. All his calculations were in ruins. His nutritional schedule collapsed. Only a week earlier my voluminous neighbour had been good-natured and cheerful, he read the newspapers out loud and joked – and now he was profoundly depressed and sighed heavily all the time. He was clearly suffering from salami withdrawal symptoms. For two days he cherished the hope that it was a mistake and he had been brought the wrong bag. He wrote a note addressed to the governor of the prison, asking him to clear the matter up. But the administration was insulted – one day the feeder was opened, not by the screw, but a sleepy, annoyed official with a bald patch, a wart and a major's shoulder straps, who explained in very clear terms that in the Lefortovo special pre-trial isolation prison, accidents do not happen: every inmate receives precisely those food products that his relative shoves in through the little window for receiving parcels.

A day later everything was made clear. The construction boss was called for interrogation.

He had been inside for more than six months and his case had been decided. The investigation had demonstrated his guilt in only half a year. There was going to be a trial. I was visiting the investigative office regularly twice a week, but Fatty had never been pulled out for interrogations.

When the controller informed him that he was wanted, the grieving glutton was naturally frightened. His hands were shaking as he changed his crumpled tracksuit trousers for a different pair, cleaner and smarter, smoothed his hair down and stepped through the opening of the door, shuddering and pulling his head down into his shoulders, like a late holidaymaker entering the cooling September sea.

He came back in time for lunch.

Frol and I had decided not to sit down to eat without our friend. He arrived to see the table laid in all its splendour: muddy macaroni soup splashing about on the bottoms of the dove-grey aluminium bowls, and lying between the bowls on crumpled pieces of newspaper, the spices and hors d'oeuvres – coarse-grained salt, several onion rings, garlic, a ration of bread. Lying separately, in the corner, were the delicacies – cheese and a couple of cucumbers.

The magnate came back in an angry mood. He cleared his throat juicily and deafeningly, exactly like Frol, and spat into the washbasin, then sat down and picked up his spoon without speaking.

'My lawyer was here,' he told us. 'He brought news. From my wife.'

He glanced into his bowl, then pushed it away in irritation and squeezed his face up as if he were about to cry.

'My money's run out,' he said. 'There's not a kopeck left in the house.'

'That's a nuisance,' Frol said with a quiet sigh.

'A nuisance!' said Fatty, turning crimson. 'I've got four houses! I won't say where, but I have! Two-storey brick cottages with slate roofs. She ought to have just sold any of them, and there would have been enough money to last a hundred years!'

'Your wife?'

'Yes! We talked about it plenty of times! And now she writes that she doesn't want to sell anything, because no one will give her a decent price!'

The construction magnate was almost sobbing. Frol and I maintained a sympathetic silence and didn't touch our food.

'I have four houses, all with garages and plots of land, and I'm sitting here without a crust of bread!'

'Listen,' I said, 'did you ever build villas?'

'Recently that was all I built.'

'But what are you inside for?'

Fatty cleared his throat.

'I'm inside,' he explained reluctantly, 'for building a villa for a certain very big man.'

'Where's the crime in that?'

'In the fact that the money he paid me with turned out to be stolen.'

'So why are you to blame?'

'Because the materials I built it with were stolen too.'

'Then they should have put both of you away. You and the big man.'

'No,' said the magnate, with a bitter shake of his head. 'That man turned out to be so big that if they put him away there'd be no point in putting any little people away. They explained that to me straight away.'

Frol smiled.

'And I thought you were a big man.'

'No,' the magnate confessed, sounding crushed. 'I'm not big. I'm just fat.'

'Why did you take the risk? Building a house out of stolen materials?'

'Not all theft is a crime,' Fatty declared with conviction. 'No matter how much you steal from the state, you can never get all your own back. I didn't steal anything from anyone. I took what was due to me!'

'Okay,' said Frol with a stern wave of his hand, 'whether you stole or you didn't doesn't concern us. You don't talk about that in the cell. Right, Brumel?'

I sucked on my teeth in a dignified manner.

'Instead,' Frol suggested, 'why don't you tell us how you got fat?'

'Getting fat and stealing are one and the same process,' the construction boss replied sadly. 'At least for me they are. Although I suppose I've been fat since I was a kid. But that didn't stop me, by the way. If someone tried to make fun of me at school, I gave him a thump on the ear straight off. Then there was the construction battalion. It was the same thing there. Only more interesting: I thumped someone's ear, then he hit me back, and it went on like that for two years ... Once I'd served my time in the army I went to the construction sites. Rose from labourer to foreman. Graduated from college by correspondence course. Joined the party, and I was moved up to head foreman engineer. Five years later I was site engineer, after seven I was deputy manager of the department. Then manager ...'

These reminiscences had clearly distracted the magnate from thoughts about his avaricious wife, and he started eating. We followed his example.

'So when you got to be the boss – you really got fat!' Frol suggested, scratching his collar bone and setting the eight-pointed thief's star tattooed on it shimmering like a star at sea.

'Not at all, brother,' Fatty replied. 'Not straight away. To be quite honest, I didn't have any subcutaneous layer at all then. Neither physical nor financial. I slaved away, didn't eat much, hardly slept at all, especially in summer, during the season when the men are at the site in three shifts. We were building from north to south right across the country then. And not rotten shops with paper roofs, like now, but factories. Any way, a year goes by, and another, and I'm the boss of an entire construction organisation. I have a car with a driver, a tie, a party card, a pretty large salary, but all the same I'm running like an errand boy round the top offices or the foundations pits, lousy mud, frost, rain, cold, heat, responsibility – in short, building work. I started getting tired, my teeth went rotten, I damaged my kidneys, and my liver too, of course.'

Frol and I chewed on bitter onion and moist cheese and nodded in agreement. In a case like this it went without saying that you couldn't get by without vodka.

'And then towards the end of the year they promise me a bonus and a paid trip to Sochi. And apart from that, at this sale' – Fatty had almost calmed down now, he was working away with his spoon, tossing bread and pieces of tomato into his mouth – 'I got myself a rare suit, made in Poland, and a pair of shoes, English …'

'Lloyd's?' I queried. 'Church's?'

'Shit knows,' Fatty responded sweepingly. 'That's not the point. Anyway, in this beautiful gear, I took it into my head to visit the site at night after an urgent operational meeting. On the way back we got stuck. It's dark, the mud's knee-deep, it's raining wet sleet, the beginning of winter. I swapped seats with the driver so he could push and I could step on the gas – the driver's a metre and a half tall, and no subcutaneous layer at all … After an hour I thought to hell with it, took my shoes off, rolled up my trousers and jumped into the mud myself. I pushed for another hour. I pushed it out. Then straight away I say to the driver: you must have some vodka around somewhere, pour me a glass quick, or tomorrow I'll come down with pneumonia. No, the driver answers, I haven't got any vodka, you banned it yourself on pain of death. All right, I answer, let's go home. When we get there I say to him: you go and check the rear wheel, my friend; I take a look under his seat. He hasn't got just one bottle in there, he's got two! I saw red and gave him one in the face. Next morning he goes to the party committee to complain. The secretary of the party committee calls me in and swears at me for two hours. I get a reprimand and an entry in my file. Behaviour unworthy of a member of the party, manhandling and humiliating an employee … They take away my trip to Sochi and the bonus. That's all. Off you go, work …'

'That's where the criminals are,' Frol cawed, then got up and headed for the container of tea. He never ate very much, after a few spoonfuls of skilly and a piece of bread and cheese he already looked full and immediately topped up on chifir.

'And that very day,' the magnate declared with a dramatic sigh, as if he were reliving the past, 'I allocated two truckloads of stone chips on the sly to the dacha of the director of a department store, and in return he gave me two Belgian suits. And that's how it went on, building up the subcutaneous reserves … Actually, I'll take a hit of chifir too, Frol.'

'That's the way, at last,' the grey-haired old lag said delightedly, expressing his approval with a complicated movement of his body that set almost all the drawings on it quivering – the Virgin and Child on his belly, and the church domes on his forearms, and his other symbolic adornments. 'Then you join in too, Andriukha.'

'No hassle,' I agreed.

'A little bit of poison won't do any harm' – the thought went flying through my mind, even though I hadn't given it permission.

After taking two noisy gulps of the black liquid, Fatty grunted hoarsely and shuddered. Now the words came tumbling out of him quickly, as if they were chasing each other along.

'In less than two years, I really woke up. Got my teeth crowned! Got a fur coat for my wife, a car for my son, a Finnish sideboard for my mother-in-law! I fired the driver. The secretary of the party committee was my best friend. I did right and shared with everyone. And they shared with me. No one stole anything! Everyone only took what was theirs. What they were entitled to! Compensation for serious damage to the nerves! My eyes were opened. I saw clearly that the scientists had built a small rake-off into all the standards! Ever since Stalin's times. From the very beginning the calculations that had been made were made with huge margins. So instead of a thousand cubic metres, I pour nine hundred and ninety, and the other ten are my share, and all without any particular damage to strength or quality!'

'I see that hit the spot, aha?' Frol interrupted, smiling.

'Definitely,' Fatty replied, embarrassed, and wiped the sweat off his forehead. After that there was *perestroika*, and it was dead easy. I managed to privatise eight dump trucks and a column crane. I rented the equipment out and built cottages. For black cash. The secretary of the Party committee looks for commissions, the accountant pays the taxes and I build up my subcutaneous layer ... But then a problem turned up. I found I was surrounded by people who liked the idea of building up their own subcutaneous layer at my expense. One came to me, borrowed some money, and disappeared. Then another. And another. And a fourth one too. All of them people close to me, relatives, friends from school, the army, college ... So then I couldn't take any more. I paid the right people and they found every one of them ...'

'The going rate?' I asked.

'What?'

'Did you pay the going rate?'

'Of course'

'And what did you do to the guys who owed you?' Frol enquired.

'What do you mean?' Fatty asked in surprise. 'I made them work off their debts! I'm a builder, after all. One smart ass worked a whole year for me, as an arc-welder! Until he'd paid everything back, right down to the last kopeck, until the last drop of fat was melted out of him ...'

'That's the way!' I put in earnestly. 'The only way! If you take something and don't give it back, then work it off!'

'I'm glad you understand that ...'

We sat there for a long time afterwards: drank chifir; smoked filter cigarettes; took tea with sugar; talked about money, about stealing, about 'black cash', the subcutaneous layer, about debtors who didn't give back what they owed; about enemies and friends; about salami and bread; about wives and children; about criminals and public prosecutors, about freedom and jail – about things that bothered us, concerned us, things that made our hearts ache.

Two days later Frol went quiet. The store of tea was melting away. One evening the old man with tattoos spread out a newspaper on his blanket, tipped the tea on to it in a neat heap, took the bottom out of a matchbox and began precisely measuring how much was still left.

'What's this, my friend,' Fatty asked in a quiet voice, 'is your stash running out too?'

'There was a man called Lenin, Vladimir Ilich,' Frol replied, concentrating on his task. 'Maybe you've heard of him?'

'I seem to remember something,' the construction magnate joked.

'Well then, he wrote that socialism is doing the accounts.'

'Have we got socialism here?'

'What's that got to do with anything?'

20

In late autumn, when it's cold and damp, it feels good sitting in a small prison cell. The heavy rain drops hammer aggressively against the barred matt-glass window. The wind howls. But inside there's yellow light, and hot tea, and the radio murmuring from a hole above the door. I have thick woolly socks on my feet and a book in my hand. It's as if I've just called into this house for a couple of hours of my own free will, to wait out the bad weather, and at any moment I can get up, drink a glass of wine for the road and go off about my business, after first taking leave of my hospitable hosts. Let them watch as I walk away and think: that guy's always on the go!

On a dank, cheerless day like this, it's good to go to the bathhouse too. To stand for a while under a stream of hot water. To warm yourself. To scour your arms and legs hard with the bundle of bast fibres. To wash your hair thoroughly. To get the dirt off your skin.

It's damp in the shower room; not hot, but really very warm. The floor is covered with slippery wooden gratings. Running along the wall above my head is a pipe full of holes, with streams of water spurting out of them. Each one of us three has taken a spot under his own personal waterfall and is luxuriating in it.

Through the clouds of steam I can make out two naked bodies moving. One is small and gaunt, covered all over with blue inscriptions and pictures. The other is huge, pale-pink and nightmarishly bloated. In comparison with these distinctive structures of meat and bone, my own dwelling of the spirit is clearly at a disadvantage. I'm not as sinewy as Frol – above all, I don't have any marks on my skin; and I'm not as ponderous and voluminous as the construction magnate.

Between the jets of water I can see two original human backsides. The first is vast and rounded. It inspires respect. It provokes thoughts of stability and permanence. The second is small and compact, but it has an inscription stretching across the buttocks: the half-effaced blue letters of Slavonic script declare laconically:

I'M TIRED OF SITTING.

In the steam of the Lefortovo prison bathhouse I behold the mature backsides of fully-formed adult men. Some time, at the beginning of life, both of them made their choice: and the owner of the first backside decided to store up his own fortune and the owner of the second decided to take other people's. Now their destinies were stamped just below the bottom of their spines.

The feeble, curved ridges grow up out of the coxofemoral joints like geraniums out of pots. One of them protrudes eloquently, the row of vertebrae sticking out of Frol's violet back, making the old lag look like some repulsive lizard. The damaged spine of the second is masked by thick folds of fat.

I lowered my eyes and looked myself over jealously. Ha! I'm nothing like them, those crooked spines. My own spinal column is as straight as an arrow, or a string, or the road ahead. My back is strong. My chest and shoulders are firm. If I stretch my arms out to the side, straighten them and tense them, fold one hand into a fist and turned it clockwise, or twist the joint through three hundred and thirty degrees in the other direction, then the dense, resilient muscle fibres stand out impressively under the skin – the fruit of persistent training.

The sight of this visible result of my efforts gave me a feeling of satisfaction and boosted my mood so much that I felt like singing. Now my body is covered with armour. With a shell as rugged as asphalt. I have changed myself, and that means the entire world too – even the prison! – merely by the exercise of my own will. Three months ago the prison swallowed a narrow-shouldered neurasthenic reeking through and through of tobacco smoke and alcohol. And now suddenly he has disappeared from its stone maw! In his place a quite different man is now soaping up his hollow belly and scraping it with his fingernails – a man with calm confidence in his own powers.

Of course, a pitiful five weeks of squats and press-ups had not transformed me into the ideal athlete. But the future was an unknown void. The red-headed lawyer had told me the case was unlikely be taken as far as a trial. But I would still have to be patient for a while longer. Possibly until the New Year. And I was going to take the maximum possible advantage of this breathing space. The alternating sessions of meditation and physical training would continue.

I was going to become strong both within and without. After squeezing my muscles with my fingers to make sure that they were real, I immediately promised myself that I would give up smoking in the next few days. Then I stretched my hands out to the sides, turned my face up towards the warm water falling down on me and realised that there was no prison, it didn't exist.

And prison really doesn't exist.

Baddies of the world! Don't believe your old friends when they brag about all the stretches they've done inside. Prison doesn't exist.

People of culture! Don't believe the gloomy epic narratives of the old writers. Prison doesn't exist.

It doesn't exist, it's a fairytale for fools. A terrifying legend that infantile blockheads use to frighten each other …

The bathhouse attendant knocked several times on the door of the shower room.

'Out you come!'

I set off towards the door, but the vast back of the construction magnate blocked the way. While I took two steps, Fatty could only shift the mass of his body slightly. I had to slow down. That was how we emerged into the corridor: first the old man with tattoos, then the magnate and right at the back – me.

Why, I wondered, does society respect fat men? And even fear them? Why are broad-shouldered, fleshy males with thick necks, massive backsides and huge bellies accepted as successful people – they can be trusted, they're good to work with (on condition, of course, that they are well dressed and behave respectably). And why, in contrast, do skinny, spry individuals like me often provoke subconscious suspicion, even if they can doll themselves up in an expensive jacket? 'Is he always nervous? A screwball. Doesn't eat enough?' society wonders. 'Probably unstable, lacks confidence, plagued by doubts and panic attacks. Someone like that might be interesting, but he's clearly unreliable …'

I suddenly felt envious of Fatty. His external dimensions, his sagging folds, the gigantic cylinders of his thighs, the way he walked, shifting one foot solidly after the other, trampling the ground powerfully and heavily, his economical, slow, almost languid gestures – they all made any observer trust a man like that, believe that his affairs and his actions are as firm and substantial as his body, and surrounded on all sides by an equally reliable layer of protective fat.

Size and scale – people will always believe in that, they turn away from people who are scrawny, fitful, skinny, they feel a liking for the owners of massive, fat-assed bodies and coarse, low voices. Where now are all the sinewy, gaunt Spartans who broke stones for their own fatties? They're gone. Washed away by the merciless tide of History. But drooping fat is in favour. Big people mean big business.

But of course, in certain places, in particular the prison bathhouse, in the cramped changing room – four metres by three – you can observe a rather uncommon picture: the immense, heavy-bellied male squeezes himself back into the corner of the small chamber, with his feet together and his hands between his knees, and waits meekly until a second male, small and covered in inscriptions and drawings, finishes getting dressed.

What then can be said of me? I had no symbols on my skin and no layer of fat under it either. In our bathhouse hierarchy I had been handed the bottom place. Frol, gaunt and small, took up half the bench and the remainder was filled by Fatty's bulky frame, while I had to make do with a narrow strip of space along the tiled wall. But anyway, I was younger, no more than a kid compared with the two of them – and I calmed myself and settled my nerves with that simple truism.

I waited patiently until both of them – the fat one and the decorated one – had rubbed the moisture off their flushed bodies, pulled their shorts up on to their loins, caught their breath and sat down on the wooden platform before I hastily scrubbed myself down, and immediately the bolt rattled and the white-painted steel door opened.

'Ready?'

On the way out there was a brief but pithy discussion with the bathhouse attendant, a very elderly warrant officer known by the name of 'Ilich'. Frol claimed that this serviceman had been working in Lefortovo since Lavrenty Beria's day. Every time I looked into the hard stare of Ilich's hard fish-eyes, I could believe the legend was true. The prison warden's pupils had absolutely no expression at all; just vigilance the colour of tin.

The legendary bathhouse attendant hands out new, clean bedding to replace the old. At this important moment every inmate of the prison is obliged to study what he has been given and request – smiling and joking as he does so, uttering various ingratiating sounds – sheets that are a little broader. The dimensions of the pieces of cloth are not all the same. If you don't look closely, you'll end up with narrow ones. You can't wrap them round your mattress properly, and the following morning you'll discover that the undersized sheet has rolled itself up into a braid (after all, at night you were tossing and turning, you had bad dreams, clammy and restless – prison dreams – and you'll discover that you didn't sleep on a clean sheet, but on the bare, dirty, prickly mattress (prison property) that has imbibed sweat from the bodies of many hundreds of prisoners.

'Now we're clean!'

The instant he was in the cell, Frol dashed over to the heating coil and the box of tea.

'Well done, Andriukha, I tell you, well done! Aha. At long last you've given up all that running and jumping. Listened to the voice of reason for real …'

I didn't answer. Why disabuse the man? I had only halted my training temporarily. Every sportsman knows that after five or six weeks of daily work-outs, you have to take a break. For about ten days. To allow the body to rest. Otherwise you get hit by over-exhaustion and all the benefit is lost. Instead of launching into an explanation, I simply said nothing.

I was keeping silent for longer and longer every day. Sometime I didn't utter a single word for days on end. I either read or sat on my bed, staring at the wall and relishing the fact that my head was entirely empty of all thoughts or ideas. In the words of Alexei Tolstoy, I dedicated myself to useful boredom. My brain was now beginning to produce conclusions only at those moments when they were needed – only when I required them. The rest of the time it rested and was dormant.

The pointless feelings had disappeared – the distress, the fears and the morbid upsurges of fantasy. I rejoiced in my self-control the way an animal-trainer in a circus rejoices in the fact that his bear has finally started to ride a bicycle. The agonizing questions – what's going to happen to me, where's my money, why doesn't my partner and boss get in touch? – now I could push them away by a simple mental effort.

I didn't speak, not even at the interrogation sessions. The latest discussion had been the twenty-fourth, Khvatov had put twenty-four sets of minutes in the CASE FILE. Every one of them registered my refusal to provide testimony.

Even when I was left alone with the solicitor, most of the time I only listened to his speeches of encouragement. I said nothing. The red-headed lawyer gazed at me in alarm, but he didn't ask any questions.

Now I cleaved through the air of Lefortovo jail like some austere Superman or Nietzschean wonder-kid – he doesn't give a fig for anything, nothing affects him, he doesn't feel hunger, or the lack of domestic comfort, or emotional pain, and the clarity of his own mind is his only concern.

As sober as a thousand confirmed teetotallers, I woke at six o'clock, spent the allotted time in doing my exercises and maintained my purity of awareness without any great effort right through until the evening.

My crooked-backed cell-mates, fat man and thin man, only fitted into all this as caricatures. Two unfortunates spending every day destroying themselves with their petty little passions. Pitiful crossword players. Embezzlers of their own fast-flowing lives. Foolish spendthrifts of precious time. There's one of them boiling water and throwing the leaves of a plant into it in order to extract the poisonous juice, consume it and be reduced to a state of artificial frenzy …

The tea was running out. Only five hundred grams had arrived with Fatty's last food parcel. Frol was economising desperately. He reduced his dose and took it less often.

'I could do with a little blast of hash,' he sighed, measuring out a meagre dose of his strong brew.

'Yes indeed,' Fatty responded. 'Followed by a nice little wine.'

'That wouldn't do it,' the old lag objected morosely. 'Two dopes don't work together.'

'You know best.'

'What about you, Buddha. What do you think about that?'

I surprised myself by confiding in him:

'One day I'm going to draw up a periodical system of poisons. I'll lay them out in order. Like in Mendeleev's table of the elements. Nicotine, caffeine, alcohol and so on. The most powerful and dangerous poison here, one that's less poisonous here …'

Frol chucked condescendingly.

'What do you know about junk, son?'

'I drank and smoked for several years.'

'Smoked, drank …' the tattooed man mocked me. 'And have you tried grass?'

'Never.'

My cell-mates broke into laughter simultaneously.

'What about hop?' Frol asked. 'Smack? Snow? Or at least dimedrol? No? And have seen the way convicts turn ephedrine into pervitine? Do you know how to knock the chalk out of tablets? And do you know what cyclodol is, kid? Or phenazepam? Phencyclidine? Alminazine? Downers? What, not even those?'

Who would have believed it, I thought and admitted honestly.

'I haven't gone that far.'

'And God forbid you ever should!' Frol declared hoarsely and started mocking me again. 'A table! Anyone who tries to draw one up will be dead before he even gets halfway through it. You've lost your marbles, Buddhist. You're thinking about the wrong things!'

Fro held his mug out to me.

'Take some chifir! Have a hit!'

'The enlightened man does not drink chifir,' I replied. 'He is in a state of equilibrium and he does not stimulate himself with poisons.'

'Grab a high, you fool,' the native inhabitant of prison said with good-natured patience. 'There's enough tea left for two days. Grab a high while you can. After the bathhouse is just the right time. Go on, grab it.'

'No thank you,' I said, frowning. 'Poisons make you dependent, and any dependence is a prison.'

'That's right,' said Frol, nodding. 'Prison on the outside and prison on the inside. Grab a high!'

I shook my head and started looking around for my textbooks.

'I'm not in prison. I'm free. And there are no prisons in nature. It's an illusion. We invent prisons for ourselves.'

Frol's eyebrows crept upwards, his pupils expanded and his nostrils flared. I got the feeling that I had offended the old man immensely with my refusal.

'If prison doesn't exist,' he said irritably, 'then what are you doing in here, philosopher? Get up and walk out!'

'Where to?'

'Out there!' A knotty finger stained brown by tobacco pointed towards the window. 'To freedom!'

'Freedom doesn't exist either,' the enlightened man said in a steady voice. 'It is also an illusion and a deception.'

Frol shuddered like a man who has heard a blasphemy uttered. He jumped to his feet and made several rapid circuits from the wall to the door and back, but then heaved a noisy sigh and stopped in front of me.

'Don't you ever,' he said, 'say that to anyone! "Prison doesn't exist, and neither does freedom" … They do! They exist, right? This is prison right here. All around us. And freedom's out there!' The finger pointed towards the window again. 'And all this' – the finger was aimed at my stubbornly inclined head – 'is just philosophy. There was a guy called Lenin, Vladimir

Ilich, maybe you've heard of him? Well then, he wrote: an idea becomes a material force when it takes possession of the masses! *Takes possession*, get it?'

Frol illustrated his own words: he stretched out his arms, squeezed his fists tight and then jerked his elbows backwards, simultaneously thrusting his hips forward for more graphic emphasis.

'It wasn't Lenin who wrote that, it was Marx,' the enlightened man objected quietly.

'The same bunch!' the old convict replied. 'And now some idea's taken possession' – the old convict repeated his obscene movement – 'of you! A periodic table of poisons! Changing your handwriting! Gymnastics in jail! You're not living in the real world, brother! You're surrounded by nothing but ideas! Philosophy! Which isn't worth anything in itself, because how can you apply it in practice, eh? If prison doesn't exist for you, walk through the wall and go back home!'

'Some day,' the enlightened man said in a steady voice, 'I'll do just that.'

'You're going to walk through the wall?' Frol howled.

'Yes.'

'Sure, I believe you!' the crooked spine shouted passionately. 'I believe you, brother! I read about things like that myself, some time way back. D'you think I'm ignorant and illiterate? No. I know that a man can do all sorts of things, that there are people in the world who really can fly, read thoughts and all the rest. Aha. Only it takes ten years to learn how ...'

'Twenty ...'

'Twenty! And while you're spending all those years mastering this tricky stuff like reading people's thoughts, sitting in jail – know what's going to happen to you?'

'Well, what?'

'You'll *rot*!' Frol's eyes glittered. 'From tuberculosis. From meningitis! From the lice! The itchy scab! The bedbugs! From the cold, the hunger and the hassle from the narks. You'll rot before you can fly ...'

I said nothing.

'Just ponder that! Think about it.' The recidivist sighed. 'I'm not your enemy. I wouldn't give you bad advice. It's the ideas, brother, they're what's destroying you!'

'Would you like,' I asked after a short pause, 'me to read your thoughts?'

'Try.'

'You're thinking it's time to light up.'

Fatty hadn't said anything so far, but now he started laughing, and all three of us lit up with delight. Reading thoughts is pretty tricky, but implanting them can sometimes be dead easy.

Just at that moment there was a metallic clang as the feeder opened.

'Rubanov! Is he here?'

'Yes,' I replied cheerfully.

'GET YOUR THINGS!'

There was a painful pause. I sniffed. The hole closed.

Frol swore quietly. Fatty sighed. Now they were both looking at me with sad regret.

In a sharp paroxysm of terror, the enlightened man suddenly broke wind loudly and clearly. The Nietzschean tough guy could feel himself trembling. Not a trace of mental equilibrium remained. His mouth filled up with sticky saliva.

'What a shame,' Frol muttered and shook his head. 'Right then, Andriukha, get packing. They're not going to wait.'

Moving despondently but hastily, I started packing away my meagre junk in plastic bags: a mug, a bowl, a towel and underwear, notebooks and textbooks, soap and toothbrush – the simple belongings of a prisoner.

My heart was pounding. What if? What if? Could it really have happened after all, could my boss suddenly have turned up, come back off the lam and presented all the interested parties with wads of cash, and now they would let me out of the gates of the fortress with the words 'you're free'? And why not? Even in the trashiest comics the hero is always lucky!

'Your food,' Fatty reminded me anxiously. 'Take your food.'

'No,' I replied sternly, deciding I would travel light into the unknown future.

'Take it!' Frol ordered me. 'Tea, sugar, smokes – take it all anyway! You never know where you might end up. Don't come the hero! Take it all. And the salami too! And the butter! And the apples!'

And so saying, Frol took a sheet of newspaper, tipped all the tea we had in the cell out on to it, rolled it into a small, very tight bundle and thrust it into my plastic bag. It was followed by the construction magnate's entire reserve of salami. All of it, down to the very last piece. With no display of emotion, with no superfluous words, with no Nietzschean display of feeling, they gave me everything that was most precious to them.

'Why?' I asked, trying to grab one of them by the wrist and the other by the shoulder. But the two grown men pushed my hands away with friendly ease.

'How will you manage without tea? Without salami?'

'Tea and salami aren't the most important things,' Frol said in a quiet vice.

'I won't take the last of everything.'

'It's all right, we've got more. Isn't that right, Fatty? Stowed away under our skin. And later the dacha will kick in …'

'Why should I take your tea, Frol? What if they're letting me go?'

'God grant,' the old lag replied in a neutral tone of voice. 'When you're out you take a hit of chifir. And remember the old vagabond Frol, aha?'

He helped me roll up the sheet into a long, thin rope and tie it tightly round the mattress that he had rolled into a tube. It was far more comfortable to lug the prison property around that way.

The key rattled as it was turned in the lock.

'Name?'

'Rubanov …'

'Out you come.'

Gritting my teeth, I grabbed up my bundles and stepped away from the people I had lived side by side with for two months.

'Turn right!'

Now where? Into the next cell? To liberty?

In my agitation I broke into a heavy sweat.

'Stop! Face the wall!'

Another clatter of keys.

'Go in!'

I turned round and found myself facing a 'kennel', a temporary holding box. One metre wide, one metre deep. Fitted with a narrow plank of wood running right across it at knee level. Stand or sit, whichever you like. Above your head, in a narrow niche, a dusty light bulb, well protected by an iron grille. Not even a grille, but heavy bars.

I hate bars, I thought.

The warder closed the door, slid the bolts shut and took a final careful look through the little hole. He closed the shutter. The light bulb went out. I was left in absolute darkness.

After a while my eyes adapted, and I could make out a faint strip of light at waist level. At one side, a metre above the floor, there was a chink in the door frame. Bending down – somehow I contrived to thrust my knees against one wall and my backside against the other – I took a peep, but didn't see anything important or useful. A small section of the opposite wall of the prison corridor. Setting my nostrils to the crack, I drew in the air – what if I could catch some rare, long-forgotten smell? No, it smelled the same as usual. Damp cement, dusty rags. Prison.

Nothing left to do but sit and wait.

'What now?' I asked myself once again. 'Where are they going to take me?'

I heard someone's confident footsteps outside the door: not a cautious screw stepping weightlessly, but someone sure of himself, clattering the heels of his shoes as if he owned the place – he came closer, pulled back the shutter, glanced in, then realised that he wouldn't be able to see anything in the dark and switched on the light. I winced. The light bulb immediately went out and the curious nobody moved on at a leisurely pace.

Just as long as they don't kill me. No, they won't kill me, they wouldn't. Times have changed. And there's no point. I'm not keeping any terrible secrets. I don't possess any compromising evidence and I'm not some political high-flyer who's suddenly fallen out of favour. I'm nothing but a banker, and even then not a real one.

They won't torture me either. They've been holding me for three months. If they wanted to, they could have ripped any confessions they liked out of me ages ago. That means they don't really want any confessions! That means they'll simply move me. To a different cell. Or to a different prison altogether. Maybe the dangerous Captain Svinets wasn't simply bluffing and I'll be transported under armed guard to the Butyrka?

As if to illustrate my alarming speculations, the sound of steps returned, accompanied by the voices of men arguing – three or even four of them. They came closer, but stopped talking before I could make out the individual words. The three (or four) of them approached my door and the visual inspection was repeated. Each of the three took a look. One – the last – even chuckled briefly: he was amused by the way I was screwing my eyes up against the sudden switch from dark to light. Then the quarrellers moved away.

Yesterday, or the day before yesterday, or a week ago, or even this morning, some important cogwheel in the administrative machine of special pre-trial isolation prison number one slash one turned. The governor of the prison, Colonel Razrez, or his deputy, or some other important official thought, carefully read his secret official instructions and gave a curt order: move him!

Enveloped as I was in silence and darkness, I could easily picture some special individual sitting somewhere in the secret depths of the Lefortovo fortress, going through the personal files and record cards of his guests and pondering who to put where, with whom and in what order.

They probably had their own style of office work in there. The Empire Style. Tea out of cheap glasses. Cardboard ashtrays on the desks – examples of the prisoners' handiwork. Cigarette smoke streaming towards the high ceilings. A game of patience pensively laid out with prisoners' record cards. In every card photographs, the charges, distinctive features. I knew that my card bore the weighty inscription: 'article one hundred and forty-seven, section three'. Embezzlement! On an exceptionally large scale! A premeditated conspiracy! By a group. Ten years of custodial confinement. For the clerks of Lefortovo this was the same kind of brand name as Valentino was for me. So the administration had to think carefully before deciding who to put in a cell with me.

Put this maniac in with the terrorist! This spy in with the bandit. This swindler with the general. We'll put the thief in here, give these villains the murderer, and these the banker …

Wherever you like, I said, adrift in the profound darkness of my tiny, one metre by one metre, universe, straining my eyes and my ears. Wherever you like! With the murderers, the maniacs, the debauchers of children – I'll remain true to my path anywhere. Work on myself. Not take any poisons. Move onwards and upwards. Hold my back straight. No caffeine. No nicotine. A sober state of awareness. Deep breathing. Oxygen. Movement. Body and mind subject to the will. That's my path to freedom.

Wherever I might end up, I know what I'm going to do. I shall train my brain to the ultimate. I shall defeat prison. I shall humiliate it. I shall practice on it my own deception, great and terrible. The choices I have at my disposal are as infinite as freedom itself. I shall learn living and dead languages. I shall become an adept of all the global religions. I shall master hypnosis. I shall study the history of world philosophy. I came in here as a primitive fool, a lover of money, I shall go out a wise man, a psychic and an ascetic.

And I shall not only perfect my mind, but my body too. I shall make myself as hard as granite. I shall learn to run up walls, jump four metres into the air, toss a lighted cigarette ten paces straight in my enemy's eye, speed up my heartbeat and slow it down. I shall make myself impervious to pain and hunger, cold and heat. The bars and walls will be transformed into weights and training equipment.

I shall come within striking distance of perfection.

No poisons. No idleness, sleep or despondency.

Working coolly and cheerfully, without sparing myself, without relapsing into despair and laziness, I shall be able to defeat prison. I shall tear the very idea of captivity to shreds. I shall make fools of those who tried to shut me up in a cell. I *shall* do it. For the road to truth has been revealed to me – as straight as an arrow, as alive as an umbilical cord.

The sound of footsteps came for the third time. Once again the light flashed on. Once again I screwed up my eyes and shuddered at the suddenness of it. Once again I was examined through the hole by someone's attentive, colourless eye.

'What?' I shouted rudely in my exasperation.

The eye disappeared. The bolts clattered. The door opened.

'Name?'

'Rubanov!'

'Out you come!'

21

All drunken evenings are alike; every awakening with a hangover is painful after its own fashion.

Three years have passed since they let me out.

And now everything in my home has been thrown into confusion. And everything in my head. And in life in general.

'You're an alcoholic and a drug addict,' my wife told me this evening. 'You're burnt out! A degenerate! You're even worse now than you used to be!'

I listened to the reproaches of my outraged help-mate in diplomatic silence.

'You've destroyed yourself with drink,' the woman asserted. 'Totally! You're at the point of no return! You're playing with fire!'

Yes, she's hit the bull's eye. It's absolutely clear. It's fortunate for her that she doesn't know *everything*. She doesn't realise how far my addiction has gone. The daily dose is a bottle of cognac or vodka. Five hundred grams. Three large glasses. Every evening. And during the day there have to be a few joints of marijuana.

Secretive and cunning, I don't advertise my quaint hobby to my wife. I carefully hide the bottles – the empties and the full ones. I keep the little plastic bags of grass, the cigarette holders, the roaches and other devices for smoking the drug in secret hiding places. I air the rooms and brush my teeth. But my woman is sensitive to smells, she is attentive to details, she notices all the oddities in my behaviour. She notes the excessive daydreaming, the absentmindedness, the groundless fits of merriment or melancholy; she knows everything. I can see quite clearly that she still loves me, but she no longer respects me. My weakness for poisons is a profound disappointment to her.

'Not so loud,' I tell her. 'Please, speak quietly. The neighbours will hear!'

'I don't give a damn!' Her voice rings out loudly, even vulgarly. 'Let them hear! Let everyone know the shameful way you treat me!'

That is followed by an emotional, absurdly melodramatic tirade about how I have mutilated and destroyed her life, her looks and her youth. Everybody knows how hard women's monologues like that are on the nerves. When the moment comes and Irma, offended and crimson faced from her inability to get through to my common sense (I simply don't have any) walks out of the kitchen (for some reason all family scandals reach their climax precisely in the kitchen), I pour myself another.

After drinking it, I sit there for several minutes. Resting. I could just do with a few drags of hash, I say to myself, and immediately put the idea into effect. A huge glass of booze and a joint – that's what helps me get through every day.

After a smoke I calmed down, got dressed, took some money and the car keys and went out, carefully closing the door behind me.

Why do I have to suffer like this? Why does my own wife treat me like an outlaw? I did my time in prison. I came back. And I'm trying to put a new life together. But I'm still mired in total and absolute poverty. No job, no money, no health, no prospects. Burdened with a family and debts. In this situation, poised on the edge, teetering on the brink of a total breakdown, don't I have the right to drink myself into a state of forgetfulness? Slump into a coma? Switch off all the damned channels of communication with the outside world?

I spent many years – all the years of my youth – with the feeling that I wasn't simply living, but running up the stairway of life three steps at a time. At twenty-two I was a penniless student; at twenty-four, a businessman with a cigar; at twenty-seven, a banker and financier. Now, at thirty-two, I'm penniless again. What am I supposed to do? What am I supposed to do?

There's only one thing left to do: cloud the brain to prevent the bitterness of defeat poisoning my reason.

I'M A PAUPER AND A SHIT!
I'M A PAUPER AND A SHIT!

Perhaps as I rode the lift down from the sixteenth floor I shouted these words out loud. It's quite possible that I broadcast my thoughts at high volume not only in the lift, but out in the street, on the way to the car. In any case, a group of young people taking it easy beside the entrance to the building fell silent when I appeared. Or perhaps it just seemed that way to me. Genuine druggies are all very paranoid – they easily fall into a state of exaggerated anxiety.

In any event, I made it to the car and got in, and then my head really took off.

I don't have a CD-player or a radio in my car. I have no self-respect and I don't allow myself to spend money on trash. What do I need music for? It will only calm me down, heal me. And in a calm state, I'll decide that my life is in perfect order. But that just isn't so.

But there and then – sitting in the car, in the yard of the high-rise apartment block on a fine spring evening – I promised myself that the next day I would buy a stereo. And then I would drive around town to the crash and whine of guitars and drums, the way I used to do in better times.

And immediately I felt immensely sad. The better times were long since over and gone. When you're always stoned on shit, it's easy to get better times and worse times confused.

I smoked a cigarette and sat there for little while, then turned on the engine and drove two hundred metres to the nearest little shop, where I bought a bottle of beer and drove back again.

Family rows are not really something that should be indulged in too often. They kill you.

I open the beer and drank it on the way back home. The leisurely journey over the smooth asphalt surface of the crooked side streets past several immense buildings (at last a thousand people living in each one) is enjoyable. Yes, it would be good to listen to some music. But I despise myself and I refuse to pamper my nerves with it. Although there was a time when I couldn't imagine life without rock and roll.

I suddenly remembered that several days before I was I arrested I changed all the CDs in my automobile. I threw out Jagger and the 'Agatha Christie' band and put in blues and ballads. From morning to evening the car echoed to the gothic baritone voices of Leonard Cohen and Nick Cave or my favourite song, an immensely sad one that I had listened to hundreds of times – ZZ Top telling the story, as I understood it, of a young guy begging his girl to give him back his blue jeans. 'Give me back,' drawled the bearded sinner, 'my blue jeans, baby.' They must have had just one pair of trousers between the two of them. The girlfriend borrowed them to wear – and she's still wearing them ... That was the kind of kids' stuff I suddenly felt I needed instead of furious drums and jangling guitar riffs. My unconscious mind had obviously already realised what kind of future was in store for me, it was preparing my psyche for the stresses to come. Restructuring itself. Demanding slow harmonies in minor keys. In other words, I had a foreboding of my own downfall.

When I finished my beer and went back into the flat, my wife was already asleep. Which was just what I needed. There was obviously no place for me in the conjugal bed today. I would have to make myself comfortable on the divan, in the end room.

That night I dreamed of myself, running with fierce intensity along the wall in the exercise yard at the Lefortovo pre-trial isolation prison.

At half past seven in the morning I got up. I woke up my son. We sat down to have breakfast.

'Dad,' my seven-year-old offspring asked, 'are you a drug addict?'

'No, of course not,' I replied. 'Where did you get that idea?'

'Yesterday evening I heard mum shouting at you ...'

'She exaggerated things.'

'But what sort of people are drug addicts anyway?'

'They're people who ...' I started thinking: it's not a simple question by any means. 'Basically, they don't want to live in the real world.'

'Then what world do they live in?'

'Their own world. One they make up.'

'That's fantastic – living in a world you've made up. Just imagine the way you want it and go and live there! Great!'

'No, it's very bad,' I replied. 'How would you like it if I started to live in my own world, and mum was in hers and you were in another one of your own? That way each of us would be all on our own.'

'Well then,' my child suggested, gnawing on a biscuit, 'we have to invent one world for all three of us, for you, me and mum, and all live together in our world! Let's invent one, dad!'

'We will, definitely,' I said with a nod. 'It's time for you to go to school. Get ready.'

Once I'd seen my child off, I lay down again for a doze. I don't have to hurry to work. I don't have a job. I live on borrowed money. A year ago I borrowed a large sum from an old friend. My family doesn't go hungry. There are clothes hanging in the wardrobes. There's food in the fridge. It's only my head that's empty.

I slept until ten and got up. By this time my wife has already gone dashing off to earn money. I'm left entirely to my own devices. I have peace, solitude and a three-room flat. I have everything I need.

Calling into the toilet for a number one, I experienced that same old unpleasant moment. Marijuana is toxic, there's all sorts of filthy muck in it, the big poison draws out all the smaller and rarer ones, and every shithead's urine has a repulsive smell, it's oily, thick, dirty-yellow. Rather saddened by this circumstance, for a while I wandered from room to room in just my shorts, scratching my bare belly.

It's a spacious flat, filled with sunshine. Three rooms, a wide corridor, an immense kitchen. Hot water, steam heating, a rubbish chute. The sixteenth floor. Outside the windows – nothing but sky and wind. The rooms seem to be soaring through the air, and from this high up I can observe almost the entire city – a writhing anthill, tormented by intense passions, fidgety, bustling, nervous. Herds of cars move along the intertwining roads, labouring along sullenly in the morning, but as night-time approaches racing in insane delight, in anticipation of pleasure, leisure and entertainment.

Since the days of my early youth I have dreamed of a place to live exactly like this – bright, high up, with currents of air blowing straight through it. This is a good place for creative work, for some kind of noble intellectual effort, for bringing up children and not getting much sleep, for despising philistines and blockheads and relaxing in the evening over a cup of tea as you chat about trifling matters with the one you love; for thinking positively and delighting in the fact that you are not old, or poor, or stupid.

In this exalted philosophical mood, I got dressed. Took a thin wad of money out of its hiding place and set off along my favourite route: bookshop, magazine stall, video rental. Intellectual shopping. The search for brain food. It's always demanding something new, my brain – I don't know why. The direct route to my goal is about three hundred metres. I can even walk there. But genuine druggies are lazy. I get into the car and drive, like a real white man. And I can have a smoke at the same time ...

The district where I live is special. Officially recognised as having the best infrastructure in the capital. Created according to all the rules of modern town-planning. Every little detail of the citizens' lives has been thought through. The shops, cinemas, restaurants and clubs jostle elbows with each other, everything's new, stylish and bright.

The world that has now admitted me into itself is one which ten years earlier I had only ever seen in illustrations in western magazines. Glittering shop windows. Bright-coloured advertisement hoardings. Roads as smooth as glass. Lawns of emerald-green grass, expertly trimmed. Brightly lit, clean streets. My building is surrounded by colossal, multi-storey shopping centres the size of sports stadiums, with car parks on their roofs, with cafes and health clubs. Drive up on to the fifth floor, expend a few calories on the fourth, go on down and restore your strength in a sushi bar and dispel your boredom in a multiplex cinema centre. When my car is washed and my face is shaved, I fit very well into this picture – a picture of bourgeois neatness and carefully planned order.

The utopian City of the Sun, the megalopolis of the future, reaching up into the sky, now accepts me as a completely legitimate resident. Only it's all pointless. I feel like a passenger without a ticket. I have sneaked into the land of happiness, a casual freeloader. I didn't build the twenty-storey buildings, and I didn't put the panes of glass in the windows. I didn't pay for all this.

To get here, all I needed to do was marry a local girl. A Muscovite. After that, it all happened without me having to do a thing. One day the local girl's family arranged an exchange. A two-room flat with a view of the Kremlin was magically transformed into two three-roomed flats – but on the outskirts. And so without even raising a finger I acquired the status – just imagine it! – of a bona fide inhabitant of the capital.

A Muscovite! My God, it's almost a joke.

These square metres of comfort were not earned by me, but by my mother-in-law. It was she, not I, who laboured for decades in factories and industrial plants in order to acquire her own accommodation. In the Land of Soviets they used to be very strict about that. If you've been honestly producing added value – here's your reward. There you are, comrade, a flat in the centre of town. All yours to live in, say thank you to the party and the government …

Anyway, all that I personally could do – as a former banker, former nouveau-riche and former workaholic – was to reject my mother-in-law's present. I didn't register myself at the flat that my wife and son had moved into.

I didn't build this house. I didn't earn the money for it. I'm an underhanded lowlife who crept in through a hole in the fence.

The bookshop is a magnificent place. An abundance of market offers facing scarce effective demand. Two or three pimply-faced girls with the ample buttocks of students of the humanities leafing drearily through volumes of either Proust or Cortazar. Pale-faced juveniles avid for mind-blowing adventures from novels by Zhelyazny or Golovachyov. A couple of simpletons rustling the pages of pocket-books from the series 'Seared by the Zone'. I look carefully at them. They'll be reading me soon too. But when?

Moving to the foreign literature section, I fish out Bukovksy and Burroughs. Success. Finding these guys outside the capital is – as the shitheads say – a non-starter. Tucking the modest editions of these geniuses under one arm, I move on down into the contemporary Russia prose department, a.k.a. the ladies' section. Here I feel as if I have accidentally wandered into the ladies' toilet: any moment now there will be fragmentary glimpses of a pink body, loud squealing and the indignant exclamation: 'What are you doing in here, aren't you ashamed of yourself!' In here it smells of creams, perfumes and various lotions. Not from the books, but from the female buyers. Actually, from the books as well. The shelves here are crammed with the opuses of highly productive female prose writers. Nothing but detective novels. I retreat, disappointed. Throwing my books on to the back seat, I drive on, with Burroughs and Bukovsky as my passengers. Less boring than most company.

I have only found one obviously dubious passage in Burroughs' book *Junkie*: the American asserts that it's not possible to combine smoking grass with driving an automobile. Indeed, novice shitheads really do avoid getting behind the wheel. It seemed to me that while Burroughs might be the real authority on hard poisons, he didn't understand grass. Having a smoke and driving off is one of the pleasures of an advanced shithead's life. I've smoked dope while driving dozens of times. I've learned how to roll a joint without taking my hands off the driving wheel. Driven around and smoked. The important thing is to maintain self-control. On the road I see myself surrounded by a multitude of sluggish, excessively cautious people, and I drive like one of them. Without hurrying.

My relationship with my second passenger is complicated. If I had been born ten years later, I might have seen the world through Bukovsky's eyes. Become an evil genius who despises well-fed consumers and relishes thrusting the blade of his wit into their lard. A puking, spitting outlaw.

But that's not the way it is. My Homeland was already covered in spit and puke long before my time. By people who hadn't a clue about Bukovsky. I love my Homeland, covered in spit and puke. I hate the spit and puke that covers it. And when I find myself in a clean, brightly lit place, I delight in it. Not in the cleanness and the beauty – I don't understand much about that – no, simply in the absence of all that spit and puke.

Leave the New Russian bourgoisie alone. Let them build up their subcutaneous layer – just as long as they spit and puke less often. That's enough. I ought to know: the philistine beer-belly, buyer of home cinemas, and his opponent, the penniless, hungry writer of prose with blazing eyes – they need each other. They're brothers. Brothers in crime, if you like. The masses of the former produce the latter. Who's the winner? Both sides are. This is where the naked truth is born, the delight of God, His goal and mine.

And now here's the second point on my route – the video rental shop. I behave rather more calmly here. I watched all the best films a long time ago. The Russian ones, and the French ones, and the American ones. And I was interested to note that the Hollywood mainstream is tending towards the psychodelic, that perversion, existential hysteria, schizoid episodes and in general all kinds of morbidity are back in fashion again. Contemporary cinema chronicles the adventures of monsters. Unstable and weak-spirited characters languish and pine in search of something new. There are voluptuous descriptions of trips and blasts, the ravings of disintegrating consciousness. In all this I find a reason not to be concerned about consuming too much poison. After all, I'm not the only one. Everybody's guzzling it! Musicians and businessmen. Lawyers and bandits, writers and their characters are all busily poisoning themselves non-stop – smoking, sniffing, drinking, injecting, they can't imagine life without it. Plots revolve around poison. A small packet of powder, a syringe full of liquid, a joint of grass are de rigueur in any film. Well then, I reckon, that means it's in the order of things, and I'm not making a mistake. New, interesting and original spiritual experience is being acquired. What if, when I'm high, I'm suddenly struck by paradoxical truths that I, and only I, am destined to proclaim, and so turn the entire universe inside out?

But no: my ego has ceased to attract ideas to itself, my imagination refuses to produce anything creative.

Thinking in this key, I travel home, cutting diagonally through the beauty and cleanliness of my district, with a light heart and a light purse. Yes, spiritual nourishment turns out to be far more expensive than the physical kind. The creative intellectuals are unwilling to sell off their products cheap. They push up the prices. Six dollars for a new book by a fashionable writer. Ten for a DVD of the latest film. Five for a glossy magazine. No change from a twenty note.

But I'm not upset. This kind of pricing policy suits me. Let society pay! Let it get used to paying. The more dollars a lazy bourgeois pays for a little book, the more rusty kopecks the author will end up with. Let them pay, screw them. And I'll pay along with all the rest. It's all right. I understand what it is I'm spending very nearly my last kopecks on.

I shall go on buying books in any case. No matter how much they cost.

Today I have gin and tonic.

I start with no haste or fuss. I start with a first dose of fifty grams – always on an empty stomach. The doctors tell us that drinking strong spirits before eating is extremely harmful. But it's effective! The next fifty grams go with a cigarette and a cup of strong coffee. By five o'clock, having dined, blissfully inebriated, I pack my joints and start smoking. Magically, sweetly, I drift away. I settle down on the divan, between the TV and the music centre, put a tray holding bottles and glasses on the floor, move up the ashtray, slowly inhale the stupefying smoke and soar off into the realms of purple phantoms. To where the sacred power of Jah will come to me.

I feel good. The way I feel is rapidly converging with the ideal.

For the time being I have money. Enough to last another couple of months. After that I'll think of something. I'll come up with something remarkable, exceptionally clever. Some absolutely brilliant plan. Every shithead is convinced that he's a genius. I'm no exception.

I observe the people on the TV screen, and laugh good-naturedly every now and then. The people seem to me to be stupid, bogged down in petty concerns. They scurry and bustle like sparrows pecking breadcrumbs. Amusing creatures, sparrows; and people too.

I grip another roll-up between my slobbery lips, in order to receive further confirmation that I am better and cleverer than everyone else.

I am farsighted and perspicacious. In intellectual terms, I have scaled unprecedented heights. In emotional terms I am stable. I am wise and laconic. I am great.

From the divan I crawl into the bathroom – I have a TV and an ashtray in there too. After prison I acquired the habit of soaking for hours in the hot water, between the bluish tiled walls.

The contact of the liquid with my body triggers a momentary shudder, and a conjecture is born in my mind: what if the urge to immerse myself in a warm substance is an indication that I am infantile? And subconsciously I am striving to return to the comfort of my mother's womb? What if I only appear to be an adult, but in fact I'm a little boy?

A grown man takes a shower; he has not time for wallowing in a trough of aromatic liquid. 'Okay,' I think, immediately granting myself permission, 'you have a moral right to that too.'

I make the water very hot. I lie down in it first, and then I turn the handles until steam starts rising from the surface. This is a compulsory ritual I have borrowed from the Strugatsky brothers' novel *Predatory Things of the Century*. The main characters in the book take narcotics with their bodies immersed in hot water. I try to recreate the original experience. Create, invent, try – that is my motto.

I have re-read all my favourite books while on a high. The Strugatsky brothers' fantastic anti-utopia simply blew me away. I have decided that when I get my million (every shithead thinks that riches are just around the corner, the million will be made or, at least, found in the street), I shall acquire the rights to the screen adaptation of *Predatory Things* and make a mid-blowing blockbuster. And become famous. A success. A celebrity. Great. Unique. Underline as required.

In Russian slang what I'm using is called 'plan'. Obviously because junkies love to make plans.

Ah, and there's the magazine. What could be more amusing than the bright-coloured pictures, the advertisements for watches, shoes, colognes? The thick pages seem to have been created especially for turning with wet hands. That classy smell of expensive printing. The 'new' section. Eight straight pages of new music albums. Another five pages of computer games. Followed by the book review: about thirty lines, in small print, at the bottom of a column.

The main feature of the issue is an interview with a rising star of the big screen. A pale-faced brunette with the sharp, pointy knees of a mean bitch. It's not clear from the text whether the star is playing in a movie or just playing the field. The photograph is set in an interior: a navel, a skinny shoulder, lips. Predatory fingers. Little breasts. The brown nipples protruding through transparent silk are gun barrels aimed at the foreheads of producers. And the boyfriend beside her, in décolleté. A sweet little boy in a little designer fur jacket.

If the glossy can be believed, the time of hairy macho men with square, stubbley chins is over and done, never to return. As an example for imitation, young men are now being offered a slender youth with plump lips, skin-tight trousers and angelic curls. I wonder what would happen if you stuck an automatic rifle in the hands of someone like that and asked him to defend the Homeland against the enemy? 'Oh, come on,' he would say, 'I don't have any enemies, and my Homeland is the entire world!' Then at least defend your own home against bandits, terrorists and evil men! 'Oh, come now, the police are there for that.'

I find the number of narrow-chested young lads with dyed curls and rings in their ears surprising, it seems excessive. Especially after prison. Everybody knows that the slightest hint at decoration of the male body is regarded quite unambiguously there. But never mind – I may have a criminal record, but there's no way I'm homophobic.

The glossy is beautiful, but fantastically banal. Once I've leafed through it, I toss it aside.

I love a different kind of periodical. An old kind, from my childhood. My yellowed folders of the publication *Technology for Young People* from the late seventies and early eighties. That magazine made me. It revealed the world to me and explained it. I have managed to preserve several complete annual sets and now, twenty-five years later, there's nothing I find more interesting than leafing through them while I smoke dope.

I immediately call to mind the ten-year-old boy Andriusha, dreaming passionately of getting into the pilot's seat in a spaceship, stabbing through the cosmos and conquering a couple of unknown planets, to the delight of all progressive humanity.

Magazines like that didn't amuse, they didn't sell brand-name trash. They prepared me for great doings. Create, invent, try – that's where I got it.

The party and the government followed little Andriusha's growth attentively. Together with the growth of several million boys in the Land of Soviets. Special books and magazines were printed for them. Writers, poets and artists laboured unceasingly on images of the bright future. Andriusha knew exactly what he had to do. He learned his social role off by heart. He understood that he was going to work cheerfully and stubbornly, despising comfort and convenience, feeling neither hunger nor cold. For people's good.

It is perfectly clear that the Lefortovo prison was not where Andriusha became an iron warrior. He had already done that by the age of twenty. By that time he had devoured hundreds of books and magazines, and they were full of the assertion that the happiest people on Earth were warriors and fighters, heroes. They were surrounded with honour, they were loved by girls, they were an example to children.

Ah, you fools! You blind fools! Back then I was ready, and so were thousands of others like me! Just say to us: lads, pack your things, you'll need your shorts and soap, we're flying to Mars, to Jupiter, up the devil's own backside, no one's coming back – and we would have gone and taken that flight! But nobody said it. There is no Party now, and all the magazines write about queers, not outer space. And the trained heroes are not sent to Mars, but to a pre-trial detention centre.

I scrambled out of the bath, walked over to one of the mirrors and studied my naked, steaming body.

That little mirror in Lefortovo has remained fixed in my mind for ever. After prison I contracted the ailment of narcissism, although only in its very mildest and most innocent form. In my home there are five large mirrors. As I wander round the flat – from the kitchen to the sitting room, then out on to balcony and back again – I can always see how I look from the outside. The only problem is that there's nothing worth looking at. The reflection in the magical looking-glass is not the nouveau-riche Andriukha or the running bull of Lefortovo and not even really a human being, but a stooped, twisted monkey with sloping shoulders.

My face has swollen up. All shitheads have excess moisture in their face, it is retained in the cheeks, below the eyes. It saddens me to see such things, and I decide to down another hundred grams.

After that I glide along, swaying, enveloped in a dense, honeyed cloud of alcoholic dreams. Sad and pensive. Reality seems no more than a flickering light, an amusing film, all about me. As I watch this film I smile in astonishment. I smoke a second joint and feel myself enveloped in a dark-grey blanket of pleasure. Reality caresses me like warm moss. I find myself exceptionally likeable. My lips fold into a thin, crooked grin, and I set out on a ravishing trip through a sequence of rainbow-coloured galaxies, through an entire garland of fun worlds.

I am as quick as the thought of a genius and relaxed as a muscle of an enlightened Zen master.

I would become as sober and resolute as stone, but I cannot see any point.

I would write a book or ten books, but the benefits of the process escape me.

I would earn millions, or create a new science, or lead humankind to the ultimate, icy, naked truth – but I am too lazy.

I want to love all human beings, every one that there is, slowly and sweetly, but they do not accept my love. They say I have lost my way, that I'm a primitive drug addict and alcoholic. They're probably right.

Ask me what happened to the furious fool positively bursting out of his cell in Lefortovo in his effort to achieve a ludicrous perfection of spirit and body, and I shall reply: nothing happened to him. He is still there. He found something, but then dismissed his discovery with easy disdain.

I remember that Lefortovo inmate now as a naïve apologist of fairytales about the perfection of human nature.

I would become great – but fuck greatness.

I would become a psychic, a hypersensitive ascetic, a master of the extrasensory. But fuck the extrasensory. Everything in the world is a transitory dream; only poisons are real.

The early evening is a difficult time. My son comes home from school. I immediately send him out into the yard – to avoid displaying my drunken features to the kid. While the boy is kicking a ball around with his friends, I drink coffee, gulp down aspirin, furiously rinse out my foul-smelling mouth with a special minty mouthwash. I apply ice to my cheeks, my nose and the bags under my eyes. At the same time I open all the windows. The ashtrays must be shaken out! The empty poison containers must go down the rubbish chute! The glasses, large and small, must be washed! Aromatic candles must be lit! The flat and its inhabitant acquire a respectable appearance.

I'm not an alcoholic or drug addict, surely? I am quite simply a laid-back shithead. A harmless consumer of colour TV.

My son comes back. I feed him his supper. I put him to bed. After all that running around n the fresh air, the little lad falls asleep straight away.

I have a gypsy family: the wife is out earning money, the husband is at home, keeping house. What's wrong with that?

And, by the way, it wouldn't do me any harm to swallow a bit of oxygen. For that all I have to do is take several steps out on to the balcony. The evening city, ablaze with points of light, is beautiful. Its citizens dash along. In a hurry to have fun. Life is short, but their purses are full. Ah, what an unbearable urge I feel to shout to all of them from my vantage point forty metres up:

'Consume poisons, gentlemen! Let your stomachs, lungs and nostrils rejoice! May the great power of Jah be with you! Consume, and the truth will be revealed. Gorge yourself on poisons – and you shall behold the meaning of all that happens to man. Man has the freedom to destroy himself. Elegantly, aesthetically, glamorously. No one can kill him better than he himself. The guillotine killed five thousand. The electric chair has killed ten thousand. Poisons kill entire peoples. All hail to that which kills us! Long live the infinitude of human fantasy! Let us destroy ourselves in the very best way possible – beautifully, like adults, usefully, with humour, with an understanding of our goals.

'It was the communists who gave birth to me. But I matured and grew strong in a collective of animals where each seeks his own benefit and his own turn-on, the best poison. I was called to penetrate the dark mystery of space, but was led to a devious gaming table. Well then, I placed my bet and I even won! How should I dispose of my winnings? Buy poisons! To consume myself and to offer to my friends. Let us gorge ourselves on them, my friends, and we shall behold the light! And the truth! The world is poison, take it and kill yourself. Snort. Shoot. Drink. Smoke. Swallow and suck. Moisten with spittle. Breathe in. Rub in. Relish. Appreciate!

'Do not hurry – the distant, icy planets will wait, the spacesuits will be patient, the meteorite showers will fall without you.'

The closer it gets to the time for my wife's return home, the more alarmed I feel. Genuine shitheads are always very sensitive. Their conscience torments them with guilt for what they do to others. Suddenly an original idea was born. I took some more money and dashed – almost at a run – to the nearest twenty-four-hour supermarket. Made the necessary purchases. When my beloved came back from work, the flat was already filled with an unusual, spicy, slightly tart smell.

'Hi there, my love,' I said. 'I have a surprise for you.'

At ten o'clock in the evening my love looked exhausted, but she was still the most beautiful woman in the world. Her husband, however, was even more exhausted. All day long he had been smoking grass, drinking and contemplating the eternal: he was exceedingly tired. He had cooked supper, as children say, when he was 'totally pooped'.

'You're drunk again,' Irma remarked without any emotion.

'Maybe so,' I declared triumphantly, tugging up my trousers. 'But anyway, today we have *fondue*!'

'What?'

'Fondue. Please come through into the kitchen! You see before you the national dish of Swiss cuisine. World famous. A classic. Made with cheese.'

My tongue suddenly stumbled treacherously. The final words sounded sluggish. It was a reminder from my friends, gin and tonic.

'With cheese?' my wife queried.

'Precisely!' I replied proudly. 'With cheese.'

'Where did you learn to cook it?'

'In prison, naturally. A certain Swiss citizen explained the subtle points to me. He taught me the theory.'

'What was a Swiss citizen doing in a Russian prison?'

'I'll tell you some other time. Later. But right now, please take a seat at the table.'

The table looked impressive. Romantic. Roses languishing in a tall vase. Lighted candles. A mixture of melted cheeses gurgling and bubbling in a nickel-plated bowl with the flame of a spirit lamp flickering intimately below it, gently warming the viands. A bottle of dry red awaiting its fate. At the sides – special forks elegantly arranged. I knew that the setting looked magnificent, and straightened my shoulders proudly in anticipation.

'There …'

'Aha,' my wife said in a funereal voice, keeping her keen eyes fixed on me. 'Fondue, then, is it? What's the occasion?'

'No occasion,' I replied modestly.

'And what am I supposed to do?'

'Sit down. Right here. It's melted cheese. You dip a piece of bread into it. We stick it on a fork like this, we dip it in like this and eat it, washing it all down with wine …'

The longer I carried on holding forth, the stonier my wife's face became. She wasn't looking at the table, she was looking at me. Her plump lower lip curled in disdain.

But she did sit down – I moved up a chair for her – and she picked up a fork.

'Can I eat it without the wine?'

'Certainly,' I assured her magnanimously. 'But it's better with wine …'

'Yes,' my wife said with a nod, surveying my puffy features. 'I can see it's better with wine.'

'No comments, please!' I blurted out drunkenly. 'With your permission, I shall continue. In this plate are the greens. Coriander, dill, parsley. A green salad. That is my own addition. To create a bouquet, so to speak, of sensations …'

'I understand.'

Sitting down facing her, I turned down the flame of the spirit lamp.

'What are you waiting for? Aren't you hungry?'

'Yes,' the woman answered in a dull voice. 'Very hungry. But all this is just another trick.'

'What exactly?'

'This,' said my wife, pointing to a candlestick. 'And this. And this. A cunning and beautiful trick. Did you think your fondue would stop me noticing that you're as drunk as a skunk again?'

I didn't answer.

'I'm not a fool any longer. I got wise while you were inside. When I had no more tears left to cry. And now I do two jobs and study in college as well. You're as drunk as a skunk. And you've been smoking grass again. I can smell it …'

I sat there without speaking, with my eyes fixed on the table, but occasionally raising my glance to admire the beauty of her wrath.

'This can't go on any longer! I married a different man. That man didn't smoke and he didn't drink vodka. He didn't wander round the flat, shuffling his feet like an old man. Only yesterday you were telling me about the crooked spines in prison, but what about you? You walk like an old-age pensioner! You stare down at the ground in front of your feet. You're a pitiful sight! You almost destroyed me and our son once – when you went into prison. Now if you carry on drinking like this, you will destroy us. I'm sorry, I can't eat.'

She pushed her chair back and stood up – erect and proud, with wondrous lightning-bolts shooting from her eyes. Suddenly the fire was extinguished and she calmed down. The flowers and candles had pleased her after all, I realised.

'The last time,' my wife said, 'you promised me you wouldn't drink any more. That was yesterday, right?'

'Yes, yesterday.'

'And it was the same the day before, right?'

'Yes …'

'And a week ago as well. Every day I hear you swear to stop, and then everything carries on in the same old way. You must think I'm a fool. All the time you're thinking: I can always wind my stupid woman, round my little finger … With a few flowers and lovely suppers … Here's some fondue for you, my darling.'

As she said that, she carefully picked up the wooden dish holding the green salad and turned it over onto my head.

Herbs and leaves tumbled down on to my shoulders in a green waterfall. The parsley got stuck on my ears. The finely chopped dill adhered to my forehead. Rivulets of cold water ran down my neck. My shirt was soaked.

'Thank you for supper,' my wife said quietly and left me there alone.

And that, gentlemen, is how it came about that in the course of a single month a certain former banker was struck on the forehead with a mobile phone and another banker of the same ilk had a plate of dill tipped over his head. And both of them thought they had got off lightly.

The evening did not end there. No sooner had I removed the little stems and leaves from my ears and the back of my head than the phone rang. The voice that began speaking in the receiver was the one I wanted to hear least of all in the world.

'Andrei?'

'Yes, it's me …'

'And this is me.'

'Hi.'

'What's happening about my money?'

'Nothing.'

'What do you mean, nothing? I lent you it for three months, and now it's almost a year already. Have you decided to swindle me?'

A genuine shithead never hides the harsh truth from anyone. I sighed and confessed:

'I can't pay you back. I don't have any money.'

'None at all, you mean?'

'Absolutely none,' I confirmed in a funereal voice. 'And nowhere to get it from.'

The other man paused before speaking.

'I see. So you've decided to build up your subcutaneous layer at my expense?'

'No,' I said, about to make excuses, but I was interrupted.

'Tomorrow morning I expect to see you here in my office!'

'I'll be there,' I replied and cut off the call.

In the morning it was, then. And let it be in the office. Everything comes to an end sometime. My carefree life as a shithead was obviously going to come to an end tomorrow.

PART THREE

22

When I stepped inside the cell, I thought at first that the prison authorities had decreed I was to be alone again. The 'hut' was virginally clean and appeared uninhabited. But only a moment later my eyes picked out a remarkably small man, seated on the corner of the blue blanket (prison property) with his sharp little knees tucked up to his chin.

The door slammed shut behind me with a resounding crash.

For a while the tiny prisoner gazed fixedly at my fists, mutilated by hundreds of blows, repeated day after day, against the stone floors of the exercise yards. I sensed a brief but powerful surge of fright that was almost panic. I knew my fists were a frightening sight, with shreds of skin dangling from the knuckles and clots of brown, congealed blood. And there were long scratches running across my wrists.

'Andriukha!' I said, declaring my identity in a vigorous manner, trying to project the sounds from the centre of my chest so that my voice would sound low and substantial.

'Gigorii Iosifovich Berger,' the man said very politely, then he got up in a rapid but dignified manner and held out a hand no bigger than a pack of cigarettes. Like a violin bow charged with rosin, his voice was spiced with an indeterminate Western European accent. 'Pleased to meet you! Do come in and make yourself comfortable …'

I instantly realised that I was not facing a vicious and aggressive man. And he was clearly a novice jailbird. Our life together promised to be conflict-free and mutually agreeable.

My new cell-mate's clothing consisted of a tee-shirt and a filthy pair of trousers – formerly light-coloured summer slacks made from an expensive cotton-polyester mix; trousers like that look great for the first few months of use, but in Grigorii Iosifovich's case they were more like an absolutely threadbare, shapeless sack with a sagging backside and a thick sprinkling of greasy stains.

The little man was scarcely more than a metre and a half tall. His little face was puffy and colourless, covered all over with a network of wrinkles and topped with sparse hair, the length and colour of which reminded me of a toilet brush.

'Where would you be from then?' I asked to get the process of getting to know each other started.

'I'm a Swiss citizen,' Grigorii Iosifovich replied simply. 'I have been here for five months. Since the middle of summer. I was picked up for smuggling drugs ...'

'Heavy stuff,' I said appreciatively. 'Five months? And in this hut all the time?'

The small man's eyes were small too. And very intelligent.

'No,' the miniature smuggler replied. 'This is my fourth cell already.'

'I don't suppose you happened to share with Frol and Fatty?'

'I'm afraid not ...'

We both said nothing for a moment.

'Am I right in thinking that they are you former cell-mates?' the Swiss citizen asked cautiously.

'Aha.'

'I beg your pardon, but would it be possible for me to treat myself to one of your remarkable cigarettes?'

'No hassle,' I said, holding out the pack. 'That is, by all means.'

The little man savoured the nicotine with obvious pleasure.

'Clearly,' he said, settling back on to his blanket and drawing his knees up to his narrow chest, 'you are unaware that this prison has a special computer and it ... uses a special program to draw up a schedule for the movement of inmates so that no two men who have ever shared a cell will ever cross paths with the previous cell-mates of their present cohabitants ... My explanation isn't too muddled, I hope?'

'No.'

'That is, this program scatters every detained suspect into the general mass of inmates and, once having encountered any individual, not only will you never meet him again, you will never meet anyone who knows him …'

'I get it,' I said with a nod. 'I twig. That is, I understand what you're saying.'

Grigorii Iosifovich from Switzerland smiled and nodded.

The relief I experienced felt just like jumping into warm water. I was lucky. My new cell-mate was a cultured man. Now I would occupy all the free space in the cell, just as Frol used to do. I would stride backwards and forwards for hours at a time. I would get washed under the tap, build up my muscles, read books, make notes on textbooks and generally do whatever I wanted. My cell-mate was a cultured man. He would understand me. He would always give way to me, he would adopt a peaceful attitude, respect my point of view. And apart from that, his physical presence was so diminutive that in principle it could be ignored.

'How, if you don't mind me asking, do you happen to know that?' I enquired cautiously. 'About the computer that "scatters" the inmates?'

'Well, you see,' my new acquaintance said rather shyly, 'as it happens, I used to be a criminal lawyer. I practiced for almost ten years. And once, a very long time ago, I came to this institution, not as a detainee, but as a defence lawyer … Of course, computers weren't in use here then … But the principle of scattering was already being applied …'

I was deliriously happy that the person I had beside me was a normal, adequate human being, unspoiled by prison, and I revelled in the most innocent and insignificant phrases that we carried on exchanging while I settled into my new place – laying out my mattress and blanket, standing my books on the shelves, setting out my notebooks. Now that I was back in a familiar linguistic environment, I realised just how barbaric I had become in only about ninety days.

Undoubtedly, during the initial minutes of our cohabitation, Grigorii Iosifovich was a little afraid of me. I was taller than him, broader in the shoulders and more athletic. But as soon as I stopped using prison jargon and went back to the best Russian language – the language of Pushkin and Gogol, the three Tolstoys, Bunin, Nabokov and Aksyonov – which, truth to tell, was the language I had used all my conscious life, then Grisha the Swiss relaxed, became animated, began smiling and asked me ceremoniously for a spoonful of instant coffee. And we started socialising.

Grigorii Iosifovich Berger had no relatives or friends anywhere in the entire Commonwealth of Independent States. He didn't receive any food parcels. In the chilly mid-autumn he was wearing the same clothes as he had in summer, at the time of his arrest. He survived on just the prison skilly. He only smoked tobacco if someone else was put in a cell with him – as in my case. Under the influence of strong tea with chocolate and a menthol-light cigarette with a double carbon filter the Swiss citizen's speech flowed in a smooth, lively stream.

The next hour passed in light, friendly conversation that imposed no obligations on anyone. We talked about Swiss cheese, about Swiss watches, about Swiss bankers, about Swiss chocolate. About Viennese opera. About Munich beer. About Dutch tulips.

The walls of Lefortovo had probably never before heard such fluent and elegant dialogues. Words and turns of phrase that I had completely forgotten over the preceding three months – 'thank you', 'please', 'with the greatest pleasure', 'bon appetit', 'pardon me', 'excuse me', 'I'm afraid I cannot agree with you' – now flew backwards and forwards from one prisoner to the other with unforced ease.

At lunch I augmented the fish soup with several pieces of salami – the very salami that Fatty had given me – and also some cheese and vegetables. That made the Swiss drugs courier really cheerful. Even the wrinkles on his pink face seemed to smooth out.

Before it was time for supper he told me his story.

When he began practicing law in the middle of the bleak 1970s, Kharkov University graduate Grisha Berger realised almost immediately that he would never earn either money or a reputation by working for thieves who stole chickens from collective farms and devotees of drunken knife fights. Undoubtedly, in the Land of Soviets there were at that time talented cat-burglars, fraudsters who had accumulated hoards of gold, major con-men and arch-crooks, and some of these actually turned up among his clients but, to Grisha's chagrin, all of them regarded prison as their natural home. Once they ended up inside, the thieves and conmen knew in advance that it was for a long stretch and no lawyer, no matter how much you paid him, would transform the statutory seven years into three. But the thieves and con-men did like to get out of their stinking cells for an appointment, to sit in a bright, cool office and chew the fat with their lawyer, while smoking the filter cigarettes that he had brought and chewing on chocolates, or sometimes even a chicken leg.

This was where Grisha discovered his own little Klondike. He began charging a small fixed fee for each visit to a client and he took in everything, including money, letters from relatives and notes with instructions from associates who were still at liberty. Naturally, such services were illegal, and if he were ever caught, Grisha would be in trouble. He already knew of one case in which a certain well-to-do criminal had a meeting with his lawyer one day and ran into him the next day in one of the prison corridors. 'What are you doing here?' the astonished old lag asked. 'Getting my mattress,' the lawyer replied gloomily ... Grisha knew he was taking a risk. But it was part of the business he had chosen! He brought in vodka – in rubber hot-water bottles – and also, in special cases, drugs, up to and including cocaine, which in those naïve times was also known in certain places as sniff. Rumours about a daring lawyer who would even carry a hydrogen bomb into prison (the neutron bomb hadn't been invented yet) for a modest remuneration spread from the White Sea to the Black. Grisha raised the prices for his services and became selective in his choice of clients. His star rose high. He shuttled between Kiev, Peter, Moscow and Tbilisi and was in great demand everywhere.

Eventually his services were requested by the extremely famous foreign currency speculator Radchenko, who was being held in the Kresty prison at the time. Many well-informed people ranked his CASE along with the CASE of Rokotov and Faibishenko, and with good reason. Radchenko was a morphine user, and on his fifth day of appalling withdrawal symptoms he ordered his personal lawyer Faifman, Ph.D (Law), in an agonised whisper to get a dose into the pre-trial isolation centre for him any way it could be done. Or to find someone else who would do it. Grisha was soon sitting facing the happy currency speculator after carrying five grams of powder through extremely strict security in his own back passage. The two remarkable professionals found that their personalities clicked and the outcome was that Radchenko invited Grisha to take part in a unique project.

The hard-currency super-hero had a fortune of about a million dollars and he had come up with the idea of using reliable people to export his entire capital into the world of hard cash, with the intention of subsequently escaping himself by calmly accepting his sentence and being sent off to the camps in the 'zone', escaping and leaving the USSR by crossing the border between Azerbaijan and Turkey. Grisha was supposed to leave the Soviet Union to settle permanently abroad, supposedly heading for Israel, taking out with him three hundred thousand dollars worth of diamonds, but stop when he reached Austria and put some of the stones in a bank deposit box, sell the rest and put the hard currency he got for them in a deposit account in the bank.

For the execution of this complex and arduous project, behind which Grisha seemed to see the shade of the Soviet literary hero Ostap Bender, the hard-currency specialist offered the Swiss lawyer a hundred thousand dollars. Grisha immediately accepted. Soon after that the millionaire was given fourteen years and left for the taiga in the Krasnoyarsk region.

Grisha took the diamonds out using a well-known convict method. Four months before his departure he took a scalpel and slit open the skin on his leg below the knee, cutting right along the bone, and set the stones into his own flesh. When the time came to cross the state border, the pink scar was no longer bothering the intrepid lawyer.

He decided not to go into any banks in frivolous Austria, but got into a bus and rode straight to Zurich, where he scrupulously carried out all of Radchenk's instructions and began living in warmth and comfort, every day remembering the literary hero Ostap and his phrase: 'The idiot's dreams have come true …'

At this Grisha Berger pulled up his trouser leg and showed me the scar on his leg: a long, narrow, old weal below the knee joint, between the bone and the flesh of the calf muscle.

I screwed up my eyes respectfully.

'Let us be friends,' the little Swiss citizen proposed.

'No problemo, bruv,' I said with a nod. 'I mean, certainly, my old mate!'

Meanwhile Radchenko suffered a crushing failure. He settled into the camp and for two years artfully disguised himself as a plain, ordinary convict, ecstatically devoting himself to the process of reform. Eventually he was moved from general work duty into the library. After he had managed to accumulate seven kilograms of sugar, he soaked several wafer towels in thick syrup for a month, fattened up a cat with choice mixed fats and then, on one desolate evening, he set off into the terrible Siberian taiga.

He ran for two days, hardly even stopping at all, clasping a glucose-soaked towel between his teeth. When his pursuers almost caught up with him and he could the barking of the dogs, Radchenko took the cat out from under his coat, clipped the claws off all four of its feet with a grinding tool and let it go. The woolly-brained dogs preferred the provocative aroma of cat to the sour smell of Radchenko, and the pursuit turned aside, just as planned. The cat ran for its life for days. With no claws, it couldn't exploit the traditional refuge from dogs up in the trees, so it was obliged to run until its strength was exhausted and it died of a heart attack, and soon after that its body was torn to shreds by the hounds. Radchenko realised he had got away. The pursuers went back to the zone, where the convicts very nearly rebelled in their delight that at last they had a criminal hero who had shafted the narks in every orifice.

Once he reached Krasnoyarsk, Radchenko turned up at the apartment of an old friend who was supposed to help him with ID and money for the journey to Azerbaijan. But then the human factor came into play. The old friend let the fugitive in, fed him and watered him and put him to bed, then phoned the KGB. Radchenko had three years added to his sentence for the escape.

When he heard this terrible news from reliable people, Grisha Berger started thinking hard. The hundred thousand that had seemed such a prodigious fortune in the Land of Soviets was clearly less impressive here. Grisha's standard of living was not much better than that of the concierge Gustav, a good-for-nothing old alcoholic who worked in the building where Berger rented an apartment. Eventually the safe containing Radchenko's diamonds was unsealed and several large stones were extracted – and they restored Grisha's finances. He began living quietly and cosily again, contriving fine holidays for himself in the form of trips to Holland, where he could freely buy and smoke super-strong dope.

Suddenly the trickle of news arriving from Moscow became a turbulent stream. One after another, as their time came, several extremely aged leaders were buried. Perestroika began. Berger now saw his former compatriots on the streets of Geneva more and more often. Surly and grotesquely dressed, they looked like savages. The only German they knew was 'Hände hoch' and their French was limited to 'Je ne mange pas six jours' (greetings once again to the great Ostap Bender). But even so, their wallets were tightly packed and there were two things they wanted in Switzerland – to buy a Swiss watch and open an account in a Swiss bank.

Grisha realised that another gold rush was begging for his attention. He opened an office, hired some smart helpers and went into business, providing the Russian visitors with consultations concerning the differences between investment banks and savings banks, or debit cards and credit cards. A year later he was already thriving, but then another piece of news totally floored him. Radchenko had made another attempt to escape, he had been caught again and had another three years added to his sentence. This is fate, Grisha realised: he took out Radchenko's money, entrusted the business to his smart assistants and began mastering the magical path of the European playboy. The snobs on France's Côte d'Azure could often see him helping girls into his snow-white Porsche Carrera and roaring off with them to Holland (six hours of furious driving along the autobahns), where he indulged ever more frequently, not only in smoking hashish, but in dropping LSD, or acid, which was becoming fashionable.

It was all just like a fairytale, until one day there came a ring at the door of Grisha's Geneva apartment. Standing there on the doorstep he saw an old, old man with an appallingly gaunt face the same colour as the bottom of a dirty ashtray and deep-sunk, piercing eyes.

'Don't you recognise me?' the old man asked in the manner of the university docent from the popular Soviet film, and hissed through his teeth in the same manner.

Although he didn't actually have any teeth, or any hair either.

'Yes,' Berger replied tersely and let Radchenko into his apartment.

It turned out that perestroika had been a benefactor, not only to the Swiss lawyer, but also to the Siberian convict. One day they had summoned him to the special section and briefly explained that in the Russian Federation the buying and selling of hard currency was no longer regarded as a crime. Then what have I been doing time for, Radchenko asked in surprise. For escaping, they told him. But now leave. You may go, as they say.

Grisha proved equal to the challenge. He instantly paid for a course of treatment in a fashionable Berne sanatorium, including a dietician, a masseur, a dentist, a solarium and so on and so forth. While Radchenko was recovering his health, the Porsche and the apartment in Zurich were both sold. Grisha paid him back in full, down to the last dollar, including interest on the deposit accounts – and was left with absolutely nothing. He still had the consultancy business, but his smart assistants had turned out not to be so very smart after all, and had gradually run the business into the ground while Grisha was drifting around the Benelux countries in a marijuana haze. The competitors spawned by a fifth wave of emigrants drove the final nails into his business's coffin.

Having received his money, Radchenko paid for a second course of treatment in the same sanatorium, and then for a third. The institution's nurses, all elderly, severe Fraus, stopped being frightened by the sight of the exotic tattoos covering the prison camp veteran's exhausted flesh. They offered to remove all of Radchenko's body art with a laser, leaving only his favourite tattoo – two ships on his arms, just above the wrists. Each ship symbolised one of his escape attempts. At the weekends Radchenko left the sanatorium – he had acquired a liking for taxi-trips to Amsterdam, where he would smoke a sweet joint in a coffee shop and then ramble through the red light district. And that was where he died – less than three months after leaving the prison camp. No doubt from an overdose of happiness.

Where his money was kept remained a secret.

This cosmic injustice plunged Grisha Berger into a profound depression and he became an acid junky. He started making ends meet by doing odd jobs and disappearing from view for six months at a time in Amsterdam. Then some of his friends introduced him to an easy way of getting rich: as well as taking acid himself, he could take it into Russia for sale.

Grisha bought the goods, got himself a ticket on a steamer to Peter and went back to the Motherland.

The Motherland welcomed the prodigal son into her stern embrace: he was picked up on the third day.

'Well, what do you think of her?' I asked

'I beg you pardon, of whom?'

'The Motherland. After so many years away from her.'

Grisha shrugged.

'I can't say that it's all total *scheise*. There are some things I like and some things I don't. It's hard to give an answer straight away … And anyway, I was high all the time until they arrested me. They tell me,' he said, suddenly brightening up, 'that I missed all the most interesting things! Is it true that tanks once actually came into Moscow and fired at the Kremlin?'

'Not just once, but twice,' I corrected him benignly, taking out the bundle of tea that Frol had given me. 'And not at the Kremlin. At the White House. That's very different. Quite different, in fact. How about a shot of chifir?'

'No thank you,' said Grisha, shaking his head. 'Caffeine is a low-class drug.'

'But I like it. It peps you up, you know … And there's no other poison to be had around here anyway.'

'By the way …' Grisha began and paused. 'There's one thing I'm curious about … Who was hanged for it, anyway?'

'Hanged?' I asked in amazement. 'What do you mean, who was hanged?'

'Well, if things went as far as tanks driving right into Moscow, the culprits must have been hanged for it afterwards ...'

I smiled, but then realised that basically Grisha was right, and I replied morosely:

'In all those years of perestroika, no one was hanged. They stood the entire country on its head, then turned it back on to its feet again, plundered it three times over, ripped it off five times over, swindled it ten times over, but they didn't hang anyone. Not a single person. They didn't cut off any heads, they didn't set anyone on the stake, they didn't rip out anyone's nostrils, or quarter anyone, or break them on the wheel, or shoot them ...'

The little Swiss settled himself more comfortably, with an expression of extreme curiosity on his face.

'*Mon Dieu*, but who answered for all of this?'

'No one.'

'That doesn't happen,' the Swiss citizen declared confidently. 'For instance, the Germans tried Honecker with great pomp and ceremony. The Czechs declared the communists outlaws. The Bulgarians installed a public toilet in Georgii Dimitrov's mausoleum. The Rumanians executed Ciaoscescu and his wife. What happened here?'

'Nothing like that,' I replied.

'What about the high priests of the party?' little Grisha persisted. 'The *führers*? The *parteigenossen*? The Central Committee of the party? The ideologists? What happened to them?'

'Well, they wouldn't go hanging and shooting each other would they? What for? They sat down calmly and came to an agreement. Now every one of them has his own bank. They bank money the same way they always did. So the Central Committee of the Communist Party of the Soviet Union is alive and well. And feeling just great ...'

I blow into my mug and took a long, noisy gulp. The taste of the wretched penitentiary high suddenly gave me a sweet, sad feeling. My heart started pounding. My vision went slightly out of focus. I frowned and took another gulp.

Such is life – yesterday you were drinking Chivas Regal, and today it's chifir. Or perhaps this isn't life, but some idiotic slapstick comedy in which you are the clown and the spectator at the same time? And also the ticket-seller for your own fiendish circus.

'But that doesn't shock me,' I went on. 'My mother and father were communists. Not fanatics. Ordinary rank and file members of the party. If not for perestroika, I would have owned a party card too. Only not, mind you, out of purely careerist considerations, but because I believe that communist ideology is progressive.'

'Yes,' Grisha said pensively. 'I probably lived in Europe for too long ...'

I took another swallow.

'Perhaps. By the way, what do you think – is Russia Europe or Asia?'

The little Swiss burst into silent laughter.

'Have you been to Europe?'

'Never,' I answered regretfully.

'Go,' Grisha advised me. 'And you'll be able to answer your own question ...'

I turned sour and gloomy.

'I have to be let out of prison first.'

'That's inevitable, *mon cher.*'

'I hope so.'

'I, for instance, am certain that they will let me go soon,' the little man said in a voice that trembled very badly. 'Or the sentence they give will only be a short one. Yes, I brought narcotics in. Yes, I'm guilty. But I know they won't give me a long sentence ...'

'But why are you telling me about the drugs,' I asked. 'What if I'm a stool pigeon? What if I'm a plant?'

Grisha gave a cautious smile.

'Hardly, *mein kamerad.* My previous cell-mate was an obvious plant ... He had nothing at all ... He didn't receive any food parcels ... Two previous convictions ... but you're wearing a five-hundred-dollar tracksuit and four-hundred-dollar shoes ... And you behave like a prosperous young man from a good family ... Don't forget that I used to be a lawyer, even if it was a long time ago. I've seen plenty of militia informers. Any educated man with some intelligence can spot an informer in three minutes, believe me! And in any case, why the hell should I be afraid of an informer, if I was caught red-handed carrying the goods? I've already told them everything they wanted to know. I made a full and frank confession … So that at least they would put me in Lefortovo … not some dirty hole like the Butyrka, that hell for idiots …'

The conversation broke off of its own accord. It was obviously a long time since Grisha had eaten salami, drunk strong tea and smoked good cigarettes. After having consumed all three in the course of a few hours, he was surfeited and fell into a doze. I lay down too. Skipping my evening meditation for the first time in many days.

'My God,' I thought, tossing and turning on the thin pancake of a mattress, 'the things that go on in the world! The wild adventures! People carrying diamonds across three borders under their own skin! And here I am planning to master the techniques of philosophical resignation! To worry about the circulation of the blood in my own brain! Doesn't that mean that I've already resigned myself to prison? That it is defeating me? Shouldn't I take the dashing hard-currency hero Radchenko as my example? Why not? What have I got to look forward to? Six or seven years of general regime? All that's left of my youth! Wouldn't it be better to drop everything and make a run for it at the first opportunity?'

I slept badly that night. And in the morning there was an unpleasant surprise waiting for me. I performed my mandatory exercise for changing my handwriting and checked the results. But it turned out that seventy days of training had got me absolutely nowhere. After spending dozens of hours covering more than a hundred pages with capital letters, I tried producing a few phrases in the usual manner, and was immediately convinced that it was all in vain. My hand instantly remembered the initial stroke and the angle and the pace and the pressure and all the characteristic features of my writing.

I went out for my walk feeling discouraged and depressed.

Fifteen steps one way, fifteen steps back. Breathing two-thirds through the nose, one third through the mouth. A hundred press-ups, with my chest touching the concrete floor and my head lifted up high – at a good pace, but without hurrying. Then more running. And then a second series of press-ups.

The little man shifted from one foot to the other in the corner of the yard, observing my activities with benevolent surprise.

Having completed my scheduled programme – forty minutes of running, four series of press-ups, ten minutes of walking on my hands – I stripped to the waist and relished rubbing myself down with snow.

'Aren't you afraid of falling ill?' Grisha enquired cautiously.

'No.'

'Have you been training for long?'

'The day after tomorrow it will be exactly sixty days.'

'Oh-la-la! And how is it? Does it do any good?'

I nodded, filled with a gloomy Nietzchean self-satisfaction, and boasted casually:

'Even when I was free I couldn't do so many press-ups! My record now is a hundred and fifty times without stopping …!'

'Is that a lot or not very much?' Grisha asked curiously. He was obviously a complete and utter ignoramus in matters of sport.

'Middling.'

'I'm not exactly keen on sport,' Grisha said without even a hint of self-criticism, 'and I've never understood the benefit of it. Now you can do a hundred press-ups. Later you'll do two hundred. Where does it all end?'

'There is no end.'

'Then, pardon, but what is the point?'

'There are two points. Developing your character – that's the first …'

'*Mon Dieu*, what do you want to develop it for?' Grisha asked in astonishment. 'At your age? You either have character or you don't. It's inherited. The scientists proved that long ago.'

'There is another benefit!' I exclaimed, hastily pulling my sweater down over my steaming torso. 'When you practice something, you want to be the leader. The champion. The very best. You move ahead of everyone else. The others will study you and copy what you do. Women will want to have your children. Men will want to imitate you.'

The Swiss shrugged:

'I haven't lived in this country for a long time. I'm a flabby European. I don't understand why anyone needs to go chasing after a leader.'

I glanced at my cell-mate. Yes, he was sloppy and provocatively unfit, his movements were not entirely precise, he was flabby, stooped, with sloping shoulders and a belly that slumped out of his pants. But even so he didn't seem too dispirited by the circumstances of his own appearance.

'Nobody chases after leaders,' I declared with aplomb, sweaty, cheerful and magnanimous. 'They arise spontaneously. Human beings are the highest level of evolution. At the same time they are also animals. And in some ways even plants, calmly sucking the juices out of reality. Every one of us is not simply a lawyer or a con man, a businessman or a public prosecutor, but also a complex organism, an animal. A herd animal that repeats the movements of its leader. People are also animals! And sometimes they're not strong enough to hold back the animal within themselves. In your beloved Holland the peaceful citizens go to specially designated places to smoke hash and buy prostitutes – they're letting out the animal. Temporarily. You know, Grigorii, I'm just as much of a humanist as you are, and I would also really like people not to rip each other's throats out in the fight for money, for women, for bread, for a buzz. But unfortunately, we can both see that's the way things are, always have been and always will be …'

'You are young, *cher ami*,' Grisha objected sadly, 'And you haven't tried that hash and those Dutch prostitutes … The reason for our beastliness is not that we are animals. It is simply that man is weak and constantly overestimates himself …'

'There is a third element too,' I confessed. 'The most important one. Perhaps it sounds pompous, but I hate bars. I don't accept captivity. I don't like it when some other guy locks me up simply because I seem suspicious, a boy too rich for my age. I'm doing what I can to spite that other guy and his friends. I'm resisting. With all my strength.'

'And is it working?' Grisha Berger asked.

'No.'

23

I had never woken as early as I did that December, in the pre-trial detention centre for the especially dangerous. At a quarter to six in the morning my eyes opened of their own accord. At first I would lie there for a few minutes without moving, thinking about nothing. Not because I wasn't able to think about anything, and not because I really liked thinking about nothing; I simply wasn't able to think about anything in particular, but I couldn't completely avoid thinking. Then I would suddenly feel an uneasy, agonizing premonition: it only lasted for a brief instant, but the sensation was very clear and distinct. Then I would hear a click from the loudspeaker – and that was all. The wake-up call. Six o'clock in the morning.

Something similar used to happen to me a long time before then, when I was a soldier in the army. The raw recruits – only two days away from home, still green, still farting the smell of their mother's pies – are first put into a separate barracks, where specially trained sergeants impress upon the eighteen-year-old novices the fundamentals of the art of war. In their pre-army days, none of the boys has ever led a life in which they woke up at six o'clock in the morning. At least not every day. The first week is genuinely painful. Woken at the crack of dawn by coarse shouting, the raw recruits are obliged to jump smartly to their feet, orientate themselves immediately, wind on their footcloths, jump into their trousers and boots and line up. And all very quickly! In forty-five seconds! They say that's how long an American missile takes to fly from continent to continent … After a while everyone gets used to it. At ten o'clock in the evening – unbelievably early for an eighteen-year-old body – their eyelids are heavy and their brains refuse to function. A young recruit's sleep is deep. But after precisely eight hours, at the crack of dawn, we woke without any command, several minutes before that hoarse, deafening screech. Huddled up in a blanket as rough as tarpaulin, every last one of the boys luxuriated in those final moments, the very sweetest, of warmth, silence and peace. Soon now, in just ten seconds, the duty orderly is going to screech in a sickening falsetto: 'Company, reveille!' Right now. In just a moment ... Just a little bit more of this magical languor ... Now, right now ...

The orderly no longer gave me my orders. I had no company commander now – only the prison governor. But I still woke ahead of time, as I had done ten years earlier. Anticipating that quiet click in the loudspeaker above the door. The prison radio system switching on in order to snatch the signal for waking out of the ether and broadcast it into my sub-cortex.

I am surrounded by semi-darkness. Forty watts of power up on a ceiling four metres high are barely capable of illuminating anything; they only create a labyrinth of dense, sinuous shadows with me at the centre – huddled up tight under my prison blanket.

Eventually the first sounds of the morning appeared. The melody of a song came floating into the cell. An extremely popular hit of the 1930s, telling me that there is not even a faint rustling to be heard in the garden. What garden, what rustling, when it's minus twenty-five degrees outside?

Meanwhile a well-trained baritone voice has congratulated me on the start of another day and immediately reminded me benevolently that the New Year celebrations are almost upon us – clearly in order to put his audience of many millions into a good mood. Life goes on, my dear friends.

My cell-mate Grisha smacked his lips sweetly and turned over on to his other side. He always went to bed in the evening fully clothed and covered himself with his pea-jacket (prison property). That way that he remained unperturbed by the command 'reveille' – the mark's clean, his bed's made, he's sleeping on top of the blanket, not breaking any of the regulations, not violating the routine. Nothing for the warder to challenge here.

I thought that the sleep process of the Swiss lawyer and smuggler from Kharkov deserved to be filmed. Grisha slept the sleep of the righteous, like an idiot without a care in the world – a deep, sweet, nonchalant sleep. Snorting quietly every now and then, uttering high-pitched little moans, drooling on his pillow. Sometimes he snored, and then I would quietly get up, take a step, reach out one hand and carefully squeeze my cell-mate's nose shut so that the hollow rumbling generated by the sleeping body's vital functions would not annoy me. So that they would not stop me doing what I had to do.

Today is Thursday, an important day. Khvatov and the red-headed solicitor will come. Today I have to be focused.

They dragged me out to the interrogation surprisingly early, almost immediately after breakfast. Grisha ignored the first meal of the day too. The usual custom was for me to accept both rations: two large pieces of soft, grey bread and sugar. I would eat half of my bread immediately, after first placing a thin piece of cheese on it. I washed down my traditional Lefortovo cheeseburger with a mug of strong, hot coffee. When the aperture in the door opened and I was told to get ready, I made another mug, twice as strong. Sensing that coffee alone would not be enough, I hurriedly prepared some chifir too. I gulped it down and delighted in the sensation of my heart beginning to beat powerfully and rapidly and my head starting to buzz.

It's very important to liven yourself up. For any serious fight you have to use dope. And apart from that, I'm feeling cold, and chifir warms the body magnificently.

As I strode along the iron gangway with my hands behind my back, from behind the rows of steel doors I caught the feeble sounds of life, the muffled voices of the isolation prison's inmates: spies, serial killers, politicians, terrorists and other remarkable criminal types. At least twice I clearly heard peals of laughter. And I smiled in response. Men don't want to suffer! Not even here, behind bars, in pre-trial isolation prison number one stroke one, where it is forbidden to pull the blanket up over your head and lie with your face to the wall, where there are searches every two or three days, where an old razor can only be replaced with the personal written permission of the prison governor, even in this most gloomy of the imperial jails living, thinking beings have no desire to wallow in misery. They laugh, they want to live, they take no notice of the walls, the bars, the constant supervision and the December chill.

That winter in that prison I felt the cold very badly. The central heating radiator was buried deep in a niche under the window of the cell and the warmth it gave out was very scant. I kept my sweater on all the time. I slept in my trousers and socks.

But outside the door, in the corridor – in a space which, judged by eye, was seven metres wide and at least twenty high (four tiers, each of them four metres) – it was genuinely freezing. The vicious, piercing draughts roamed at will. The iron railings bordering the gangway were covered with white hoarfrost. My guard flaunted a pair of woollen gloves. The low temperature had reduced his professional zeal to a basic minimum: he patted my thighs and forearms carelessly, merely for form's sake, and beat a hasty retreat, evidently wishing to drink hot tea or warm himself up in some other manner unknown to me.

The investigator's cheeks, ruddy from the biting December frost, provoked my envy, and his voice seemed to have an excessively cheerful ring to it. Like any living organism that has moved into a warm building from an icy street blasted by damp winds, Khvatov was agitated, rubbing his hands together, breathing noisily through his nose and squirming on his chair.

I drew in a cautious breath of the air in the office – dry, stagnant, fusty, with an indeterminate hint of something rotten – and then hastily lit up, in order to kill the smell with one that was not quite so bad. The floor in here had clearly been washed the day before with a piece of old, decaying sackcloth, and then the window and door had been firmly closed, and so now the room was impregnated with the sharp odour of rotten rags and dried-out wood.

Khvatov clearly sensed the same thing that I did. He frowned discontentedly, muttered something about it being stuffy and hastily opened the small upper windows – first on the inner window-frame and then on the outer, deftly bending his hand and sticking it between the bars.

From the other side, the side of freedom, there came an instant whiff of the new-born winter. I almost tuned in to its energy. Almost managed to remember wet mittens on elastic, ice skates and hockey sticks, felt boots with rubber galoshes, country snowdrifts many metres long, and the flame humming in the stove, and my own ice-cold, bright-pink palms that had to be warmed by holding them under a stream of cold water, it had to be cold, if it was hot, the tips of my fingers would start hurting so badly that tears welled up in my eyes; and my six-year-old sister with a fluffy shawl wrapped cross-wise round her chest; and my mother in the doorway, handing out an old birch switch, the one we were supposed to use for brushing the snow off our shoes; and my lips curling up from the cold; and the mandarins at New Year, and the smell of fresh fir needles on the New Year tree, and the patterns on the windows, and the lumps of black coal in the cavernous iron bucket with dents in its sides – but I instantly shook my head hard, driving away the pictures of childhood that had come to me so inopportunely.

Meanwhile a few soft snowflakes came flying in through the window. They fell on to the broad window-sill and were instantly transformed into murky drops of moisture.

I was absolutely sick and fed up of this office and the air in it, of the entire atmosphere of this big, ghastly building. It was a bestial, biological revulsion. My excursion to prison – the rich idler's piquant adventure – had turned out to be a descent into a pit of fear, despair and loneliness. With each new day the menacing walls closed in further around me, the ceiling pressed down on me, the bitter-tasting skilly stuck in my throat. Chifir didn't help (I drank it three times a day now), nor did meditation (an hour every morning and evening), nor did dreams about how one fine day I would catch up with my former business associate Mikhail, who had so cold-bloodedly betrayed me.

'And just what did you expect?' the cynical moneymaker Andriukha sneered somewhere inside me, half-pissed. 'You were obviously counting on mutual fraternal support and assistance, then? Dreaming of superhuman efforts being made in order to give you back your freedom, the freedom of such an extraordinary and absolutely unique young man? No, you soppy kid!' Andriukha took a long swig of prestigious booze, relishing it, drew in the tart smoke of his cigar, adjusted his cufflinks and spat out brutally: 'You're nothing but the canon-fodder of business! Just one of a hundred thousand fools who are exploited every day and every hour in this cruel city! The fools are duped and set up for a fall! They have always been duped and set up! They always will be duped and set up! That's the way life is! Accept it, bro!'

'I won't accept it!' I protested vehemently, but not out loud. Just at that moment Khvatov was taking out of his bag the assorted wires designed to bring his computer to life. 'I won't accept it! Never. The prison for me hasn't been built yet …'

'Why are you so pale?' the investigator asked in concern. 'And your eyes are glittering … Are you ill?'

I should think so, I thought. After swallowing a dose of caffeine like that!

'Pale?' I asked. 'Pale, you say …' I filled my chest with air. 'I'll tell you why I'm pale! This is the time for my walk. I should have been taken out to go walking, and instead of this I'm being questioned! It's the third time this has happened in a month! Didn't I ask you only to drag me out for interrogation in the afternoon! And here you are again at ten o'clock in the morning! If I'm late for my walk because of you, we'll have a falling-out!'

'I'm sorry, Andrei,' Khvatov said peaceably. 'I forgot.'

'Well, you ought to remember!' I rebuked him haughtily. 'The walk's sacred! It means precious litres of oxygen! Why, instead of taking in the fresh air, do I have to sit in this stuffy, dusty place with you, discussing subjects that we're both absolutely sick and fed up of?'

I started snorting indignantly through my nose. I even tossed my pen down on the desk in a rude gesture. I'm sick of being there. I'm sick of searching for a way out. You bloody bastards, let me go. I haven't done anything. I'm a good man. I'm a useful member of society. I won't do it again …

'So what's it going to be today?' Khvatov asked, indifferently ignoring my psychopathic outburst. 'The usual thing? We don't say anything? No, you know, testimony?'

'That's exactly right!'

'Are we going to wait for the solicitor?'

'Absolutely not!' I snapped. 'Let's start without him, so as not to waste time! If we can be finished in half an hour, then I'll still have time to go for a walk ... What do we have today?'

'A warrant to take samples of your writing in capital letters.'

I shuddered.

'Why on earth do you want my writing in capital letters?'

'I don't want it,' Khvatov corrected me, 'the investigation requires it. And the investigation knows best. The boss has spoken, and I obey, you know, unquestioningly. By the way, you have a legal right to refuse ...'

'I refuse!'

'I see,' said the patient man from Ryazan with a conciliatory gesture. 'Then we'll just quickly draw up the appropriate minute, and you can go back ... How are you getting on, in general? Is everything all right? They've not mistreated you in the cell?'

'Let yourself be mistreated and you'll get yourself fucked,' I said, citing a crude but accurate prison saying. 'Listen, Stepan Mikhailich! I'm sick of your prison. I'm wasting my time in here. I intend to get out, quick. I don't like it in here any more. What do I have to do, eh? Confess to something I didn't do, is that it?'

Khvatov frowned severely.

'No, Andrei. You need to tell me everything. Answer the questions in detail. Help us establish the truth about your little episode. Clarify a few points that are, you know, unclear to us ...'

'Out of the question,' I snapped. 'It's much safer for me to keep my mouth shut. I could cause trouble for too many people on the outside with my loose tongue. That's my reason for refusing. There won't be any testimony. Anything else – by all means.'

'Testifying is your ticket back home. Only, you know, testimony, that's all.'

'Listen, Mr Investigator! I've been inside for more than four months! In that period of time just before I was put in prison, I earned half a million!' In a furious outburst of frustration, I punched my own head so hard that it started ringing painfully. 'If I were free, I'd have another half million now! And I'd be happy to give that money to you, to the Public Prosecutor's Office! To make good the harm I've done to the country! And I'd still have something left in my own pocket! Everything that's happening is irrational! I'm losing my future in here, the means to feed my son!'

'Calm down.'

'I can't! I'm not capable! It's beyond me! It's all right for you – you can be calm!' I took my face in my hands. 'It's the New Year in two weeks! You'll put your presents under the tree in your own home! But I won't! I won't put my presents under the tree! On the first of January my son won't get a present from his daddy! All the children will get presents from their daddies and only my son will be left without a present! He'll wake up and feel about under the tree – and there won't be any present! Not even the tiniest little present! Because his daddy's in prison! Do you know, Citizen Investigator, what it's like when a little human being, a child, is left without a present on the first of January? Why, I'd demolish the entire world just to have a chance to put my present under the tree! Why are they keeping me here? What for? Who's to blame for it? You! You're the one to blame!'

'No,' Khvatov replied. 'I'm not. You're the one to blame.'

'Yes,' I agreed with a heavy sigh. 'That's true. In the first place, I'm the one to blame … But you shouldn't pretend that you have nothing to do with it!'

'By the way, I'm in a bad mood today as well,' Khvatov declared, screwing up his eyes. 'And your rudeness is, you know, starting to get on my nerves. Stop honking your horn, okay? If you raise your voice just one more time I'll put in, you know, a report, and you'll be punished …'

'Sorry,' I said, shrugging and immediately backing off. 'You know what it's like, winter depression, prison, bars and all the rest … But what's got you down? Are the headaches bothering you again?'

'Yes, they are,' the man from Ryazan confessed.

He took out a large, clean handkerchief that was neatly folded into a square, removed his thick horn-rimmed spectacles from the bridge of his nose and started deliberately polishing the lenses with regular, precise movements of his fingers. His fingers were trembling slightly.

'I tell you what I think,' he said in a low voice. 'I think I'll just unravel this racket of yours and go back home. To Ryazan.'

'It's not my racket,' I immediately responded in severe voice. 'I'm innocent.'

'You're guilty,' the investigator pronounced benignly, without even looking at me. 'You helped to, you know, legalise stolen money. It's very simple. We only have to unravel you all the way to the end. Take a good sniff at every one of the documents that were confiscated from your office. Back home I'd have unravelled you in a month – or two months at the outside …'

Having polished one lens, Khvatov looked through it at the light, then simply breathed for moment, exposing his small, yellow but regular and very healthy teeth – the ivory keyboard of a well-balanced man who grew up in the fresh air and now lives in it, far from any big cities.

'But I've been scrabbling away here for almost half a year now,' he went on in annoyance. 'It's hard for me to work in this Moscow of yours. It's impossible, you know, to concentrate on anything. You know, Andrei, I started in the Department for Countering the Theft of Socialist Property and Speculation. I unravelled dozens of swindles. I have a penchant for, you know, analytical work. I like working with documents. Do you like the way Svinets works with you? All those jokes and that psychology, shouting, kicking up a ruckus … That's because he works *with people*. But I work with material evidence …' Khvatov set to work on the second lens. 'I'm not so good with people,' he went on. 'What I'm good at is sitting down at home in the evening, on the veranda, in summer … opening the windows … switching on, you know, the lamp on the table … laying out the files with the invoices and the other clever bits of paper – and thinking. Comparing, you know, the facts … Writing down the conclusions on a piece of paper … And then comparing one conclusion with another – and so on …'

Outside the window in the prison yard I heard the sound of a car engine and a long squeal of brakes, follow by a harsh, piercing blast on a klaxon horn. The investigator started as if he'd suffered an electric shock. The lens in his fingers crunched. Thin, curved slivers of glass jangled pitifully as they fell to the floor. Khvatov looked up at me, then lowered his eyes again, grabbed his ruined spectacles with both hands, snapped them in two with a sudden, sharp movement and flung them away.

'They're honking again!' he exclaimed furiously. 'They're always honking! They can't live without it here! Always honking, honking! Why do they always have to honk here? Why is it so noisy here? Why do the drivers always have their hands on the horn, as if the damned horn was the most, you know, important part of their car?'

He lifted his cut index finger up to his eyes, squinted short-sightedly and disgustedly wiped away the blood that had appeared on it with his handkerchief.

'Tell me this, Andrei, answer me a simple question! Here in this stupid city you're always in a hurry! Always dashing somewhere – and honking! Why can't you drive calmly, without honking? Why do you need all this honking? Why, eh? Answer me!'

The investigator was trembling. There was a hint of angst in the expression of his eyes. Those big fingers – the fingers of a peasant, a farmer never pampered by generous harvests, a beekeeper, a connoisseur of apples and cucumbers – plucked nervously at the blood-stained handkerchief.

What is it, neighbour of mine, are you feeling bad? I feel even worse.

'I'd have unravelled someone like you in a month!' Khvatov exclaimed sadly. 'In three, you know, weeks! But your friends, other people just like you, come dashing to help you! They go racing past my windows honking! Distracting me! Preventing me from thinking! Honking all day and all night! If it wasn't for those honking friends of yours, you'd have gone to trial ages ago and been given your five years, and I'd have gone back home to my veranda and forgotten all about your damned big-city honkers.'

I didn't know what to say to that.

Five months earlier, in a former life on the outside, the jovial nouveau riche Andriukha used to honk himself, and how! He hurtled implacably along the jam-packed streets, he rushed like a lunatic, he kept his thumb on the button of the horn all the time, and if there was some creep driving in front of him with only seventy horse-power, then Andriukha honked for all he was worth. And he honked at creeps driving a hundred horse-power as well. And the other creeps, driving a hundred and fifty horse-power, and the creeps on two hundred horse-power. Andriukha's herd was bigger, and he honked voluptuously at the pitiful fools with too few horses. Andriukha was firmly convinced that Moscow was not a European capital at all, that the place was a hundred per cent uncompromising Asia. In this city, just like in the Mongolian steppe, the biggest honcho was the one with the biggest herd of horses. Smug Andriukha honked at plenty of creeps. And as they were moving up on him from behind, equally smug creeps whose herd was bigger than Andriukha's honked at him. Some of them had as many as five hundred horses or more neighing triumphantly under the bonnet. When he spotted a herd like that in his rear-view mirror, Andriukha gave way. He moved over. He diverted his herd into another lane of the traffic. And if he was too slow in doing it, the owner of the bigger herd honked.

At this point Khvatov finally pulled the CASE FILE out of his bundle, and I suddenly felt mortified by shame. I have to work for what I want, and not listen to the complaints of a provincial who has given up in the face of the raw energy of the megalopolis. I have a simple goal: to get a glimpse of at least a couple of pages from that plump, grey file. And preparatory to that – wind up my opponent's nerves. That's how I will distract his attention. It was precisely in order to distract him that I made such a fuss about the walk. Of course the walk could wait.

At the previous interrogation I'd managed to read almost an entire paragraph. And I wasn't planning to stop at that.

'Unless I'm mistaken, your son is only two years old,' the investigator said politely, opening the file.

I squinted cautiously, trying to pick out at least something. The CASE FILE was lying awkwardly, at an angle. But I had been practicing every morning for two months.

'Yes,' I replied. 'He'll be two in January.'

'So he doesn't understand yet, you know, where his daddy is, right?'

Again and again I lower my eyes to the sheets of paper. Squinting sideways. Pretending to be examining my nails. Khvatov checks first one page in the CASE FILE, then another, as he draws up one more set of minutes, tapping on the keyboard with his bent index fingers. I recognise the words 'solicit', 'refuse', 'appoint' and also the formula 'bearing in mind the seriousness of the offence committed'. None of this interests me. I wait for what comes next.

'They told my son that his daddy was away on business ...'

Take a book, any book, open it, put it down on the table in front of you, then turn it through a hundred and eighty degrees and push it away from you to arm's length. Sit down sideways on to the table. Turn your head slightly to the side. Behave casually. Pick your nose, smooth down your hair, sniff, whistle the song 'Vladimir Central' – everything has to make it look as if the contents of the book are of no interest to you at all. And now try to read it. At first glance it seems like madness. But after five weeks of practice success is guaranteed.

So far I hadn't managed to discover anything that would seriously interest me. But there was still time. The investigation would go on for at least six months. My brainy friend Khvatov would visit me at least fifty times. And little by little I would extract from the CASE FILE everything that I needed. I would draw out all the necessary information, word by word, phrase by phrase.

Now every time I was visited by the man from Ryazan – and he was still coming twice a week, like before, tormenting me by taking more samples of my handwriting and performing other tests – I managed to read ten, or even fifteen lines. Unfortunately the information was no use to me at all – it was all long, tedious paragraphs of pure bureaucratic jargon.

But one day I saw a minute from an interrogation of my 'associate' in the case – the minister. And I made out the words 'I demand', 'I refuse', 'I request', 'I reserve the right'. From what I read I concluded that, just like me, the minister wasn't talking. At least, he wasn't singing and giving away all the details. That meant I should keep my mouth shut too, I told myself.

Of course, I would have preferred Khvatov to open his interesting volume at pages that concerned me directly. But I hadn't been that lucky even once.

'Sign,' said the Ryazan neurasthenic, pushing the freshly typed minute towards me. He put his pen down on top of the sheet of paper.

'I have my own,' I said gloomily.

Businessmen always use their own pens for everything. I didn't depart from the rule of etiquette even in Lefortovo – that was at least one victory over the prison for me. I casually tugged the sheet of paper out from under the investigator's thick black fountain, took out my own stylo and was on the point of adorning yet another procedural document with my autograph, when I suddenly remembered that you should never sign anything without your lawyer being present, and I said:

'Let's wait.'

'Ten minutes ago you were all het up, desperate to go out for your walk,' Khvatov pointed out indifferently, 'and now you're in no hurry to go anywhere …'

I was spared the need to come up with a reply by Red's arrival.

The lawyer hadn't got as badly chilled as the investigator. He had undoubtedly driven to work in a warm car, with the additional warmth of his excellent long sheepskin coat – it was now hanging on a hook in the corner of the room, clashing diabolically with the crudely plastered wall: a tuxedo in a boiler room would have looked the same way.

'Not late am I?' Red asked, shaking both our hands with equal nonchalance.

'Andrei's in a hurry to go for his walk,' Khvatov told him. 'So sign, gentlemen, then I'll go, and you can stay here without me. You have ten minutes. Or even, you know, fifteen. But if there's such a big hurry and you crave oxygen so badly, I'll call the guard right now …'

'Twenty minutes,' I said in a wooden voice, feeling furious with myself.

Khvatov now had one more reason for thinking of me as a lying scumbag. But the way I wanted to look was perfectly honest.

Gathering up his instruments of torture – laptop, printer, wires – the investigator walked out without even saying goodbye.

The lawyer immediately sat down in his place, deftly hitching up his beautifully ironed woollen trousers. This young guy has everything under control, I thought enviously yet again. He has his winter shoes and gloves and a warm jacket. The cold weather's barely set in, and he's already dressed for the season in the best possible taste. Everything bought and altered to suit his figure in advance. He's only starting out as a solicitor, probably doesn't even make a thousand a month. And look at me – not so long ago I was making fifty thousand, but I never had such excellent winter shoes, with little metal studs set in the soles, and gloves like that, they look really comfortable, soft, light-brown leather. How could I have found time for going round the shops? And what do you need winter clothing for, anyway, if you live and work in a city and you have a car? I had my first car at the age of twenty, but I didn't have any winter shoes until I was twenty-four.

The moment the door closed, I gestured to Red to get everything ready. Hastily, but with a certain distinctive lightness of movement typical of people unfamiliar with physical labour, the lawyer put his briefcase on the desk, and took a stack of paper and two thick felt-tip pens out of it. The briefcase was left standing open. I immediately moved half of the stack of paper over in front of myself. Speaking in a hoarse whisper, with my head lowered, I said:

'I've obviously overstayed my time in here. I should have been heading home by now. I intend to take action. This is what I need ...'

I wrote down the word 'information' on the first sheet of paper, showed it to the lawyer, set the paper aside, immediately took hold of the second sheet and scrawled 'Misha Moroz' on it.

'I need news from here.'

The word 'strategy' appeared on the third sheet.

'We can't just sit here and wait, without knowing if it's the right thing to do ...'

The lawyer nodded understandingly and asked, also speaking very quietly:

'What do you want me to do?'

I thought for a moment. Then scribbled something down.

'What do you think about this option?'

'Stupid,' the lawyer whispered and pulled a sour face, setting his elbows on the table and folding together his white hands with the well-tended nails.

'Then how about this?'

'It's impossible.'

'And this?'

'Irrational.'

'Shall we involve these?'

'It won't do any good. Totally ineffective. I know from experience.'

'Then this is what we'll do.'

The lawyer picked up his felt-tip pen and also resorted to the use of paper.

'Then they'll do this.'

'I agree. But we'll gain on this side …'

'Then this will be their answer. They'll send him here.'

'They won't!'

'They certainly will! And if that happens, then you're …'

With obvious relish the lawyer traced out a short, six-letter word signifying the total and absolute collapse of everything in the world. I swore loudly and expressively into every corner of the office. Let them hear what I think of them!

We had to break off and meticulously destroy the paper we had used. Every sheet was torn into at least thirty-two little pieces. With our four hands energetically working in unison, Red and I produced a heap of formless rubbish, stirred it all up together and loaded it into the briefcase with precise haste. When one tiny little piece suddenly leapt out of my hand and glided under the table in a slovenly fashion, I took the trouble to bend down, run my hand over the lino and locate the lost fragment.

I won't give them even the slightest chance. I won't let them have even a single scrap of information. They won't get even a single letter out of me! But I'll get absolutely everything I want from them.

'All right,' I went on. 'Let's forget it. Contact this man …'

'He doesn't answer my calls.'

'Then this one.'

'He told me he'll do everything he can to help you, but not in the immediate future.'

'He said that? "I'll help, but not in the immediate future"?'

'Yes.'

'The bastard …'

The lawyer sighed sternly.

'Listen, I phoned all of them ages ago. We're going round in circles here …'

I gestured in annoyance.

'Then contact … Contact … Then find … Just a moment, I'll tell you who … Let me think.'

'Think,' Red said, nodding.

I suddenly had the feeling that he was almost indifferent. It made me furious. The solicitor has an obligation to exert his brain too! Isn't the counsel for the defence supposed to put every possible effort into finding ways to save his client? Perhaps I should take him by the scruff of the neck, give him a good shaking and snarl a classic phrase from some gangster movie, something traditional like: 'Get me out of here!', 'I don't give a damn how you do it!' or 'You're costing me a bundle!' – some simple sentiment that would normally be yelled by a furious Mafioso wearing an excellent tie, who has ended up in prison, grabbing hold of the front of his lawyer's jacket while he does it …

Eventually I painstakingly spelled out several words expressing the thought that was tormenting me, added a big, round question mark and held the phrase up to Maxim's eyes: 'What are you getting paid for?'

The lawyer lowered his eyes. And immediately wrote out an answer. I liked his writing – rapid, clear and easy on the eye. 'I haven't been paid for a long time.'

'Four months,' he added out loud, holding up four fingers to help me grasp this news.

I froze in amazement.

'Why didn't you tell me straight away?'

'What point was there in upsetting you? Don't worry, everything will work out.'

'Ring this number,' I said, my felt-tip pen running over the paper again, 'or this one …'

Red looked sad:

'In both those places they do nothing but make promises.'

'Then go to these people … they'll pay you for sure …'

'Don't be nervous.'

'What does that mean, "don't be nervous"?' I said, getting carried away again. I felt a sudden powerful burning sensation in my chest, like an electric shock. I thrust my jaw out. 'You won't work for nothing!'

'We'll think of something. I'll ring round everybody one more time …'

'And will this one more time really happen?'

I tried to summon up a bleak, bitter laugh, like a genuine convict. Like an experienced inmate of a political prison. Like a genuinely enlightened man. But from the outside it all must have looked very pitiful and forced, because Maxim Stein shot me a glance of sympathetic commiseration

'Stop that!' he said very quietly, but with a firmness that surprised me, compressing his lips into a narrow line. 'I'll come next week. Without fail.'

I frowned disdainfully:

'Why should you bother? Doing charity work now, are you? Favours and noble gestures are no good to me. They only make me feel worse. If someone does me a favour, I sleep badly afterwards.'

'Let's drop this subject.' Red stood up. 'You have to have someone who comes and looks at you, who sees what kind of state you're in. This is a prison, after all! If I drop your CASE now, I'll lose my self-respect …'

'I don't like bombastic phrases!' I replied, borne along on a flood of despair. 'And I don't want to join in any games played by noble musketeers! All work should be paid for at the appropriate rate! But now I can't guarantee that. It's over. You're not going to come here any more.'

'I shall come, Andrei. Without fail.'

'And how am I going to pay you?'

'We'll decide that later. When you get out.'

'I can't promise.'

'No need. Believe me, I have my own reasons for coming to see you without being paid.'

'What reasons?'

The lawyer smiled.

'I can't tell you. Later, maybe ...'

'And why's that?'

Red began neatly pulling on his extremely comfortable sheepskin coat.

'Because I have a lot of respect for you, Andrei. And I want to do something for you. As simple as that. Help you. You'll get out of this hole soon, believe me. And then you can be useful to me.'

'Soon?' I asked, also getting up. 'How soon?'

'Well, a year and a half. Two at the most ...'

'Two years!' I screamed. 'You call that soon, do you?'

'In your situation, it's an excellent result. Ah yes, by the way!' The lawyer held out his elegant, narrow hand. 'Happy New Year!'

I was in time for my walk after all. But I didn't feel like running and jumping any more. I spent an hour sloping miserably from one corner of the yard to the other, with my hands stuck in my pockets, trying to overcome my agitation.

Red had been paid an advance in summer, when my boss and I were both still free. Now it turned out that it was the only money he had received. The first and the last. My boss had been let out a long time ago, but he hadn't been in touch, and he wasn't paying my solicitor! And the solicitor had only just let me know that the advance had run out ages ago and all his subsequent actions had been motivated by a fit of altruism ...

And all this now, at the very moment when I have realised that the only thing that has so far prevented me from defeating prison is a belief in foolish ideals – in friendship, decency or spiritual strength. Now, when I have decided that the time has come to reject romantic fantasies, bury my plans, forget about my dear boss Mikhail and start trying to save my own skin. It might be mangy, but it's still mine. Now, at the very moment when I need reliable contacts with the outside world and reliable people out there, my own solicitor tells me that he's not being paid! Now, at the very moment when I have decided to arrange a few articles in the newspapers, and to write a couple of letters to especially close business friends, asking them to put pressure on the investigation, to intercede for me. Now, at the very moment when I have realised that it's time to take action on my own account, without concerning myself about the people who have betrayed me, they betray me again, and my own solicitor tells me to get used to the idea of two years in prison! What exactly do I have to do to save myself?

The legendary currency speculator Radchenko was way ahead of me. He didn't addle his brains with meditation and read books on training the attention and the memory. He immediately got his lawyer involved and set about saving himself, without relying on anyone else. Why hadn't I done the same?

'Aren't you running today?' Grisha asked me.

'No.'

Why run? Where to? What for? Everything's gone wrong. My plans have collapsed. I can't even read a single page of the CASE FILE properly. My boss has done a runner. And my money has disappeared with him. My lawyer has admitted that he's not getting paid for visiting me …

'That's right,' the Swiss citizen said cheerfully. 'You can't run away from them. Or from yourself.'

I started. In my furious agitation I had spoken the final phrases of my internal monologue out loud.

'What are you talking about?' I asked, going down my knees and starting to punch the ground.

You have to hit hard, so that it hurts really bad. That calms the nerves.

Grisha paused before he replied:

'Excuse me,' he said. 'I was thinking about something else …'

24

Every year on the thirty-first of December I feel myself drawn back to the Land of Soviets. Back to its heart-rending accordion music and damp strawberry beds. Back to the soya sweets, the boiled potatoes, the processed cheese, the freshly ironed ties of the Young Pioneers, the ice creams, the rustling tapes of reel-to-reel tape recorders, the portraits of smiling, bright-eyed cosmonauts, the black and white TV serials about fearless secret agents, the songs about the Baikal-Amur Railway. Back to the truck drivers' greasy padded jackets, to the fortified wine, to the journals in the collective farm library, falling apart from being read so many times. Back to the damp soldiers' leg-wrappings, the worn gun-butts of the guards' carbines and the demob photo albums.

Back to a sense of pride in your immense, absurd, frozen, awkward, skewed, drunk, terrible and great Motherland.

It's foolish to dream about what can never happen. I can never go back to my childhood, never.

But I'm not old yet, after all. I'm not even fully grown up. I'm only twenty-seven.

I'm experienced, rational, serious. I'm not poor. But I'm not grown up! My childhood is somewhere close by, not far behind me, only twelve years away. It costs me no effort at all to recall any detail, any little thing, any momentary experience of the past.

Some day I shall grow up, become an adult, turn hard, become grey and insensitive – then the emotions of boyhood will be drowned in the depths of memory. But as long as I'm not grown up, I remember everything.

Under the rainbow sky of the Land of Soviets there was no day brighter or holiday merrier than the thirty-first of December. Never mind the pompous, flag-waving anniversaries of the revolution, for me the very finest and most warm-hearted holiday will always be the New Year, that slightly pagan family festival when the citizens all try sincerely to convince each other that nothing but good lies ahead for everyone. But those years are behind me now. The Land of Soviets is dead. My childhood was spent in a country that no longer exists on the map – that's the whole problem.

Throughout the final day of the old year my cell-mate and I hardly even spoke to each other at all. A holiday in prison is not a holiday, it's more of a pretext for pondering and editing, I suppose you could call it, your opinion of yourself, and we pondered sadly, listening to the radio.

At eleven o'clock in the evening I took a hit of chifir. Grisha declined. He lay down, turned to face the wall and said nothing. Perhaps he was recalling his adventures in Switzerland, his trips to Monte Carlo and Amsterdam. I didn't disturb him – right up until midnight I amused myself by listening to the words of old, familiar songs about love and friendship, about the conquest of the land, about sailors and airmen, about geologists, miners and other glorious heroes.

Then came the midnight chimes.

On the final stroke of the Kremlin bell, Grisha and I heard a dull pounding.

To the right and the left, in the neighbouring cells, there were men exactly like us – especially dangerous criminal suspects under investigation. They were wishing us a happy New Year by hammering their fists on the wall. And I drummed back furiously in reply.

'Happy New Year, Grisha!'

'Happy New Year,' the little Swiss replied glumly. 'What should I wish you?'

'No need to wish me anything. I have everything.'

'Maybe luck?'

'I don't believe in luck.'

'Freedom then?'

'My freedom is always with me.'

On the occasion of the holiday the prison authorities left the radio switched on until half past midnight. And then there was a quite unprecedented incident – they changed the wavelength! The Lefortovo receiver was retuned to FM. For almost an entire hour the inhabitants of the cells revelled in the melodies of dance music. As I lay there motionless, the chords of a different, previous life leapt out on me from the hole in the wall. The chords of a free life.

At least three songs gave me real pleasure, when they played me 'I shot the sheriff', 'Imagine' and 'The show must go on'. Songs full of beauty and energy, the songs of my reckless youth that I knew by heart. They were my accompaniment when I acquired my first experience of life and earned my first bumps – painful, never forgotten, but completely healed now. But when would these new prison bumps ever heal?

In the year just past I had reached the peak of my commercial career. Risen to mind-boggling heights, to a stupendous level of income, to unprecedented opportunities. And that same year I had fallen; slumped right back to the very bottom. Into prison! What next? Surely the new year of 1997 was bound to bring me changes for the better? Surely I would break free of these walls and these bars? The questions hung in the air, swaying like the branches of a New Year tree.

Somewhere out there, beyond the walls of the cell, in a warm, brightly lit apartment, the people I love are sitting round a festive table. My wife. My mother. Feeling sad. Drinking sparkling champagne. My son – he will be two in a week's time – has been asleep for a long time already. He is still too small to understand where his father is. In that, at least, fate has been kind to me.

The feeling that filled my heart was so dark and heavy, the gloom that swept over me so all-consuming, the icy sorrow so agonizing as it seared deeper into my chest, penetrating into the very deepest nooks and crannies, heedlessly ripping open the intimate recesses where the love for those nearest and dearest to me was kept – the love for my wife, my son, my mother, my father, my sister, for the warm, living human beings who had once been forgotten for the sake of a chance to play at *business* and *big money*; my breathing was so tightly constrained as the sharp, curving, barbed claws sank in, ripping my self-assured ego to shreds, that in my panic I started looking for something to poison myself with, to dull my brain. But I couldn't find anything or come up with any ideas except to brew more damned chifir.

I drank an entire mug full, but it didn't help. I repeated the dose. I started feeling unwell. The pain didn't pass.

The yellow walls came to life and started swirling around. The floor went rushing to the left, the ceiling to the left. I grabbed the cigarettes and tried lighting up, but the smoke didn't save me, the poison didn't ease my suffering.

My little cell-mate was saying something, gazing sympathetically into my face, but I was incapable of hearing anything. There was only one thing I wanted desperately: to cry. But instead I was sick.

I spent the first, the purest and brightest, minutes of 1997 leaning over the gaping throat of the toilet pipe, puking bitter bile into the prison sewerage system.

25

Red turned out to be a decent human being after all. A right-on legal macho. Hardly even deceived me at all. He did turn up, not one week, but twenty days later and he brought me a three-page letter from my wife. He told me that he had sent four complaints on my behalf to four important legal structures, including the Supreme Court and the Public Prosecutor's Office.

Then there was a pause that lasted for a month. It wasn't until mid-February that I once again sat facing the round, freckled face of my solicitor. But by that time everything had changed. I had become different, and so had the prison. I had grown weaker and the prison had grown stronger. It had almost chewed me up and swallowed me. Forced me on down into its innards. It had become clear that very soon I could simply fall apart and suffer final defeat.

As God is my witness, I fought with all my strength. I put everything I had into the fight. I was stubborn, cunning, patient. I was prepared for absolutely anything: humiliation, beatings, hunger, fits of despair, terrible illnesses, darkness – anything but this cotton-wool silence, this monotony, this yearning for my family that was gnawing at my insides.

February 1997 was grey and sunless. To me in my cold yellow cell, the entire world seemed to be immersed in a murky, freezing twilight and roofed over with an ashen, lead-grey sky. The entire universe seemed like a labyrinth of narrow, dimly lit cells, and in every one there were men cheerlessly eating their rations, leafing through stupid newspapers, drinking chifir, washing their shorts, quarrelling and waiting lethargically, joylessly for something to change in their destinies …

I came to my next meeting with the lawyer straight from my latest fit of prison blues. The attack had lasted several days. I hadn't combed my hair or shaved or brushed my teeth. What for? Six months inside, and what did I have to look forward to? The end of the initial investigation, a trial, a prison camp, skilly. Convict lifers for my friends. Bars across the sky. And on and on like that for many long years.

'You're not looking too good,' the solicitor stated circumspectly, peering into my face.

'Neither are you,' I said honestly.

Red's appearance really was curiously picturesque. It was the first time I'd seen him like that – with his hair cropped short, thinner and more sombre than before, and wearing a leather jacket and jeans held up by a wide belt with a massive buckle. A two-day stubble the colour of old copper covered the lower part of the lawyer's face and ran up over his temples – the hairs on his head and his chin were the same length, which lent Maxim Stein's appearance a certain brutal charm: and what's more, I was astonished to spot a tacky gold bracelet on his wrist.

But on the other hand, the expression on the advocate's face testified quite clearly that he was struggling to resolve some vitally important problem and felt rather awkward dressed up like a bandit.

'How's tricks?' I asked.

'How can you ask a lawyer a question like that?' Red asked with a humourless grin. 'As it happens, my cases are all going differently. Some have been closed, some have been referred for court hearings, in some charges are only just being initiated …'

'I withdraw the question,' I said seriously. 'By the way. Don't you think that expression "initiate a charge" has an oddly Freudian ring to it?'

The lawyer scraped at his prickly cheek with his fingers.

'That's something I've been thinking about more and more often, just recently' he replied in a serious voice. 'And I've actually come to a conclusion …'

'What's that?'

'My work doesn't give me a charge any more.'

'You just need to stop coming to this prison,' I advised him. 'Forget about Andrei Rubanov. That's all.'

'You're not the problem,' the advocate said with a weary frown. 'I've got other clients inside like you ... I visit prisons almost every day ... The Butyrka. The Matrosskaya Tishina. Pre-trial isolation centre number five. Kapotnya. Once every two weeks I even go to the Kashira ... And everywhere' – at this point the lawyer's voice took on a more neurotic tone – 'I see dirty people with crazy faces, in tattered tracksuits, they want to break out, they hand me notes, telephone numbers ... They tell me to phone someone and tell them something, get some money from their tearful, red-eyed wives and mothers ... It's not for me. I've decided to give up practicing law. Completely.'

I shook my head disapprovingly.

'And where are you going to go?'

Maxim reluctantly confessed:

'I've been invited to join a commercial bank, as a legal consultant, but I haven't made my mind up yet ...'

'What bank is it?'

Red told me the name.

'I've heard of it,' I said, nodding. A decent enough outfit. The owners are strong, talented guys. You'd have every opportunity for professional growth and building a career.'

'As it happens, you influenced my decision too,' the lawyer said suddenly, scratching his unshaven cheek once again with relish.

That gave me such a surprise that the lighted cigarette almost fell out of my mouth.

'Pardon me, but I don't quite catch the drift of your patter ... What have I got to do with this?'

'It's a long story.'

'Why not give it a go? I've got time.'

Red smiled sadly, but then immediately took a firm grasp of his belt's heavy trade-mark buckle and drew his breath in sternly through his nose.

Exactly the way a man should behave when he's put ten years of his life into achieving professional success and then suddenly becomes disillusioned with his work.

'I envy you,' he said eventually in a soft voice.

'Me?' I almost burst out laughing. 'Bloody hell, I'm in prison! I'm all washed up! I'm looking at doing a serious stretch! And you envy me?'

'Yes.'

'Why?'

'Because you're always cheerful, calm and stable, and you're not afraid of prison.'

'You're wrong,' I replied sadly. 'That's the way I'd like it to be, but it isn't. I am afraid. And every day it gets worse. Prison's a terrible place. It's impossible not to be afraid of it.'

'Why are you pretending?' Red protested. 'It doesn't suit you. You'll soon be out. They won't give you a heavy sentence. Your time inside will be just an exotic episode in your life. You'll make money again …'

Flattered, I lowered my eyes.

'People like me,' the lawyer continued in a quiet, pensive voice, jabbing one finger into his chest in disgust, 'will always be nothing but service personnel for you. Lawyers, solicitors, accountants, consultants, managers – they're all just *menials* to people like you … You're in prison and I'm free, but even so I'm a menial! Instead of becoming a millionaire, a master of life, I go running round the pretrial prisons, scribbling complaints, wasting my energy on small talk with fools who stole three kopecks in a drunken fit and are prepared in advance to accept three years of standard regime for it! No, I don't want that. I want to move through life like a metal bulldozer!' The lawyer's eyes glinted and the gold bracelet clattered against the wooden table top. 'That's why I come here. To get charged up from you, like plugging into the mains!'

I gave a short, sad laugh. It's a good thing this naïve resident of the capital doesn't have a chance to observe the tough guy, the master of life, snarling in the evenings with his face stuck into the pillow (prison property) that's as hard as the sole of a shoe, grinding his teeth in his helplessness and mentally imploring all the gods he knows to grant him just two or three tears – but his eyes remain dry, and there's no moisture in his throat either, as if the one-time banker, the one-time honest man, is gradually drying out completely. Like a shrub forgotten by the gardener …

'Listen, friend,' I whispered mysteriously, 'could you – only don't be surprised, okay? – slit open your own skin, plant diamonds in your own flesh and take them out of the country?'

Red shuddered. Demonic green sparks that I'd never seen before suddenly appeared in his eyes.

'Do you need to get some stones out to the West?' he whispered back in a serious, business-like tone of voice.

'No,' I said with a smile. 'Where would I get stones from? I just thought I'd ask.'

'Personally speaking, I could,' the lawyer replied, without even pausing for thought. 'Slit the skin and put them in – what's so hard about that? What's the commission?'

'Fifty per cent.'

'I agree. When do we start?'

I smiled again and brought him back down to earth:

'I'm sorry, I only asked out of simple curiosity.'

I managed a short, suggestive laugh, as if somewhere, there on the outside, I really did have a secret hiding place full of diamonds and emeralds. But unfortunately I hadn't stashed away any stones. I hadn't put anything away for a rainy day. Or stored up a hundred or so thousand for unforeseen difficulties. All my money, right down to the last kopeck, had been invested – a financial policy that used to bring in constantly increasing revenue for the banker Andriukha; why pickle your money by buying stones? Shares and securities – they were what brought a banker his gold. On the financial market money circulates with the greatest possible speed, flying like a bullet from owner to owner, and the smart player who is quick at getting his bearings can always rely on a profit. What good are stones? Investment in them is secure, but the returns are low. Only a hapless foreign currency speculator from the old days of the Land of Soviets would go for such a dead option as diamonds. When you could end up facing the firing squad in the land of university equality (i.e. poverty), what option do you have but to start buying up anything you can sell for a good price in the West?

Now I regretted not having created a secret reserve of freely convertible valuables. And I swore to myself that from now on I would definitely start putting aside part of the money I earned. From the viewpoint of the active businessman this is ridiculous and naïve, but there are other opinions on this question … the only thing that bothered me was that I didn't know when I was going to start earning again … I had a prison term coming up … God only knew what lay in store for me …

'But to be serious,' I said to Red, speaking in a normal voice, 'you would be an absolute idiot to give up practicing law and go to work in a bank! Bankers are the greatest criminals in the whole wide world. Some day they'll trick you the same way they tricked me. And you'll end up in jail.' I took out a cigarette with a trembling hand. 'Forget about bankers. Just do your own job. Don't get despondent. Walk away calmly. And don't come to see me any more. I'm a hopeless case. And in addition, I'm bankrupt. I've sunk into prison like I would into a swamp. I don't know what I ought to do. I see prisons everywhere. I wanted to defeat prison by my own will-power, but I couldn't. Now it seems to me that desire to defeat prison is itself a prison! Do you understand me?'

The lawyer nodded, but I knew that he didn't realize, he wasn't capable, he didn't know how – he couldn't see his own prisons yet, but I'd already perceived every last single one of them.

'Any desire is a prison!' I told him passionately. 'And there is no end to these prisons!'

The advocate looked at me as if I were mentally ill – with pity. But he listened carefully, without moving or even blinking. I carried on, speaking in a hoarse, breaking voice, like some mentally unstable hysteric who is uncertain of himself:

'Our desires are our prisons, get it? Megalomania – there's a prison for you! The mother of all prisons! I want money! I want power! I want success! I dream of making good! Making something of myself! I want the most beautiful wife and the most obedient children! I want new trousers! A gold watch! I want mansions in Malibu, I must have canvases by Matisse on the walls! I want three women in one bed! I want a multitude glorifying my genius! That's where the prisons are. The terrible attachments, the cells that are so difficult to leave. Every one of us is stuck inside thousands of prisons at once! In order to understand that, I had to wind up in the simplest one of all …'

'I understand,' the red-headed lawyer said, nodding with an expression that told me quite clearly he didn't understand a single thing.

'Prisons fit inside each other, like Russian *matryoshka* dolls,' I continued patiently. 'The prisons of delusions. The prisons of pride and arrogance. And I regarded the poverty I tried to run away from for so many years as a prison too …'

'You escaped from that prison,' Red objected, adjusting his buckle again.

'Escape from one prison and you end up in another! The rows of cells are infinite. Our prisons are always with us. Remember that. Look at me and draw your conclusions …'

Afterwards I walked, with my hands behind my back, along the narrow iron catwalk beside the wall, striking the soles of my shoes against the rag carpet laid over the top of the fluted metal surface and thinking I was following this route for the fiftieth time already. Every Tuesday and Thursday, twenty-four weeks, six months – no doubt about it, it was time to celebrate the anniversary...

I walked with a long, rapid stride, but the guard didn't ask me to slow down. The screws like it when the suspects walk fast. I noticed that a long time ago. A prison warden's job is wearisome. Take one man for interrogation, then a second, a third, a tenth, frisk them all thoroughly, then escort them back again – this doleful labour requires skill and dexterity, the entire process is like an assembly line, and if one of the prisoners moves faster, so much the better for those players on the market of prison services. The sooner you get one client back, the sooner you can go to fetch the next one. Everybody's happy – the supervisors and the prison inmates.

And then, walking quickly is a highly reliable way of warming yourself up …

The hut was empty. The Swiss from Kharkov had gone for interrogation today as well. In silent solitude I approached the wretched little mirror and received further confirmation that the lawyer had not been mistaken in his assessment of my appearance.

I really did look bad. Prison had defeated me. The skin of my face had turned an unhealthy, sallow colour. Leo Tolstoy once compared this colour to that of the shoots of sprouting potatoes. The great classic of Russian literature scored a bullseye in the numerator, but a bad miss in the denominator. People aren't potatoes, they don't grow in prison, they wither. I was now observing with my own eyes the process of my own living tissues withering away. The muscles of my forehead and cheeks had lost their elasticity: the features that only recently had easily metamorphosed into every possible kind of expression and grimace, had turned into a frozen mask of mourning. The corners of the colourless, cracked lips had turned down. The look in the eyes was barbed and directed into emptiness.

That's the way a man looks when he has played out his game and failed completely, and is well aware of it. The look of the thorough-going loser who has ossified and sunk down to the very bottom, lost all faith in himself. A man who has lost even the slightest interest in the categories of success and victory. A man who has become as self-sufficient as stone.

My sense organs were tired. My eyes from the monotony of the colours, the endless combinations of grey, yellow and green (all muddy and dull, arousing feelings of alarm and discomfort). My tongue from the same old taste combinations of tea, bread and cigarettes. Food had turned into a dreary obligation. I chewed the food, mechanically ground it down and swallowed it like medicine. My hearing betrayed me: I would suddenly hear shouting in the distance, but who could possibly shout anything to anyone in the supremely quiet, supremely disciplined institution number one point one? Or just the opposite, my ear drums would be struck by a cotton-wool silence, too deep, with an icy, coppery resonance.

Victory over imprisonment seemed a pitiful self-deception to me now. How could I triumph here? My prisons were always with me. If not one, then another.

* * *

The key jangled as it was inserted in the lock. My cell-mate had come back from his interrogation. In January and February they took him out almost every week, usually on Fridays, for three or four hours at a time, and he always came back in exactly the same condition: excited and angry, with red eyes and puffy eyelids.

He would lie down on his bed and sigh quietly, sometimes even sob, then start to tell me – for some reason in a whisper – just how lucky he was. He'd ended up in the cleanest, most civilized prison anywhere in the former USSR. But he could have landed in the filthy, overpopulated Butyrka – a hell for fools. And so on.

I would immediately recall the leaden captain – Svinets – who had promised me a rapid move, and wince.

Asking questions in prison is bad form, so I didn't say anything. After all, my Swiss friend Grisha had real reasons for suffering. He was facing a stiff sentence, he had no relatives, no lawyer, he didn't get any food parcels. He had no one else to rely on. He was battling prison single-handed. But today I suddenly felt so indifferent to prison etiquette that I went straight ahead and asked my little friend:

'What is it, do they beat you?'

'No, of course not,' he replied, and all the wrinkles in his face began moving.

'You look as if you've been crying ...'

'You're probably right there, *mein kamerad*.'

'Will you have some chifir?'

'No thanks, I'll abstain. How can you drink that *scheise*?'

'It's the only high there is around here.'

'Ah, *cher ami*, if only you knew the highs they sell in Europe!' my cell-mate declared wistfully. 'Openly! All different varieties. You go into the coffee shop, and standing there behind the counter is this clever, grown-up guy, and lying in front of him he has thirty joints already filled, and he asks you with real feeling: "Vat do you vant, friend?" I want to fly away! And he holds out to me the fattest, most tightly packed joint and laughs: "Special for you, friend!" I go off into the far corner, sit down on a little divan and light up – slowly, savouring it, aware of just how right everything is that's happening … And I really do fly away, really fly … how can I explain all this to you?'

I felt disgusted, and I said:

'Don't explain. Poisons are just more prisons. That's as clear as day. Tell me instead why they beat you.'

'They don't beat me,' said Grisha, dismissing my concern. 'Why would they. I've told them everything. I've given everybody away. I'm not a fool, I used to be a Soviet lawyer, I understand everything that's going on. I was caught with a kilogram of hash and three thousand tabs of ecstasy. Caught red-handed.'

'Dostoevsky claimed that cultured people make the least successful criminals.'

Grisha smiled ruefully.

'I'm looking at twelve years of imprisonment in the Russian system, and it's really appalling, I know that, I've seen it, I wouldn't lie to you, mon cher … It will kill me, that's absolutely clear … And I wrote a full and frank confession! On one condition – until the end of the investigation and for the period of the trial I stay here, in Lefortovo. I won't go to any other prison. I hate Russian prisons. Believe me, I've seen plenty of them. I've been everywhere. And I got the message. I don't want to go there. It's horrendous there. The stench, the filth, the ghastly criminal faces, the crowded conditions, the sicknesses, the hunger … Hell! Hell for fools!'

Unexpectedly the lock rattled again. A figure appeared in the doorway, a man wearing a brown jacket, pink shirt and grey tie. The insignificant face bore the heavy imprint of exhaustion.

'Good day, comrades,' he said in an official tone of voice. 'I'm the supervisory prosecutor. Do you have any complaints?'

'No,' I replied, clearly discerning all the prosecutor's prisons. His neck was languishing in the prison of his tie knot, his extensive, sloping stomach in the prison of his belt. The prosecutor's crimson nose and cheeks, covered with a network of fine veins, clearly indicated the prison of a partiality to alcohol, and the despondent, incurious gaze that slid indifferently over me and Grisha, testified that the official's very occupation, his work and his means of earning his bread, were a burden and a bother to him, they had become repulsive and were also experienced as a prison.

On hearing my answer, he immediately turned round and left – he was stuck fast in his own prisons, a man drained of energy, tired.

26

'**A**t last!' Captain Svinets said contentedly and smiled. A blithe, spring-like smile. 'At last. As it happens, I always believed in you! I knew that one day you'd tell me everything. You've done the right thing. It's not in your own interest to keep your mouth shut ...'

I smoked drearily, thinking how from the outside I must look as if I fitted into the situation perfectly, just right, from head to toe: pale, skinny, with a dead, dull look in my eyes, in a dirty tracksuit and trainers without any laces. An abject prison inmate. A man caught in his own trap, who had lied himself into a corner, a talentless bonehead who had overestimated his own strength.

'It probably seems strange to you,' the happy detective continued, strolling round the office at a leisurely pace, 'that I've been trying so stubbornly for a whole six months to drag what I want out of you. The explanation's simple. As well as this ... what's his name, Feferonov ...'

'Farafonov.'

'Yes. That's it' – Svinets paused – 'as well as him, a member of the militia was killed. An officer. And if that wasn't already enough, a good friend of mine. A comrade-in-arms ... And that, as you know yourself, transforms an ordinary criminal case into a matter of principle! A case that has to be solved no matter what ... and it will be solved!'

The captain carefully put his notebook away in his pocket – the notebook in which he had written down the name I had given him – and started walking backwards and forwards again, as massive and impressive as a concert grand piano.

The first-class suit of fine, dark-blue woolen cloth sat on him like a second skin. The snow-white shirt fitted snugly across his chest. His perfectly shaved cheeks had a lustrous gleam. The sharp, fresh smell of expensive toilet water tickled my nostrils, arousing memories of better times – of the days when the crafty and fortunate wheeler-dealer Andriukha, stylishly dressed and sweetly scented, used to turn over mind-boggling deals worth millions, delighting in the fullness of life.

'By the way, how do you like my little suit?' the man from Moscow CID asked smugly, following the direction of my gaze.

'The very thing,' I said quietly, forcing out the words.

Svinets sat down on the corner of the wooden table. The item of furniture gave a subtle creak.

'That time, in August, when we first met, you probably really thought I didn't know a thing about clothes, right?'

I shrugged.

'I had to trick you,' the square-cut captain admitted and gave me a charming wink. 'I hired those leather jeans specially. From my cousin. I know you really liked them. They're a good pair of trousers. Practical … It was important for me to make sure you really were who you claimed to be. So you see, you're not the only smart trickster around!'

'Just what makes you think I'm a trickster?' I protested feebly, feeling my cheeks burning as if they'd been slapped hard.

'It's written on your forehead,' Svinets informed me briskly. 'In big letters. You think you're better than everyone else, that's what. That you're the cleverest, the most cunning. The champion. But just between you and me, you're still a long way from championship standard …'

The square-cut captain slipped his hand inside the flap of his jacket in a laid-back gesture and brought out a flat cigarette case that glinted yellow in the light – obviously gold. He took out a Captain Black cigarette and lit up, politely blowing the smoke away into the corner.

'I have to bust your kind almost every day,' he boasted. 'This last month alone I've busted five. All of them bandits, murderers, swindlers and thieves. And every one, as it happens, has his own little secret apartment. To hide from their wives. Or the militia. And all the things there are in those apartments!' The CID man's round face took on a dreamy expression.

'Televisions, computers, stereos, video-players, faxes with photocopiers, all sorts of fancy clothes, watches, gold … Drugs too – hash, cocaine, tablets for getting the girls excited, acid, amphetamines and so on … And money. In sacks, in boxes, in plastic bags, in suitcases, in pillow cases … Kilograms of it!'

I felt ashamed. The boisterous, rich Andriukha once used to have an apartment pretty much like that.

Just at that moment a brown sparrow jumped on to the frame of the small window that was standing open. He gave a melodic little chirp, fluttered his wings and disappeared. The message was easy enough to follow: It's spring outside, sunshine, fresh air. What are you sitting in here for, in the dust and the semi-darkness? Hurry up, live, move, enjoy!

'Every time I bust one of those bastards,' Svinets continued with obvious pleasure, 'the first thing I do is find out the precise address of the secret apartment. The keys to it are always lying in the bastard's pocket. Lying there so the wife won't find them. Or they're hidden in the car. When it comes to clothes and cash in pockets, I know what I'm doing, believe me …'

'Steal what was stolen?' I asked.

'Well, you could put it that way,' the captain agreed readily enough. 'Just between the two of us, I'm not the squeamish or shy type. And I know my own worth. I've solved eight murders. I've been in Chechnya three times. Been wounded twice. As a reward my country gave me a little iron medal and two little stars on my shoulder straps. And a little bit of money. The grand total would be just enough for one pair of shoes like these …'

Svinets pointed with a short, strong finger at his own gleaming fashion footwear, and his face suddenly hardened, turning stern and very manly, seeming to express some deep-rooted sense of protest against injustice. He went on:

'You respect strong people, right? And you think you're strong too. Am I right? That strong lad Napoleon once said: "The people that does not wish to feed its own army will feed someone else's". Do you agree with Napoleon?'

'Yes,' I whispered.

'Good man,' the detective said approvingly. 'Well, it's the same with cops! If you don't want to feed the militia, then you'll feed the bandits ... But I personally don't want the citizens of my country to feed bandits ... As it happens, I don't bear the country any grudge. I love it. It's my country. One day it gave me a pistol and an identity card. A little gentleman's set, so to speak. And basically, that's enough for me ...'

A large, sleepy fly circled slowly around just below the ceiling in turn after turn after turn, none of which made any sense to anyone but the fly.

In the office and in the corridors, in all the spaces inside the prison and outside it – everywhere – spring was in the ascendant. Even the guard who had brought me to the interrogation today had looked exhilarated and his eyes had sparkled: he had searched me without any real zeal, quite clearly not thinking at that moment about his immediate responsibilities, but about his plans for the evening.

'Don't feel too bad, okay?' Svinets slapped me on the shoulder. His hand was heavy and firm. 'And don't go imagining that you're some kind of Judas or something of the sort ... He dropped you in it. Right in deep! He slipped you a hot document. Not just hot, red hot! To be quite honest, I didn't expect you to cover for such an unscrupulous bastard. But you wouldn't budge for six whole months, my friend! What am I saying, six months, longer! How long have you been inside now?'

'Eight months,' I forced out.

'Quite a while. But it's no real time, of course. What made you keep needling me like that for eight whole months? What for? Dragging it out, trying to be cunning ... What for, eh? Thought you'd try playing at Sterlitz, did you?'

I didn't answer. I didn't feel like talking. That trick with the change of clothes had shocked me. I'd been duped. Cleverly and neatly. With suave professional ease. With the kind of skill that I could probably never match.

'But I, sinner that I am,' the captain said pensively, 'was thinking it was time to ask for you to be moved to the Matrosskaya Tishina, the hell for fools ...'

'Where?' I asked, turning cold.

'The hell for fools. Why, haven't you heard the expression before?'

'No,' I lied, hearing a ringing sound somewhere inside my head and remembering little Grisha Berger's crumpled face.

The detective paused.

'By the way, pardon me, but I always stand when I talk with suspects under investigation.'

'I've noticed.'

'It's good. It's a way of demonstrating my respect for people and in general ... I feel more comfortable working like that.'

'Does that mean,' I began timidly, and cleared my throat, 'that I can count on staying here? At Lefortovo?'

'Definitely,' Svinets assured me. 'In any case, for the period of the preliminary investigation into your CASE. After that – we'll see ... Okay ...' He deftly tugged up his shirt cuff and glanced at his watch – it was obviously gold. 'Time for me to go. A date. There's a woman waiting.'

'Double D bust, right?' I asked immediately. 'A blonde?'

Svinets chuckled.

'Exactly right. As it happens, double D blondes all adore armed men in good suits.'

'Nothing surprising about that,' I muttered. 'If I was blonde and female I'd act the same way.'

The captain laughed, emitting a series of manly, April, springtime sounds. The sound of a male laughing as he catches up with a female who has taken his fancy.

I felt a sharp pang of envy.

'So you do understand the logic of life!' the detective declared.

'I try to ...'

'The sparrow came back, this time not alone, but with two companions. The reckless chirping of the disheveled little hooligans filled the entire room. Svinets narrowed his eyes mischievously and flicked his cigarette butt at the birds. They scattered and retreated in panic.

There was a knock at the door.

'Come in!' the detective who was so excited by spring shouted in his deep bass voice.

Khvatov had a pair of brand new spectacles sitting on his nose. The lenses reflected the bright light outside the window.

'We're just saying goodbye,' Svinets told him. 'And as it happens, we're parting almost friends. Isn't that right, Andrei?'

I wiggled my shoulders and neck in an indefinite gesture that could have been taken for agreement or its opposite. The man from Moscow CID slapped me on the shoulder again and made for the door.

'Your tie still doesn't match your shirt!' I said to his square back. 'And shoes with toes like that stopped being cool two years ago!'

Never let your opponent have the last word.

Svinets slowly turned round.

An offended expression had appeared on his face. He shook his head disapprovingly, stuck his hands in his trouser pockets and went out.

I lowered my eyes. I felt dizzy. Obviously this was exactly the kind of day – sunny and fresh – when the most inveterate criminals capitulate. Real life bursts in on them, through their ears, their nostrils, their eyes, in bright colours and strident sounds, in the smells of dampness, mould and melt-water, blended with the scents of expensive perfumery from the people who come to interrogate them but then go back out into freedom, into April, to where there's water dripping from the roofs and everybody's smiling, where the blondes are out hunting for champions.

But the criminals, having come clean and given away their accomplices, are left behind to rot in their dank cells, gnashing their teeth with envy and dreaming of defeating prison one way or another.

All through March, spring infiltrated my cell and me, gradually, taking its time – in the yellow beams of sunlight, in the voices of the birds, in the damp breath of the warm wind. When I went out into the exercise yard, I just couldn't force myself to start my mandatory run – I stood there for a long time with my head thrown back, looking up at the sky: heavy and bright-blue, filled with shapeless, fluffy clouds that were sometimes straw-yellow, sometimes matt-turquoise, sometimes pearly-violet. They seemed to me like the plumage of some immense, all-powerful bird of happiness that had flown into my city. But not to me personally. Not to me.

Galled by my defeat at the hands of the captain, I decided to balance out the situation with an immediate victory over the investigator. During the final interrogations in March I had achieved unprecedented success. Every time Khvatov opened up the plump CASE FILE again, I was already reading entire paragraphs, grasping the sense instantly.

Now I knew that apart from me there were four others involved in the CASE and another individual was wanted. I had learned that three of the four were inside, like me, shut way in the pre-trial prison, and one was being questioned under the terms of a recognizance not to leave the area. The three who were inside (including the minister) were not providing testimony, but the one who came to his interrogations from his warm, comfortable home had given a full and frank confession. The case against me was founded on his testimony.

I had succeeded in extracting much useful information from that thick grey volume. I knew that the investigation was on the point of being concluded, that the body of evidence had basically been assembled, that I was not the most important defendant, and was only involved in one of the episodes. The sum stolen from the state treasury was close to fifty billion roubles. I had been involved in the theft of six billion of them – about one and a half million American dollars.

I even knew the details. I had read dozens of pages. I had mastered the knack. This victory had been achieved as soon as I perfected my method. First I chewed up bread to make glue, then used the blade of a razor to cut about twenty columns of text out of the first book that came to hand and stuck them on paper. The document I produced in this way was a precise imitation of a page in the CASE FILE. It was the same size, with lines the same length, letters the same size and about the same spacing of the text. It took me a week to prepare my training device.

Grisha, like my two previous cell-mates, slept to excess, as much as he possibly could, and never emerged from the kingdom of Morpheus before ten in the morning. But I, recalling that the God of the Christians incites us to be ever-vigilant, woke up at six. Then I sat down with my back to the door, took out my training device and worked away on the sly.

The very first day the guard, observing through the spy hole, noticed that his client was engaged in some important task, opened the embrasure and asked bluntly:

'What that you're doing?'

'Making notes on the Code of Criminal Procedure, comrade boss!' I replied briskly.

The screw cleared his throat dubiously and closed the feeder hole.

The bread glue came straight from my own mouth. I broke the blade out of a razor.

'How's your health, Stepan Mikhalich?' I asked Khvatov. 'Are your enemies still honking?'

'And how!' the investigator replied, sitting down at the table and connecting up his equipment. 'I had to go to the doctor last week …'

'And what did the doctor say?'

Pale and considerably thinner than before, the man from Ryzan sniffed sadly.

'He advised me, you know, to do more walking. In the fresh air …'

For a few minutes we exchanged meaningless remarks. I was waiting.

But Khvatov dashed my hopes. He didn't take the CASE FILE out of his bag. When he needed to glance into it he hid his eyes from me and pulled the voluminous file out for only a few seconds, until he realized what he was doing and left it on the table instead, but *closed*. Even in doing this, he gave himself away with the posture of his body and the meaning implied in all his small movements – the way he deliberately looked straight past me, the casual, almost nonchalant way he slammed the file shut, the haste with which he immediately turned back to his keyboard.

He could only have learned that I was trying to read the CASE FILE from one source. I was horrified to realise that my cell-mate, the drug-running lawyer, little Grisha Berger, could be an informer.

When Khvatov hastily slammed the CASE FILE shut once again, and even tapped his palm down on it, while gazing straight past me, I remembered about the 'hell for fools', put two and two together and realized that Grisha *was* a grass. And I decided that the moment I arrived in the cell I would hit him. With my fist. In the face. Several times.

In general, such radical action could have three consequences for me: first, the punishment cell; second, a guaranteed move away from the quiet, cultured Grisha to the company of some stupid idiots; and third, a new charge against me, and an extra year on my term. Only I'd already almost served that year and the prospect of the punishment cell didn't frighten me. But to move away from such a convenient cell-mate as the European Grisha … I didn't want to change my surroundings for the worse. And I found it easy to abandon the idea of physical violence against the stranded Swiss citizen.

If Grisha's an informer, I realized, that means his entire story about the diamonds is a bluff. The bold hero Radchenko never existed and he never made that run across the tundra. And perhaps Switzerland didn't exist either, or even Grisha Berger himself.

Back in the cell, I found the stool pigeon reading the newspapers. Grisha was so small that the only parts of him protruding from behind the unfolded sheet of newsprint were his tiny pink fingers and his feet – in the woolen socks that I had given him. The sight of the chunky knitting on socks that my wife had sent me suddenly made me furious.

I could have crushed the rat with one hand. Strangled him. Broken his back. How else do you deal with rats? But I managed to restrain myself. With Andriukha's help. 'Don't be a hothead,' he advised me. 'Remember the teaching of the great deceiver Machiavelli: "Never act in accordance with the first prompting of the soul, for it is the most noble".'

'What's in the paper, Grigorii?' I enquired in a smarmy voice.

'I'm reading the TV guide,' the Swiss drug-runner replied amiably.

'Nothing but criminal news, right?'

'That's right. There's even a show called "Full and frank confession".'

'Yes,' I blurted out. 'That's a subject close to your heart …'

The stranded *Monsieur* put the newspaper down.

'I suppose you despise me, don't you?'

'What for?'

'For my full and frank confession.'

'Your confession's absolutely no business of mine,' I replied rather rudely.

But was it ever made, that confession? The thought flashed through my mind, hot and furious. Maybe I should give him a good kick right here and now?

'I have almost fifteen years experience of practicing law,' Grisha said in a very quiet, apologetic voice. 'You probably know the old criminal saying: "A full and frank confession lightens the punishment, but increases the sentence"?'

Last time he said he had ten years' experience, and now it's fifteen. It's all lies and deception. I've been deceived. On the outside and here on the inside. My boss Mikhail deceived me, General Zuev deceived me, the detective Svinets deceived me. And now my cell-mate has deceived me. And in addition, I have deceived myself. Curses on deception and deceivers. Curses on falsehood in all its forms!

'Yes,' I croaked. 'I know that saying.'

'Well, it's wrong.'

'Possibly …'

'By confessing,' Grisha declaimed in a whisper, as if he were delivering a revelation, 'a man chooses the least difficult road for himself. He unfetters himself psychologically. Unburdens his soul …'

Any moment now he'll start quoting Dostoevsky.

'Having purged his conscience at the preliminary investigation stage, the criminal finds it easy to go through the painful procedure of a trial and accepts his punishment not as an act of vengeance, but as the start of a new life …'

'Back to freedom with a clear conscience,' I quoted.

'Yes!' the little stool pigeon exclaimed passionately. 'That's it exactly. Surely freedom and a clear conscience are what every man seeks? You're seeking your own freedom, aren't you?'

'My freedom is always with me,' I replied. 'In here, behind bars,

I'm as free as on the outside. But a conscience isn't a saucepan. It's never entirely clean.'

Why the hell am I discussing matters of conscience with a prison nark?

'Stop trying to educate me, Grisha.'

'I'm not trying to educate you,' the grass said with a radiant smile. 'I just want to help you.'

You've already done that. And how! Ruined all my plans. How can I live with you now? I'll have to look into your eyes! Say good morning to you! Give you cigarettes! Tell jokes. How am I going to co-exist under the same roof with an informer? How am I going eat with him at the same table? How will I be able to bear the rat's presence?

But a minute passed, then another – and I received a clear reply to my question. The door embrasure suddenly opened.

'Rubanov!' someone called outside. 'Is Rubanov here?'

'Yes.'

'GET YOUR THINGS!'

I took this third repetition of the laconically cruel order calmly. Philosophically. Not like an enlightened man and not like a fighter waging war on the idea of prison, but like an ordinary, experienced prisoner.

Yes, I quite distinctly hated that phrase 'Get your things!' – it brusquely shattered the routine of my life, uprooted me and carried me away further, deeper into the prison, into an uncertain future; but at the same time I had wearied long ago of feeling afraid of uncertainty, and I met this new blow with a measure of healthy indifference. The modern prisoner submits easily to training. They tell him: 'Face the wall!' – and he instantly turns into the required position. They order him: 'Get your things!' – and he obediently gathers up his underwear. Deftly and quickly, with no unnecessary movements.

I was ready in five minutes. The shorts, socks, books and notebooks all fitted into a single plastic bag. The food was left for the stool pigeon to eat. Remembering the noble gesture made by my old friends, Frol and Fatty, I didn't take the tea, or the butter, or the smokes – let them all stay to remind that rat Grisha about me when the next victim of his treachery moves into the cell. Let them. I'm not greedy.

The mattress was rolled up into a tube and tied, the bag was buttoned shut. There was enough time left for a final conversation.

'Goodbye, Grisha,' I said, sitting down facing the Swiss. 'I know you're a grass and a bastard. And I want you to know I know it. I'll always know and always remember ...'

Grisha wasn't surprised by my words. His eyes took on a stern, kind expression, like a schoolteacher's. His chin twitched forward and to one side.

'Goodbye, Andrei,' the little nark replied calmly. 'When we meet on the outside you can cast a stone at me ...'

'Be sure of it,' I warned him. 'That stone's definitely going to strike home! And what a stone it will be – the stone to end all stones, yeah? It will fly true, all right!'

Grisha didn't answer.

'How could you do it?' I asked quietly. 'You ate my bread, then went to the cops and ratted on me! You always came back so cheerful and excited! Because they gave you a dose! They treated you to a high, right? You smoked, or snorted, or shot up, or whatever you drug addicts call it! And you grassed me up! How could you?'

'What would you have me do, *mon ami*?' Grisha protested. 'I'm looking at twelve years. I don't have any family or friends in this country. How will I survive in the hell for fools? I'll be fifty soon! How can I hold out to the end of my term? What will I be like when I get out? A toothless old man? With TB? An impotent invalid? Has what I did really done you that much harm? You're young. You'll be out again in three years. Am I supposed to rot here until I die?'

'How could you do it?' I groaned, ignoring the villain's tirade of self-justification. 'How could you deceive me? You know, I *trusted* you. And you deceived me! I *trusted* you! Shared every last thing with you! I felt for you! Scrubbed your back in the bathhouse! Told you about my plans! And you ratted on me! How could you?'

'I could,' Grisha admitted. 'I just could. It's not so hard ...'

They led me out. Without being reminded, I turned to face the face. And I guessed its secret. Understood it. Unmasked that wall's identity – it was the very same wall after which the narrow, crooked little street in New York was named. The legendary Wall Street. Russian businessmen still rave about it deliriously, even now. Every second one of them dreams of a vertiginous commercial career, concluding in an office on the street named after a wall, millions of dollars, a sweet life and a wife who's a Hollywood movie star.

In fact, however, instead of millions of dollars and the stars from the sky, all we have is the brisk, brassy instruction: 'Face the wall'.

Facing the wall *is* Wall Street, Russian-style.

My things caught up with me at the exit, in the frisking room. Eight months earlier this was where I'd been told to spread my buttocks. I'd just moved in then – now I had no idea where I was going.

'There's a delivery for you.'

They brought in the sack. Laid out the plastic bags of food and clothing on the table. The apples gleamed brightly through the plastic.

'Check it and sign.'

An hour later I left special pre-trial detention centre number one point one. I was fully equipped. Loaded down with tea, sugar, cigarettes, fruit and underwear, I barely managed to fit into the metal kennel of the prison van. The guard in camouflage gear even had to press the door shut in order to close the bolt, leaving me face to face with all the things gathered together by my wife so that I would survive, be saved.

All I had to do was carry out the plan. Survive and be saved. And even, perhaps, win my freedom.

27

Moscow – if you look at the plan of its roadways, it's like a crooked wheel. Immense blocks of thousands of buildings, sliced through by the rings and radiuses of the streets and avenues. This traffic arrangement is always liable to remind anyone – long-time resident or newcomer – of the centrifugal and centripetal order of life here; but then, the entire country lives according to the same rule. People, money and information move from its border regions to the centre; moving at breakneck speed in the opposite direction, out to the periphery, is a stream of governmental decrees, glossy magazines, TV shows and, sometimes, columns of tanks. Close to the centre the mass of humanity is denser and more solid, the tension is higher. But at the edges there is the silence of a peaceful half-doze.

These were my thoughts at shortly after six in the morning as I studied a map of the city's roads in an attempt to decide exactly which route I should take to the meeting place. The creditor who had made an appointment with me the evening before had an office on the opposite side of the megalopolis. I would have to travel almost seventy kilometres through streets crammed with crowds of thousands of pedestrians, cars big and small, trucks, trams and buses.

So how should I travel? Through the centre, overloaded with traffic, or round the edge? No doubt at all that any smart Asiatic type would choose the long road as the simplest and calmest. Although it's almost three times as long. A naïve European, on the other hand, would measure the distance from A to B with a ruler, calculate the relative advantage, jump into the driving seat and have no more doubts about anything.

On that grey, entirely sunless spring morning I – unemployed, with a criminal record and no money to my name – suddenly wanted to feel like a European, and I drove off into the centre shortly after seven. At the same instant another ten million greater and lesser beings officially resident in the capital also stirred into motion, as well as several million visitors, gastarbeiters, illegal immigrants, unregistered individuals and tourists.

Tens of thousands of trucks drove in from the surrounding regions. Thousands of buses and hundreds of suburban electric trains brought in cheap labour power from the same area. The city awoke. The wheel started turning.

I drove straight into the centre, right into the mincer. After all, this is my city, why should I have to go around, if there's a short, direct route?

'I want to be a European!' I muttered 'I want to be a European!'

I had prepared for the conversation with my creditor. Put on my best suit. The one I had worn twenty days earlier to go to the final meeting with my former boss Mikhail. Now the two-piece in a colour something between sandy beige and lettuce green had come in useful again.

As always, memories of my former friend roused pain and a feeling of dull resentment. Poor Mikhail, unfortunate Misha Moroz! What was he going to do now? He ruined everything himself. Of course, I hadn't believed his story about losing the million. The million was definitely safe and sound. Hidden. Stashed away in secret hiding places. Only what use was that? In some Hollywood action movies – not the biggest box office hits – the final, entrancing scene shows the hero disappearing with a suitcase full of dollars. The hero – a negative character, but devilishly charming – picks up the suitcase with his right hand, always puts his left arm round a young blonde, and disappears … Where to? Into what kind of life? What is he going to do? How is he going to spend the large sum of money represented by that plump, luscious word?

Keep looking round as you walk, dear Mikhail. Sit quiet and don't stick your head up. Spend what you stole a little bit at a time. You'll never scrape another million together. Never rise any higher. The past will weigh your feet down like ton weights. You betrayed and sold out first one man and then several more; now live, breathe and spent your bundle of capital.

A miserable fugitive, burdened with neuroses. Do you think a million will take the place of love and peace for you? I doubt it. Hiding it and hiding it again, all the time trembling with fear, counting and recounting it, quaking – that's your future, my dear former friend.

As I composed this monologue in my head, I walked out of the house and launched into the colourless, difficult start of a hazy Moscow Friday. I settled down comfortably inside my rusty but frisky auto that reeked of tobacco. After several attempts I got the motor started – and I set off.

My car, manufactured on the banks of that Asiatic river, the Volga, simply couldn't bear fine clothes. As soon as I, its owner, set out on a journey clad in light-coloured trousers, it immediately broke down: something trivial, not serious, just being awkward, exclusively in order to make me stop it in the middle of the dirty, uproarious street, open the bonnet and tug on some wire or hose, getting dirt on my knees and elbows. To make me stroke its withers. But on the other hand, if I defiled myself with tatty, crumpled jeans and stained tee-shirts, my idiot motor functioned perfectly. The headlights sparkled, the engine purred and even the small defects, like the door handle that was stuck, suddenly corrected themselves.

As I set out today, there was no way I could afford to be delayed, I had to deceive the machine. I put my shirt and suit in a cover and laid them on the back seat, intending to change before I arrived. And I took my seat at the controls, dressed in a pair of singularly democratic tracksuit trousers with stretched and baggy knees. Failing to spot my cunning trap, my motorised carriage started off and carried me almost without any delays right as far as the Garden Ring, into the initial precincts of the centre. Here, like everyone else, I was obliged to submit to the severe traffic conditions: I waited patiently, crept forward two or three metres, sometimes politely allowed other drivers to pass and sometimes cut in rudely right in front of their noses.

The capital's newly begun day was dim and muggy: the dirty cotton wool of the low clouds wound itself around the spires of the Stalin skyscrapers. The hot air trembled and shimmered above the asphalt, above the steel, aluminium and plastic bodies of thousands of cars – red and blue, expensive and cheap, ultramodern and long out of date. Their owners – all of them – were dreaming of getting into the centre.

For me the morning had also begun with a vile hangover sucking at my soul and my stomach. I banished its physical consequences immediately after waking up. A hot-and-cold alternating shower and two cups of coffee with aspirin quickly got rid of the headache and the nausea. But the mind is not so easily deceived. The previous day's bottle of gin had given me two hours of euphoria. But now the see-saw had swung in the other direction: as soon as the effect of the poison ceased, depression set in.

While I stood, covered in goose-bumps under the icy streams of water, chewed on tablets, brushed my teeth, ironed my shirt and started up the car, I didn't notice the acid indigestion of my nerves, or perhaps it was still gathering within me. But after half an hour of exhausting travelling, moving in spurts, close to the Kremlin, on the totally jammed quayside just before the Kamenny Bridge, I felt myself trembling in fury.

The tension suddenly became unbearable, and I swore out loud. Yelled at the top of my voice. The people in nearby cars looked at me in amazement. Especially the young, exceptionally fresh girl riding along side-by-side with me in a Japanese sedan from the upper price range. That is, the girl was from the upper price range, as well as the car. Brushing back a platinum lock of hair to reveal a suntanned ear, the owner of the ultra-fashionable auto (either a kept mistress or the beloved daughter of a daddy who was doing well: perhaps even both at the same time) opened her eyes wide in amazement, raised her perfectly plucked eyebrows and shrugged a petite shoulder, unable to understand what had so infuriated her neighbour in the stream of traffic, this guy with the puffy face and the premature wrinkles.

I felt ashamed. I raised the tinted window and hastily lit up. 'You're a loser,' I told myself mournfully. 'You're right down on the bottom again. Your health's ruined, you don't have a job. You're on your way to a place where you'll be asked to pay back a debt. But you don't have any money. You're a nobody. A shit with a criminal record. A pitiful neurasthenic. Look around – the people riding along smoothly beside you are confident and neatly dressed. Their faces are full of Asiatic tranquility. Their lives are all fine-tuned. The air-conditioned coolness caresses their bodies. They are the inhabitants of the centre. But you, you disorderly fool – what are you seeking among them? You're out of place here and you always will be. You're too nervous and skinny. You don't look right here. They won't accept you into this kingdom of the well-balanced, in any case. The most they'll do is use you and then throw you away. It's already happened once, and now here you go poking your head back in again, trying to learn how to elbow others out of your way.

Gradually I began feeling worse again. I could feel a hot, rough lump stirring in my chest. Darkness welling up from beyond the edge of reality. I tossed out my cigarette, pressed the right pedal down to the floor and overtook several absentminded competitors by driving right up on to the pavement. Then, by committing another crude breach of the rules of the road, I managed to advance again: I darted out on to the junction against a red light, speeded up and stopped just in front of the entry to the bridge.

There were another twenty or so sly dogs perched there all around me. The entire stream of traffic was divided in two. Some preferred to wait for a while and cross the dangerous spot according to all the rules, others attempted to slip across any way they could, even under the threat of a militiaman's whistle and a fine.

As I tried to steer into a convenient position, I got in someone's way and heard the indignant honking of a horn.

'Sorry!' I muttered to the aggrieved party. 'It's the law of the jungle here, my friend. If you want to drive according to the rules, get in line with the well-balanced folk!'

But my 'friend' demonstrated astonishing persistence and actually succeeded in overtaking me. The battered, swaying poop of an absurd dreadnought manufactured on the banks of that Asiatic river, the Moscow, appeared in front of my eyes. The rough lump in my chest exploded in a thousand sparks of fire. I forced my engine to roar. There was a piercing squeal of rubber giving off stormy clouds of smoke. Starting off at full throttle, I overtook the impudent jerk, blocked his way and made my tyres squeal again – this time in triumph – before dashing away. Unfortunately, the insolent manoeuvre didn't do me any good. Fifty metres further along, on the hump of the bridge, the flow of traffic halted again, and my stubborn rival ended up in the next line, just five metres away from me; I saw him lower the glass in his door and shout something in my direction, rolling his eyes in fury. Intrigued, I also opened my window and stuck my head out.

'Why you ... why I'll ... you'll ...' the offended party yelled, showering me with obscene hints and menacing threats.

This adult male about forty years of age, wearing a funny cap, laid particular emphasis on potential sexual contact between us, with me playing the passive role. Emerald-green stars glittered in front of my eyes. My head, full of stale alcohol fumes, was not working too well. The insult, unbearable for any man who has done time in jail, was not absorbed by my brain and my reason, but by my entire being, already so tense that it was bursting apart.

'What?' I roared in a deep bass. 'What? What did you say?'

I yanked on the handle, smashed my shoulder against the door and leapt out into space. My opponent, clearly stung to the quick, came dashing towards me, his large, meaty ears wiggling aggressively. His outfit consisted of the same sort of tracksuit trousers as I had, with extremely stupid stripes and the same kind of old, stained tee-shirt. The only real difference was that my clothing bore no slogans (I find them irritating), while my enemy's chest was decorated with a large invitation in English:

WELCOME TO SWITZERLAND!

When I made out the letters, I felt myself turning cold with hate.

'Come here!' I shouted. 'Come on, then!'

Fisticuffs were no part of my plan. Such conflicts, even the very lightest and briefest, always end in bruises, blood and direct material losses in the form of torn clothing. As I was hurrying to an important meeting with an important man, there was absolutely no way I could allow any of that to happen. If I wanted a fight, I would definitely have tried to jump out of my car before my enemy. In order to catch him as he was straightening up from a sitting position, with the door of his own car. I would have attacked first, immediately, with all my strength, without wasting precious moments on threatening interjections.

On this occasion the moment had been missed. More than that, when my enemy and I moved closer, I discovered that he was a head taller than me and clearly stronger, and his arms were much longer than mine.

'Why, I'll ... you!' my enemy roared, extending his sinewy upper limbs towards me. 'I'll ... you!'

In reply I spouted a string of the most convoluted, most horrific obscenities of which an inmate of a Russian prison is capable. But mere acoustic means were not sufficient to defeat the enraged citizen. He pushed me hard, then again, and again.

There was a time when my fighting weight used to be seventy-two kilograms. Unfortunately the most important of those – the flesh, the muscles on the shoulders and arms and the fat on the stomach – had been left behind me in prison. In other words, the participants in this fight belonged to different weight categories. On the other hand, my fists remembered very well the sensation of thousands of blows against the concrete floors of the Lefortovo exercise yards, the pink and crimson scars were still clearly visible. Deciding that I would at least break the fool's lower ribs, two on the left and two on the right, I waited for the moment to launch a counter-attack. Now I could blind the hothead with a but to the bridge of his nose, I calculated, then stick my knee into his groin, and then knock him down and finish him off with a series of kicks ...

But at the decisive instant, when my entire body was already tensed for the first, most important onslaught, the rational prison inmate in my head – the chifir-soaked philosopher, the habitué of the cells – awoke and quietly reminded me that for causing moderately serious bodily harm I could face a minimum of three years low-security regime. Bearing in mind my previous record, it could be the full four! This realization instantly cooled my ardour. I demonstratively lowered my hands.

In addition, as the two sweaty, poorly dressed blockheads clumsily played out a fight in the very centre of the capital, a cavalcade of government limousines drove past them – dark-blue, gleaming, with their expensive tyres rustling grandly, and as I yelled out obscenities, men with greying hair and solid, powerful chins looked out at me irritably from behind the greenish-tinted glass – high-ranking officials hurrying on their way to work.

I thought better of it. My opponent was breathing heavily in my face. Cars were driving round the scene of battle, honking furiously. We had created a traffic jam. I have to end this stupid little scene, I thought. Those words on his tee-shirt, that Switzerland, that instantaneous trip into the depths of memory, a flash-back featuring the stool pigeon Grisha – that was what had really made me furious.

'Don't you know the rules?' the long-armed man menaced me, with spittle splashing from his mouth. 'You little pup!'

'You drive according to the rules, do you?' I roared in reply. 'That's your problem! You Swiss!'

'We'll sort this out at the militia station!' the aggressive stooge barked.

The mention of the militia cooled me right off. Bracing my wide-set feet against the ground, I pushed the hot, angry body far away from me and hurriedly dusted off my dirty trousers. In the heat of a battle that never quite happened, I had actually touched the ground with my knee two or three times. There was no denying that my opponent had strong arms.

'Threatening me with the militia?'

'Yeah, I am!'

'Okay,' I hissed. 'The militia it is then! Let's go!'

'Let's go!' My opponent tugged off his cap to let the air get to his broad, bright bald patch, got into his car, pulled sharply into the flow of traffic and drove off down the bridge.

I drove after him, still submerged in a wave of adrenalin.

I knew I would get a special reception at the militia station. I couldn't count on any special indulgences. An idle loafer with a criminal record, a suspicious type with no definite form of employment had started an outrageous fight under the very walls of the Kremlin, in full view of peaceful citizens and the employees of the British embassy. A hooligan like that was guaranteed fifteen days straight away, and after that – we'd see … I couldn't just disappear: the offended blockhead was sure to have memorized my number …

They would put me inside again! Because of my stupid lack of self-control at a moment when my mind was clouded by a hangover, they would put me inside again. Stick me behind bars, where I would sleep with the light on, defecate in front of my cell-mates and hate myself. My bronchi would suck in the stench of tuberculosis. My wife would bring me tea and sugar, scraping the kopecks together. My son would think his daddy was 'away on business'. My mother and father would go grey. My soul would turn as black as pitch. The triple fool would hurt the very people he loved. Poison their lives ...

But I was lucky. I was saved.

I suddenly remembered that there was always a traffic cop on sentry duty at the very end of the bridge. Round the clock. The gates into the Kremlin were on the square, the President himself drove inside the red battlements at this spot. Everything happening here was monitored! My vicious rival might fail to see the militiaman and drive on past. But I would stop and report the incident first.

It happened just as I wanted: the enemy's scratched vehicle went trundling on upwards, towards Pashkov House and the mouth of New Arbat street.

'What's wrong, Swiss, not in such a hurry to meet the militia?' I laughed soundlessly as I stopped and switched on the emergency lights. 'Here's one! Right here! Why are you so inconsistent? If we're on our way to the militia, we should stop at the first representative of authority! The very first employee of the agencies of security! At this captain in the dove-grey uniform. To report and lodge a complaint!'

I got out and started waving my arms to my opponent, but he was hopelessly caught up in the dense mass of vehicles. Either he had cooled off too, or he really didn't know about the militia post by the entrance to the red brick tower. He might simply have put off writing his complaint until later. But I didn't put it off. I immediately reported the unlawful incident. If you want to report something, then do it quickly, setting aside all doubts and emotions.

'Comrade captain. I have a conflict to report!'

'Aha!' the captain said in delight, squinting at my dirty knees. 'And they tell me over the radio that there's a fight on the bridge! They want me to stop it ... So that was you, was it?'

'That's right!' I declared, flinging my arms out. 'An absolute disgrace! Believe me, some villain insulted me, tried to give me a beating, waved his fists about, and then just drove off! That's his car there, the white Moskvich, see it? Fleeing the scene of the incident! It's appalling! In the centre of the capital city of my homeland I get insulted and they try to provoke me to fight! Outrageous! The hooligans are running riot! Stalin's what they need! I won't leave it at this!'

'Calm down,' the traffic cop told me. 'We'll sort this business out!'

'People like that ought to be put in jail!' I shouted, offering the militiaman my cigarettes (he politely declined). 'This is absolute anarchy!'

'These things happen,' the guardian of the law told me reasonably. 'Go on about your business.'

'What business, when my nerves are shattered first thing in the morning?'

'We'll take measures,' the traffic cop said reassuringly, clearly already losing interest in me. 'There are security cameras installed everywhere around here. The criminal's number plate has been caught on video tape. Don't get upset. All the best.'

Acting as if my feelings of civil justice had been restored, I went back to my car and hurriedly drove away, knowing that I had done everything just in time and just right. I had outplayed my enemy both as a European – by reporting a crime to the authorities in a timely manner – and as an Asiatic – by doing everything with sagacious flexibility. Now, if the enemy tried to lodge a complaint with the agencies of the interior ministry, it would very soon become clear, that *I had told them earlier*! I reported first! That was a victory. I had proved cleverer and more worldly-wise than the naïve man with the stupid slogan on his chest.

Pleased with the rapid solution of a big problem I had just shifted into second gear when, a second later, I stepped on the brake. On my right, road-workers were breaking up the asphalt with crowbars. The bus trundling along ahead of me changed direction sharply as it drove round them. A stone shot out, spinning furiously, from under the hot, black rubber of the bus's rear wheel. As if it had been fired out of a sling, the small piece of road-metal smashed into my windscreen and a crack immediately appeared from top to bottom. I shuddered. Braked again. A second flying stone followed, then a third, and a fourth, clattering against the bodywork and bouncing back off.

In the very centre of a big city, on the joyless morning of a joyless day, I was being stoned, and suffering unendurable, superstitious terror – as if the veil of eternal darkness had stirred and suddenly parted to reveal images of inhumanly cruel executions.

Drop everything. Forget the past, the sweet life, the millions. Calm down. Start all over again. From where you started before. From nothing. Work off the debts. Reject the vodka and the drugs. Thirty-two years old – fine, that's okay. You have a family, you have a home, you have a head …

I had to stop. To catch my breath. But they started honking impatiently behind me. Come on, kid, keep the traffic moving. No time, no time for reflection! You'll have time later to think about the stones that were thrown. But for now – forward.

PART FOUR

28

They drove me off again.

On one of the sharp turns in the city the luxurious high-tech meat-wagon jolted violently. Oranges spilled out of a bag and went rolling across the steel floor, diffusing the scent of the New Year holiday. I carefully picked up the soft orange cannonballs and stuck them in my pockets. Fruit was one thing I was going to need.

I was tormented by uncertainty and furious with the penal system. Why hadn't I been told the purpose of the journey? It was humiliating. As it happened, I hadn't even been convicted, I was only a suspect under investigation. That is, officially *an innocent man*. My guilt would be established by the court. But they treated me – an innocent man! – as if I were an animal. Why couldn't they tell me, in just a single short phrase, what the destination of this journey was?

'Cool it!' said Andriukha, pulling me up sharply. Perfectly sober this time, he said: 'You must have known what you were in for. You're not a little boy any more. You could have guessed for yourself that it's written on your forehead. Life often sends young men with inscriptions like that to prison, sometimes even to the graveyard. Any full-grown adult who's not stupid can read that writing, and a professional servant of the law, whether he's a dick or a screw, can decipher it quite clearly. Do you know what you have written on your forehead?'

I know. I realised the whole thing without you anyway. You can't make out any individual letters, naturally. And the words merge into each other. But this is the meaning:

YOU CAN'T TOUCH ME.

Maybe it reads 'I'm the smartest' or 'champion of the world' or 'the coolest' or even 'the slickest'.

'You must agree that it's good for a young man with that sort of thing written on his forehead to get put behind bars!' said Andriukha, picking the foie-gras out of his teeth. 'Inside, they'll shuffle the cocksure young lad from interrogation to interrogation, from cell to cell, from prison to prison, without asking him about it, until he realises his mistake. Then they'll put him away in a camp and advise him to concentrate on making cast-iron manhole covers for the heating mains. Get ready, brother!'

The door of the vehicle slid aside with a dull screech. I jumped down on to a surface of brown asphalt dotted with dark gobs of spittle. Very close, on the right and the left, grey walls with flaking paint rose high above me. I drew the air in through my nose and discovered dampness in it. Somewhere nearby there was a large river or other body of water.

Suddenly, just above my head, someone started bawling in an appallingly loud, hard, young voice that grated savagely:

'One! One! Nine!'

I turned to the right and the left, but couldn't find anyone. Only the walls, only the windows in those walls, covered with a system of close-set parallel metallic strips.

'One! One! Nine!'

'Speak!' I heard a voice say in the distance.

'Brother! Ask! Mityukha! Sedoi!' At this the invisible yeller coughed hoarsely from the strain of his efforts. 'Mityukha! Sedoi! The load! Is it home?'

A few seconds the dull reply arrived.

'Home, home, brother! Home, home! Got that?'

'Got it! Got it! So long!'

I was shoved roughly in the back.

'Heard enough?'

A person dressed in dirty khaki, with bandy legs, black hair and a pock-marked face, no more than a metre and sixty centimetres tall, showed me a rubber truncheon and grinned, revealing small, brown teeth.

'Go through,' he ordered, nodding at a door in the grey wall.

All the saliva suddenly disappeared from under my tongue. I unglued my lips and wheezed:

'Tell me, boss! Where am I? What is this place?'

'A fine place!' the cadaver said and repeated his grin. 'The best in the world! Move on!'

'Where am I? Where have they brought me?' I insisted as I picked up my bags.

' Matrosskaya Tishina!'

It actually had a proud ring to it, a certain grand swagger, as if we were talking about a golf club.

I went in. My nose was assaulted by a pungent odour of urine and the barracks-room. In the dim electric light I surveyed the peeling walls and the yellow tiles of the floor. The cadaver stomped along vigorously behind me.

After the compulsory procedure to establish my surname, first name, patronymic and year of birth, and also the charge against me, I found myself in the frisking section, where I was dealt with by a second cadaver, dressed more cleanly. With his elbows propped on the tin-covered table, he rummaged half-heartedly in my bundle.

'From Lefortovo?'

I nodded.

'Been inside long?'

'Eight months.'

'That's no time,' cadaver number two stated definitively. 'Ah, sod you. Go on. Move it, move it!'

As it happens, my rear passage was not inspected. This wasn't the terrible Lefortovo fortress, I twigged that straight away. The manners here were obviously a bit less sophisticated. They didn't look up your back passage here.

When I found myself in a suite of rooms illuminated by the feeble glow of dusty light bulbs, with walls covered in a spongy concrete overcoat, I realised that the building I had arrived in was itself a back passage, the anus of civilisation. The smells were right, and so were the sounds. The entire character of the dark-green corridors and rooms – dirty, damp, dark, fouled with vomit and sprinkled with bleach, echoing with the screeching of obscenities and the tramping of heavy boots, simply cried out that this was the spot where civil society relieved itself, expelling its human waste. Right now it was expelling me. Briskly, even with a certain humour. Forcing me further on along its intestines.

On reaching the end of the section, I turned left after my escort and walked up a staircase – as broad as the one in Lomonosov Moscow State University – to the second floor. Here there was a second section of intestine, a long corridor; the metal extraction box of the ventilation system stretched along the ceiling; in the walls there were massive steel doors that had once been painted black, but time and the vapours breathed by many thousands of men had made the paint flake off and in places the metal itself was tainted by rust. The embrasures in the doors were all wide open, and in every one there was a pale, inquisitive young face with eyes that watched intently as I walked by.

My escort stopped and took out a bundle of massive keys, selected the one he needed, put it in the lock and turned it twice with an effort. He pulled the door towards himself.

'Go in,' he invited me, and for some reason winked at me with a mischievous black eye.

Clutching my bags, I took two steps that carried me inside, and immediately ran into a mass of human bodies crowded tightly against each other. It was like trying to force your way into a bus during the early morning rush hour. Only people in a bus wear clothes, they don't smoke, and there are some women among them. Here the clothes and the women were completely absent.

'Why here?' several hoarse voices began protesting around me, and the cry was immediately taken up by other, more numerous voices, further away. 'Why here, boss? It's chock-a-block already! Where's the space?'

In reply the warder gave vent to a vehement shower of obscene abuse.

'How many of you are there?' he shouted.

'A hundred and thirty-five already!'

'So what?' the screw retorted with a chuckle. 'Over in one nineteen there are a hundred and fifty, and it's okay, no one's beefing! Cut the racket!'

The door slammed shut behind my back.

After the twenty square metres of the cell in Lefortovo, I saw the space in front of me here as absolutely vast. I tried breathing in, but that proved not to be so simple – instead of air, some rotten, disgusting substance flowed into my lungs. Streams of sweat instantly began trickling down my temples.

Through a whitish murk, I made out the figures of dozens upon dozens of semi-naked and completely naked men, their bony, angular limbs in constant motion, the sickly skin of their shaved and scratched heads constantly puckering into wrinkles. Inflamed eyes turned the blaze of their feral glances on me – and were instantly extinguished. The noise of voices grew louder and after a halt of a few seconds, the movement of arms and eyes was renewed.

'Listen …' a fleshless, sharp-nosed individual, covered all over in patches of iodine, touched my sleeve, 'Listen, I'll tell you … leave your things here and you go over there, further in. The *supervisor's* in there, have a talk with him …'

I turned sideways on and squeezed between the bodies, took one step, then a second and a third. The crush was appalling. There were naked creatures sleeping on their sides, pressed up against each other, on two-storey steel bunks. There were massive bundles of things dangling from the ceiling in shapeless stalactites: travel bags, bundles, sacks and plastic bags. There was grey laundry drying on taut-stretched strings. In the centre of the space I discovered a long table, crammed with chipped enamel mugs. There were heating coils stuck into some of them. The bluish steam streamed up into the air.

Protruding on all sides were bony, tattooed shoulders, knees and elbows. Some of the men watched me go by with a hostile glance, some gave a predatory laugh, some greeted me as if I were an old acquaintance – but

I took one step and then another without speaking, sometimes stooping to avoid catching my head on the feet of men sleeping on the upper bunks. By now the sweat was streaming down over my stomach as well as my temples.

I tried once again to take a gulp of air and once again realised that the process of breathing here involved certain difficulties and required a special skill. On my third step into the cell I wanted to turn and bolt. It became manifestly clear to me that my appearance here was a mistake, a misunderstanding, an oversight on the part of the administration: I shouldn't be here, I couldn't be here; I had to get out of this nightmarish menagerie immediately and demand special conditions for myself.

I slowed down and decided to go back. The thought appeared on my fifth step, when yet another sleeping prisoner's brown foot emerged from the sour fog of tobacco smoke. The human limb above it was covered in sores and was half-yellow, half-green from the furacillin or Vishnevsky ointment or other remedy that had been used to treat them: its little toe stuck out obscenely, there were half-moons of dirt in all the hollows between the toes, the nails had grown disgustingly long and were infected with mould. The foot appeared right in front of my eyes, about ten centimetres in front of me. I stopped and decided to go back. Turn chicken.

'Turning chicken's risky,' Frol had told me once. 'Go to the door and rap on it with your fist and ask the goon to take you out of the cell – and you're a goner. You'll never have authority or respect, you're doomed to live in the herd, you're a passenger. You're chicken. Never hammer on the door with your fist. Solve every problem on the spot. Yourself. Take a good look around, get your bearings, mingle with people. Don't be in any hurry to look for a place to sleep. You'll be all right, you're a lad with a head on your shoulders, plucky. But never rap on the door with your fist!'

'Sorry Frol,' Andriukha put in politely, but with extremely ugly cynicism, pulling a wry face, 'sorry, but I can't stay here, this is a pigsty. I'm going to go to the prison authorities and buy myself a better spot. I'll pay the going rate. Let the other cretins choke in this hellhole and smell the stench that they've all created, the gas from a hundred and thirty sets of intestines. Let the others breathe the smoke of dirt-cheap cigarettes.'

I'm going to ask the screw to take me out into the relatively cool corridor and there I'll offer him any amount of money to take me to the people in charge, and then I'll promise them any amount of money to get me out of here! After all, I'm not just anybody! I'm a major criminal! I was picked up for the theft of one and a half million American dollars! I'm a Moscow businessman! A banker! I'm big-time, rich, what am I going to do in this messy jumble of bodies, in this anthill, in this cesspit?

But even so I took a step forward.

At this point a person with thin arms, very fierce and serious, and immensely short of sleep – his badly swollen cheeks kept slumping downward, but he immediately forced his intent, staring eyes open – appeared in front of me and punched the dirty foot swaying in front of my nose. He didn't hit it really hard, just hard enough for the owner of the rotten trotter to feel it and draw his leg up, groaning pitifully in the depths of his bright sleep. I tried not to notice the two very large, brownish testicles, covered with a bright-red rash, that slipped out through the opening of a pair of old, dirty shorts with burn holes in two places and the waist elastic sticking out and knotted back together, and in addition it was obvious that the penis was in a state of extreme excitation, sticking out hard and stretching the thinning fabric tight.

Once again I thought it was time to turn back. But the exhausted man smiled cheerfully at me and I changed my mind. The exhausted man raised his eyes higher and sought out a woebegone individual with the appearance of a native son of central Asia – he was balancing skilfully, sitting with his short legs drawn up under him on the edge of the upper row of bunks.

'Listen,' the exhausted man called quietly but distinctly.

The Asiatic individual woke from his semi-slumber.

The exhausted man pointed out the sleeper's state of intimate disarray.

'Give him a shake … Tell him to make himself decent …'

Beaming with joy, the Asiatic delightedly shook his neighbour by the knee, almost waking him. The man rolled over, received a few weak pokes in his sleep from the men pressed against him on the right and the left and covered his exposed privates.

'Just come in?' asked the exhausted man, turning his red eyes on me. He parted his dry lips with an obvious effort.

'Yes.'

'Come with me …'

Deftly carving a way through the naked crowd with his shoulder, he led me out into the air and the light at the far side of the room, where there were two long windows in the end wall, both with bars and, beyond those, 'eyelashes' – long strips of strong metal welded into the frame close together at an angle, so that the air could pass through. But there was no direct view though.

Under the windows there were several very sweaty, dirty young men in baggy shorts bustling about, talking quietly between themselves as they deftly manipulated the thick ropes dangling from the windows. Hanging on the wall between the windows was a large television. Below it, set on a makeshift electric hot plate standing directly on the floor, was a metal basin with something unappetising frying in it. The nearby section of the wall was an impressive iconostasis, with several rows of images of saints. Their faces were grave. The eyes of the man with me regarded me in exactly the same probing, piercing manner: grey face, hollow cheeks, wild stare.

Suddenly the exhausted man drew back a bright-coloured rag that turned out to be a curtain – and I saw a rectangular den with two beds, closed off on three sides by blankets stretched taut vertically. This prison tent was held in place by an entire system of ropes and pieces of string. On the fourth side were the wall, the bars and the icons.

'Have a seat,' said the exhausted man, sitting down facing me and pulling the curtain shut. Casting a quick, keen glance over my five-hundred-dollar track suit he bit his lip, pondered something for a brief moment, knitted his brows and enquired:

'Where are you from?'

'From Lefortovo.'

'Lefortovo?' My companion was astonished. 'A terrorist? A maniac? What are you inside for?'

'Financial fraud.' I reached into my pocket and took out a cigarette.

The exhausted man made a gesture of warning.

'Please,' he said. 'Don't smoke in front of the icons. All right?'

I nodded hastily.

Outside the cloth walls the sounds of a hundred voices made a smooth hum, like a swarm of bees.

'So this fraud of yours must be serious, if they put you in Lefortovo … Been inside for long?'

'Eight months.'

'That's no time.'

'That's the third time I've heard those words today,' I confided. 'Is eight months really so little?'

'That all depends … For instance, I've been inside for four years.'

It was my turn to be astonished.

'Four years – in a pre-trial prison? You've been convicted then?'

'No. I'm under the court.'

The exhausted man was young, but his manner of speaking and his facial expressions seemed extremely mature to me, more appropriate for a forty-year-old.

'What does "under the court" mean?' I asked.

'It means I'm being tried.'

'They've been trying you for four years?'

'Exactly.'

'That doesn't happen, surely!'

'That's not even the half of it,' my companion said dourly. 'I'm Stanislav. Stas. You can call me Slava, as in the Russian word for "Glory". My moniker's "Glory to the CPSU". Pleased to meet you.'

The exhausted Slava pointed with his thumb to his forearm, on which there was a tattoo: two S's written in the form of jagged downward strokes of lightning.

'I did that out of youthful stupidity,' Slava Glory-to-the-CPSU explained. 'Three years ago. Now I regret it.'

'Why?' I asked, curious.

'Drawing pictures on yourself is a sin,' Slava declared sternly. 'Paganism.'

'So these,' I said, nodding at the icons, 'are all yours?'

'Yes,' Slava replied simply.

'So tell me,' I enquired politely, 'does God help you? Does he give you what you ask for?'

'God isn't Father Christmas,' Slava answered even more sternly. 'Asking Him for things is pointless. There's only one prayer he can really answer.'

'Which one is that?'

'If you ask him for strength.'

There was the sound of excited exclamations outside the taut woollen rags and my new friend stuck his head out through the curtain, leaning his hand amiably on my knee as he did so.

'What's happening there?'

'They've brought in another one,' the men standing nearby informed him.

'Aha. All right, let him come over too. Just see what they're doing!' Slava grumbled, returning to his comfortable seat on the patterned bedspread. 'A hundred and thirty-seven in thirty-two places!'

'Is it always like that here?' I asked, horrified.

'No, of course not,' my new friend reassured me. 'Right now it's not too bad. Last summer they packed in almost a hundred and fifty. And the summer before that …'

A loud, coarse baritone spoke on the other side of the curtain:

'Where? Here? Or here? Eh?'

The worn material, darned in many spots, was thrown aside. A man the same age as myself, with a round face, broad shoulders and a lumbering manner sat down beside me and wiped the sweat off his forehead.

'Joyful greetings, outlaws!' he declared deafeningly. 'Peace to your home! Who's the supervisor in this hut?'

'Just come in?' Slava Glory-to-the-CPSU enquired amiably.

'Aha! I'm Dima the Rookie! And you're the supervisor, right?'

'The supervisor?' Slava repeated cautiously. 'What's that, a "supervisor"?'

'Listen,' Dima the Rookie said challengingly. 'I'm one of the right lads, as it happens. So don't joke like that with me. In any normal hut there's always a supervisor, and I want to have a word with him …'

Slava paused before calling out:

'Johnny!'

A well-proportioned, extremely muscular figure appeared from behind the curtain.

'There's someone here looking for the supervisor!' Slava declared.

The athlete's full, shapely Slavic lips spread into a cautious smile.

'And what's that?'

'I don't know.'

'Neither do I.'

Dima the Rookie looked around shiftily.

'Lads, what's this bullshit you're giving me? Give it to me straight, no more jokes!'

'Straight …' Slava repeated pensively, casting a rapid glance over the right lad who had just come in: dirty black jeans and a shirt unbuttoned down to the navel, with a multitude of metal buttons and other fastenings. The abundance of gilded metal on this item of clothing was an unmistakable indication to me – and obviously also to Slava – of the bad taste of its owner and his low social status. Under the shirt I could see a stale singlet, soaked right through.

'I tell you what …' Slava began slowly. 'Friend! Why don't you just wait for a moment? I have to finish talking with this man here …'

He nodded at me.

'It's all right,' the red-faced newcomer said condescendingly. 'I'll just sit here in the meantime, on the side. The whole place is crowded out there, packed solid, nowhere you can put your feet down …'

The athlete observing the conversation started breathing through his nose with menacing loudness.

'No,' Slava retorted firmly. 'Don't sit here on the side. Go out for the time being. Mingle a bit out there, in the hut. As soon as I'm finished, I'll call you.'

'Ah, come on,' Dima the Rookie protested gracelessly. 'I won't get in the way. Or have you got some mysterious kind of secrets here?'

'No secrets,' said Slava, wrinkling up the thin, grey skin on his forehead. 'What secrets can there be in prison? Go on. Go on. Take a stroll, brother.'

'No space for it, brother,' the new boy replied in the same tone. 'There's a crowd out there, all covered in sores, I'm afraid to touch them ...'

It was the first time I'd ever observed a display of such colossal insolence and offhand impudence, and I thought it best to keep quiet – the way I did seven months earlier, during those first hours with Frol, my very first cell-mate.

'Yes, there are a lot of men,' Slava declared warily. 'But it can't be helped! This is a prison! Take a stroll round the hut, wait five minutes. Go.'

'There's no space!' Dima the Rookie declared boorishly, sweating profusely, and I realised that when he entered the cell he had suffered just as powerful shock as I had, only ten minutes earlier. 'No space! I want a parley with the supervisor.'

Slava nodded. His eyes narrowed.

'All right. I'll arrange that meeting for you. Later. But right now you shouldn't be here. Understand, friend, I hardly know you. You came in a minute ago – and straight away you're climbing on my blanket, asking about a parley with someone. Cool it. Calm down. If you want to have a talk with people, go into the hut and talk, mingle a bit, get to know them, come to your senses ...'

'I am in my senses,' Rookie objected with sullen force.

'Of course you are!' Slava corrected himself amicably and rested his gaze on the newly arrived lad's shoes, patched and grey with mud.

The broad-shouldered athlete made a noise in his nose again.

Meanwhile Slava shifted his gaze from Dima the Rookie's footwear to my two-hundred-dollar Reebok basketball boots – massive, but with excellent air circulation, made of natural leather; every bit as bright as the life for which they are made.

'Listen, chum,' the athlete said in a deep voice, looking Dima the Rookie up and down, 'if you've been told to take a stroll, then you'd better take a stroll for real. Right now.'

'No sweat!' Dima the Rookie suddenly said with a nod and a smile that revealed a surprisingly expensive white-gold filling. 'No sweat ...' he repeated more slowly and emphatically, and went out.

The muscular blond man shook his head and also disappeared behind the curtain. Left alone with me, Slava said:

'There are some cretins like that ... So, you're from Lefortovo?'

'Yes.'

'What did they get you for? What's the charge?'

'Fraud.'

'And what's your damage?'

'How do you mean?'

'What sum is the charge for?'

'For the episode I was involved in,' I confided modestly, 'one and a half million dollars. But for the entire CASE – ten million ...'

'Ten million dollars,' my companion repeated quietly, without the slightest sign of emotion, then he thought for a moment and told me in an even quieter whisper: 'By the way, I'm the supervisor in this hut. I'm in charge, that is, I keep an eye on the situation. Do you understand what that means?'

'Yes.'

'Excellent. This is my fifth year inside, and for four years I've been the supervisor in this hut.'

Slava suddenly changed. The person looking at me was no longer a gaunt criminal type, but a life-loving boy.

'I keep things steady in here,' he remarked casually. 'Things don't get out of hand, not ever. We have the Common Way here. So don't you worry about a thing. Stay here beside me for a while.'

I didn't object.

29

When I woke from sleep, I lay there for a long time with my eyes closed (or rather, squeezed tight shut), unable to make myself look at my new reality.

I had a dull headache. Warm sweat covered my thighs, my stomach, my sides; my hair was matted; the uncomfortable position had made my neck numb and now it ached disagreeably.

My hearing was gradually invaded by the dull rumbling of a hundred voices. Sophisticated obscenities; mirthless, cackling prison laughter; the jangling of metal tableware; the buzz of a tattooing tool; the glugging of boiling water; the muttering of the television – no, I didn't want to open my eyes, get up and insert myself into this complicated, chaotic mass of movement. On the contrary, the first few seconds of the new morning were spent in hoping that the communal cell in Matrosskaya Tishina would turn out to be a nightmare, and my real awakening would once again take place, as it had yesterday and the day before, in the clean, comfortable box at the Lefortovo pre-trial detention centre …

The two-tier steel construction for fifteen sleeping places swayed heavily at times, evidently barely able to support its triple load. When someone jumped up on to the second level, the metal pipes and strips quaked ominously. Suddenly afraid that the whole heap of scrap would collapse, I sat up on my narrow, dirty prison bed.

From the height of two metres the cell looked like an ark, a lifeboat crammed to overflowing with the victims of a shipwreck. The naked men on the second level lay on their sides, packed together like sardines in a tin, with their heads to the wall and their feet sticking out into the passage.

Others made their way between the rows of sleepers, treading carefully – they wanted to get to their things: to the bags, sacks, bundles and plastic bags dangling from the walls and the ceiling. One reached for his bread ration, another for a piece of soap, yet another for his toothbrush and many more for various household articles.

Lower down, on the first level, life was concealed behind makeshift curtains. The entire lower storey was divided into so-called 'compartments'. I assumed that was where the more prosperous lived, fenced off from prying eyes by vertically stretched pieces of bed sheets. The faces were just as pale as on the upper level, but their jaws were in a constant state of sluggish movement. The men on the lower level at least had some kind of food.

Sleeping on the lower level was more comfortable and more prestigious, and there was more air. I'd realised that the day before, my very first day. The fact that I was offered a place on the second level for the night was by no means an indication of my high status in prison society. On the other hand, although I went to bed on the upper level, at least I was close to the window, beside that barred opening that bestowed oxygen and coolness. From the glances of several of my pale, gaunt neighbours I realised that the square metre I occupied was the height of their dreams and an object of envy.

However, I found the process of descent from the second storey to the first humiliating. After freeing myself from the embrace of the damp, torn sheet I sat up, banging my head against the rag bundles of possessions dangling from the ceiling, and moved across to the edge of the precipice, only to discover that I couldn't simply climb or jump down. There was a solid mass of bodies shifting about below me.

The narrow space between the two sleeping units set along the side walls of the cell was occupied by a long table that was all of a piece with wooden benches in metal frames. Men were crowded right up against each other here, with some sitting sideways, supported on just half a buttock. Someone was chomping with relish on something disgusting, someone was drinking transparent tea, someone was darning incredibly crude and shapeless slippers with a rusty needle; at least three groups were playing card games with homemade decks; one pair, surrounded by a group of supporters, was moving figures across a chess board.

'Hey!' I called politely. 'Hey, do you hear? Brother? Look out! I'm going to jump!'

Two or three dozen half-crazed, unhealthy eyes glinted as they looked up enquiringly. In some the whites were yellow and bright, in others – red and dull: the irises were all different colours: blue, grey and green for the Slavs; lilac and brown for the Asiatics; coal black for the Caucasians.

'Do you hear!' I called more insistently. 'Let me get down!'

Finally one moved to the right and two others to the left. A section of bench half the size of a plate was exposed. I managed to make the jump accurately.

Of the many gazes directed at me, one stood out as the most intent.

'Woken up?' asked Slava.

'Yes indeed. Good morning.'

'And to you.'

This very young guy, Slava Glory-to-the-CPSU, looked like the miner Stakhanov just back from the coalface, like the flyer Chkalov just after he flew over the North Pole; like the cosmonaut Gagarin just after he landed from orbit. Like a man who is deadly tired, staggering from extreme exhaustion. He looked as if he were held up by nothing but willpower and was about to collapse into the arms of his faithful friends and comrades.

'How are you feeling?' Slava enquired.

'Fine.'

'We're waiting for you to have lunch.'

'What do you mean, lunch?' I asked in surprise. 'What time is it? How long have I been asleep?'

'I've no idea,' Slava replied frankly. 'Go get washed and join us ...'

Two other faces – young, serious, healthy and sensible – appeared out of the whitish-brown tobacco haze, framing Slava's narrow, colourless face on the right and the left.

'Don't look for your bag. It's here.'

They pushed my bag over to me across the chipped tiles of the floor. It was as capacious as the saloon of a high-class limousine. I tore the fastenings open and smiled as I caught the smell of oranges – the smell of home and family, the aroma of those who remembered me. I took out everything I needed and went to perform my morning ablutions.

There were seven men languishing in the queue for the washbasin. Another five wanted to take a leak. I politely took places in both queues.

I took out my cigarettes and lit up, but immediately a dozen quiet voices full of hope started speaking:

'Can we have a smoke?'

I had to give away the entire pack.

I was immediately allowed through to the front of the queue. Bemused, I went behind the curtain and speedily vented my superfluous liquid down the toilet hole then, standing at the washbasin, I seared my face with cold water and rinsed off my teeth.

What now? I wondered. What was I going to do all day long – until the moment when I could lie down again, close my eyes and hide from the nightmare?

On my way back from the washbasin my path was blocked by the smiling athlete who had been with Slava the previous day. The smiler's wrists were mutilated by bruises and scars. He introduced himself.

'I'm Johnny. A roadman.'

'Aha,' I replied.

'Come this way.'

Shoving his way through the crowd – sometimes brusquely, sometimes with polite interjections – Johnny very deftly circled round me, drew a curtain aside and gestured for me to follow him. I leaned down and went in. Inside the den all was order and comfort. The lighted lamp had a makeshift wire shade. Slava was sitting on the neatly made bed with his legs crossed, Turkish-style.

Johnny sat down beside him without any ceremony. Nodding towards me, he said:

'He's shy.'

'Never mind. That won't last long.'

The head jailbird, as white as an underground mushroom, gave me a wink full of lively mischief.

'You're just in time for lunch,' he told me.

Suddenly my nose caught the aroma of frying meat. I shuddered.

I hadn't eaten hot meat in all the time I'd been behind bars. Eight months. From August 1996 to April 1997.

'How long did I sleep?'

'What's the difference?' Johnny replied philosophically, stretching his full lips into a smile once again.

'But even so?'

'You came in yesterday after lunch. You woke up today, after lunch again. That makes it about twenty hours.'

I felt ashamed.

'Put your toothbrush, soap and razor in a separate plastic bag and hang them here,' Johnny advised me in a simple tone of voice. 'Don't keep them in your bag. It's not convenient.'

'And in general, relax,' Slava appealed to me. 'You're among friends here. Here, have some salami ...'

I remembered Fatty, a man from my past, and laughed.

'That's it!' Slava said with a smile. 'A bit more lively, brother! Calm down! You're in prison! In the Common Hut! Everything bad that could happen to you has already happened. Go ahead! In God's name!'

The salami and onions fried in butter seemed to me the most exquisite delicacy of all that are known in this sublunary world. I gulped down three scorching hot pieces, hardly chewing at all, followed them with bread and mayonnaise, and felt my strength come flooding back to me.

We dined hastily, despatching pieces of hot, salty salami into eager mouths filled with saliva, chewing rapidly, savouring the food and swallowing it down, dunking our bread and soaking up the juices: we rounded off the meal with strong tea and caramel sweets, and then lit up.

'And now,' Slava said, stumbling over his tongue, 'we can talk about serious matters. If you don't object.'

I shrugged my shoulders.

Johnny jumped off the bed and went out into the passage, carefully closing the makeshift curtain behind him. A moment later the roof of our compartment swayed – the young guy with the ready smile had settled down to sleep in the very place where I had woken up half an hour earlier. Meanwhile Slava lit another cigarette and sighed.

'I don't like to talk a lot. And I don't know how. Anyway, there's no need right now. You understand everything for yourself. And you can see. Prison. A crowded cell. People dying. Meningitis, jaundice, the tube everywhere. A hundred and thirty-seven of us! And a hundred and twenty are down-and-outs on their last legs, drug addicts, homeless bums, all sorts of trash, freaks, and there are imbeciles too – three of them right now, in short, a real rag-bag assortment. Not a rusty kopeck between them. We're going crazy. I'll ask you directly: how can you help?'

'With money,' I said firmly.

'Excellent,' my companion said with a nod. 'Have you got a lawyer?'

'No.'

Slava was seriously surprised.

'How can you manage without a lawyer?'

'I don't have money for a real one, and a free one's no use to me.'

'But you say you've got money …'

'Not for a lawyer, but there's a bit left with my family. I figured I'd rather see the money in my wife's pocket than my lawyer's …'

'Very honorable!' Slava said approvingly. 'You understand, I'm not asking for myself. I personally have everything I need. I've been inside for four years, and I've got everything sorted. Tea with sugar, filter cigarettes and so on. I'm asking for the Common Way! We'll be grateful for every kopeck, brother! You've seen what the crowd in here's like! Every three months one in ten of them brings fifty roubles – and that's all the cash there is … How can you set up the Common Way with people like that?'

'You don't need to explain these things to me,' I put in demurely. 'You're talking as if I'd only just moved in yesterday!'

Slava smiled.

'And when did you move in?'

'I've been inside for eight months already!'

'You've been in Lefortovo,' the pale-faced supervisor spelled out condescendingly. 'There isn't any Common Way there. Call that a prison?

This here is a real prison!' Slava gestured round the space of his den, hung on all sides with tightly stretched fabric. 'The only way the prisoners here can survive is if they organize mutual assistance. If every man only looks out for himself, the goons will crush everyone. We'll all be marching in line. And shout in chorus: "Good morning, Mr Boss!" As if we were on Fire Island, not in the Matrosskaya Tishina. Have you heard about that island?'

'Naturally.'

'Good,' said Slava and suddenly frowned. 'Anyway, what was I talking about?'

'About the Common Way.'

'No. About money. In short, if you can help, spare even five hundred roubles, we'll do all the rest ourselves. Write a letter and give it to me. There are people who will carry your letter out. Then other people will deliver it, hand it directly to your relatives – wife, sister, brother. They'll take any load from them, get it in here, and hand it directly to you. It's all set up, brother!'

'That's what we'll do,' I said with a nod. 'Is two hundred dollars all right for a start?'

Slava closed his eyelids gravely.

'Ideal! Only no dollars. The same amount all in roubles, in fifty-rouble notes ...'

'Easy.'

'I see you're not very thrifty with money.'

'I used to have an income of five thousand dollars a month.'

'How much?' Slava cried out, opening his eyes wide.

'Five thousand ...'

I deliberately reduced the figure by a factor of ten in order not to confuse the naïve young man.

Suddenly the voices behind the curtain, which had so far merely burbled gently, became louder. There were cries of outrage. Slava's face took on a concerned look.

'You stood on my foot!' said a voice at the table. 'Where do you think you're going?'

'Let me get through!' a powerful throat roared in reply. 'Move over, come on!'

'Don't shove!'

Slava started moving, about to leave the compartment, but a fleshy face was thrust in through the crack between the curtains. I recognised Rookie – the man who had joined the cell the day before, straight after me.

'Good day to you!' he said churlishly, casting a quick glance over the two of us and all the finery of the den: his gaze rested for a moment on the bowls with the remains of our feast. 'Can I come in? There's something I want to talk about …'

'Come in,' said Slava, instantly transformed once again from a young man full of the joy of life into an exhausted prison inmate. 'We don't have any secrets here … What's the problem?'

The large, strong-smelling body sniffed, lowered itself heavily on to the bed and exclaimed loudly:

'No problems! Just something I don't understand …'

'Please,' Slava interrupted politely, 'don't talk so loud. There are a hundred and thirty men in the hut, if we all start shouting, we'll go out of out heads …'

'No sweat,' said Rookie, nodding and began wiping his bumpy forehead with the edge of his own undershirt.

The fleshy shoulders of the loud-voiced newcomer were adorned with complex tattoos – not convict tattoos, but Celtic decorations created in a tattoo parlour.

'So what is it you don't understand?'

'You're the supervisor, I guessed right, didn't I?' the sweating rookie asked.

'You could say that,' Slava replied with dignity.

'Look here,' Rookie began bumptiously, turning up the volume again. 'I came into this hut yesterday, and I still don't have anywhere to sleep. I can't even sit down. Even taking a piss is a problem. Everywhere's crammed and crowded, human trash, lice. But I've been an outlaw ever since I was a kid! I earn my bread the criminal way! I know lots of the brothers and the right lads on the outside! I was thick with the Kunstsevo mob, and the

Tanganka mob and Orekhovo mob! Now I end up in here, and I'm no one, with nothing. I tell you straight, for God's sake, find me a spot where I can get at least a couple of hours' sleep!'

'Yes, there are a lot of men,' Slava agreed quietly. 'But you think for yourself about a place to sleep. I can't show you your place. You can only show a nark his place. You ought to know that, if you were thick with the brothers on the outside.'

'There isn't anywhere!' Rookie protested in a hysterical baritone. 'There's nowhere to sleep! There isn't even anywhere to sit! Fifteen hours I've been on my feet, I'm fit to drop!'

Slava sighed.

'A hundred and thirty men found a place to sleep, you find one too.'

'In four shifts, six hours at a time?'

'Yes, for the moment,' said Slava, shrugging peaceably. 'Like I said, there are a lot of men. Later, if you show willing and support the Common Way, the men will appreciate that, and conditions will improve by themselves. We don't know yet what kind of man you are. Everyone here claims to be outlaws and thieves. But words have to be backed up by the whole of your life, agreed?'

'I'm not going to sleep in four shifts with trash!' Elephant declared with intense malice.

'Be careful talking about trash … Words like that can't just be thrown around. Have you been inside long?'

'It's my fourth day,' Rookie admitted, continuing to ooze liquid. 'Three days in the holding cells and then straight here …'

'That's no time,' I said cautiously.

Rookie shot me a glance full of hate. I was annoyed with myself. I ought to have kept quiet. In a single moment, with a single word, I had earned myself an enemy. We had entered the cell at the same time, but I had been put in a clean corner, where there was air, and slept for as long as I needed, while he – a brother-in-arms of the bandits of Kuntsevo and the Taganka – had spent all that time on his feet, in the dirty crowd riddled with psoriasis; I had dined on fried meat, and he had quite possibly not even drunk tea.

'Yes, that's no time,' Slava agreed. 'Tell me, I've forgotten, what's your name?'

'Rookie!'

'Rookie,' Slava repeated pensively and surveyed the streams of sweat running down the temples and neck of the indignant outlaw. 'Do you have an ordinary name?'

'Dima!'

'Basically, Dima, it seems to me that I've answered your question. This isn't a hotel, it's a prison. Everyone who comes in defines his own place. He finds friends for himself, he looks for a place to rest and food to eat himself. What are you inside for?'

'For drugs.'

Slava livened up a little.

'I see. Can you get some good stuff in here, into the Central? Write a letter to your friends and we'll do all the rest. We have people on the outside, they'll fetch and carry, deliver straight into your hands …'

Rookie sighed.

'That's difficult. Right now my entire stash is lying in the investigator's safe …'

'Aha,' said Slava in an expressionless voice. 'Well, all right, then … Perhaps money? Help us with at least a couple of roubles.'

'Where would an outlaw get money?'

Slava didn't say anything.

Rookie lowered his decorated hands on to his knees, and the moisture began dripping straight from his face on to the floor.

'Well then, Dima,' Slava summed up, taking a general exercise book and several pens out from under his pillow. 'Pardon me if we break off the conversation now. I've no time for more talk. Don't be sad. Handle yourself right, the real way, the right lad's way – and you'll have everything. It's possible to live anywhere, even here in the Common Hut …'

'All right,' Rookie replied in an indefinite tone of voice. He jerked open the curtain and left the supervisor's den.

'Let me get through!' he demanded rudely again, addressing the men standing nearby.

'An addict,' Slava summed up quietly. 'The genuine article. And what's more – a total bonehead. He's coming down now. Got the shakes. This evening he'll come running back again, you'll see …'

'It's time for me to go too,' I said politely. 'I wouldn't want to get in your way.'

'Stay there,' said my new friend. 'Where would you go to? We'll have some tea, then do something else. Do you play backgammon?'

'No.'

'Then here, take this.' Slava thrust his skinny hand under the pillow again and took out a small cassette player. 'Do like music?'

'Of course.'

'Relax,' Slava advised me magnanimously. 'Don't worry. Listen to some music.'

'Thank you …'

I really didn't have anywhere to go. Behind the curtain, outside Slava's small, rather stuffy, but quite comfortable residence, there was a compressed mass of humanity waiting for me – puffy, yellow or grey faces, bodies covered in sores, unfamiliar customs and practises.

As I surveyed the squirming anthill from behind the curtain, I thought with grim humour how only the day before, in Lefortovo, I had been making plans for victory over prison. That prison had turned out to be a health resort. The real prison had only just swallowed me up. I had been tilting at windmills. But prison had been biding its time.

Here, in the common cell, it was impossible even to read a book, because there weren't any books, and even if I were sent some from outside, where would I keep them? Here there was an agonizing war going on for every square foot of space. Here people spent immense efforts on scraping a little hollow in the ceiling, fixing a hook made from a toothbrush into it and hanging their bits and pieces on the hook. Who has time for books here, I thought bitterly, hooking on the earphones and letting the hoarse, cracked voice of some criminal crooner I didn't know fill my head. Books? Exercises? Training? Concern for your purity of perception? Here? Is that really what your freedom consists of? So men are going to rot alive all around you, slowly die of hunger and disease, and meanwhile you're going to pump up your biceps, meditate and read textbooks. Who will you turn into then?

After the fourth cassette, I realised it was already evening. In the space of several hours, I had only once left my lair in order to go to the toilet, and then hurried back to the safety of Slava's compartment.

Close by, right beside the wall and the bars, a feverish performance was being played out by two young men. They were deftly and expertly manipulating several lengths of strong, shaggy rope that ran out through the windows. The ropes would suddenly disappear, snaking into the gaps between the bars, then stretch taut; there would be a knocking on the walls and the heating pipes, and from the other side of the wall the semi-naked, bustling prisoners would pull in bundles of notes tied with special knots and parcels wrapped in paper and plastic. The Road, I guessed. The prison post.

After supper Slava withdrew into the corner that had been turned into a chapel and prayed for about an hour, with his head and shoulders bowed. Then he came back to his place, pulled a cardboard box full of medicines out from under the bed and rummaged around in it for a long time, fingering the different-coloured packages, bottles and tubes of ointment. He stuck his head out into the passage and spoke to the men standing nearby:

'Call Rookie. The rowdy one who moved in yesterday.'

The tattooed Celt appeared immediately – as if he had been waiting.

'Sit down,' said Slava. 'I see you're in a bad way.'

'You got that right,' my new enemy admitted with real feeling.

His appearance reminded me of the punishment inflicted by nature on all lovers of unnatural pleasures. His shoulders, chest and neck gave off waves of an acrid stench. There was a wild look in his eyes. His hair stuck out. There was a pitiful twitching in his temples. His vest was soaked through and stuck to his body. Every now and then the unfortunate consumer of poison scratched his sides and his stomach with his nails.

'It's the shakes,' he said, wincing. 'I got them bad.'

'Here.' Slava gently took hold of the outlaw's shaking hand and placed a few tablets in it. 'Take them all at once. That will be enough for two or three hours … Then we'll think of something else …'

'Thanks from the heart,' Rookie blurted out gratefully, blinking his tear-filled eyes. 'From the heart, brother! From the heart!'

'Prisoners don't abandon each other in misfortune.'

'From the heart, Slava,' Rookie repeated, touched, and slipped out.

Once again Slava cast off his mask of exhaustion and smiled at me mischievously.

'That's how we make our enemies into our friends, understand?'

'Yes.'

I had another four hours to wait before Johnny would leave his narrow mattress free for me.

And I made a mistake – my first and only, serious, unforgivable mistake. I rummaged in my bag and found a volume of Hegel, *The Philosophy of Law*. I left the den. Waited for the moment when a gap appeared in the solid row of men sitting at the table, slipped in smartly and immersed myself in reading.

'Oho!' the men on the right and the left of me remarked. 'Philosophy! A philosopher, are you?'

'No,' I replied with a friendly smile. 'I'm just interested, that's all ...'

There was loud, sarcastic laughter. However, the irony directed at me only went so far – the entire cell had already realised that for reasons unknown the newcomer in the expensive trousers had become a member of the supervisor Slava's small inner circle, with a seat at the boss's table.

The wouldn't let me read. Where are you from? What are you in for? How long have you been inside? From Lefortovo? And how is it there? And what you do on the outside? Anybody else in your case? What kind of stretch are you looking at? Is this your first time in prison? Having more or less satisfied my neighbours' curiosity, I nonetheless opened the book and even took out a pencil to underline the key points. That is, I confused a pre-trial prison with a library reading hall.

A heavy hand fell on my shoulder. I raised my head. Rookie, whose suffering had clearly been eased by the tablets Slava had given him, smiled at me with his ugly mouth and tightened his fingers slightly; but then he immediately released his grip.

'You're Andrei, right?'

'Andrei,' I confirmed, tensing up.

'And what's your moniker?'

'I don't have a moniker,' I admitted.

The large, heavy-boned man in a dirty singlet looked at my book and then turned his glance back to my face.

'A student?'

'Why do you think that?'

'It's a clever book.'

'Yes, it is that.'

'All right,' Rookie said seriously. 'Sorry for interrupting. Only don't forget, Andrei – you'll slip up all the same. Understand me? You'll slip up all the same, I tell you straight. You'll slip up …'

The circles and angles of the Celtic patterns ran through a brief, menacing dance; their owner turned his back on me and began walking away.

'Dima!' I called. 'Wait! Dima!'

I wanted to resolve everything peacefully. Get to know the drug adddict. Give him a cigarette. Smooth things over. Rookie was no longer an enemy for Slava – but he had clearly chosen me as a target.

My enemy ignored me and merged into the mass of bodies.

My adaptation to the new place was rapid, taking about three days. I even felt a little proud of how quickly I settled in and grew accustomed to the sights, sounds and smells. But what was so surprising about that? Firstly, I had prepared myself morally a long time before – at the time when I was still sharing a cell with the old convict Frol. And secondly, on many occasions at various times and in various places, in the towns and villages of my great Homeland I had seen rooms that were fouled with excrement and vomit, and lice, and faces skewed out of shape, and human limbs covered with rotten scabs, and blue veins scorched by heroin. It was another matter that in the Matrosskaya Tishina pre-trial prison all of the above were present side by side, in appalling abundance, all mixed up together into a single putrefying lump.

Having a hundred and thirty-five cell-mates is not the same as having one or two, as in the five-star Lefortovo castle. Life at the Matrosskaya Tishina 'Central' was ebullient. Everyone in there was young. The national fringes of the Empire were generously represented: Uzbeks, Kazakhs, Turkmens, Chechens and Ingushes, Georgians, Azerbaijanis, Armenians, Moldovans, Chukchas and Yakuts – all stewing in the same pot. In different corners at different levels of the small universe known as the 'Common Hut' you could hear torrid speech sprinkled with clicking sounds as associations, groups, coalitions and enclaves were formed and fell apart and quarrels flared up.

Every day five to seven men disappeared from the cell. Once they received their sentences, they left to be transported to the camps. At the same time, new men came in. The dirtiest newcomers, who had lost all dignity even before prison, were immediately sent to a special section known as the 'depot', where their confreres initiated the neophytes into the prisoners' faith by cutting their hair and giving them soap. They didn't progress far beyond the depot. The square metres of space around it were populated by those who wanted to work – wash other people's laundry, sew pillow cases and slippers, mend clothes – in exchange for sugar, tea or cigarettes. Those who did not wish to work, or could not find an employer among the small number of their rich cell-mates, formed the morose mass of prisoners in a constant state of witless jitters, covered in scabs and devoured by lice, who were known as 'passengers'. The hunger, lack of sleep and constant need to stand in a vertical position drove these men half-insane. They led a feeble, sluggish life – looking for a friend with a spare lump of sugar, fighting among themselves for the chance to sit at the table for a few minutes, or staring at the television for hours over the tops of dozens of heads.

In here, semi-literate peasants slept side by side with the owners of diplomas from the capital's colleges, murderers played chess with burglars, Christians shared bread with the devotees of bizarre pagan cults. A pulsating mass of suffering, laughter and tears. A varicoloured, multiracial body of a hundred and thirty living beings, squeezed into a space scarcely larger than a school class room, surviving in the best way it knew and could manage.

Tea and tobacco circulated like currency, a pair of socks without holes or a piece of butter was regarded an item of substantial value. Mortal enmity could be triggered by a needle, a pencil, a soap-dish or, as in my case, a sleeping place beside the window.

On the third day my money arrived. Just how the currency that was specifically banned inside the pre-trial prison found its way into the cell, I didn't know. But to judge from Slava's face, this brain-teaser of an operation was no problem for him.

In addition to a wad of small bank notes, the package contained a letter from my wife and even several photographs. We looked at them together: Slava, Johnny and I. The letter was quite short, composed in haste. A clear picture appeared before my eyes: some suspicious-looking types turn up at the apartment, hand my wife a letter from her husband and wait at the door, while my beloved hastily scrapes her pen across the paper, trying to gather her thoughts …

I hadn't had any news from my family for more than three months. The latest had been delivered by the red-haired lawyer on his final visit to me in February. Now I ran my eyes greedily over the lines of large, rounded letters, and even raised the notebook page to my nostrils in an attempt to catch the smell of my woman. But I couldn't. The note had obviously passed through the dexterous hands of many of Slava's trusted associates and lingered for a long time in their dirty pockets.

My wife hinted in passing that the sum I had asked for seemed very lavish to her. But that was merely a short phrase that slipped out.

Never mind, my beloved, have patience, I whispered, cautiously pressing my fingers to the glossy image in the photo, looking hard at those stern eyes, those tightly compressed lips, that light hair. I won't ask for so much again. I know myself that money's getting short. Thank God that at least some survived. Thank God that you and our son have bread on the table and a roof over your heads. Soon I'll come back and put everything right.

Yes, the family's money was melting away, I understood that. Life in the capital of the Empire isn't cheap.

Compared with my former boss Mikhail, who had divested me of my capital, I was quite definitely a poor man. And I thought of myself that way. An impoverished, bankrupt, deceived blockhead who had lost everything, whose pitiful savings consisted only of the sums that he given to his wife for safekeeping at various times.

But even in that condition, having lost hundreds of thousands of dollars and held on to a pitiful few kopecks, I was still incredibly rich compared to those who surrounded me here, in the common cell at the Matrosskaya Tishina. Two hundred dollars – until only very recently that had been an insignificant sum, pocket money that could be drunk away in a single evening. But here, behind bars, it had grown into inconceivable riches, a gleaming treasure trove, a source of joy.

'My respects!' Slava told me in a satisfied tone, gently fondling the bills in his fingers. 'You're a monster, Andriukha! A real gangster! A high card! If we had more like you, just another couple, we'd turn the entire Central upside down!'

I couldn't take my eyes off the sight of this young man, as skinny as death, tenderly caressing the rainbow-coloured pieces of paper. He caught my glance.

'You, Andriukha, must be thinking – what is this place I've ended up in? Am I right?'

'Absolutely not,' I lied.

'Don't be sad! You'll get used to it. The way I got used to it.'

'I still can't believe you've spent four years in here,' I admitted frankly.

'I'm doing my fifth already,' Slava corrected me. 'I came in when I was eighteen and now I'm twenty-three.'

'You look older …'

'Prison,' Slava explained. 'Not enough food or oxygen. Back on the outside – can you believe it? – I weighed eighty kilos … But that's all in the past. To be honest, I've already forgotten what it's like on the outside. Cars, girls, kebabs, green trees – it's all so far away … Sometimes I doubt that the outside even exists. It feels like I've been here since I was born. My entire adult life has been spent in here. Let me out now, and I'd go insane, for real… God only knows what I'd do out there, what kind of work … But here in the Central, everything's clear to me, down to the finest detail. I'm like a fish in water here. I grew up here. Learned everything about people. Found my way to God. Learned how to live. Learned to believe in my own strength. Johnny here will tell you it's the truth …'

That night I couldn't get to sleep for ages. I re-read my wife's letter several times. I gazed at the photographs trying to guess all the small details, all the things that weren't in the letter. How was she out there? I had eight months behind me already – and how many still to go? Would she wait for me? Would she hold out?

I suppose it's a banal cliché – sitting in a pre-trial prison and worrying about whether your woman will wait for you. But then every cliché, as it develops, is transformed into its direct opposite.

On top of everything else, at night the temperature rose sharply. The cell was filled with a dense fug that was especially distressing at a height of two metres above the floor. I was streaming with sweat. The sheet underneath me was soaked through.

Just before morning I realised that I wasn't going to get any proper sleep. And then a familiar harsh voice suddenly began muttering directly below me, in my patron's compartment.

The words weren't spoken loudly, but I was only separated from the speakers by a makeshift mattress and a metal sheet: I could even hear the speakers breathing, even hear Rookie occasionally scratching his body.

'Only don't go thinking,' the tattooed bandit said morosely, 'that I'm here to propose any kind of challenge or beef …'

'Speak, speak,' Slava said benevolently.

Rookie began with emphatic slowness:

'Of course, I've pretty much guessed why you took in that businessman straight off …'

'What businessman?' Slava asked in surprise.

'You know.'

'Ah, that Andriukha? Is he a businessman, then? Did he tell you *himself* that he's a businessman?'

'No, he didn't,' Rookie admitted. 'But you can tell just by looking at him. I'm no fool.'

Slava switched to a mysterious whisper. I strained my ears to hear.

'Just don't tell anyone … That Andriukha's a con man and a shark. He took a million bucks in that fraud of his, get it? They kept him in Lefortovo for almost a year for that. That's the first thing. The second …' – Slava started speaking more loudly, with more emphasis and aggression – 'I don't understand what you said about "taking him in". Maybe you're trying to hint that I get money from him? Eh?'

'Of course not,' Rookie protested hastily. 'How could you think that? But then what's he done to deserve the sweet life and a seat at the boss's table, while worthy lads sleep in four shifts? This is my fifth day in the hut. I understand everything here now. I've talked to everyone. Lots of them aren't happy, Slava. I'm not the only one. Don't you go thinking I want to make any kind of challenge …'

'That's enough,' the supervisor interrupted in a harsh, metallic tone of voice. 'You … what's your name, I've forgotten?'

'Dima.'

'Dima, you can't challenge me about anything!' Slava snapped. 'Not a thing. Everything in the hut's regular. I answer for that. While I've been here not a single man has been killed, or lowered, or broken without good reason. No brawls and no bedlam. There are some who aren't happy, I know them all and I see their lives. Tell me, why do these ones who aren't happy whisper in the corners? And never say anything to my face? Eh?'

Rookie scratched himself deafeningly.

'Because they're mice,' Slava declared, 'and they live mousy lives …'

I heard the click of a lighter, and then Rookie boomed 'thank you' – obviously he had been offered a cigarette.

'Here,' Slava went on, 'all around us, everything's right. It's convict order, pure penal, just the way it ought to be. Get it? I personally haven't taken anyone in, or moved anyone up or back. I haven't given anyone a nice cosy spot. In a worthy hut the prisoners find their own place. This con man you're obsessed with, I keep him beside me for just one reason:

I, Slava Glory-to-the-CPSU, personally find him interesting and likeable. Personally. I want to pull a certain stroke with him, but what it is – sorry, that's nobody's business but mine and his …'

Rookie breathed out heavily.

'I'm not convinced,' he said. 'Let's cut the crap here, Slava, I'll tell you one thing before I go: that student of yours should thank God that he found a place under your wing. I'd shake his million out of him in half an hour. Along with his guts. I used to do that on the outside – and I can do it here …'

'I understand you,' Slava replied indifferently.

'Then I'll be off.'

There was a metallic creak.

'If you have questions, call round any time,' Slava said nonchalantly in farewell.

Several seconds passed in silence. I made out the click of the cigarette lighter again.

'Andriukha,' my protector called quietly from below. 'You're not asleep, are you?'

'No.'

'Did you hear everything?'

'Almost everything.'

'Come down. There's something we need to discuss. Only not right away. In about ten minutes. Or fifteen. Or even longer. Take a look, where's that meathead?'

'He's gone to drink chifir.'

'Aha. Okay, make a crafty pause – and then call in.'

Fifteen minutes passed in wearisome, hot anticipation. Eventually I sat up, yawned strenuously and jumped down – on the fifth day I could manage it deftly and precisely – and ducked straight into the supervisor's den.

Slava was a picture of unconcern. The blanket in front of him still bore the imprint of my enemy's heavy backside.

'Feeling nervous?' Slava enquired immediately.

'Not at all,' I lied

'Don't lie,' Sasha rebuked me and smiled. 'Don't get uptight over anything. Just keep your cool. Relax, get used to things. I've been in this hut for four years. I've met a thousand like this Rookie – and seen them off. On the outside he'll smash some oaf over the head, take a hundred roubles off him, get smashed on heroin, and he's happy. But once he moves into prison, he starts getting cocky: I'm tough, I'm a real bandit, I know everyone ...'

'If he gets pushy,' I exploded, 'I'll rip his throat out.'

'He won't touch you. And he'll sleep in four shifts. Until I want things to be different. And if need be, we'll give him a sharp shock that he won't forget in a hurry ... By the way, have you got any coffee?'

'Yes. In the bag.'

'Don't keep anything in the bag. Bring it here, we'll boil up some water and cheer ourselves up a bit.'

Slava thought for a moment and his face brightened. He laid a gaunt, weightless hand on my shoulder.

'You know, God sends everyone on his own path. For this rookie and his kind, it's a short one. But our path is a little bit longer. Agreed?'

'Agreed.'

'Let's invite our roadmen to drink coffee too. And Johnny, and Givi Sukhumsky. By the way, do you know anything about the Road?'

'I've heard a thing or two ...'

'That's good.'

30

During the first days of summer the temperature in the city rose to twenty degrees, and in the Common Hut to thirty-five, with one hundred per cent humidity.

The men, stripped to their shorts, turned quiet. The ceaseless twenty-four-hour motion of four hundred gaunt limbs slowed down. A weary tension hovered over the angular bodies rubbing up against each other, over the water glugging as it boiled in dozens of mugs, over the sleeping and the wakeful, the sated and the hungry. The air turned liquid, transformed into a sour broth that failed to nourish.

One morning the hot, shimmering atmosphere suddenly vibrated to the sound of some familiar words. I listened. Deprived of oxygen, my brain wasn't working too well. I had to think for a long time before I realised they were shouting my name:

'What is it?'

'Rubanov! Is he here? You're wanted, urgently!'

In five weeks I had completely found my feet, settled into my new place. The Common Hut no longer seemed like a cave inhabited by terrifying goblins. With a shake of my head, I managed to concentrate and quickly squeezed my way sideways through the crowd – unceremoniously elbowing some men aside, rounding others at a tangent, with polite exclamations, winking at some and disassociating myself from others with a dark glance

I pushed my way through to the open rectangle of the 'feeder', eager to find out from the screw what kind of summons this was, where to and what for.

But the warder did not wish to exchange pleasantries with me. Although only the day before yesterday, he had accepted one of my cigarettes.

'You're wanted means you're wanted!' he roared. 'You ready or not? Get a move on! There's a lot of you and only one of me!'

In the overcrowded Matrosskaya Tishina prison, the procedure for taking prisoners out to meet the requirements of the investigation tended towards extreme simplicity. Swearing stentoriously, a special duty officer wearing a camouflage shirt unbuttoned down to the navel collected about twenty men from the entire floor and drove the entire crowd, shuffling along in their beach slippers, through staircases and corridors into the next section – the investigative block. Constantly increasing the intensity of his obscenities, he crammed his wards into the 'tram' – a tiny box three metres by three. In there the murderers, bandits, hooligans and other criminals swore obscenely at being so cramped, lit up cigarettes from each other and exchanged news until they were taken, one at a time, to the offices.

There was no question of a search. The 'take-out' duty officer was only acting rationally. Why frisk a crowd of dirty, hungry, angry men on the way *there*? What forbidden items would a prisoner take into the investigative block? A knife, maybe? To cut the prosecutor's throat? Nonsense.

But a prisoner going in the opposite direction was a different matter. After a meeting with his lawyer, he carried things in his pockets, in his sleeves, in his shorts and socks – rolled up and disguised newspapers, magazines, books, cigarettes, cigarette lighters, matches, sweets, chocolate, bouillon cubes, exercise books, pens, felt-tip markers, batteries, needles, nail files, plastic bags, rolls of sellotape, thread, a sticking plaster, aspirin, other painkillers, deodorants, substances for killing cockroaches, lice and itch mites, glue, scissors and a thousand other little items that it was forbidden to use, but which were absolute essentials of life in prison. A prisoner like that was just begging to be frisked.

What a pity my lawyer isn't my lawyer any more, I thought sadly. Johnny, now, he's called out to see his advocate every week, and he never comes back empty-handed. Red-headed Maxim would come in very handy now. All the useful things he could bring in for me! Who says lawyers are needed to defend their clients in court? What naïve stupidity! A prisoner in the Matrosskaya Tishina needs a lawyer for a reliable supply of valuable household items. If a prisoner in the Matroska has a pack of filter cigarettes, he's a big man. What has a defence in court got to do with anything? First you have to survive until the trial.

Remembering the ginger lawyer, I smiled bitterly and lowered my chin onto my chest, so that the men squeezed up against me – a Chechen from Petersburg, a Tajik from Moscow and two Georgians from Siberia – wouldn't see my momentary weakness. Ah Maxim, you bright spark! Where have you got to, my friend? And you said you came to get charged up from the socket. Why haven't you come for a fresh charge in four whole months? Why did you flatter me, if you knew it was the last time you were going to come? Why didn't you say straight out: 'Goodbye, let's part friends!' A shameful, unmanly way to act.

And there waiting for me in the investigative office, sitting at the table and drumming his fingers on its top, was my former lawyer – obviously materialised directly from my mental reproaches.

'Hi,' I said, feeling greatly ashamed.

Maxim Stein's appearance astounded me.

The copper-haired young man sitting at the table was shaking badly. Although he had repeatedly informed me with pride that he hated tobacco, the moment the door closed behind the guard, he pulled out a pack of Gitanes and tossed it onto the table. It was followed by a lighter. The lawyer then immediately grabbed up both items again with his trembling hands and took out a cigarette, lit it and blew out the smoke from under his upper lip. His pupils were distended, his cheeks were overgrown with untidy stubble that was grey in places. An absurd gold bracelet dangled pathetically on his wrist. The third button of his jacket, the bottom one, was only held on by a few fine threads and clearly intended to drop off at any moment.

'I'm sorry,' he muttered, 'for not coming for so long.'

'It's nothing,' I said magnanimously.

'How are things? I didn't even know that they'd transferred you to the Matroska … I phoned your wife, and she told me … I'm in shock too …'

'What's wrong with you?' I asked, frowning. 'What's happened, eh?'

'Everything's fine,' the lawyer replied, thrusting a half-smoked cigarette into the ashtray and clearly holding himself back from grabbing another. 'Everything's just great …'

'Then give me a cigarette.'

'Of course.'

'And now tell me what's happened. Some bad news with my CASE?'

'Everything's fine with your CASE.'

'What then?'

Maxim breathed in and out.

'I need your advice.'

'Gladly.'

'Andrei!' the lawyer immediately shouted. 'They're bringing down the bank. They've dragged me into a fraud. My signature's on all the documents! They gave the big depositors their money back and dumped the small ones! I initialled every single contract! I'm being followed! I get threats over the phone! I've been questioned three times! Yesterday they planted drugs in my safe!'

'What kind of drugs?' I enquired with interest.

'Cocaine …'

'Did you snort any?'

'Are you insane! I flushed it down the toilet.'

'You're the one who's insane. You should have snorted it.'

'You think it's funny!' Red flung his arms up in the air. 'But I'm right on the brink!'

'Don't get so hot under the collar. Control yourself.'

'You told me! Back then, in February! You said it was a strong firm! And the guys there were talented and sound!'

'Yes,' I nodded, taking another tasty cigarette. 'I could have said that the people there were sound, or that there were talented people there, but I never told you that the people there were *honest*. Can you give me all the details?'

Red gulped noisily

'Back then, in February,' he began, 'when you were still in Lefortovo … when I came to see you the last time … I wasn't entirely honest with you … I'd been working with them for a month already. I started as the deputy manager of the legal department ... Three thousand dollars a month – can you imagine it? Plus a quarterly bonus ... At the very beginning of spring, my boss resigned, he was supposed to be ill, and I took his place ... Five thousand a month ... Truckloads of work. People pouring in. We were taking deposits at fifty per cent annual interest ...'

'What's that? Fifty?'

'Fifty per cent annual interest.'

'Fifty per cent!' I grabbed hold of my head, like a footballer who has just missed the goal from three metres. 'You should have gone running straight to the public prosecutor's office.'

Red sniffed.

'I didn't know! I didn't have a clue! That's why they took me on! They wanted a fool! A man from the outside, who didn't understand anything about finance! I initialled every deposit document! Mine was the second signature, the first belonged to the chairman of the board ... He turned out to be a phoney. Fictitious. And his signature was written for him by someone unknown ... Anyway, the first deputy chairman disappeared next. Almost all the heads of department resigned ...'

'I get it. The rats left the sinking ship ...'

'The rats, and the sailors, and the captain! The second deputy chairman and I are the only ones left ...'

'You run too!'

'Too late!' the lawyer exclaimed. 'The second deputy chairman beat me to it. The day before yesterday he went off to his dacha, but yesterday he phoned me from Tel Aviv ...'

'All the better for you. It makes you almost the only member of management who didn't run, but stayed. It's a clear indication of your innocence ...'

Red suddenly leaned over and spat on the floor – awkwardly, like a woman. Then he ground it in with the toe of his shoe. He was clearly in shock.

'What can I do? They'll put me away! They'll put me away! What's your advice, as a banker?'

I shrugged.

'Calm down. Take a sonapax tablet. By the way, do you happen to have any on you?'

'No.'

'Pity. Then how do you get rid of stress?'

'I guzzle vodka.'

'That's really bad! My advice to you is: don't guzzle vodka. Go to the interrogations. Lose the tail that you've spotted. Bring the cocaine you found to me … I'm joking. There's a great demand for poisons like that in here … Record the threats over the phone on your dictaphone. You didn't run for it like the rest, you stayed to clear up the shit – that's a plus for you. In addition, you're an objectively honest and decent man who only joined the bank very recently – that's another plus. No right-thinking cop will ever put you away.'

'What about you?' the lawyer asked. 'Did right-thinking cops put you away? Without a single piece of evidence?'

I remembered the piercing gaze of General Zuev's watery eyes and nodded seriously:

'Yes. I was put away by exceptionally right-thinking men. I would say they were right thinking personified. And in their place I would have done the same. And as well as that, one of them, one of these right-thinking men, recently demonstrated to me, as clearly as two times two makes four, that the most important piece of evidence is written on my forehead.'

Red gaped incredulously at the bridge of my nose, but was obviously unable to see anything and grabbed his pack of Gitanes again. His hands were shaking.

'But the most important thing,' I said, suddenly remembering, and the lawyer shuddered, dropped the cigarettes and leaned bodily towards me, preparing avidly to drink in the wisdom of the great shark of Russian business for which he obviously took me (at this point, I started feeling genuinely sorry for him), 'the most important thing of all is – never try to deceive anyone!'

Red didn't say anything. I picked up the cigarette he had dropped on the table and carefully put it back in the pack – then put the pack in my pocket.

'I'll take the lighter too.'

'Yes, yes, of course …'

'Have you got a pen?'

'Here, take it …'

'And another thing,' I added casually, 'I'd like to borrow some money from you …'

'How much?' Red exclaimed, hastily taking out his wallet.

'About five hundred roubles. If possible in small bills …'

The lawyer immediately counted out the cash and I put it away in a safe place that everyone knows about.

Red watched my manipulations in disgust.

'Don't worry,' I told him with a farewell smile. 'Prison isn't made for people like you, it's for people like me. For the man who thinks he can't be punished, that he's the most cunning of all the cunning. This isn't your place. You're tormenting yourself unnecessarily. Resign from the bank, get your nerves back in shape, change your phone number and the place you live … Go back to practicing law. My trial will be starting soon – perhaps you'll be able to help me again …'

The thick metal, sawn untidily round the edges, had been welded to other metal by human hands. After some time other, patient hands had torn it off, disconnected one from the other. Loosened what had been fastened, straightened what had been bent. A hole had been formed, a gap. Now, looking through it, I saw what it was forbidden to see: freedom.

Such was the privilege of my new, improved status: to climb up on the prison windowsill and feast my eyes on freedom through the gap.

But only a narrow strip out of the whole of freedom. Directly opposite, fifty metres away, was the massive grey bulk of the next building, the special block (in the local jargon, simply 'the special'). To the right was the hospital building. Directly below was the roof of some auxiliary structure. But between the two grey prison buildings, there it was – freedom. Blue sky, a fragment of the embankment, a small stretch of a grassy slope with a few trees. A tall apartment building. How did people like living there – in that house with a view of the prison?

'Don't get nervous,' Johnny advised me briskly. 'I'll tell you everything and show you. I've been on the Road for a year already.'

'Aren't you bored with it?'

'This sort of thing doesn't get boring,' my trainer said quietly and flexed his impressive deltoids. 'The Road's a sacred business. It's the foundation of the Common Way. Of course, sometimes you get hot and hassled or tired and suchlike. But I get a kick out of it. The best thing is that you're busy all the time … Oh! Hear that? That's them tapping from the side. Pull! Not like that, not like that … You have to pull quickly, but without jerking. Now untie the knot and unwrap the cloth. Give me the scrips here … In short, here on the road, things are okay. It's a twelve hour shift. You're moving all the time. That's the important thing. You're busy, you're always on the run, you've got work to do, you eat with the boss. Nobody touches you, but you can tell almost anyone where to get off …'

A single prisoner with scabies on his stomach surfaced out of the common wave of humanity and handed Johnny a note. The prison letter, carefully sealed into plastic, precisely repeated the shape and size of a stick of chewing gum. I took the missive, looked at the address – 'To H. 135' – realised that it had to be sent upwards, and was just about to tie the knot, but Johnny stopped me.

'Don't set the "horse" running just for one scrip! It's been working for three weeks already. By the way, start every shift by checking all the horses to make sure they won't break. If a horse can't bear the weight of your body, throw it away and plait another one.'

'And what do I do with the scrip?'

'We'll wait until we have at least three or four and get rid of them all at once. Exceptions are only made for urgent missives and missives of Common importance.'

'But where do I put it now?'

'Wherever you like. You took it, so now you answer for it with your life. Put it in your pocket and close the zip. If you lose it or – God forbid – let the goons grab it, you'll be off the Road like a shot … And I'll follow you. Usually the entire shift is sacked. We've had that happen twice in a year. I wasn't involved, of course …'

'That's drastic.'

'That's the way it has to be,' said Johnny, raising one finger sternly. 'This is prison! Every scrip could decide someone's fate. Although ninety per cent of all the post is garbage. "Brother, send us over some sugar and cigarettes when you get a chance." Sometimes they just write because they've got nothing to do. But you're still answerable anyway … Oh, there's another tap. Pull. Not that one! The top one! What?'

'It's stuck.'

'Jump up. Put your hand through. Not like that! Stick it through the bars!'

I started panting.

'It won't go through.'

'Of course not! You have to roll up your sleeve. Then it'll go through.'

With an effort I squeezed the load that had got stuck in through the eyelashes and jumped back down.

'Don't forget that in different huts the holes in the "eyelashes" are different sizes. Sometimes the load will go through your gap, but stick solid at the next place. You have to remember about that. Look, they've brought another two missives … Don't hurry. Check that they're sealed properly! Don't reseal them yourself – just give them back, that's all. The person who sends a missive or a load always seals it. If anyone in the hut comes and asks for matches, a lighter, cellophane – don't give them any. They have to have their own … Put the missives together. Wrap them in the cloth. Tighter. Not like that! Here, let me do it … Now tie the knot. Now tap. Don't knock loud. There are some amateurs who hammer so hard the goon can hear it in the corridor. There, it's gone …'

'It's got stuck again.'

Johnny slapped me on the shoulder.

'Up you go, roadman! Push it through! And look smart! What if the filth breaks in all of a sudden – and you've got a load stuck in the bars! Let the load get taken and they'll knock your head off. You'll be jumping like that the whole twelve hours. Up and down. What are doing perched up there? Jump, they're tapping on the other side again.'

There are two windows in the cell. We handle the post that goes sideways through the window on the left, and the post that goes up and down through the one on the right. The windows are set two metres above the floor, and the distance between them is ten paces. After running to and fro several times and making dozens of leaps up and jumps down, I was soaked in sweat, I'd sprained my foot, scratched my hand and I was out of breath.

Johnny simply found it amusing.

'You'll get used to it. By the way, take your slippers off. Stand on the Road in your socks. It's easier to jump like that. Basically, right now, during the day, there's next to no post. At night it'll come flooding in. There are ten thousand prisoners in the Central, and they all want to keep in touch. The nights are tough. You don't even have the time to light a cigarette. That's why the shifts rotate: this week we're on days, and Givi Sukhumsky and Kolya the File are on nights. Next week it's the other way round. Oh, they're tapping! Pull the side horse. No, let me pull it, you'll get it stuck again. You get it stuck because you don't pull it right. I told you – quick and smooth. There's a drainpipe outside on the wall, and the load always gets hooked on it …'

'What sort of address is this?'

'Aha,' Johnny replied after examining this latest note. 'That's for the other block. Send it up, to "HR".'

'Where?'

'The High Road. Have you seen that cable stretched between the blocks? That's the HR. The lads there are worth ten of you or me. Five to seven of them on a shift. The horse is a hundred metres long …'

'But why …'

'Quiet!' my partner suddenly interrupted. 'Hear that?'

In a single bound, Johnny flew up two metres and pressed his ear against the bars. He froze. Then he turned round and roared deafeningly:

'Quiet in the hut! Turn off the television!'

The babbling murmur of a hundred prisoners' throats stopped instantly and a tense silence descended. Only now could I make out a distant, hoarse howling:

'Goon under the bars!'

'Quick!' Johnny leapt down. 'Stretch the horses tight! All of them! Tie them to the radiators! Or else they'll snap them! Pull them tighter. Signal the neighbours! Quick, brother, quick!'

'Goon under the bars!' we heard the voice say again, but we had already halted all movement and secured our ropes firmly – now they were pressed tight against the walls of the building on the outside.

'Sometimes when they've got nothing to do,' Johnny said after he'd caught his breath, 'they take a walk along the wall. Every one has a cable with a hook on the end. If he throws it, snags the horse and pulls off the load, he'll take it to the godfather, the bastard. So remember, Andriukha, you have to check out the clearing. Take a mirror, jump up, stick your hand out and look to see if there's a screw down by the wall. A good roadman checks out the clearing every time before he sends a load. And when it's Common post – that's always at night – you can even light a newspaper and throw it down so you can see …'

'It sounds tricky,' I confessed frankly.

'Nothing tricky about it. Work hard, use your head, take it seriously, and you'll soon master the whole business. The worst thing is when there's some fool standing on the neighbours' Roadway. Like now. Why do you think our loads are getting stuck? Because he's not tying the knot right! You have to make the knot flat, and tie the load along the "horse", not across it – then it'll slip straight through … Let's write them a line, while the heat's off and the Roadway's frozen … You can write it yourself. Get a pen and paper …'

'But what do I write?'

Johnny smiled.

'Want me to dictate? Write: "Joyful greetings, outlaws! Peace and prosperity to your home and the whole Common Way". Common Way with capital letters. Got that down?'

'Yes.'

'Next: "One of your men has been tying the loads wrongly for the whole shift today. They get stuck in the bars. Please correct the situation. Cordial convict greetings. The Road in hut one one seven." Road with a capital letter.

Ah, I forgot! Add this underneath: "Outlaws! When you get the chance send in a pack of good cigarettes, we're right out of them over here".'

'I've written it.'

'Fold it up and seal it.'

'There's no polythene left.'

'So?'

'Where do I get some?'

Johnny heaved a sigh.

'Andriukha, use your head. There are a hundred and thirty-five men in the hut! Go get some from any of them. Everyone who receives parcels always has cellophane bags. Go for it!'

The curtain of the nearest compartment was drawn back, and I saw Slava's creased and crumpled face. Our supervisor had his own ideas about time. The twenty-three-year-old boss usually stayed awake for two or three days at a stretch. Paying no attention to the alternating sequence of day and night, he composed dozens of missives to his numerous friends and acquaintances, sent and received dozens of loads, talked at length with the new arrivals in the hut, played cards, backgammon, chess and draughts, settled the inevitable conflicts between cell-mates, prayed, watched the television – and he did all of this for fifty or seventy hours. Then he swallowed several dimedrol tablets and slept like a log for another fifty hours. His day and night extended over an entire calendar week.

'Johnny, how are things?' he asked in a surly, sleepy voice.

'Everything's fine,' Johnny answered. 'There's a smartass blocking the Roadway.'

'Are you out of plastic bags?' Slava asked – he must have heard our last exchange.

'We'll find some,' Johnny assured him.

'Andriukha,' Slava admonished me, 'you're a roadman, understand? Go into the hut and take whatever you need! The Road has to run like clockwork. Cellophane, matches, paper – anything. Only don't get heavy, do it politely. And while you're at it let those slobs know that every worthy prisoner gives the Road everything it needs without having to be asked or reminded!'

The final words were spoken loudly. The sound flew up to the ceiling and bounced between the walls. A hundred and thirty-five men – apart from those who were asleep – lapsed into an uneasy silence.

Slava emerged into the passage, rubbed his face with one hand, took his towel and strolled through the entire cell to the washbasin. The men made way for him. The more experienced and smarter ones tugged on the arms and shoulders of those who were slow on the uptake. The supervisor's bleary-eyed, aggressive gaze slid over their faces.

'A hundred and thirty men!' Slava lamented in disgust. His voice swelled with power. 'Does a roadman really have to go chasing after every one of you, asking for every last trifle? Give him the thread! Give him matches! All right? What else?'

Slava fixed his stare on the nearest man, daubed with iodine from head to foot.

'What's your name?'

'Lantern …'

'Lantern, I know you're never away from the tattoo man, you take tea and sugar in by the kilogram, just to get your next job done! But you never go near the Roadway. You never ask the lads how things are going, or if they need anything. And you, Ali-Baba? Yesterday you got a delivery, but you didn't even come across with a cigarette for the lads! And you, Fedot? Have you decided to live like a passenger?'

'I don't get any deliveries,' said eighteen-year-old Fedot, with his pockmarked face and shaven head, trying to make excuses in the deafening silence.

'Take a needle!' Slava shouted in a deep bass voice. 'Sew a pillow case! Take some glue and make a box for the Common fund! The old one's fallen to pieces! But you didn't know that, right? Do something at least! Join in the Common Way! If you don't know how, ask the men! They'll tell you! Don't be a passenger! Do something! Show what you can do! What sort of life is it, hiding away in a corner, guzzling your rations? Passengers! Every last one of you is a passenger! Doing nothing, guzzling your rations, waiting to see how things turn out – that's your life! No God, no conscience! Rookie! Where are you?'

'Here,' Rookie boomed from behind the other mens' backs.

In a month inside, Dima the Rookie had settled in and pretty much got his life in order. We didn't meet very often, though. I rarely left my favourite cosy corner in Slava's compartment. I stayed in there twelve hours a day, watching the television screen, fenced off from prying eyes by the curtain, only going out in order to relieve myself. My enemy had attached himself first to one group, then to another that was richer, and eventually even found himself a place on the first level – although he still slept in four shifts.

'Tell me, am I right?'

'Yes,' Rookie confirmed morosely. 'No arguments, Slava. You're right.'

'There, you see!' Slava looked round the men nearest to him. 'In other words, please! If anyone has polythene bags, spare what you can for the Road. That's all.'

While he was getting washed, they brought dozens of small bags, large bags and pieces of polythene to the wall for Johnny, as well as three exercise books with square-ruled pages, two pens, one cigarette lighter, fourteen filter cigarettes and one lump of sugar

Even Fedot with the pockmarked face, who didn't get any deliveries, thrust the stump of a pencil into my hand. Although his gesture was accompanied by a rapid glance of envy.

31

'**W**ell now, Andrei,' Khvatov said, and sighed. 'The investigation's finished. We're handing you over for trial.'

'Congratulations,' I replied warily and sat down on the windowsill.

While the windows in the investigative offices at Lefortovo overlooked the inner courtyard, under the democratic arrangements at the Matrosskaya Tishina prison, I could glimpse genuine freedom through the grimy glass – a city street, parked cars, citizens hurrying about their business. However, in a year nothing appeared to have changed. The same citizens. The same cars. The same check cowboy shirt on the investigator from Ryazan.

'Shall we say goodbye, then?' I suggested.

Khvatov laughed. It was a long time since I'd seen him in such a genial mood.

'There's a long way to go until it's goodbye,' he replied. 'You've still got the "two hundred and one" to come. Before they start to try you, you and your co-defendants have to, you know, familiarise yourselves with all the prosecution materials. Article two hundred and one of the Criminal, you know, Procedural Code.'

'You're going to let me read the CASE FILE?'

'All fifty-seven volumes of it.'

'How many?' I asked in amazement.

'Fifty-seven,' the native son of Ryazan repeated, putting his hand into his bag and pulling out a plump cardboard folder. 'This is for you today. It's volume one.'

Volume one – incredibly massive, grey and tidy – crashed down on to the table top.

I had to laugh despite myself.

'So you tied it all up after all.'

'Yes we, you know, tied it up.'

'You took your time getting there.'

'Yes, it took a long time,' Khatov agreed. 'But it's all according to the letter of the law. We got it, you know, done within eleven months.'

As I admired the grey cardboard monster, I experienced a complex gamut of emotions. A year before I had been dreaming of reading just one page. In my sleep I used to see myself feverishly leafing through the terrible sheets of paper. I was planning to pay a bribe. I was trying to master the skills of inconspicuous spying. And now I had the right to read all the papers quite legally. But I honestly didn't really want to any longer.

Now I'll glance under that grey cover and learn if I did the right thing by refusing to talk to the investigation and not answering questions. Now I'll start reading – and I'll discover that the minister did talk, so did the pharmaceutical chemist, and my former boss Mikhail, and the other witnesses. Now I'll open the book of fate and see my own future in it.

Awed by the importance of this historical moment, I made myself comfortable on the stool, pulled the CASE FILE towards me with a decisive movement and began greedily devouring its contents – but I was disappointed.

Volume one contained official resolutions concerning the instigation of criminal proceedings and other special prosecutor's documents. Every last one of them verbose to an extreme and overflowing with bombastic bureaucratic terminology.

The dozens of resolutions were filed in chronological order. The resolution concerning the instigation of the CASE. The resolution concerning the transfer of the CASE, once instigated, to higher authorities. The resolution concerning the bringing of charges against the major suspects. The resolution concerning the bringing of charges against the secondary figures. Including A. Rubanov. The resolution concerning the detention of suspects under arrest. The resolution concerning the allocation of a new number to the CASE. The resolution concerning the establishment of an investigative team. The resolution concerning the inclusion in the team of investigators such-and-such, police operatives such-and-such, specialists such-and-such.

Everywhere there were illegible signatures in blue ink. Menacing stamps. The Municipal Prosecutor's Office. The Republican Prosecutor's Office. The General Prosecutor's Office. The Deputy General Prosecutor, Senior Legal Counsellor such-and-such. Acting General Prosecutor such-and-such. Menacing faxes. Round seals with two-headed eagles. Crisp formulae. Taking into account the particular danger! And also the seriousness of the offence! To be arrested!

Eventually I closed volume number one in disgust and sighed.

'Nothing much there.'

'It will get more interesting,' Khvatov promised.

There's something missing, I thought. Some usual detail of my investigator's appearance is missing. I suddenly realised what it was.

'Where are your painkillers?' I enquired politely. 'Surely the cars haven't stopped honking, have they?'

'No, they haven't stopped,' Khvatov remarked casually.

'Have you got used to it?'

'Of course not. How can you get used to something like that?'

'But your head doesn't hurt any more?'

'No.'

'How did you manage to beat your complaint?'

The man in the check shirt laughed.

'I went to the pharmacy,' he confided, 'but instead of buying tablets I bought, you know, a brochure. *How to defeat stress.* A very useful, you know, little book! It's all in there.'

'Aha, I see. The pharmacy. And a little book. All very simple. And what does medicine recommend for removing stress these days?'

The investigator gave me a cunning, suggestive glance through his spectacles. He really didn't look depressed or tired at all. Although only recently, at our last meeting, he'd had purple patches under his eyes and he'd kept swallowing aspirin all the time. He stuck his hand into his bag again.

'How about that?' he declared proudly. 'That's my medicine!'

'I saw a CD player. Delighted with himself, Khvatov carefully set down several boxes containing disks beside it.

'That's what I listen to! Look. This is the sound of tropical, you know, rain. Nothing else for a whole hour, nothing but water pouring down and birds calling. This is the sound of the ocean waves on the shore. Another hour-long recording. And this is a really remarkable thing: the mating songs of whales …'

'May I listen to some?' I asked.

'By all means,' Khvatov agreed. 'Only, you know, quickly …'

I put the tiny plastic buttons in my ears and pressed play.

My head was filled with deep rumbling and ringing and rustling sounds. Streams of water came pouring down out of a low, cloudy sky, billions of heavy drops pattering on broad, emerald-green leaves. I heard the shrieking of a parrot, or a monkey, or an elephant, or some other denizens of the jungle unknown to me. Coarse, freakish howls, calls and other signals coming from the distance, or sounding very close.

The living cacophony of nature pacified me. I squeezed my eyes shut and pictured a forest, water, flowers, green stems. I imagined luscious tropical aromas, cool freshness, the atmosphere of a festival. When I opened my eyes again, I saw the investigator from Ryazan looking at me and saying something with a smile of satisfaction on his round face. He was obviously telling me how he had used the recordings to overcome his health problems and forget about the unmerciful honking of the big city's inhabitants.

I cautiously stroked the CD player's plastic case. It looked very alluring. And so did the disks in plastic boxes with colourful pictures on their covers. In a sombre pre-trial prison that positively stank of misery, these were alien objects. They belonged to a different world, one that was festive and glossy. Free. I felt sadness and envy.

I had a sudden brainwave. Yes, there was a CD player in our cell – a creaking, battered little device that had been handed round from one prisoner to another many times over and survived dozens of searches.

Sometimes, during especially vicious searches, the player had been confiscated, but every time we had managed to ransom the precious object afterwards. In fact, there was a device for listening to music in every decent hut in the Central. Or almost every one.

The only problem was the music itself. The top spots in the hit parades at the Matroska were unvaryingly occupied by prison songs. I personally can't listen to a three-chord chanson for very long. At one time I even wrote off to my neighbours, friends and acquaintances in the Central, asking them to send something apart from 'gangster music', if they had any. But the answers from everywhere were disheartening. They had Krug, Kuchin, Nagovitsyn and lots of other solo performers, but apart from that, nothing.

And now here in front of me I had the sound of tropical rain! The mating songs of whales! Ocean breakers! This was it! This was what I needed! This was the experience my soul was thirsting for! This was what would save me from the daily nightmare, from the sight of that churning, parasite-ridden mass of humanity! The sound of a tropical downpour! The mating songs of whales!

'Sell me the music, Stepan Mikhalich!' I suggested resolutely.

Khvatov shook his head smugly.

'Are you kidding?'

'Sell it to me, Stepan Mikhalich!' I said, putting into my voice all the conviction that I could muster. 'Sell me the disks! Sell me the songs of the whales! And the tropical rain! And the ocean waves! And the player too! Sell them to me, Stepan Mikhalich!'

The man in the check shirt dismissed the request with an austere wave of his hand. Gathering up his magical equipment from the table, he hastily put it back into his bag, where it was followed by the mating songs and all the rest.

'Stop talking, you know, nonsense. How can I sell it to you? What are you going to do with it? You won't get it through to the cell ...'

'I will!' I exclaimed passionately. 'You just agree, and I'll get it through, don't you worry! I'll get it through three searches! We have it all set up!'

'Are you going to pay the going rate, then?'

'Maybe I will. That's my business. But I'll get it through, no hassle, I tell you! Sell it to me, Stepan Mikhalich!'

'Stop it,' muttered the man from Ryazan. 'You haven't even got any money.'

'Not with me, it's true,' I agreed. 'But the next time, when you bring me volume two, I'll have the full amount!'

After a rapid mental calculation, I realised I could get together seventy dollars in a day. From my neighbours, friends and acquaintances. And I attacked again:

'Sell me it, Stepan Mikhalich! Sell me it! Be a friend! Help me out here! Put yourself in my place! There are a hundred and thirty men in the same cell as me! Tuberculosis, scabies, lice, meningitis, dropsy, hunger, fainting fits! Vagrants, drug addicts, squabbling and fighting! The nervous strain of it! Sell it to me, Stepan Mikhalich! Sell me the whales and the rain of the tropics! No one will find out! I'll get it through on the quiet! And in the evening in the hut I'll sit down, close my eyes, put on the earphones – and relax! Settle my nerves! I'll feel freedom, life, air! Well? Go on!'

As I elaborated, I imagined myself listening to the mating songs of whales in the middle of a common cell in the Central with such vividness that the tears sprang to my eyes.

'Stop it,' Khvatov replied. 'I can't. It's out of the question.'

Maintaining my patience, I paused for a while and tried a different approach.

'That's your first player, isn't it?'

'What of it?'

The investigator from Ryazan didn't react to the new, more familiar tone in my voice. Perhaps he simply didn't notice it.

'You bought it,' I went on ingratiatingly, 'learned how to use it, figured out all the buttons, and for a while you were delighted, but very soon you realised that for the same money you could have bought yourself *much better* technology! Am I right?'

Khvatov thought about it.

'Pretty much, yes,' he replied. 'The main reason was that I had no one to ask. I'm surrounded by respectable people, and a CD walkman is an amusing, you know, toy for young people …'

'Now you'd buy a better model, wouldn't you? One with the controls on the wire as well as the case. Right?'

The man in the check shirt thought about it and immediately admitted that I'd hit the, you know, bull's eye. Inspired, I took out my prestigious cigarettes (not everyone in our Central smokes Gitanes, and those who do, don't smoke them every day), energised myself with the expensive smoke and continued coolly:

'Sell it to me, Stepan Mikhalich. Do it. I'll pay you the full value. The same as if it was a new player. And you'll buy yourself another one, only better! You spent your money, but it was only later, as you pressed the little buttons, that you realised which functions and options you needed and which were useless! It was only in the course of using technology that was new to you that you developed the taste of a consumer. And now you've reached the stage when you're ready to exchange the item for a better one! If not a more expensive one, then at least one that's a better match for your specific personal requirements! It's time to move on! Towards new horizons! Sell it to me, Stepan Mikhalich! Sell me your player! Get yourself a better one! Respect yourself and your own needs!'

'You're quite, you know, right,' Khvatov muttered. 'But what you suggest is out of the question. And you know it. That's it. I'm calling the guard. Be ready.'

Disappointed, I pushed volume number one away from me and cast a regretful, caressing glance at the earphone cable dangling out of the investigator's bag. Then I made one last, desperate, pitiful appeal.

'Sell it to me, Stepan Mikhalich! I beg you, as a fellow country-boy! As a man of feeling! Sell it to me, eh?'

'The apparatus is not for sale,' the investigator replied. He paused and then added. 'Like its owner.'

The figure of a warder appeared in the doorway.

'I'll come tomorrow,' Khvatov warned me. 'I'll bring, you know, volume two. Be ready.'

'Please don't forget the disks,' I said, switching back to a more formal tone of voice as I got up off the uncomfortable prison stool. 'I'll read the CASE FILE and listen to the sound of ocean waves. All right?'

The following day, the check-shirted campaigner against stress brought volume two – but not the CD player. He was obviously frightened that this totally crazed prisoner would somehow manage to persuade him.

But as it turned out, reading the CASE FILE was a far more emotional experience for me than listening to the sounds of tropical rain.

The first time I laughed as I studied the latest volume, the investigator from Ryazan looked at me with apprehensive suspicion.

'What's so funny?'

'Oh,' I replied. 'it's just something that makes me laugh.'

'Are you reading your own testimony?'

'No. I'll weep over my own testimony.'

In July Khvatov started visiting me frequently again, just like the previous autumn, at the very height of the investigation. He came two or even three times a week, bringing one volume after another – and I read them and laughed.

The pages of the CASE FILE, those neatly typed minutes, gave off a strong whiff of abject, pitiful fright and grotesque, naive falsehood, both typical of the cultured intellectual.

My Boss Mikhail was up there in the front line. He had been interrogated three times, and each time he changed something, made something up, invented something, rejected his previous opinions and judgements, tried to be cunning and generally, in my view, did absolutely everything possible to make the investigation suspect him of direct involvement in the theft of billions of roubles from the state. It was a good thing that while the minor character Rubanov was being questioned in the next office, he kept his mouth shut – or instead of getting out a month later, my boss Mikhail would still have been enjoying the state's hospitality.

Mikhail immediately ruined his story of being the 'office supplies manager'. In one place he called himself 'the firm's business manager'. The next day he defined himself as 'the office manager'. A week later, at the third interrogation, he declared: 'I dealt with everyday practical matters, and also carried out other instructions from Andrei.'

Why? – I thought in horror, and took my head in my hands. What other instructions? The office supplies manager – full stop! Maybe, as he sat there in side profile, my boss Mikhail had decided at the last moment that they wouldn't believe a young man with an imposing appearance like him? Maybe he suddenly doubted his own acting abilities?

If you have more than a million dollars in your pocket, if you have a servant in your home and your car is driven by a chauffeur, if you long ago stopped thinking about petty matters such as screwing in light bulbs, washing dishes, putting petrol in your tank or paper in your fax machine, paying the utility bills and so on – then playing the part of an office supplies manager in the prosecutor's office is by no means as easy as it might seem.

One way and another, Mikhail gave objectively bad testimony. Confused, incoherent, full of contradictions. He said a lot more than he should have done.

I found certain passages absolutely stunning. 'For some time I used to trade in parts at the radio market.' What market? What radio parts? What was he trying to do, win the investigator's pity?

'When I graduated from university I was left without any means of support.' I laughed out loud at that. What a way to put it! Without any means of support. Perhaps a sympathetic tear fell on the minutes at that point? Go work on a building site, in a factory, join the army under contract! Live there! What do you think you're doing, complaining about a lack of means to a militia investigator, with his measly salary? Sweep streets! Tighten bolts! Working hands are needed everywhere. You, Mikhail, made a serious mistake. From your millionaire's point of view, to live you need an income of at least one or two thousand dollars a month. And anything under that amount doesn't even count as living.

The others were not far behind my boss. Those involved in the case as witnesses, that is. My own assist, Semyon, declared: 'My relations with Andrei were friendly, with a hint of superiority on his side.' What hints are you talking about? You're giving testimony in the office of the General Procurator of the entire country! Who's interested in your hints here? General Zuev? This is a matter of a serious criminal offence! Express yourself clearly, stick to the substance, the main point. Nobody's going to ponder all your hints and analyse all the subtle vibrations of the soul of a member of the intelligentsia. I worked for Andrei. Full stop. Hints of superiority aren't going to amuse anyone here, in offices with homemade paper ashtrays – but they will show you, my friend in a negative light.

The other important witness for my episode of the drama wasn't exactly laconic, either. When he was caught, this young guy – the very same supplier of other people's passports and ID whose name the cunning Captain Svinets finally dragged out of me – spouted over thirty pages. He dictated an entire novella! Told them everything. Even made up a few things. Starting with 'It seems to me', and following it with ponderous paragraphs of conjecture and surmise.

But that wasn't enough for the seller of passports: he drew *illustrations*! He sketched diagrams of urban courtyards and secluded passageways, drawings of all the places where he and I had met. He made detailed drawings, with explanatory inscriptions, little arrows and the names of major local landmarks set in quotation marks. Each sketch plan was grandly completed with the refrain: 'Drawn by my own hand'; then signature and date.

As I read the effusive outpourings of my former friends and partners, I just had to laugh. There was a time when same these people, manfully compressing their lips and knitting their brows, squaring their shoulders and performing various other convincing corporeal manipulations, used to swear their profound devotion – naturally, not to me in person, but to our work, to the business. I had been given to understand that confidentiality would be maintained even under the most terrible torture.

And now here I was reading their testimonies, full of redundant details, references to 'hints' and sheer idle fantasy.

My merriment was not long-lived. Of the fifty volumes of the CASE FILE, only the first few folders contained the minutes of testimony from witnesses and the accused. The fundamental bulk was taken up by expert opinions. The prosecution demonstrated irrefutably that it was I, and no one else, who bought the fly-by-night firms, and I was the one who applied the round seals to the paper, the one who signed the financial documents with my own hand. The minutes of accounting audits asserted that my firms had accumulated astronomical debts to the budget. The analyses of other experts clearly revealed the entire path followed by the stolen billions – from the treasury accounts, via several transit points in the provinces, and later in the capital, and on to banks in Estonia, Cyprus, Austria, Switzerland …

The testimony provided by foreign bankers had a fine ring to it as well. General Zuev personally travelled to Europe, where he searched doggedly for the stolen money, moving from country to country. In some places they were helpful and made all the information available to him. The statements and copies of payment instructions were included in the CASE FILE – the much-vaunted bourgeois secrecy of deposits proved to be a fiction. The European bankers didn't want to quarrel with the General Prosecutor's Office of the mighty nuclear Empire. The bankers in Cyprus made a special effort. The documentary evidence removed from the banks in Limassol was exhaustive. And the industrious Estonians were quick to get their calculators out too.

There was only one country where General Zuev was not told a single thing, let alone allowed access to clients' accounts – in that small state of gnomes that everyone knows about, the land of chocolate and cheese.

As I read about how the embezzlers had taken the budget's money out of the country and the routes they had used, as I followed the experts along the chain, I laughed once again at the surprising discovery that my position in the chain of intermediaries was sixth.

That could play well in the court, I thought. I'm only number six! It would sound very good. I'm not the main criminal, not the organiser, not the ideas man, only a middle man. A lowly minion, used but kept in the dark. I'm only number six!

First the minister, then his brother, then a major businessman closely associated with the minister's brother, and another businessman, of middling size, closely associated with the major one. After that a smaller businessman, closely associated with the middling one. The next link was the pharmacist. And finally – me.

The banker was a stooge.

32

'**F**ilth under the bars!' I screech in a wild falsetto, moving my mouth right up close to the gap between the eyelashes, so that the whole Central can hear, including the common block, and the special, and the TB clinic, and the hospital, so that all movement on the Road will stop. 'Filth under the bars!'

The horse is stretched as tight as a bowstring, but it doesn't break. It's a first-class horse, absolutely new, strong, four woollen sweaters went into making it and as well as that several strands of thick fishing line were woven in: to make it stronger and allow it to slide more easily, it has been smeared with wax and plasticine, and so far it's holding. Despite the fact that down in the street a warder is tugging the horse towards him and on our side three strong roadmen are holding on tight to it; I'm one of them. All the loads tied on to the horse are outside the cell. I can see them, but I can't reach them.

I can hear the warder swearing smugly to himself. Only a minute ago he spotted the loads on the move and flung his 'cat' – a steel hook on a strong string – and now he's determined to get his hands on the prisoners' post.

'Maloi, Johnny, pull, pull!' I yell, and my friends strain, tighten their grip and hang on. I am sitting hunched over in the window aperture, more than two metres above the floor, holding on to one of the bars with one hand, with my other arm thrust out through the gap between the pieces of metal, trying to reach the loads and save them – and together with them my own reputation. There's a crash that sets the steel bars and strips ringing. The warder had spotted my hand and thrown something heavy at it, evidently a stone – but he has missed.

'Bring some hot water!' Johnny shouted into the hut. 'And sod it, let's have a knife here, quick!'

A hundred and thirty pale faces – apart from those whose turn it is to sleep – tensely observe the course of events. The last time we poured down three litres of boiling water, and that decisive response put the screws off their habit of attacking the road for a whole month. But they keep coming back over and over again. Our cell, number one hundred and seventeen, is on the second floor, not very high, and so the loads that pass through us seem like easy prey to certain especially zealous warders.

Another two volunteers come dashing over – I recognised one of them as puny Fedot – and now eight thin but sinewy hands repeatedly jerk on the horse, trying to pull at least part of it back into the cell. The warder is yielding. After all, there is only one of him and there are five of us. The time before last we pulled so hard that we lifted the greedy goon up into the air, and he fell from a serious height.

We jerk hard and an entire metre of rope slides back inside. Then another metre. I can almost reach.

'Again! Again! Is that water ready yet? And sod it, let's have a knife here, quick!'

They throw me up a homemade knife, I stick my naked arm out through the hole again and start cutting the taut fibres.

The horse snaps with a dull twang, and I go somersaulting down from on high, smashing my knee and shoulder against the sharp corners of the nearby bunks and making them bleed, but clutching the rescued packages firmly in my hand. There are only two of them. The third and last slipped out of the knot when the horse snapped and has fallen into our enemy's hands after all. The four men who were pulling below me also fall, but suffer less damage.

'Maloi,' I said, gasping for breath and streaming with sweat, my hands covered in blood, my chest and brain filled with hatred for all the window bars in this sublunary world, 'do you know what you're doing? Why didn't you spy the meadow?'

'I did spy it!' Maloi protested.

'We can see how well you spied it!' Johnny boomed angrily, showing the young lad the frayed and tattered end of the horse. 'The load's been taken! Give me that mirror!'

I have to jump up to the bars again. A hole has been worn in the wall by many generations of prisoners, there's a length of iron rod sticking out of it and tied to the rod is a special kind of noose, a strap made of tightly twisted rags. Bracing my foot in it, I go flying upwards, stick my arm out again and try to use the mirror to spot the warder standing down below.

'Boss,' I call to him quietly. 'Listen, boss…'

'Go on,' a quiet voice tells me from below.

'Give back the load.'

'The load?' The warder is up for a bit of bravado. 'Your *load's* going straight to the godfather's desk, got that?'

'Who needs the godfather here?' I protest politely. 'Let's strike a deal, ah? I'll pay the going rate!'

'Do you know what the rate is?'

'Don't insult me, boss!'

The negotiations last about ten minutes. It's already clear that no one really intends to go to the godfather. There's no point. The prison administration knows all about the Road, but is obliged to accept the existence of the makeshift ropes stretched between the windows of the cell blocks. They could snap them off, organise massive searches, find them and confiscate them – but the next day ten thousand prisoners would just repair and restore everything. They could even arrange punitive actions every day of the week. The gaunt inmates of the pre-trial isolation prison would still come up with some solution.

Eventually I give the sign, and Johnny hands me up a reel of thin but strong string – the 'failsafe'. Whereas a 'horse' is made out of sweaters, the failsafe is made out of socks, especially for occasions like this.

'You won't cheat us, boss?'

'No.'

'Then catch this.'

I tie a weight made out of several small stones wrapped in a piece of rag to the end of the 'failsafe', attach a fifty-rouble note a little bit higher, lower the money down, and a couple of minutes later I hoist up the rescued load. I come down off the windowsill. I twirl the cause of my sufferings in hands that are trembling with tension and then in furious annoyance fling it down on the blanket spread out at the bottom of the wall.

The load is a pack of cheap cigarettes without filters (the kind that only cost three roubles in the prison shop), crudely wrapped in paper and carelessly sealed in polythene. The address is on the front:

KALYOK SARATAVSKY IN H. 138

I can't help swearing – avoiding, nonetheless, any dangerous obscene expressions, after all, there could easily be friends or acquaintances of the respected Nikolai from the town of Saratov present, and they would be sure to bring my insulting remarks to his attention. That's the way they do things here.

'Right, Maloi,' I say, 'half the Central was thrown into uproar for the sake of this useless garbage! Draw your own conclusions!'

Maloi nods repentantly.

It's also true that the pack of lousy smokes could be a hiding place for drugs, a thousand roubles, a plan of escape from the prison or instructions for an accomplice on what to say and how to say it at the next interrogation session. So for the roadman all loads are equally valuable, and he is equally answerable for the disappearance of any one of them. If he makes a mistake his punishment is very simple – he's taken off the Road, and that's all. Then Slava Glory-to-the-CPSU will choose another strong, gutsy young guy out of the hundred men available. And the culprit will find himself stuck back in the depths of the hut, sleeping in four shifts. Perhaps later, after several months, he might manage to restore his position by unimpeachable purity of conduct, but the misdemeanour will remain on his record.

In here any misdemeanour always remains on your record. That's why Maloi, Johnny and I pant in relief, wipe the streams of sweat off our faces and shoulders with towels and light up some of my Gitanes. The humidity is so high that the cigarettes barely even smoulder.

The right thing now would be to give Maloi the tongue-lashing for being so sloppy and idle – after all, he was the one who'd been too lazy to spy the meadow before we despatched the loads. But from the door on the opposite side of the cell a loud shout announces that in ten minutes there will be a walk. That means it's time to put the Road on ice.

At that moment a lowlife, covered in spots of green ointment and totally out of his skull, squeezes through the compressed mass of naked bodies, clutching in his dirty fist a sloppily sealed scrip, which he holds out to Johnny.

'Listen, brother,' my partner explodes, 'have you completely lost it? Can't you see what's going on? There's uproar on the Roadway, and you come trying to pass on a missive! And when there's a walk too! Stick with the others for a while! We'll send off your scrip when we get back, all right?'

The lowlife looks at Johhny without understanding a thing. His pupils are like two match heads – he must have dosed up no more than ten minutes ago. He mumbles something and disappears, swaying, into the depths of the hut. I've never seen him before. Who is he? Where did he get heroin from? I must remember to have a word with him in a free moment …

Wasting no time, we put the Road on ice. Signal to our neighbours by giving the coded knock on the walls and the heating pipes, untie the horses, coil them up and store them away in their hiding places. Everyone knows how to hide three coils of homemade rope in a Common Hut so that they won't be found if there happens to be a search.

August, 1997. In the Common Hut it's about forty degrees. It's practically impossible to breathe. A walk is a sacred ritual. A hundred and thirty-five suspects under investigation are gasping for oxygen. Many of them promptly take out plastic buckets and start jostling around the water tap. Someone stands on someone else's foot or face, a few feeble wrangles flare up, someone is almost scalded with hot chifir. Eventually the door rumbles open.

'Out you come!'

The excited mass makes a dash for the corridor. The only ones left behind are sleepers and 'fatiguers' – the cleaners – they'll take advantage of the fact that the centre of the hut is empty and sweep up at least some of the dirt. The others hurry out into the main corridor and on up the stairs. All in their shorts and plastic slippers, their necks covered with towels and handkerchiefs used to wipe away the constant streams of sweat. They carry soap, wisps of bast and buckets with them. There is loud talk and swearing. A guard dog jerks on its lead and barks, sending echoes resounding along the corridor. The staircases are as wide as in the Lomonosov Moscow State University.

The human stream flows upwards. On the fourth floor everyone is already short of breath. Some can hardly even put one foot in front of the other. From time to time every third man breaks into a spasm of hoarse coughing. Ah now, there's the yard!

'This is the little yard, boss! Open up the other one! We're not going into this yard! We won't fit!'

The yard next to ours is several metres wider, and everybody knows it. The duty guard is paid his fee at the going rate and the crowd joyfully flows from the little yard into the spacious one next to it, where the air flows pleasantly, dry and delicious. The bright sunlight hurts their eyes. The ones who brought buckets of water have taken off their shorts and started soaping themselves. The others observe them enviously. Not everyone has a bucket. In the summertime in our prison the owner of a plastic bucket is a big man.

Some men sunbathe, turning their faces up to the rays of the sun. In one corner some low-lifes set fire to a piece of rubber sole from a shoe in order to make soot – the tattooist needs it to use instead of ink. But sensible men immediately put the brainless gorillas right, and they rapidly extinguish the fire, agreeing that it's almost impossible to breathe anyway, and we can all do without the stench and the soot.

Two or three of the younger ones have jumped up to grab hold of the bars of the overhead grille and are trying to do pull-ups. The old hands mock and sneer. In summer in the common block any kind of exertion is tantamount to suicide. There's no food, or air, or space. Exercising like that is a quick way to death.

I squat down on my haunches beside the wall. We roadmen have our own, separate bucket, but Johnny's the one getting washed today – it will be my turn the next time. Leaning my fleshless back against the wall, I think in silence.

Did I really believe not so long ago that it is possible to train the body and the mind in prison? Is it only four months since I used to boast to myself that prison was no problem for me? Now it turns out that I was doing time in a five-star hotel, not a prison. It's only now that I find myself in a real prison. Of course, there is one prison that I have already left behind – my naivity. I cover my face with my hands so that no one will see me laughing

Before even ten minutes have passed, the door of the yard swings open with a long, drawn-out creak and I hear someone shout:

'Rubanov! Rubanov, is he here? You're wanted, urgently!'

Totally bemused, I wander across to the exit, wondering who could possibly want to see me and why.

'Move it, move it!' says the screw, raising his voice.

I recognise him – it's cadaver number one in person, the very first overseer I met at the Matroska, a squat Mordovian with brown teeth and a lock of hair as black as tar sticking out at a rakish angle from under a prodigiously filthy uniform cap.

'Cool it, boss,' I protest calmly. 'Don't want to take me to a meet in just my shorts, do you? Let's go back to the hut, then at least I can put my trousers on!'

'Move it, at the double!'

The hut is unusually empty. There are seventy-something men lying in motionless repose on the thirty-two sleeping places. Their gaunt, grey legs, covered in sores and boils, dangle from the bunks, their knees protrude, painfully sharp, their pale mouths, half-open, greedily suck in the air.

Most of these men stand for eighteen hours in a row, packed tightly together in a crowd of sad cases like themselves, only sitting down at the table for a few minutes twice a day to eat transparent cabbage soup, or drink a mug of *vtoryak* – tea brewed from the same leaves for the third or fourth time; they couldn't give a damn for the walk – six hours in a horizontal position is the only rest they get.

I hastily pull on my trousers and tee-shirt and go back out into the main corridor, only for some reason I am not led upstairs to the investigative block, but down to the ground floor. I am even more puzzled now. What for? Where to? Slithering my beach slippers over the cool tiled floor, I gloomily run through the options in my mind.

We go down some steps. Walk past the sequence of prodigiously foul and filthy rooms stinking of excrement where the huge mass of prisoners arriving at the prison and departing from the prison is sifted, filtered and split up. At the very end of the corridor I am pushed into a small room with no windows or furniture. I feel a twinge of alarm. It could be that they are going to beat me. Last month I scalded a screw with boiling water and the month before that I insulted the block supervisor, so there's always some reason for me to get a rubber truncheon across the ribs ...

Standing there in the middle of the empty, dusty room, his feet firmly planted in a wide stance, was the one man I least expected to see: Captain Svinets. In one hand he was holding a pack of LM cigarettes and a bar of Toblerone chocolate.

His light, blindingly white suit of excellent-quality linen and his suede sandals entrance me, summoning forth vague snatches of half-effaced memories of a past life. Of cool, air-conditioned rooms, of leather armchairs, of sparkling mineral water and still mineral water, of cigars, of compact disks, of veal cutlets, of dewy glasses of whisky with ice, of rustling sheets, of laughing, smooth, male and female faces, of bank notes – green American ones and rainbow-coloured Russian ones – and of various other delights which once used to surround me on all sides, but the very existence of which is now disputed on a daily basis by my inflamed reason.

'Hi, Andrei,' the sleuth said amiably, extending a broad palm in my direction. I shook it cautiously.

'I came especially,' Svinets said, looking to one side, 'in order to apologise.'

'For what?'

'Back there in Lefortovo ... I had to tell you a little untruth.

You see … it's none of my doing that you've been moved here to the hell for fools. It's absolutely nothing to do with me. So if you think …'

'I don't think anything. And I don't bear a grudge.'

'I knew a long time ago that they were going to transfer you. Last year, in fact. As long as the preliminary investigation was going on, you were kept in Lefortovo. In conditions of maximum isolation. But now the investigation's finished, keeping you in there is an expensive luxury …'

'The Marquis de Sade,' I replied, scratching my stomach, 'paid his own money for his own prison quarters. That was how it was done then. The French aristocrats paid out of their own pockets to be kept in the Bastille. Look at history, learn from the experience of your great predecessors …'

'So now you've decided,' the snow-white detective asked with a frown, 'that you're an aristocrat? A Marquis?'

'No. I'm not in his league. The Marquis used to masturbate eighteen times a day, simultaneously making a detailed record of his sensations on paper. But I thank God if I can manage it once a week.'

'Stop fooling about. Take the chocolate. I brought it especially for you.'

'Thank you,' I replied, putting both hands behind my back.

Captain Svinets sighed.

'Anyway, you understand, do you? I had nothing to do with it. It wasn't me who decided to let you rot here. I only took the chance to get what I needed. Information.'

'And was it useful?'

'What?'

'The information.'

The detective gestured dismissively.

'No. It turned out that the murder victim Farafonov's passport was sold by his own wife after he was already dead. For a hundred and fifty dollars. She said she needed money urgently. And where would a widow get money? So it was all pointless. And your stubbornness was pointless …'

'No, it wasn't,' I objected, 'I did it on principle. And for general training purposes. Do you understand?'

'Absolutely.'

'Let's put an end to this conversation,' I said simply. 'If you came to apologise for lying to me, then consider your apology accepted, and it's over. I don't have much time …'

'Not much time?' Svinets asked, amazed. 'You're in prison. Where could you be going in a hurry?'

I smiled condescendingly. I couldn't tell this man in white trousers, who was so far removed from prison life and, moreover, was a servant of the law, that any time now, when the hut came back from its walk, I had to set the Road up again, then spread the word among the socially conscious prisoners that they should donate their sweaters, then pull the threads apart and plait a new horse to replace the one that had been snapped. And then I would certainly have to help Slava Glory-to-the-CPSU weigh and recount the Common holdings that had been accumulated over the week – several kilograms of tea and sugar – and for that I had to write upwards, to the brothers in one two eight, to ask them to lend us a spring balance, since ours had disappeared during the latest search. And after that I was planning to scribe a short missive to Fatty. My former cell-mate from Lefortovo had also been transferred to the Matrosskaya Tishina, but he had ended up in the special, not the Common Block. He was in a small, six-man cell, doing comfortable time in the company of two light-fingered generals and two narcotics barons who had been pronounced skunks, and for the pleasure of living in relative peace and quiet he was paying three hundred dollars every month into the pocket of one of the top officials in the prison administration.

Fatty – in this prison he was known by the more respectable moniker 'Stout' – never refused my requests. He sent in coffee and soup cubes and good cigarettes. And salami as well. It's a convenient and useful thing to have a rich friend like that in the Central. Real estate prices had gone up, and one of the construction magnate's dachas had been sold after all, a fact of which the delighted salami fanatic had informed me in his very first note.

As well as all that, I intended to compose a letter to my wife – it would be taken out by reliable people. And finally, the remainder of the day was set aside for repairing the cassette player – the reliable Japanese device had completely stopped working after a cockroach found its way into the tape-tensioning mechanism.

What could this sleuth in a white suit, this lover of busty blondes, understand about my life? And did he really need to know all the details?

'I've got a lot to do?' I replied evasively. 'All sorts of different things. Black ones and red ones.'

'Let's talk like friends.'

'By all means. That is, no worries.'

'Who did you want to be when you were a kid?'

'A cosmonaut. And after that – a writer. And you?'

'A polar explorer.'

'Great.'

We said nothing for a while

'Well, cosmonaut, why didn't you become who you wanted to be? Why did you turn out a swindler?'

'I'm not a swindler, I'm a knight of fortune. There's a difference.'

'You're a fool, not a knight!' Svinets declared pityingly, taking out his handkerchief and mopping the sweat off his low, pink forehead. 'I know about you! I know how you pumped up your muscles. How you tried to read the CASE FILE that Khvatov left open on the table. I know you want to change your handwriting. To train your memory. I went on a dozen searches of your hut in Lefortovo. I looked through all your textbooks. I looked through the exercise books with your notes in them. And there's one quote, as it happens, that I even copied for myself … as a keepsake …'

Svinets took out his notebook and looked for something in it – his face set in a tense expression, like a billiard-player's at the moment of the decisive strike – and he cited with feeling:

'"When you are going with your opponent to court, make an effort to settle with him while you are still on the way; otherwise he may drag you before the judge, and the judge hand you over to the constable, and the constable put you in jail. I tell you, you will not come out till you have paid the last farthing." The Gospel according to St Luke, chapter twelve, verses fifty-eight and fifty-nine ... so you read the Bible, do you?'

'I don't have time for it now. But yes, in Lefortovo I read it. Many times.'

The detective closed the little book and tapped the edge of it against his chin.

'I'm aware,' he stated with emphasis, 'that you have joined the criminals' community, the "thieves way" ... That's what it's called, if I'm not mistaken?'

'I don't know anything about that.'

'I see. So it would be stupid to offer you the chance to do some work for us ...'

'Aha,' I laughed, 'so that's why the polar explorer came to see the cosmonaut! To make an offer of collaboration!'

Svinets paused for a moment.

'Don't be like that,' he told me disapprovingly. 'You shouldn't be against us.'

I shook my head.

'I'm not against you! Not against you! You still haven't understood a thing, polar explorer! I'm against those fools who invented the idea of punishing a man by taking away his freedom. And also against those who part with this freedom of theirs too easily. The militia, the law, the law enforcement apparatus – that has always existed and always will exist, it has to, for sure. But it is physically impossible to take my freedom away from me! It's mine! A part of me! Always with me! No, it's even more than just a part of me – it *is* me! It ...' I pondered for a moment and quickly found the word I needed. 'It's like a name. You can even take away my life. Shoot me in the head and you'll take it. But the name remains. Andrei was alive – now he's dead, but still Andrei ... Apart from that, I'm strong and I will always take the side of the weak. That's what I was taught in the Land of Soviets. That's what my mother and father told me to do. That's what it says in the books I read in my childhood ...'

'Clear enough,' said the sleuth, brusquely interrupting my soliloquy. 'Let's change the subject.'

'As you wish.'

Svinets unbuttoned his quite excellent light jacket and showed me his tie. His face lit up with pride.

'How do you like that? Your actual Christian Dior. Confiscated from an individual who committed an especially serious crime. The individual concerned has already confessed, fully and frankly. So he won't be needing his tie. But I can find a use for it ...'

'How's your blonde? Are you married yet?'

'What are you talking about?' exclaimed the man in white from Moscow CID. 'Married? To that untidy slut? We split up ages ago. She's stupid. And a fool as well. No taste and no education. Wears a red blouse with a blue skirt. Doesn't shave under her arms. Guzzles beer, as it happens, by the litre. Why would I want someone like that?' Svinets carefully buttoned his jacket and ran his hands down its sides. 'No, I'll find myself a more presentable girlfriend than her ...'

'Good luck to you.'

'And you too.'

'But I don't believe in luck.'

'That's because you're still young. Don't forget the smokes and the chocolate ...'

'I won't take the chocolate.'

'What am I going to do with it?'

'Give it to Farafonov's widow.'

Captain Svinets smiled rapaciously.

'Farafonov's widow is a blonde with long legs and a size E bust. She'll be all right. I'll keep an eye out. Take the chocolate. To sweeten the bitterness of defeat ...'

I gave a superior smile, as if my companion were the one doing time, not me.

'You don't get it, Mr Polar Explorer. Defeat and victory are the same thing. Prison and freedom are the same thing. The criminals and the men who put them away are the same people. It's all a matter of words! Words are nothing more than little prisons, and life goes on outside them ... Goodbye, it's time for me to go. I'm a busy man.'

'Go then, busy man. And don't be surprised that I dragged you down here, not into the investigative block. Someone could have seen you there and spread the rumour that you're the godfather's man, an informer and all the rest ... You should appreciate my prudence, Andrei. If we meet on the outside, we'll take a glass of vodka ...'

At nine in the evening, having handed over the shift to Givi Sukhumsky, I went to get washed.

In summer only the roadmen have the privilege of splashing under the tap. The others make do with the weekly visits to the bathhouse. In the cell itself any sanitary procedure involving water is absolutely excluded during the summer. Damp is our deadly enemy. Every month about a dozen prisoners take their things and move out of our hut – to the TB clinic. Koch's bacillus is ever vigilant. It is constantly active, killing us, and we try to resist. In summer, in the heat, washing yourself or your clothes in the hut is not allowed. For the common good.

But an exception is made for the roadmen, jumping from one barred window to the other for twelve hours in a row. And I go to wash off the dirt and sweat. Past the chifir-soaked blacks imprisoned for smuggling heroin, past the tattooist, who has orders for a month ahead, past the station, through the swaying, dirty mass of passengers, devoured by lice and tormented by scabies, indifferent to everything – the ones who simply couldn't care.

Today's a good day: we have dope. Standing on the Road when you're high is not really desirable and the two of us, Johnny and I, decided immediately that we would only light up after we had handed over the shift. There's very little dope, barely enough for a tiny joint, a couple of drags each. But that doesn't worry us. We drop a few phenazepam tablets – that will strengthen the hit.

Maloi knows we've got grass and he wants some very badly, it's clear from that yearning look in his eyes, but a sense of guilt for the fracas that took place in the afternoon holds him back and he sullenly keeps his distance from Johnny and me. We, however, are philanthropically inclined, and I call the boy over to share our pleasure with us. Maloi instantly throws his slim, fifty-kilogram frame on to the bunk and sits down beside us.

'Well Maloi, you made a real mess of things today, eh?' Johnny says.

Bickering and settling scores are impermissible when you're high. But we have no bad feelings for each other – after all the loads survived; everything's fine. On the other hand we have to make it clear to our brother just who he is and where his irresponsible actions could lead.

'You've already got one black mark!'

'What?' Maloi protests warily.

'Wasn't that you a week ago who guzzled aminazine and slept for two whole days? While the other lads broke their asses for you at the bars?'

'Why two days? It was only nineteen hours! That's nothing like two days. Two days is forty-eight hours. And it was only nineteen …'

We're sitting there with our legs crossed, Turkish-style, and smoking.

Someone's socks have a very pungent smell – obviously Johnny's, but then mine can't be totally discounted either, since the washer who contracted to process our laundry with soap and water has been smashed on relanium since the previous evening and neglected his duties. Where he got the rare tablets from is still a mystery to everyone.

In the opposite corner I can see Slava's back. He's praying, standing facing the icons. He prays the same way I once used to meditate: mornings and evenings. Sometimes in the middle of the day. Prayer is the only means of maintaining a state of relative calm amidst the seething, swirling world of the Common Hut. No one will ever call out to a prisoner who's praying, or disturb him. To improve his concentration Slava plugs his ears with pieces of cotton wool. He's holding the *Prayerbook for Laymen*, but the small volume is closed. Slava knows the entire canon off by heart.

We politely wait for our leader. He crosses himself three times, performs the stipulated number of bows, leaves his chapel and comes over to us.

'Have a drag, Slava,' Johnny invites him.

After the act of communion with the Almighty, Slava Glory-to-the-CPSU is quiet and pensive. He sits down without saying anything and takes a drag. Then we three others smoke.

The poison doesn't take effect immediately. For some time we say nothing and wait. Eventually I feel dizzy and hear a light ringing in my ears, the picture before my eyes starts flickering, the colours become more intense and the sounds do the opposite, fading away and seeming to come from behind a soft, thick wall. Johnny and Maloi start talking about something, but I have no desire to take part in the conversation or even to listen to my brothers. This part of the comic strip is boring, and I turn the page.

The next page is more interesting altogether. Here the former boy-banker tries to leave his own body and look at himself from the outside. At a certain moment he actually succeeds. He hovers above the floor of the prison cell and observes. Somewhere close by he senses the presence of the nouveau-riche Andriukha, but he isn't saying anything. Soon I'll probably stop having any contact at all with my double from the past. His appearances are getting less and less frequent. He realises that he's not needed any more.

Separated from myself, I observe a self-satisfied idiot who is not yet middle-aged. He is clever, educated, cultured, totally stoned, he has started thinking about some idea of his own and he has a fastidious grimace on his face. He was searching for adventures, money, freedom, and now look at him, accepted as a fully fledged member of a mob of villains suffering the consequences of serious and exceptionally serious criminal charges, sitting under a window fitted with iron bars.

'Why have you gone so quiet?' Slava suddenly asks me.

'I hate bars.'

'That's not good,' Slava rebukes me gently. 'Hate is a great sin. You shouldn't hate. You shouldn't hate anything. Not even bars. Or prison in general. Nobody's forcing you to love it. But you shouldn't hate it. God will punish you for that …'

'How?' I asked in amazement. 'How can he punish me any more? I'm already in prison.'

'He'll make you love.'

'Who? What?'

'The thing you hate …'

'I doubt that …'

I suddenly feel I want to lie down. The drug's not very strong, it's a stupid poison, a plaything for dull-witted juveniles. But I have grown weaker too. Tomorrow will be the anniversary. I shall have been inside for a year – without light or air, without any decent food.

I'm feeling sleepy. Through the general hubbub I hear a familiar coarse baritone voice. In four months Dima the Rookie still hasn't learned to talk quietly, as prison etiquette requires. But he has learned a great many other things. He lives very close now – right on the other side of the vertically stretched blanket. Now he has sugar and butter, and even white powder for injecting into his veins. Dima the Rookie aspires to a better life. We say hello, even sometimes exchange a couple of words, but my opponent's eyes are always cold, and his smile promises nothing good.

'Lads,' I declare, my tongue slurring the words as I struggle to keep my eyes open. 'Lads! I most humbly beseech your forgiveness, but the use of excessive dosages of poisons, and also their various combinations, induces in me relapses into a chronic state of sociophobia, misanthropy and even – I shall not fear the term – autistic withdrawal. I am obliged to leave you. If anyone has failed to cop my spiel, let him breathe easy, insofar as I have not communicated to you anything repugnant and have not in any way infringed your prisoners' dignity.'

Johnny takes a close look at me and gives his diagnosis:

'He's out of it. Maloi, move over, let the con man lie down.'

I immediately assume a horizontal position and gradually fall asleep, but just before the final descent into oblivion I start dreaming that the periodical table of poisons will be revealed to me in my sleep.

The same way that a different table – of the elements – came to the chemist Mendeleev in a dream. But the poisons do not wish to line up in due order, they flicker on and off and spin rebelliously, and I abandon my attempts to make a great discovery.

33

Starting from the middle of the day, I travelled in the cold metal box alone. Then the vehicle stopped at one district court, a second, a third and a fourth – until it was completely packed. The long, narrow cage, furnished with a bench for eight compact backsides, held seventeen men. Still seated, I was pressed right into the very corner. I had to squeeze my legs tight together and turn them sideways, and later even let a taciturn, obviously very tired old man in a grubby cloth cap sit on my knees. His face looked remarkably like Frol's. Prison rapidly makes people look like each other.

Other men hung over the old man in every possible sort of freakish pose – some had the backs of their heads pressed against the ceiling, some were hanging on to their neighbours, some were balancing on one leg. The driver of the van definitely seemed to think of himself as the pilot of some kind of racing fireball, taking steep turns, forcing the engine to roar like a space rocket, clashing the gears with an infernal screeching. When he braked too sharply or did the opposite and pulled away too sharply from a traffic light, everybody fell on to each other, slamming their elbows and foreheads into the bodies of their neighbours and setting the inner space of the box ringing with deafening obscenities.

'Great!' said my neighbour on the bench – a pockmarked boy in very clean trousers and a very dirty padded jacket – speaking right into my ear in a deep bass voice. 'October! Autumn! Not too hot, not too cold! Just the right season for a drive!'

'When isn't it the right season?'

'In winter and in summer,' my neighbour informed me authoritatively.

'In winter it's a non-starter. Frost. In summer it's a double pain: too hot and you can't breath. But now it's autumn! Great! It's a buzz, outlaws!'

'You know where you can put your buzz ...' someone at the side objected irritably in a Caucasian accent. 'Where do you think you're going, boot-polish?'

Among the twenty or so pale-grey faces there was one that stood out for being completely dark. The semi-darkness made the African's features quite distinctly violet – exactly like in that song of Vertinsky's. Of course, that particular lilac-skinned black was a habitué of a dive in San Francisco, and this one was a prisoner of the Russian militia.

'I want to sit,' the dark-skinned man replied shyly in broken Russian, and then added in smooth English: 'Sit down.'

'Impossible, brother!' was the curt answer from beside the door.

The extremely bright whites of the African prisoner's eyes glinted in annoyance.

'What's your name?' my pockmarked neighbour asked, tugging at the black man's knee.

'Bobby.'

'Where are from Bobby?'

'From Jamaica ...'

The name of this green island in a green ocean elicited a romantic exclamation from the pockmarked boy. He repeated it like some magical charm:

'Jamaica! That's really something! And what did you do there, in Jamaica?

'Played Jamaica soccer,' lilac Bobby confided sadly.

'What's that?'

'Football on a volleyball court,' someone explained. 'Two on each side. They smash the ball over the net with their feet ...'

'Fantastic,' the pockmarked boy exclaimed. 'And what are you in here for, Jamaica?'

'Cocaine ...'

'What in hell's name brought you here, Bobby?' a hoarse voice groaned out of the jumble of bodies. 'Jamaica soccer! People here save money for a whole year to fly to Jamaica and gape at them kicking a football over a net. But you've done everything backwards, you fool! Why did you drag yourself all the way from there to here, when all the normal people flock from here to there?'

The Afro-prisoner didn't say anything. He was clearly embarrassed.

'So what's happening?' the same voice asked. 'Where are we going, boss?'

'Shut up,' the indifferent guard advised him from behind the barred door.

'Too much trouble to tell us, is it? Where are we going?'

'Stop talking!'

'Listen, just do me a favour! Where are we going?'

'Home.'

The crowd howled in joy.

Windows are not provided in prison vehicles. We could only guess at the direction of movement and the destination – or ask the guard directly.

'We'll get there before the change of shift,' the pockmarked boy commented.

'And what if we don't?' I asked cautiously.

'We'll spend two hours standing just outside the prison. Waiting for the new shift to start taking people in. They won't take us up to the huts before ten in the evening …'

I wanted really badly to eat, sleep and get warm.

A few days earlier Khvatov – during one of his visits – had warned me that I was obliged not merely to read the fifty-seven volumes of the CASE, but also to acquaint myself with the associated video material. 'Of course, the viewing won't take place in the Matrosskaya Tishina, but in the, you know, public prosecutor's building. They can't go dragging a video player and TV into the investigative block just for your sake, can they? So get yourself ready, be prepared, tomorrow or the next day they'll, you know, tell you "dress for the season".'

They did tell me – at four in the morning. At half past four they led me out of the cell – half-asleep, with a bad head. Together with about fifty other travellers (the overwhelming majority were on their way to the courts), I was escorted to the ground floor. And locked in an assembly cell.

The puke-stained room stank of chlorine bleach and excrement. It had black walls and a vaulted ceiling. Its corners were polluted by tubercular phlegm, and it was soon so crowded that I couldn't risk squatting down on my haunches and just stood there, choking on the cigarette smoke and blinking my watering eyes, until nine in the morning. At one point they gave us rations, but an absolute majority refused to take either the bread or the sugar. I acted in solidarity with all the others. Chewing anything, consuming food in that kind of crush, surrounded by the odours of excrement, seemed an absolutely inconceivable thing to do.

When I had absolutely no more strength left to stand there vertically, all the time submitting to the heavy swaying of the tight-packed crowd of a hundred men, the door opened. The general sigh of relief was instantly replaced by a tense silence. The lead-out guard started shouting out names.

My name was one of the last spoken:

'Name?'

'Rubanov.'

'Article of charge?'

'One hundred and fifty-nine – part three, one hundred and ninety-nine – part two, three hundred and twenty-seven – part one ...'

'Enough, enough!' the lead-out guard laughed and checked my prisoner's file card. 'Which court?'

'I'm not going to court. I'm going to the public prosecutor's office. The General Public Prosecutor's building.'

'The General Public Prosecutor's building? Terrorism?'

'Fraud.'

'Go to the end of the corridor!'

Right beside the way out there was a second assembly cell, extremely small and cold; a group of ten bodies languished in it for another half hour before the command came to get into the meat wagon.

Late in the autumn morning, having been to four of Moscow's district courts and gradually emptied, the prison van delivered me to the city centre.

Handcuffed to a young sergeant, I jumped down on to the pavement at almost exactly the same spot where fifteen months earlier I had all but puked from agoraphobic shock. This time I didn't feel anything of the kind. I was in a big cell, after all – not the nine-square-metres stone box in Lefortovo. This time I didn't feel blinded, or deafened, or crushed to the ground. On this cool October day Vorontsovksy Lane, which leads the pedestrian from Tverskaya Street towards Patriarshie Prudy, looked as grey and dull as the cheap sets for a TV serial.

At this point I started feeling concerned. What if everything that was happening to me was not, after all, a bright, glossy comic strip featuring an invincible super-hero, but a dreary, rubbishy TV serial, a cheap, histrionic soap, in which all of the characters' actions have been preordained?

The lane – a crooked little relic of old Moscow – had two bends, although it was only a hundred metres long. In addition, it was set on a steep slope. Twisted in all three dimensions, it had a very Asiatic look,

'Fifteen hours of recordings,' Khvatov declared, grandly indicating a pile of video cassettes. 'Where shall we start?'

'Anywhere at all.'

Bearing in mind the ride back – in a metal box, in a tangle of human bodies – as well as the 'gatherer', where I would have to spend several more hours in torment that evening, I felt quite certain that I wouldn't survive fifteen trips. I decided that this very day I was going to affix my signature to the special prosecutor's document: I have acquainted myself with the materials!

Then the prosecutor from Ryazan would file the document in the final volume of the CASE FILE. That would put an end to my period of subjection to article two hundred and one, which had lasted from June to October.

During the viewing of the first (and last) video cassette I laughed merrily again.

'I remembered the name of Andrei Rubanov's firm,' the main witness for the prosecution – also known as the 'chemist' and the 'pharmacist' – declared candidly, 'from reading the sign …'

God Almighty, what sign, I wondered in amazement. Where and when did I ever hang any kind of sign on my door? The whole point of my business was to work *without* any sign. The pharmacist is lying through his teeth. And his lies are brazen, completely undisguised! Look how greedily he's smoking! Those dark marks his wet fingers leave on the cigarette! Listen to the way his voice trembles! He's lying. Obviously going for it. Making it up as he goes along. Of all the things to invent – a sign! Ha!

Suddenly nouveau-riche Andriukha appeared beside me.

'Laugh, laugh, you wanker,' he said. 'The pharmacist is walking around free. He testified – and they let him go home. Home, got it? And you, the great tough guy, went to prison. Now you'll be feeding the lice and the bedbugs. You macho shithead. Which one of you should be laughing?'

This time the smug jerk was probably right, I sighed as I arranged the little old man's weightless body on my knees. He had just been sentenced to three years of general regime for stealing two sacks of animal feed from the Motherland's storehouses. Somehow I didn't feel like laughing. I haven't been able to cry ever since I was a kid, and soon I'll forget how to laugh as well.

Another series of happy exclamations rang out just above my ear:

'We made it! The Matroska! We're driving in, thank God …'

'We're here!'

'Home! Home, lads!'

'Great!'

'Keep your chin up, Jamaica!'

Everything was repeated in the reverse order. From one scruffy, filthy 'gatherer' to another just like it. Again the crowd, the puffy faces, the hollow cheeks of a hundred men who had once been young, strong, passionate, but now were stooped and feeble, incapable of doing anything more than encouraging each other with nervous laughter and swearing obscenely.

By evening my legs simply couldn't hold me up. I wonder what will happen to me when the trial starts? How long will it go on for? Will I survive the daily journeys? They say men have fits of hysterics in the gatherer. They also say that many prisoners, having made the trip a couple of times, offer full and frank confessions right there in the courtroom and cry, pleading with the judge to pronounce sentence there and then, give them any prison term at all, just as long as they don't have to make any more of those journeys.

After finally reaching my cell, I realised why a prisoner will always say 'home' instead of 'to the prison' or 'to the hut'.

Home! I really had come home – to the place where I can wash the dirt off my face, drink tea and assume a horizontal position. I was home. After fifteen hours spent in a smothering crush, without having drunk a single mouthful of liquid or swallowed a single bite of food, standing almost all the time, finally I am home! I have come back home – to my own pitiful, clammy, crushed little world, divided up by rags, cut across by homemade ropes, buzzing with the din of a hundred dry, chifir-scorched throats. Stinking of tobacco, iodine, socks, foot wrappings, fish soup and millet, as well as fish soup and millet excrement. Such, now, is our home, my home – as disgusting as I myself, as everything that is happening to me.

After eating some bread and drinking some tea and afterwards even smoking some excellent grass (or maybe it just seemed like that because I was exhausted), I slumped onto the bunk and instantly fell asleep. Set sail on a cruise through the bays and shallows of the ocean of freedom, as wide as a dream.

A sleeping man is always free, in any prison.

I woke up with someone shaking me by the shoulder.

Waking a sleeping prisoner for no reason is a great sin. All ready to express my indignation in crude terms, I opened my eyes. And saw Givi Sukhumsky's Abkhazian nose quivering in alarm.

'Get up Andriukha! Listen, get up. It's a disaster!'

Tugging the curtain aside, I jumped out of the compartment and immediately collided with several solid backs.

'Bring him here! Carry him over here! Closer to the air! Careful with the head! Quickly!'

In the very centre of the boss's meadow someone semi-naked was lying on the floor with his arms flung out to the sides. Men were bustling around him.

'A lemon! Is there a lemon? Give it here! And wet a towel! With cold water! Move it! Move it!'

Suddenly I recognised the person who was shouting out instructions. Dima the Rookie – the one-time neurasthenic streaming with foul sweat – had become a brisk, stern commander. He issued coarse directives while simultaneously skilfully manipulating the motionless body: punching the narrow, still chest, slapping the cheeks in a regular rhythm – right, left.

The semi-naked man didn't move.

'He's not moving!' the front rows of men sighed anxiously.

'Quiet! Where's the towel? Have you brought the lemon? Get me a sharp edge! Slice the lemon! Quick, come on!'

I tried to understand what was happening. Sedated by marijuana, my brain wasn't working at all. Everything around me was floating in a thick, purple-and-red mist. Sounds were either barely audible or seemed unbearably loud. The semi-naked young man lying on the floor with his waxy chin pointing upwards was dying from a narcotics overdose.

'Wake the head lads!' I howled. 'Wake Slava, urgently! Wake all of them!'

'We're trying! It's not working! They're not getting up!'

'Too much dope, that's why they don't get up,' Rookie remarked acidly. 'Well, have you found a lemon? Fedot, help me!'

Shoving somebody aside, I jumped right across to the man on the floor.

Then my head finally cleared and I realised that I had no idea what to do. I had no experience. Everything I knew about the procedure for saving someone from an overdose came from the film *Pulp Fiction*, where they gave the girl who was a drug addict an adrenalin injection directly into the heart. With a huge needle, as long as the sole of a shoe. The scene was supposed to be comic. I broke into a sweat. Of course there was no suitable needle or suitable substance in the cell in a pre-trial prison. How could there be? Any moment now the wretched drug addict's time on this sinful earth would come to an end! How could the unfortunate fool be saved? He was going to die within the next two minutes. It was obvious from the yellowish-purple colour of his face and the exaggerated sharpness of his cheekbones.

Then all hell would break loose. It wasn't just the dying addict that I felt sorry for. I knew him. Nineteen years old. An anaemic youth, none too bright. For the last year and a half he'd been solidly hooked on heroin. That was what he had been arrested for. Every month his good mother and father always sent their son a food parcel and a money order. In our prison a prisoner like that was a really big man. He could always find himself experienced friends. And they would tell him where and how to get drugs in the Common Block. Now this young boy had tried to fly too high and any moment he would move on from the stage of clinical death to the next stage. The final one. The finish.

The death of a prisoner is a serious emergency. Especially if the cause is drugs. Tomorrow the administration would organise a thorough general search of the cell. And then interrogations. What, where, how? Where did he get the powder? Who were his friends? Who were his enemies?

And then they would *split up* the cell. That was the usual practice. A hundred and thirty-five men would be distributed in groups of five or seven to the other forty-something huts in the Common Block. They would bring new men to the empty cell – gathered from all over, a motley assortment of men shocked by the sudden changes in their lives and their daily round.

I personally would lose everything. In my new place, I would be obliged to start all over again. Try once again, as they say, to prove that I am not a camel. To win the essentials of life. To make new friends and contact. To put my life in order. As God is my witness – it wasn't just the dying fool I felt sorry for, I felt sorry for myself as well.

'Block the peepers!' I shouted, straightening up. 'Block the peepers!'

Several men close to the door formed a compact group and pressed their backs against spy hole. They blocked the peepers. Concealed what was happening from the warder's eyes.

Out of the corner of my eye I saw skinny Givi Sukhumsky shaking the sound-asleep Slava Glory-to-the-CPSU by the shoulder.

After smoking grass with us, the supervisor had enhanced its effect with a few tablets of dimedrol. He was absolutely out of it. Unable to surface from his heavy slumber.

'Fedot!' Rookie commanded in the meantime. 'Open his mouth!'

A stream of lemon juice was poured in between the drug addict's bluish lips. Then he was beaten on his purple cheeks again, his face and chest were scrubbed intensively with the wet towel. It was a matter of seconds. Even I, who knew nothing about the realities of a junkie's life, the life of that high-flying crowd, heroin addicts, realised that death would arrive at any moment.

'Out of the way!' Rookie suddenly shoved me rudely, so that he could get at the breathless body from the other side. And he gave me a dark look.

He had shaved his head, and now he wore black trousers and a black singlet that exposed his tattooed shoulders. I could easily believe that on the outside this young man was capable of inspiring real terror in any salesman in a cigarette kiosk.

'Got any ice?' Rookie asked me furiously. 'You've got a fridge! Have you got any ice? Bring it here quick!'

I dashed off and grabbed a plastic bag full of pieces of ice out of the fridge. Realising as I did so that I had completely lost face. I had been pushed, then shouted at and, to cap it all, sent to fetch something.

Rookie grabbed the searingly cold bag out of my hands and flung it to Fedot.

'Rub his temples with ice! And his forehead! Give me another lemon! And you,' the muscly villain said to me, 'move, out of the way!'

I filled my lungs with air, feverishly trying to think of what answer I ought to give. Here, beside the Road, on the boss's own meadow, in my territory, I couldn't allow anyone to talk like that. I had to offer a rapid, sharp rebuff. One that would stop my rival dead in his track. But riding round the city in a metal box since early morning had tired me out, and then I'd smoked grass and afterwards only slept for two hours. I couldn't pull myself together quickly enough. I opened my mouth, still not really knowing what exactly I was going to say to my enemy.

The argument over the half-dead man never took place, His chest suddenly trembled. A low wheeze emerged from his throat. His face turned pink. A sigh of relief ran through the cell.

'Come on!' Rookie shouted, continuing his rough shaking of the head. The man lying on the floor was alive now, returned from the next world to this one.

From the look on the saved man's face it seemed clear that this world was not much different from that one. The reanimated corpse started moving his limbs and opened his brown eyelids.

'You're a fine one!' Rookie told him. 'When you recover, I *personally* will make you pay for almost dropping the hut in it ...'

The rescuer straightened up. Looked round triumphantly at the men surrounding him. Breathing heavily and twitching his Celtic ornamentation. A hundred and thirty-five pale faces – apart from those who were sleeping, and myself – watched him admiringly. Fedot handed the hero a towel, and he triumphantly wiped the sweat off his short neck.

At that moment Givi Sukhumsky finally managed to bring round Slava Glory-to-the-CPSU. Waking the supervisor had taken almost longer than the epic struggle to save the dying man.

'Ah? What's going on?' Slava wheezed, making his appearance with eyes that were still vacant. 'An overdose, right? An overdose? Again?'

'Everything's fine, Slava!' Rookie boomed in his deep voice. 'While your gang were sleeping, I just saved a cretin's life ... Everything's fine! Take it easy! And I'm going for a piss. Move aside, outlaws!'

The men made way as the angular designs cut diagonally right across the cell.

'What a hut!' Rookie declared. 'Just see what happens when outsiders creep into the brotherhood.'

At the sound of these words, Slava shuddered. His face contorted in fury. With precise, bird-like glances, he looked round at me – the crowd catching its breath – and the boy who had been saved. He looked at the triumphant victor's back. Rookie was getting washed, snorting as he threw handfuls of water on to his naked torso.

Slava waited for passions to cool. It didn't take much time. After a few minutes, a hundred and thirty men went back to their interrupted business, they wanted to drink chifir, eat breakfast or supper, play a game of cards, read the old newspapers. It was only then that Slava summoned the proudly smiling Celt. He caught his eye and beckoned to him.

Suddenly the other man was not alone. There beside him was Fedot, daubed all over with green ointment, puny, but in determined mood.

'What's that racket you're making in the hut?' Slava asked straight away, staring wild-eyed at Rookie's chest or the bridge of his nose. 'What sort of slogans are those?'

'I'm not making any racket,' Rookie replied, jauntily rebuffing the attack. 'I spoke from the heart. I've just saved the hut from disaster. For that mess, for a dead body, the goons would have come down heavy on us …'

'Everybody knows that,' Slava interrupted sharply. 'So who is it that's an outsider in the brotherhood? Out with it.'

'Your businessman,' Rookie replied immediately. 'And I'm not the only one who thinks so.'

'Who else thinks so?'

'I do,' said Fedot, forcing the words out.

'And will you tell him so to his face?' Slava asked flintily.

'I told the entire hut,' said Rookie, still smiling. 'And I'll tell him to his face.'

'You too!' Slava asked tensely, turning to Fedot.

'Me too.'

'Andriukha!' Slava called. 'Come here.'

I'd heard the entire conversation – I was installed behind the cloth wall of the compartment. In order to join in the discussion, all I had to do was pull the curtain aside from in front of my face and throw it behind my back.

'There's a question that's come up here,' Slava said in a quiet voice. 'They're calling you a businessman.'

The sounds of voices quivered in the stale atmosphere between the dirty blanket walls of the prison wigwam – bouncing off each other, drifting and hanging in the air like chords clumsily played on an old, poorly tuned guitar.

'Who is it that says I am?' I asked, sitting down.

'He does.' My patron pointed a finger at the Celtic designs.

'Let him say it again!'

Rookie looked me in the eyes.

'Why do I need to say it again? You know it all anyway, don't you? People like you sit beside their safes, behind their iron doors and their alarms, and when I come with my sawn-off and say "give me the money", they go running to the cops and write statements … A businessman is the victim. There's no place for him with the right lads.'

Shall I kill him? – the original idea flashed through my mind. Stick a finger in his eye? Crush his throat?

I threw myself forward, but discovered that Johnny and Givi Sukhumsky were standing on the right and the left of me. They grabbed me by the elbows. It's very easy to prevent a seated man from jerking forward rapidly.

'Quiet!' Slava commanded in a terrible whisper. 'Control yourself, con man! Any violence is out of the question here! This is a serious subject. We'll get to the bottom of it, brothers.' He rested his wild gaze on Fedot. 'Do you think Andriukha's a businessman too?'

In stead of replying, Fedot suddenly exclaimed:

'Slava, why did you call me a "passenger" and a "mouse" that time?'

Slava shook his head with a baffled expression.

'Me? You say I called you a "passenger"? What's your name?'

'Fedot …'

'I called you a passenger? When?'

'You did!' Fedot whimpered, and the smell of iodine that he gave off became even stronger. 'You did, you did! The men heard it!'

Slava sighed repentantly.

'Listen carefully, Fedot,' he said, almost separating out each syllable. 'You – are – not – a passenger! You're a sound lad, a worthy prisoner. Is that clear? You're not a passenger and you never were one! And now, go with God. Go, all right. And we'll have a talk. Go.'

Fedot disappeared behind the curtain without another word.

'Now brothers,' Slava declared very quietly, in a steely baritone, 'with God's help we'll seek the truth until we find it …'

'Slava,' voices unexpectedly started muttering politely behind the cloth partition. 'Slava, do you hear?'

'What the hell?' the supervisor exploded. 'What do you want?'

'They've just called you for court, the screw came and called your name ...'

'What?' asked Slava, amazed. 'For court?'

'Yes. They're going to take you out at five.'

'What time is it now?'

'Half past four, Slava. I've already cleaned your jacket.'

'Court ...' Slava repeated in a trance, instantly losing interest in the conversation about businessmen. 'Well, well, well. Are they really going to start? Are they going to try me after all?'

Seeming suddenly to come to his senses, he looked at Rookie, then at me, trembling with stress and sighed.

'We'll have to postpone our business, brothers. Agreed? When I get back this evening, we'll finish talking. Get everything clear, with God's help. What do you say?'

Neither I nor my enemy moved an inch.

'No, that won't do!' said Slava, raising his voice. 'Step down, lads! Step down! You, Andriukha, get on that Road! Johnny, you make sure the guy who nearly died gets a chance to recover. Givi, you too ... don't sit there doing nothing. Step down! We'll finish this in the evening! No talk, no arguments until I get back!'

Submitting to our leader's authority, we stood up and set about our business. Slava began hastily searching for his special court shoes, I frenziedly grabbed hold of the nearest rope, Johnny disappeared into the depths of the cell to search for the drug addict who had just been saved and had hidden himself out of harm's way.

Life resumed its usual, repetitive daily round.

Throughout the day that followed, Dima the Rookie hardly ever left the boss's 'meadow'. He used to appear there often enough before that, but only in order to watch the television. Now, however, the heroic reanimator of the dead did not look at the blue screen, but in the opposite direction. Along the line of sight into the hut. The anticipation of power contorted the features of his round face. From time to time he cast a special kind of glance – full of mocking contempt – in my direction. But I had no difficulty withstanding it. And I even smiled in reply. Baring my teeth. Demonstrating my belief in my own strength.

And then I actually went off to sleep, having stood my twelve-hour shift on the Road, having despatched another two or three hundred notes and packages from prisoners, and almost having managed to forget all my alarm concerning forthcoming events.

'When I woke up again, Givi Sukhumsky immediately informed me:

'Listen, Slava's not here. Listen, he's gone to court again. He said they're really going to work on him, they're going to drive him out every day until he gets his sentence ... Your dispute's been put off ... For the time being ... Until Saturday. That bonehead, Dima the Rookie, doesn't seem to mind too much ... Slava said you wouldn't mind either ...'

'Of course not,' I replied. 'I'll wait as long as necessary. It'll give me time to get myself psyched up.'

To be quite honest, I don't much like beating a man about the face. And apart from that, I'd read plenty of books, but not one of them gave instructions on how to bite your enemy to death in front of the entire pack.

34

Once it finally started moving, the trial of Slava Glory-to-the-CPSU set off at a gallop.

The God-fearing bandit's last five years had passed as follows: arrested for attempted armed robbery, eighteen-year-old Slava had appeared before the court six months later. But neither the victims nor the witnesses had turned up for the trial. They were too afraid. When they were eventually found and brought in, they gave confused and contradictory evidence. The principal judge referred the CASE for further investigation.

The investigation was completed in double-quick time. After another six months, the court was due to convene, but while one of Slava's co-defendants was being familiarised with the materials of the CASE, unnoticed by the investigator, he managed to tear several extremely important sets of minutes out of the volume and destroy them. The documents had to be restored.

As little time as possible was wasted on that. Another six months later the trial almost began again, but an unpleasant complication suddenly occurred: the third member of the gang fell ill with hepatitis.

In the prison hospital they put him back on his feet immediately. Another six months later the bandits came up for trial again. By this time the main victim, a young woman cashier from a bureau de change, had married a citizen of the state of Israel, and moved away forever from 'that madhouse', as she herself called it in a telephone conversation with the judge. Another important figure in the case suffered a stroke.

The lawyers acting for the accused lodged a protest. The principal judge once again referred the CASE back to the investigative agencies.

After another six months Slava was back in the dock again, but not for long. This time a prisoner in his cell died of meningitis; a quarantine was declared immediately and no one could leave the infected cell. The trial was postponed, then again, and again.

Time passed. Slava was still inside. He had got well used to the idea of travelling to court three or four times a year – only for the judge to inform him in person of the latest postponement of the hearing.

But now our criminal authority left the cell every night. He came back dark in the face with exhaustion, but with his eyes gleaming.

'How's it going, Slava?'

'The trial goes on,' he replied curtly.

We understood: his fate was about to be decided at any moment. Obviously, word of the outrageously protracted criminal proceedings had reached some important judicial functionary and he had issued instructions for the hearings to be brought to a rapid end, no matter what. In order to avoid spoiling some fancy performance statistics or other.

Slava travelled on Monday, and on Tuesday, and on Wednesday, and on Thursday. He left at five in the morning and came back at nine or – more often – ten in the evening; he got washed, ate something and fell asleep immediately. And six hours later he set out again.

The atmosphere in the cell changed imperceptibly. The majority failed to react in any way to the fact that the supervisor was suddenly so busy with his trial. The vast majority of clients in the Matrosskaya Tishina pre-trial isolation prison were there for a month or two, maybe three – they were all arrested for petty theft, for possession of small amounts of narcotics and other insignificant offences. These men were given their sentences quickly, within one or two months, and then they disappeared, after 'getting their things', to make way for new victims of the legal conveyor belt. I didn't even have time to get to know many of them by name. But the old-timers – Johnny, and Maloi, and me, and Givi Sukhumsky, and Fedot, and Kolya the File, and another dozen or so, were only too well aware that the immediate future promised important changes.

Dima the Rookie was totally transformed. Now he was a benign beast who sauntered at a leisurely pace wherever his fancy took him. By Friday more than twenty men had left the cell, and the same number of newcomers had been brought in – they all clearly regarded the tattooed bully as the most terrifying of the hundred and thirty villains. This young guy, heavily decorated with blue squiggles, who had once hysterically demanded a place to sleep, was now making an all-out bid for the top boss's place. He laughed easily as he chatted with first one, then another new arrival. He handed out cigarettes to those who wanted them. He pulled strings for people. He cultivated his own authority. He wrote several notes and sent them off to various addresses. He received replies.

I realised that an enemy like this would be hard to defeat. I probably wouldn't be able to handle him. I had ascended the steps of the prison hierarchy with the support of a mentor, but he was doing it on his own, relying on nothing but his own strength.

Finally Saturday arrived. The day Slava had set for the decisive conversation. But early in the morning of the first day of the weekend, Dima the Rookie received a load. And the load contained a dose.

The settling of accounts never took place. The triumphant reanimator of the dead spent all Saturday and Sunday lying motionless in his personal bed. Five times at least they tried to bring him round, including two attempts by Slava Glory-to-the-CPSU. But the only response from the tough guy was inarticulate groaning.

'Draw your own conclusions,' Slava said to me when, following yet another unsuccessful attempt, we sat down for a smoke and a drink of tea. 'Look at him, and look at you! You're a serious man, you've been trusted with the Road. And he's a junkie. What's the point of talking to someone like that? We'll bring him down according to all the rules, then you'll smash his face in and we'll throw him out of the meadow. And tell him not to show his face here again. Only when are we going to do it? On Monday I'll go off to court again. You'll have to be patient a bit longer, con man.'

On Sunday night I took over the shift from Givi Sukhumsky. Early in the morning the 'court men' left, Slava among them. Half an hour later, there in front of me was that familiar, saffron-coloured cranium, once again carefully shaved, and those naked, tattooed shoulders. At first I tried not to notice the probing glance trained on me. Then I grew fed up of pretending. I turned away from my ropes and raised my eyebrows questioningly.

'I want to send some money,' Rookie declared in a sullen voice, looking me in the eyes. 'To one-two-zero. Let it get lost and you'll answer for it.'

'Go fuck yourself!' I shouted. In my mind, of course.

Number one hundred and twenty was the home cell of the *dealer*, who sold everyone the coveted white powder. Whether or not to use it was each individual prisoner's private business. It was none of my concern who consumed poisons. My job, as a roadman, was to ensure the rapid and safe passage of any load, whether it was money, heroin or an innocent pinch of tea. I snorted sharply in reply:

'What does that mean – "you'll answer for it"? If your money's lost, I'll answer for it in any case. The way it always is in such cases. Only where did you get the idea that it'll get lost?'

'You know what I meant,' said Rookie, baring the filling behind his blue lip. 'Make sure it doesn't get stuck in the bars ...'

'It won't get stuck,' assured him. 'And if it does, we'll do everything right.'

'And you know how to do things right?'

'Do you doubt it?'

'I'm sending a thousand roubles, get it? Make it perfect! I'll be tough for you trying to pay it back!'

He's trying to hint that it's too much, I guessed, and returned his serve:

'Don't push so hard. Your thousand will get there.'

'Yeah?' the tattooed man asked, with a sneering laugh. 'Well, you said, it, not me ... I know the goons are in a fierce mood ... They're breaking off Road horses every night ...' He raised his voice. 'Make it a perfect job, got it?'

'Got it!' I growled. 'I'll do it right! Only don't forget – I don't answer for the entire Roadway!'

'How's that?'

'It's very simple. If your load disappears between one-two-six and one-two-five or between one-two-five and one-two-four – where the lads have the medical assistant's window between their bars and the horse gets stuck every second time – or if your load is taken between one-one-nine and one-one-eight, where there's a projection in the wall – then I don't answer for it …'

Rookie bared the metal in his foul mouth once again, but this time less confidently. Fedot was watching me carefully over his shoulder.

My backup was better: behind the vertically stretched blanket, Johnny and Givi Sukhumsky hadn't fallen asleep yet, and they were listening to the verbal altercation, lying there with their eyes closed, but clearly noting everything that was being said, and from the way Givi's Caucasian nostrils were flaring, I could tell that he was ready to join in at any moment.

'You don't answer for it?' Rookie asked.

'No.'

'Well, for crying out loud,' my enemy said skittishly. 'Just what do you answer for?'

Six weeks before my arrest my boss Mikhail brought in another client.

'You have a word with him.'

The meaning of my boss's phrase was as follows: 'This client is nothing special, not particularly important. Middling. A man who doesn't have a million. Not someone like my boss.'

The flabby eyelids of an alcoholic, shoes with buckles, a ring with a small diamond on his finger – the client looked exactly like Mikhail's opinion of him. A run-of-the-mill businessman, who through intense labour had earned the right to decorate his fingers with gold.

His wife had gone to Los Angeles. Either to work, or on holiday. With well-off women it's sometimes hard to tell the difference. Her husband wanted to send her three thousand dollars each month from Moscow.

'Shit, she had a credit card!' the gilded gent informed me. 'Shit, and with thirty thousand dollars on it. Shit, I thought it would be enough, But shit, she phones me every second month and asks for more money, shit!' He took out a wad of greenbacks. 'There, shit, that's the full amount. Here's the number of the account, the name of the bank. All the details.' The wife's husband paused and then added: 'If the money gets lost – you'll answer for it!'

I waited for a moment, then started drumming my fingers on the desk. Who did he take me for, this lover of cheap gemstones? My shoes cost five times as much as all his finery! Send three thousand dollars to America – what could be simpler than that? I'd deputised that kind of operation to Semyon and Sergei ages ago. I myself only worked with large sums. Even if three thousand should happen to disappear halfway from Moscow to America, somehow mystically dissolve in the digital web – I'd make good the loss out of my own pocket money. I might get drunk, but I wouldn't get upset.

However, every banker is obliged to remain stable. No one and nothing should ever be allowed to disrupt his equilibrium. The symbol of this equilibrium is the tie that divides the banker's chest into two equal halves.

'What does that mean – "you'll answer for it"?' I'd asked politely. 'If your money's lost, I'll answer for it in any case. Only where did you get the idea that it will get lost?'

'Shit, you understood what I told you,' said the Russian husband of the American wife. 'Just make sure it doesn't get stuck halfway there ...'

'It won't,' I assured him. 'Only bear in mind that I don't answer for the entire process.'

'How's that?'

'I only answer for the transfer of the money from my bank to the recipient's bank. If I transfer the funds today, and the recipient's bank fails tomorrow – I'm not answerable for that ...'

'I only answer for the passage of your load from our hut to the next one,' I snapped, staring hard at Rookie's grinning features. 'If I send a load now, and in five minutes the horse in the next hut snaps – I'm not answerable for that.'

Dima the Rookie sudden broke into a smile.

'For crying out loud!' he repeated in a loud voice. 'You look just like you're sitting behind the desk in your office! Think you're swinging a deal, do you? The only thing missing is the tie!' He broke into laughter, and his purple shoulders shook.

No doubt, at such a moment any enlightened man is obliged to recall the lines in that popular manuscript, *The Art of War*. Do not hinder your enemy when he thinks that he is strong. Or something of the sort. However, although it did come to mind, the centuries-old Asiatic wisdom failed to imbue me with strength. Perhaps because I'm not an Asiatic. There were others who laughed along with Rookie. Not only Fedot – other incidental witnesses to the conversation, men I didn't know, who perhaps had only joined the cell yesterday and didn't understand a thing about the real nature of this fierce skirmish between two old-timers – started smiling and subconsciously took my shaven-headed enemy's side. His Celtic patterns were dancing again.

Never let your opponent have the last word, I thought.

'So you still think I'm a businessman?'

'Why,' Rookie asked casually, cutting short his laughter. 'Are you saying it isn't so?'

'If I was a businessman,' I countered, 'that is, a man with money, I'd be sitting in the special now, relaxing in comfort? Agreed?'

The bright metal glinted between his lips for the third time.

'We'll talk again. Later. Here's the money. Send it.'

Grasping the crumpled bills in my hand, I turned away and noticed Johnny beckoning silently to me from behind the blanket. I went over.

'You do talk like a businessman, for real,' my partner rebuked me in a whisper. 'Keep the spiel simple! And to the point! "The passage of your load"… You should have told that no-good bum where he could go straight off! Worried about your money – no problem, take it to one-two-zero yourself! That's what you should have said! But you flim-flam like some sort of trusty! Sort yourself out! Otherwise, without Slava they'll have you and me in a flash! This bonehead's already got half the hut on his side!'

'Do you think Slava will leave soon?'

'No thinking needed,' Johnny replied gloomily. 'It's just a matter of days. You've seen the way they're working him. Dragging him out every day!'

'And what are we going to do?'

My partner tensed a substantial bicep, slapped it with his other hand, and sighed.

'I don't know.'

Suddenly I heard a familiar voice.

'But I know.'

Strolling jauntily though the crowd with his hands in his pockets, there was Andriukha the nouveau riche coming towards me. My nostrils were titillated by the intoxicating scent of Issei Miyake.

'Go away,' I said. 'I haven't got time for you …'

'Who are you talking to?' Johnny asked me.

'Myself.'

'You've got a friend in the special, Fatty,' Andriukha carried on in the meantime. 'Write to him. He'll help you. Pay the going rate, and they'll move you from this cell to another. Or better still, move out of the Common Block altogether. What are trying to catch here? Without the support of authoritative friends, your life is worth nothing in this bunch of aggressive idiots. Assess your own strength more realistically. You've got lost in all these bandits' games. If you're not careful, they'll rip your head off your shoulders!' I lowered my eyes. The spineless financier lowered his voice. 'Maybe you are a smart guy, but you'll always be an outsider here. You're too cultured and too soft. You speak too correctly and you're vocabulary's too rich. The skin on your face is too clean. You smile is too open. After a year and three months inside, you still haven't really grown into prison. You don't seek the friendship and respect of its half-wild inhabitants. You haven't turned into a raw-boned old lag, with a malicious leer on his face for everyone. You have remained yourself. Run from this place. Slip the prison governor a bribe and go and join the decent people in a decent six-man cell!'

'You're right,' I replied. 'Fatty will help me. I'll write to him in the special today. Today …'

'I thought about that too,' Johnny murmured quietly.

I must have spoken those last words out loud.

* * *

'That's it, brothers!' Slava Glory-to-the-CPSU heaved a sigh, walked up to the icons and crossed himself with broad, sweeping movements. 'The film's over! The day after tomorrow I get sentenced. The prosecutor's asked for seven years maximum security.'

'That means they'll give you six,' said Johnny. 'Or even five ...'

Slava plucked pensively at the grey skin of his cheek.

'It'll be six,' he declared, following the old prisoner's habit of immediately preparing for the worst case. 'Six years in maximum security! And for what? For smacking some fool over the head and taking the money that he would have drunk away in two days in any case? For firing a shot into the ceiling? For what, eh? For what, brothers?'

'It's a good thing it's max security,' Johnny remarked. 'They say they keep order better in max.'

'But,' I put in, 'what if they only give you five? Then you'll see the New Year in as a free man!'

'Everything's in God's hands,' Slava sighed, carefully slipping a makeshift clothes hanger into the sleeves of his crimson jacket a la New Russian. 'I'll catch up on my sleep, then I'll go ...'

You were expected to go to court in decent clothes. The court costumes – a few pairs of trousers and some shirts and jackets – were carefully stored in a special cover, beside the television. These items could be used by any worthy prisoner – a principle that was observed religiously.

In my opinion, all the jackets were terrible. Double-breasted, Mafioso-chic style items with huge lapels and gold buttons and, in addition, terribly badly worn. But in some magical manner even these garments sometimes managed to transform dirty, narrow-shouldered young crooks into tidy youths from cultured families. On numerous occasions a neat suit had helped to slice a year, or even two, off a sentence. At least, that was what everyone believed.

The court collection was replenished with due thought from the garments of new arrivals.

'So how many outings to court have you made?' I enquired.

'Thirty-two,' Slava replied.

Johnny sucked in his breath respectfully.

Suddenly there was a sound of hasty knocking from the end wall, and he hurried off to haul in the side horse. Slava and I were left alone together.

'It'll be six,' Slava said. 'I'll be out in less than a year.'

'Well, aren't you glad?'

Slava thought about it.

'Yes,' he replied glumly.

'Then how come you look so sad?'

'I don't know. What am I going to do there, on the outside? What do people do out there anyway, eh?'

'I don't know,' I answered. 'I've been inside for over a year myself. I lost the plot a long time ago.'

'Me too,' the godly bandit admitted.

I was alarmed and confused. Slava was leaving! The day after tomorrow my mentor would learn his sentence. Become a convicted criminal. The very next day he would be ordered out 'with his things'. Five minutes after the door closed behind Slava, a coup would take place in my cell. The place of supervisor would be taken by another authoritative prisoner. And, of course, it wouldn't be me. What sort of authority would I make? On the contrary, my own life would take a sharp turn for the worse.

Moving aside the edge of the curtain, I looked at the opposite compartment, from which every now and then the gruff voice of Dima the Rookie could be heard. I knew that in a moment Rookie would send one of his sidekicks – most likely the little, insolent Fedot – across to us, to find out how Slava was doing, how his case was coming along.

For the last few days Rookie had been behaving in an emphatically friendly manner with me, he had called a halt to the war of nerves and stopped provoking me, hadn't made any malicious comments or jokes. Every day the bandit covered in Celtic designs had sent two or three bank notes along the Road to a certain address, and the same day received back several doses of white powder. Money is sent down the Road quite openly, and Rookie's traffic in drugs was no secret to me. After mainlining a shot, my hulking enemy would fall quiet for a long time, remaining inside his compartment for many hours. Fedot, who was kept by Rookie as his stooge, brought skilly, chifir and clean sheets to him behind the curtain.

But by now I was too well versed in the customs and habits of prison community life not to guess that the lover of poisons and aggressive body art was waiting for his hour to come. He knew very well that, once left without its leader, the supervisor's team of henchmen – Johnny, me, Maloi, Givi Sukhumsky – wouldn't be able to keep things under control.

None of us was suited for the role of leader. Maloi was too small. Givi was in the middle of being tried himself and he would soon be leaving. Johnny, physically strong and experienced, had been inside for a long time, he knew prison, but even so, he wouldn't be able to keep order in the hut: he lacked the authority required for that and, even more importantly, he lacked the slyness, cunning and strength of will.

'What are we going to do without you, Slava?' I suddenly blurted out.

Slava put his hand on my shoulder.

'You stand firm as a rock, and everything will be steady. Show any sign of weakness, and they'll gobble you up.'

I lowered my eyes dejectedly.

'This is prison, brother,' Slava went on quietly. 'You have to be very clever and very cunning to survive in here. Forget all about decency, about justice, about culture, about your books. The only thing you mustn't forget about is God. Live in the real world. Look out for yourself in the first place, and in the second place, and in the third place, then after that look out for your neighbour … When you do things, act tough! I'm not going to give you a lesson – you know it all yourself, you've been in here with me for half a year.'

'I won't be able to do things like you. I'm not experienced enough.'

'Then you learn from Rookie. He's got even less experience, but just look at him go.'

'Something has to be done about him.'

Sasha smiled, exposing a fresh gap in his front teeth. He had lost another tooth during the last month. On average, a prisoner in our 'Central' lost two teeth a year.

'You worry too much about that meathead. He's weak. He won't bring you down. He's a nobody. A junkie. He's a long way from the Common Way. When they order me out of the hut, I'll have a special word with him, warn him off, up front. And apart from that, I'll write to someone about him … If that fool gets out of line and you can't handle him, some people will come in here and stop him dead in two seconds flat … But you understand, it would be better not to take things that far …'

'He'll start throwing his weight about the moment you leave. The very same day.'

'No, he won't,' Slava snapped. 'He's already well off as it is. He's got his smack and he's got his stooge. What more could he want? What are you quaking and shaking for anyway?' Slava frowned in annoyance and mimicked me in a thin, high voice. 'Ah, what's going to happen, what will we do without you … You'll be leaving soon yourself! Or am I wrong?'

'Not soon,' I objected. 'I've got almost a hundred witnesses, without all the rest of it. And the trial hasn't even started yet. I'll be driving backwards and forwards for a long time yet. Two years for sure …'

'If you're afraid,' Slava advised me irritably, lowering his voice, 'then get off the Road! Hide away in a corner, live like a passenger! Just hand the hut to Rookie on a plate, let that junkie destroy everything! Or clear out of here altogether, slip the goons some money and move across to the special! Well, have you thought about it already?'

'No,' I lied.

'Then stop trembling and complaining! Quit whining! Otherwise something very unpleasant will happen.'

'What?'

'I'll change my opinion about you.'

Ashamed, I fell silent.

Late that evening the reply from Fatty arrived.

As well as the page from an exercise-book covered with small letters, there was a load: a pack of imported cigarettes.

'Hi, Andriukha!' my old friend, the salami fanatic, wrote. 'I'm glad you remembered about me. What you asked about can be done. I agree with you, you don't belong there in the General Block. They say you have almost a hundred men in a cell there! You could end up with no subcutaneous layer at all like that, and that's certain death. Break out of that zoo, move to the special! We have seven men for five places here. You can get by all right ... now down to business. This is how we'll solve your problem: you send me your wife's address and telephone number. My lawyer will meet her. She'll give him three hundred dollars, and he'll take the money to the right person. You know who. In a week, or maybe two, they'll transfer you. I can't promise it will be to my cell. But you will be moved into a small cell, with normal, respectable people who are worthy of you – that's guaranteed. So that's the way of it. I await your reply.

Warm prisoner's greetings – Vadim the Stout.

P.S. If you need anything, write, don't be shy.

P.P.S. By the way, you have to pay the above-mentioned sum every month. I hope you're prepared for that. Cheers! Yours tr. – Vadim.'

Of course I'm prepared for that, I thought sadly as I tore the note into little pieces. I've been prepared for a long time. I'm prepared to hand over the money all right. Only I don't have it. I'm willing to pay, but I don't have anything to pay with. I don't have three hundred dollars. And I don't have any time either. 'In a week, or maybe two' – the term doesn't suit, as the bankers say.

The day after tomorrow Slava Glory-to-the-CPSU will come back to the cell as a convicted criminal. From then on it will be illegal to hold him with suspects under investigation. They'll allow him a bit of time to pack everything up, then they'll lead him out, 'with his things'.

I had fifty hours left to come up with a way out.

35

A November night is an excellent time for the modern prisoner. Cool. Quiet. A blissful atmosphere of relaxation reigns below the vaults of the immense hall where once, a hundred years ago, wounded mariners who were fortunate enough to have survived some bloody battle of Tsushima or other were treated for their ailments. The present occupants of the former military hospital might be less reputable – but they were certainly no less fond of life.

Almost as soon as darkness fell, the distinctive life of prison life was in full swing. The Roads were stretched taut along the walls and loads began slipping along them. Thieves and thieves' bosses set about writing the many, many replies to the scrips they had received the day before with requests to settle some argument or another. Speculators and drug barons took money and heroin out of their hiding places in order to send them to the suffering. The brothers took their seats to pass an hour or two in a game of cards. The drug addicts carefully boiled their simple accessories in mugs.

Small machines hummed into action, covering bodies with tattoos. That season the subject of the audacious rebel was all the rage. Buxom mermaids and faces of the Saviour gave way to ugly swastikas and other Nazi symbols. It was an expression of protest from men in total despair, driven insane by hunger and cramped conditions, a protest against the criminal law, humane in form but essentially cruel in content.

More or less instantaneously, roll-ups were filled, salami was fried, home brew was filtered, tape-decks were switched on, scores were settled, informers were made to pay, transgressors were brought to strict justice, and the prisoners let the good times roll right through till morning.

And we arranged a banquet.

In prison the very presence of drink is usually sufficient reason for drinking. Good-quality alcohol is a rare visitor to the Central. But today we had a good reason. An excellent reason, the very best. We were seeing a friend off, back out to freedom. Slava Glory-to-the-CPSU was all set to go home. By the time the verdict in his CASE was announced he had already done a full five years inside, and the judge, the third already, who was absolutely exhausted by the trial, had decided to give the jailbird a sentence 'for time served'. The haggard bandit's guilt had clearly not seemed obvious to the judge, and the seven-year stretch demanded by the prosecutor had been cut back severely.

When he returned late at night following the pronouncement of sentence, Slava hadn't said a word to anyone, and his face – an assemblage of bones tautly covered with grey skin – was expressionless: his eyes were looking down at the floor.

He took a long time getting washed, generously soaping his neck, and shoulders, and elbows. A hundred and thirty-five men – with the exception of those who were sleeping – fell silent. Everyone knew that Slava had brought back his sentence. Many had been in here for a year, or two, or three. By spending five years in pre-trial prison, Slava Glory-to-the-CPSU had set one of the Central's records. After he finished getting washed, Slava prayed for a long time, reciting the Penitential Canon several times. Then he summoned several of the slightly richer prisoners and asked them to lend him money. I put in a hundred roubles, Johnny did the same. Even Rookie, who happened by chance to emerge from his heroin-fuelled visions, shelled out two crumpled ten-rouble notes, only to withdraw immediately back into his junkie trip.

Gathering up the bundle of notes, Slava crossed the cell, walked up to the door and stuck his head through the feeder. He spent about an hour sitting by the hole in the door. Screws came up from the other side and talked to him about something for a long time. When they went away, others appeared. Having finally come to an arrangement, the patient Slava walked across the cell again, this time in the opposite direction, and right there, under the bars, beside the wall, on the boss's meadow, he informed Johnny and me that he had five days left to serve.

We were jubilant.

There and then Slava announced his farewell party.

'They'll bring it and we'll just enjoy ourselves,' he said with a wink.

They only brought it two days later. In addition to vodka, meat arrived, and even pepper (which is strictly forbidden in prison; you can throw it in a guard's face, or his dog's nostrils, and make a run for it).

At two in the morning the cell was filled with the aroma of roasted beef seasoned with spices. After he finished cooking the main dish, Slava borrowed two packs of tea from the Common Fund, on his own personal account, promising to make good the shortfall as soon as he could. No one dared to refuse a man who had done five years inside. The tea was tipped onto a newspaper and placed in the centre of the table under the gaze of a hundred pairs of eyes belonging to naked, hungry men.

'Chifir for anyone who wants it …' Slava announced in a clear voice.

In a second five to eight groups of five to eight men formed and the heating elements ripped into the water in the mugs like automatic weapons; the extremely strong tea – not actually chifir – was drunk before it was fully brewed. It would mature in the belly.

After downing our first shot of vodka and swallowing a piece of scorching hot meat each, we fell silent. The forgotten tastes and smells aroused cherished memories for every one of us.

'Now I'm going to drop a few downers,' Slava announced. 'I'll pray for a while and go to bed! And I'll sleep the whole three days and three nights, until they send for me …'

We drank a second shot, and a third. We ate the meat: try hard as we did to savour it, chewing slowly, relishing every tiny piece – the kilogram disappeared in a few minutes. After the fourth shot there was a slight mishap. A warder came up to the door of our cell and told the men standing nearby to call Johnny to the opening.

My partner had long ago become chummy with several members of the lower ranks of the administration. One such acquaintance, having nothing to do during the night, had come to ask for a cigarette and have a chat. The tipsy prisoner was more than happy to swap a couple of phrases with the sober jailer – he stuck his head out through the feeder into the corridor, lit up, laughed, shared the news.

At that very moment the DAGPTIS – Duty Assistant Governor of the Pre-Trial Isolation Prison – happened by chance to enter that very corridor. The most senior and important prison officer, directly responsible for everything that happens at the Central. Not a rank-and-file warder, not a cell-block supervisor, but the man over them all, Screw Number One.

On catching sight of the red, jocular features of the prisoner, the important officer with the red armband and the rank of a full major immediately suspected that something was amiss, ordered the subordinate warder 'to attention' and then determined that the prisoner's head protruding form the rectangular aperture was diffusing into the air the smell of entirely fresh alcohol. After asking the man's name, the big boss ordered him to summon the supervisor.

So then Slava Glory-to-the-CPSU – no less merry – stuck his head through the embrasure. He made an effort to explain himself somehow. But the big boss flew into a furious rage. Fixing tipsy Slava with his piercing glance, Number One declared in a voice of thunder:

'I'm calling out the reserve! Open up the cell! Everybody out!'

Everyone knows that any boss, even if he's lazy and slipshod, or even if he's a democrat, or simply obliged to close his eyes to breaches of the rules … in other words, any boss whose department is a zone of infinite, eternal disorder must, at least occasionally, assert himself. Show who's in charge. Otherwise everything will slide into chaos!

The country's a bloody shambles! – that was evidently what the top man told himself bitterly. A total shambles! But I'm not going to have any shambles in here. In here, at least, I shall root it out. I won't allow suspects under investigation to go guzzling vodka with impunity!

The huge door swung out into the semidarkness of the corridor.

'Out!' yelled the screw who only five minutes earlier had been making amicable small talk with Johnny. 'Wake the ones who are asleep! The entire hut – out, and quick!'

Has the man ever been born who could observe with indifference, without a shudder, as a stream of bodies smelling of iodine and tobacco, shuffling their sandals along the floor, flows out of the gaping maw of a prison cell? As somebody's sons, husbands and fathers come creeping out, hitching up the trousers that are slipping down, sniffing and swearing at each other, scratching their privates, coughing convulsively and screwing up their eyes, driven on by cries of foul abuse, moving out of the small space into a large one, stumbling into each other in their confusion, and finally squatting down in a row with their forearms resting on their knees?

When I went out, the corridor was already humming. Several commandos in camouflage gear, masks and gigantic boots with high tops were there, shifting from one foot to the other. There were dogs wheezing and choking on their leads. A hundred and thirty semi-naked creatures were squatting down along the wall. In the dirty, egg-yolk-yellow electric light the protruding backbones were like crooked lines of perforation on the hunched-over human backs. Limbs bent awkwardly, faces drained of colour, cracks for mouths, gristly protruding ears – the men before me were like images out of Bosch.

Alarmed and curious faces appeared in the door-holes of neighbouring cells. What's happened? What's all the row all about? What if they're searching the whole floor?

After walking along the long row of knees and shaven heads, the loudly swearing Number One identified those who had consumed the forbidden poison by smell. There were four of them, including me.

No, we weren't seriously drunk. The state we were in is known to the tender-hearted Russian individual as a little under the weather. We weren't swaying, we weren't bawling out songs, we weren't behaving aggressively – but the uncertain movements of our hands, our stumbling tongues, glittering eyes and foolishly curved, moist lips were unmistakable evidence of offence.

'Put these ones in the hold!' Number One ordered, looking at us in disgust. 'Put the others back inside.'

The commando nearest to me immediately prodded me in the back with his truncheon.

'Move!'

I started walking. Exuding fragrant alcohol fumes, we were escorted to the ground floor.

While we were still on the stairs I heard a dialogue in low voices behind my back. Slava Glory-to-the-CPSU, who was walking last in line, and the DAGPTIS, who was still swearing, had separated off from the procession and fallen behind. I heard Slava quietly remonstrating and trying to demonstrate something, and the head goon snarling furiously – but only under his breath. Soon their voices faded away completely.

I started feeling more cheerful. Slava had squirmed his way out of it! No doubt now they would take him back now, and then we would be saved, all of us! The supervisor, and me, and Johnny, and Maloi. We weren't afraid of the hold, that is, the punishment cells. But there was no way we could all go there at the same time. Then who would keep order in the lives of a hundred and thirty hungry, deranged men? Who would rein in the fights, the stealing and the rest of the disorder? There could be no doubt that these were the very arguments the cunning Slava was whispering in the outraged major's ear.

But I really ought to spare a thought for my own fate. If word got out in the Central that all the roadmen in our cell had been put in solitary for drinking, that the Common Load had been abandoned to the whim of fate – that would be the end of Slava Glory-to-the-CPSU as an authority. And I'd be completely finished. My reputation as a prisoner would be dead and buried. And unlike Slava, I still had a lot of time to do. I still had the trial to come, and then the convict holding prison, transportation and prison camp …

Finding myself in the centre of an empty room with a tiled floor, I realised that a certain event – not crucially important, but long-awaited, and repeatedly anticipated, was about to take place. The guy who got away with everything was about to receive his comeuppance. But then, it was long overdue. Once, a long time ago, in the middle of summer, in this same little room with dirty walls, Captain Svinets had tried to induce me to collaborate.

I was followed into the room by three men with broad shoulders, wearing masks, but they immediately pulled the black rags up over their heads and turned out to be young men of my own age – ruddy-cheeked, massive clones of Captain Svinets; only their eyes didn't look as intelligent look. The atmosphere thickened.

'Where'd you get the vodka?' one of the ruddy-faced young guys asked, slapping his rubber truncheon into an immense palm.

'I haven't been drinking vodka,' I replied.

'Then what have you been drinking?'

'Headbanger.'

'Moonshine, you mean?'

'That's it, boss. Moonshine.'

'Okay … What about the meat. Where's the meat come from?'

'I haven't eaten meat for two years.'

'The hut smells of roasted meat.'

'It wasn't meat we were roasting.'

'So what were you roasting?'

'Bread steaks.'

'What are they?'

'You take some bread,' I explained, 'slice it thinly – and roast it …'

The ruddy-faced guys exchanged glances.

'Cocky,' the one who was standing on my right said succinctly.

'Why don't we slice him thinly,' suggested the one who had stationed himself facing me.

I took a step backwards. It would be good to feel the wall with my elbows. Sometimes they stand you with your face to the wall. Sometimes rock musicians sing about a wall. Sometimes the main street of the entire financial world is referred to as Wall Street. And sometimes a wall just happens to be good, not as a song or a business symbol, but as protection against a blow from behind.

But I was too late. I received a kick to the ankles, from the side, and at that very moment I was grabbed by the shoulders and jerked sharply downwards. My flip-flops went fluttering rapidly through the air like black butterflies. My bones slammed against the tiles of the floor. They laid into me with feet clad in heavy artificial leather boots. Then again. And again.

'That's for your head banger! And that's for your bread steaks!'

And so the goons beat the shit out of our banker after all, gentlemen. This is absolutely essential in a comic strip. They beat me without any particular enthusiasm. If they'd wanted to, they could probably have crippled me for life; but they didn't want to. Possibly in that place they practiced various different categories of beatings, and what was handed out in my case was the gentle, educational kind, strictly for form's sake. They didn't beat me, they hit me with their feet: they didn't sink their heels into my ribcage, didn't aim for my head, and the massive laced boots were never swung at full force

I received two or three dozen blows to the soft tissues, on my buttocks and the backs of my thighs. I took repeated hits from a rubber truncheon on my shoulders and elbows – it was all painful, it stung and smarted, but in general it was almost bearable. I was given powerful slaps and punches to the back of my head, my temples, my ears – but not to my face: I protected it with my open hands and my knees drawn right up to my head. In addition, while in this embryonic position I rolled about on the cool tile floor as I attempted to avoid each incoming blow. And I also yelled like a stuck pig. I almost squealed. Not in pain, but entirely out of considerations of self-defence. It's a well-known fact that when the victim of a beating screams loudly, it embarrasses the people beating him. Who knows if some outsider, or even one of their fellow security officers, walking along the corridor on some official business, might not overhear, start thinking and go and report to the man at the top?

I tried to give my howls verbal form, that is, I didn't just howl 'A-A-A!' or 'O-O-O!' – I croaked with expression, threatened and swore, took the Lord's name in vain. After all, gentlemen, we should not forget that I was in a state of inebriation; it's all water off a duck's back to a drunk: alcohol deadens pain, that's a well-known fact.

Attracted by the smell of poison, the nouveau-riche Andriukha put in an appearance. 'Too late, gentlemen!' he laughed in the faces of the camouflaged goons (they didn't hear a thing, but I heard). 'Too late to thrash him now! You ought to have given him a good battering much earlier than this, much earlier! A year and a half ago! The very first day he was arrested! At Lefortovo. While he was still warm and soft, wearing his Kenzo suit and his crocodile sneakers! Ah, your kicks and punches would have done him so much good then! But it's a waste of time now! You're just wasting your efforts, gentlemen!' Unheard and unreal for everyone but me, the flickering, insubstantial Andriukha sank back into his empty void.

Even the conclusion of the educational procedure, when they shoved me into the punishment cell, I was still conscious. And despite the sharp pain in certain parts of my body, I even felt a certain satisfaction, seasoned with a hint youthful audacity: I had been scorned, humiliated and beaten but I was alive and still in one piece, almost cheerful in fact.

The real pain came through later, after several hours. In the cramped, damp little cell, lying on bare boards, longing to drink, eat and get warm, naked to the waist, trembling from the sensation known in prisoners' circles as 'cold turkey', I as made acutely aware of my condition.

36

At eight in the morning they brought food. I leapt up off my planking bed. Hobbled and limped over to the door.

'Give me your bowl,' said the skilly man.

'Haven't got one.'

The boy from domestic services rummaged in his trolley and held out a dented aluminium container.

'Tea,' I requested in a loud whisper. The brown, steaming liquid exuding the intense smell of life gushed into the bowl. I grabbed hold of the aluminium rim and immediately jerked my hands away – it was hot. The skilly man waited patiently. Evidently, while distributing food in the hold, he had seen plenty of beaten and bloody men. He was very familiar with their reactions. Finally I contrived somehow to take hold of the precious vessel and hastily set it down on the wooden bunk. The hole in the door slammed shut.

The tea was steaming hot. My mind was clouded by thirst. I tried to raise the bowl it to my lips – it was too hot, too hot. Aluminium, that damned aeroplane metal, conducts heat perfectly. I had to lean over, lower my swollen face, and start lapping like a dog.

Soon after that the warder of the hold appeared, smelling strongly of cheap deodorant. He led me off to the supply room and took away the trousers that had saved me from the cold during the night. A prisoner in the punishment cell was given official issue clothing: a grey cotton jacket and trousers with black horizontal stripes.

'Kenzo?' I asked, crumpling the coarse material in my hands. 'Versace?'

'Versace's been blown away,' the hold warder responded to my jibe, demonstrating his understanding of the basic trends of the fashion business. 'Put them on, lad. Know what your stretch is?'

'No.'

'Fifteen days.'

All dolled up, I plodded back to the cell, every inch the prisoner in a classical cartoon. The hold warder fastened the plank bed up against the wall, locked it with a special key and left me alone.

I searched for a place to sit. But in the square box of the punishment cell, three paces by three, no provision was made for sitting. Or for lying, naturally. I couldn't stretch out on that damp floor, as cold as the grave. The free choice remaining to me was either to stand, or walk about, or squat down on my haunches. In any case, my legs were my only means of support.

Pulling off the striped suit, I inspected my damaged limbs, then tore a long scrap of cloth off my shorts, urinated on it and wiped down the bleeding grazes on my elbows and knees. The bad smell didn't matter, the important thing was to avoid inflammation. One week in the local prison climate could turn any scratch into a huge, suppurating boil. Take proper care for your own health, cleanliness and hygiene – that's one of the basic rules for a prisoner in the Matrosskaya Tishina – the *Sailor's Rest*.

I spent several hours in complete idleness. My broken ribs, tenderized backside and back all ached. I would have paid any rate at all for a tablet of painkiller, for a little white cylinder of analgesic. But I had slipped all my money – a few fifty-rouble banknotes, rolled up into a tight tube – into my 'washer's' hand just before I left the cell, in the commotion at the door, where no one could see.

This puny little man, who had been picked up at the Cherkizovo market for brazenly snatching two hamburgers out of the hands of a student from Moscow's Bauman Higher Technological University, was about as far removed from any form of cash liquidity as any man in prison could be. The weedy 'washer' was daubed all over with green antiseptic and furacillin, and the only personal property he possessed was a pair of shorts with a flowery pattern. He had lost the clothes in which he was arrested playing cards during the very first days of his stretch inside. Now, in order to survive, he washed sheets for me and Johnny, receiving sugar and tobacco in exchange. I knew the washer was a decent prisoner, he'd keep my wealth safe and return it as soon as I got back home to the cell.

But right now my assets were frozen, they were in someone else's hands. I had nothing at all to take away the pain. Not even any cigarettes. Smoking in the punishment cell is forbidden. So is wearing any kind of clothes except official prison issue. You can't have any personal things at all. Your only amusement is walking from one corner to the other. Five steps one way, four and a half back. Half a step goes on the turn. Everything exactly like in the cell at the Lefortovo fortress, where I started out – still arrogant, rich, self-assured.

In the evening a miserable-looking screw I didn't know showed up. He opened the lock, lowered the bunk and told me to come out – to collect a mattress. I went to the same store room where I'd been issued the stripy threads that morning, grabbed up a shapeless heap of rags that unravelled in my hands, went back to my cell, made up my bed and fell on it.

I learned the best way to use the mattress immediately. You shouldn't actually sleep on the mattress – you get cold on top; and you don't sleep under the mattress, either, but *inside* it. The fabric was torn in many places by the hands and feet of previous inhabitants of the hold. I thrust my arms and legs into these holes and after a brief period of discomfort, I fell asleep.

Half of the night went by. At its precise mid-point, in the dead hour just before dawn, an iron lock squeaked. The door embrasure opened. A bundle thudded on to the black floor. My aid parcel, I thought triumphantly, jumping to my feet. My parcel! My parcel's arrived!

After unravelling the threads and unfolding several sheets of newspaper, I took out ten caramel sweets, some sugar, cigarettes and matches. Now life would be bearable.

After relishing a long smoke, I settled in as comfortably as I could between the lumps of crumpled wadding held together by stitching and fell into thought.

I knew perfectly well how much these cigarettes, caramels and grubby sugar lumps had cost. They had been bought for money set aside out of old men's pensions and women's meagre wages. Brought to the prison by mothers and wives. Handed in at the food parcel reception window. And then they had reached the trembling hands of a hungry prisoner. After painful deliberation, calculation, hesitation and licking of lips, the cigarettes and caramels – one out of ten or one out of fifteen – had been donated to the Common Fund. Tipped or packed into a special cardboard box. Weighed on a simple balance. Carefully recounted over and over again. Packaged into loads. Sent from several different cells to one, where they were repacked more conveniently. By dint of great effort, risk and cunning, by means of deception and bribery, the cigarettes and sweets had followed a route that ending beside a man in the punishment cells.

At this hour of the night, other cigarettes and caramels were being delivered to men coughing up blood in the TB clinic, men herded together into the special cell AIDS sufferers – to all who were suffering in adversity.

The community of prisoners never forgets those who are in adversity. They will always pay the going rate to the warders in the hold, and at night the warders will deliver the loads themselves, tossing a tightly wrapped bundle into every narrow stone box.

These hungry, ragged, tormented creatures want to live. They will invent a thousand means to help themselves and their companions in misfortune. In each separate cell they will patiently gather the means together: a pinch of tea, a lump of sugar, a rouble. Working like ants, they will transport all the loads together to a single cell. They will employ bribery, persuasion and cunning to squeeze food and tobacco through into the very deepest of holds. They will stretch the thread of life right down to the very bottom.

Perhaps, in some other comic strip, the boy banker did not live in Asia, but in Europe. In some neat little country where on holidays the women dress up in their great grandmothers' starched skirts and dance their great-grandmothers' dances.

Over there, in Europe, they would have put the boy banker away in an aseptic institution with good food, a gym, workshops to keep him busy and telephone booths for regular business calls. A European prison.

But in that European prison he would never have found himself in a filthy kennel in the basement, and the poverty-stricken warder, bribed by the even poorer prisoner, would never have delivered a lump of sugar and a cigarette to the banker's kennel.

And the banker would not have chewed that lump of sugar. Or smoked that cigarette. And so he would never have learned how a man can affirm his freedom.

It's a good thing that we live in Asia.

Thanks to these sublimely doleful thoughts about the dramatic journey taken by the sweets and cigarettes, I failed to perform one simple and essential action; that is, I failed to hide the tea, tobacco and other items securely. After chewing and smoking my fill, I nonchalantly stuffed the remains of my riches into the ventilation shaft. There were numerous crumpled pieces of paper, some kind of stones and other rubbish lying there in the narrow tunnel. I hoped that the bundle would escape the hold warder's attention. But I was mistaken.

In the morning he came into my box and looked me up and down – he reeked of sickly, suffocating, cheap perfume – and immediately made straight for my hiding-place. He found everything. The hold warder had a funny habit of biting his chapped lips with rapid movements of his teeth: first with his lower teeth, then the other way round.

'Where'd you get it?' he asked in a low voice, examining the bundle.

I kept silent.

The master of the punishment cell cast another critical glance over my striped personage and toyed with his rubber truncheon. In principle, he could have immediately reported confiscating foodstuffs and cigarettes that it was forbidden to consume in his jurisdiction and added another five or ten days to my sentence. But this fragrant junior penitentiary official turned out to be a humanitarian.

'If you smoke, I'll punish you,' he told me, then he put my tobacco and sugar in his pocket and strode rapidly out into the corridor. The incredibly greasy cloth of his trousers gleamed across his backside.

I immediately cursed myself. Thanks to my own heedlessness, thanks to my inherent intelligentsia tendency to soar high in the empyrean, thanks to the *habit of thinking* – I had been left without any cigarettes.

The day passed in suffering. I wanted a smoke so badly, I kept grating my teeth and my spleen was quivering. I inspected the entire cell. The walls and the floor. Centimetre by centimetre. Looking for even the tiniest little fag-end. And I found one, two in fact. The first would be good for at least one full-blown drag, the second (it even still had the 'Yava' logo on it) for at least two. But how could I light them, where could I get a flame?

The search continued. Looking in the corners and in the cracks, I finally found everything else. The inflammable match-heads were squeezed into their hiding places, rubbed into the dirt with fiendish cunning. In other cracks I even discovered special paper for lighting up, torn into tiny little squares. At the fifth attempt I managed to produce an orange flame and I smoked the big butt, then the small one.

Naturally, the dose wasn't enough; by the evening I'd started feeling out the walls and the corners again, wondering if a new parcel would arrive that night.

At eight in the evening the hold warders changed shifts. A new overseer appeared. Unlike the morning one, who smelled of soap and violets, this one smelled of tarpaulin, socks and – naturally – tobacco. Unable to restrain myself, I avidly breathed in the remnants of the poison from his crumpled camouflage jacket: my nostrils could even sense the smoke that had survived in the bottom of his lungs.

That night no aid parcel arrived.

The beginning of the second day without tobacco was hard. Every smoker knows that the morning cigarette is the most important of the entire day. It's almost impossible to get by without it.

I spent the time until evening in torment, covering at least five kilometres walking from corner to corner. I fell asleep, but slept very shallowly and immediately heard the quiet squeak of the lock opening and the sound of the heavy load falling. Dashing across to my long-awaited present with feral rapidity, I tore the paper and threads open with my teeth (every load is wrapped and tied very tightly and securely) to discover everything that a man needs to relieve his suffering – and immediately smoked two cigarettes one after the other.

The effects of a two-day break in tobacco consumption made themselves felt: my head started spinning, and I began feeling nauseous, but even so I smoked the cigarettes to the end, down to the filter, with one hand propped against the wall and my head lowered. I staggered back across to the mattress, fell on it and lay there, running my paper-dry tongue over my equally dehydrated gums.

In addition to the cigarettes, tea, sugar and even vitamins – a few small yellow peas of ascorbic acid – had arrived. Sure, I would have liked to drink some fresh, hot, strong tea. But a man incarcerated in the punishment cell is not supposed to have any hot water.

The unusually large dose of poison set my head booming like a drum. In its hollow space the question that had been tormenting for the last few days was exposed, as large as life: what was going to happen to me next? Tomorrow would already be the third day – and that was already a fifth of my sentence. Not far left to go to a third. From a third to a half was only another two days. Before I could even glance over my shoulder, the sentence would be past the halfway point. Fifteen days and night would fly past in a moment – that was the conclusion produced by this prisoner's algebra. But what then?

I tried to assess my prospects soberly. Everything indicated that I had no prospects, none at all. The scenes that appeared before my eyes were each worse than the other: there was the cell supervisor, the legendary Slava Glory-to-the-CPSU, saying goodbye to his subjects; there he was casting his final glance over a hundred and thirty-five faces turned in his direction; there was the door closing behind him, there was the uneasy silence hanging in the air, there was one day passing, then another – and everything was changing. Slava wasn't there, he was on the outside, free. Johnny's wasn't there, and neither was Andriukha. They were both in the punishment cells, incarcerated for drinking. Who was going to pull on those tricky road ropes now? And most important of all: who was going to instil fear in a crowd of a hundred hungry, naked men, half-dead from overcrowding and lack of sleep?

Then I would come back. Shrouded, as it happens, in an aura of disgrace. He abandoned the Roadway because he was drunk! He damaged the Common Way! They'd accuse me for that straight away. Rookie would. He did thing things by the thieves' rules, didn't he? All three of us would get it: Johnny, me and Maloi.

It probably wouldn't go as far as a fight. But every worthy prisoner would learn an important piece of news: apparently, the men who had only recently been standing right here beside them, on the Road, were outsiders who had no understanding of the rules. People like that shouldn't be allowed to have anything to do with the Common Way! My friends and I would immediately be thrown out of the boss's meadow.

I lit up my third cigarette.

Never mind, I thought, there are still ten and a bit days to go. But meanwhile I have to do the most urgent and important thing. Hide the contents of the aid parcel. Over a period of two hours, sometimes crawling on my knees, sometimes jumping to the dirty ceiling, working unhurriedly, I dissolved a whole pack of cigarettes and box of matches in the cell. Shoved them into all the holes and cracks, making putty out of my own spittle and dust, and using it to complete the camouflage.

'That's a better trick than hiding someone else's billions from the tax police!' laughed the nouveau-riche Andriukha, who had suddenly appeared out of nowhere.

'Go to hell!' I barked: maybe even out loud.

'Whatever you say,' the boy banker replied indifferently, and disappeared. But all the same, he was right.

When the hold warder came in next morning, he drew the air in through his nose, bit his lips and said:

'Come out into the corridor.'

A lightning search was immediately carried out. I lost all the sugar and nine of the twelve cigarettes that I'd hidden.

'I see you're a cheeky one,' the appallingly fragrant hold warder declared. 'Do you like it in here, then?'

'Not a bit.'

'I think you do,' the punishment cell supervisor continued. 'You got fifteen days, right?'

'Precisely.'

'I'll make it thirty for you,' the hold warder promised. 'But in general, just so you know, your type usually does forty-five in here for me. Did you get that, lad?'

This lad was twenty-eight years old.

'Unambiguously, boss,' he replied, making all the movements required of a 'lad': he extended his lips in an ingratiating smile, spread his fingers, threw his hands up in the air, and lent his eyes a quite extraordinary law-abiding expression. Meanwhile, in his own mind he cursed both the wily screw for guessing where his hiding-places were, and himself, for failing to show enough ingenuity.

'If I catch just one more whiff of smoke,' the hold warder warned me, 'I'll stick on another fifteen days! For violating the regulations. Got that?'

The lad repeated his ceremonial response.

The hold warder fastened the lock on the bunks. I began slowly figuring out how I could manage to stretch out the three surviving cigarettes over two days. I would probably simply have decided to give up smoking and turn the entire stupid war with the deodorised overseer to good effect, if my old life had been waiting for on my return from the hold. But I couldn't even dream about that. And to search for a way out I required all the resources of my brain. I couldn't manage it without smoking.

I spent the whole of the fourth day in doleful reflection. Today was the day when the man who was more important to me than any other had left the Sailor's Rest pre-trial prison.

Somewhere up there, two storeys higher, in hut number one hundred and seventeen, this morning someone had shouted out:

'Slava! You've been ordered out!'

A hundred poor devils – apart from those whose turn it was to sleep – had craned their necks avidly, trying to catch a glimpse of the man this phrase was addressed to, so that they could remember the moment of triumph on the face of this prisoner who had done five years inside, the fleeting glint in his eyes, the sparing gesture of triumph with his hand.

Some day they would say the same thing to me. But meanwhile things were bad. Really bad.

My friend had gone. And my enemy was waiting for me, to attack and destroy me.

I decided to realise the next tranche of cigarettes with a yield of fifty per cent. That is, to save at least half of what was hidden from the hold warder. I broke the filter – an unnecessary indulgence in my circumstances – off each cigarette. I broke all twenty of the paper cylinders into two halves to make them easier to conceal. After that, with deliberately carelessness, I stuffed some fat butts into places that the overseer was bound to glance into. He'd find them, decide that the job was done and not bother to look any further. That way I'd save the bulk of them.

The search for the most cunning hollows in the floor and cracks in the walls continued until dawn.

But when the job was nearing completion, I stopped. Through the ventilation opening the sounds of morning reached my ears: the distant tramping of many feet. The clomping of heavy boots, the slightly lighter and subtler sound of the soles of officers' shoes, the resounding blows of ladies' high heels against asphalt. It was the prison's staff hurrying on their way to work: warders, security officers, medical assistants, the women who received the food parcels, store men, ancillary workers, dog kennel caretakers, financial office workers and other toilers of the key and the truncheon.

There's no point, I told myself. There's no point in hiding the forbidden tobacco and sugar. No need to conceal anything. On the contrary.

'Well, blow me!' the hold warder exclaimed ominously when he saw me sitting on the mattress, enveloped in clouds of smoke. 'You've got everything backwards!'

'Not at all, boss,' I objected.

'You're openly smoking!' the warder screeched. 'I'm giving you extra time today! To start with – five days! Give me those cigarettes! And everything else.'

'You want them – you take them.'

Grabbing the soft packet – I'd deliberately left it in open view – the hold warder turned his back on me and walked away.

'Don't forget,' I told him.

'What?'

'To add on the five days. Don't forget.'

The fragrant overseer stuck his teeth into his lips once again.

'You're cheeking me, lad! Watch it, or else five days will suddenly be ten!'

I could have pushed the conflict even further. Raised the stakes to fifteen. But I decided that was enough for the first time. Let my sweet-smelling friend add on the extra. Five days or ten. Better still, a month straight away. Here in the punishment cell it was cold and there was nothing to eat – but at least it was calm. In a few weeks up there above me, at home, all the passions would have cooled. Many eyewitnesses to events – those who could remember the reanimation of the juvenile junkie, and the drinking session I was involved in – would have left. Their places would have been taken by novices. And you could never tell – maybe even Rookie would be tried and move on to the convict prison, transportation, and a prison camp, somewhere far away from me …

It didn't matter that I would see the New Year in below ground level, embracing a tattered mattress. No problem. At least I would get a break. That's how the trainer of a volleyball team does things. When the opposing team gets it spirits up during a match and its attackers start hammering home one ball after another, building up a devastating score – the trainer immediately takes a break, a time-out. To undercut the impetus of the attack …

Throughout the second half of my time in the punishment cell I smoked openly. The loads arrived once every two days. Now the cigarettes and matches, sugar and vitamins lay openly in the corner, on the floor, on a clean sheet of the *Moscow Komsomolets* newspaper. Every morning the hold warder indifferently collected up the forbidden riches and left without saying a word – he just fixed me with his gloomy gaze and bit his lips.

On the final night, the fifteenth, I couldn't get to sleep. I was too agitated.

When there was a squeak and the plate over the opening in the door swung out, I leapt towards the door. But the benefactor I couldn't see managed to shove the new bundle through the half-open feeder and hastily close the opening – obviously, he didn't want the guests in the punishment cells to see his face. I only caught the lingering remains of a powerful smell of cheap men's deodorant.

Then the nouveau-riche Andriukha condensed out of the yellow gloom.

'Still inside?' he asked in a mocking tone of voice, lighting up a hefty Havana.

'Yes.'

'And how is it?'

'The same as it is for everyone.'

'Ha! And I thought you were different from everyone else ...'

'That's just it. I was wrong.'

'Draw the conclusions from your mistakes and move on,' Andriukha exhorted me casually. 'You know yourself that experience is born of hard mistakes! It was Pushkin who said that, the great Afro-Russian! Learn the lesson and pick yourself up! A glass of cognac?'

'No.'

'Cigar?'

'No, thank you.'

'As you wish. It's a classy smoke with cognac ... So, do you understand everything now? You picked yourself up once, set to work and got rich – and you'll pick yourself up again and set to work ...'

'I picked myself up all right!' I said, mocking him. 'I set to work! And where's that guy who picked himself up now? In prison! And not just any ordinary prison, but the dirtiest, darkest and foulest, and not even in a normal cell, but down in the basement! In the hold! In the absolutely lowest place of all. Is that what you mean when you say I "picked myself up"?'

The nouveau-riche didn't answer.

'All right, never mind about prison,' I sighed. 'It'll come to an end some day. Prison and freedom – they're two names for the same condition. But what am I going to do afterwards? I'm a pauper! No partner, no business, no money, no prospects!'

'Start all over,' Andriukha repeated. 'Pick yourself up. Start from the bottom. You'll do it, because you have no choice.'

Looking from out of the cold, hunger and constant silence, I saw the flunky banker in especially sharp focus. Many details of his character that I hadn't noticed before were suddenly revealed to me. The young financier's hands were trembling slightly. His nails were bitten. Andriukha lived in fear. That was what was revealed to me. Basically, he only even made money in order to in order to stop feeling afraid. Sure, Andriukha was a rich guy, but a weakling. This thought manifested itself in my mind with such piercing clarity that I laughed quite merrily.

'Does something amuse you?' the boy banker asked in surprise.

'Yes.'

'Why?'

'Stop trembling,' I advised him.

'I'm not trembling.'

'You are. You're shaking. And how. Look: I'm wearing a striped uniform, I'm a pauper, I'm hungry, I'm stuck in a punishment cell – I'm not trembling. But you, all tarted up in Kenzo, well-fed, drunk, with your nose drenched in tobacco – you're trembling. You're afraid.'

'Ah, go to hell!' shouted Andriukha, stung to the quick, and he choked on thick cigar smoke. 'Go to hell!'

'You go to hell,' I replied calmly.

Andriukha instantly disappeared.

If I had known that I was talking to the boy banker for the last time, then I probably wouldn't have been so hard on him, I wouldn't have beaten the boy on his sore spot, wouldn't have hinted that the surrounding world made him afraid and hence his passion for multiplying capital: the boy only required money in order to shield himself against frightening reality.

But nothing frightened me any more. Or almost nothing.

In the morning the hold warder didn't bother to enter my smoke-filled box. After swinging the door open, he stopped on the threshold, stuck his teeth into his lips and said:

'Let's go.'

'Where?'

'Home. Out!'

I started trembling.

'What do you mean, home? What are you saying, boss? We have an agreement! You promised!'

'I didn't promise you anything,' the hold warder declared, turning away. 'Out you come, hand in your clothes and the mattress. Your time's up.'

'I won't go,' I said quietly. 'Add on the extra time.'

'Out you come, lad! Move it!'

'Lad yourself! Add it on.'

The screw raised his truncheon. A black rubber dildo with a convenient handle on the side. A good device for demonstrating that you're right.

'Out, or you'll be crawling out instead of walking!'

'Listen, boss,' I said quietly and amicably, but with passion. 'I can't go back to the hut! Leave me here.'

'It's not allowed. Out, come on!'

I obeyed.

The familiar figures of Johnny and Maloi were already out in the corridor, clutching their mattresses in their arms. Both with a flicker of alarm in their eyes. Johnny was still holding up. But Maloi looked frankly frightened.

'What are we going to do?' I asked my friends bluntly.

'Go to the hut,' Johnny replied seriously, and flexed his biceps. He smelled strongly of sweat.

I realised that Johnny was preparing for the return to our home cell in his own way. By strengthening his muscles. He was expecting the worst.

'Yes!' Maloi said in a trembling voice. He sniffed. 'We'll go to the hut!'

Silent and tense, we were led upstairs.

In the main intestine on the ground floor I saw a group of new arrivals, looking around like cornered animals as they crowded together in front of the open door of the store room, where some new inmates – one out of five – managed somehow to get an official issue bowl or bed sheet from the administration.

And at that point I slowed down. One of the novices – plump, red-haired, wearing a smart tracksuit, far too smart for this filthiest of all the filthy place in the whole wide world – looked familiar to me. As I walked by, I struck him on the shoulder, and he shuddered and looked round. In that same instant I felt a shudder of amazement too.

'What the hell are you doing here?' I exclaimed.

'Getting a mattress,' the red-headed lawyer replied with a pitiful smile.

I was so astounded that at first I couldn't think of what to say to the unfortunate fool.

'What are you in for?'

'Embezzlement, narcotics … you know it all already.'

I caught the intense beam of fear and despair radiating into space from my former defender's face, and despite myself I almost felt glad. Perhaps for the first time in his life this refined native son of Moscow was giving off the smells of a grown man who has fallen into serious misfortune – his body didn't smell of antibacterial soap, or sweet eau de colognes and lotions, but of tobacco and mucous. And there I was standing facing him, a gaunt, spiteful monster with exposed elbows covered in bruises, risen up from the very bottom of the hell for fools. A craggy, verminous body that had expended all its strength in its attempts to survive, but was still prepared to make ever new attempts.

'When you get into a hut, write to me,' I said hastily. 'One seventeen, the Road, Andriukha the con man!'

Red nodded feebly. He looked crushed, twisting his lip, not knowing where to put his hands. My heart ached in pity for him. I grabbed him by the sleeve.

'Repeat it!'

'One seventeen,' the former lawyer mouthed obediently. 'The Road … Andriukha the con man …'

Someone hit me a painful blow on the shoulder from behind.

'No talking! Move on!'

With an encouraging smile at Red, I glided on along my way. Going home.

In the cell nothing had changed. The same sour smell of ammonia, the same pall of smoke. The same compressed mass of bodies right beside the door: two or three Kazakhs, a Kalmyk, an Ingushetian, a Turkmenian, an Uzbeki, about ten Ukrainians, a citizen of Uganda and a citizen of Costa-Rica. People I understood, friendly, my kind of people.

'Andriukha! Andriukha!' declared a few scrawny men who were well-disposed towards me.

'Where?' I heard a very familiar-sounding voice say.

'Andriukha's back! And Johnny! And Maloi!'

'Where?'

The voice belonged to Slava Glory-to the-CPSU. As he emerged from the naked crowd, he smiled.

I froze, not understanding a thing, and Johnny, walking behind me, ran into my back.

'Slava!' I shouted. 'How did you get here? What are you here for? You are here?'

'Yes,' said Slava, clearly savouring my astonishment.

All my insides plummeted downwards, then soared back up again, then plummeted back down; my legs turned weak; my mouth stretched out in a stupid, happy smile. I squeezed through between the bodies and hugged my friend.

'Didn't they let you out?'

'Let me out?' Slava laughed. 'Just let them try not letting me out! I didn't go. Come on, come through. There's still a drop of vodka left ... Let's have a drink ...'

We sat down in the boss's meadow, right beside the wall. In the same place where we had eaten meat fifteen days earlier.

'What happened? Why didn't you go?'

'You mean you don't understand?' Slava asked severely.

'No.'

'How could I go? Just drop everything? The hut? The Common Way?

The Road? They'd make me answer for that! You're not here, there's nobody here … Anway, I tipped the godfather the necessary amount, and stayed. Until you came back …'

'Why do you want with this hut? And the Road?'

Slava suddenly became furious.

'Have you lost your mind? This is *my* hut! I've been in here four years! Just to get up and leave would be an ungodly thing to do!'

'What about Rookie?' I said, asking the question that had been tormenting me. 'Didn't he come on to you?'

'What Rookie?' Slava asked in surprise. 'Ah, Rookie … he's not here any longer. They took him away. With his things.'

I didn't say anything.

'And for that,' Slava Glory-to-the-CPSU added quietly, 'I tipped the Godfather the necessary amount.'

'At the going rate?'

'No,' my friend replied tersely. 'I gave him everything. Down to the last kopeck. Everything I'd saved up, all the pocket money I'd put aside for life outside.'

'But how can you go out there, into freedom, without any money?'

'My freedom won't go anywhere. It's always with me.'

'And mine,' I said immediately.

'And mine,' Johnny repeated like an echo.

'And mine,' whispered Maloi.

Our voices had a hollow echo.

And then each of us made the same movement, reaching a hand towards his pocket, as if he were about to extract his freedom from his tattered trousers, or from under his shirt, or from behind his belt, or from some other secret place – his very own freedom, carefully preserved, cherished, surrendered to no one – and show it, if not to the entire world, then at least to his close friends.

It sang. It is mine. Ours.

It is and it shall be.

In the morning Slava Glory-to-the-CPSU left for freedom.

A hundred and thirty-five faces – apart from those whose turn it was to sleep – lit up as he walked towards the door. Many sad eyes followed the stooped figure of the man leaving prison for a different life on the other side of the bars.

Slava presented the icons and holy images to me. He donated his blanket to the Common Way.

37

'**G**ive me your right hand!'

I squatted in the doorway of the van and reluctantly took my hand out of my pocket. The vicious January frost immediately grabbed me by the fingers.

The guard did the same. He clicked the icy-cold, scorching metal round my wrist.

The vehicle had driven right up close to the porch. The journey from the meat wagon to the door of the court would take one, maybe two seconds at most. On the right and the left, cutting off the route to any possible escape, four masked men with machine guns stood, shifting from one foot to the other. The black cloth round their mouths was covered with white patches of frost.

A crowd surrounded the van. Several doze people had come to get a look at the arrested dignitary and his accomplices. Wives and mothers. Daughters. Relatives. And also reporters and newspapermen. The trial of the gang of embezzlers had created a great stir in the media. After all, it wasn't every day that a minister, even a provincial one, was tried for a criminal offence. The crowd shouted words of support to the accused who had just been delivered. When the minister appeared, the noise became so loud that several startled ravens flew up from the branches of trees round about. They began circling between the buildings, above the grey box of the prison van, above the occasional people walking by at this midday hour in winter.

I walked second in line – behind the minister. Like him, I had time to pause for an instant on the very edge of the hatch and take a look around from the full height of the van.

'DADDY!'

Instantly guessing exactly where the clear, childish shout had come from, I turned my head and saw a tiny little figure in a bright-coloured jumpsuit. The look of those wide-open child's eyes pierced straight to centre of my consciousness.

Red cheeks. A thick scarf under a tiny chin.

My wife was holding my son by the hand.

My family was standing apart from the minister's noisy supporters, but higher than all of them: they had clambered up on to a snowdrift.

Two weeks earlier my son had turned three.

I gulped in a mouthful of icy air.

'Move, move!'

A jump down. The sweetish smell of exhaust fumes tickled my nostrils. One and a half hasty steps – and I was inside, in those chambers where a free man simply never finds himself. And God forbid that he ever should.

And so, today's the important day. The start of the trial. I'll finally get to meet the members of my gang. And the judge.

But that's not the most important thing. I've seen my family, they're all right, they came to support me – that's the real event! My son, in a brand-new winter outfit. A plump-cheeked, sturdy Pokemon. My wife, not wearing cast-offs either. A fur coat, a bright headscarf, kid gloves. My dear ones aren't going hungry. They're doing just fine. They're holding on, they love me.

But it could all have been different! My friend Johnny's so-called fiancée got tired of waiting after only six months. Other friends had wives who worked at two jobs, for mere kopecks, obliged to support not only themselves and the children, but also their husbands, taking it easy behind bars …

The guard room of the Kuzminsk intermunicipal court reminded me in every detail of the changing room in the bathhouse at Lefortovo. It was just as cramped – two metres by two and a half. The same white steel door. The round opening of the spy hole covered on the outside with a special shutter. By the far wall – a wooden platform. Penal interiors are simple and cheap.

But then, everything that's necessary is here. You can even have lie down. It's almost warm. Dry. Quiet.

'Smoking's forbidden! Hand in your cigarettes and matches! You'll get them back on the way out. Your shoelaces too.'

'How can I manage without laces?'

'The same way everyone else does.'

It was only now that I realised why the footwear of many of my neighbours' in the meat wagon footwear had been held on their feet by short piece of rag twisted into cords. Laces like that – ten-centimetres-long ribbons – were not confiscated, while I had to pull my real ones out of their holes and hand them over to the duty guard.

'Boss, take me to the toilet.'

'In an hour.'

'Can't we go sooner than that?'

'No talking!'

'Boss, I can't wait! Take me!'

'I said, no talking!'

Never mind, I decided. I'll wait as long as I have to. There was something worse. That morning, in the assembly cell, in a dense crowd of a hundred and fifty men, I had broken into a copious sweat in my pullovers, sweaters and long johns. During the next two hours, spent shut inside the van, the damp underclothes had turned cold. Instead of warming me, they had given me a fit of shakes that had lasted the entire journey. Prison transport is heated by the same economical method as the Moscow metro – by the warmth of human bodies.

There was a smell of fresh paint in the guardroom. The metal door had obviously been touched up no more than three or four days before. But already its surface was once again covered by numerous examples of prisoners' petroglyphs. Deep in his soul every jailbird is a great criminal, craving glory. He is prepared to record his story, compressed into a few brief words, on any even surface.

'Grisha, Syzran. Three years minimum security. Home soon!' 'Rashid, Turkmenia. Seven and a half years. May Allah help me!' 'Petrukha, Peter. Six months for a joint. The day after tomorrow – freedom. Hold on, you tramps!' 'Nadiukha. Four years maximum security for theft!' Even more frequent were the names of judges, accompanied by the most varied abusive epithets.

And finally – a little to one side of the main group of aphorisms – my eye was caught by something familiar, learned off by heart long ago, read hundreds of times on the walls and doors of cells, gatherers, trams, kennels and other prison rooms, in every place where a prisoner was left alone with his thoughts for even a moment:

CURSES THOUGH THE AGES ON THE MAN WHO FIRST DECIDED TO CORRECT MEN WITH PRISON!

Perhaps I ought to leave my autograph too? Make my mark among the other victims of the system with a few crucial words? Not out of vanity, but as a piece of intellectual mischief. Why not? But then, what should I scratch, exactly what phrase, what revelation should I offer? What would be my telegram from the heart?

Perhaps this:

DID TIME FOR TWO. NOUVEAU-RICHE ANDRIUKHA.

No, it was petty. Taking on someone else's guilt is no heroic feat. It's normal. As they say, in my place anyone would have done the same. I scratched my unshaved neck with my nails. Maybe not anybody.

Better something like this:

MY FREEDOM IS A PART OF ME.

That's bad too, I thought. Pathos is no good. I've had enough of those high-flown intellectual slogans: enough of those highly significant little placards, hung out for no obvious reason on the walls of consciousness, blotting out the glittering horizon. Prison is also a part of me. Prison, freedom, wealth, poverty – mendacious brand names, tricks, tasty worms on sharp little hooks. The two sides of a single coin.

I sighed, for a single sad moment regretting the lost illusions of youth, then suddenly realised what my inscription would be. I know, I know! I know what I'm going to write on the door of my cage! While I'm waiting for judgment to be passed on me! Before the one who always got away with everything finally gets his punishment! I have the words – the most crucial, simple, precise, short words that everyone understands, weighty and easy to remember! I have them!

I pulled out my pen and searched for a free space on the vertical metal surface. I sighed as I tried to formulate more precisely. But just then a bolt clanged and the door swung wide open.

'Name?'

'Rubanov.'

'Out you come!'

And so the stone kennel for the temporary holding of criminals on trial never did become the repository of my personal prisoner's truth. And afterwards I even forgot it myself.

Stepping through the doorway, I saw several figures dressed in the blue-grey of uniforms. And another two in civilian clothes.

Here, in the corridor of the Kuzmino court of the city of Moscow, the gang of embezzlers that had been under investigation for a year and a half had finally been brought together.

The minister proved to be a large man, far from old, broad-chested and extremely charming, even charismatic.

'How are you?' he asked me.

'Never better,' I responded.

The minister laughed in a deep, brassy voice.

'No talking!' an armed escort shouted.

'Calm down, sergeant,' the minister advised him gently.

'No talking!'

The sad pharmacist was standing beside him, sighing. He was in a far worse state than the minister and I. The poor unfortunate had been taken a lot later than us. A year after the investigation began. My former business partner had seriously been counting on maintaining his status as a witness. Or perhaps an accused, but one who remained at liberty, under written recognisance not to leave the city. He had given exhaustive testimony. Told General Zuev all the details. But the cautious general had still put the pharmacist away under lock and key anyway. Although he had been indulgent with him. The poor soul was still being kept in the comfortable Lefortovo prison. That was where they had just brought him from. But we – the minister and I – had long ago joined the ranks of the prisoners in the Sailor's Rest.

The last time I'd seen the pharmacist was two and a half years earlier, and he had deteriorated badly. Let his beard grow. Lost weight. His tweed jacket dangled pitifully on his shoulders. But when I looked into the quick, lilac eyes of my old acquaintance, I realised that the old man image and the stooped posture were no more than a mask. In prison many people are inclined to play the part of old men for purposes of self-protection.

Of course, somewhere here, in among the intent armed guards, the other members of the gang of embezzlers of state funds ought to have been waiting to learn their fate. The minister's brother. And also the major businessman closely associated with the brother. As well as the smaller businessman closely associated with the major one. And of course, my former boss, Mikhail. But all these people had somehow squirmed their way out of it. Some had left the country in good time. Others, like Mikhail, had been shielded. Now the three of us would answer for the actions of the entire organised criminal gang.

They attached each of us to his own personal militia officer. The procession lined up in pairs. The senior escort – a broad-faced, handsome man with blond hair and vicious-looking eyes – looked the tense criminal threesome over carefully and announced:

'I will now explain the procedure for proceeding into the hall of the court session! No talking on the way! Maintain strict order while moving! Obey all orders from the commander of the escort! In case of disobedience the escort will use gas and rubber truncheons – without warning! Is that clear to everyone? Let's go …'

The bolt rattled open. Another heavy metal door – how many of those had there already been in my epic adventures as a prisoner – swung aside.

The glare of TV floodlights stung my eyes. Screwing them up, I saw that the other half of the corridor was crammed with people. Several cameramen were holding TV cameras above the peoples' heads. The black pears of microphones protruded on long metal poles.

I didn't really know how I ought to behave. I didn't exactly feel like flashing a thirty-two-teeth smile, like the minister. I paraded past the noisy crowd with my eyes lowered and my lips sternly pressed together.

Deprived of laces, the tongues of my shoes were dangling out. It suddenly seemed to me that the cameramen were not aiming at the face of the minister – the obvious newsmaker for today's evening bulletins – but at my footwear, ready to slip off my feet at any moment.

The hall turned out to be small, with only three windows. To the right of the entrance there was a steel cage, painted white. Inside it was the proverbial bench. The old wood had been polished by many thousands of human posteriors.

The first man shoved into the cage was the minister, followed by the pharmacist. I found myself in the place furthest away from the judge. I wasn't first, or even second. That was probably a good thing.

The trial was to be held on camera. Apart from those taking part in the court session, no one was allowed into the hall. Reporters, relatives, friends and other curious citizens remained in the corridor. Already seated at the long table facing the cage were the lawyers, six of them. Three were defending the minister; two, the pharmacist. Ties, distinguished grey hair, an expression of professional calm on their faces.

I had only one defender. I hardly even knew him. He had been hired by my wife, despite my protests. Now he winked at me, but immediately turned away and started whispering with his colleagues. The door in the far corner of the hall squeaked as it opened. An ugly young woman with a bored face appeared. Thin hair gathered into a bun. A neat blouse. A large bureaucratic bum.

'Miss Kuzmino Court' cleared her throat delicately.

To a man, the lawyers settled themselves more comfortably in their chairs, pulled over their leather folders and adjusted their jackets.

'Please stand. The court is in session.'

38

The comic strip breaks off here.

Those thin, glossy books of bright-coloured pictures don't last for long. As a rule, once having leafed through them, people use them a stand for a hot saucepan of macaroni. Or they roll them up into a tube ands swat flies.

The final page is frayed and worn, it's useless now. If you look closely, you can make out that it is devoted to the trial of a gang of swindlers and embezzlers of state funds.

The minister was considered to be the head of the gang. The pharmacist was classed as his assistant. I was declared the actual doer of the deed. The examination of the CASE lasted a long time. For the whole of 1998 I left the prison almost every day.

Our Russian criminal trial procedure is monotonous. Unlike, for instance, the American one, familiar from many Hollywood court dramas. The basic difference between the two ways of administering justice lies in the fact that in Uncle Sam's kingdom the truth is established right there in the courtroom, in the course of an open hearing. But our native jurisprudence learns all that it needs in advance. In the prosecutors' offices. Where the suspects sit sideways on. A convenient, Byzantine system.

In the spacious room with light-brown walls no incendiary lawyers' addresses thundered out, no spine-chilling revelations were made by witnesses. Everybody already knew everything. The testimony had been given. The minutes had been bound and numbered. The evidence had been gathered. The quiet, drowsy, exceptionally cautious judge – a young man with round ears that looked as if they were made of plush – painstakingly read out one page of the CASE after another.

The endless sequence of witnesses – especially the women – amused the morose criminal threesome at first. And indeed, to leave a stinking prison cell and some to admire the well-dressed, sweet-smelling female inhabitants of freedom through the bars of your cage is one the few pleasures of a prisoner on trial.

On the other hand, leaving home in the dead of night, followed by five hours in the crowd at the assembly room, waiting to be loaded into the meat wagon, and another three hours driving round the city in a metal box, just in order to look at some fragrant female witness for ten minutes, is stupid.

This became especially clear in January 1999, in temperatures of thirty degrees below zero, when the metal walls of the van scorched my hands even through woollen gloves. Jammed in between twenty other frozen and furious poor souls like myself, shuddering, shivering and shaking, dreaming of a mouthful of hot water, pulling the collar of my sweater up over my nose, I realised that I was dreaming of hearing a sentence, any sentence. It was five years – so be it. Seven years – let it be seven. As long as these exhausting journeys finally came to an end.

But they drove me back and forth all of January. And February. And all of March.

Naturally, my former boss did not come to the trial. Nor did the seller of passports. In fact, not a single one of the most important witnesses for the prosecution turned up. I realised then why General Zuev had decided to transform the pharmacist into a suspect and put him behind bars. If the pharmacist had retained his status as a witness, he would also have avoided any involvement in the trial. Fled to Europe or somewhere even further away. Maybe I would have done the same.

The absence of the important eye-witnesses failed to unnerve anyone involved in the performance. During December, somewhere about the forty-fifth session, all of them – including the judge, the lay assessors, the accused, the lawyers, the secretary, the escort, the reporters and the relatives – felt extremely tired. All present were seized by a single burning desire: to get it over with as soon as possible.

The most colourful soldiers in the large brigade of witnesses proved to be my fake company chairmen. They were all boys, eighteen to nineteen years old. One actually brought his father, leading him by the hand. The faces of these chairmen and directors radiated the fresh fright of youth.

The company chairmen came from the lower levels of society. It was precisely a total lack of money that had driven these unfortunate young kids into the clutches of financial swindlers. In the court room, in the presence of serious people discussing serious matters, the juvenile, spotty-faced directors, in their dirty, crumpled jackets, felt intimidated. They completely avoided looking at the three villains in the cage.

I didn't know any of them. I had paid a middleman three hundred dollars for each blockhead. A company president's complete term in office had been ninety days, after which the life of the firm came to an end; a new chairman was hired for a new company.

It emerged unexpectedly that of the money paid by me, only twenty or thirty dollars at most actually reached the pockets of the chairman himself. The remainder was pocketed by the middleman. I laughed again at this, and the judge admonished me.

By the way, I did become a champion after all.

The total amount of time I did in the Central (twenty-four months, not counting another eight months in the Lefortovo fortress) placed me firmly in the middle of the field in our cell. There weren't very many who had been inside under investigation and 'under the court' for a whole two years, but there was Johnny (three and a half years), and Slava Glory-to-the-CPSU (five) and Givi Sukhumsky (two and a half), and a few more men with complex, multi-volume cases, facing grave charges involving many different episodes.

But in terms of the actual number of *trips* I made to the court – almost sixty – I outstripped everyone else by a long way. I was flaunting the leader's jersey. And, in addition, I was promoted to the status of a TV star. On five or six occasions I had the pleasure of seeing my own pale, sharp-nosed face on the television screen. Mostly in the evening news on Channel Two or NTV. Instead of fresh footage they always showed the same thing: the courtroom corridor. The cameramen had only been able to catch the criminal trio, accompanied by the escort in their taut camouflage suits and masks, as they made their hasty passage from the door of the guard room to the entrance of the courtroom. I was always walking at the back, after the minister with his broad smile and the pharmacist, and I didn't raise my eyes even once. Walking into a court with your hands shackled and camera lenses trained on you, squinting at the flashlights, is a rather dubious pleasure.

Just look at me, a real Charles Manson they've made me! I thought in annoyance. Next thing, people will start thinking I really am a dangerous criminal …

The reporters' remarks accompanying the visuals were neutral in tone. The commentators and experts were united in the opinion that at the edge of the patchwork blanket of the empire, in a small and unstable mountain republic, a minister carries too much political weight. It was far from easy to put him away in jail.

My humble personage was of no interest to the journalists. But nonetheless I was able in someone else's reflected glory. On discovering that I had become the hero of the criminal chronicles, my one hundred and thirty-five cell-mates were inspired with serious awe for me. When I came back from my latest court session, pulled off my stinking sweaters and walked towards the washbasin, the mass of humanity parted before me as it once had before Slava Glory-to-the-CPSU.

Despite my apprehensions, without the authoritative Slava, the life of the cell did not come to a halt. Of course, I myself now hardly took any part in it. On days that were free from exhausting travelling, I slept like a log.

My place on the Road was taken by Fedot.

The minister – the head of the criminal group – maintained a cheerful manner at the trial. He did not conceal his confidence that he would be acquitted. At the decisive moment the high official's defence presented a large number of new documents for consideration by the court and demanded that a whole group of new witnesses be summoned. The veterans of the bar claimed that even if the stolen money had been transferred to foreign bank accounts, it had subsequently been returned to the state in the form of goods of one kind or another: medicines, clothing, food products, etc., which said medicines and food products had disappeared from the warehouses and storehouses through no fault whatever of the minister. Here are the bills of materials with seals and signatures – by your leave, Your Honour …

This was a good move. The dozy judge became concerned. And he hinted that in connection with the newly revealed circumstances he would refer the CASE for further investigation.

The accused were downcast. They were facing catastrophe. Further investigation! Several more months of interrogations and expert analysis, a new 'two hundred and one' – and a second trial, everything all over again from the very beginning, with different court personnel! More cells, meat wagons, 'assemblers' and 'guard rooms'! Another year, perhaps even eighteen months, of drudgery!

The minister became thoughtful. In the event the new documents were not added to the CASE – and in March the trial began moving towards its final conclusion.

Alexander Kaplan, the lawyer hired by my wife, acted precisely and radically. The target he chose was not the twenty-eight-year-old judge, but the state counsel for the prosecution. My lawyer yawned openly during the proceedings. But when each session came to an end and the participants in the trial all ran off for a smoke, my defender moved into action. He took the prosecutor by the elbow, led him off to one side and began admonishing him.

Nothing brings grown men so close together as the joint consumption of poisons. At the beginning of spring the prosecutor, led off to one side yet again, admitted to the lawyer that, yes indeed, the lad really had nothing to do with the whole business, that was as clear as day, there was no room for argument.

Undoubtedly, the prosecutor was also being cunning. He regarded taking a smoke with the lawyers of the minister or the lawyers of the pharmacist as a risky business. He only smoked with the defender of the most harmless member of the gang on trial.

The fact that I was the most harmless and I would get less time than the others had become clear more or less automatically. The judge showed minimal interest in me. The two lay assessors knitted their brows in sympathy when they turned towards me. The minister winked cheerfully at me. The closer the conclusion came, the faster my heart beat. What if they let me go?

That was when I sent a letter out into the free world, to my wife. I tried to prepare her psychologically for further ordeals. Expect five years, I wrote to her. I've done almost three – there's not long left. I'll be sentenced and go to a camp. Things are better there, there's air, trees. I'll come back to life, grow strong. And I'll come back. I'll definitely come back. From wherever I am – from prison, from camp, from the 'zone', from the very jaws of the devil – but I will come back to you, my beloved.

Probably I needed this note more than my wife did. Undoubtedly she at least had long ago prepared herself for the worst. Such is the defensive reaction of the human psyche.

In April the prosecutor addressed the court. For the minister he demanded six years, and for the pharmacist – five. He suggested I should be released. In the state counsel's opinion, I had nothing at all to do with the theft of money from the state budget. This turn of events meant that I would, certainly, be convicted – but only for non-payment of taxes. I had, after all, set up the fly-by-night firms and put through illegal transactions. I still had to answer for my crimes.

And the just punishment followed.

During the final days of April, standing with my fingers squeezed against the metal rods, I heard my sentence. Three years of imprisonment. The judge immediately applied some minor amnesty and released me from custody there and then, in the courtroom.

In all, I was inside for two years, eight months and thirteen days. Including two hundred and forty days in the Lefortovo pre-trial prison and another two years in the Sailor's Rest isolation prison. I was released on 28 April 1999.

39

The bars – powerful and heavy, the thick rods set close together, with braces of steel strip between them. A strong, slightly cluttered structure. Not as massive as in the Lefortovo fortress, and not as crude as in the Sailor's Rest prison – but nonetheless a genuine set of bars. An arrangement that prevents you from getting in. Or getting out. Which is basically the same thing.

I have to fabricate them. First take the measurements of the window aperture. Then protect my eyes with a special transparent mask and cut the metal. Put two of the parts on the welding table. Carefully measure them with a tape measure. Change my mask for a different one, with dark glass. Weld them solidly together. Use a hammer to beat the clinker off the fresh welds. Use an electric hacksaw to remove the barbs sticking out here and there. Finally, call over my assistants – Ahmed, Said and Kerim – to help me set the article upright, lean it against the wall of the building and paint it.

While the paint is drying, I waste no time, but grab the aluminium ladder and the Makita percussion drill, wind several coils of power cable on to my shoulder and clamber up to the window.

The order is for twenty-four sets of bars for twenty-four windows on the ground floor of some minor building in some minor factory that produces complex parts required for use in such a narrow sector of industry that I would be prepared to wager my own head that there are times when the manufacturers themselves doubt that the sector even exists.

But anyway, there's the new red-brick building. The factory has started working. Perhaps not in its own sector. However, the men here don't wander about aimlessly around the grounds in idle, drunken groups, they run across them briskly, shout at each other (a good sign) and demonstrate how busy they are in all sorts of other ways too.

Naturally, I don't actually work at the factory. It's all much more serious than that. I am a representative of a private construction company that has been given a contract for metalwork. I have nothing to do with the factory. My job is bars. I set up the ladder, clamber up, make myself comfortable (don't work without support!) and make four holes in the side walls of the window aperture with the drill. We'll drive the support hooks into them with a sledge hammer and then attach the entire structure.

The drill bit goes deep into the mass of brickwork, about forty centimetres. It has to. Otherwise some dark night, in the quiet hour before the dawn, evildoers will drive up in a truck, throw in a hook on a cable and tear my bars out bodily. Or they'll choose a less noisy method and force them out of the wall with crowbars. They'll gain entry to the premises and commit the theft of valuable items. I know all about the skills of forced entry. In the common cell at the Sailor's Rest prison, under the influence of bracing chifir and a tasty cigarette, any prisoner is willing to share his original experience as a thief.

The work is simple and heavy. The pay for it is middling. A temperature of thirty degrees heightens the intensity of my sensations. While I wield the welding rod, I throw on a thick tarpaulin jacket for protection against splashes of metal, and immediately throw off this armour, remaining naked to the waist, if I have to climb up to the window. The sweat streams off me, brick dust settles on my wet body.

My eyes hurt. When you work with an arc-welder, you can't avoid catching one or two bright flashes during a shift. I have to use special eye drops.

My three assistants – Said, Ahmed and Kerim – grab the completed set of bars and lift it up along two ladders. I don't have three assistants because I'm an important specialist, it's simply that lifting the bars requires the strength of four men. At the very least.

If Said, Ahmed and Kerim knew how to weld metal, the work would go much faster. But they are unskilled labourers and, what's more, they're gastarbeiters. The boss pays them a pittance. As a welder and foreman, I have to be paid serious money. Every month I get four hundred and fifty dollars in cash from the boss.

In our company there is no standard working day, but at five o'clock in the evening I cease all my manipulations, lock up the equipment and go home. Of course, I could carry on for all the hours of daylight, as late as ten o'clock, do two days' worth of work. But then the next day my hands would be trembling and I wouldn't complete even half of the jobs planned. No one needs 'labour heroism' – that old chestnut from the Land of Soviets – any more. And in any case, the boss doesn't give me the daily allowance of milk that the law specifies for harmful work. That makes me angry.

And apart from that, if I'm injured – for instance, if a speck of molten metal damages my eye – no one will pay me while I'm off sick. No contributions are paid into any pension fund either. I receive my salary in 'black cash' – the kind that I know so much about.

If an electric welder in my country was officially registered in his job and all the taxes and contributions to state funds were paid, then the entire rapidly developing construction sector would simply collapse. It would be totally bankrupted. The sector has always been, and always will be based on black cash, disenfranchised gastarbeiters and unfortunates like me.

The conclusion to the working day is usually fast and furious. The four ragamuffins – Said, Ahmed, Kerim and the former banker who has joined forces with them – start hurrying and get nervous. Eventually, to the sound of stentorian swearing and heartrending howls of 'Ally-oop!', 'Harder!', 'One-two, heave!' the final set of bars is fitted into the window aperture, leaving behind traces of wet paint on our hands. Said thrusts a crowbar through it, leans down on the steel shaft with his full weight and the bars lift a little. Ahmed slips some pieces of wood underneath them and Kerim runs back ten metres to asses the horizontal and the vertical alignment by eye. Then, armed with a sledgehammer, I climb up the ladder for the hundredth time. I hammer four hefty metal pins into the holes. I grab the welding unit that Ahmed helpfully hands up to me. I weld the pins to the body of the article. I hammer out the wooden wedges. I paint the points of attachment. It's done. The daily norm has been fulfilled. We can have some tea and get changed.

The factory management has allocated us construction workers a separate basement room, which is where we keep our own things and our tools. There is even a shower cabinet and, in addition, a table, a bench and an electric socket. Everything we need for working and for relaxing afterwards

Wiping the sweat and dust off their faces, the three comrades sit down at the wooden table and whisper for a long time in their native language. There is the sound of liquid gurgling. Glass clinking.

'Hey!' Kerim calls. 'Take a drink with us, chief? Vodka?'

The basement is as dark as the punishment cell in the Sailor's Rest. And just as damp – despite the heat of August. And there's the dirty walls are impregnated with almost the same smell. And the light is similar – yellow and dim.

Every time I go down into the basement I experience a slight frisson of deja vu.

'I don't use alcohol, nicotine or caffeine,' I say.

'Hey! Please yourself.'

I laugh and climb into a pair of linen trousers.

The smart item of clothing is a left-over from my former life. Bought for huge money; before prison, in the year ninety-five of the previous century, i.e., the trousers are seven years old already! A good age! Designer pants last well, the material hasn't thinned, they're not torn. They're still helping to protecting my body against humidity and high temperatures.

'What the hell are you doing drinking alcohol?' I ask severely, putting on an expression of profound disgust. 'You're Muslims!'

'Hey! Allah's far away,' Kerim remarks philosophically. 'Almost as far away as my home …'

'So at home you'd smoke hash, right?'

The Asiatics all laugh together. The poison splashes again.

'Hey!' Kerim's face turns dream and even more swarthy. 'It doesn't say anything about that in the Koran.'

'By the way, I've read the Koran,' I observe. 'I remember it has the following lines in it: "There is not one of you without a place appointed to him". Sura thirty-seven, verse one hundred and sixty-four.'

'Hey!' Kerim raises his black eyebrows in surprise.

Like all Asiatics, he gets drunk quickly and becomes aggressive.

'What's this, chief, are you trying to put me in my place?'

The Tajik Kerim has also done time in prison. Almost six months. This son of the mountains was arrested on suspicion of storing narcotics. Then released. For lack of evidence. He did the time in the same place as I did, the Sailor's Rest. And even at the same time as me. We might even have met somewhere deep in the bowels of the capital city's overpopulated pre-trial isolation prison. Seen each other at the 'gatherer', during a trip to court. Or in the 'tram' – hurrying to an interrogation with the investigator. The native son of Dushanbe had done his time right above my head, in cell number one-three-nine. Two storeys up.

Now he thinks I live by the thieves' rules.

'Kerim, do you know what is the most important condition for the brain to function properly?'

'Hey! How should I know?'

'A straight spine!'

All three of the children of the mountains involuntarily straighten their backs. It looks very funny.

'Kerim,' I say with a smile, 'I've no need to put you in your place. When you, Kerim, consume poison, you define yourself. You, Kerim, put yourself your own place. Got that, have you?' I pronounce the phrase 'got that' the prison dialect way, like a single word.

The Tajik is puny and skinny, a head shorter than me. Physically weak. He has no future as a gastarbeiter. From his eyes I can tell that he is insulted, but obliged to swallow the comments that offend his vanity. But even so, his natural Asiatic optimism wins out and the quick-eyed southerner smiles mischievously, winks at me and says in a quiet voice:

'Hey! By the way, I've got hashish. I could warm some up. What do you say, chief?'

'Stuff your hashish up your ass,' I reply in a cultured manner. 'Poison yourself there, brother. I've already left that prison behind …'

'Hey!' the Tajik continues ingratiatingly. 'I guarantee you won't find resin like it anywhere. It's Afghani – for real. They say its from Osama's people .. Take two drags and you're away …'

Kerim isn't a gastarbeiter at all, I realise, combing my hair, wet from the shower. He's a drug dealer. Construction site work is his cover, it's only temporary. As soon as he builds up his client base and starts earning at least fifty dollars a month from his risky business, he'll forget all about the hard life of the subcontractor. Rent a separate flat. Start sending his family a monthly allowance. Through the 'Anelik' interbank money transfer system. Meanwhile, he walks round in torn trousers and an absolutely ridiculous short jacket of synthetic material, what used to be known in the Land of Soviets as a 'bologna'. Makes out that he's poor. In actual fact, Kerim has a brilliant future ahead of him. His hashish is superb. The Tajik even treats the director of our firm to his valuable narcotic. The director is his most important potential customer. Hash is extremely popular in Moscow.

'I don't want anything to do with that Osama of yours,' I reply. And then, raising my voice, I address all three of them: 'It's time I was off. Drink your vodka, you Asiatics. It will make you feel good.'

GORGE YOURSELF ON POISON, ASIATICS!

It's easier for you – you've lived in Asia all your lives. But I'm trying to live in Europe.

'Drink alcohol,' I say. 'Smoke dope. That's why it's called "dope", after all. You smoke it, and there's one more dope in the world … And in Russia they call it "plan" too. Smoke it, and you just sit there, making plans. Smoke dope. Put money in Osama's pockets. Chase it with nicotine. It's your life. But I'm going home. Tomorrow at eight, I want everyone on-site. A clear head is compulsory. Do I make myself clear?'

'Hey!' replies Kerim, rolling his brown eyes cunningly. 'Good health to you, chief. See you tomorrow!'

I shake the narrow hands of the tipsy black-haired workers, walk out of the basement – the hot air strikes me in the face – get into the car and drive away.

As it happens, I shan't be here tomorrow. The three comrades have seen me for the last time. I have achieved my goal. I'm quitting. And I'm not going to weld any more steel frameworks. I've done enough of that. No more. I've clambered out of the pit. Worked off my debt. I'm a free man now. My prisons have all pegged out, every last one. I have conquered them.

I looked through the comic strip from start to finish. I studied the pictures and the words carefully. I entirely agree with the idea of the work. Freedom is relative. So is prison. Prison can be interesting, happy, useful: freedom sometimes turns into drudgery, problems, stress, family quarrels, debts. There are fools like that – they live their freedom as if they were in a prison cell.

Me, I'm trying not to be one of them any more.

They built a road right round my city. It's actually called the 'Ring Road'. At one time it was famous as a terribly dangerous route: narrow, poorly lit, with lots of holes in the asphalt. While I was doing time in two prisons, they re-built it, widened it, put up signposts, installed modern streetlamps and generally gave the entire transport facility a European look.

The summer is very hot, like the one when they came for me. I'm driving through the city with all the car windows open, dressed in linen trousers and a tee-shirt. With leather sandals dangling on my feet.

Unlike me, a live human being, the car is unable to tolerate the high temperature. Strictly speaking, this vehicle is not entirely unsuitable for travelling in hot weather. Its engine has a tendency to overheat, like a recidivist with a tendency to escape. To avoid a break-down, I turn on the heater – it extracts excess heat from the cooling system and pumps hot air into the car. The superheated jet strikes me on the feet, scorching my bare toes. The windscreen acts like a lens, refracting the sun's rays and gently roasting the upper half of my body.

The only reason I am not streaming with stinking sweat is that I avoid drinking while I travel. But those of my fellow-drivers who carry bottles of drinking water with them are constantly mopping salty liquid off their foreheads, creating the preconditions for an accident to happen.

Every year during the very hottest weeks of summer, especially after heavy rain, when the hot asphalt is steaming, when you can take a handful of air and squeeze it out like a towel from the bathhouse, I remember the common cell in the Sailor's Rest. It helps me understand where prison really is, and where freedom lies.

On days like this the sweltering heat under the vaults of the Common Hut is unbearable. The men squat motionless on the floor, with their heads lowered. The lowest layer of air, right down at the bottom, is not so empty and hot. On the upper bunks it's quite impossible to breathe.

Cigarettes won't burn. Any attempt to move a hand or a foot induces copious sweating. No one eats their rations or their skilly. Experienced prisoners, old-timers, advise their fellows to keep their strength up by mixing sugar with a small amount of water and swallowing this solution. The moisture escapes through the pores of the body, but the useful glucose remains inside ...

I am distracted from my painful reminiscences by a traffic inspector's whistle. I stop the car and get out.

'Good health to you, comrade senior lieutenant!'

It really is impossible not to be charmed by these fat-bellied guys with their advanced years and low ranks.

'What are you smiling at?' the guardian of order enquires suspiciously.

'I'm just having a good day!'

The traffic cop peers at a spot above the bridge of my nose. But I know the distinctive inscription disappeared a long time ago. The lieutenant relaxes. Then suddenly he leans towards me, drawing the air into his tanned nostrils, and raises his bleached eyebrows.

'Been drinking?'

I prop one elbow against the door of the car in a dignified manner.

'I don't use alcohol, nicotine or caffeine!'

'Then what's that smell?'

'Acetone,' I have to explain. 'I'm a welder. Window bars, fences, railings, doors, gates … Weld it and paint it! Today I've been painting all day long. And I diluted the paint with acetone … Got to dilute it if you want to improve your pay…'

The elderly lieutenant nodded understandingly.

'True enough,' he remarked. 'So where are your documents?'

'Here you are! Licence. Log book and service record. Insurance. The car's in perfect working order …'

Driving with a full set of documents gives me genuine satisfaction. For five years I didn't have a driving licence. I've only got one now, after serving my time inside; after suddenly realising that I don't wish to pay the going rate any more. After doing the sums once, out of sheer curiosity (not on a calculator, like a business man, but on my fingers, like an ordinary human being) I discovered that in five years, since I was caught on average once a week, I had paid about seven thousand dollars at the going rate. This seemed such a hefty figure to me that I went off to the appropriate institution, filled out the papers, paid a few kopecks at the savings bank and the state generously issued me a little permit.

I had to stand in queues for hours to reach the little official windows. I put up with it. I read *Helter-Skelter* with an impassive air. In all I spent three days queuing – but now I'll save seven thousand dollars in five years!

Driving past a figure with a baton without experiencing any panic or nervous stress, without feverishly calculating in your head whether you have enough cash to pay the baksheesh – that's a really great feeling.

After fingering the small pieces of laminated cardboard, the guardian of order hands them back to me, takes another close look at my face (split by a smile from ear to ear) and can't help chuckling.

'So you don't drink?'

'I gave it up.'

'Well, well!' the guardian is astonished. 'How long were you drinking?'

'Three years.'

'That's no time! How'd you give up?'

'I can tell you.'

'Go ahead. Only hang on just a second ...'

The senior lieutenant proves to be a great master of his trade. He performs a 360° revolution and in a split second picks out with his truncheon the most suspicious car in the dense stream of traffic – dirty, rusty and battered, but with dark windows and menacing stickers on its sides. There is the sound of a whistle, and yet another vehicle has been halted for checking. Quickly and decisively, without a single superfluous movement.

'What's the problem, commander?' the driver, clearly nervous, enquires plaintively through the half-opened window. He is a large-nosed native son of the empire's high mountain territories.

'Stay there and wait!' the guard orders him casually, then turns to me and mutters. 'Commander ... They have commanders in the army! But I'm standing at the crossroads ... Come on, tell me quickly how you gave up drinking.'

'I went to the chemist's,' I tell him briefly. 'I bought a booklet: *How to Conquer Alcohol*. It's all in there.'

'I could do that myself,' the traffic cop says irritably. 'All right, on your way. Some method that is ...'

After leaving the lieutenant, I smile even more broadly.

I had to deceive the red-faced master of the striped stick slightly after all. Not seriously. Only over a petty detail, but I still deceived him. My car's not in absolutely perfect working order: the horn doesn't work.

It broke one day. Some fine wire that I know nothing about became detached. A connection parted, a terminal burned out, or something of the sort. And I didn't bother to get it fixed. I left it as it was. I don't honk any more. Not at all. Never.

'By the way, you've slipped back into deception again,' I tell myself, 'and you're feeling good about it again! It's about time to grow out of this childish passion, like masturbation! The enlightened man does not deceive anyone. Especially not himself. And he doesn't guzzle poisons. Don't lie, don't drink vodka – what's so hard about that?'

I step on the pedal and speed up, but then some flashy yuppie lights me up from behind with the unbearably bright beam of his headlights.

Hinting that I'm in his way. I have to turn the wheel and politely move over. A gigantic coal-black automobile goes hurtling past.

Through the open window I can see person sitting inside the powerful jeep, securely protected by the dark windows, alarms, cunning permits and special passes, as well as the cash in the pockets of his expensive threads. He is young, a mere youth, with narrow shoulders and well styled hair. A clone of myself in the year ninety-six of the previous century.

Sitting there in the leather saddle of the off-road vehicle, casually clutching the steering wheel like the bridle of a thoroughbred mare, flaunting his wealth with a comfortable air of extreme preoccupation, is none other than nouveau-riche Andriukha. The boy banker from my distant past. I smile condescendingly.

I know the boy is in a hurry to get to the office. Moscow time is six fifteen p.m. The end of the working day. Heavy traffic. The law-abiding citizens are all going back home. But the youthful businessman is still doing battle. After a series of business meetings he is rushing back to the office. Everybody is hurrying home, but he's moving against the flow. He's going *to work*.

He himself will personally lock up his office. Leave after everyone else, the very last. He will grab a bunch of keys and start. Acting as his own turnkey. He will close the safe, and the office, and the second office, and the first outer door, and the second door, and the intermediate barrier. And he won't forget about the metal shutters on the windows, or about the alarm system. He'll start jangling the keys for ages, sorting through the bunches with his fingers and swearing. He's in a hurry. He has a problem: an absolute shortage of time. But soon – you can tell from just looking at him, he'll make the break-though to a different status. Hire himself a driver. And a guard too. The driver will drive him around, and the guard will do night duty in the office and remember which key to stick in which lock.

But even when he's sure that everything is closed, that the bars are strong and the safes hermetically sealed, Andriukha won't be able to get to get a calm night's sleep. In the evening his wife will make a scene about his not paying enough attention to the family. That will cause stress, and

Andriukha will drink heavily. And he will sink into sleep, in a hysterical state, complaining to himself that being in his family feels like being in prison, and being at work feels the same.

Where is my freedom? How did I lose it, and when? Andriukha will fall asleep, perplexed and drunk, still tormenting himself with these questions.

But at six o'clock in the morning his special alarm clock – a pager – will start to squeak. Words will appear on the emerald-green display: 'Money never sleeps'. This is Andriukha's favourite phrase. A quote from the Hollywood film *Wall Street*. Nouveau-riche Andriukha will wake up, gloomy and heavy-headed, wash his face, take a strong dose of caffeine (two cups, one after another, freshly ground, brewed with mineral water, with added salt water and a tablet of aspirin). This may not really invigorate Andriukha and improve his muscle tone, but it will at least give him the nervous edge he needs. The he will hurry off to make money.

Gunning his engine appallingly, nouveau-riche Andriukha goes flying past without even looking in my direction. And in principle, that's exactly how it should be: after all, he's a man from the past.

As it happens, I am also not on my way home, but to the office. My present boss is waiting for me there. He has no family and he likes to stay on late at work.

The boss's office is finished in green plastic panels more or less the same as in the reception box at the Lefortovo pre-trial isolation prison. I experience a vague frisson of déjà vu.

The boss's subcutaneous layer inspires a degree of respect. The lard has built up thickly on his shoulders, his sides, his backside and his thighs – absolutely everywhere, in fact. The fingers have turned into plump sausages. The cheeks are comparable in shape and size to table-tennis rackets. The gigantic armchair groans pitifully under the weight of the huge body.

Standing on the right of the armchair, at arm's length, is the safe – a capacious, dark-blue box with nickel-plated handles. Located on the left, also close at hand, is the fridge. Fatty turns according to his need, either to the right, for money, or to the left, for food.

I approach without speaking, take some money out of my pocket and put in on the desk in front of the boss.

'What's this?' he asks suspiciously.

'There's five hundred dollars there. We're even.'

Fatty has the crimson, sickly face of an old client of the alcohol prison. He gives me suspicious looking-over.

'That can't be right!'

'Ten months,' I declare, savouring the words, 'at three hundred and fifty dollars a month – that makes three thousand five hundred. That's another five hundred. A total of four thousand. We're even, Vadim! Even!'

Fatty picks the green notes up off the desk, lovingly folds them in half and sticks them in his breast pocket.

'Where did you get the money from?' he enquires suspiciously. 'I suppose you stole paint?'

I pause before answering his question with a question.

'Do you keep accounts?'

'Of course.'

'And how are they? Do the debit and credit columns match up?'

'Yes, I think so?'

'In that case, Vadim, no one has stolen anything from you.'

'That's logical … So you're debt's paid off, then?'

'Precisely.'

'All four thousand?'

'Aha.'

I sigh.

'What's wrong?' my former cell-mate asks kindly.

'There was a time when I earned that much money in a single day.'

Fatty gestures feebly with his hand.

'That's all in the past …'

I nod submissively; there's no point in arguing; seven years have gone by since the time when I used to earn four thousand dollars in a day. And all that big, fast money debauched me. Which is precisely what my companion was hinting at.

'By the way,' he went on in a low voice, 'close the door will you, please.'

I obediently carry out his request. Today I have paid off my debt in full and intend to hand in my notice and get the hell out of Fatty's firm. He can't order me to do anything any more, only ask.

Turning towards the fridge, he extracts a bottle of poison from it, then reaches into the safe and lays some papers down in front of me.

'Sign right here,' the boss says even more quietly. 'Only not with your own name.'

Without any superfluous comment, I take the pen he holds out to me and inscribe a fussy monogram on the receipt for a purchase order.

'You're a master,' says Fatty.

I frown and say:

'Even so all your documents have been signed by the same hand. It's obvious. Even to the naked eye.'

'And who's going to look into my documents with an eye that isn't naked?' Vadim pushes across another receipt. 'Now scribble something on this one too. In different handwriting.'

'It won't work,' I object authoritatively. 'You can't change your handwriting. I practiced for almost three years. And I got nowhere.'

'There, you see,' Fatty laughs condescendingly. Back then, in the cell, there was no way the two of us could convince you that your exercises were useless …'

'Not all of them,' I reply, and move closer to Fatty's desk. He is sitting right in front of me, facing me.

Looking at the knot in the construction magnate's tie, I point at the papers lying on the desk.

'This … is an application for credit … to the local branch of the Savings Bank,' I read. 'Dated yesterday. This … is a letter … from an officer of the court. This …'

'That's enough, I get the idea,' Fatty interrupts. 'So you developed your peripheral vision, did you?'

'I practiced for seven months, an hour and a half every day. I read lots of interesting papers on the prosecutor's desk.'

'I believe it.' Fatty anxiously hides the documents in a folder. 'So you're handing in your notice, then?'

'Yes.'

'Where will you go now?'

'I don't know. I've got two hands, two feet, a head – I'll get by.'

'All right. How about a shot, fifty grams?'

'I don't use alcohol, caffeine or nicotine.'

'Well, I'll have a drink … remember Frol?'

'Of course.'

'He died.'

'How do you know?'

Fatty looks into the fridge again – but I can see that there's nothing but salami in it. Three or four kinds. Semi-smoked. After glancing inside, the magnate gives a wry grin and closes the white door of his comestibles depository.

'The day before yesterday,' he informs me, 'I got drunk. I had fit of depression. Why don't I call him, I thought – so I did, and I found out. His mother told me … I'll miss him …'

'Aha.'

The boss pauses for a moment.

'Stay and work for me.'

'That's out of the question.'

'Not as a welder,' Fatty says hastily. 'Better than that. You'll come in three times a week for two or three hours and write fake invoices. The way you know how …'

'I've done enough of that. I'd better write a novel instead. I've been dreaming about it ever since I was a kid.'

'You know best.'

My one-time cell-mate and present employer tips a dose of the Moldavian cognac Kvint into himself and follows it with a sniff at his Trodat stamping pad.

'Have a bite of salami,' I suggest.

'I can't bear the sight of it …'

'I sympathise …'

Fatty says nothing for about a minute.

'I know,' he says, speaking slowly, 'that you've got a grudge against me.'

'For what?'

'For forcing you to work off the debt.'

'You didn't force me,' I protest politely. 'If you recall, I was the one who suggested the arrangement.'

'All the same, you've got a grudge!' the magnate repeats stubbornly. 'Well, so be it. If you want, you can throw a stone at me.'

'Never,' I say sincerely.

Fatty sniffs.

'Why did you come to me at all, eh? You're clever, you have experience. You could have got a job in some bank, the pay there's five times as much and it's clean work. You could have settled up with me in three months …'

'No, I won't go into a bank. A certain friend of mine, a lawyer by profession, a criminal lawyer, once took a job in a bank too. For a big salary.'

'And?'

'He's still doing time. The bank no longer exists, but they gave the lawyer four years. Low security.'

'Then your lawyer's a fool.'

'He's no more stupid than I am.'

'And do you think you're clever?'

'In principle, yes.'

'You're the same kind of fool as the rest of us. Only very lucky. And blessed.'

The boss drinks every day. After a hundred and fifty grams of poison he gets sentimental.

'Why's that?' I ask in surprise.

'You're young.'

'Only I have a criminal record.'

'I have a record too.'

'But you're rich.'

'Only I did five years, and you did less than three …'

'But now you're a big-shot company director, and I'm a pauper.'

'Only you're thirty, and I'm fifty.'

'I'm thirty-three.'

'But not fifty-one …'

'Only you saved you're money! But I didn't.'

'You fool! You saved your family!' Fatty pours another drink. 'Your wife waited, but mine ran off. After selling four of my houses. Believe me, son, a wife who waited for you is worth all the money in the whole wide world. Anyway, go, leave the job. As a mater of fact, I would have fired you anyway.'

'What for?'

'You're a bad worker. Too slow.'

I laugh. I realise Fatty's trying to be cunning. My window bars are extremely good. They're welded securely, with thin welds. Primed properly. Painted carefully. Installed solidly. I derive a sensuous satisfaction from working with my hands. I like the very act of producing a material object – when a heap of parts, lumps of iron, scraps and strips of blue-grey metal is transformed into a complicated item that is socially useful.

'Right, Vadim. Time I was going. My wife's waiting.'

'She's waiting?' Fatty echoes drunkenly. 'Then you really are lucky, brother …'

I left him alone with the prison of his subcutaneous layer and walked out.

Getting out of prison's easy. You sit there and count the days. The months. The years. One day they let you out. It's harder to climb out of a deep pit. But I managed it.

And now – home.

When I'm driving, I like to chat on my mobile phone. The main conversation partners are my wife and son.

In 1995 the boy banker acquired a mobile phone for five thousand dollars. He walked down the street, pressing the black device to his ear, and people turned to look at him. Now, eight years later, every schoolboy has a magic handset.

But there is no good without evil. A conversation on a mobile phone is terrifying. People can't see each other, they can't sense the currents of electricity given off by the body and the mind, they can't detect the odours of agitation, alarm, excitement or dislike. Instantaneous long-distance communication has destroyed an entire thousand-year-old culture of human contact. Nowadays people talking on the phone communicate with each other through the expressive modulation of the voice, the intonation, the volume; but at the same time the mental effort makes their features flabby, their eyes turn glassy and stare into empty space, their mouths become shapeless – in other words, the beauty, the supreme sensitivity and the special magic of conversation are lost. Nowadays conversations are possible in which one person whispers sensuously, while the other strains to hear and shouts, with the handset pressed against his ear, in the middle of some workshop or foundation pit:

'Eh? What? Yes, I love you too! What the fuck are you putting it here for? Put it there, in the stack! No, I wasn't talking to you. Of course I love you! Eh! Said! Kerim! Ahmed! In the stack, fuck you, in the stack!'

Sometimes the most amazing people get in touch. For instance, an old friend of mine has just called, Slava Glory-to-the-CPSU. He's back in the Sailor's Rest again. For aggravated assault and the use of a firearm.

The mobile phone revolution has even affected the inmates of prison. In the new millennium every worthy lad on the inside has a small phone in his pocket.

'Hi, brother,' Slava said in a very hollow voice. 'How are you doing?'

'Couldn't possibly be better,' I say.

My voice sounds cheerful and confident. Anyone on the outside, any free man is obliged to make life-affirming sounds. After all, he's out enjoying life, fresh air, the smell of women's perfume, the taste of roasted meat. He's flying high, on a roll. He's enjoying himself.

From the prisoner's point of view, that's the way life is outside the walls of the pre-trial isolation prison: an exuberant carnival, a colourful panoply of sensual delights – women, food, filter cigarettes, tea with sugar.

'How are you getting on there,' Slava asks, 'on the outside?'

'The same as usual. And how are things in prison?'

'The same as ever.'

'May God be your support, brother!'

The radio waves transmit a bitter sigh through space.

'Leave it out. There is no God, brother! There is no God! If there was, how could he allow something like this to be done to someone who believed in him, eh?'

'Don't be sad,' I reassured my friend. 'They'll get you out.'

'I'll get myself out. Good luck.'

'I don't believe in luck …'

'Why so late?' Irma asks when I enter the flat.

This is my wife's standard opening.

'I was working,' I report laconically. 'I have the documents to prove it.'

'Show me.'

I take out two bank notes. Straighten one out and hand it to my wife. My eyes take an instantaneous snapshot of the archetypal picture: a slim woman's hand with long manicured nails firmly clutching a rainbow-coloured piece of paper.

My wife smiles and then points with her eyes to the second banknote that is still held in my fingers.

'And who's that for?'

'That's for a rainy day. I'm going to build up my subcutaneous layer.'

'You're trying to trick me.' This woman doesn't trust me. 'You'll drink it away.'

'I don't use alcohol, caffeine or nicotine,' I declare quietly.

My spouse smiles again.

Just recently she has put on quite a lot of weight. Her earnings overtook mine a long time ago. She works for four hundred dollars a month as a make-up artist in one of the capital's TV studios and in addition she earns twice as much again from her private clients. Ladies who wish to improve their hairstyle, dye their hair and drink a cup of coffee while they listen to a lecture on maintaining a healthy scalp come to her home every day and leave hundreds and thousands of roubles in her purse. My wife pays house visits to the very richest ladies, in her own car. There were times she supported herself and me and our son. She dressed like a film star, but paid for her glossy façade by clipping away with scissors ten hours a day.

'All right,' I say after a moment's thought. 'Take this too.' And I hand over the second banknote.

Extremely pleased, Irma puts both pieces of paper away in her purse with a precise movement.

She bore me a son, she waited for me to come back from prison – why shouldn't I now give her all the money there is in my pockets?

I myself don't need money. That is, I do, but not a lot. Or rather, I do need it a lot, but not so badly as to give myself a nervous breakdown over it.

For me, the present me, the best way to spend money is to buy books. Literature is the only commodity in the world that is truly worthy of my money. And anybody else's money.

There can be no doubt that mankind only invented these rustling pieces of paper with watermarks in order to pay for the writing of books, the creation of ever more new works of art. As soon as money stops flowing into the pockets of writers and poets, actors and artists, musicians and sculptors, the world will immediately collapse, civilisation will start to degenerate.

There was a time when I made a lot of money, but spent it primarily on buying trousers, alcoholic drinks and metal boxes for driving along asphalted roads. In three years in the banking business I never read a single page of prose.

They say that businessmen have no time. They're too busy to read. That's nonsense. Every man is obliged to read books, just as a prisoner in the Common Hut is oblige to donate a box of matches to the Road – otherwise he will no longer be a worthy prisoner – and the man will no longer be a worthy man.

I stride round the flat, the very image of a worthy prisoner – tee-shirt tucked into baggy shorts, socks and flip-flops on my feet, a neatly folded handkerchief tucked into my waistband. When I catch a glimpse of my reflection in a mirror, I get a brief twinge of déjà vu.

Everything's all right at home. My wife's gluing on her new nails. My son's playing. My help isn't required anywhere. I go out on to the balcony. Greedily draw the tasteless but perfectly fresh air of the Moscow evening in through my nose. I have a hiding place out here: a half-bottle of whiskey, already opened, and half a pack of cigarettes.

When I feel sad; or I remember my old boss, Mikhail, who ran off with my money; or I remember just the money, without Mikhail; or I remember something else that has no connection with either Mikhail or money – some bright detail of a rich youth, wasted so absurdly on superficial trifles – then my hand reaches out for the poisons of its own accord. They help me to forget.

But today I'll manage without. I don't want alcohol or nicotine. I don't want to forget. What I want is not to deceive myself.

A banker, or a welder, an alcoholic, or a teetotaller, a writer, or a falsifier of commercial documents – I look around and down from my balcony.

And before me I see Europe or Russia; prison or freedom; the dead Land of Soviets or the living Russia.

The book is finished, gentlemen.

You are all free.